*S*ister on the Street

The story of Mother Teresa

Sam Godwin

Illustrated by
Tony Morris

Mother Teresa

Mother Teresa was born Agnes Gonxha Bejaxhiu to Catholic Albanian parents in 1910. She grew up in Skopje, a town in Serbia (now called Macedonia) in Eastern Europe. Agnes was a religious child, spending a lot of time in prayer. At the age of 18, she travelled to Ireland and joined the orders of the Sisters of Loreto as a novice nun. It was then that she took the name of Teresa. Before long, she went to India to continue her studies and to do missionary work. After taking her final vows, she became the principal of a Catholic school for wealthy girls in Calcutta. But the poverty that Mother Teresa saw outside the convent in Calcutta, led her to set up her own order, The Missionaries of Charity.

As her work spread to the far corners of the world, Mother Teresa became a spokesperson for the poor, sick and unfairly treated. She was awarded the Nobel Peace Prize in 1979 and died in 1997. Even after her death, the work of the Missionaries of Charity continues to help the poor of the world.

Chapter 1

It was nearly going-home time and I felt
tired and hungry. Geography was my
favourite lesson and Mother Teresa my
favourite teacher, but today was too hot
for lessons and I was desperate to get
home so I could have some cold mango
juice. The end of lesson bell rang,
interrupting Mother Teresa in
mid-sentence, and everyone started
putting their books in their satchels. I
placed my atlas under my arm, where
everyone could admire it. It was brand
new, with colourful maps and pictures.

As I was walking to the door, Mother Teresa stopped me. 'Could you help me with the map, Sunita?' she asked.

Mother Teresa had pinned a huge world map to the blackboard for the lesson and she needed help with putting it away.

'I heard your sister Aisha is back in Calcutta,' she said as we folded the map.

'She got back yesterday,' I said. 'I'm sure she'll come and see you soon.'

'I'd love to see her,' Mother Teresa smiled. 'She was a very good pupil and a credit to St. Mary Entally School, just as you are, Sunita.'

I blushed. It's nice to be praised by a teacher, especially one who also happens to be the school principal, but I was glad that all the other girls had gone out of the classroom.

Mother Teresa placed the folded map in a drawer. Then she started arranging the books neatly on her desk. 'Is your sister still working at the lawyer's?' she asked.

'Yes,' I said. 'But she is giving her work up soon, to get married. She's going to live in Delhi with her husband's family.'

Mother Teresa smiled. 'It must be nice to have a home of your own, and children. But we are not all called to the same vocation.' She finished tidying up the books and sighed. 'Have you given any thought to your future, Sunita?'

'I want to travel,' I said. 'Like you, Mother. I want to go from one country to another, seeing all there is to see. I want to visit Ireland to see your Mother House, and England to see Buckingham Palace. And perhaps I'll go to Egypt too, to visit the pyramids you told us about.'

'Travel broadens the mind,' agreed Mother Teresa kindly. Perhaps she was thinking of her own travels around the world, from her own home in Serbia to Ireland, and then to India on a boat. Mother Teresa had often told us about her journey to India, how sick she had been on the boat and how miserable because there was no Catholic priest to say Mass.

I had no intention of suffering during my travels. I wanted to ride in the first-class coaches of trains, in the best cabins on fantastic cruise liners. I wanted to eat the most delicious food and wear the most fabulous gowns from Paris. I dreamt of being rich.

Mother Teresa looked out of the window, past the neat lawns and playgrounds of our school. Beyond the walls, lay the slums of Calcutta, where the poorest people lived. Only a few girls from there had ever come to our school, and only two had stayed for more than a term. 'We go where God asks us to go,' Mother Teresa said. 'Some of us to enchanted places faraway, some of us to undiscovered worlds closer to home. There are wonderful things to experience everywhere, even in the bustees.'

Her words puzzled me. The bustees outside the school walls were not a place anyone in their right mind would want to visit. What wonderful things could you possibly find there? Sometimes I didn't understand Mother Teresa at all.

Chapter 2

'Are you going to see Mother Teresa?' I
asked my sister Aisha as we sat in our
living room, drinking tea.

'Why would she bother to go and see
that nun for?' scoffed my brother Sunil.
'She's not a pupil at St. Mary's anymore.'

'Mother Teresa would like to see her,'
I argued. 'She likes to keep in touch with
her old pupils.'

'Nuns don't care about their pupils,' Sunil said. 'They only care about their convent and their religion. They're European, after all. When did white people ever do anything for us? They're only here to grab what they can.'

I flared up, 'Mother Teresa isn't like that. She genuinely cares about people, any people, including Indians. Sometimes she goes unnoticed into the slums and helps the poor and the sick. She comforts them and gives them medicine. That's more than you will ever do for your own people.'

I thought that my brother would be impressed with Mother Teresa's work, but he wasn't. 'If she likes Indians so much, why does she keeping on wearing European clothes in this hot weather? Why doesn't she wear a sari?'

'Because she is a nun,' I shouted, losing my patience, 'and nuns have to wear habits, like soldiers have to wear uniforms.'

Sunil grinned. Like most brothers, he enjoyed upsetting his younger sister. 'No,' he said. 'Your precious Mother Teresa wears a habit because she thinks she is superior to us all.'

Aisha put down her tea. 'Sunil has a point,' she said. 'It's better not to get too close to Europeans, no matter how caring they seem to be. In the end they always go back home and leave the poor of India to suffer on their own.'

'Mother Teresa would never leave India,' I said stubbornly. 'She's different.'

Chapter 3

But was she different? The Friday following my argument with Sunil, I met my friend Shamila in the playground. 'Have you heard the news?' she gasped. 'Mother Teresa is leaving St. Mary's.'

I looked at her in shock. Mother Teresa had been principal at our school ever since anyone could remember. No one could imagine St. Mary's without her.

'Where is she going?' I asked.

Shamila shrugged. 'No one knows for sure. Some say she is going to the convent in Darjeeling. Others say she is going back to Ireland. Bimla from the third year thinks she's leaving the Order to marry an English doctor.'

'Never,' I said. 'Mother Teresa is far too old to get married. She's thirty-eight years old.'

But many of the other girls had heard the rumour too. Some asked the teachers and other sisters if they knew what was going on, but it was all news to them too. I decided to ask Mother Teresa myself, just so I could tell everyone the truth, so I offered to take the attendance register to her office.

'Mother's not in for the day,' said another sister, taking the register from my hands. 'She's visiting some sisters on Lower Circular Road. She won't be back till late.'

As I walked back to my classroom, my head was filled with doubt and Aisha's words echoed in my mind… 'It's best not to get too close to Europeans. In the end they all go back home and leave the poor of India to suffer on their own.'

Was Mother Teresa really going to desert us after all? Was she going back home to Europe? I was soon to find out.

Chapter 4

It was late on Sunday afternoon. Shamila and I had been helping out at the boarding school, which shares the same grounds as St. Mary's. The younger children there were putting on a play for the end of term and we had volunteered to help make costumes and paint scenery. As we were walking towards the main gate, Shamila noticed a light in the convent chapel.

'What's going on in there, I wonder?' she asked. 'The chapel is not normally open at this time of the day, not even on a Sunday.'

'I have no idea,' I said, 'and we're not finding out. The chapel is out of bounds for us.'

That was the wrong thing to say to Shamila. She's easily the most curious person on earth. She started walking across the lawn and I followed her, so I wouldn't be left alone.

There was someone in the chapel. We peeped in and saw Mother Teresa standing

in the sacristy with Mother Du Cenacle, the former school principal and her superior. There was a priest too, one we had often seen at school but had never talked to. He spoke in a different accent from Mother Teresa's or Mother Du Cenacle's. To our astonishment, Mother Du Cenacle was crying into her handkerchief.

'Here they are, father,' said Mother Teresa. She picked up three white saris with blue borders and placed them on a table. The priest blessed them.

'That's curious,' said Shamila who saw mystery and intrigue in everything. 'Who are the saris for? Do you think Mother Teresa is going to turn Indian and marry a Bengali doctor?'

'Don't be silly,' I said, 'maybe they're a gift for someone. They're only cotton saris.'

The priest finished the blessing and Mother Teresa folded the saris away in a cardboard box. 'Thank you, father,' she said. 'Now I must go and prepare some lessons. We have so much to do this term.'

'Did you hear that?' I said to Shamila as we hurried back across the lawn to the school gates, 'Mother Teresa is preparing lessons for next term. She can't be leaving after all.'

Chapter 5

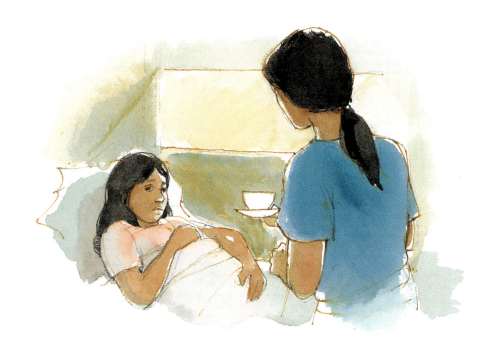

On Monday morning I woke up with a cold.
Ma told me to stay in bed and Prya, our
servant, made me lots of hot, herbal tea.
By Wednesday my cold had developed into
full-blown flu. I was bedridden for days.
Shamila came to see me every day, mostly to
fill me in on local gossip.

Then, one afternoon, she stumbled into my room, wide-eyed with excitement. 'You've missed the biggest event of the century,' she said. 'Mother Teresa HAS left St. Mary's after all. She's gone to Patna, to study nursing.'

Patna? Nursing? I couldn't believe my ears. 'Are you sure?' I said.

Shamila sat on the edge of my bed. 'Of course, I'm sure. There was a presentation at the boarding school and a farewell concert with Bengali songs. Everyone was crying their eyes out.' She stood up again, 'Perhaps she is going to marry an English doctor after all.'

'Don't be ridiculous,' I said. 'Mother Teresa is too dedicated to give up her work; she must have some other plan.'

Just then Sunil came into the room,
looking like the cat that had got the
cream. 'Heard the news?' he said. 'Your
precious nun has gone and dumped you.
I bet she'll go back to Europe, to live in
some fancy convent where they get good
food and nice cool weather.'

Sunil didn't finish the sentence because
I threw a pillow at him. He ducked but it
hit him.

'Why do you defend the old nun?' he
said. 'What is she to you?'

30

'I don't know,' I said. And it was true, I had no idea why I felt such a connection with a school principal, especially one that had let me down and was leaving us.

Chapter 6

It was a hot Sunday in December. Shamila and I were sitting on the verandah drinking tea and chatting. Prya, our maid, interrupted us. 'You wouldn't happen to have a spare workbook for my Ravi, would you, Miss Sunita?' she asked.

'I think I do,' I said.

Shamila looked up from her teacup. 'I didn't know your Ravi went to school, Prya,' she said.

'Oh yes,' replied Prya proudly. 'My Ravi goes to the new school in Motijhil.'

Shamila and I looked at each other. Motijhil was the terrible slum outside our school. There were hardly any decent buildings for people to live in there, let alone a school. The people lived out on the streets, wrapped in ragged blankets. What was Prya talking about?

'It's not much of a school, yet,' she continued. 'We have no building with classrooms, just a big tree for the children to sit under. We're going to buy slates and a blackboard soon, so the teacher won't have to write the lessons on the ground with a stick. But my Ravi's learning the alphabet already. He has milk every day and he's learnt a lot about cleanliness too. Yesterday he won a bar of soap for getting his sums right. Now the principal says she might get a hut for five rupees. I said to her, I said, 'Mother Teresa I'll…"

'Hold on a second,' I said.
'Did you say 'Mother Teresa?'.

'Oh yes,' said Prya, her eyes shining
with pride. 'I think she used to be
principal at your school, but she's my
Ravi's principal now. She went to Patna
for a few months, to learn how to care for
the sick and the dying. But she's back in
Calcutta now, teaching again.'

I looked at Shamila in triumph. So my beloved Mother Teresa hadn't deserted India after all. She hadn't gone back to Europe like Sunil had insisted. On the contrary, she'd given up her cushy life at our school, to work just around the corner, looking after the really needy. Because Mother Teresa cared. I stood up and turned to Prya.

'Tell Ravi he can have all my spare copybooks,' I said, 'and all my pencils and rubbers too. And there's something else I want to give your school principal. But I want to give it to her in person.'

Chapter 7

Shamila and I ventured into Motijhil,
followed by five of our classmates.
Although we'd been to Entally every day,
we'd never ventured into the bustee. Of
course, we saw poor people all the time,
huddled on the side of the streets, begging
for a rupee or two. But we'd never seen
the poverty we saw that day in Motijhil.

The huts were small and crowded. There was a terrible smell in the air, which came from the open sewers that ran into the tank they called 'the lake'. There were naked, dirty children everywhere, some of whom had a leg or an arm missing.

Then we saw Mother Teresa, our former principal who had lived in an immaculate convent surrounded by neatly cut lawns, teaching ragged children under a tree. At first we didn't recognise her. She wasn't wearing a nun's habit but a sari – one of the saris Shamila and I had seen the priest blessing in the chapel. Most of my friends gasped. They'd never seen a European woman in a sari before, only Indians. And what's more, Mother Teresa was wearing sandals. She was practically barefoot. That shocked us too, for Europeans never showed their toes, not even in the hottest of summers. For the first time in her life, Shamila was speechless.

Mother Teresa looked up from her
pupils and saw us. She smiled the old,
comfortable smile I knew so well.
'Sunita,' she said. 'Welcome to our school.'

I ran forward, leaving the others
behind. 'I've brought you something,'
I said, 'for your lessons.'

'What is it?' asked Mother Teresa.

'My atlas,' I said. 'You're going to need an atlas for your geography lessons.'

'But *you* need the atlas,' said Mother Teresa. 'You're going to Ireland and England and Egypt, remember?'

'Oh no, I don't need an atlas any more,' I said, for I had suddenly realised why I felt such a connection with my old school principal. I too wanted to help change the world, to make the slums a better place for people to live in. My future had nothing to do with luxury trains and cruise liners. I wanted to spend my life helping to sort out the unfairness in the world. I could learn to teach, nurse, bring hope into people's lives. Like Mother Teresa, I wanted to be a sister on the street.

Glossary

bustees an Indian word for slums in which very poor people live

habit a cloak-like garment worn, mostly in the past, by religious people, especially nuns and monks.

Mother House the head house of a religious order

missionary a person who travels to another country to do good work, usually of a religious nature.

novice a new member of a religious order, before they have taken their final vows.

order a group of people, usually religious, who have the same leader and are united by their beliefs and vows.

rupee the unit of money used in India

sacristy a special part of a church where the priests dress for ceremonies. Sacred objects used for worship are also kept there.

sari a long, cotton or silk dress traditionally worn by Indian women.

vocation a call, usually considered to be from God, to spend one's life helping others through action and prayer.

I
J. R. a Millie
DIOLCH

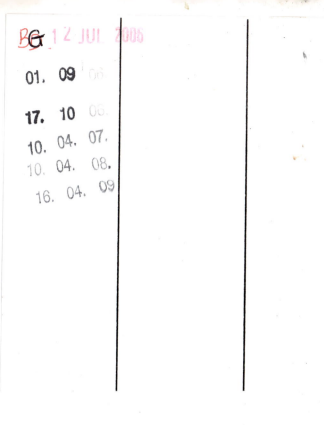

Argraffiad Cyntaf – Mawrth 2006

© Testun: Catherine Aran
© Darluniau: Eric Heyman

ISBN 0 86074 226 1

*Cyhoeddwyd ac argraffwyd
gan Wasg Gwynedd, Caernarfon*

Os gwelwch chi fynyddoedd
Eryri rhyw dro, yn enwedig ar
brynhawn niwlog, gwlyb, mi
fyddwch
chi'n siŵr
o deimlo'n
ofnus.
Mynyddoedd
uchel iawn a
thywyll ydyn
nhw, gyda niwl y
cymylau'n chwyrlïo
drostyn nhw a glaw yn
llifo i lawr y llethrau.
Maen nhw'n edrych fel
byddin fawr wlyb o
gewri ar eu ffordd i ryw ryfel
pell. A rhwng y creigiau mae'r ogofeydd
duon i'w gweld fel cegau mawr ffyrnig.

Erstalwm, roedd 'na wrach yn byw yno, meddan
nhw. Hen wrach gas a milain o'r enw Ganthrig
Bwt, oedd yn hoffi bwyta plant.

Doedd Ganthrig Bwt ddim yn ddel. O nagoedd, ddim yn ddel o gwbl!

Gyda'i chroen llwyd fel papur gwêr, ei llygaid duon a'i thrwyn hir cam, cefn fel pont, traed fel cychod a gwallt hir llwyd fel cortyn bêls yn llithro i lawr at ei phengliniau, doedd hi ddim yn ddel.

Ond roedd Ganthrig Bwt yn meddwl ei bod hi'n ddel iawn; yn ddelach na'r un wrach na'r un ferch ifanc a gerddodd drwy'r mynyddoedd erioed.

Bob bore mi fyddai'n dringo i lawr at y llyn ac yn ymolchi, gan daflu dŵr oer dros y creithiau, y blew a'r swigod ar ei bochau, dan grawcian,

'Dyma'r ffordd i olchi wyneb, i olchi wyneb, i olchi wyneb . . .'

Yna byddai'n neidio ddeg gwaith i wneud siâp seren gam yn yr awyr, ac wedyn, gan anadlu'n drwm, byddai'n tanio sigâr hir a'i smocio cyn dringo'n ôl i'r ogof i gysgu.

Un prynhawn, wrth iddi gerdded tuag at bentref Llanberis, ar ei ffordd i farchnad Caernarfon, mi welodd rywbeth a fyddai'n newid ei bywyd yn llwyr. Poster lliwgar oedd o, wedi ei ludo ar bolyn ffens:

YDACH CHI'N DLWS?
YDACH CHI'N SLAPUS?
YMUNWCH YN
Y GYSTADLEUAETH!

CYSTADLEUAETH
FFAIR LLANBERIS
I DDOD O HYD I'R FERCH
DLYSAF YN Y PENTREF
DYDD SADWRN
13EG O FEB AM 1.00YP
GWOBR - BUNCH

Ydach chi'n dlws? Ydach chi'n siapus?
Ymunwch yn y gystadleuaeth!
Cystadleuaeth Ffair Llanberis i ddod o hyd
i'r Ferch Dlysaf yn y Pentref!
Dydd Sadwrn 13 o Fedi am 1.00 o'r gloch
Gwobr: Buwch

'Wel, wel, dyma ni!' chwarddodd Ganthrig. O'r diwedd, dyma fy nghyfle i brofi i bawb mai fi ydy'r ferch dlysaf yn y lle 'ma!'

Yna, gan godi'i bag a'i hysgub, rhuthrodd yn ôl am yr ogof i roi mwd ar ei chroen.

Ar y bore Sadwrn cododd yn gynnar, a gan chwibanu iddi hi'i hun, aeth at geg yr ogof a chodi'r twmpath o lysiau a phlanhigion yr oedd wedi eu hel y diwrnod cynt. Aeth i gynnau tân ac i nôl dŵr o'r llyn. Arllwysodd ef yn ofalus i grochan seimllyd a'i hongian ar gangen uwchben y tân. Wedi i'r dŵr ferwi, rhoddodd y llysiau i mewn yn y crochan, un ar y tro, a disgwyl.

Rhyw awr wedyn, roedd y gymysgedd yn barod. Llusgodd y wrach swp gwlyb o ganol y crochan â'i llaw, a'i daflu'n glewt i ganol ei hwyneb.

'Aw . . . aw! . . . Rargol, ma' hwnna'n boeth!' gwaeddodd wrth ei esmwytho'n ofalus dros ei bochau blewog, gan osgoi'r defaid ar ei thrwyn.

Wedi i'r potes sychu, roedd ei chroen yn disgleirio'n wyrdd ac arogl sur yn codi oddi arni.

'Perffaith . . . rŵan ta, beth i'w wisgo?'

Aeth i gefn yr ogof at focs pren anferth, ac wedi stryffaglio i agor y caead, tynnodd allan ffrog hir o felfed coch. Gwisgodd yn ofalus, ac wedi ailosod ei het ddu bigog ar ei phen, brasgamodd ei ffordd i lawr y mynydd tuag at y pentref.

Roedd Llanberis yn fwrlwm o bobl, a rhes ar ôl
rhes o fyrddau'n dal nwyddau o bob lliw a llun.
Llestri blodeuog, blancedi streipiog, rhubanau pob
lliw, a ffrwythau a llysiau o bob siâp a maint.
Llanwyd y lle â phobl yn siopa, yn sgwrsio, yn
gweiddi a chwerthin, nes i rywun weld Ganthrig
Bwt – yna, yn sydyn, dechreuodd pawb sgrechian
a rhedeg i guddio.

Cerddodd y wrach yn urddasol a balch heibio'r
stondinau nes iddi weld llwyfan bychan yn y pen
draw ac arwydd 'Y Ferch Dlysaf' mewn hanner
cylch ar hyd y cefn.
    'Aha! Dyma ni!' meddai gyda gwên, a dringodd
y grisiau'n drafferthus, gyda llygaid pawb yn y
pentref wedi'u hoelio arni. Cerddodd ar hyd
blaen y llwyfan a sefyll yn stond ar ôl dewis y lle
gorau i ddangos ei hun yn grand i gyd.

Doedd yna ddim smic o sŵn yn unman ac roedd
cegau'r pentrefwyr ar agor fel llond tanc o bysgod
aur. Edrychodd pawb ar ei gilydd gan geisio
dyfalu beth ar y ddaear roedd y
wrach yn ceisio'i wneud. Yna,
camodd y Prif Dderwydd yn ei
flaen.

'Ydach chi'n aros am rywun?'
gofynnodd.

'Ydw, y beirniad,' atebodd
Ganthrig Bwt gan wenu.

'Y . . . b . . . beirniad?' holodd y
Prif Dderwydd.

14

'Ia, fydd o'n hir?' gofynnodd hithau.

'Wel . . . y . . . na fydd. Ym . . . 'dach chi ddim yn bwriadu cystadlu, ydach chi?"

Dechreuodd trigolion y pentref biffian chwerthin.

'Wel, wrth gwrs!' atebodd Ganthrig Bwt, gan chwarae â'i gwallt yn swil.

Tawelodd y pentref yn sydyn. Yna, ar ôl distawrwydd hir, chwarddodd un, yna un arall, ac un arall nes roedd pawb yn rowlio chwerthin, yn dal eu boliau mewn poen a dagrau'n llifo i lawr eu bochau.

'Oes 'na rywun wedi dweud rhywbeth digri?'
gofynnodd Ganthrig Bwt yn flin. Trodd bochau
pawb yn goch wrth iddynt ysgwyd eu pennau.

'Y . . . y . . . 'sa'n well i ni ddechrau'r
gystadleuaeth,' meddai'r Prif Dderwydd. 'Musus
Enfys Mefus, ddowch chi a Brochwel Tŷ Brain i
feirniadu, a gawn ni'r cystadleuwyr i'r llwyfan, os
gwelwch chi'n dda?'

Brysiodd Musus
Mefus a Brochwel Tŷ
Brain i eistedd yn
eu cadeiriau, a
gwthiwyd
merched ifanc,
gwragedd tŷ a neiniau
i sefyll mewn llinell i
gael eu beirniadu.

'Fysa fiw i ni roi'r
wobr i neb heblaw
Ganthrig Bwt!' sibrydodd Musus
Mefus wrth y ddau arall.

'Ond allwn ni ddim rhoi'r wobr iddi hi, Enfys;
mae'n amlwg i bawb ei bod hi'n rhy hyll!'
atebodd Brochwel dan ei wynt.

'Arhoswch funud,' meddai'r Prif Dderwydd
rhwng ei ddannedd, 'mae gen i syniad . . .'

Safodd y Prif Dderwydd yn bwysig ar ben ei gadair.

'Drigolion Llanberis, er fod llawer iawn o ferched del iawn gennym ni yn y pentref, rydym ni'r beirniaid, ar ôl meddwl yn ofalus, wedi penderfynu eleni, er mawr clod i'r Tywysog, i roi'r wobr i'w ferch fach, y Dywysoges Gwenllïan, a gafodd ei geni'r bore yma.'

Clywyd 'Hwrê!' fawr gan y dorf, a dechreuodd pawb guro dwylo'n frwd. Ond trodd wyneb Ganthrig Bwt o wyrdd i goch i ddu ffiaidd.

'Efallai fod y dywysoges fach yn ddel,' meddai, 'ond chaiff hi byth weld golau dydd! O'r eiliad hon ymlaen, os bydd pelydrau'r haul yn cyffwrdd ei chroen, bydd yn llosgi a marw, oni bai bod rhywun . . . ha!' meddai gan edrych ar y bobl o'i blaen, 'yn ei charu hi ddigon i grio a'i chusanu cyn iddi syrthio!'

Ac ar hynny, cerddodd Ganthrig Bwt oddi ar y llwyfan, trwy'r pentref, ac yn ôl i'r mynydd.

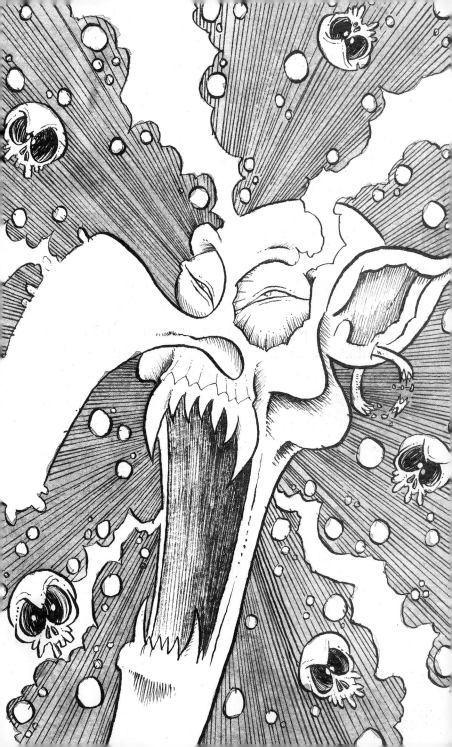

Wedi cyrraedd ceg yr ogof,
cerddodd yn ei blaen nes
iddi gyrraedd y llyn.
Eisteddodd yno am oriau yn
cwyno a bytheirio.

'Ddim digon del iddyn nhw, nacdw?'
gofynnodd iddi'i hun, wrth droi i edrych ar ei
hadlewyrchiad yn y dŵr. Ond wrth iddi edrych
yn fanwl, gwelodd wyneb gwelw, prydferth yn
syllu'n ôl arni, drws nesaf i'w hwyneb ei hun,
wyneb tlws oedd yn goleuo'r dyfnderoedd.

Edrychodd o'i hamgylch, ond welodd hi ddim nes iddi edrych i fyny, ac yno, yn yr awyr, fe welodd yr wyneb hyfryd. Wyneb y lleuad.

Maen nhw'n dal i alw'r llyn yn Llyn Lloer hyd heddiw!

Yr eiliad honno, penderfynodd Ganthrig Bwt y byddai'n rhaid iddi ddwyn y lleuad, a'i gwisgo ar ei hwyneb ei hun. Fyddai neb yn medru ei galw'n hyll byth wedyn! Felly, heb oedi, rhedodd yn ôl i'r ogof i nôl ei hysgub, neidio arni a hedfan yn uwch nag yr hedfanodd yr un wrach arall erioed. Hedfanodd drwy'r cymylau a heibio'r sêr, a chyn i neb sylweddoli beth oedd yn digwydd, roedd Ganthrig Bwt wedi dwyn y lleuad. Aeth y ddaear i gyd yn dywyll iawn.

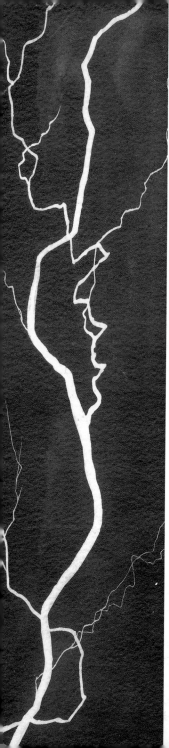

Oherwydd fod y lleuad wedi diflannu mor sydyn, trodd y byd yn lle cymysglyd dros ben. Cododd storm fawr gan orchuddio'r awyr â chymylau du nes iddynt guddio'r haul, a doedd dim goleuni i'w weld yn unman. Roedd sŵn y gwynt a'r glaw yn fyddarol! Doedd neb yn gwybod y gwahaniaeth rhwng dydd a nos, ac felly doedd neb yn gwybod pryd i gysgu na deffro a dechreuodd pawb droi'n flin a chas efo'i gilydd. Roedd pobl yn gweiddi a chwffio yn y strydoedd, a throdd y trefi a'r pentrefi yn llefydd peryglus iawn.

Doedd yr adar ddim yn gwy
pryd i ddechrau canu chwait
felly roedd pob aderyn yn canu
drwy'r amser nes eu bod mor
flinedig fe ddechreuon nhw
gwympo fel glaw o'r awyr.

Ac oherwydd fod y lleuad yn
rheoli'r môr, cododd y tonnau'n
uchel fel mynyddoedd a dryswyd
y llanw'n llwyr: dechreuodd lifo
i mewn yn bellach dros y
traethau gan fwyta mwy a mwy
o dir nes bod yr afonydd a'r
nentydd bychain yn llawn halen,
gan wenwyno'r pysgod am nad
oeddynt wedi arfer â dŵr hallt.

Mewn un afon fechan, roedd criw o bysgod wedi casglu at ei gilydd yn frysiog i drafod y sefyllfa. Ond roedden nhw'n cael trafferth mawr i siarad, gan ei bod hi mor anodd iddyn nhw anadlu.

'Rhaid i ni wneud rhywbeth, yn sydyn!' dywedodd pysgodyn bach arian.

'Beth fedrwn ni wneud? Sut allwn ni adael y dŵr i wneud unrhyw beth?' atebodd slywen hir.

'Oes 'na rywun sy'n 'nabod y wrach nath ddwyn y lleuad?' gofynnodd brithyll sâl iawn.

'Dwi'n 'nabod rhywun sy'n 'nabod y lleuad yn dda iawn . . . Idris y Cawr . . . fo ydi cariad y

lleuad . . . efallai y bydd o'n medru helpu!' meddai pysgodyn lliwgar.

'Wrth gwrs! Rhaid i ti ddod o hyd iddo, y funud yma!' gwaeddodd y slywen.

Trodd y pysgodyn lliwgar ar ei union a nofio i fyny'r afon. Cofiodd fod Idris yn ffrindiau mawr â Carwyn y Carw, a phan nad oedd yn rhannu'r gofod efo lleuad, mai at Carwyn y byddai'n arfer mynd. Roedd Carwyn yn byw ymhellach i fyny'r afon, felly brysiodd yn ei flaen gan deimlo'n well ac yn well wrth i'r dŵr fynd yn llai hallt.

O'r diwedd, roedd y pysgodyn yn medru gweld Idris a Carwyn yn eistedd wrth lan yr afon o flaen tanllwyth o dân ac yn hel atgofion rhwng ffitiau o chwerthin.

'A phan eisteddaist ti ar y to . . . Hi, hi, hi . . . !' chwarddodd Carwyn.

'A dylet ti fod wedi gweld dy wyneb di pan dorrodd o'n deilchion . . . hw, hw, hw . . . !

'Ahym!' pesychodd y pysgodyn â'i ben allan o'r dŵr, ond roedd y ddau'n rhy brysur yn rowlio ar y llawr i'w glywed. Dechreuodd wneud twrw wrth droelli yn y dŵr ond methodd hynny â thynnu'u sylw nhw chwaith, felly dechreuodd neidio allan o'r dŵr gan droi ei hun yn yr awyr cyn glanio ar wyneb yr afon â sblash!

'Be gebyst?
Rargol . . . 'Sgodyn
sy'n meddwl ei fod
o'n acrobat!' meddai
Idris.

'Ia, Idris, pysgodyn
sydd mewn trafferth!'
atebodd y pysgodyn.

'Y Creadur Di-droed!'
meddai Idris mewn
syndod.

'Ia, a rŵan dwi angen
dy help di!' Peidiodd
Idris â chwerthin yn
sydyn.

'Be sy'n bod?' gofynnodd
mewn llais difrifol iawn.

'Ti'm 'di sylwi ar y tywyllwch?' holodd
y pysgodyn.

'Wel do, wrth gwrs, ond mae hi'n ganol nos!'

'Wel, nacdi, ddim a deud y gwir, mae hi i fod
yn ganol dydd,' meddai'r pysgodyn.

'Mae hi wedi bod yn noson hir, rhaid i mi
gyfaddef, ond roedd Idris a minnau'n cael y fath
hwyl . . . ' dechreuodd Carwyn esbonio, ond
torrodd y pysgodyn ar ei draws.

'A'r rheswm am y fath lanast ydi fod Ganthrig Bwt wedi dwyn y lleuad, ac yn ôl pob sôn yn ei gwisgo hi fel masg yn lle gorfod dangos ei hwyneb hyll ei hun!'

'Lleuad? Fy Lleuad i?' gofynnodd Idris, a'i lygaid yn llenwi.

'Wel toes 'na'm ond un, y jolpyn!' atebodd y pysgodyn yn swta.

Cododd Idris ar ei draed yn benderfynol.

'Tyrd, Carwyn! Mae'n rhaid i ni achub Lleuad!' meddai, gan droi a cherdded tua'r gogledd.

'O na, ddim eto!' meddai Carwyn yn wan.

Roedd Idris y Cawr ar frys, ac wrth iddo gerdded rhwygai'r coed oedd o'i ffordd allan o'r pridd a'u taflu bob sut, felly roedd Carwyn yn gorfod bod yn ofalus iawn i beidio â chael ei waldio gan y brigau.

'Aw, gwylia . . . ow! Idris . . . wff! fy mhen i!'

'Tyrd, Carwyn,' meddai
Idris, gan danio brigyn i greu ffagl danbaid, 'does
'na ddim amser i gwyno!' ychwanegodd, a golwg
flin a phenderfynol ar ei wyneb.

Erbyn yr amser y dylai hi fod wedi nosi, roedd Idris a Carwyn wedi cyrraedd y gogledd. Roedd popeth yn dywyll, a phrin roeddynt yn medru gweld cysgodion y mynyddoedd yn y düwch.

'Fy nghoesau bach i . . . ' dechreuodd Carwyn.

'Sssht!' sibrydodd Idris wrth fodio'i ffordd rhwng y creigiau. 'Does gen i'r un syniad lle'r ydan ni, na lle i fynd i ddod o hyd i'r hen wrach 'na, ond dwi'n trio gwrando!'

'O . . . am be?'

'Wel . . . ym . . . dwn i'm, jest rhywbeth, unrhyw beth i roi cliw i ni!'

'O . . . 'dan ni ar goll ta?' gofynnodd Carwyn
dan ei wynt.

'Wel na . . . wel . . . ydan!' ochneidiodd Idris
gan eistedd yn y fan a'r lle.

Chafodd ei ben ôl ddim amser i swatio. Wrth
iddo ollwng ei bwysau ar y creigiau dechreuodd
pob carreg o fewn canllath rowlio a llithro i lawr
ochr y mynydd, gan gario Idris a Carwyn yn y
llif. Sgrechiodd y ddau gan gydio'n dynn yn ei
gilydd nes iddynt gyrraedd y gwaelod, a cherrig
yn tasgu i bob cyfeiriad.

'Wff! Aw! AAAAAAAAAAA! Aw! Wff!'

Eisteddodd y ddau mewn distawrwydd yn y tywyllwch am oes, yn gleisiau ac yn friwiau drostynt.

'Alla i ddim credu mod i'n gwneud hyn eto!' meddai Carwyn. 'Bob tro dwi'n dy ddilyn di mae 'na bethau od yn digwydd. Mae 'nghoesau i'n ddrwg fel maen nhw heb i mi syrthio i lawr ochr mynydd hefyd.'

O'r tywyllwch clywsant lais swynol yn canu,

'Dyma'r ffordd i fro gogoniant . . .

Ar . . . hyd . . . y nos!'

'Sssh, Carwyn!' meddai Idris rhwng ei ddannedd.

'Helô, pwy sy na?' sibrydodd i'r tywyllwch. Clywodd y ddau sŵn adenydd yn curo, ac ar ôl swish hir, glaniodd rhywbeth yn ysgafn ar lin y Cawr.

'C-C-C-Carwyn, mae 'na rywbeth byw yn sefyll ar fy nghoes i!' sibrydodd Idris.

Cododd Carwyn ddarn o bren o ganol y cerrig, a mwg yn codi ohono.

'T'isio hwn?' gofynnodd yn betrusgar.

Ymbalfalodd Idris yn y tywyllwch gan afael yn y pren a'i danio. Wrth i'r golau dyfu'n araf, edrychodd Carwyn ac Idris yn syn ar lygaid crwn eos fechan yn rhythu'n ôl arnynt.

'I ble rwyt ti'n myned, fab annwyl dy fam?' canodd yr aderyn.

''Dan ni'n chwilio am Lleuad,' atebodd Carwyn yn syn.

'Ble'r ei di, ble'r ei di?' canodd yr aderyn eto.

'I lle bynnag mae Lleuad! Sgen ti ryw syniad lle mae hi?' gofynnodd Idris yn flin.

'Dau gi bach yn mynd i'r coed!' canodd yr eos gan godi i'r awyr a dechrau hedfan o'u blaenau.

'Hei, aros amdanon ni!'
gwaeddodd Idris.

Hedfanodd yr eos yn ôl
ac ymlaen wrth arwain y
ddau drwy'r coed ac at
droed mynydd uchel. Yn
sydyn, o'u blaenau
gwelsant danllwyth o dân
ac wrth ei ymyl, ar gadair
siglo, rhywbeth yn
gorwedd fel llwyth o
gadachau. Ar ben y
cadachau, roedd Lleuad.

'Lleuad!' sibrydodd Idris wrth symud yn agosach
ar ei bedwar.

Agorodd Lleuad ei llygaid, a sylweddolodd Idris
fod y llwyth o gadachau yn perthyn i gorff –
corff y wrach – ac roedd Lleuad yn sownd i'w
hwyneb.

'Ssssh, Idris! Mae Ganthrig Bwt yn cysgu!'
rhybuddiodd Lleuad.

Ceisiodd
Idris afael yn Lleuad a'i
thynnu'n ofalus. Griddfanodd
y wrach a symud ychydig.
Arhosodd pawb yn
hollol lonydd.

'Does dim pwynt trio,' sibrydodd
Lleuad. 'Dwi'n gwbl sownd!'

'Ond mae'n rhaid i ni dy gael di'n ôl!' mynnodd Idris.

'Does 'na ddim ond un ffordd – mi fydd rhaid i ti addo rhywbeth iddi,' meddai Lleuad.

'Addo be?'

'Addo ei gwneud hi'n ddel am byth.'

'Be? Sut ar y ddaear mae gwneud rhywbeth mor hyll yn ddel?' gofynnodd Carwyn.

'Dach chi'n cofio pan oeddech chi'n fach, ac yn gwneud stumiau hyll y tu ôl i'ch mam?'

'Wnes i rioed ffasiwn beth!' wfftiodd Carwyn.

Gwenodd Lleuad gan fynd yn ei blaen, 'A hithau'n dweud wrthych chi am beidio, achos tasa'r lleuad yn gwibio drwy'r awyr yr eiliad honno, byddai'ch wyneb chi'n aros fel'na.'

'O ia, cofio rŵan!' chwarddodd Carwyn.

'Wel, mae'n medru gweithio'r ffordd arall hefyd. Felly, y cwbl sydd raid i chi wneud ydi addo i Ganthrig Bwt y byddech chi'n medru ei gwneud hi'n ddel am byth, dim ond i chi 'nghael i'n ôl yn gyntaf!'

'Cael pwy yn ôl yn gyntaf?' sgrechiodd y wrach wrth godi, wedi deffro wrth glywed ei henw.

'Y Lleuad,' atebodd Idris gan godi ar ei draed.

'A pham y buaswn i'n ei rhoi hi'n ôl i ti? Am dy fod ti mewn cariad, ia?' chwarddodd Ganthrig Bwt, gan ddangos rhes o ddannedd melyn, budr.

Edrychodd Idris i lawr arni, ac ar ôl meddwl am funud, plygodd a gofyn,

'Wyt ti eisiau bod yn ddel?'

'Dwi yn ddel!' atebodd y wrach.

Plygodd Idris yn nes ati i geisio gweld ei hwyneb yn fflamau'r ffagl, ond roedd wyneb hyfryd Lleuad yn ei chuddio. Bu bron iddo gyfogi wrth arogli ei harogl sur, ond yn lle gwneud hynny, sythodd a sibrwd,

'Nagwyt, wrach fach, wyneb Lleuad sy'n ddel! Wyt ti eisiau bod yn ddel? Os gwnei di roi Lleuad yn ôl i mi, dwi'n addo defnyddio pob hud o fewn fy ngallu i dy droi di'n ddel am byth.'

'Ond Cawr wyt ti, nid dewin!' atebodd Ganthrig yn wyllt.

'Falla wir, ond mae o'n gynnig eitha da, on'd ydi o?' atebodd Idris mewn llais tyner.

'Wel . . . '

'A fysat ti byth yn maddau i ti dy hun am golli cyfle mor dda.'

'Nafswn, ond . . . '

'A mater bach fyddai i rywun fel ti gael y Lleuad yn ôl.'

'Ac mae'n bechod i ti aros mor hyll am weddill dy fywyd!' ychwanegodd Carwyn.

'Iawn! Be 'dan ni'n ei wneud gyntaf?' crawciodd y wrach yn gyffro i gyd.

'Awn ni i lawr at y llyn wrth y pentref. Mi ddechreuwn ni yn fan'no.'

Cododd Carwyn frigyn o'r tân i oleuo'r ffordd
hefyd, ac aeth y tri i lawr y mynydd mewn rhes
gan basio defaid, sgwarnogod, cŵn, cathod a
llwynogod oedd wedi clywed y newyddion ac a
oedd yn ysu i weld sut aflwydd roedd Idris am
lwyddo i wneud gwrach mor hyll yn ddel.

Wedi cyrraedd y llyn roedd
trigolion Llanberis i gyd wedi
clywed y newyddion hefyd ac
yn eu disgwyl gyda ffaglau,
llusernau a chanhwyllau ar
ochr y llyn. Aeth Ganthrig
Bwt i sefyll ar ochr draw'r
llyn a safodd Idris ar ochr y
pentref, ynghanol y dorf. Yn
araf, rhwygodd y wrach y
lleuad oddi ar ei hwyneb gan
gwyno a chrio gyda'r boen, a
Carwyn yn cwyno a chrio
wrth weld wyneb hyll y
wrach yn dod i'r golwg.

Rhoddodd Ganthrig Bwt y lleuad i Idris, a gan edrych i fyw llygaid ei gilydd yn heriol, taflodd Idris y lleuad fel ffrisbi llachar i ganol y nos.

'Wwwwwwwwwwww!' oedd ymateb y dorf.

Wrth i Lleuad hedfan yn ôl am adre, tasgodd gwreichion fel cynffon tân gwyllt y tu ôl iddi, gan lanio ar Ganthrig Bwt. Yn sydyn clywyd . . . crac, Crac, CRAAC! Dechreuodd y croen ar wyneb Ganthrig Bwt droi'n llwyd a newidiodd ei thrwyn, ei llygaid a'i gên eu siâp.

44

Diflannodd y defaid, y blew a'r creithiau nes
bod y dorf yn edrych ar wyneb newydd,
prydferth ac urddasol – ac oer – Ganthrig Bwt.
Roedd hi wedi cael ei throi yn graig!

'Hwrê! Hwrê!' gwaeddodd pawb. 'Mae'r hen wraig yn graig! Mae Ganthrig Bwt yn graig!'

Dechreuodd pob person ac anifail neidio, dawnsio, chwerthin a chanu ac aeth y parti ymlaen ac ymlaen, hyd yn oed wedi i Haul godi. Edrychodd Lleuad ac Idris ar ei gilydd a gwenu, a diflannodd y ddau yn ddistaw dros y gorwel.

Ac os ydach chi am weld wyneb y wrach, ewch ar gwch i ganol Llyn Padarn. Ynghanol y llyn bydd y Capten yn dweud wrthych chi am edrych ar y graig er mwyn gweld wyneb rhyw ddynes hardd . . . ond rydan ni'n gwybod wyneb pwy sydd yno go iawn, tydan?

HUMAN REPRODUCTIVE DECISIONS

THE GALTON INSTITUTE

The Galton Institute is concerned with the interdisciplinary study of the biological, genetic, economic, social and cultural factors relating to human reproduction, development and health in the broadest sense. The Institute has a wide range of interests which include the description and measurement of human qualities, human heredity, the influence of environment and the causes of disease, genetic counselling, the family unit, marriage guidance, birth control, differential fertility, infecundity, artificial insemination, termination of pregnancy, population problems and migration. As a registered charity, the Institute does not propagate particular political views, but it does seek to foster respect for human variety and to encourage circumstances in which the fullest achievement of individual human potential can be realised. More generally, the Institute seeks to advance understanding of biosocial matters by enabling biologists, clinicians, demographers, sociologists and other professionals to work together in a mutually productive manner.

The Galton Institute was formed in 1988 as the successor body to the Eugenics Society, which in turn derived from the Eugenics Education Society founded in 1907 by Sir Francis Galton, FRS. Membership of the Institute is international and consists of fellows and members. Fellows are those who contribute by their work and writings to the advancement of knowledge in the biosocial sciences. Members are drawn from a wide area of biosocial interests. Amongst its activities the Institute supports original research via its Stopes Research Fund, sponsors the annual Darwin Lecture in Human Biology, co-sponsors the biennial Caradog Jones Lecture, and publishes the journal *Biology and Society*. Each year, the Institute mounts a two-day symposium in which a topic of current importance is explored from differing standpoints, and during which the Galton Lecture is delivered by a distinguished guest.

Information about the Institute, its aims, activities and publications may be obtained from: The General Secretary, The Galton Institute, 19 Northfields Prospect, Northfields, London SW18 1FE, England.

Human Reproductive Decisions

Biological and Social Perspectives

Proceedings of the Thirtieth Annual Symposium of the Galton Institute, London, 1993

Edited by

R. I. M. Dunbar
Professor of Psychology
University of Liverpool

St. Martin's Press in association with
THE GALTON INSTITUTE

First published in Great Britain 1995 by
MACMILLAN PRESS LTD
Houndmills, Basingstoke, Hampshire RG21 2XS
and London
Companies and representatives
throughout the world

This book is published in Macmillan's *Studies in Biology, Economy
and Society* series
General Editor: Robert Chester

A catalogue record for this book is available
from the British Library.

ISBN 0–333–62051–8

10	9	8	7	6	5	4	3	2	1
04	03	02	01	00	99	98	97	96	95

Printed in Great Britain by
Ipswich Book Co Ltd, Ipswich, Suffolk

First published in the United States of America 1995 by
Scholarly and Reference Division,
ST. MARTIN'S PRESS, INC.,
175 Fifth Avenue,
New York, N.Y. 10010

ISBN 0–312–12436–8

Library of Congress Cataloging-in-Publication Data
Galton Institute (London, England). Symposium (30th : 1993 : London,
England)
Human reproductive decisions : biological and social perspectives
: proceedings of the thirtieth annual symposium of the Galton
Institute, London, 1993 / edited by R. I. M. Dunbar.
p. cm.
Includes index.
ISBN 0–312–12436–8
1. Human reproduction. 2. Fertility—Human. 3. Birth control.
I. Dunbar, R. I. M. (Robin Ian McDonald), 1947– . II. Title.
GN235.G35 1995
304.6'32—dc20   94–32721
                                                              CIP

Contents

List of Tables

List of Figures

Notes on the Contributors

John A. Bock, Department of Anthropology, University of New Mexico, Albuquerque, New Mexico, USA.

John Cleland, Population Studies Unit, London School of Hygiene and Tropical Medicine.

R. I. M. Dunbar, Department of Psychology, University of Liverpool.

Jeanette Edwards, Department of Anthropology, University of Manchester.

Peter T. Ellison, Department of Anthropology, Harvard University, Cambridge, Massachusetts, MA, USA.

P. R. Andrew Hinde, Department of Social Statistics, University of Southampton.

Sara E. Johnson, Department of Anthropology, University of New Mexico, Albuquerque, New Mexico, USA.

Hillard S. Kaplan, Department of Anthropology, University of New Mexico, Albuquerque, New Mexico, USA.

Jane B. Lancaster, Department of Anthropology, University of New Mexico, Albuquerque, New Mexico, USA.

John Landers, All Souls College, Oxford.

Alan S. McNeilly, MRC Reproductive Biology Unit, Centre for Reproductive Biology, Edinburgh.

Máire Ní Bhrolcháin, Department of Social Statistics, University of Southampton.

Sara Randall, Department of Anthropology, University College, London.

Alan R. Rogers, Department of Anthropology, University of Utah, Salt Lake City, Utah, USA.

Lyliane Rosetta, Department of Biological Anthropology, University of Cambridge.

Eckart Voland, Department of Anthropology, University College, London.

1 An Interdisciplinary Approach to Human Fertility

R. I. M. Dunbar

Seen from a biological perspective, reproduction is the central problem around which all else hinges. It is that to which all cellular and mechanistic processes lead, and from which all population and evolutionary consequences follow. Its pivotal role in the life of the organism places it in a unique position to provide a focus for the exchange of views between those biologists whose interests lie with the mechanisms of reproduction and those whose primary interests focus on the consequences of reproduction.

While reproduction is obviously of intrinsic interest to biologists, it is also a subject of interest to many social scientists. Most obviously, demographers are intimately concerned with the decisions that individuals make about when and how often to reproduce. But reproduction is also of interest to social anthropologists precisely because individuals find themselves at the centre of a web of social influences that may include immediate family as well as society as a whole. In a social species like our own, the reproduction of one member is often a matter of personal interest to many other individuals, all of whom may seek to influence the outcome.

The past decade, in particular, has witnessed a number of major advances in our understanding of the biology of reproduction. On the one hand, reproductive endocrinologists have developed a very much more sophisticated view of the mechanisms that control and regulate fertility. In large measure, this has involved extending the range of factors considered out beyond the more conventional feedback loops involving the reproductive hormones and the brain to include the influence of external factors such as the infant's sucking on the breast, the work loads that women bear in traditional societies and the role of seasonal food shortages. The emerging picture is one of increasing complexity that involves a web of interactions between intrinsic and extrinsic factors. The relationships out of which this web of casual processes is built usually involve fairly simple deterministic effects. Put together, however, they yield sufficient complexity to allow the reproductive system to respond

1

with infinite flexibility to subtle changes in the local conditions in which an individual woman finds herself.

This growing understanding of the machinery of reproduction has been matched by an equally dramatic growth in our understanding of the teleonomic aspects of behaviour. Advances in evolutionary biology have revolutionised our understanding of the functional aspects of animal behaviour in ways that could not have been anticipated as little as two decades ago. The principal thrust of much of this work has been to point to the central significance of genetic replication (genetic *fitness*) as the guiding factor in the behavioural decisions that individuals make.

Naïve interpretations often misconstrue the functional approach in biology as constituting some form of genetic determinism. Such a view makes little biological sense. Of course, there must be genes in the system somewhere, but they may be buried so deeply that the behavioural strategies they generate are completely flexible and involve fine-tuned adjustments in response to subtle changes in the environment in which the individual lives. If this was not so, higher organisms like mammals would not be able to survive. At the level of actual behaviour, however, it makes no difference to the nature of the decision being made by an organism whether its decision rules are learned or dictated by its genes: the decision rule itself is independent of the machinery that allows it to be manifested.

Evolutionary (or functional) considerations of this kind are necessarily mediated by physiological and neural mechanisms that provide the machinery necessary to implement the organism's fitness-oriented decisions. Conventional wisdom within organismic biology has always insisted that function and mechanism are logically distinct questions that should be answered separately. None the less, with half a century or more of independent progress on these issues, a degree of convergence is beginning to emerge. Understanding the mechanisms can tell us a great deal about the constraints that act on the functional decisions that individuals make. Conversely, understanding the function that mechanisms subserve within the individual's life strategy may clarify just why the machinery is structured in the way it is.

This broadening of the relevant context brings biology into direct contact with the more conventional social sciences. Demographers have been intimately concerned with the processes of human reproduction for a very long time, but their emphasis has been primarily on the proximate mechanisms that guide the decisions that humans make. These have tended to focus either on the economic aspects of fertility (the value of children as labour in the family production system or as providers of a form of social security for parents in their old age) or on the social and cultural pressures that serve to dictate how individuals should behave. In the latter respect, demographers broach a common ground with social anthropologists who, working within a framework traditionally dominated by Durkheimian thinking, have tended to focus their interests increasingly on the ways in which individuals respond to and view the pressures that society places on them.

Interaction between biologists and social scientists has undoubtedly been frustrated by a prevailing ethos that has viewed biology and culture as two opposing (indeed, irreconcilable) features of human behaviour (for a succinct review of this see Tooby and Cosmides, 1992). This view seems to have been predicated on views of biology that can no longer be legitimately sustained. The primary lesson of the developments in evolutionary biology over the past decade or so has been that the traditional narrow view of biology (that biology means neither more nor less than genetics or endocrinology) is simply untenable. The scope of organismic biology, in particular, spreads far beyond the mere machinery to encompass the context within which the organism lives. And, in the human case, the social and cultural context is as much a part of the biological system as the ovaries and brain. On the one hand, cultural processes provide the mechanism whereby rules of behaviour are passed on from one generation to another, while on the other hand they also constitute an important component of the costs and benefits that individuals need to evaluate when deciding how to behave (see below).

Above all, then, it has been a shift to a systemic view that has characterised the history of organismic biology (in particular) within the past few decades. This broadening perspective, however, brings with it further dangers of misunderstanding. It is thus important to appreciate from the outset precisely how the different disciplines relate to each other. Failure to do so in the past has often resulted in presumption that explanations being offered by one discipline are in direct competition with those of another discipline, when in reality they are complementary.

Biologists have long recognised (Huxley, 1942; Tinbergen, 1963) that there are a number of logically distinct levels at which a particular phenomenon can be approached. These are now known as *Tinbergen's Four Why's*. Essentially, when we ask 'Why did this individual conceive?' we can answer the question at four different levels: proximate mechanisms (the physiological or psychological mechanisms that make a given behaviour possible), functional consequences (the objectives that the behaviour in question is designed to achieve), ontogenetic explanations (involving the interaction of genetic and environmental factors in the unfolding processes of development and enculturation) and, finally, phylogeny (historical explanations about the changes at the species' level that have taken place in the sequence leading up to the behaviour as we see it now). These different types of explanation are logically distinct, yet all are simultaneously necessary if we are ever to claim to have provided a complete explanation for any given phenomenon.

The problem has been that most disciplines concentrate on just one of these levels of explanation. Physiologists, psychologists and social anthropologists focus on various sub-types of proximate mechanism (endocrinological processes, motivations, economic and social considerations); evolutionary biologists emphasise function (and not, as is commonly assumed, questions of evolutionary history, which are largely the province of palaeontologists and taxonomists); developmental biologists concentrate on ontogeny. Failure to recognise these differences of level have generated disputes that have been largely pointless and wholly unproductive and which have served only to obscure the lessons that each discipline has to offer the others.

This book, then, represents an attempt to break through some of these interdisciplinary barriers in order to facilitate a more profitable systemic approach to problems of general social and biological concern. It will not attempt to look at all the possible levels in the system – that would be too large a task at the present time. However, profitable inroads can be made by tackling the interface between functional and mechanistic explanations, and between the various sub-layers within those larger categories. Biologists themselves have recently undertaken similar attempts to bridge the gulfs that exist within biology itself in this particular respect (see Bateson and Gomendio, 1992).

Our focus here, then, is on the kinds of functional and mechanistic explanations that are relevant to the facts of reproduction in humans. In answer to the question 'Why did X conceive?', we might offer an explanation in terms of the endocrinological processes involved (weaning the previous infant reduced the level of nipple stimulation below that required to block the production of the gonadotrophins that trigger ovulation) or one in terms of the contextual variables (work loads were reduced below the level needed to suppress the production of gonadotrophins such that cultural prohibitions against the use of contraceptives resulted in the woman falling pregnant the moment this happened). These are two different kinds of proximate or mechanistic explanation, both of which may simultaneously be true. We can also, however, answer the question in terms of the goals that individuals seek to achieve. These functional explanations can also take a number of forms because there are a number of increasingly inclusive goals involved in biological systems. Maximising economic output may be one such objective. But, biologically speaking, this cannot be the end of the story because maximising economic output ultimately has implications for how the individual's genes are represented in future generations. Evolution is simply a consequence of differential reproduction; and if some individuals can consistently manage to reproduce more often than others do, then selection can and must operate. This is an unavoidable fact of the way the biology of reproduction works. Functional questions thus always eventually come down to: Will reproducing now add to or detract from this individual's genetic fitness (the frequency with which her genes are represented in the next generation)?

Biologists have learned to use functional considerations to guide the kinds of questions they ask about animal and human behaviour in ways that identify crucial questions at the level of the mechanisms and the ontogenetic processes involved. But functional questions are surprisingly difficult to ask because we are not used to asking them in normal life. When we ask 'Why did *X* happen?' we normally expect either an explanation in terms of motivations (the kinds of answers that we habitually deal with when discussing our own behaviour) or in terms of the machinery that scaffolds that behaviour (the physiological processes, the genes that underpin it, etc). Functional questions seem counter-intuitive by comparison. Yet they provide the *raison d'être* of both the proximate mechanisms and the ontogenetic processes that give rise to them. For this reason, they form an important part of any attempt to understand why organisms behave as they do.

One final point needs to be made to avoid unnecessary confusion. The title of this book places emphasis on the word *decision*. It may be tempting to assume that this implies conscious forethought because of the connotation this word has in everyday usage. I use the term here in the way evolutionary biologists now conventionally use it. That usage emphasises only the goal-directedness of functional explanations in much the same sense that computer scientists use the term in systems analysis: the organism (or computer) encounters a choice point at which it must go in one of two (or more) mutually incompatible directions (in this case, to reproduce or not to reproduce at that particular moment). In line with Tinbergen's emphasis on the separation of levels of explanation, this usage remains neutral on the mechanisms involved. The behavioural outcome may be a consequence of genetically controlled processes or it may be a consequence of cogitation, or even simple acquiescence in a culturally imposed norm. From a functional point of view, which emphasises the fitness *consequences* of behavioural decisions, the nature of the machinery is irrelevant. This does not mean to say that questions about the way the machinery works are uninteresting or unworthy of investigation; it merely asserts that they are not directly relevant to the functional consequences of those decisions.

Social scientists may be tempted to argue that an individual acting under social pressure does not do so out of choice. However, the situation is in fact more complex than this and it is important to tease apart its components with care. In evolutionary time, the organism does, in effect, have that choice (and in one sense at least may actively be implementing it if its decision to acquiesce to social pressure is guided by the decision to prefer conformity to social isolation, an option that it always has available to it). In this respect, cultural rules acquired during socialisation may simply be a psychological short-cut that saves the individual time and effort trying to work out the best thing to do on each and every occasion. Emphasis on the lack of choice arising out of the processes of socialisation is, of course, a (quite legitimate) question about ontogeny, but it should not be confused with questions about function. Seen from the perspective of the individual at the moment of its decision, socialisation (and the lack of choice this implies) is simply a constraint within the system. Conversely, if the individual makes any kind of active choice, then those pressures placed on the individual by the other members of its social group are part and parcel of the costs of the decision process.

This brings into sharper focus the relationship between the Durkheimian view favoured by the social sciences (the individual's behaviour is dictated by society via the processes of enculturation during childhood) and that of evolutionary biology (society is the creation of individuals). One interpretation is that these are simply opposite sides of the same ontogenetic coin. Of course, the individual's behaviour is dictated by its upbringing, with many of its behavioural rules instilled by society during childhood. But the fact that these rules exist does not mean to say that they have always existed in that form: societies do change and when they change they invariably do so at the behest of individuals. Social rules as we see them now may thus be the outcome of long periods of social negotiation in a past that we cannot see and which have long been forgotten. This does not mean that ideologies may not be important in driving social change or that cultural institutions are not limited in the number of forms they can take by internal structural coherence. Such ideas have received considerable attention from evolutionary biologists [examples include Dawkins' (1976) analysis of memes and Boyd and Richerson's (1985) models of cultural evolution]. But it does mean that there may be grounds for reinterpreting the relationship between Durkheim and Darwin as one of differences in time-frame or perspective rather than one of epistemology.

As the title for this book, the use of the term *decision* emphasises the fact that functional questions provide the one feature that serves to unify all four senses of *Tinbergen's Four Why's*, thereby unifying the interests of the various disciplines represented in this volume. Behavioural decisions (the fact we have to explain) have evolved (a phylogenetic answer when interpreted in contrast to some ancestral condition) in order to allow individuals to maximise their genetic fitness (a functional answer), a process that is made possible by endocrinological mechanisms and subject to social and other contextual variables (different forms of mechanistic answer) mediated via processes of inheritance that involve either genes or learning or both (an ontogenetic answer). Only once we have managed to specify each of the steps in this chain will we be able to claim that we have understood the business of reproduction.

I can do no better than end by endorsing Cosmides *et al.*'s (1992) plea for a more sensible understanding of what neighbouring disciplines might have to offer each other:

> By calling for conceptual integration in the behavioural and social sciences we are neither calling for reductionism nor for the conquest and assimilation of one field by another. Theories of selection pressures are not theories of psychology; they are theories about some of the causal forces that produced our psychology. And theories of psychology are not theories of culture; they are theories about some of the causal mechanisms that shape cultural forms. ... In fact, not only do the principles of one field not reduce to those of another, but by tracing the relationships between fields, additional principles often appear.
>
> (Cosmides *et al.*, 1992, p. 12)

I hope that this book signals that we have at last begun to pull down the barricades and set about the exciting task of developing a genuinely unified theory of human behaviour. I can think of no better place to start than with the business of reproduction, with its central role in biology and the immediacy of its interest in all our lives.

ACKNOWLEDGEMENT

I thank Eckart Voland for his comments on the original draft of this chapter.

REFERENCES

Bateson, P. P. G. and Gomendio, M. (eds) (1992), *Behavioural Mechanisms in Evolutionary Perspective* (Madrid: Juan March Institute).

Boyd, R. and Richerson, P. (1985), *Culture and the Evolutionary Process* (Chicago: University of Chicago Press).

Cosmides, L., Tooby, J. and Barkow, J. H. (1992), 'Introduction: evolutionary psychology and conceptual integration', in J. H. Barkow, L. Cosmides and J. Tooby (eds), *The Adapted Mind: Evolutionary Psychology and the Generation of Culture* (Oxford: Oxford University Press) pp. 3–15.

Dawkins, R. (1976), *The Selfish Gene* (Oxford: Oxford University Press).

Huxley, J. S. (1942), *Evolution: The Modern Synthesis* (London: Allen and Unwin).

Tinbergen, N. (1963), 'On the aims and methods of ethology', *Zeitschrift für Tierpsychologie*, vol. 20, pp. 410–33.

Tooby, J. and Cosmides, L. (1992), 'The psychological foundations of culture', in J. H. Barkow, L. Cosmides and J. Tooby (eds), *The Adapted Mind: Evolutionary Psychology and the Generation of Culture* (Oxford: Oxford University Press) pp. 19–136.

2 Breastfeeding and the Baby: Natural Contraception

Alan S. McNeilly

INTRODUCTION

Although it had been recognised for centuries that breastfeeding could delay the resumption of menses and the timing of the next pregnancy, the potential use of breastfeeding as a reliable means of spacing births was not accepted. It was Roger Short while Director of the MRC Reproductive Biology Unit in Edinburgh who was one of the first to recognise the potential practical importance of resolving the mechanisms involved in suppressing fertility in order to maximise the use of breastfeeding as a reliable birth-spacing method, and so coined the phrase Natural Contraception (Short,1976). Breastfeeding is the only natural and reversible mechanism which inhibits fertility in women (Howie and McNeilly, 1982; McNeilly, 1988, 1993, 1994). In many other mammals, including primates, there are periods of reproductive inactivity usually related to factors associated with seasonal change, be it day length, temperature or nutrition and in the majority lactation also delays either conception by inhibiting ovarian activity, or implantation of the conceptus to create an interbirth interval allowing maximum chance of survival of the newborn infants (McNeilly, 1988, 1994). In Man, the breakdown of the natural delay in birth of children leads to an increase in morbidity and mortality of siblings which is as high as 40 per cent in some parts of the world (Thapa *et al.*, 1988).

Our research has been and is directed towards understanding the components of breastfeeding which control the length of the infertile period not only to develop practical guidelines for women to maximise the reliability of breastfeeding as a contraceptive, but also to determine whether we could devise more natural methods of contraception based on the only natural inhibitor of fertility in women. It became apparent in the early 1980s that in the majority of clinical studies on breastfeeding and fertility, most emphasis was placed on endocrine changes with time postpartum, with little or no appreciation of the essential input of the baby.

9

Indeed, even in papers published now, the pattern of suckling related to changes in endocrinology is either only briefly mentioned, or in some cases, completely ignored! This is an extraordinary situation, akin to studying the function of an engine while ignoring the changes in fuel input.

Our first studies in Edinburgh, with Peter Howie, concentrated on documenting accurately the changes in ovarian activity in relation to the suckling activity of the baby, including the pattern of suckling and effects of supplements (McNeilly et al.,1981; Howie et al., 1981a, 1982a,b). This type of study has now been replicated world-wide and for the first time has accurately documented the changes in ovarian steroid secretion indicating ovarian activity in relation to suckling activity of the baby. It became apparent that the pattern of suckling was extremely important and that the suckling activity of the baby, more than time postpartum, was the major factor influencing the duration of lactational amenorrhoea, a time of almost total ovarian inactivity and maximum protection from pregnancy. It then became apparent that, at least in Edinburgh, addition of supplementary food to the baby's diet could result in a resumption of ovarian activity and return of fertility (Howie et al.,1981a). This was related to a reduction in the duration of suckling without necessarily a reduction in the number of breastfeeds each day and emphasised the importance of the suckling activity of the baby in controlling the return of fertility. We further discovered that a large number of the menstrual cycles occurring while the mother continued to breastfeed were associated with a poor luteal phase (McNeilly et al., 1982). This may explain the low incidence of fertility in menstruating women who continue to breastfeed in some societies (McNeilly et al., 1983a).

What did become increasingly apparent was that the large variation in the time to resumption of fertility was related to the suckling behaviour of the baby and was probably not a controllable variable. Indeed, each mother–infant pairing was unique and the time to resumption of fertility in the same mother in a subsequent lactation was not predictable, depending instead on the baby. In some instances, where the duration of infertility was short, this was related to a poorly established lactation. In our own studies, regular visits by a midwife with knowledge and ability to help mothers breastfeed properly led to a natural extension of the period of suppression of fertility, but only where the baby wished to continue suckling (Howie et al., 1981a). In a controlled study in Chile where mothers were encouraged to increase the number of times a baby was breastfed each day, there was no effect on resumption of fertility (Diaz et al., 1988). In this case, the babies reduced the duration of each suckling episode such that the total suckling input per day remain unaltered. Our studies in Edinburgh illustrated that both the suckling frequency and the duration of suckling were important, allowing us to determine minimum criteria for both which would protect against fertility (McNeilly *et al.*, 1983a). These were similar in other studies of Westernised women. However, the pattern of suckling activity in different societies varies enormously, from very frequent suckling for very short periods as in the !Kung hunter-gatherers to the standard Western pattern of five or six times per day (see McNeilly, 1993, 1994). It has been very difficult to establish clear and universal guidelines for women to predict the time of onset of fertility by monitoring changes in the pattern of suckling. In part, this was due to inconsistent definitions of full and partial breastfeeding, supplements, etc. which have now been defined but the definitions may not be universally accepted (Labbok and Krasovec, 1990). In addition, where mothers sleep with their babies, or suckling occurs frequently, keeping accurate records becomes impractical or impossible.

In an attempt to determine whether any guidelines could be drawn up to allow breastfeeding to be included as a contraceptive with a degree of predictability, a meeting was held in Italy in 1988 in which all the available evidence world-wide was assembled and the Bellagio Concensus developed (Kennedy *et al.*, 1989). It was concluded that precise definitions of suckling patterns were not possible because of the difficulty in ensuring both correct collection of the information and consistency in defining a breastfeeding episode. Thus three easily defined criteria were evaluated: the continuation of lactational amenorrhoea, full or nearly full breastfeeding without addition of supplements and a lactation duration of 6 months. It was concluded that if all three criteria were fulfilled, then the efficacy of breastfeeding as a contraceptive was equal to that of most contraceptives. More recently it has been shown that there is only a small increase in pregnancy rate if only lactation amenorrhoea up to 6 months is used (Kennedy and Visness, 1992).

Thus in spite of the immense variation in the pattern of breastfeeding throughout the world, it has been possible to define circumstances which will allow women in at least some parts of the world to use breastfeeding as a reliable means of birth spacing. It also allows women to delay using other methods of contraception until necessary during breastfeeding. However, the major variability in breastfeeding remains the pattern of suckling of the infant. Since this is directly related to the availability of milk, and the pattern of suckling controls the resumption of fertility, it is clearly important to discuss briefly some of the elements essential for the establishment of successful lactation.

MAKING MILK

During pregnancy, the breast undergoes remodelling from predominantly connective and adipose tissue with limited glandular tissue to a gland dominated by alveoli containing hypertrophied cells (see Glasier and McNeilly, 1990). These changes are co-ordinated by steroids which also inhibit milk secretion until delivery. Plasma concentrations of prolactin increase through pregnancy and delivery stimulates milk production by the alveolar cells when plasma concentrations of progesterone fall after delivery of the placenta (Howie *et al.*, 1980; Glasier and McNeilly, 1990). The increase in milk production is gradual and is completely dependent on prolactin since suppression of prolactin causes total inhibition of milk production. Suckling causes the release of prolactin throughout lactation and occurs at the initiation of lactation. However, plasma concentrations of prolactin are normally extremely high, some 10- to 100- fold higher than during the menstrual cycle, allowing the initiation of milk production (lactogenesis) without the need for an increase in prolactin secretion during suckling (Howie *et al.*, 1980). However, suckling is required to remove milk from the breast since a homeostatic mechanism appears to exist whereby factors accumulated in milk can prevent further milk secretion (Wilde and Peaker,1990). It appears that there is rarely an endocrinal reason for a failure to establish lactation. It is possible that a delay in the onset of suckling may lead to a reduction in, or even failure of, milk production. However, in a study in Thailand where breastfeeding is the accepted way of feeding the baby, a delay of up to three days before suckling was established did not affect the subsequent lactation (Amatayakul *et al.*, 1991).

Although milk may be produced, the majority remains in the breast unless it is actively ejected by the release of oxytocin which contracts the myoepithelial cells surrounding the alveolar cells and run longitudinally along the ducts causing expulsion of stored milk (Glasier and McNeilly, 1990). Without oxytocin only about 20 per cent of the milk in the breast is available to the baby. While oxytocin is released in response to suckling, there is also a substantial release before nipple stimulation (McNeilly *et al.*, 1983b) and spontaneous release of oxytocin in the absence of the baby (McNeilly and McNeilly, 1978). The release of oxytocin can be inhibited by stress (Wakerley *et al.*, 1988). Since oxytocin is essential for milk let-down, stress-induced inhibition of release will lead to failure of delivery of milk to the baby, increasing the stress on the mother, further failure of oxytocin release and failure of lactation. Intervention using nasal oxytocin to ensure milk ejection has dramatically improved lactation (Ruis *et al.*, 1991).

The speed of delivery of milk, estimated by the time a baby suckles to achieve a complete feed, varies considerably. We found mother–infant combinations who were very fast feeders having a full feed within 6–7 minutes while others required up to 30 minutes (Howie *et al.*, 1981b). Since the amount of suckling is the controller of the duration of infertility, it is not difficult to appreciate the unpredictability of the effect of breastfeeding on fertility. Thus the use of a marker ovarian inactivity, the lack of menses, is a more reliable index of resumption of fertility since this is a bioassay of ovarian activity.

During lactation, milk production is maintained by prolactin released in response to every suckling episode. Within a few weeks postpartum the normal increase in prolactin during sleep resumes and the amount of prolactin released at night is greater than during the day (Glasier *et al.*, 1984a; Tay *et al.*, 1992). The amount of prolactin released is very variable. While it has been suggested that more prolactin is released during each suckling episode in women with a long duration of amenorrhoea (Diaz *et al.*, 1989, 1991), we have been unable to confirm this (Tay *et al.*, 1992). The amount of prolactin released appears to relate to the intensity of suckling and a greater release of prolactin may, therefore, reflect a greater suckling stimulus, i.e. it is secondary to a direct inhibitory effect of suckling on ovarian activity. Prolactin release during lactation remains under dopaminergic control but is not apparently controlled by opiates in women, in contrast other species including primates (Tay *et al.*, 1993; McNeilly, 1994). Increasing prolactin concentrations by giving dopamine antagonists can improve lactation and would potentially prolong lactational infertility by maintaining suckling. Interestingly, in malnourished women (Lunn, 1985) and underfed red deer (Loudon *et al.*, 1983), basal levels of prolactin are higher than normal. This appears to be due to an increase in suckling frequency required to obtain adequate quantities of milk when the rate of milk production is reduced.

In summary, there is little or no endocrinal or physiological reason for lactation failure in most women. The most vulnerable mechanism appears to be stress-induced failure of oxytocin release and this can be overcome by the use of oxytocin. The duration of suckling is very specific to each mother and baby and attempts at increasing suckling activity are probably doomed to failure. The baby controls suckling to maintain a reasonably steady intake of milk. Provision of nutrient other than breast milk will reduce the requirement of milk and reduce suckling time, if not frequency. Similarly, increasing frequency will usually result in a decrease in the duration of each suckling episode to maintain the same overall level of milk intake.

SUCKLING SUPPRESSES THE RESUMPTION OF FERTILITY

The reproduction changes which make up the interbirth interval are illustrated in Figure 2.1. Only two components have a finite time period, the initial phase of recover of the hypothalamo-pituitary-ovarian-uterine system after pregnancy, and the pregnancy before the birth of the next child. During breastfeeding there is a period of amenorrhoea of variable duration before a further variable period of menstrual cycles. In fact, mothers can ovulate and become pregnant during amenorrhoea (McNeilly *et al.*, 1983a) so that they do not have a menstrual period at all between births, even though there may be a prolonged interbirth interval. In most cases, pregnancies occurring during lactational amenorrhoea rarely occur before 6 months postpartum (Kennedy *et al.*, 1989; Kennedy and Visness, 1992) and are often related to an abrupt decrease in breastfeeding (McNeilly *et al.*, 1983a).

During the normal menstrual cycle the hypothalamus controls reproduction by regulating the release of gonadotrophin-releasing hormone (GnRH), released in pulses 1–4 hours apart, and reaching the pituitary via the hypophyseal portal blood system where GnRH maintains synthesis of luteinising hormone (LH) and follicle stimulating hormone (FSH). Each pulse of GnRH also releases a pulse of LH and FSH which

Components of the Interbirth Interval

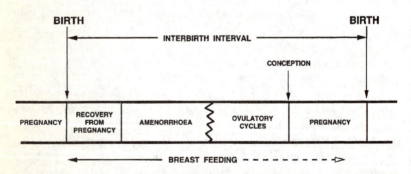

Figure 2.1   Ovulatory menstrual cycles may resume while breastfeeding continues, although fertility rates tend to be lower during these menstrual cycles than in non-breastfeeding women. Conception may occur during lactational amenorrhoea though rarely before 6 months postpartum, and is often associated with an abrupt decline in suckling activity before ovulation and conception

act in concert to stimulate the growth and steroid secretion of the follicle. Growth is principally under FSH control while LH promotes androgen secretion by the theca of the follicle which is then converted to oestradiol by the granulosa cells. The preovulatory Graafian follicle is 18–120 mm in diameter and at this size produces sufficient oestradiol to trigger the preovulatory LH surge to induce ovulation and release of the egg. The follicle transforms into the corpus luteum and secretes principally progesterone under the influence of LH pulses released at a frequency of four to ten per 24 h, considerably slower than the follicular phase frequency of one per hour.

During pregnancy the high concentrations of placental steroids inhibit GnRH release resulting in an inhibition of LH synthesis such that at term the content of LH is only 1 per cent of normal (De la Lastra and Llados, 1977). Only small follicles are present in the ovary at term (Govan, 1970). In the absence of suckling, normal secretion of LH and FSH recovers gradually and is normal by 4–6 weeks postpartum (see McNeilly, 1993). The increase in FSH and resumption of pulsatile LH release results in follicle growth and ovulation with luteal function which is often inadequate, followed by menses at around 9 weeks postpartum. In contrast, in women who breastfeed, pulsatile secretion of LH is almost absent (Tay *et al.*, 1992) or of very low amplitude (Nunley *et al.*, 1991) at 4 weeks postpartum. By 8 weeks, the majority of women show pulsatile release of LH but from this time and throughout lactational amenorrhoea, the pattern of pulsatile LH release is irregular, only returning to a regular pattern of hourly pulses around the time of first ovulation (Tay *et al.*, 1992). In contrast, plasma concentrations of FSH return to within the normal range by 4 weeks postpartum, although there is no evidence of follicle growth at this time (Glasier *et al.*, 1984b, 1986). Oestradiol secretion (the major product and indicator of follicle growth) remains low throughout most of lactational amenorrhoea, although there are occasional increases in oestradiol during this amenorrhoea (McNeilly *et al.*, 1985). While this has been interpreted as indicating an absence of follicle growth, this may not be the case. Ultrasound scanning of the ovaries during lactation has shown the presence of follicles up to preovulatory size in some women even though oestradiol remains low (Flynn *et al.*, 1991). These results suggest that FSH is sufficient to stimulate follicle growth but that the slow pulsatile release of LH is insufficient to maintain high levels of steroid production by the follicle. Replacement of GnRH by hourly administration by pulsatile pump results in the growth and normal pattern of secretion of oestradiol in breastfeeding women (Glasier *et al.*, 1986). This confirms that the lack of normal steroid production is due to a lack of LH and not due to an intrinsic lack of sensitivity of the ovary to gonadotrophins. Indeed, ovarian activity can be stimulated during lactation by amounts of exogenous gonadotrophins similar to those of non-lactating women (Zarate *et al.*, 1972).

These results suggest that suckling prevents the normal growth and development of the ovarian follicle by disrupting the normal regular hourly pattern of GnRH release from the hypothalamus and hence the pulsatile release of LH from the pituitary. This limits follicle growth by reducing androgen production by the follicle and hence oestradiol production. Only when suckling declines below a threshold does near-normal pulsatile secretion of GnRH and LH release resume and normal follicle growth resume.

Once follicle growth has resumed, ovulation may take place but is often accompanied by abnormal or reduced corpus luteum function (McNeilly *et al.*, 1982, 1983a). The failure of normal luteal function, or even lack of ovulation, appears to relate to a suckling-induced alteration in the positive feedback effect of oestradiol. During the normal menstrual cycle the preovulatory LH surge is released in response to the progressive increase in plasma concentrations of oestradiol from the developing preovulatory follicle. This generates a large release of GnRH from the hypothalamus and the production of the preovulatory surge. Injection of oestradiol, which mimics the normal preovulatory oestradiol rise, will induce the release of an LH surge positive feedback. However, during lactation, exogenous oestradiol fails to release an LH surge (i.e. positive feedback is inhibited) and there is a greater than normal suppression of LH release (i.e. increased negative feedback) (Baird *et al.*, 1979). We have recently shown that this is related to an oestradiol-induced inhibition of pulsatile GnRH release. Therefore, it appears that even when pulsatile release of LH resumes during breastfeeding, resulting in an increase in oestradiol secretion, this oestradiol will then feedback and reduce or inhibit further GnRH release (McNeilly *et al.*, 1985). Thus while suckling remains above the inhibitory threshold the disrupted pattern of GnRH/LH release continues to be maintained by both the suckling stimulus and the enhanced negative feedback effects of oestradiol. Once the suckling stimulus drops below the inhibitory threshold, the increased sensitivity to oestradiol diminishes and a normal pattern of pulsatile GnRH/LH can continue. Even when a preovulatory LH surge occurs and ovulation resumes, inadequate luteal function may be caused by the release of a reduced amount of LH during the preovulatory LH surge (Poindexter *et al.*, 1983; McNeilly *et al.*, 1985).

MECHANISMS INVOLVED IN THE INHIBITION OF OVARIAN FUNCTION

The mechanism(s) responsible for relaying the suckling stimulus to the GnRH neurones remain unclear. Opiates will inhibit LH release by reducing GnRH release. In some animals suckling may operate by increasing hypothalamic opiate tone (McNeilly, 1988, 1993, 1994) but there is no evidence for such an effect in primates or women (Gordon *et al.*, 1992; Tay *et al.*, 1993). Dopamine may also inhibit GnRH/LH release but blockade of dopaminergic systems with dopamine antagonists, while releasing prolactin, does not affect LH release (Tay *et al.*, 1993). Prolactin-secreting tumours are associated with reduced gonadotrophin secretion and infertility, and reduction of prolactin by treatment with dopaminergic drugs results in a return of fertility. However, it has not been possible to link suckling-related release of prolactin directly to the inhibition of LH release. Pulsatile release of LH occurs at times when suckling is or is not occurring and when prolactin levels are low or high (Tay *et al.*, 1992). In the absence of any clear relationship between prolactin and pulsatile LH release it is not possible to implicate prolactin as a causal agent.

Thus at present there is no clear pathway by which the suckling stimulus causes inhibition of the normal pattern of GnRH release. It is probable that it will involve direct neuronally-induced alterations in expression of genes within the hypothalamus associated with GnRH release such as *galanin* or *c-fos*. Clearly it will not be possible to determine whether this is the case in women.

SUMMARY

Suckling delays the resumption of ovarian cycles by disrupting the normal regular pulsatile secretion of GnRH from the hypothalamus and hence LH release from the pituitary. The reduced LH input to the ovary results in reduced ovarian steroid production but when oestradiol levels do increase there appears to be a suckling-induced increase in sensitivity to the negative feedback effects of oestradiol with subsequent reduction in GnRH/LH release. Only when suckling is reduced below a threshold can pulsatile GnRH be sustained and normal follicle growth and steroid secretion be maintained. When ovulation occurs during lactation the subsequent corpus luteum may not be normal. Thus, while menses may resume, there is an unpredictable period when luteal function may be insufficient to maintain a pregnancy. All these changes are dependent on the suckling stimulus.

The very nature of the suckling stimulus and its variability explain the difficulty in accurately predicting the duration of infertility associated with breastfeeding. It is probably not possible to alter the pattern of suckling established by the baby. Attempts to prolong infertility by increasing suckling frequency would only succeed if the duration of suckling also increased. This does not occur. Thus it appears that the optimum way of maximising the period of infertility associated with breastfeeding is to recognise when it is over and then either accept a variable period of relative fertility or use a contraceptive. Recognising that there is a very low risk of pregnancy during the first 6 months postpartum while amenorrhoea persists, at least delays the time when a contraceptive is necessary. This may not be a wise option in some societies where it is important that long interbirth intervals are maintained but the mothers are lost to follow-up after delivery. If this is the case, it may be preferable to introduce contraceptives early and not rely on breastfeeding alone unless prolonged breastfeeding is the norm.

ACKNOWLEDGEMENTS

It is a pleasure to acknowledge my collaborators with whom I have worked on lactational infertility over the years, particularly Peter Howie, Anna Glasier, Clem Tay, Peter Illingworth and Mary Houston.

REFERENCES

Amatayakul, K., Wongsawasdi, L., Munglaprukus, A., Imong, S. M., Jackson, D. A., Tansuhaj, A., Suwannarach, C. , Chiowanich, P., Woolridge, M. M. and Drewett, R. F. (1991), 'Successful sustained lactation following postpartum tubal ligation', *Advances in Contraception*, vol. 7, pp. 363–70.
Baird, D. T., McNeilly, A. S., Sawers, R. S. and Sharpe, R. M. (1979), 'Failure of estrogen-induced discharge of luteinizing hormone in lactating women', *Journal of Clinical Endocrinology and Metabolism*, vol. 49, pp. 500–6.
De La Lastra, M. and Llados, C. (1977), 'Luteinizing hormone content of the pituitary gland in pregnant and nonpregnant women', *Journal of Clinical Endocrinology and Metabolism*, vol. 44, pp. 921–3.

Diaz, S., Miranda, P., Brandeis, A., Cardenas, H. and Croxatto, H. B. (1988), 'A study on the feasibility of suppressing ovarian activity following the end of postpartum amenorrhoea by increasing the frequency of suckling', *Clinical Endocrinology*, vol. 28, pp. 525–35.

Diaz, S., Seron-Ferre, M., Cardenas, H., Schiappacasse, V., Brandeis, A. and Croxatto, H. B. (1989), 'Circadian variation of basal plasma prolactin, prolactin response to suckling, and length of amenorrhoea in nursing women', *Journal of Clinical Endocrinology and Metabolism*, vol. 68, pp. 946–55.

Diaz, S., Cardenas, H., Brandeis, A., Miranda, P., Schiappacasse, V., Salvatierra, A. M., Herreros, C., Seron-Ferre, M. and Croxatto, H. B. (1991), 'Early differences in the endocrine profile of long and short lactational amenorrhoea', *Journal of Clinical Endocrinology and Metabolism*, vol. 72, pp. 196–201.

Flynn, A., Docker, M., Brown, J. B. and Kennedy, K. I. (1991), 'Ultrasonographic patterns of ovarian activity during breastfeeding', *American Journal of Obstetrics and Gynecology*, vol. 165, pp. 2027–31.

Glasier, A. and McNeilly, A. S. (1990), 'Physiology of Lactation', in S. Franks (ed.), *Ballière's Clinical Endocrinology and Metabolism, Endocrinology of Pregnancy* (London: Ballière Tindall) pp. 379–95.

Glasier, A. F., McNeilly, A. S. and Howie, P. W. (1984a), 'The prolactin response to suckling', *Clinical Endocrinology*, vol. 21, pp. 109–16.

Glasier, A. F., McNeilly, A. S. and Howie, P. W. (1984b), 'Pulsatile secretion of LH in relation to the resumption of ovarian activity post partum', *Clinical Endocrinology*, vol. 20, pp. 415–26.

Glasier, A. F., McNeilly, A. S. and Baird, D. T. (1986), 'Induction of ovarian activity by pulsatile infusion of LHRH in women with lactational amenorrhoea', *Clinical Endocrinology*, vol. 24, pp. 243–52.

Gordon, K., Hodgen, G. D. and Richardson, D. W. (1992), 'Postpartum lactational anovulation in a nonhuman primate (*Macaca fascicularis*): endogenous opiate mediation of suckling-induced hyperprolactinaemia', *Journal of Clinical Endocrinology and Metabolism*, vol. 75, pp. 59–67.

Govan, A. D. T. (1970), 'Ovarian follicular activity in late pregnancy', *Journal of Endocrinology*, vol. 48, pp. 235–41.

Howie, P. W. and McNeilly, A. S. (1982), 'Effect of breastfeeding patterns on human birth intervals', *Journal of Reproduction and Fertility*, vol. 65, pp. 545–57.

Howie, P. W., McNeilly, A. S., McArdle, T., Smart, L. and Houston, M. J. (1980), 'The relationship between suckling induced prolactin response and lactogenesis', *Journal of Clinical and Endocrinology Metabolism*, vol. 50, pp. 670–73.

Howie, P. W., McNeilly, A. S., Houston, M. J., Cook, A. and Boyle, H. (1981a), 'Effect of supplementary food on suckling patterns and ovarian activity during lactation', *British Medical Journal*, vol. 283, pp. 757–59.

Howie, P. W., Houston, M. J., Cook, A., Smart, L., McArdle, T. and McNeilly, A. S. (1981b), 'How long should a breast feed last?', *Early Human Development*, vol. 5, pp. 71–7.

Howie, P. W., McNeilly, A. S., Houston, M. J., Cook, A. and Boyle, H. (1982a), 'Fertility after childbirth: infant feeding patterns, basal PRL levels and postpartum ovulation', *Clinical Endocrinology*, vol. 17, pp. 315–22.

Howie, P. W., McNeilly, A. S., Houston, M. J., Cook, A. and Boyle, H. (1982b), 'Fertility after childbirth: postpartum ovulation and menstruation in bottle and breast feeding mothers', *Clinical Endocrinology*, vol. 17, pp. 323–32.

Kennedy, K. I. and Visness, C. M. (1992), 'Contraceptive efficacy of lactational amenorrhoea', *Lancet*, vol. 339, pp. 227–30.

Kennedy, K. I., Rivero, R. and McNeilly, A. S. (1989), 'Consensus statement on the use of breastfeeding as a family planning method', *Contraception*, vol. 39, pp. 477–96.

Labbok, M. and Krasovec, K. (1990), 'Toward consistency in breastfeeding definitions', *Studies in Family Planning*, vol. 21, pp. 226–9.

Loudon, A. S. I., McNeilly, A. S. and Milne, J. A. (1983), 'Nutrition and lactational control of fertility in red deer', *Nature*, vol. 302, pp. 145–17.

Lunn, P. G. (1985), 'Maternal nutrition and lactational infertility: the baby in the driving seat', in J. Dobbing (ed.), *Maternal nutrition and lactational infertility* (New York: Raven Press) Nestlé Nutrition Workshop Series, vol. 9, pp. 41–50.

McNeilly, A. S. (1988), 'Suckling and the control of gonadotropin secretion', in E. Knobil and J. Neill (eds) *The Physiology of Reproduction* (New York: Raven Press) Ch. 59, pp. 232–49.

McNeilly, A. S. (1993), 'Lactational amenorrhoea', in J. P. Veldhuis (ed.), *Endocrinology and Metabolism Clinics of North America, Neuroendocrinology II* (Philadelphia: W. B. Saunders) pp. 59–73.

McNeilly, A. S. (1994), 'Suckling and the control of gonadoptropin secretion', in E. Knobil and J. Neill (eds) *The Physiology of Reproduction*, 2nd edition (New York: Raven Press) in press.

McNeilly, A. S. and McNeilly, J. R. (1978), 'Spontaneous milk ejection during lactation and its possible relevance to success of breast-feeding', *British Medical Journal*, vol. 2, pp. 466–8.

McNeilly, A. S., Howie, P. W. and Houston, M. J. (1981), 'Relationship of feeding patterns, prolactin and resumption of ovulation post-partum', in G. I. Zatuchni, M. H. Labbok and J. J. Sciarra (eds) *Research Frontiers in Fertility Regulation* (Mexico City: Harper Row), pp. 102–16.

McNeilly, A. S., Howie, P. W., Houston, M. J., Cook, A. and Boyle, H. (1982), 'Fertility after childbirth: adequacy of post-partum luteal phases', *Clinical Endocrinology*, vol. 17, pp. 609–15.

McNeilly, A. S., Glasier, A. F., Howie, P. W., Houston, M. J., Cook, A. and Boyle, H. (1983a), 'Fertility after childbirth: pregnancy associated with breast feeding', *Clinical Endocrinology*, vol. 18, pp. 167–73.

McNeilly, A. S., Robinson, I. C. A. F., Houston, M. J. and Howie, P. W. (1983b), 'Release of oxytocin and prolactin in response to suckling', *British Medical Journal*, vol. 286, pp. 257–9.

McNeilly, A. S., Glasier, A. and Howie, P. W. (1985), 'Endocrine control of lactational infertility', in J. Dobbing (ed.), *Maternal Nutrition and Lactational Infertility* (New York: Raven Press) Nestlé Nutrition Workshop Series, vol. 9, pp. 1–16.

Nunley, W. C., Urban, Evans, W. S. and J. D. Veldhuis, (1991), 'Preservation of pulsatile luteinizing hormone release during postpartum lactational amenorrhoea', *Journal of Clinical Endocrinology and Metabolism*, vol. 73, pp. 629–36.

Poindexter, A. N., Ritter, M. B. and Besch, P. K. (1983), 'The recovery of normal plasma progesterone levels in the postpartum female', *Fertility and Sterility*, vol. 39 pp. 494–9.

Ruis, H., Rolland, R., Doesburg, W., Broeders, G. and Corbey, R. (1991), 'Oxytocin enchances onset of lactation among mothers delivering prematurely', *British Medical Journal*, vol. 283, pp. 340–2.

Short, R. V. (1976), 'Lactation — the central control of reproduction', in *Ciba Foundation Symposium 45 Breast-feeding and the Mother* (Amsterdam: Elsevier/Excerpta Medica) pp. 73–86.

Tay, C. C. K., Glasier, A. F. and McNeilly, A. S. (1992), 'The twenty-four hour pattern of pulsatile luteinizing hormone, follicle stimulating hormone and prolactin release during the first eight weeks of lactational amenorrhoea in breastfeeding women', *Human Reproduction*, vol. 7, pp. 951–8.

Tay, C. C. K., Glasier, A. F. and McNeilly, A. S. (1993), 'Effect of antagonists of dopamine and opiates on the basal and GnRH-induced secretion of luteinizing hormone, follicle stimulating hormone and prolactin during lactational amenorrhoea in breastfeeding women', *Human Reproduction*, vol. 8, pp. 532–9.

Thapa, S., Short, R. V. and Potts, M. (1988), 'Breastfeeding, birth spacing and their effects on child survival', *Nature*, vol. 335, pp. 679–81.

Wakerley, J. B., Clarke, G. and Summerlee, A. J. S. (1988), 'Milk ejection and its control', in E. Knobil and J. Neill (eds), *The Physiology of Reproduction* (New York: Raven Press) pp. 2283–321.

Wilde, C. and Peaker, M. (1990), 'Autocrine control in milk secretion', *Journal of Agricultural Science*, vol. 114, pp. 235–8.

Zarate, A., Canales, E. S. and Sorio, J. (1972), 'Ovarian refractoriness during lactation in women: Effect of gonadotropin stimulation', *American Journal of Obstetrics and Gynecology*, vol. 112, pp. 1130–5.

3 Understanding Natural Variation in Human Ovarian Function

Peter T. Ellison

INTRODUCTION

At the sociocultural level human reproductive decisions are exceedingly complex. Individual motivations are influenced and constrained by partners, peers and family, by religious values and legal statutes, by individual psychology, national economic trends and geopolitical conflicts. Yet reproductive 'decisions' of a certain sort are also made at a physiological level. To an extent these physiological 'decisions' may be easier to comprehend than those at the sociocultural level in that the patterns they present may be more consistent and easier to describe, although they are not without subtleties of their own. This paper will concern itself with a subset of these physiological decisions, those that are made in the form of natural variations in female ovarian function which in turn, modulate female fecundity. It will not consider the role of lactation in modulating human ovarian function, as that will be the subject of a separate paper in this volume. Rather it will only consider ovarian function in non-pregnant, non-lactating women. Yet within this restricted context considerable variation exists that can be understood not as a pathological failure of homeostasis but as a functional adjustment of female fecundity to the likelihood of a successful reproductive outcome and the balance of competing reproductive and physiological investments.

Much of the evidence that will be presented comes from studies that I and my colleagues have conducted among populations in the United States, Zäire, Nepal, Poland and Bolivia using measurements of salivary steroids to monitor the ovarian function of ambulatory female subjects even under remote and logistically difficult conditions. The methodological aspects of these techniques have been presented elsewhere (Ellison,1988, 1983, 1994; Lipson and Ellison,1989;

22

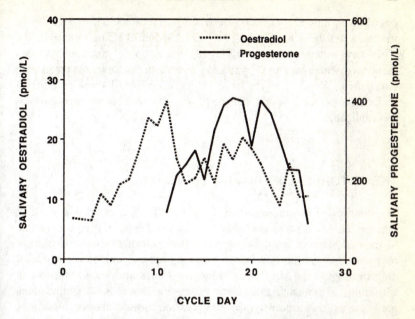

Figure 3.1 An example profile of salivary oestradiol and progesterone from a single subject aligned on menstrual onset (O'Rourke, 1992)

O'Rourke and Ellison, 1993). The information that they provide takes the form of fine-grained profiles of the principal ovarian hormones, oestradiol and progesterone, across the menstrual cycle (Figure 3.1). These profiles contain both qualitative information, for example concerning the presence or absence of an active corpus luteum, and quantitative information, such as the length of the follicular and luteal phases and the attained levels of circulating hormones. Because salivary steroid levels reflect the unbound, biologically active fraction of the total circulating steroid complement (Riad-Fahmy *et al.*, 1982), they convey more relevant information than plasma or urinary steroid measurements. Due to the very low levels in saliva, oestradiol is considerably more difficult to measure than progesterone, and our assay for oestradiol in saliva has been developed more recently (O'Rourke and Ellison, 1988; O'Rourke, 1992; O'Rourke and Ellison, 1993). Hence we have more information at present concerning variation in progesterone profiles than oestradiol profiles.

Three nested levels of variation in ovarian function will be considered in this paper: (1) variation within individual women over time and under different conditions; (2) variation between women within the same population; and (3) variation between populations. Three sources of variation will be considered as well: (1) 'random' variation unassociated with any independent variable; (2) variation in ovarian function associated with age; and (3) variation in ovarian function associated with energetics. We do not yet have information on all three sources of variation at all three levels, but the patterns we do observe appear robust and replicable.

THE CONTINUUM OF OVARIAN FUNCTION

The concept of natural variation in ovarian function is relatively recent vintage. This is in part a consequence of the disciplinary perspectives that historically have been brought to bear on the study of human reproduction. Social scientists – demographers, sociologists, social anthropologists – have been concerned primarily with the social regulation of human fertility since the time of Malthus. The Malthusian paradigm is in fact built on the idea that the 'natural checks' on human population only work through increasing mortality rates, while fertility must be constrained by social and behavioural means. If there were effective natural regulation of fertility, of the sort envisioned by Wynne-Edwards and the group selectionists, then the 'principle of population' would not hold. Rather, Malthus explicitly assumes that human fecundity is high, constant and not a limiting factor on human fertility. Where variation in fecundity is built in to proximate models of human fertility (Davis and Blake, 1956; Bongaarts and Potter, 1983), it usually appears as a potential distribution between dichotomous states; fecund, infecund; ovulation, anovulation. Rarely, if ever, does one encounter in the demographic literature a notion of underlying female fecundity as a continuous variable. Only recently have the results of waiting time to conception studies made evident the inability of dichotomous models of variation in human fecundity to adequately account for the observations (Wood *et al.*, 1992).

Medical and epidemiological research also employ a predominantly dichotomous model of variation in ovarian function. In the clinical view, the human organism exists in either of two alternative states, health or disease. Discrimination of these states is the basis of diagnosis and treatment. Human ovarian function according to this view is either normal or abnormal, healthy or pathological. Variation in function within the normal state, although perhaps acknowledged, is regarded as inconsequential. At least two unfortunate consequences follow from the adoption of this model. One is the enshrinement of the ovarian function observed among healthy, western women as a rather idealised notion of 'normal' ovarian function. The other is the use of the term 'dysfunction' to encompass almost all departures from this idealised norm.

Recent research indicates that ovarian function is more usefully considered as occurring along a graded continuum ranging from fully fecund cycles with high steroid profiles to chronic amenorrhoea and the absence of cyclic ovarian activity (Figure 3.2) (Ellison, 1990). Individual women may traverse this continuum as part of the normal processes of reproductive maturation (Apter *et al.*, 1978; Vihko and Apter, 1984; Ellison *et al.*, 1987) or ovarian senescence (O'Rourke and Ellison, 1993), or during the return to regular ovarian function after pregnancy or lactation (Howie and McNeilly, 1982). As will be detailed below, certain behavioural, constitutional variables are also associated with variation in ovarian function along this continuum. In every case, where a more extreme level of one of the variables is associated with more profound suppression of ovarian function, more moderate levels of the same variable are associated with milder, often more subtle, suppression of ovarian function.

Two features of this model of variation in ovarian function deserve particular mention. First, much of the continuum of ovarian function lies 'below' the clinical 'horizon'. That is, considerable variation in ovarian function is possible without obvious variation in menstrual function of the sort that would be apparent to a woman or her physician. Detection of this variation requires regular monitoring of follicular development and/or hormonal profiles. Second, although variation along the continuum of ovarian function may be associated with variation in fecundity, it does not

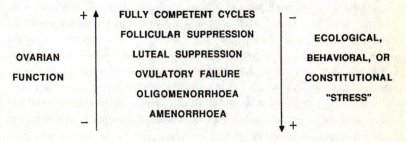

Figure 3.2 The continuum of ovarian function (Ellison, 1990)

necessarily represent 'dysfunction' in the sense of the failure of homeostatic mechanisms under stress. Rather, as I will hope to show, the consistent pattern of graded modulation of ovarian function in response to specific behavioural, constitutional and environmental variables has all the characteristics of a dose–response relationship designed by natural selection to achieve appropriate physiological regulation.

Ovarian function has two important dimensions: the production and maturation of gametes and the production of steroid hormones. The relationship of gamete production to female fecundity is perhaps obvious. But the relationship of steroid production, particularly of the two principal ovarian hormones, oestradiol and progesterone, to female fecundity is also extremely important. Oestradiol stimulates gamete maturation and follicular development, regulates activity of the hypothalamus and pituitary through feedback, stimulates endometrial proliferation and promotes the production of progesterone receptors in both granulosa and endometrial cells (Eissa, *et al.* 1986; Fritz *et al.*, 1987; Maslar, 1988; Shoham *et al.*, 1991; Dickey *et al.*, 1993). Follicular oestradiol levels are significantly correlated with the size of the dominant follicle (Apter *et al.*, 1987) and the subsequent fertilisability of the oöcyte (Yoshimura and Wallach, 1987). Levels of follicular oestradiol prior to ovarian stimulation also have been found to have a significant independent effect on the success rates of ovulation induction in achieving pregnancy (Dickey *et al.*, 1993) as well as the success of *in vitro* fertilisation procedures (Liu *et al.*, 1988). The crucial importance of luteal progesterone to the success of implantation and the maintenance of ongoing pregnancy has been underscored by the effectiveness of the synthetic progesterone antagonist, RU486, in terminating pregnancy and inducing menstruation at any time from the early luteal phase through the late second trimester (Baulieu, 1989). Short luteal phases, low luteal progesterone production and luteal phases which are poorly synchronised with follicular development and gamete maturation are all associated with low fecundity and high rates of embryonic loss (Liu *et al.*, 1988; Maslar, 1988; Stouffer, 1988; McNeely and Soules, 1988). Comparison of conception and non-conception cycles indicates that conception cycles which result in ongoing pregnancies are associated with higher progesterone both before and after implantation than are non-conception cycles, or those that result in embryonic loss (Lenton *et al.*, 1988). The characteristics of ovarian steroid profiles can thus serve as useful indices of ovarian function which can be monitored longitudinally with minimal inconvenience to study subjects.

'RANDOM' VARIATION IN OVARIAN FUNCTION

Although it would seem to be basic information, relatively little is known about the degree of 'random' variability in ovarian function within a woman over time, that is, variation not related to any other independent variable. The paucity of this information often makes clinical assessments of ovarian function difficult or ambiguous, since it is not clear to what extent a certain level of ovarian function in one cycle is predictive of ovarian function in the future (Walker *et al.*, 1984; McNeely and Soules, 1988).

Some feel for this level of variability can be gleaned from a data set drawn from one of our ongoing studies of salivary progesterone profiles. This data set consists of daily progesterone values over six consecutive menstrual cycles in each of eight Boston women. All the women are between 25 and 35 years of age, a period during which, according to our previous studies (Lipson and Ellison, 1992), there is little age-associated variation in progesterone profiles. All the subjects were within normal ranges of weight for height and were subjects in an ongoing study of waiting time to conception.

Repeated measures analysis of variance was used to compare the distribution of variance in monthly progesterone profiles within and between women. The variance between women was approximately three times as great as the variance within women, even within this relatively limited data set, and was statistically significant beyond the 0.001 level. This implies that women tend to have individually characteristic progesterone profiles and that different cycles from the same woman will tend to resemble each other more than cycles from different women. A visual impression of this distribution can be gained from Figure 3.3.

Indices of ovarian function reflecting different aspects of the overall progesterone profile and derived from the daily values can also be compared within and between women using factorial analysis of variance. Both average luteal progesterone level and average mid-luteal progesterone level (over the interval 5–9 days after the onset of the luteal progesterone rise) show significantly greater variance between than within women, although the ratio is much greater for mid-luteal progesterone (average luteal progesterone, $p < 0.05$; average mid-luteal progesterone, $p < 0.01$). The variance in the rate of rise in progesterone is also much greater between than within women ($p < 0.01$). The initial rate of rise in progesterone is significantly correlated with mid-luteal progesterone level ($r = 0.721$, $p < 0.001$), suggesting that cycles with slow initial progesterone production will also have low peak levels.

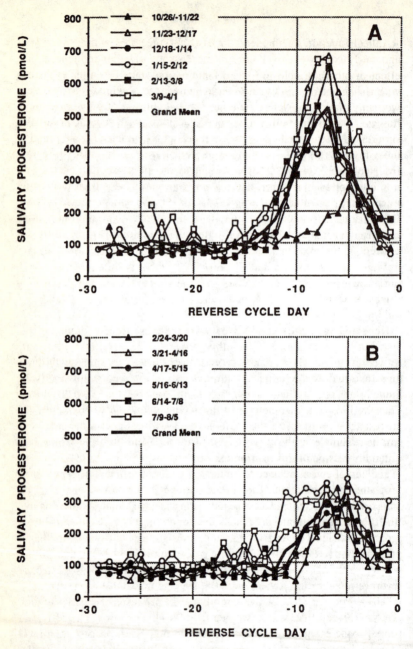

Figure 3.3 Salivary progesterone profiles for six consecutive cycles, plus the average of those cycles, for two different individuals: (A) a subject with characteristically high progesterone profiles and (B) a subject with characteristically lower progesterone profiles

Luteal function thus appears to be fairly integrated within individuals and fairly consistent over time in the absence of other influences. The effect of other variables on luteal function may thus be easier to discern within than between individuals. The significance of within- and between-woman variation in ovarian function for fecundity is not fully understood, however. In some clinical studies, women with characteristically suppressed luteal function (so-called luteal phase deficiency) are found to have higher rates of spontaneous abortion and early embryonic loss (McNeely and Soules, 1988) and comparisons of conception cycles with non-conception cycles indicate higher progesterone levels in the former even before implantation (Lenton *et al.*, 1988). The data presented here are in fact drawn from an ongoing study of the effect of variation in ovarian function within and between women on the monthly probability of conception designed to address these issues directly.

AGE VARIATION IN OVARIAN FUNCTION

In his original analyses of natural fertility, Louis Henry drew attention to the fact that the age pattern of marital fertility in natural fertility populations is remarkably constant, despite significant differences in level (Henry, 1961). He also noted that the decline in age-specific fertility rates after age 30 was associated both with an increase in the frequency of women who fail to have any subsequent birth and with increasing time intervals between births in those women who continued to bear children. This age-specific decline in natural female fertility has often been explained as a function of declining frequency of intercourse (Bongaarts and Potter, 1983; Menken *et al.*, 1986). But recent research indicates that the role of age-associated declines in underlying female fecundity may be greater than that of declining coital frequency (Weinstein *et al.*, 1990). The age-specific decline in female fecundity has been particularly apparent in age differences in the success rates of various assisted reproductive technologies, including artificial insemination by donor (Fédération CECOS, 1982), ovulation induction (McClure *et al.*, 1993; Dickey *et al.*, 1993), *in vitro* fertilization (FIVNAT, 1993) and ovum donation (Levran *et al.*, 1991), with most data indicating significant declines in female fecundity by age 35. Less attention has been given to patterns of increasing fecundity before age 25, although increases in marital age-specific fertility rates in this age range are also characteristic features of natural fertility populations.

We have studied age patterns in the salivary progesterone profiles of 136 Boston women between the ages of 18 and 48 (Lipson and Ellison, 1992; Lipson and Ellison, 1994). All the subjects were experiencing regular menstrual cycles, were of stable weight, were within normal ranges of weights for height and none engaged in regular strenuous exercise. The overall progesterone profiles showed significant differences between age groups by repeated measures analysis of variance ($p < 0.001$) and all indices of luteal function showed relationships to age that were well described by second order polynomial regressions (Figure 3.4).

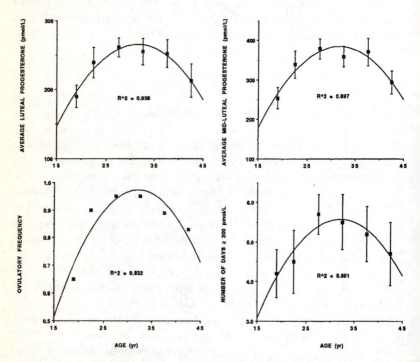

Figure 3.4   Mean (±SE where appropriate) values by age group for four indices of ovarian function from 126 Boston women (Lipson and Ellison, 1992): average luteal progesterone over the 16 days preceding menstrual onset, average mid-luteal progesterone over the interval 5–9 days before menstrual onset, ovulatory frequency and the number of days per cycle with progesterone readings $\geq$ 300 pmol/l. Regression lines are second-order polynomial regressions. In all cases both linear and quadratic terms were significant, $p < 0.001$

We have also studied age patterns of salivary oestradiol by age in 53 Boston women over 25 years of age meeting same criteria as the subjects in the progesterone study (O'Rouke and Ellison, 1993). In this case it is useful to divide the menstrual profile into three divisions aligned on the mid-cycle peak of oestradiol: a mid-follicular phase from 5 to 10 days before the mid-cycle peak, a late-follicular to mid-cycle phase from 4 days before to the day of the mid-cycle peak, and a luteal phase from 1 to 10 days after the mid-cycle peak. Declines in mid-follicular and luteal oestradiol levels are apparent in our study subjects after age 30 and are significant by repeated measures analysis of variance ($p < 0.05$) (Figure 3.5). There are no significant age differences in mid-cycle peak oestradiol levels, however, perhaps reflecting the constancy with age of the positive feedback threshold for stimulating a luteinising hormone surge. Although we do not yet have data on salivary oestradiol patterns in younger women, Apter *et al.* (1987)

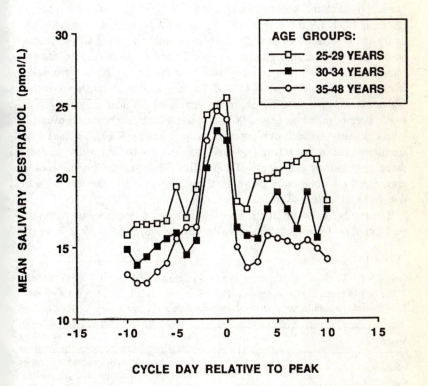

Figure 3.5   Average profiles of salivary oestradiol in 53 Boston women by age group (O'Rourke and Ellison, 1993)

have found that Swedish women in their teens characteristically have smaller dominant follicles and lower oestradiol levels than older women.

Thus it seems that ovarian function as a whole follows a parabolic trajectory with age with increasing function lasting until the early to mid-twenties and declining function evident as early as the mid-thirties. It is notable that this pattern occurs in subjects who are menstruating regularly. Indeed, the data of Treloar *et al.* (1967) on cycle length and regularity have long been cited in support of the view that ovarian function is fairly constant outside the immediate post-menarcheal and pre-menopausal years. New data such as these on variation in ovarian function with age together with the compelling evidence of declining fecundity with age in assisted reproductive technology procedures now require us to view ovarian function as a more continuous function of female age.

The very same parabolic trajectory of ovarian function by age is also displayed by women in quite disparate populations, widely divergent in geography, culture, genetic background and basic subsistence economy (Ellison, 1994; Ellison *et al.*, 1993b). Table 3.1 presents the results of an analysis of variance of average mid-luteal salivary progesterone levels across seven 5-year age groups between 15 and 50 in three populations: middle class Boston women ($n = 136$), Lese subsistence farmers from the Ituri Forest of Zaïre ($n = 144$), and Tamang agro-pastoralists from the highlands of Nepal ($n = 45$). There are significant differences by age group in all three populations ($p < 0.001$) and significant differences in average levels at every age between populations ($p < 0.001$). The absence of any significant interaction effect, however, indicates that the age patterns in the three populations are essentially parallel. This parallelism is readily apparent if a second-order polynomial regression is fit to the data in each population (Figure 3.6).

The parabolic pattern of age variation in ovarian function thus seems to be a common feature of human biology even though the average level of

Table 3.1 Two-way analysis of variance of mid-luteal salivary progesterone levels across seven 5-year age groups (15–19, 20–24, 25–29, 30–34, 35–39, 40–44, 45–49) in three populations (Boston, Lese, Tamang)

Source	F	P
Population	68.28	0.0001
Age	4.20	0.0004
Population X Age	0.35	0.9796

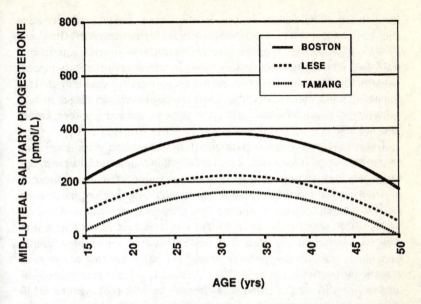

Figure 3.6   Best fit-quadratic regressions of mid-luteal salivary progesterone on age in three populations, middle-class Boston women ($n = 136$ cycles), Lese horticulturalists from Zaïre ($n = 144$) and Tamang agropastoralists from Nepal ($n = 45$). In each case both linear and quadratic terms were significant, $p < 0.001$. Overall regressions are also each significant, $p < 0.001$ (Ellison, 1993b)

ovarian function may vary widely between different populations. In fact, the combination of a constant age pattern together with differences in level is extremely reminiscent of Henry's original observations of natural fertility. In the Boston sample, other potential sources of variation in ovarian function, such as workload and energy balance, have been controlled. Similar control was not possible in Zaïre and Nepal, yet the consistency of the age pattern suggests that it is due to underlying processes of maturation and ageing common to all three populations and not to the acute effects of ecological variables that happen to be proportionately distributed by age in all three populations. It also seems likely that this consistent age pattern of ovarian function contributes to the consistent age pattern of female fertility seen in natural fertility populations.

One may also inquire concerning the functional significance of this parabolic age trajectory of ovarian function that seems such a constant feature of our species' reproductive biology, presumably the product of natural selection. In many ways it seems a counter-intuitive trajectory.

Wouldn't it better serve a woman's evolutionary fitness for her ovarian function to rise rapidly after menarche to its highest attainable level and then to maintain that level as long as possible? Why such a protracted period of increasing ovarian function over the first half of a woman's reproductive lifespan? And why such an early onset of declining ovarian function, more than a decade before menopause? Are these merely necessary constraints of the system that natural selection has been unable to overcome?

The possible functional significance of the parabolic age trajectory may be more apparent if we think of ovarian function as a variable contributing to the intensity and distribution of maternal reproductive effort. Ovarian function should be a determinant of the length of the interbirth interval, in particular a determinant of waiting time to ongoing pregnancy. Although waiting time may not be as important a determinant of total interbirth interval as the length of lactational amenorrhea, it is functionally significant as a period of reduced energy demand separating two heavily demanding periods, lactation and gestation – a brief period of 'metabolising for one' separating two periods of 'metabolising for two' in the reproductive career of a woman in a natural fertility population. Goldman *et al.* (1987) have demonstrated with World Fertility Survey data that inter-pregnancy interval durations in fact have the expected U-shaped relationship to maternal age across a broad array of populations even after correcting for the duration of lactation.

From this perspective, the parabolic trajectory of ovarian function with age seems more compatible with the standard predictions of life-history theory. Increasing ovarian function with age over the first half of the reproductive career represents a trend of increasing reproductive effort, a shift of resources in the direction of reproduction at a cost to a mother's own maintenance. The period of 'metabolising for one' shortens in the service of hastening the next pregnancy. This pattern of increasing reproductive effort is predictable as a woman's own reproductive value declines with advancing age. In mid-reproductive career the trend reverses and ovarian function begins to decline steadily, associated with longer waiting times to conception (Goldman *et al.*, 1987). This shift of resource distribution in favour of maternal maintenance is not a consequence of increasing reproductive value, which in fact continues to decline, but rather of the dependency of children already born on the continued survival of their mother. In the hypothetical instance that human offspring became fully independent at weaning, a woman would optimise her fitness by continuing to increase her reproductive effort progressively with age as her own probability of surviving to reproduce again monotonically decreases. The continued dependency of human offspring through infancy and childhood, however, renders the same strategy less than optimal, as a woman might be sacrificing the survival probabilities of children already born in the pursuit of yet another pregnancy. If mechanical constraints related to ageing oöcytes and dwindling follicular reserve further diminish the expected fitness of offspring born late in a woman's reproductive career, the scales will be tipped even more in favour of investment in children already born rather than investment in further reproduction.

Hypotheses such as these regarding the significance of life-history traits are most appropriately tested in cross-taxonomic, comparative studies beyond the scope of this paper. Yet it is perhaps worth noting that gradually declining fecundity with age is a common feature of large mammals with prolonged periods of parental investment, but not of reptiles and fish with minimal periods of parental investment.

ENERGETICS AND VARIATION IN OVARIAN FUNCTION

The preceding discussion has already introduced the notion of reproduction as an energetically demanding process. Rose Frisch deserves credit as the primary proponent of the importance of energetic constraints in human reproduction, although, as she herself notes, similar ideas are present in Darwin's own writings (Frisch, 1990). Frisch's ideas have often been expressed in rather dichotomous terms, focusing on the presence or absence of menstruation and corresponding threshold values of associated energetic variables, primarily stored body fat. This presentation resembles in its form a familiar clinical model whereby pathological or dysfunctional states are distinguished from healthy or functional ones by key diagnostic criteria. However, even for Frisch's own data the diagnostic power of body fat or other related measures to predict the menstrual status of individuals is very low (Reeves, 1979; Trussell, 1980; Ellison, 1981). Although the evidence is strong that ovarian function varies with energetic stress, it appears to do so in a continuous rather than a discontinuous fashion.

Energetic demands on human physiology can be manifest in many ways. Net energy balance or simple weight change are perhaps the best indicators of acute energetic stress, while body composition provides a more cumulative indication. Energy intake and energy expenditure also can each be assessed separately. In the present context any variable reflecting constraints on the organism's ability to invest energetically in reproduction is of interest.

Our own studies have focused on energy expenditure and weight change as correlates of ovarian function. In two studies of recreational runners in Boston we have found significantly lower salivary progesterone profiles in women who run 10–15 miles a week on average than in age-matched, sedentary controls of similar weight and height even though both runners and controls were menstruating regularly with cycles of comparable length (Ellison and Lager, 1985, 1986; Bledsoe *et al.*, 1990). Similar effects have also been reported by Shangold *et al.*, (1979). We have also found moderate weight loss of 1–1.5 kg/month in sedentary Boston women of normal weight for height to be associated with lower salivary progesterone profiles, both within and between women (Lager and Ellison, 1990). The magnitude of the weight loss is significantly correlated with the relative degree of progesterone suppression in the month following that in which the weight loss occurred, indicating a lag time in the full effect of this level of energetic stress. Studies of German women have also documented changes in ovarian function associated with voluntary dieting (Pirke *et al.*, 1985; Schweiger *et al.*, 1987).

Moderate energetic stress of this nature is also clearly associated with suppressed fecundity in American women. Epidemiological studies in the state of Washington have demonstrated that an hour a day of aerobic exercise (Green *et al.*, 1986) and a weight less than 85 per cent of standard for a given height (Green *et al.*, 1988) are both associated with an increased risk of clinical infertility in nulliparous women (relative risk = 6.2 for exercise and 4.7 for low body weight). Bates *et al.* (1982) report that simple weight gain was associated with a successful conception in, 19 of 26 patients with unexplained infertility who were also below 85 per cent of weight for height standards. Three other patients in this category declined to follow the advice to gain weight.

Energetic stresses are not limited, however, to cases of idiosyncratic and self-imposed regimes of dieting and exercise among well-off women in developed countries. In many populations energetic stresses are unavoidable consequences of subsistence economics. It is in such contexts that the ecological significance of physiological responses to energetic stress can be best appreciated. Nor is it clear, in the absence of direct evidence from such populations, that extrapolations from aerobic exercise to subsistence workloads, or from calorie restriction diets to chronic undernutrition, are valid. We have studied ovarian responses to energetic stresses related to subsistence patterns in three quite distinct populations: Lese horticulturalists of the Ituri Forest in Zaïre (Ellison *et al.*, 1986, 1989; Bailey *et al.*, 1992), Tamang agro-pastoralists of the Nepalese highlands (Panter-Brick *et al.*, 1993) and rural Polish farm women in the countryside outside Krakow (Jasienska and Ellison, 1993). Despite the differences in genetic background, geography, culture and life-style the patterns of ovarian response to energetic stress observed in all three populations are strikingly similar.

The Lese inhabit the centre of the Ituri Forest in northeast Zaïre, living in dispersed settlements loosely organised along patrilineal kinship lines located on the remains of a Belgian road transecting the forest from north to south. They practice shifting cultivation of manioc, maize, dry rice and peanuts, annually clearing, burning and planting patches of late-succession, second-growth forest. The dilapidated condition of the road has eliminated virtually all commercial trade in the central Ituri. The Lese do trade in kind with the Efe, short-statured, semi-nomadic Pygmies who cohabit the Ituri. The Efe trade meat, forest products such as honey, and labour for Lese garden produce, tobacco and occasional manufactured goods. The brief dry season during December and January provides the only opportunity for preparing new garden sites, so that the horticultural activities of the Lese, and the associated workloads, are highly synchronised in a tight seasonal pattern. The synchronised harvest, beginning with peanuts in June and extending through rice in October, together with poor environmental conditions for long-term storage of produce, results in a strong seasonal pattern of food availability as well, with a 'hunger season' preceding each year's harvest in March through May.

The regular occurrence of energetic stress in the spring, when food availability is lowest and the daily workload associated with garden cultivation is (for women) high, results in a regular seasonal pattern of energy balance observable as seasonal fluctuation in weight. In addition, the severity of the seasonal energetic stress can vary year to year depending on climatological and ecological conditions. If the rains ending the dry season begin earlier than usual, new gardens are smaller, or old gardens of reduced fertility may have to be replanted. If the rains begin later than usual, germination of the new crops may be adversely affected resulting in reduced yields. Other unpredictable circumstances, such as the locust infestation that affected the entire Ituri region in 1989, can also produce large year-to-year differences in the intensity of the energetic stress faced by the Lese population.

We have observed that ovarian function among Lese women is reduced in response to periods of negative energy balance (Ellison *et al.*, 1989; Bentley *et al.*, 1990; Bailey *et al.*, 1992). Because of the poor harvest in the summer of 1984 many women lost weight during the period from July to November (Ellison *et al.*, 1989). Women who lost 2 kg or more during this period had lower progesterone levels and lower frequency of ovulation than women who lost less than 2 kg or gained weight during the same period. Similarly, women with poorer nutritional status at the beginning of this period, as assessed by weight for height, displayed poorer indices of ovarian function than those with better nutritional status. Overall, the ovulatory frequency among all Lese women decline steadily throughout the period of weight loss (Figure 3.7). During the hunger season of 1989 a similar suppression of ovarian function was observed (Bentley *et al.*, 1990; Bailey *et al.*, 1992). Average body weight declined

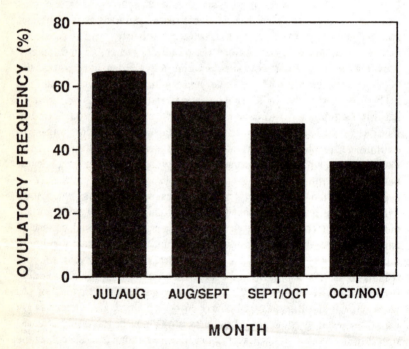

Figure 3.7   Ovulatory frequency by month among Lese women in 1984, assessed from salivary progesterone profiles (Ellison *et al.*, 1989)

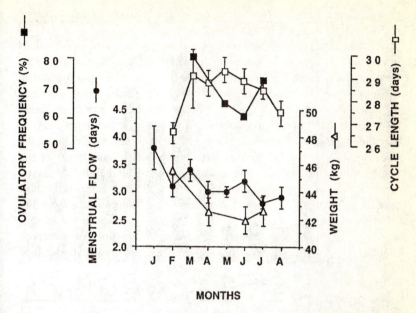

Figure 3.8   Mean values (±SE where appropriate) for ovulatory frequency, days of menstrual flow, weight and cycle length for Lese women by month in 1989 (Bailey *et al.*, 1992)

steadily from February through June with slight increases evident by July. Parallel to this trend in energy balance was a decline and rebound in ovulatory frequency, a decline and slight increase in the duration of menstrual bleeding (a bioassay of endometrial thickness reflecting oestrogenic stimulation) and an increase and subsequent decline in average cycle length (Figure 3.8).

The impact of these seasonal effects on Lese fertility is apparent from the analysis of 10 years of vital event data (Bailey *et al.*, 1992). Births among the Lese are significantly seasonal. The monthly conception rate drops during the late spring, rebounding again after the June harvest (Figure 3.9). The dearth of conceptions in this period is significantly stronger in those years with the most profound weight loss than in those years with milder hunger seasons. Thus both the seasonal and the annual variation in conception reflect the distribution and severity of energetic stress suffered by the population. Interestingly, the Efe, who are subject to all the same meteorological and environmental conditions as the Lese, do not show either a seasonal pattern of energetic stress or a seasonal pattern

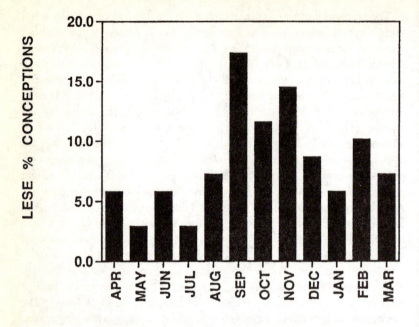

Figure 3.9 Monthly distributions of conceptions (birth dates minus 9 months) for Lese women between January 1980 and August 1987 (Bailey *et al.*, 1992)

of conceptions. Presumably their mobile, hunting and gathering life-style buffers them to a certain extent from the variable energetic stresses that are a consequence of the Lese subsistence regime.

The Tamang are the largest ethnic group of the central highlands of Nepal, inhabiting an altitudinal zone between 1350 and 3800 m above sea level. They cultivate wet rice, maize, wheat, barley and millet on terraced fields and keep herds of goats which are moved among different grazing zones according to season. Workload for Tamang women is both heavy and seasonal and the demands of seasonal subsistence labour often constrain the time available for all other activities, including childcare and the nursing of infants (Panter-Brick, 1993). The monsoon season is a period of particular constraint as female participation in group labour is necessary for the transplanting of rice seedlings in the paddies.

The seasonal pattern of energetic stress in the Tamang population is not highly synchronised, as it is among the Lese. Although the summer monsoon season appears to be the most energetically demanding (Panter-Brick, 1993), the average weight change among all adult Tamang women between the winter of 1990 and the summer of 1991 was not significantly different from zero (Panter-Brick *et al.*, 1993). Yet indices of average ovarian function decline over the same period. The absence of any change in average weight, however, obscures considerable individual variance in energy balance. Individual changes in ovarian function are associated with individual energy balance, with significant suppression of progesterone profiles and associated indices among women who lost weight and no significant change among women who gained weight (Figure 3.10). Age differences in the distributions of both energy balance and ovarian function were also observed. Young women under the age of 23 years were the least likely to lose weight or show suppression of ovarian function, women in the mid-reproductive years (23–35 years) the most likely.

In the southern Polish countryside agriculture is still largely unmechanised. Family fields are scattered across a hilly landscape, planted with rye, oats and potatoes, with others used for hay and pasturage. The preparation of the fields is largely done with draft animals while many tasks, such as haying, are accomplished manually. All able-bodied adult members of the family of both sexes are involved in agricultural labour. During the winter, the agricultural workload is much lower, though domestic tasks still keep women employed from before dawn until after sunset.

Thus for Polish farm women, as for the Lese and the Tamang, subsistence workloads are heavy with pronounced seasonality. Yet unlike the Lese and the Tamang, the nutritional status of Polish women is quite high and food availability is more or less constant year-round. We have initiated a study of energetics and ovarian function among this population as well in order to determine whether effects similar to those observe in Zaïre and Nepal are observable even under generally favourable energetic conditions, or whether they only occur in situations of chronic nutritional stress (Jasienska and Ellison, 1993). In a pilot study, daily saliva samples were collected from 20 women for one summer month. Women were repeatedly interviewed and categorised into high and moderate workload groups on the basis of the temporal distribution of daily activities. Workloads varied considerably between women depending on the size and location of family fields and the amount help available. Women in the high workload category had progesterone profiles significantly lower than those in the moderate workload category (Figure 3.11) despite being of

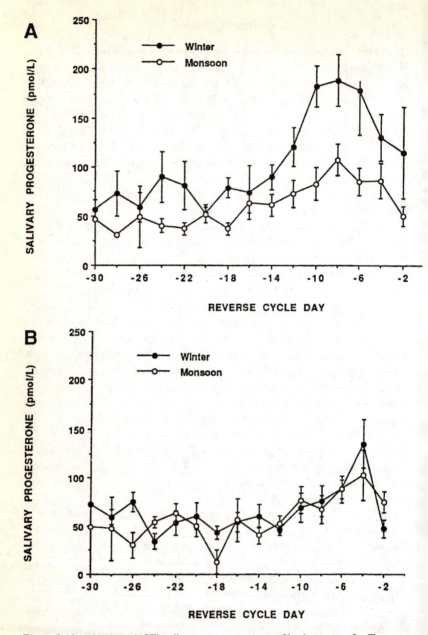

Figure 3.10 Average (±SE) salivary progesterone profiles by season for Tamang women in 1990–91. (A) Profiles for women who lost weight between the winter and the monsoon. (B) Profiles for women who gained weight between the winter and the monsoon (Panter-Brick *et al.*, 1993)

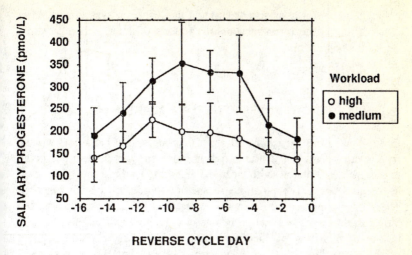

Figure 3.11   Average (±SE) salivary progesterone profiles for 20 rural Polish farm women categorised by the intensity of their subsistence workloads (Jasienska and Ellison, 1993)

similar age, weight and weight for height. We are currently analysing samples from the definitive phase of the project which will enable us to compare ovarian function within and between women both during the agricultural season and during the winter.

Results from these three distinctly different populations indicate that human ovarian function does vary with energetic stress, whether that stress is occasioned by variations in food availability and energy intake, variations in workload and energy expenditure, or a combination of the two. Variation in ovarian function in each population is relative to the level of ovarian function typical for that population and does not appear to be limited to situations of chronic undernutrition. In functional terms it is hard to avoid the hypothesis that the modulation of ovarian function in response to energetic constraints represents an adjustment of reproductive effort in relation to the fraction of total metabolic energy available to invest in reproduction. The studies of Prentice and Whitehead and their colleagues in the Gambia have demonstrated elegantly that substantial energetic investment begins from the moment of conception (Prentice and Whitehead, 1987), so that acute energy balance during the periconception period can be crucial to reproductive success as well as predictive of energy availability in the near future. Phenomena like the birth seasonality of the Lese should thus not be interpreted as the consequences of a system designed to synchronise births with a particular season, but as an epiphenomenon of a subsistence system that causes a synchronisation of conception failure by synchronising periods of acute energetic stress across the population.

INTER-POPULATION DIFFERENCES IN OVARIAN FUNCTION

In addition to the variation in ovarian function within individual women from cycle to cycle and the variation between women within a given population associated with age and energetics, there are significant differences between populations in average indices of ovarian function. These inter-population differences are apparent in the comparison of the trajectories of ovarian function by age in Figure 3.6 and can also be seen in the comparison of the composite average progesterone profiles presented in Figure 3.12 (Ellison *et al.*, 1993a). Differences also exist between Boston and Zaïre in average levels of salivary oestradiol and average duration of menstrual bleeding, which itself may reflect the degree of oestrogenic stimulation for endometrial proliferation in the follicular phase (Bentley *et al.*, 1990). Similar differences in levels of ovarian steroids have been noted between British and Thai adolescents by Danutra *et al.* (1989). It appears that in different populations different baseline levels of ovarian function are established and that other patterns of variation, associated with age or energetics for example, are observable relative to these baselines. This is similar to the way that individual women differ in their characteristic hormonal profiles with individual variation occurring relative to these baselines.

However, neither the significance nor the aetiology of inter-population differences in ovarian function is well understood. It is tempting to speculate that population differences in ovarian function reflect differences in underlying fecundity, but the data on comparative waiting times to conception necessary to test this hypothesis are lacking. The consistency of the differences in level of ovarian function across different ages (Figure 3.6) makes it seem more likely that they reflect differences in established features of adult ovarian function rather than acutely generated differences that happen to be proportionally distributed by age. This could occur as a consequence of differences in chronic conditions during growth and development that might lead to the establishment of different adult setpoints for feedback regulation within the hypothalamic-pituitary-ovarian (HPO) axis, for example. Evidence from Sweden (Apter and Vihko, 1983) and Italy (Venturoli *et al.*, 1987) suggests that the late-

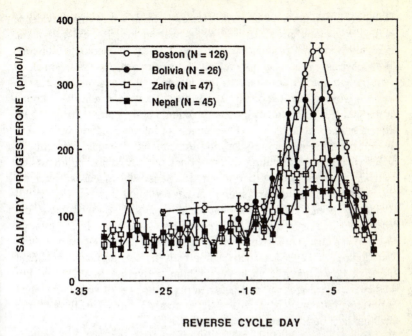

Figure 3.12   Average (±SE) salivary progesterone profiles for women from four
populations, middle-class Boston women, Quechua Indians of
highland Bolivia, Lese horticulturalists from Zaïre, and Tamang
agro-pastoralists from Nepal (Ellison *et al.*, 1993a)

maturing women within these populations continue to have lower indices
of ovarian function well into their adult reproductive years. If similar
developmental effects also pertain to inter-population differences in
reproductive maturation they might help account for differences in
baseline levels of adult ovarian function. Evidence has also been presented
to suggest that population differences in steroid metabolism might exist
(Bentley, 1994). By themselves, however, these differences could not
generate the observed baseline differences in ovarian steroid profiles
unless feedback relationships within the HPO axis were also altered. More
rapid steroid turnover would lead to a weaker level of negative feedback at
the hypothalamus and pituitary which would in turn result in stimulation
to increase steroid production until target circulating levels were achieved.
Yet it may be that altered steroid metabolism is one of a suite of changes
in reproductive physiology that together produce inter-population
differences in ovarian function.

At this point, the most important lesson to be drawn from the evidence is that inter-population differences in ovarian function exist, that the idealised hormonal profiles presented in medical textbooks to illustrate 'the menstrual cycle' may only reflect observations that have been made in western women. A corollary to this lesson is that ovarian function in western women, such as our Boston subjects, may represent one extreme of the global distribution of ovarian function, not the norm (Ellison, 1994; Ellison *et al.*, 1993a, b). The consequences of inter-population variation in ovarian function may ramify beyond the context of female fecundity as well, potentially contributing to inter-population differences in breast and ovarian cancers and other oestrogen-sensitive diseases such as osteoporosis and cardiovascular disease (Cummings *et al.*, 1985; Henderson *et al.*, 1988; Kelsey and Gammon, 1991; Barret-Connor and Bush, 1991). Progesterone differences may affect levels of immune function and susceptibility to sexually transmitted disease (Su *et al.*, 1988; Tau-Cody *et al.*, 1988). Understanding both the aetiology and functional significance of natural variation in human ovarian function, within women, between women, and between populations, will very likely shed important light on general issues of women's health as well as on the physiological basis of 'reproductive decision'.

ACKNOWLEDGEMENTS

I thank Robert Bailey, Gillian Bentley, Alisa Harrigan, Grazyna Jasianska, Catherine Lager, Susan Lipson, Deborah Lotstein, Mary O'Rouke, Nadine Peacock, Sara Sukalich and Virginia Vitzthum for their many substantive contributions to the work reviewed here. I also thank the women of Boston, Zaïre, Nepal, Poland and Bolivia who have graciously aided us in our studies. This work has been supported by the National Science Foundation, Washington, DC.

REFERENCES

Apter, D. and Vihko, R. (1983), 'Early menarche, a risk factor for breast cancer, indicates early onset of ovulatory cycles', *Journal of Clinical Endocrinology and Metabolism*, vol. 57, pp. 82–6.

Apter, D., Viinkka, L. and Vihko, R. (1978), 'Hormonal pattern of adolescent menstrual cycles', *Journal of Clinical Endocrinology and Metabolism*, vol. 47, pp. 944–54.

Apter, D., Raisanen, I., Ylostalo, P. and Vihko, R. (1987), 'Follicular growth in relation to serum hormonal patterns in adolescents compared with adult menstrual cycles', *Fertility and Sterility*, vol. 47, pp. 82–8.

Bailey, R. C., Jenike, M. R., Bentley, G. R., Harrigan, A. M. and Ellison, P. T. (1992), 'The ecology of birth seasonality among agriculturists in central Africa', *Journal of Biosocial Science*, vol. 24, pp. 393–412.

Barret-Conor, E. and Bush, T. L. (1991), 'Estrogen and coronary heart disease in women', *Journal of the American Medical Association*, vol. 265, pp. 1861–67.

Bates, G. W., Bates, S. R. and Whitworth, N. S. (1982), 'Reproductive failure in women who practice weight control', *Fertility and Sterility*, vol. 37, pp. 373–8.

Baulieu, E. E. (1989), 'Contragestion and other clinical applications of RU486, an antiprogesterone at the receptor', *Science*, vol. 245, pp. 1351–7.

Bentley, G. R., Harrigan, A. M. and Ellison, P. T. (1990), 'Ovarian cycle length and days of menstruation of Lese horticulturalists', *American Journal of Physical Anthropology*, vol. 81, pp. 193–4.

Bentley, G. R. (1994), 'Ranging hormones: do hormonal contraceptives ignore human biological variation and evolution?', *Annals of the New York Academy of Sciences*, vol. 709, pp. 201–3.

Bledsoe, R. E., O'Rourke, M. T. and Ellison, P. T. (1990), 'Characterization of progesterone profiles of recreational runners', *American Journal of Physical Anthropology*, vol. 81, pp. 195–6.

Bongaarts, J. and Potter, R. G. (1983), *Fertility, Biology, and Behavior: An Analysis of the Proximate Determinants* (New York: Academic Press).

Cummings, S. R., Kelsey, J. L., Nevitt, M. C. and O'Dowd, K. J. (1985), 'Epidemiology of osteoporosis and osteoporotic fractures', *Epidemiologic Review*, vol. 7, pp. 178–208.

Danutra, V., Turkes, A., Read, G.F., Wilson, D. W., Griffiths, V., Jones, R. and Griffiths, K. (1989), 'Progesterone concentrations in samples of saliva from adolescent girls living in Britain and Thailand, two countries where women are at widely differing risk of breast cancer', *Journal of Endocrinology*, vol. 121, pp. 375–81.

Davis, K. and Blake, J. (1956), 'Social structure and fertility: an analytic framework', *Economic Development and Cultural Change*, vol. 4, pp. 211–35.

Dickey, R. P., Olar, T. T., Taylor, S. N., Curole, D. N. and Matulich, E. M. (1993), 'Relationship of endometrial thickness and pattern to fecundity in ovulation induction cycles: effect of clomiphene citrate alone and with human menopausal gonadotropin', *Fertility and Sterility*, vol. 59, pp. 756–60.

Eissa, M. K., Obhrai, M. S., Docker, M. F., Lynch, S. S., Sawers, R. S. and Newton, R. R. (1986), 'Follicular growth and endocrine profiles in spontaneous and induced conception cycles', *Fertility and Sterility*, vol. 45, pp. 191–5.

Ellison, P. T. (1981), 'Prediction of age at menarche from annual height increments', *American Journal of Physical Anthropology*, vol. 56, pp. 71–5.

Ellison, P. T. (1988), 'Human salivary steroids: methodological considerations and applications in physical anthropology', *Yearbook of Physical Anthropology*, vol. 31, pp. 115–42.

Ellison, P. T. (1990), 'Human ovarian function and reproductive ecology: new hypotheses', *American Anthropologist*, vol. 92, pp. 933–52.

Ellison, P. T. (1993), 'Measurements of salivary progesterone', *Annals of the New York Academy of Sciences*, vol. 694, pp. 161–76.

Ellison, P. T. (1994), 'Salivary steroids and natural variation in human ovarian function', *Annals of the New York Academy of Sciences*, vol. 709, pp. 287–98.

Ellison, P. T. and Lager, C. (1985), 'Exercise-induced menstrual disorders', *New England Journal of Medicine*, vol. 313, pp. 825–6.

Ellison, P. T. and Lager, C. (1986), 'Moderate recreational running is associated with lowered salivary progesterone profiles in women', *American Journal of Obstetrics and Gynecology*, vol. 154, pp. 1000–3.

Ellison, P. T., Peacock, N. R. and Lager, C. (1986), 'Salivary progesterone and luteal function in two low-fertility populations of northeast Zaire', *Human Biology*, vol. 58, pp. 473–83.

Ellison, P. T., Peacock, N. R. and Lager, C. (1989), 'Ecology and ovarian function among Lese women of the Ituri Forest, Zaire', *American Journal of Physical Anthropology*, vol. 78, pp. 519–26.

Ellison, P. T., Lager, C. and Calfee, J. (1987), 'Low profiles of salivary progesterone among college undergraduate women', *Journal of Adolescent Health Care*, vol. 8, pp. 204–7.

Ellison, P. T., Lipson, S. F., O'Rourke, M. T., Bentley, G. R., Harrigan, A. M. Panter-Brick, C. and Vitzthum, V. J. (1993a), 'Population variation in ovarian function', *Lancet*, vol. 342, pp. 433–4.

Ellison, P. T., Panter-Brick, C., Lipson, S. F. and O'Rourke, M. T. (1993b), 'The ecological context of human ovarian function', *Human Reproduction*, vol. 8, pp. 2248–58.

Fédération CECOS, Schwartz, D. and Mayaux, M. J. (1982), 'Female fecundity as a function of age', *New England Journal of Medicine*, vol. 306, pp. 404–6.

FIVNAT (1993), 'French national IVF registry: analysis of 1986 to 1990 data', *Fertility and Sterility*, vol. 59, pp. 587–95.

Frisch, R. E. (1990), 'Body fat, menarche, fitness and fertility', in R. E. Frisch (ed.), *Adipose Tissue and Reproduction* (Basel: Karger) pp. 1–26.

Fritz, M. A., Westfahl, P. K. and Graham, R. L. (1987), 'The effect of luteal phase estrogen antagonism on endometrial development and luteal function in women', *Journal of Clinical Endocrinology and Metabolism*, vol. 65, pp. 1006–13.

Goldman, N., Westhoff, C. F. and Paul, L. E. (1987), 'Variations in natural fertility: the effect of lactation and other determinants', *Population Studies*, vol. 41, pp. 127–46.

Green, B. B., Daling, J. R., Weiss, N. S., Liff, J. M. and Koepsell, T. (1986), 'Exercise as a risk factor for infertility with ovulatory dysfunction', *American Journal of Public Health*, vol. 76, pp. 1432–6.

Green, B. B., Weiss, N. S. and Daling, J. R. (1988), 'Risk of ovulatory infertility in relation to body weight', *Fertility and Sterility*, vol. 50, pp. 721–6.

Henderson, B. E., Ross, R. K. and Bernstein, L. (1988), 'Estrogens as a cause of human cancer: the Richard and Hilda Rosenthal Foundation Award Lecture', *Cancer Research*, vol. 48, pp. 246–53.

Henry, L. (1961), 'Some data on natural fertility', *Eugenics Quarterly*, vol. 8, pp. 81–91.

Howie, P. W. and McNeilly, A. S. (1982), 'Effect of breast feeding patterns on human birth intervals', *Journal of Reproduction and Fertility*, vol. 65, pp. 545–57.

Jasienska, G. and Ellison, P. T. (1993), 'Heavy workload impairs ovarian function in Polish peasant women', *American Journal of Physical Anthropology Supplement*, vol. 16, pp. 117–8.

Kelsey, J. L. and Gammon, M. D. (1991), 'The epidemiology of breast cancer', *CA-Cancer Journal for Clinicians*, vol. 41, pp. 146–65.

Lager, C. and Ellison, P. T. (1990), 'Effects of moderate weight loss on ovarian function assessed by salivary progesterone measurements', *American Journal of Human Biology*, vol. 2, pp. 303–12.

Lenton, E. A., Gelsthorp, C. H. and Harper, R. (1988), 'Measurement of progesterone in saliva: assessment of the normal fertile range using spontaneous conception cycles', *Clinical Endocrinology*, vol. 38, pp. 637–46.

Levran, D., Ben-Shlomo, I., Dor, J., Ben-Rafael, Z., Nebel, L. and Mashiach, S. (1991), 'Aging of endometrium and oocytes: observations and conception and abortion rates in an egg donation model', *Fertility and Sterility*, vol. 56, pp. 1091–4.

Lipson, S. F. and Ellison, P. T. (1989), 'Development of protocols for the application of salivary steroid analyses to field conditions', *American Journal of Human Biology*, vol. 1, pp. 249–55.

Lipson, S. F. and Ellison, P. T. (1992), 'Normative study of age variation in salivary progesterone profiles', *Journal of Biosocial Science*, vol. 24, pp. 233–44.

Lipson, S. F. and Ellison, P. T. (1994), 'Reference values for luteal progesterone measured by salivary radioimmunoassay', *Fertility and Sterility*, vol. 61, pp. 448–54.

Liu, H. C., Jones, G. S., Jones, H. W., Jr and Rosenwaks, Z. (1988), 'Mechanisms and factors of early pregnancy wastage in *in vitro* fertilization–embryo transfer patients', *Fertility and Sterility*, vol. 50, pp. 95–101.

Maslar, I. A. (1988), 'The progestational endometrium', *Seminars in Reproductive Endocrinology*, vol. 6, pp. 115–28.

McClure, N., McDonald, J., Kovacs, G. T., Healy, D. L., McCloud, P. I., McQuinn, B. and Burger, H. G. (1993), 'Age and follicular phase estradiol are better predictors of pregnancy outcome than luteinizing hormone in menotropin ovulation induction for anovulatory polycystic ovarian syndrome', *Fertility and Sterility*, vol. 59, pp. 729–33.

McNeely, M. J. and Soules, M. R. (1988), 'The diagnosis of luteal phase deficiency: a critical review', *Fertility and Sterility*, vol. 50, pp. 1–15.

Menken, J., Trussell, J. and Larsen, U. (1986), 'Age and infertility', *Science*, vol. 233, pp. 1389–94.

O'Rourke, M. T. (1992), *Human Ovarian Function in Late Reproductive Life*, PhD dissertation, Harvard University (Ann Arbor:University Microfilms).

O'Rourke, M. T. and Ellison, P. T. (1988), 'Salivary estradiol in the human menstrual cycle', *American Journal of Physical Anthropology*, vol. 75, p. 255.

O'Rourke, M. T. and Ellison, P. T. (1993), 'Salivary estradiol levels decrease with age in healthy, regularly-cycling women', *Endocrine Journal*, vol. 1, pp. 487–94.

Panter-Brick, C. (1993), 'Seasonality of energy expenditure during pregnancy and lactation for rural Nepali women', *American Journal of Clinical Nutrition*, vol. 57, pp. 620–8.

Panter-Brick, C., Lotstein, D. S. and Ellison, P. T. (1993), 'Seasonality of reproductive function and weight loss in rural Nepali women', *Human Reproduction*, vol. 8, pp. 684–90.

Pirke, K. M., Schweiger, U., Lemmel, W., Krieg, J. C. and Berger, M. (1985), 'The influence of dieting on the menstrual cycle of healthy young women', *Journal of Clinical Endocrinology and Metabolism*, vol. 60, pp. 1174–9.

Prentice, A. M. and Whitehead, R. G. (1987), 'The energetics of human reproduction', *Symposium of the Zoological Society of London*, vol. 57, pp. 275–304.

Reeves, J. (1979), 'Estimating fatness', *Science*, vol. 204, p. 881.

Riad-Fahmy, D., Read, G. F., Walker, R. F. and Griffiths, K. (1982), 'Steroids in saliva for assessing endocrine function', *Endocrine Reviews*, vol. 3, pp. 367–95.

Schweiger, U., Laessle, R., Pfister, H., Hoehl, C., Schwingenschloegel, M., Schweiger, M. and Pirke, K. M. (1987), 'Diet-induced menstrual irregularities: effects of age and weight loss', *Fertility and Sterility*, vol. 48, pp. 746–51.

Shangold, M., Freeman, R., Thyssen, B. and Gatz, M. (1979), 'The relationship between long-distance running, plasma progesterone, and luteal phase length', *Fertility and Sterility*, vol. 31, pp. 699–702.

Shoham, Z., DiCarlo, C., Patel, A., Conway, G. S. and Jacobs, H. S. (1991), 'Is it possible to run a successful ovulation induction program based solely on ultrasound monitoring? The importance of endometrial measurements', *Fertility and Sterility*, vol. 56, pp. 836–41.

Stouffer, R. L. (1988), 'Perspectives on the corpus luteum of the menstrual cycle and early pregnancy', *Seminars in Reproductive Endocrinology*, vol. 6, pp. 103–13.

Su, T., London, E. D. and Jaffe, J. H. (1988), 'Steroid binding at sigma-receptors suggests a link between endocrine, nervous, and immune systems', *Science*, vol. 240, pp. 219–21.

Tau-Cody, K. R., Campbell, W. F., Dodson, M. G. and Minhas, B. S. (1988), 'Progesterone markedly enhances *Chlamydia trachomatis* inclusions *in vitro* and results in increased inflammation and productive infection *in vivo*', *Fertility and Sterility*, vol. 50, p. S29.

Treloar, A. E., Boynton, R. E., Behn, B. G. and Brown, B. W. (1967), 'Variation of the human menstrual cycle through reproductive life', *International Journal of Fertility*, vol. 12, pp. 77–126.

Trussell, J. (1980), 'Statistical flaws in evidence for the Frisch hypothesis that fatness triggers menarche', *Human Biology*, vol. 52, pp. 711–20.

Venturoli, S., Porcu, E., Fabbri, R., Magrini, O., Paradisi, R., Pallotti, G., Gammi, L. and Famigni, C. (1987), 'Postmenarchal evolution of endocrine pattern and ovarian aspects in adolescents with menstrual irregularities', *Fertility and Sterility*, vol. 48, pp. 78–85.

Vihko, R. and Apter, D. (1984), 'Endocrine characteristics of adolescent menstrual cycles: impacts of early menarche', *Journal of Steroid Biochemistry*, vol. 20, pp. 231–6.

Walker, S. M., Walker, R. F. and Riad-Fahmy, D. (1984), 'Longitudinal studies of luteal function by salivary progesterone determinations', *Hormone Research*, vol. 20, pp. 231–40.

Weinstein, M., Wood, J., Stoto, M. A. and Greenfield, D. D. (1990), 'Components of age-specific fecundability', *Population Studies*, vol. 44, pp. 447–67.

Wood, J. W., Holman, D. J., Weiss, K. M., Buchanan, A. V. and LeFor, B. (1992), 'Hazards models for human population biology', *Yearbook of Physical Anthropology*, vol. 35, pp. 43–88.

Yoshimura, Y. and Wallach, E. E. (1987), 'Studies of the mechanism(s) of mammalian ovulation', *Fertility and Sterility*, vol. 47, pp. 22–34.

4 Nutrition, Physical Workloads and Fertility Regulation

Lyliane Rosetta

INTRODUCTION

In both men and women the major steps in the endocrinological mechanisms underlying a successful reproductive issue are now well understood, even if there are still several aspects in its regulation and impairment under scrutiny.

In human beings, men are generally able to produce adequate sperm quality and quantity at any time of the year, and the ecological pressures and/or their life-styles are unlikely to decrease fecundity to a critical level. Even if there is seasonal variation in sperm quality whatever the climate or the nutritional status (Levine *et al.*, 1990), these variations are in a range which does not jeopardise the fertility potential of a given couple (Rosetta, 1993a).

On the other hand, women have to cope with very different limiting factors: first, they are able to produce only a single ovum, exceptionally two, per menstrual cycle. Second, even for a normally fertile couple the rate of fecundability is estimated at 25 per cent (Schwartz and Mayaux, 1982). Then, even after successful conception, several conditions need to be fulfilled before a successful and normal pregnancy giving birth to an healthy infant results. The early steps of each pregnancy, which are the implantation and nidation of the ovum, are at high risk of failure, entirely dependent on an adequate production of progesterone, both in timing and in quantity.

This paper focuses on the two main limiting factors of fertility in normal healthy couples, which are both in women: first of all, they have to have an ovulatory cycle and secondly, the ovulation and conception must be followed by a normal luteal phase. During the first half of the normal menstrual cycle in primates and human females, the follicular development is stimulated by the pulsatile secretion of both gonadotrophins, the

luteinising hormone (LH) and the follicle stimulating hormone (FSH) by
the adenohypophysis, themselves under the control of the pulsatile
secretion of the gonadotrophin releasing hormone (GnRH) produced by
the mediobasal hypothalamus. According to Knobil (1988a) the
neuroendocrine control of the menstrual cycle in primates or humans is
compared to an oscillator having a period of approximately one pulse every
hour during the follicular phase. Several factors have been shown to be able
to disturb the oscillator, either in frequency or in amplitude (Thalabard,
1992). These modifications are immediately followed by a modification in
the release of the gonadotrophin, with possible modification in the ratio of
FSH/LH and their impact on the ovarian function.

This paper examines the factors, in terms of nutritional intake, physical
activity and personal characteristics of body composition and energy
storage, suspected to play a role in the regulation of the menstrual cycle. It
describes the effects of nutrition, both in quantity and in quality, at the
central and peripheral level of regulation of reproductive function. The
possible effects of strenuous physical activity are discussed, as well as the
complementary effect of nutrition and energy expenditure, in terms of
energy balance and its possible impact on the normal ovulatory process
and hormonal welfare.

NUTRITION

In mammals, including primates, there is now evidence of the effect of
nutrition on the regulation of reproductive function. In a review, I'Anson
et al. (1991) have identified the possible sites of action of nutrition within
the reproductive system, even in humans. Nutrition influences
reproduction at different stages of life: either during maturation when the
onset of puberty is delayed by undernutrition (Foster and Olster, 1985) or
during the reproductive life in adults. Several modifications in the
regulation of the reproductive function can be attributed to nutrition, some
of them related to dietary composition, others to the adequacy of the daily
food intake required to satisfy the needs of each individual. Pubertal
development and postpubertal maintenance of the ovulatory cycle are
under nutritional control: a comparison of the progesterone activity in
adolescents living in Britain and Thailand, respectively, have shown a
significantly greater progesterone activity in British girls compared to their
Thai counterparts when matched for chronological and gynaecological
ages (Danutra *et al.*, 1989).

Focusing on women during their reproductive life, experimental studies have been carried out to investigate the role of the quality of the diet on the menstrual cycle. Hill and coworkers (1984) compared the duration of the menstrual cycle after a change in the usual diet with and without meat among omnivorous Caucasian women and vegetarian South African women. In the latter group, the women were poor to middle class Black urban hospital employees, eating a typical rural diet supplemented with bread, sugar, milk and vegetables cooked in lard. In both groups the women involved in the study had regular ovulatory menstrual cycles and a proven fertility. After 2 months of transfer from their normal diet (to a vegetarian diet for the group of Caucasian, and to a diet complemented with meat each day for the group of urban Black South African women), the duration of the follicular phase was altered. The meatless vegetarian diet was associated with a shortening of the follicular phase during the second menstrual cycle among Caucasian women, with a decrease in the pulsatile release of LH and FSH, and with a decrease of the pituitary response to GnRH stimulation. Among the South African women, the 2 month transfer to a Western diet resulted in an increase in the duration of the follicular phase. In both groups, body weight was not modified at the end of the experiment, their diet having been carefully established to match the usual caloric intake in each group. Other evidence is suggestive of the impact of the vegetarian diet. For instance, Pedersen *et al.* (1991) compared traditional vegetarian women with non-vegetarian premenopausal healthy women and found a significantly higher percentage of menstrual irregularities in the group of vegetarian women compared to the non-vegetarian women.

During the last 10 years several teams of epidemiologists have compared the level of circulating steroid hormones in female populations with different habits of food consumption all over the world in an attempt to identify risk factors of breast cancer. They have shown that, in Asian populations eating a traditional mostly vegetarian diet, levels of plasma oestrone, oestradiol, testosterone and androstenedione were significantly lower than in Western omnivorous controls from Boston (Goldin *et al.*, 1986), even with small sample sizes. In addition, the ratio of urinary-to-faecal oestrogen excretion was higher for oestriol, oestrone and oestradiol measured in Oriental women compared to their Western counterparts. Similar findings have been clearly established in an epidemiological survey carried out among 3250 rural Chinese women recruited in 65 counties in China and compared with British controls (Key *et al.*, 1990); the mean concentration of oestradiol was 36 per cent higher and the mean concentration of testosterone 48 per cent higher in the group of 35–44-

year-old British controls than in the same age group of Chinese women. The differences were even more dramatic in older groups of women. The difference in testosterone concentration between the two groups was attributed mainly to the lower average body weight in Chinese women, whilst the differences in oestradiol or oestrone concentration seemed to be positively correlated with the level of fat intake and negatively correlated with the quantity of dietary fibre.

A complementary aspect generally linked to the low level of fat intake is the high level of fibre and carbohydrate intakes of a vegetarian (or at least meatless) diet. These characteristics are likely to increase the excretion of active metabolites whilst the conversion of androgens to oestrone and oestradiol is possibly altered in relation to the level of fat intake. Another possible mechanism involved in this regulation is a higher rate of conversion to inactive metabolites producing 2 α-OH-catechol-estrogens after a shift from the normal 16-hydroxylation towards a 2-hydroxylation. 2 α-OH-catechol-oestrogens are inactive analogues of oestradiol competing with the active metabolite so reducing the positive feedback at the pituitary level (Warren, 1983). Whatever the exact mechanism, all of those hypotheses implicating oestradiol metabolism are situated at the peripheral level of the regulatory mechanism (Rosetta, 1992a). Is there any aspect of food quality which possibly interferes directly or indirectly at the central level of regulation? In the last decade animal experiments have shown that at least some neuropeptides and a few amino acids called excitatory amino acids (such as glutamate and aspartate) suspected of being concurrent to inhibitory neuromediators like β-endorphin, interleukin-1β or neuropeptide-K, may act at the hypothalamic level. *N*-methyl-d-aspartate (NMDA) is an analogue of the amino acid aspartate. In the rat, NMDA injection can prevent the central inhibition induced by one of the inhibitory neuromediators tested (Bonavera *et al.*, 1993). In juvenile monkeys, prolonged NMDA stimulation can lead to precocious puberty. In addition, glutamate receptors have also been identified (Plant *et al.*, 1989).

The role of a low fat diet on the metabolism of oestradiol has already been tested in an experimental modification of the diet of Western sedentary women. Women given a controlled high fat diet followed by a 2 month low fat diet with the administration of radio-labelled oestrogen during the corresponding follicular phase of their menstrual cycle showed a decrease in 16α-hydroxylated metabolites 'without any measurable change in the actual amount of E2 being produced or metabolised' (Longcope *et al.*, 1987).

Conversely, the comparison between the quality of food intake in amenorrhoeic runners compared to eumenorrhoeic runners matched for height, weight, per cent fat and training distance has highlighted the significantly lower fat and zinc intakes, higher quantities of crude fibre and a slight difference in protein intake in the diet of amenorrhoeic compared to eumenorrhoeic long distance runners (Deuster, 1986). It is interesting to note that great similarities have been found between the diet of these amenorrhoeic runners and the characteristic food intake of rural Senegalese women with long duration postpartum amenorrhoea (Rosetta, 1989).

The effect of voluntary restricted caloric intake on the duration and the quality of the menstrual cycle associated with a vegetarian or non-vegetarian diet has been tested experimentally by Pirke *et al.* (1986). Eighteen omnivorous sedentary women with a normal menstrual cycle were randomly assigned over 6 weeks to either a vegetarian or a non-vegetarian diet. In addition, the caloric intake in both groups was calculated to induce a weight loss of approximately 1 kg body weight per week. Seven out of nine in the vegetarian group became anovulatory while only one became anovulatory in the non-vegetarian group. Anovulation was associated with a decrease in LH, oestradiol and progesterone values. In this experiment two different aspects of food intake (quality and quantity) have been tested and the major finding is probably that the sensitivity of the central regulation of the menstrual cycle to an inadequate caloric intake has been increased by the vegetarian regime.

Other studies carried out in female athletes have often considered nutrition as a whole. Two different aspects of their nutritional intake, quantity and quality, been investigated at the same time, regardless of the very different physiological process induced by each of them. It is only recently that major advances have been made in the investigation of the role in reproduction of the quantity of food intake.

In a series of very elegant studies, Cameron and her coworkers have answered most of the questions about the role of short-term food shortage in the regulation of reproduction in primates and humans. In 1991 they published the results of experimental short-term food restriction on the reproductive system in adult male rhesus monkeys (Cameron and Nosbish, 1991). The animals were routinely fed once a day with a 600–700 calorie meal, provided between 11.00 and 12.00 h. On the day of the experiment, they were not fed their daily meal, though they always had access to water. The loss of weight was minimal (1–3 per cent body weight/ 0.1–0.2 kg), but the effect on the reproductive axis was an immediate reduction in LH pulse frequency (but not amplitude) and a concomitant decrease in the pulsatile secretion of testosterone. To determine whether the changes in pulsatile secretion of LH and testosterone were induced by frequent blood sampling, four monkeys were sampled in the same way as the preceding experimental design but given a normal diet: they showed no modification in LH or testosterone pulsatile secretion. The next problem was to discriminate between the hypothalamus and the pituitary as the site of action: the sensitivity of the pituitary in response to exogenous GnRH stimulation was compared in the same animals after a day of normal feeding and after a day of fasting. The responsiveness of the pituitary was even higher after a day of fasting than after a day of normal feeding suggesting that a decrease in the release of GnRH is induced by short-term food restriction and reflected by the decrease in gonadotrophin secretion at the pituitary level. The phenomenon was immediately reversed by feeding the animal a normal meal.

In men, similar findings resulted from 48 h of fasting in voluntary normal healthy adults. A significant decrease in mean LH, FSH and testosterone concentrations was found, compared to days when they fed normally and the LH pulse frequency was significantly lower after fasting than during a day of normal feeding in each subject, even though LH pulse amplitude was not modified (Cameron *et al.*, 1991).

Another study was performed in normal male adult monkeys 'to determine if graded changes in nutrient intake can cause graded changes in LH and testosterone secretion' (Parfitt *et al.*, 1991). After a day of fasting, when the same decrease in LH and testosterone pulsatility was found as in previous experiments, the animals were fed varying sized meals, from 0 (which meant another day of fasting) for eight animals, 100 calories for six animals, 200 calories ($n = 6$), 300 calories ($n = 6$) or 600 calories ($n = 8$) which is their normal size meal. The monkeys that continued to fast showed no change in the low pulse frequency of LH and testosterone on the second day but the increase in the frequency of pulsatile LH and testosterone secretion was directly proportional to the size of the meal in all other animals.

In an attempt to investigate the physiological mechanism involved in this regulation, attention focussed on the role of the hypothalamic-pituitary-adrenal (HPA) axis. This was prompted by the fact that elevated levels of cortisol and adrenocorticotrophic hormone (ACTH) have been reported in men after a short period of fasting (Beer *et al.*, 1989) and the fact that several hormones secreted at different levels of the HPA axis are already known to interfere with the pulsatile secretion of GnRH (Dubey and Plant, 1985; Williams *et al.*, 1990). In monkeys, on the day of fasting both cortisol and ACTH significantly increase at the time of the normal distribution of food. Both hormones, cortisol and ACTH, return to their normal levels in the afternoon, the time at which the striking decrease in the LH pulsatility occurs. In addition, the behaviour of each animal was recorded and scored continuously over 30 min three times each day. All fasting monkeys exhibited agitated behaviour at the time of normal feeding, but no difference in behaviour occurred when they received a day of normal feeding in the second period (Helmreich *et al.*, 1993). An exogenous increase in cortisol was simulated by a hydrocortisone acetate injection administered to monkeys fed a normal diet, but their secretions of LH and testosterone were not modified. The suppression of corticotrophin releasing hormone (CRH) by dexamethasone treatment also failed to show any modification in the effect of a day of fasting on the release of LH. This demonstrated that the activation of the adrenal axis following a missing meal is not the causal agent in the disruption of the GnRH pulse generator.

Nevertheless, as the fasting monkeys displayed a high level of agitation at meal times the hypothesis that stress was a causal agent was tested against a metabolic signal (Schreihofer *et al.*, 1993a). Overfeeding the animals the day before fasting prevented the decline in LH pulse frequency during the 6 h following the suppression of the meal, whilst all the animals none the less exhibited high levels of agitated behaviour. This result suggested that a metabolic rather than a psychological stress signal was involved. This finding was confirmed in another experiment in which the monkeys were fed by intragastric nutrient infusion instead of by their normal pellet meal after 1 day of fasting. They showed the same agitation on the second day at the normal time of feeding as they did during a real period of fasting despite receiving a normal amount of nutrient by intragastric infusion. The release of LH and testosterone was immediately restored just as if they had received a normal meal (Schreihofer *et al.*, 1993b). The next step in this research was to identify the metabolic signals involved in the regulation of the GnRH pulse generator during short-term food restriction. It had been suspected that a peptide hormone released from the gastrointestinal tract in response to meal consumption, cholecystokinin (CCK), was involved. So this was tested using a CCK receptor-type A antagonist which prevents LH release after a meal whilst the blockage of CCK receptor-type B does not (Schreihofer *et al.*, 1993c). That CCK can stimulate LH secretion in adult male rhesus monkeys has been confirmed by other researchers (Perera *et al.*, 1993).

PHYSICAL WORKLOADS

Our knowledge of the way in which physical workloads may interfere with fertility comes mainly from female athletes' reproductive physiology.

In a recent review of this question (Rosetta, 1993b), it was found that:

(1)　The risk of impairment of the menstrual cycle is clearly associated with the level and characteristics of training (i.e. endurance, recurrence of daily session of training in a week and intensity of each session).

(2)　The impairment of the reproductive function is not an all or none process but is gradual and reversible and involves the hypothalamic pulsatile secretion of GnRH.

(3)　The frequency of the pulsatile secretion of GnRH seems to be significantly decreased above a certain level of training. The question of the nature of the signal is still a matter of debate, although endogenous opioid peptides, mainly β-endorphins, are serious candidates (Knobil, 1993) and have been shown to slow down the hypothalamic pulsatile oscillator, then suspected to be the causal agent in the effect of physical endurance training.

In rhesus monkeys, there is clear evidence from a series of experiments (Ferrin, 1987; Knobil, 1988b) that the release of β-endorphin by the neurones of the medio-basal area of the hypothalamus in response to physical stress is immediate and appears even after a light stress. These studies have also shown that the β-endorphin release interferes with the pulsatile secretion of GnRH. In humans, where the hypothalamic-pituitary portal blood system cannot be assessed, there is an increase in the plasma blood concentration of β-endorphins above an intensity and duration of physical exercise estimated at 70 per cent of maximum oxygen consumption maintained for at least 40 min. The delay in appearance of the increase in β-endorphin in the general blood system can be reduced by increasing the intensity of exercise (Goldfarb *et al.*, 1990). Moreover, it is generally believed that the secretion of endogenous opioids is much more rapid and intense in the portal hypothalamic-pituitary blood system than is its release into the general blood circulation.

The hypothesis was then considered that above a specific threshold in intensity and duration of physical exercise, the release of neuromediators like β-endorphins may interfere at the hypothalamic level with the pulsatile secretion of GnRH in the reproductive axis (Rosetta, 1992b). To what extent can these findings be applied to sedentary women living in various socioeconomic and cultural contexts? Obviously, there are very different life-styles in developed and developing countries; in the former, mechanisation, automatisation and transport facilities have reduced considerably the levels of physical activity for men and women, whereas there is usually a great deal of physical activity in developing countries.

Furthermore, in developing countries, there are significant differences between people living in urban and rural settings; the poorest people are usually those with the highest physical workloads, both in order to produce or collect the resources necessary to feed their families and to run the daily routine of the household. If we concentrate again on the situation of the women in such contexts, the highest workloads are borne during their reproductive lifetimes (Hurtado and Hill, 1990; Durnin *et al.*, 1990; Ferro-Luzzi, 1990). This can be widely observed in Africa, Asia or South America, where women are generally in charge of collecting water and fuel for the consumption of the whole household. They participate in agricultural work or, in non-agricultural populations, they quite often search for roots, vegetables and wild fruits or hunt for small animals or fish. They carry with them the produce they have collected as well as the youngest child of the family, and the load may account for 20–70 per cent of their own body weight. Distances travelled while so burdened may be several kilometres and may include mountainous terrain.

Over the past 10–20 years, physiologists have made considerable efforts to assess the energy costs of a large number of physical activities (Ainsworth *et al.*, 1993). These measurements have been carried out in experimental conditions, either in the laboratory or in the field. Most of the detailed surveys carried out to estimate the mean daily energy expenditure in free-living populations were based on a careful record of activities using a minute-by-minute activity diary, recorded either by an independent observer or by the subject. The cost of the successive activities was then computed from the estimated unit cost of each multiplied by its duration. These surveys are extremely time-consuming for the researcher and disruptive for the subject. Some authors have questioned their reliability and suggested the use of the assessment of energy intake as an indicator of energy expenditure, based on the assumption that, in the mid to long term, each subject must be in energy balance (Durnin, 1990). Other researchers considered that there are more difficulties in recording food intake than in the estimation of energy expenditure as there are now less invasive and even more reliable techniques that we could apply in the field (Goldberg *et al.*, 1991; Ulijaszek, 1992a). These methods are based on the relationship between the harshness of a task and the increase in heart rate (Ceesay *et al.*, 1989). They have been tested among sedentary people as well as among sportsmen and women (Schulz *et al.*, 1992) and it may be possible to apply them in free-living populations (Ulijaszek, 1992b).

Can we relate heavy physical workloads to endurance training? To answer this question we need to assess the daily routines of women, including both the pattern of their daily energy expenditure related to their physical activities and the total amount of their energy expenditure over 24 hours. Then we will question the recurrence of their activity pattern.

What we need to know in this hypothesis is the effect of physical load on the reproductive axis, i.e. are the duration and intensity of physical activities , at some time during the day, sufficiently high to stimulate the secretion of a neuroendocrine signal which will interfere at the hypothalamic level with the GnRH pulse generator? In other words, when a woman spends 30 min pounding millet enthusiastically, we would like to classify the intensity of the task as low, moderate or high and if it is high, we would like to calculate the total energy expended during this task (Livingstone *et al.*, 1990). Consequently, we need to calibrate the relationship between oxygen consumption and heart rate during standardised exercises for each subject. Then we equip each subject with a non-invasive device to record her heart rate frequency over 24 h and we will probably need to get a record of her activities on the same day to allow for the possibility of increases in heart rate being due to emotional events.

Besides the detection of significant bursts of intense activity during the day, the second aspect of physical activity that we would like to assess is the mean daily energy expenditure. The range in mean daily energy expenditure shown for female adults in various subsistence patterns (Strickland, 1990) is from 150 to 220 kJ/kg/day with an exceptional 300 kJ/kg/day for a small sample of young women (18 years old). Moreover, there is evidence of marked seasonality in most of the agricultural populations, which is not the case in non-agricultural populations. Studies of Amazonian (Dufour, 1984), New Guinean (Norgan *et al.*, 1974) and Sahelian West African women (Bleiberg *et al.*, 1980) revealed that, except for a small number of activities classified at high cost of energy expenditure, most of the daily activities were classified as low to moderate. However, the duration of sustained moderate activities may lead to high level of total energy expenditure: 'the activities with "moderate" rates of expenditure 3.2–4.9 kcal/min are manioc planting, grating and sieving, rapid walking, and carrying burdens of 25 kg or more' (Dufour, 1984). The same observation has been stressed recently in Nepalese women (Panter-Brick *et al.*, 1993) and in childbearing Gambian village women (Lawrence and Whitehead, 1988). The low cost of transport of loads in traditional rural populations is one of the most surprising findings for a Western observer. The phenomenon was first studied in East African women where it was found that women were able to carry loads up to 20 per cent of their body weight without any increase in their rate of energy consumption; for heavier loads, the energy consumption was proportional to the load (Maloiy *et al.*, 1986). Others have questioned the mechanical efficiency of walking in traditional populations (Ferretti *et al.*, 1991), but even with economical ways of moving, with or without loads, the overall energy expenditure probably only makes sense in relation to energy intake (Jones *et al.*, 1987).

ENERGY BALANCE AND POSSIBLE MECHANISMS OF ADAPTATION

What are the components of energy balance? Energy intake is essentially food intake, but energy expenditure can be divided into different components. The amount of energy needed for the maintenance of tissue metabolism and the energy needed for physical activity are the two main subdivisions, given that the energy needed for the maintenance of tissue metabolism comprises the basal metabolic rate (BMR) together with amounts needed for the replacement of tissues lost as a result of turnover, the thermic effect of food (TEF) and the minimal amount of physical activity required for survival. The minimal survival energy expenditure has been estimated in the last few years at $1.5 \times$ BMR. Others have shown that resting energy expenditure (REE) accounts for two thirds of the total energy expenditure (TEE), the other third being the result of TEF and the energy required by physical activity (Astrup *et al.*, 1992).

If there is any change in energy balance, either in the short-term or in the long-term, there are two questions we can ask. First, which components are the more likely to be modified and, second, are there any adaptive mechanisms to compensate for these modifications in order to allow the maintenance of a positive energy balance (Norgan, 1983)?

Regarding energy intake, there are a number of possibilities, both in the day-to-day food consumption and in the long-term. The well-known seasonal food shortage in many developing countries is an example. It is important to note that, in the context of a non-catastrophic situation (as opposed to famine), the head of the family may carefully manage food distribution during the period of shortage which may last several months. The daily allowance of millet or other staple food of the household may be gradually reduced in order to avoid a complete disruption in daily food intake before the next harvest. Is there a threshold in the reduction of daily intake that might be related to a change in energy balance (McNeill *et al.*, 1988)?

Alternatively, what aspects of energy expenditure can be varied significantly and are there energy-saving behaviours or other adaptations (Myerson *et al.*, 1991)? Many authors have looked for adaptation in BMR and have concluded that there is no evidence for a significant modification in BMR (Ferro-Luzzi *et al.*, 1987; Bingham *et al.*, 1989) or in energy required for thermogenesis. 'The proposition that some groups have remarkably low energy requirements ... is not backed by any objective measurements' (James and Shetty, 1982). These conclusions leave us with the last component of energy expenditure, namely the energy required for physical activity. In order to maintain a positive energy balance, two different responses to a decrease in energy intake have been suggested: a modification in the total amount of non-essential activities (more rest, less walking, etc.) to compensate for an increase in activity at high cost in energy. This may be the case during periods of intense agricultural work for example or during periods of scarcity (which are usually at the same time of the year) or during pregnancy and lactation (McNeill and Payne, 1985). Another possible way of saving energy may be a more efficient mechanical output for those activities considered by observers as costly and only found to be moderate after assessment. It is well known that individuals who have not been physically trained for a task expend much more energy in doing an exercise than people who are accustomed to the task.

Attempts to estimate the discrepancies between energy intake and expenditure in physically active women have yielded conflicting results, a point that stresses the difficulties of making these measurements in free-living populations and the high percentage of error generated by both assessments, even in carefully conducted studies, 'estimates of total error being as high as 20 per cent' (Mulligan and Butterfield, 1990; Wilmore *et al.*, 1992). The cost and accuracy of the different methods in use have to be weighed in relation to the aims of the study and the choice of the relevant methodology has to focus on the questions raised in the context. Then, besides the estimation of the pattern of activities and the estimation of the 24 h energy balance, can we report on indirect indicators to assess the change in energy balance in individuals like the seasonal variation in body weight and/or in body composition? As long as there is no evidence of significant loss of weight, we are presumed to be in positive energy balance (Waterlow, 1986). However, although many surveys have failed to show a significant change in body weight associated with a change in physical activity or in food intake, this does not prove that the subjects were in negative energy balance (Adair *et al.*, 1984). Women have long been considered as being well-buffered, compared to men, against seasonality, probably because of their higher and differently partitioned body fat as energy reserves. It has been shown recently that they are not systematically affected by maternal cumulative depletion, body mass index (BMI) and triceps fat increasing with parity in women from rural Lesotho (Miller and Huss-Ashmore, 1989).

Nevertheless, women with the lowest BMI are often those at high risk of menstrual impairment among Western sportswomen and they are also those with the longest period of postpartum amenorrhea in developing countries. They are all characterised by low weight for height and low body fatness, which means low energy stores and possibly different fat distribution than their fatter counterparts. They are also those with the highest levels of physical activity endurance. The causality of weight change and body composition in the regulation of ovarian function is still debated. It seems that any significant decrease in body weight in women is a side-effect of a serious decrease in energy balance and if there is a causal effect it might be indirect and correlated with the low level of energy reserves. It is tempting to explain this physiological effect using catastrophe theory: most of the women seem able to cope with several successive adjustments when they have to face slight seasonal decrements in food intake or sustained increase in physical activity, but there is apparently a limit when the environmental change becomes significant and precipitates a sudden catastrophic change in physiological response. This may correspond to the threshold between a positive and a negative energy balance. It has been argued by Ferro-Luzzi *et al.* (1987) that : 'the overlap and interaction of several seasonal events confound the picture and may precipitate a marginal situation into imbalance in areas with low seasonality index'. If there is a causal role for energy balance in this regulation, it seems reasonable to think that women with low weight for height, and a concomitant low body fatness, are more at risk of ovarian impairment: they live in a narrow window of physiological safety and any significant change in either energy intake or physical activity may result in a dysfunction in their reproductive axis.

This hypothesis has to be tested and this calls for the use of anthropological indicators in fertility surveys. The recording of height, body weight, arm circumference and the estimation of body fatness from skinfold thicknesses are widely accepted in field conditions and will certainly be recommended (Norgan, 1992). Moreover, it has already been shown that differences in body composition account for 82 per cent of the variance in sleeping energy expenditure in premenopausal women (Astrup *et al.*, 1992).

The role of energy balance in the regulation of reproductive function has long been hypothesised, but is still not understood (Bentley, 1985; Rosetta, 1990; Ellison, 1991; Bailey *et al.*, 1992). Is there a threshold in the level of energy balance able to initiate a metabolic, neuroendocrine or electrical signal to the reproductive axis? Although it has never been proven, the idea of negative energy balance is commonly used implicitly in discussion of the loss in body weight. If there is a permissive effect from a positive energy balance, does it mean that a negative energy balance will be able to suppress the system or, as suggested recently by Knobil (1993), is it mainly the negative effect of a shortfall in caloric intake? More research is needed to answer this question, but there is no doubt that the recent findings on the central suppression of the reproductive axis during short-term food shortage are of major importance in this respect.

DISCUSSION

In a number of studies carried out to assess the return to fertility after pregnancy it has been established that the return of ovulation may occur before the first menses in a high proportion of women, both in breastfeeding (Brown *et al.*, 1985) and non-breastfeeding women (Gray *et al.*, 1987). More recent studies in urban Chilean women have shown that the full recovery of ovulation and a normal luteal phase increases rapidly after the return of menses (Díaz *et al.*, 1992). In this sample, the probability of ovulating during breastfeeding was approaching 40 per cent before 6 months postpartum and 100 per cent before the end of the first year. The majority of women showed a long follicular phase and a short luteal phase during the first ovulatory cycle; the normality of the luteal phase was usually apparent after the third cycle. The same trend has been described in non-breastfeeding postpartum women in which 32 per cent of the first cycles were anovulatory, the rate decreasing to 15 per cent during the second cycle, with a normal luteal phase in most of them by the third cycle. The 24-hour pattern in LH secretion underlying the return of fertility during lactational amenorrhea has recently been assessed in fully breastfeeding amenorrheic women at 4 and 8 weeks postpartum (Tay *et al.*, 1992). The suppression of LH pulsatility was almost universal at 4 weeks postpartum, whereas LH pulse was detectable in the majority of subjects at 8 weeks. This gives us an indication of the likely time lag between the first sign of activity of the central drive of the reproductive axis and the occurrence of the first ovulation, followed by the progressive return to normal luteal and follicular phases even in fully breastfeeding women. The results of these hormonal studies emphasise the fact that, once the first menses start during the postpartum period, regardless of the degree of breastfeeding (fully, partly or none), the return to fertility is almost the same in all groups with the likelihood of an ovulatory cycle following the return of menses after 6 months being even higher than before 6 month postpartum (Eslami *et al.*, 1990). The major difference between groups is in the duration of postpartum amenorrhea (Hennart *et al.*, 1985). Some individuals are more fertile than others: there is evidence in men for inter-individual variability in semen quality and among women the difference between individuals seems to lie more in the tendency to resume fertility earlier or later after a pregnancy, both in lactating or non-lactating women (Díaz *et al.*, 1991), or to be more successful throughout reproductive life. The relationship between later age at menarche and longer amenorrhea has been mentioned in some studies (Liestøl *et al.*, 1988); others have found a higher percentage of fetal loss in the first pregnancy among Moroccan women with late menarche (Varea *et al.*, 1993). All these relationships probably reflect different aspects of the same individual variation in fertility among healthy women, possibly accentuated by environmental factors (Laurenson *et al.*, 1985).

In the few hormonal surveys that have involved large samples, individual variability is considerable. Among well-nourished Australian women, who breastfed for at least 6 months postpartum, less than 20 per cent (n = 89) ovulated and less than 25 per cent (n = 101) menstruated earlier than 6 months postpartum. However, the range of hormonal profiles was extremely wide, from 24 days for the first ovulation (35 days for the first menstruation), to 750 days for the longest first ovulation (698 days for the longest first menstruation) (Lewis *et al.*, 1991).

Among non-pregnant non-lactating women, unusual hormonal sex patterns have been recorded in populations of hunter-gatherers in Botswana (Van der Walt *et al.*, 1978) and the Philippines (Goodman *et al.*, 1985), in tribal horticulturalists from Papua New Guinea (Wood *et al.*, 1985) and in two different populations living in the Ituri forest of Zaire (Ellison *et al.*, 1986). All of them exhibit low levels of plasma gonadal hormones compared to Western female controls, with evidence of high incidence of anovulatory cycle and frequently inadequate luteal phases. In women of Highland New Guinea, the duration of the menstrual cycle for 36 cycling subjects was 40 per cent longer than the median estimated for US controls matched for gynaecological age (Johnson *et al.*, 1987).

Longitudinal surveys on lactational performance in breastfeeding women from different cultural and socioeconomic levels reported by Prentice *et al.* (1986) indicate that the composition of the milk does not vary significantly with the availability of food of the mother, although the volume and the daily mean intake of milk by the infant may vary dramatically according to the season, as shown in the Gambia (Lunn, 1992). They have also stressed the complexity of the relationship between environmental seasonality and lactational performance in this group of women, as it seems that the variability in milk output is mainly related to the number of feeds rather than to the intake per feed. In such societies, where the mother's activity interferes with the amount of time she can spend with the baby, there is an additional stress component to the nutritional and physical stresses already existing: the baby may have to suckle more strongly to satisfy its nutritional needs than when both mother and milk are more accessible. It is interesting to note that similar interactions have already been suggested for monkeys in order to interpret the observed variability in female fertility (Lee, 1987). In humans, other attempts to quantify the breastfeeding pattern in relationship to the duration of postpartum amenorrhoea have highlighted the wide difference in postpartum duration between two different socioeconomic groups in the same rural Andean community from Peru (Vitzthum, 1989). The median was 21.6 ± 3.1 months in the poorest group, and 8.8 ± 3.8 months in a group of wealthier women. This underlines the fact that access to a market economy may have an impact on the quality and quantity of food supplement given to the baby and may explain the dramatic decrease in nursing duration (Vitzthum, 1992). If the women have access to commercial baby food they are also likely to have access to more diversified food for themselves and the other members of the household, as suggested by a survey of poor Iranian lactating women (Geissler et al., 1978). This is probably also correlated to a decrease in manual work or the amount of exhausting walking and load-carrying that are additional sources of impairment to the reproductive axis.

Similar significant decreases in the mean duration of postpartum amenorrhea have been found in the historical records of fertility in Norway during the period 1860–1964. A dramatic decrease from 12 months prior to 1900 to 6 months postpartum duration for the women who have given birth after 1900 has been reported from the medical records of a large sample of women (Liestøl et al., 1988). The authors attributed the decrease mainly to a change in breastfeeding pattern, although it seems difficult to completely discount a change in breastfeeding pattern due to other factors such as the pattern of workload and physical activity, nutritional status, access to better food, etc. An experimental attempt to provide a nutritional supplement to lactating mothers in the Gambia, for example, resulted in a mean reduction of 6 months in the resumption of menstrual and ovulatory activity even though the pattern of breastfeeding remained unchanged (Lunn et al., 1984).

Even if the physiological role of energy balance in the regulation of the reproductive axis in primates and humans is not yet fully understood, we can accept the fact that nutrition has a real effect at both the qualitative and quantitive levels. At the same time, the possible suppressive effect due to long bursts of intense physical activity raises the question of whether there is a trend in fertility across the populations that correlates with life-style. Recently, Bentley *et al.* (1993) have compared the fertility of agricultural and non-agricultural peoples. There is a significant difference between intensive agriculturalists (as compared to extensive agriculturalists) and all other non-agriculturalist groups, with an increase in fertility for the group of agriculturalists. It might be fascinating to continue this comparison. We can hypothesise from our actual knowledge of endocrinology, that hunter-gatherers and other populations living in precarious environments who are totally dependent on their own physical capacity to survive are the most at risk of reproductive failure because they live in a state of fragile equilibrium due to high levels of daily endurance activity (Leslie and Fry, 1989). With sedentarisation, there is a trend to a less diversified food regime that is more reliable in the short-term than is the case for the previous group, even though in the long-term seasonal food shortages might be important. With an agriculturalist lifestyle, the physical activity levels of women are still close to those typical of sportswomen. Because these involve patterns that better match their normal energy intakes most of the time, they may be reproductively more successful than non-agriculturalists. The next decisive step seems urbanisation. When people first arrive in towns from rural areas in developing countries, they use the same basic foods as they did in their villages, but this diet is progressively supplemented with typical urban food such as bread, milk, sugar, etc. Except in the slum areas, where the precarious life-style is rather different from that found in villages (and may even be worse), the nutritional constraints and the risks of heavy physical workloads are likely to persist only at the poorest socioeconomic levels. These constraints probably disappear quite rapidly in the middle classes among whom the risk of food shortage is usually minimal and the women have much reduced levels of physical activity. On these grounds, we might predict an increase in physiological fertility from the village to the town and from the very poor to the middle classes in urban settings in developing countries. However, in the middle and upper classes in developing countries or at any socioeconomic level in developed countries, the nutritional and energetic constraints are less likely to play a role in the regulation of fertility except in cases of voluntary dieting or repetitive endurance training.

REFERENCES

Adair, L.A., Pollitt, E. and Mueller, W. H. (1984). 'The Bacon Chow study: effect of nutritional supplementation on maternal weight and skinfold thickness during pregnancy and lactation', *British Journal of Nutrition*, vol. 51, pp. 357–69.

Ainsworth, B. E., Haskell, W. L., Leon, A. S., Jacobs, D. R., Montoye, H. J., Sallis, J. F. and Paffenbarger, R. S. (1993), 'Compendium of Physical Activities: classification of energy costs of human physical activities', *Medicine and Science in Sports and Exercise,* vol. 25, pp. 71–80.

Astrup, A., Buemann, B., Christensen, J. N., Madsen, J., Gluud, C., Bennett, P. and Svenstrup, B. (1992), 'The contribution of body composition, substrates, and hormones to the variability in energy expenditure and substrates utilization in premenopausal women', *Journal of Clinical Endocrinology and Metabolism,* vol, 74, pp. 279–86.

Bailey, R. C., Jenike, M. R., Ellison, P. T., Bentley, G. R., Harrigan, A. M. and Peacock, N. R. (1992), 'The ecology of birth seasonality among agriculturalists in central Africa', *Journal of Biosocial Science,* vol. 24, pp. 393–412.

Beer, S. F., Bircham, P. M. M., Bloom, S. R., Clark, P. M., Hales, C. N., Hughes, C. M., Jones, C. T., Marsh, D. R., Raggatt, P. R. and Findlay, A. L. R. (1989), 'The effect of a 72-h fast on plasma levels of pituitary, adrenal, thyroid, pancreatic, and gastrointestinal hormones in healthy men and women', *Journal of Endocrinology,* vol. 118, pp. 337–50.

Bentley, G. R. (1985), 'Hunter-gatherer energetics and fertility: a reassessment of the !Kung San', *Human Ecology,* vol. 13, pp. 79–109.

Bentley, G. R., Goldberg, T. and Jasieñska, G. (1993), 'The fertility of agricultural and non-agricultural traditional societies', *Population Studies,* vol. 47, pp. 269–81.

Bingham, S. A., Goldberg, G. R., Coward, W. A., Prentice, A. M. and Cummings, J. H. (1989), 'The effect of exercise and improved physical fitness on basal metabolic rate', *British Journal of Nutrition*, vol. 61, pp. 155–73.

Bleiberg, F. M., Brun, T. A., Goihman, S. and Gouba, E. (1980), 'Duration of activities and energy expenditure of female farmers in dry and rainy seasons in Upper-Volta', *British Journal of Nutrition*, vol. 43, pp. 71–82.

Bonavera, J. J., Kalra, S. P. and Kalra, P. S. (1993), 'Evidence that luteinizing hormone suppression in response to inhibitory neutropeptides, β-endorphin, interleukin-1β, neuropeptide-K, may involve excitatory amino acids', *Endocrinology,* vol. 133, pp. 178–82.

Brown, J. B., Harrison, P. and Smith, M. A. (1985), 'A study of returning fertility after child-birth and during lactation by measurement of urinary oestrogen and pregnanediol excretion and cervical mucus production', *Journal of Biosocial Science*, vol. 9 (Supplement), pp. 5–23.

Cameron, J. L. and Nosbisch, C. (1991), 'Suppression of pulsatile luteinizing-hormone and testosterone secretion during short-term food restriction in the adult male Rhesus-monkey (*Macaca mulatta*)', *Endocrinology,* vol. 128, pp. 1532–40.

Cameron, J. L., Weltzin, T. E., McConaha, C., Helmreich, D. L. and Kaye, W. H. (1991), 'Slowing of pulsatile luteinizing-hormone secretion in men after 48 hours of fasting', *Journal of Clinical Endocrinology and Metabolism,* vol. 73, pp. 35–41.

Ceesay, S. M., Prentice, A. M., Day, K. C., Murgatroyd, P. R., Goldberg, G. R., and Scott, W. (1989), 'The use of heart rate monitoring in the estimation of energy expenditure: a validation study using indirect whole body calorimetry', *British Journal of Nutrition*, vol. 61, pp. 175–86.

Danutra, V., Turkes, A., Read, G. F., Wilson, D. W., Griffiths, V., Jones, R. and Griffiths, K. (1989), 'Progesterone concentrations in samples of saliva from adolescent girls living in Britain and Thailand, two countries where women are at widely different risk of breast cancer', *Journal of Endocrinology*, vol. 121, pp. 375–81.

Deuster, P. A., Kyle, S. B., Moser, P. B., Vigersky, R. A., Singh, A. and Schoomaker, E. B. (1986), 'Nutritional intakes and status of highly trained amenorrheic and eumenorrheic women runners', *Fertility and Sterility*, vol. 46, pp. 636–43.

Díaz, S., Cárdenas, H., Brandeis, A., Miranda, P., Schiappacasse, V., Salvatierra, A. M., Herreros, C., Serón-Ferré, M. and Croxatto, H. B. (1991), 'Early difference in the endocrine profile of long and short lactational amenorrhea', *Journal of Clinical Endocrinology and Metabolism*, vol. 72, pp. 196–201.

Díaz, S., Cárdenas, H., Brandeis, A., Miranda, P., Salvatierra, A. M. and Croxatto, H. B. (1992), 'Relative contributions of anovulation and luteal phase defect to the reduced pregnancy rate of breast-feeding women', *Fertility and Sterility*, vol. 58, pp. 498–503.

Dubey, A. K. and Plant, T. M. (1985), 'A suppression of gonadotropin-secretion by cortisol in castrated male rhesus monkeys (*Macaca mulatta*) mediated by the interruption of hypothalamic gonadotropin-releasing hormone release', *Biology of Reproduction*, vol. 33, pp. 423–431.

Dufour, D. L. (1984), 'The time and energy expenditure of indigenous women horticulturalists in the Northwest Amazon', *American Journal of Physical Anthrophology*, vol. 65, pp. 37–46.

Durnin, J. V. G. A. (1990), 'Low energy expenditures in free-living populations', *European Journal of Clinical Nutrition*. vol. 44 (supplement 1), pp. 95–102.

Durnin, J. V. G. A., Drummond, S. and Satyanarayana, K. (1990), 'A collaborative EEC study on seasonality and marginal nutrition: the Glasgow Hyderabad (S. India) study', *European Journal of Clinical Nutrition*, vol. 44 (supplement 1), pp. 19–29.

Ellison, P. T. (1991), 'Reproductive ecology and human fertility', in G. W. Lasker and C. G. N. Mascie-Taylor (eds), *Applications of Biological Anthropology to Human Affairs* (Cambridge: Cambridge University Press) pp. 14–54.

Ellison, P. T., Peacock, N. R. and Lager, C. (1986), 'Salivary progesterone and luteal function in two low-fertility populations of Northeast Zaire', *Human Biology*, vol. 58, pp. 473–83.

Eslami, S. S., Gray, R. H., Apelo, R. and Ramos, R. (1990), 'The reliability of menses to indicate the return of ovulation in breastfeeding women in Manila, The Philippines', *Studies in Family Planning*, vol. 21, pp. 243–50.

Ferin, M. (1987), 'A role for the endogenous opioid peptides in the regulation of gonadotropin secretion in the Primate', *Hormone Research,* vol. 28, pp. 119–25.

Ferretti, G., Atchou, G., Grassi, B., Marconi, C. and Cerretelli, P. (1991), 'Energetics of locomotion in African pygmies', *European Journal of Applied Physiology*, vol. 62, pp. 7–10.

Ferro-Luzzi, A. (1990), 'Seasonal energy stress in marginally nourished rural women: interpretation and integrated conclusions of a multicentre study in three developing countries', *European Journal of Clinical Nutrition*, vol. 44 (supplement 1), pp. 41–6.

Ferro-Luzzi, A., Pastore, G. and Sette, S. (1987), 'Seasonality in energy metabolism', in B. Schurch and N. Scrimshaw (eds), *Chronic Energy Deficiency: Consequences and Related Issues* (Lausanne: IDECG) pp. 37–58.

Foster, D. L. and Olster, D. H. (1985), 'Effect of restricted nutrition on puberty in the lamb: patterns of tonic luteinizing hormone (LH) secretion and competency of the LH surge system', *Endocrinology*, vol. 116, pp. 375–81.

Geissler, C., Calloway, D. H. and Margen, S. (1978), 'Lactation and pregnancy in Iran: II. Diet and nutritional status', *American Journal of Clinical Nutrition*, vol. 31, pp. 341–54.

Goldberg, G. R., Prentice, A. M., Coward, W. A., Davies, H. L., Murgatroyd, P. R., Sawyer, M. B., Ashford, J. and Black, A. E. (1991), 'Longitudinal assessment of the components of energy balance in well-nourished lactating women', *American Journal of Clinical Nutrition*, vol. 54, pp. 788–98.

Goldfarb, A. H., Hatfield, B. D., Armstrong, D. and Potts, J. (1990), 'Plasma beta-endorphin concentration: response to intensity and duration of exercise', *Medicine and Science in Sports and Exercise*, vol. 22, pp. 241–4.

Goldin, B. R., Adlercreutz, H., Gorbach, S. L., Woods, M. N., Dwyer, J. T., Conlon, T., Bohn, E. and Gershoff, S. N. (1986), 'The relationship between estrogen levels and diets of Caucasian American and Oriental immigrant women', *American Journal of Clinical Nutrition*, vol. 44, pp. 945–53.

Goodman, M. J., Estioko-Griffin, A., Griffin, P. B. and Grove, J. S. (1985), 'Menarche, pregnancy, birth spacing and menopause among foragers of Cayagan Province, Luzon, the Philippines', *Annals of Human Biology*, vol. 12, pp. 169–77.

Gray, R. H., Campbell, O. M., Zacur, H. L., Labbok, M. H. and MacRae, S. L. (1987), 'Postpartum return of ovarian activity in non-breastfeeding women monitored by urinary assays', *Journal of Clinical Endocrinology and Metabolism*, vol. 64, pp. 645–50.

Helmreich, D. L., Mattern, L. G. and Cameron, J. L. (1993), 'Lack of a role of the hypothalamic-pituitary-adrenal axis in the fasting-induced suppression of luteinizing hormone secretion in adult male rhesus monkeys (*Macaca mulatta*)', *Endocrinology*, vol. 132, pp. 2427–37.

Hennart, P., Hofvander, Y., Vis, H. and Robyn, C. (1985), 'Comparative study of nursing mothers in Africa (Zaire) and in Europe (Sweden): breastfeeding behaviour, nutritional status, lactational hyperprolactinaemia and status of the menstrual cycle', *Clinical Endocrinology*, vol. 22, pp. 179–87.

Hill, P., Garbaczewski, L., Haley, N. and Wynder, E. L. (1984), 'Diet and follicular development', *American Journal of Clinical Nutrition*, vol. 39, pp. 771–7.

Hurtado, A. M. and Hill, K. (1990), 'Seasonality in foraging society: variation in diet, work effort, fertility, and sexual division of labor among the Hiwi of Venezuela', *Journal of Anthropological Research*, vol. 46, pp. 293–346.

I'Anson, H., Foster, D. L., Foxcroft, G. R. and Booth, P. J. (1991), 'Nutrition and reproduction', in S. R. Milligan (ed.), *Oxford Reviews of Reproductive Biology* (Oxford: Oxford University Press) vol. 13.

James, W. P. T. and Shetty, P. S. (1982), 'Metabolic adaptation and energy requirements in developing countries', *Human Nutrition: Clinical Nutrition*, vol. 36C, pp. 331–6.

Johnson, P. L., Wood, J. W., Campbell, K. L. and Maslar, I. A. (1987), 'Long ovarian cycles in women of highland New Guinea', *Human Biology*, vol. 59, pp. 837–45.

Jones, C. D. R., Jarjou, M. S., Whitehead, R. G. and Jequier, E. (1987), 'Fatness and the energy cost of carrying loads in African women', *Lancet*, vol. xii, pp. 1331–2.

Key, T. J. A., Chen, J., Wang, D. Y., Pike, M. C and Boreham, J. (1990), 'Sex hormones in women in rural China and in Britain', *British Journal of Cancer*, vol. 62, pp. 631–6.

Knobil, E. (1988a), 'The neuroendocrine control of ovulation', *Human Reproduction*, vol. 3, pp. 469–72.

Knobil, E. (1988b), 'The hypothalamic gonadotrophic hormone releasing hormone (GnRH) pulse generator in the rhesus monkey and its neuroendocrine control', *Human Reproduction*, vol. 3, pp. 29–31.

Knobil, E. (1993), 'Editorial: Inhibition of luteinizing hormone secretion by fasting and exercise: "stress" or specific metabolic signals?', *Endocrinology*, vol. 132, pp. 1879–80.

Laurenson, I. F., Benton, M. A., Bishop, A. J. and Mascie-Taylor, C. G. N. (1985), 'Fertility at low and high altitude in central Nepal', *Social Biology*, vol. 32, pp. 65–70.

Lawrence, M. and Whitehead, R. G. (1988), 'Physical activity and total energy expenditure of child-bearing Gambian Women', *European Journal of Clinical Nutrition*, vol. 42, pp. 145–60.

Lee, P. C. (1987), 'Nutrition, fertility and maternal investment in primates', *Journal of Zoology, London*, vol. 213, pp. 409–22.

Leslie, P. W. and Fry, P. H. (1989), 'Extreme seasonality of births among nomadic Turkana pastoralists', *American Journal of Physical Anthropology*, vol. 79, pp. 103–15.

Levine, R. L., Mathew, R. M., Brandon Chenault, C., Brown, M. H., Hurtt, M. E., Bentley, K. S., Mohr, K. L. and Working, P. K. (1990), 'Differences in the quality of semen in outdoor workers during summer and winter', *The New England Journal of Medicine*, vol. 323, pp. 12–6.

Lewis, P. R., Brown, J. B., Renfree, M. B. and Short, R. V. (1991), 'The resumption of ovulation and menstruation in a well-nourished population of women breastfeeding for an extended period of time', *Fertility and Sterility*, vol. 55, pp. 529–36.

Liestøl, K., Rosenberg, M. and Walløe, L. (1988), 'Lactation and post-partum amenorrhea: a study based on data from three Norwegian cities 1860–1964', *Journal of Biosocial Science,* vol. 20, pp. 423–34.

Livingstone, M. B. E., Prentice, A. M., Coward, W. A., Ceesay, S. M., Strain, J. J., McKenna, P. G., Nevin, G. B., Barker, M. E. and Hickey, R. J. (1990), 'Simultaneous measurement of free living energy expenditure by the doubly labeled water method and heart-rate monitoring', *American Journal of Clinical Nutrition*, vol. 52, pp. 59–65.

Longcope, C., Gorbach, S., Goldin, B., Woods, M., Dwyer, J., Morrill, A. and Warram, J. (1987), 'The effect of low fat diet on estrogen metabolism', *Journal of Clinical Endocrinology and Metabolism*, vol. 64, pp. 1246–50.

Lunn, P. G. (1992), 'Breast-feeding patterns, maternal milk output and lactational infecundity', *Journal of Biosocial Science*, vol. 24, pp. 317–24.

Lunn, P. G., Austin,S., Prentice, A. M. and Whitehead, R. G. (1984), 'The effect of improved nutrition on plasma prolactin concentrations and postpartum infertility in lactating Gambian women', *American Journal of Clinical Nutrition*, vol. 39, pp. 227–35.

McNeill, G. and Payne, P. R. (1985), 'Energy expenditure of pregnant and lactating women', *Lancet*, vol. ii, pp. 1237–8.

McNeill, G., Payne, P. R., Rivers, J. P. W., Enos, A. M. T., John de Britto, J. and Mukarji, D. S. (1988), 'Socio-economic and seasonal patterns of adult energy nutrition in a South Indian village', *Ecology of Food and Nutrition*, vol. 22, pp. 85–95.

Maloiy, G. M. O., Heglund, N. C., Prager, L. M., Cavagna, G. A. and Taylor, C. R. (1986), 'Energetic cost of carrying loads: have African women discovered an economic way?', *Nature*, vol. 319, pp. 668–9.

Miller, J. E. and Huss-Ashmore, R. (1989), 'Do reproductive patterns affect maternal nutritional status? an analysis of maternal depletion in Lesotho', *American Journal of Human Biology*, vol. 1, pp. 409–19.

Mulligan, K. and Butterfield, G. E. (1990), 'Discrepancies between energy intake and expenditure in physically active women', *British Journal of Nutrition*, vol. 64, pp. 23–6.

Myerson, M., Gutin, B., Warren, M. P., May, M. T., Contento, I., Lee, M., Pi-Sunyer, F. X., Pierson, R. N. Jr and Brooks-Gunn, J. (1991), 'Resting metabolic rate and energy balance in amenorrheic and eumenorrheic runners', *Medicine and Science in Sports and Exercise*, vol. 23, pp. 15–22.

Norgan, N. G. (1983), 'Adaptations of energy metabolism to level of energy intake', in *International Workshop: Energy Expenditure Under Field Conditions* (Prague: Charles University) pp. 56–64.

Norgan, N. G. (1992), 'Maternal body composition: methods for measuring short-term changes', *Journal of Biosocial Science*, vol. 24, pp. 367–77.

Norgan, N. G., Ferro-Luzzi, A. and Durnin, J. V. G. A. (1974), 'The energy and nutrient intake and the energy expenditure of 204 New Guinean adults', *Philosophical Transactions of the Royal Society of London, B.*, vol. 268, pp. 309–48.

Panter-Brick, G., Lotstein, D. S. and Ellison, P. T. (1993), 'Seasonality of reproductive function and weight-loss in rural Nepali women', *Human Reproduction*, vol. 8, pp. 924–30.

Parfitt, D. B., Church, K. R. and Cameron, J. L. (1991), 'Restoration of pulsatile luteinizing hormone secretion after fasting in rhesus monkeys (*Macaca mulatta*): dependence on size of the refeed meal', *Endocrinology*, vol. 129, pp. 749–56.

Pedersen, A. B., Bartholomew, M. J., Dolence, L. A., Aljadir, L. P., Netteburgh, K. L. and Lloyd, T. (1991), 'Menstrual differences due to vegetarian and nonvegetarian diets', *American Journal of Clinical Nutrition*, vol. 53, pp. 879–85.

Perera, A. D., Verbalis, J. G., Mikuma, N., Majumdar, S. S. and Plant, T. M. (1993), 'Cholecystokinin stimulates gonadotropin-releasing hormone release in the monkey (*Macaca mulatta*)', *Endocrinology*, vol. 132, pp. 1723–8.

Pirke, R. M., Schweiger, U., Laessle, R., Dickhaut, B., Schweiger, M. and Waechtler, M. (1986), 'Dieting influences the menstrual cycle: vegetarian versus nonvegetarian diet', *Fertility and Sterility*, vol. 46, pp. 1083–8.

Plant, T. M., Gay, V. L., Marshall, G. R. and Arslan, M. (1989), 'Puberty in monkeys is triggered by chemical stimulation of the hypothalamus', *Proceedings of the National Academy of Sciences USA*, vol. 86, pp. 2506–10.

Prentice, A. M., Paul, A. A., Prentice, A., Black, A. E., Cole, T. J. and Whitehead, R. G. (1986), 'Cross-cultural differences in lactational performance', in M. Hamosh and A. S. Goldman (eds), *Human Lactation 2: Maternal and environmental factors* (New York: Plenum).

Rosetta, L. (1989), 'Breast-feeding and post-partum amenorrhea in Serere women in Senegal', *Annals of Human Biology*, vol. 16, pp. 311–20.

Rosetta, L. (1990), 'Biological aspects of fertility among Third World populations', in J. Landers and V. Reynolds (eds), *Fertility and Resources* (Cambridge: Cambridge University Press), SSHB Symposium, vol. 31, pp. 18–34.

Rosetta, L. (1992a), 'The relation between chronic malnutrition and fertility', *Collegium Anthropologicum*, vol. 16, pp. 83–8.

Rosetta, L. (1992b), 'Aetiological approach of female reproductive physiology in lactational amenorrhoea', *Journal of Biosocial Science*, vol. 24, pp. 301–15.

Rosetta, L. (1993a), 'Seasonality and fertility', in S. J. Ulijaszek and S. S. Strickland (eds), *Seasonality and Human Ecology* (Cambridge: Cambridge University Press) SSHB Symposium, vol. 35, pp. 65–75.

Rosetta, L. (1993b), 'Female reproductive dysfunction and intense physical training', in S. R. Milligan (ed.), *Oxford Reviews of Reproductive Biology* (Oxford: Oxford University Press) vol. 15, pp. 113–41.

Schreihofer, D. A., Golden, G. A. and Cameron, J. L. (1993a), 'Cholecystokinin (CCK)-induced stimulation of luteinizing hormone (LH) secretion in adult male rhesus monkeys: examination of the role of CCK in nutritional regulation of LH secretion', *Endocrinology*, vol. 132, pp. 1553–60.

Schreihofer, D. A., Parfitt, D. B. and Cameron, J. L. (1993b), 'Suppression of luteinizing-hormone secretion during short term fasting in male rhesus monkeys. The role of metabolic versus stress signals', *Endocrinology*, vol. 132, pp. 1881–9.

Schreihofer, D. A., Amico, J. A. and Cameron, J. L. (1993c), 'Reversal of fasting-induced suppression of luteinizing-hormone (LH) secretion in male rhesus monkeys by intragastric nutrient infusion. Evidence for rapid stimulation of LH by nutritional signals', *Endocrinology*, vol. 132, pp. 1890–7.

Schulz, L. O., Alger, S., Harper, I., Wilmore, J. H. and Ravussin, E. (1992), 'Energy expenditure of elite female runners measured by respiratory chamber and doubly labeled water', *Journal of Applied Physiology*, vol. 72, pp. 23–8.

Schwartz, D. and Mayaux, M. J. (1982), 'Female fecundity as a function of age. Results of artificial insemination in 2193 nulliparous women with azoospermic husbands', *New England Journal of Medicine*, vol. 306, pp. 404–6.

Strickland, S. S. (1990), 'Traditional economies and patterns of nutritional diseases', in G. A. Harrison and J. C. Waterlow (eds), *Diet and Disease* (Cambridge: Cambridge University Press) SSHB Symposium, vol. 30, pp. 209–39.

Tay, C. C. K., Glasier, A. F. and McNeilly, A. S. (1992), 'The 24 h pattern of pulsatile luteinizing hormone, follicle stimulating hormone and prolactin release during the first 8 weeks of lactational amenorrhoea in breastfeeding women', *Human Reproduction*, vol. 7, pp. 951–8.

Thalabard, J. C. (1992), 'The female reproductive axis and its modifications during the post-partum period', *Journal of Biosocial Science*, vol. 24, pp. 289–300.

Ulijaszek, S. J. (1992a), 'Estimating energy and nutrient intakes in studies of human fertility', *Journal of Biosocial Science*, vol. 24, pp. 335–45.

Ulijaszek, S. J. (1992b), 'Human energetics methods in biological anthropology', *Yearbook of Physical Anthropology*, vol. 35, pp. 215–42.

Van der Walt, L. A., Wilmsen, E. N. and Jenkins, T. (1978), 'Unusual sex hormone patterns among desert-dwelling hunter-gatherers', *Journal of Clinical Endocrinology and Metabolism*, vol. 46, pp. 658–63.

Varea, C., Bernis, C. and Elizondo, S. (1993), 'Physiological maturation, reproductive patterns, and female fecundability in a traditional Moroccan population (Amizmiz, Marrakech)', *American Journal of Human Biology*, vol. 5, pp. 297–304.

Vitzthum, V. J. (1989), 'Nursing behaviour and its relation to duration of post-partum amenorrhea in an Andean community', *Journal of Biosocial Science*, vol. 21, pp. 145–60.

Vitzthum, V. J. (1992), 'Infant nutrition and the consequences of differential market access in Nunoa, Peru', *Ecology of Food and Nutrition*, vol. 28, pp. 45–63.

Warren, M. P. (1983), 'Effects of undernutrition on reproductive function in the human', *Endocrine Reviews*, vol. 4, pp. 363–77.

Waterlow, J. C. (1986), 'Notes on the new international estimates of energy requirements', *Proceedings of the Nutrition Society*, vol. 45, pp. 351–60.

Williams, C. L., Nishihara, M., Thalabard, J. C., Grosser, P. M., Hotchkiss, J. and Knobil, E. (1990), 'Corticotropin-releasing factor and gonadotropin-releasing hormone pulse generator activity in the rhesus monkey. Electrophysiological studies', *Neuroendocrinology*, vol. 52, pp. 133–7.

Wilmore, J. H., Wambsgans, K. C., Brenner, M., Broeder, C. E., Paijmans, I., Volpe, J. A. and Wilmore, K. M. (1992), 'Is there energy-conservation in amenorrheic compared with eumenorrheic distance runners', *Journal of Applied Physiology*, vol. 72, pp. 15–22.

Wood, J. W., Johnson, P. L. and Campbell, K. L. (1985), 'Demographic and endocrinological aspects of low natural fertility in Highland New Guinea', *Journal of Biosocial Science*, vol. 17, pp. 57–79.

5 For Love or Money: the Evolution of Reproductive and Material Motivations

Alan R. Rogers

TWO QUESTIONS

What reproductive strategies are favoured by natural selection in a world where wealth can be inherited? Heritable wealth introduces several interesting wrinkles. First, there is the trade-off between the number of one's children and their wealth. A parent cannot simultaneously maximise both. Second, there is the question of how fitness should be defined. It makes no sense to equate fitness with the number of children, because the parent whose children are many may lose in competition with parents whose children are fewer but wealthier.

These observations suggest two questions. First, Is it true that at evolutionary equilibrium the wealthy must out-reproduce the poor? An affirmative answer would follow the assumptions that (1) selection favours those who produce the most offspring and that (2) a wealthy person has all the opportunities available to a poor person and more. If this were true, then selection should lead to an equilibrium at which the wealthy produce at least as many offspring as the poor. Yet human females do not behave this way and this has been a source of consternation for evolutionary ecologists (Vining, 1986). But I have already suggested that assumption (1) need not hold when wealth can be inherited. Thus, there may be no cause for consternation.

A second question involves the psychology of motivations. I shall distinguish *reproductive motivations* (the desire for children) from *material motivations* (the desire for wealth). I will assume without proof that (1) the strength of selection for reproductive motivations depends on the correlation r_{kids} between fitness and the number of one's surviving offspring, and that (2) the strength of selection for material motivations depends on the correlation r_{wealth} between fitness and wealth. These assumptions imply that if $r_{wealth} \gg r_{kids}$, then selection should favour a psychology dominated by material

76

motivations, while the opposite should be true when $r_{\text{wealth}} \ll r_{\text{kids}}$. In the absence of heritable wealth $r_{\text{kids}} = 1$ and $r_{\text{wealth}} < r_{\text{kids}}$. Thus, selection should favour a psychology in which reproductive motivations were dominant. It is not clear what to expect when wealth is heritable. Thus, I shall ask: Under what circumstances, if any, is r_{wealth} large relative to r_{kids}?

PREVIOUS WORK

Henry Harpending and I have written two previous papers on this subject. In the first (Rogers, 1990), I calculated optimal reproductive strategies in a model with heritable wealth. I will not describe that model in detail, since it differs from the one described below in only one respect: the earlier model assumed clonal inheritance: that each individual was genetically identical to her single parent. The clonal model was convenient because the fitness of an individual could be equated with the ratio of increase of the clone comprising her descendants. Under mild assumptions, this ratio converges to a stable value λ. The optimal reproductive strategy is the one that maximises λ.

λ can also be interpreted as the dominant eigenvalue of a matrix $\mathbf{G}$, whose ijth entry is the expected number of offspring of wealth i per parent of wealth j. The procedure for calculating $\mathbf{G}$ involved assumptions similar to those in the sexual model described below and will not be repeated here. Once an optimal strategy has been found, the clonal assumption also makes it easy to calculate the *stable wealth distribution h* (the vector whose ith entry is the equilibrium proportion of the population in wealth category i), and the vector w of *long-term fitnesses* (whose ith entry is proportional to the number of descendants that an individual of wealth i will produce in the long run, that is in the limit as time goes to infinity). These vectors are, respectively, the column- and row-eigenvectors of $\mathbf{G}$ that are associated with λ, the dominant eigenvalue. They are analogous to the *stable age distribution* and the vector of *reproductive values* from classical demography (Keyfitz, 1968).

The optimal strategy under one set of assumptions (see the original paper for details) is described in Figure 5.1. That result provided surprising answers to both of the questions raised above: even at evolutionary equilibrium, fertility need not be a non-decreasing function of wealth, and r_{wealth} may greatly exceed r_{kids}. In a world such as that described in Figure 5.1, fertility would be a poor measure of fitness, and selection should favour a psychology dominated by material motivations.

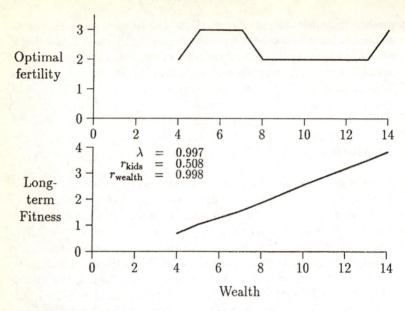

Figure 5.1   An evolutionary equilibrium under clonal inheritance
Source: Figure 2 of Rogers (1990)

The paper went on to show that $r_{wealth} > r_{kids}$ in harsh environments, whereas $r_{wealth} < r_{kids}$ in harsh environments, whereas $r_{wealth} < r_{kids}$ in mild ones. Thus, selection should favour material motivations most strongly in harsh environments.

The model underlying these conclusions was unrealistic in many ways, but two of these seem especially important. The first is that of clonal inheritance. Under this system, my descendant ten generations hence would – apart from the minor effect of mutation – be genetically identical to me. Under sexual reproduction, on the other hand, this descendant would share few genes with me. Thus, increasing the wealth of this descendant would increase my fitness more in the clonal case than in the sexual case. My assumption of clonal inheritance probably inflated the importance of heritable wealth.

A second assumption introduced an opposite bias. I assumed that, in addition to inheriting wealth, each individual earned some wealth on her own. This earned wealth was a Poisson random variable, with a distribution that did not depend on the wealth inherited. Thus, offspring of rich parents earned the same amount on average as the offspring of poor parents. In reality, inherited wealth often facilitates the acquisition of additional wealth. It would have been more reasonable to assume a positive regression of earned on inherited wealth. Thus, my independence assumption probably reduced the effect of heritable wealth.

Since the two false assumptions produce opposite biases, it is not clear whether their net effect makes heritable wealth more or less important than it should be. To find out, we need a model that incorporates sexual reproduction. Harpending and I (1990) extended the linear mathematics of the first paper to the sexual case. However, that algebra holds only at demographic equilibrium and does not provide a means of finding this equilibrium. Thus, we were unable to calculate optimal reproductive strategies.

The next section will extend the earlier model to deal with sexual reproduction and to make earned wealth depend on inherited wealth. The subsequent section will describe the algorithm used for finding evolutionary equilibria. Results are presented and discussed in the final two sections.

MODEL OF A MONOECIOUS SEXUAL POPULATION

The model incorporates sexual reproduction, but has only one sex: each individual is able to mate with any other. I am assuming, in other words, monoecious sexual reproduction. This allows me to incorporate the effects of sex while neglecting the complexities that are introduced by separate sexes. In addition, I assume that generations are discrete and non-overlapping. Individuals of each generation are classified into a finite number K of discrete wealth categories.

In order to find optimal reproductive strategies, we must be concerned with two kinds of equilibria: demographic and evolutionary. A population at demographic equilibrium is one within which the relative frequencies of individuals within wealth classes do not change. This demographic process is described in the next subsection. A population is at evolutionary equilibrium when its members have a genotype with higher fitness than any other genotype would have when rare. The evolutionary process is described in a later subsection.

A Genetically Homogeneous Population

A homogeneous population can be described by the number $n_i(t)$ of individuals of wealth i in generation t, where $i = 0, 1, ..., K - 1$. The column-vector whose ith entry is $n_i(t)$ will be denoted by $\mathbf{n}(t)$. The total population size in generation t is

$$N(t) = \sum_k n_k(t).$$

To describe the production of each of each new generation, I extend Pollak's (1990) birth–matrix–mating-rule model to deal with the case in which offspring are classified into K categories. The expected number of wealth i in generation $t + 1$ can be written as

$$n_i(t+1) = \sum_{jk} b_{ijk} u_{jk}\big[\mathbf{n}(t)\big] \tag{1}$$

where b_{ijk} is the expected number of offspring of wealth i produced by a mating between parents of wealths j and k, and $u_{jk}[\mathbf{n}(t)]$ the expected number of such matings, a function of $\mathbf{n}(t)$. A demographic equilibrium is defined by a vector $\mathbf{n}(t)$ such that $\mathbf{n}(t + 1)$ is proportional to $\mathbf{n}(t)$. The conditions under which such equilibria exist can be specified under restricted versions of this model (Caswell, 1989; Pollak, 1990), but are unknown in the general context considered here. In later sections, equilibria are found numerically using an algorithm based on recursion 1.

To show how this recursion relates to the linear mathematics of clonal populations (Rogers, 1990, 1992) (or of classical demography), I re-express it as

$$\mathbf{n}(t + 1) = \mathbf{G}\mathbf{n}(t) \tag{2}$$

where $\mathbf{G}$ is a matrix whose ijth entry g_{ij} is the expected number of offspring of wealth i per parent of wealth j. Equating the two recursions shows that

$$g_{ij} = \sum_k b_{ijk} \frac{u_{jk}\big[\mathbf{n}(t)\big]}{n_j(t)}. \tag{3}$$

In general, $\mathbf{G}$ is a function of $\mathbf{n}(t)$ and will change each generation. Thus, we cannot project the population into the future simply by iterating (2) with constant $\mathbf{G}$. The familiar linear mathematics of classical demography no longer apply.

On the other hand, if the population does reach an equilibrium, the linear mathematics become useful. It is reasonable to assume that the mating function $u_{ij}[\mathbf{n}]$ is homogeneous of degree 1, i.e. that

$$u_{ij}[a\mathbf{n}] = au_{ij}[\mathbf{n}]$$

for any scalar a.[1] This says, for example, that doubling the number of individuals will double the number of matings between each pair of wealth categories. When this assumption holds, g_{ij} will depend only on the relative frequencies of individuals within wealth categories. At equilibrium, these relative frequencies do not change and therefore neither does g_{ij}. Equation (2) is then linear, and the standard results of stable population theory apply (Rogers, 1990, 1992). Given particular assumptions about b_{ijk} and $u_{jk}[\mathbf{n}]$, we can use numerical methods to find equilibria and then interpret them in the ordinary way. We can, for example, use the methods described above in the previous section to calculate the ratio λ of increase, the vector w of long-term fitnesses and the stable wealth distribution h. What we cannot do is specify, in general, the conditions under which equilibria will exist.

Adding sources of variation to a model usually makes it harder to study, rather than easier. Yet adding genetics to this model provides a way around its non-linearity. The trick is to ask a slightly different question. Rather than seeking demographic equilibria, we seek to determine the circumstances under which a rare allele can invade a population dominated by some other allele. A strategy that cannot be invaded is an 'evolutionarily stable strategy' or ESS (Maynard Smith, 1982).

When Can a Rare Allele Invade?

Consider the dynamics of a rare allele B in a population dominated by a common allele A. Superscripts 1, 2 and 3 will indicate genotypes AA, AB, and BB, respectively. For example, $n_j^{(2)}(t)$ denotes the number of AB individuals of wealth j in generation t, and $u_{jk}^{(2,1)}[\mathbf{n}^{(1)}(t), \mathbf{n}^{(2)}(t)]$ is the expected number of matings in which one parent has genotype AB and wealth j while the other has genotype AA and wealth k.

Since B is rare, we need consider only two genotypes (AA and AB), and two types of mating ($AA \times AA$ and $AA \times AB$). The other genotypes and mating types are negligibly rare. Prior to the introduction of B, all individuals were of genotype AA and I assume that this population was at equilibrium. At this equilibrium, the relative frequency of individuals of wealth i is a constant $p_i^{(1)}$, and in each generation the population increases by a constant ratio $\lambda^{(1)}$, i.e $N^{(1)}(t + 1) = \lambda^{(1)}N^{(1)}(t)$. While B is rare, its effect on the demographic parameters of AA will be small. Thus, any departures of AA from this equilibrium will be small enough to neglect. The AA component of the population will continue to increase by a factor of $\lambda^{(1)}$ each generation.

The *AB* component of the population reproduces itself via matings of type *AA* × *AB*, whose offspring are evenly divided between genotypes *AA* and *AB*. Of these, the *AA* offspring can be ignored since they are rare compared with the offspring of *AA* × *AA* matings. The *AB* offspring, on the other hand, are of central concern: their number in each generation is approximately equal to the number of copies of the *B* allele. Thus, if *AB* increases at a ratio faster than $\lambda^{(1)}$ then the *B* allele will increase when rare. This ratio of increase is determined from the equation,

$$n_i^{(2)}(t+1) = \frac{1}{2} \sum_{jk} b_{ijk}^{(2,1)} u_{jk}^{(2,1)} \left[\mathbf{n}^{(1)}(t), \mathbf{n}^{(2)}(t) \right]. \tag{4}$$

The factor of 1/2 here arises because only half of the offspring produced by an *AA* x *AB* mating are of genotype *AB*. This factor does not appear in equation (1), a fact that seems to impose a 2-fold disadvantage upon the *AB* component of the population. However, this apparent disadvantage is exactly offset by a less obvious advantage: the number of unions (i.e. the sum of u_{jk}) equals half the number of individuals in equation (1), but equals the total number of *AB* individuals in equations (4) (see equations (7) and (11) below).

Equations (4) can also be expressed as

$$\mathbf{n}^{(2)}(t + 1) = \mathbf{G}^{(2,1)} \mathbf{n}^{(2)}(t) \tag{5}$$

where $\mathbf{G}^{(2,1)}$ is a matrix whose *ij*th entry

$$g_{ij}^{(2,1)} = \frac{1}{2} \sum_k b_{ijk}^{(2,1)} \frac{u_{jk}^{(2,1)} \left[\mathbf{n}^{(1)}, \mathbf{n}^{(2)} \right]}{n_j^{(2)}} \tag{6}$$

is the expected number of offspring of wealth *i* per parent of wealth *j*. So far, the algebra is identical to that of the homogeneous population considered above. The important difference here is that equation (5) is approximately linear when allele *B* is rare, provided that $u_{jk}^{(2,1)}$ is homogeneous of degree 1 and is a function only of $n_j^{(2)}$ and $n_k^{(1)}$.

To see why this is so, expand $u_{jk}^{(2,1)} [n_k^{(1)}, n_j^{(2)}]$ in Taylor series about $n_j^{(2)} = 0$, drop terms in $(n_j^{(2)})^{(2)}$, and note that $u_{jk}^{(2,1)} [n_k^{(1)}, 0] = 0$ since there can be no matings involving *AB* when this genotype is absent. This gives

$$g_{ij} \cdots \frac{1}{2} \sum_k b_{ikj} \frac{Ju_{jk}^{(2,1)}\left[n_k^{(1)},0\right]}{Jn_j^{(2)}}.$$

Since $n_j^{(2)}$ does not appear here, it is clear that g_{ij} does not vary with the number of AB individuals. Neither does it vary with $n_k^{(1)}$. This follows from the fact that, since $u_{jk}^{(2,1)}$ is homogeneous of degree 1, the derivative here is homogeneous of degree 0 (Varian, 1984, p. 330).

For example, if mating is at random and all AB individuals find mates, then

$$u_{jk}^{(2,1)} = n_j^{(2)} p_k^{(1)} \tag{7}$$

and

$$g_{ij}^{(2,1)} = \frac{1}{2} \sum_k b_{ijk}^{(2,1)} p_k^{(1)}. \tag{8}$$

The relative frequencies $p_k^{(1)}$ are approximately constant, since the AA component of the population is at approximate equilibrium.

The constancy of $g_{ij}^{(2,1)}$ implies that the AB component of the population will converge to a stable distribution of wealth categories given by the leading right-eigenvector of $\mathbf{G}^{(2,1)}$ and will then grow at a ratio given by the corresponding eigenvalue $\lambda^{(2,1)}$ of this matrix. Since the AA component of the population is still increasing at ratio $\lambda^{(1)}$, it follows that B will increase in frequency when rare if and only if

$$\lambda^{(2,1)} > \lambda^{(1)} \tag{9}$$

This argument applies also to the case in which B is common and A is rare. In that case, B increases when

$$\lambda^{(2)} > \lambda^{(1,2)} \tag{10}$$

where $\lambda^{(2)}$ is the equilibrium growth ratio of a pure BB population, and $\lambda^{(1,2)}$ the ratio of increase of AB in a population dominated by BB.

Inequalities analogous to (9) and (10) are widely used within evolutionary ecology for populations structured by age (Charlesworth, 1980, section 4.3). The present results generalise these to the case of populations structured by arbitrary categories, such as social class or levels of wealth.

Mating

I assume that mating is at random, both with respect to wealth category and genotype. Under this assumption, the unions matrix $u_{jk}^{(2,1)}$ for rare individuals of genotype AB is given by equation (7). In a homogeneous population, the unions matrix for AA individuals is

$$u_{ij}[\mathbf{n}(t)] = \frac{n_i(t)n_j(t)}{2N(t)}. \tag{11}$$

The denominator $2N(t)$ is chosen to make

$$\sum_{ij} u_{ij}[\mathbf{n}(t)] = N(t)/2$$

as is appropriate if all individuals form pairs.

Reproduction

A reproductive strategy will be represented as a vector whose ith entry determines the allocation to fertility when the bearer's wealth is i. For example, if there were only $K = 3$ levels of wealth, one feasible reproductive strategy is $v = (0, 0, 1)$. An individual with this strategy would allocate 0 units of wealth toward fertility if her own wealth was either 0 or 1, and 1 unit if her own wealth was 2.

I assume that the two individuals in a union make independent allocations to fertility, as determined by their own wealth and strategy and independent of the allocation made by their partner. These assumptions serve simplicity more than realism and might usefully be revised in future work.

A family's allocation to fertility is the sum of the allocations made by the two partners. For example, consider a union between two individuals who share strategy v, but who have wealth 1 and 2 respectively. According to strategy v, the first parent's fertility allocation will be 0, that of the second 1. The family's fertility allocation will be the sum of these, or 1. The wealth not allocated to fertility is inherited by the children produced. Our example family has wealth $1 + 2 = 3$ and bequeaths 2 units of wealth to its children. Inherited wealth is divided among the children as evenly as possible.

A family that allocates x units of wealth to fertility will produce

$$m(x) = \begin{cases} 0 & x < s \\ \text{Round} \left[m_+ (1 - e^{-a(x-s+1)}) \right] & x > s \end{cases} \qquad (12)$$

children. $m(x)$ is called the 'fertility function' and is graphed in the upper panel of Figure 5.2. No children are produced at all if the family allocation is less than s, the 'starvation threshold'. Above this threshold, fertility increases with allocation at a decreasing rate toward a maximal value, m_+. The rate of increase is determined by a third parameter, α; $m(x)$ is rounded to the nearest integer for computational convenience.

I assume that heterozygous *AB* individuals exhibit, with equal probability, either the strategy of *AA* or that of *BB*.

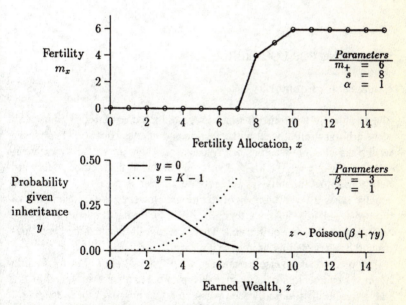

Figure 5.2   The upper panel shows how many offspring are gained for given investments of wealth. The lower panel shows the truncated Poisson probability distribution of earned wealth. The solid line there applies to all individuals when $\gamma = 0$, and to those who inherit nothing when $\gamma > 0$. The dotted line shows the distribution of earned wealth given the maximal inheritance, $K - 1$, in the case when $\gamma = 1$

Earned Wealth

In addition to inherited wealth, each offspring earns some wealth on her own. The wealth y earned by an individual who inherits x units of resource is a Poisson random variable with mean

$$E\{y\} \equiv \beta + \gamma x$$

γ can be interpreted as the regression of earned on inherited wealth. When $\gamma = 0$, earned and inherited wealth are independent as my earlier paper assumed.

If $x + y \geq K$, then the individual's wealth is truncated back to $K - 1$. This truncation models nothing in the real world and is done solely for computational convenience. In the earlier paper (Rogers, 1990), I showed that it made little difference.

These assumptions are sufficient to determine all of the quantities defined in the first two parts of this section.

SEARCHING FOR EQUILIBRIA

Demographic Equilibria

The simplest algorithm for finding demographic equilibria begins with some arbitrary initial wealth distribution and iterates equation (1) until the wealth distribution becomes nearly constant. Then, the ratio of increase is calculated as $\lambda = N(t + 1)/N(t)$. I will refer to this as the method of forward iteration. Unfortunately, if an accurate answer is desired, this method usually takes a large number of iterations. However, a small number of iterations – I use no more than six – is usually sufficient to reach the neighborhood of an equilibrium. Then, the equilibrium can be 'polished' using the faster method of inverse iteration.

The method of inverse iteration is a well-known algorithm for finding selected eigenvectors of a matrix. Given initial estimates of λ and of the stable wealth distribution, each inverse iteration improves these estimates. I modified the standard algorithm (Press *et al.*, 1988, pp. 394–395) only slightly, by using equation (3) to recalculate **G** at the beginning of each iteration. The resulting algorithm usually converged rapidly.

When the inverse iterations did not converge, the two-stage process was repeated again with a new, randomly chosen, initial vector. As many as five initial vectors were tried. This algorithm nearly always converged. Furthermore, extensive experimentation failed to identify any cases in which different initial vectors lead to different equilibria. Thus, the demographic equilibria in this model appear to be unique.

Evolutionary Equilibria

For each set of parameter values, the goal is to find an *evolutionary stable strategy*, or ESS (Maynard Smith, 1982). An ESS is a strategy whose fitness is higher, when common, than that of any possible invading strategy. My search algorithm begins with an arbitrary initial strategy and pits this against each possible one-step perturbation. Here, a one-step perturbation is a strategy that differs from the old by ±1 in exactly one position. When a better strategy is found, the new strategy replaces the old and the process begins again. The search ends when it finds a strategy that cannot be improved by any one-step perturbation.

In comparing an old strategy A with a new one B, I calculate four ratios of increase:

$$\lambda^{(1)} = \text{ratio for pure } AA \text{ population}$$
$$\lambda^{(2,1)} = \text{ratio for rare } ABs \text{ with } AA \text{ common}$$
$$\lambda^{(1,2)} = \text{ratio for rare } ABs \text{ with } BB \text{ common}$$
$$\lambda^{(2)} = \text{ratio for pure } BB \text{ population.}$$

I will say that AB invades AA if $\lambda^{(1)} < \lambda^{(2,1)}$ and that AB invades BB if $\lambda^{(2)} < \lambda^{(1,2)}$. In comparing two strategies there are four cases to consider.

First, if AB invades AA but not BB, then BB is an ESS but AA is not. In this case, the search algorithm replaces A with B and continues.

Second, if AB invades BB but not AA, then A is retained and B rejected.

If neither of these cases holds, then there is at least one internal equilibrium which may be either stable or unstable. In these cases, the search algorithm accepts B if $\lambda^{(2)} > \lambda^{(1)}$ and rejects it if this inequality is reversed. Ties occur when $\lambda^{(1)} \approx \lambda^{(2)}$, to within the limits of numerical precision. When an upper bound on optimal investment is sought, ties are decided in favour of the strategy investing more. The reverse is true when a lower bound is sought.

This procedure ignores internal equilibria (mixed ESSs), and consequently may stop at a strategy that is not an ESS. However, in practice this seldom happens. Almost always, the upper and lower bounds on optimal investment enclose a region that is stable against invasion from outside the region.

RESULTS

Figures 5.3 and 5.4 illustrate optimal reproductive strategies calculated
from two sets of parameter values. The second differs from the first in that
β is reduced from 3 to 1 and γ increased from 0 to 1. Thus Figure 5.4

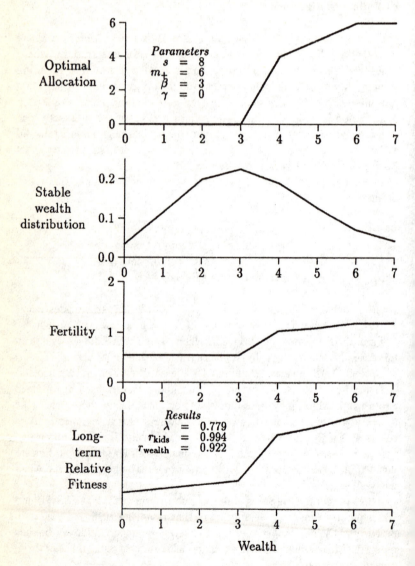

Figure 5.3   An optimal strategy with $\gamma = 0$

describes a world in which wealth is harder to earn for those who inherit little, but easier to earn for those with an ample inheritance. The two optimal reproductive strategies are identical for wealth levels 0–4. At higher wealth levels, less is allocated to fertility in Figure 5.4 than in Figure 5.3. This makes sense: inherited wealth has become more

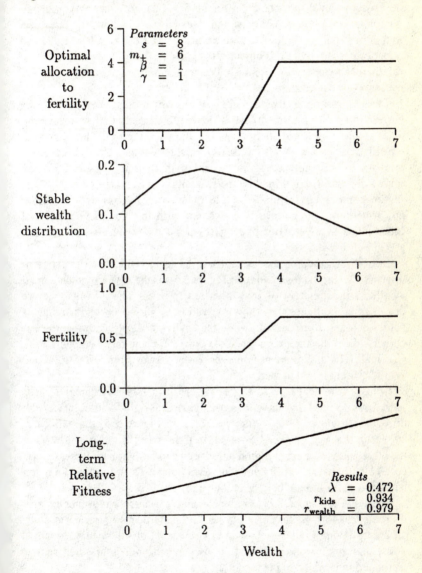

Figure 5.4   An optimal strategy with $\gamma = 1$

important, so wealthy parents are emphasising quality at the expense of quantity.

Note that fertility is a non-decreasing function of wealth in both figures. With sexual reproduction, I have been unable to find parameter values that generate a decreasing or non-monotone relationship such as that shown for the case of clonal inheritance in Figure 5.1. I cannot guarantee that non-monotone equilibria do not exist under sexual reproduction, but I have yet to find one. This provides a tentative negative answer to the first of the two questions with which I began. It seems unlikely that the negative relationship observed in many Western countries can represent an evolutionary equilibrium.

Let us turn now to the second question, which asks when, if ever, the correlation of long-term fitness with wealth exceeds that with fertility. The stable wealth distributions in the two figures show that at equilibrium, mean wealth is lower in the second. Thus, Figure 5.4 appears to describe a harsher world than than in Figure 5.3 – an impression that is confirmed by the two values of λ. Note that $r_{wealth} > r_{kids}$ in the harsher environment, while the reverse is true in the milder environment. This pattern is consistent with that found under clonal inheritance in my earlier paper (Rogers, 1990) (see also the second section of this chapter).

But before reaching any conclusion, let us examine a wider range of parameter values. This is done in Figure 5.5 for the case in which earned wealth is independent of that inherited ($\gamma = 0$). The two perspective drawings in the figure show how r_{kids} and r_{wealth} vary over a wide range of values of s and β. In each drawing, the environment is harshest at the left corner, where the starvation threshold (s) is large and mean earned wealth (β) small. The environment improves as one moves from left to right and is mildest in the right corner.

In my earlier paper, r_{kids} was near zero in harsh environments, near unity in mild ones and undefined at the extreme right-hand corner of the drawing (Rogers, 1990, Figure 5). Here, in Figure 5.5, the pattern is similar in that r_{kids} increases from left to right, but it is never as low as in the other analysis. Sexual reproduction seems to have greatly increased the correlation between fertility and long-term fitness. Thus, fertility is a much better proxy for fitness than the earlier study implied.

In the earlier paper, r_{wealth} was near unity in harsh environments and decreased to low values in mild ones. Its pattern in Figure 5.5 is quite different, having highest values in environments of intermediate quality. Thus, the conclusions of the previous paper do not hold when sexual reproduction is added to the model.

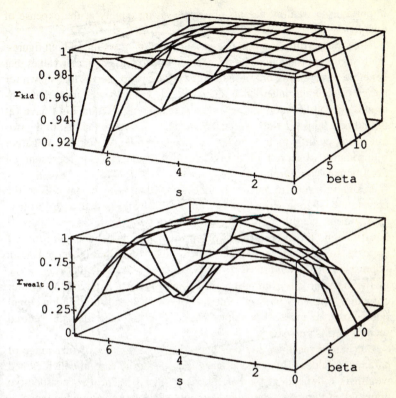

Figure 5.5   Response of r_{kids} and r_{wealth} to s and β. Parameters: $m_+ = 6$, $\gamma = 0$

But as I suggested above, the original model was unrealistic in two important respects and only one of these is corrected in Figure 5.5. This figure, like my original analysis, assumes that earned and inherited wealth are independent. This second problem is corrected in Figure 5.6 which assumes that the regression of earned on inherited wealth is $\gamma = 1$. This figure exhibits a pattern much like that of the original analysis. The correlation r_{kids}, between fertility and fitness, is highest in mild environments, while the correlation r_{wealth} between wealth and fitness, is highest in harsh environments. Thus, harsh environments may in fact select for material motivations and mild environments for reproductive motivations.

But although the present analysis does confirm the pattern detected earlier, it has different implications concerning the magnitude of the correlations. This is seen most easily in Figure 5.7. There, panel A graphs

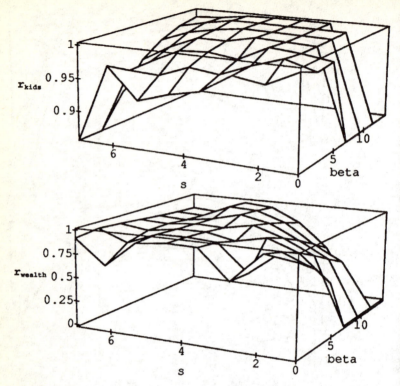

Figure 5.6   Response of r_{kids} and r_{wealth} to s and β. Parameters: $m_+ = 6$, $\gamma = 1$

the correlations in Figure 5.5 against λ, the ratio of increase, and panel B does the same for the correlations in Figure 5.6. What is impressive about these correlations – especially those in panel B – is that most of them are very large. The range of λ here is unrealistic. We can safely ignore all but the region near $\lambda = 1$. In this region, both correlations are always large. Thus, the present model implies that fertility and wealth are *both* excellent proxies for fitness. In a world such as that described here, there is no reason to expect either kind of motivation to dominate.

DISCUSSION

Modern economics recognizes a variety of motivations, including the desire for children (Becker, 1981). None the less, many economic models accord primary importance to material motivations. For example,

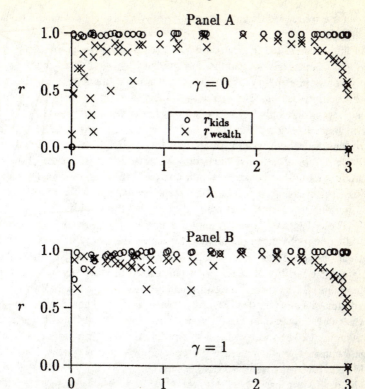

Figure 5.7 r_{kids} and r_{wealth} against γ

Friedman (1953, p. 171) observes that the assumption of 'single-minded pecuniary self-interest . . . works well in a wide variety of hypotheses in economics bearing on many of the mass phenomena with which economics deals'. Both the intuitive appeal of this theory and its predictive success argue that material motivations are important. Yet it does not follow that their importance is paramount.

Human sociobiology would explain material motivations in terms of their effect on short-term reproductive success. Those who acquire more resources are able to devote more resources to producing offspring and thus gain higher fitness. In this theory, material motivations are subordinate to reproductive ones. We desire material goods only in order to facilitate reproduction. Thus, we should not desire more resources than we can use for reproduction. The very wealthy should not desire additional wealth.

In this account, the theory of reproductive motivations is more general than that of material motivations, for it tells us when the latter theory will apply. Thus, the theory of reproductive motivations subsumes that of material motivations. The latter is a simplified approximation to the former, applicable only in a restricted set of circumstances.

But there is evidence contrary to this view. The very wealthy go on increasing their own wealth, in spite of the negligible effect this has on their own reproduction. Data from Western countries often show a negative relationship between wealth and the fertility of females (Vining, 1986). This is easy to understand in a theory of material motivations, since the opportunity cost of child care is higher for the wealthy than for the poor. These data are, however, hard to reconcile with a theory that makes reproductive motivations paramount. Similarly, the theory of reproductive motivations struggles with the 'demographic transition', a historical decline in the fertility of developed countries. As productivity increased in these countries, the limits to fertility must have relaxed. Thus, a theory of reproductive motivations implies that fertility should rise with productivity, rather than falling as it did in fact. The theory of material motivations makes short work of this problem: the rising productivity of these countries would increase the opportunity cost of time devoted to child care, favouring a shift to smaller families.

The results presented here suggest a way to reconcile these data with the supposition that human motivations evolved by natural selection. In a world with heritable wealth, wealth has value over and above its effect on the number of one's offspring. By continuing to earn, a rich person can increase the wealth of descendants several generations removed. Thus, the marginal effect of wealth on fitness may remain positive even among the very wealthy. Furthermore, the model suggests that wealth and fertility may be of roughly equal value in estimating fitness. At evolutionary equilibrium, material and reproductive motivations should both be important. In such a world, material motivations would be in no sense subordinate to reproductive ones. Resources should be valued even when they have no immediate effect on reproduction.

ACKNOWLEDGEMENTS

I thank Eric Charnov, Jack Hirshleifer, and Steve Josephson for comments. Steve Josephson suggested the paper's title.

NOTE

1.   A rationale for this assumption is discussed by Pollak (1990, p. 406).

REFERENCES

Becker, G. S. (1981), *A Treatise on the Family* (Cambridge, MA: Harvard University Press).
Caswell, H. (1989), *Matrix Population Models* (Sunderland, MA: Sinauer).
Charlesworth, B. (1980), *Evolution in Age-Structured Populations* (Cambridge: Cambridge University Press).
Friedman, M. (1953), 'The methodology of positive economics', in M. Friedman (ed.), *Essays in Positive Economics* (Chicago: University of Chicago Press).
Harpending, H. C. and Rogers, A. R. (1990), 'Fitness in stratified societies', *Ethology and Sociobiology*, vol. 11, pp. 497–509.
Keyfitz, N. (1968) *Introduction to the Mathematics of Population with Revisions* (Reading, MA: Addison-Wesley).
Maynard Smith, J. (1982), *Evolution and the Theory of Games* (Cambridge: Cambridge University Press).
Pollak, R. A. (1990), 'Two-sex demographic models', *Journal of Political Economy*, vol. 98, pp. 399–419.
Press, W. H., Flannery, B. P., Teukolsky, S. A. and Vetterling, W. T. (1988), *Numerical Recipes in C: The Art of Scientific Computing* (New York: Cambridge University Press).
Rogers, A. R. (1990), 'The evolutionary economics of human reproduction', *Ethology and Sociobiology*, vol. 11, pp. 479–95.
Rogers, A. R. (1992), 'Resources and population dynamics', in E. Smith and B. Winterhalder (eds), *Evolutionary Ecology and Human Behavior* (Hawthorne, NY: Aldine de Gruyter) ch. 12.
Varian, H. R. (1984), *Microeconomic Analysis* (New York: W. W. Norton) 2nd edition.
Vining, D. R. (1986), 'Social versus reproductive success – the central theoretical problem of human sociobiology', *Behavior and Brain Sciences*, vol. 9, pp. 167–260.

6 Fertility and Fitness Among Albuquerque Men: A Competitive Labour Market Theory

Hillard S. Kaplan, Jane B. Lancaster, John A. Bock and Sara E. Johnson

INTRODUCTION

The reduction in fertility accompanying modernisation poses a scientific puzzle that has yet to be solved. Despite the fact the problem has received a great deal of attention from economists, sociologists, demographers, anthropologists and biologists, no discipline in the social or biological sciences has offered a fully developed and coherent theory of fertility reduction that explains the timing and pattern of fertility reduction in the developed or developing world. The inability to offer an adequate theory raises fundamental questions about the theoretical foundations of those disciplines. For example, although economics has made great strides in explaining consumer behaviour, time allocation and labour force participation through the recognition that the household is a fundamental organisational unit of human action, there is no adequate explanation of why households are mostly composed of men and women who marry and have children. There is no economic theory of why reproductive partnerships form such a fundamental organisational principle in human societies nor of why people have and want children in the first place. The very modest progress of economists in explaining long-, medium- and short-term trends in fertility highlights this weakness.

Evolutionary biology in its application to human fertility has fared no better. The core theoretical foundation of modern evolutionary biology is that differential reproductive success is the principal driving force determining evolutionary change and stability. A corollary proposition is that competition for the resources for reproduction is the primary determinant of differential reproductive success. Thus, the fact that

96

people in modern, industrial societies obtain access to and utilise more resources than ever before in human history and yet evidence the lowest fertility rates ever recorded presents a particularly critical challenge to evolutionary biology, at least in its application to humans. Vining (1986) has argued that modern human fertility behaviour provides strong evidence that evolutionary theory as it is currently understood is incapable of providing adequate answers to the causes of human behaviour.

This chapter presents the first results of an in-depth study of fertility in a representative sample of men from Albuquerque, New Mexico, designed to evaluate the empirical force of Vining's critique. We present a simple three-generational model of optimal fertility based on maximising number of grandchildren and test it with data from a sample of 7107 men. On the basis of these largely negative results, we consider the empirical and theoretical requirements of an adequate theory of human fertility and one possible solution to the problem. We briefly outline a new theory of modern fertility reduction, based on changing returns to human capital investment in the context of competitive labour markets. The chapter concludes by discussing the kind of selection on the psychology of decision-making processes that could have produced optimal fertility regulation under traditional conditions and generates non-adaptive low fertility under modern industrial conditions.

A SIMPLE MODEL OF OPTIMAL FERTILITY

Both biological and economic models of optimal fertility are based on the assumption that there is a tradeoff between quantity and quality of children (Lack, 1968; Smith and Fretwell, 1981; Becker, 1987; Easterlin, 1974). This tradeoff is presumed to result from the fact that parents have limited resources they can invest in offspring and that each additional offspring necessarily reduces average investment per offspring. Most biological models operationalise this tradeoff as number versus survival of offspring. However, since about 97–98 per cent of children in modern industrial societies survive to adulthood, even among the poor, it is unlikely that reduced investment could significantly impact survival. Nevertheless, it is possible that reduced investment does affect adult competitiveness of offspring and thereby lowers their reproductive value. Therefore, the model we attempt to test here operationalises the tradeoff as between completed fertility of parents[1] and reproductive value of offspring, with the outcome measure being number of grandchildren produced (cf. Rogers, 1990). Since number of grandchildren is equal to the fertility of parents times the expected or mean lifetime fertility of each offspring produced (i.e. reproductive value at birth[2]), we can represent the fitness function as:

$$G = F_0 \cdot F_1 \qquad (1)$$

where G is number of grandchildren, F_0 is the completed fertility of parents and F_1 is the average completed fertility of children. The variable to be optimised in this model is F_0. The model assumes that the fertility of parents has both direct and indirect effects on fitness. It has a direct positive effect through the number of offspring born but a negative indirect effect through lowering the expected reproductive value of offspring. This is illustrated in Figure 6.1. To solve for the optimum level of parental fertility, we can find the total derivative of the number of grandchildren in terms of parental fertility, set that derivative equal to zero and solve for the optimum. Thus we have:

$$0 = \frac{\partial G}{\partial F_0} + \frac{\partial G}{\partial F_1} \cdot \frac{\partial F_1}{\partial F_0}. \qquad (2)$$

On the right-hand side of the equation there are three partial derivatives, the first representing the marginal effects of parental fertility on number of

Direct and indirect effects of fertility on fitness

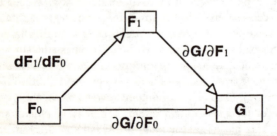

Figure 6.1   Direct and indirect effects of fertility on fitness

grandchildren, the second the marginal effects of children's fertility on number of grandchildren and the third the marginal effects of parental fertility on children's fertility (the product of the second and third term is the indirect effect of parental fertility on number of grandchildren through its negative effect on fertility of children). We refer to those effects as partials in recognition of that fact that other factors also affect number of grandchildren. The model expects the first and second terms to be positive and the third term to be negative. Using equation (1) we can take the partial derivatives of first and second generation fertility on number of grandchildren, respectively, and substitute them into equation (2) to obtain:

$$0 = F_0 \cdot \frac{\partial F_1}{\partial F_0} + F_1. \tag{3}$$

Solving this equation in terms of fertility in the first generation to obtain its optimum or equilibrium value, we have:

$$F_0^* = -F_1^* \cdot \left(\frac{\partial F_1}{\partial F_0} \right)^{-1} \text{ or } \frac{F_1^*}{F_0^*} = -\left(\frac{\partial F_1}{\partial F_0} \right) \tag{4}$$

where the asterisk represents the equilibrium values. This equation has intuitive meaning. Since, at the optimum, the fertility in the second generation must be positive, the partial marginal effect of first generation fertility on second generation fertility must be negative in order for there to be a meaningful optimum[3]. If there is no effect (i.e. the partial derivative is equal to zero), infinite fertility (or a corner solution, if first generation fertility is constrained) is expected. Another interpretation of equation (4), obtained by algebraic rearrangement, is that the ratio of children's fertility to parents' fertility must equal the negative of the derivative of the former with respect to the latter. This means that the larger the difference between reproductive value at adulthood and reproductive value at birth (which would be due primarily to pre-adult mortality), the smaller will be the marginal effect of parental fertility on children's reproductive value at equilibrium. Under modern conditions of low mortality, the ratio of second generation reproductive value at birth to first generation reproductive value at adulthood should approach one and the derivative of the former with respect to the latter should approach negative one. This means that at equilibrium each additional child that parents have should decrease children's fertility by one child.

In considering the applicability of such a model to modern conditions, we have specified one possible causal pathway for parental fertility to affect the reproductive value of offspring. This causal pathway is illustrated in Figure 6.2. Both parental resources and parental fertility should affect total parental investment received, with wealth affecting it positively and fertility negatively. Total parental investment is expected to affect educational attainment of offspring directly and income both directly and indirectly through its effects on education. The model then predicts that income and education affect an individual's desirability as a mate and fertility through the routes specified in Figure 6.2. Thus the tradeoff between first and second generation fertility in this model is mediated through the effects of parental investment on education and income.

We test the applicability of this model as a possible solution to the problem of low fertility in modern societies with data from the sample of Albuquerque men below. Those data were collected specifically to test the applicability of this model. Men were chosen as study subjects for two reasons. First, the measurement of the relationship between parental investment and income and between income and reproductive outcomes is somewhat more direct for men, because of many women's role as a 'homemaker' throughout much of the twentieth century. Second, the relationship between income and mating opportunities is likely to be stronger for men and, if parental fertility affects children's fertility through effects on mating success, those effects should be easier to detect with men as study subjects.

METHODS

The Short Interview

The instrument was designed to obtain the following information on the respondent: place and year of birth, ethnicity, education, religion, income,

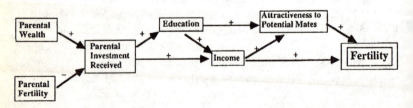

Figure 6.2   Factors that influence fertility

current mate's income, years in Albuquerque, number of years he lived
with each biological parent, number of half and full siblings, the fertility
and age of siblings, number and age of biological children, years lived
with biological children, number of spouses and women with whom he
had children, and the number of step and foster children he parented.
Information on the respondent's parents' place and year of birth,
education, ethnicity and income were also collected.

The Short Interview Sample

The total short interview sample of 7107 men included 2789 Hispanics,
3762 Anglos and 556 others. The composition of the sample by ethnicity
and birth cohort is presented in Table 6.1.

Potential respondents for the short interview were contacted at the
Bernalillo County Motor Vehicle Division (MVD) which serves all of
Albuquerque. All men who appeared to be over 18 years of age were
considered eligible for initial contact and were contacted as they received
their driver's license photo. If they agreed to the short interview, which took
about 7 min to administer, it was immediately conducted in a private area.

Sampling men who are renewing or obtaining driver's licenses and
photo IDs at the MVD provides a highly representative sample of the male
population in Albuquerque. It is the largest city in the State of New

Table 6.1   The sample of Albuquerque men by birth cohort

From (≥)	To (<)	Anglos	Hispanics	Others	Total
1895	1900	3	0	0	3
1900	1905	29	4	0	33
1905	1910	67	12	4	83
1910	1915	234	44	14	292
1915	1920	187	61	12	260
1920	1925	176	78	22	276
1925	1930	208	112	21	341
1930	1935	234	152	30	416
1935	1940	287	188	40	515
1940	1945	419	314	52	785
1945	1950	603	442	71	1116
1950	1955	581	519	113	1213
1955	1960	734	863	177	1774
	Total	3762	2789	556	7107

Mexico with a population of 455 000; approximately 35 per cent of the state's population lives in greater Albuquerque. Over 95 per cent of all New Mexican males over age 20 have a current driver's license (US Department of Transportation, 1987), compared to an estimated 92 per cent telephone availability (of which 30 per cent are unlisted numbers) for the Albuquerque area (US Department of Commerce, 1980). In addition, individuals who do not drive utilise the MVD to obtain valid photo IDs. Drivers' licenses and IDs must each be renewed every 4 years. By sampling only men who are waiting for license and ID photos, men who visit the MVD more frequently (i.e. those who do not have checking accounts and cannot register vehicles by mail, those who frequently pay fines, those who frequently sell and purchase vehicles, etc.) are not over-represented in the sample. Groups who are likely to be absent or under-represented among the licensed drivers include the elderly, disabled, institutionalised, transient, extremely poor and criminal. These groups are also likely to be under-represented or uncooperative in most other sampling frames as well.

Evaluation of sample bias
The sampling methods employed in this study provided several avenues for evaluating potential biases in the composition of the sample. First, after the first 850 interviews were collected, we compared the demographic characteristics of the sample we obtained with data from other sources such as the census. We examined the age and ethnic distributions of our sample compared to licensed drivers and to census population data for males. There were no significant differences in any of these comparisons. In fact, the ethnic breakdown of the sample obtained at the MVD is almost identical to that obtained from the 1980 Census (see Figure 6.3).

We also examined refusals. About 78 per cent of all men approached agreed to the short interview. One factor that predicted refusals was whether the potential respondent was alone or accompanied at the MVD; accompanied men refused 28 per cent of the time whereas men who were alone refused only 18 per cent of the time. No other biases such as age or time of day were detected. Refusals decreased steadily through time because of improved interviewer training.

Following this phase of unbiased sampling, we increased the proportional representation of Hispanics and others by not interviewing Anglos on about 20 per cent of sample days. In this way, we obtained a sample that was 53 per cent Anglo, 39 per cent Hispanics and 8 per cent other ethnicities.

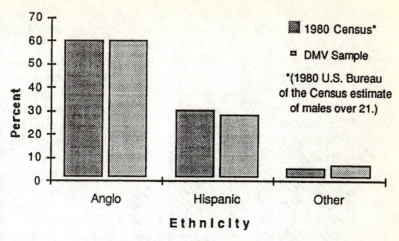

Figure 6.3   Ethnic distribution of men in sample obtaining drivers licenses versus frequencies for Albuquerque SMSA

RESULTS

Descriptive Results

Data on the fertility of Albuquerque men are presented in Figures 6.4–6.8. Figures 6.4a and 6.4b show the mean completed fertility of 5-year cohorts of men born between 1900 and 1960 among White (Anglo) and Hispanic men, respectively. The cohort labelled 1920 includes all men born before 1920, with the oldest man in our sample born in 1897. The men born after 1945 may not yet have completed their fertility (our analysis showed that over 90 per cent of men completed their reproduction by age 45, at least in the older cohorts for which we have data). These results show clear effects of both cohort and ethnicity on reproduction. White male fertility is low for men born in the early part of the century (many of whom reproduced during the Great Depression) and increases to a maximum for men born between 1935 and 1940. This peak corresponds to the Baby Boom. Among Hispanics, reproduction is highest for men born before 1935 and decreases thereafter, possibly representing a later demographic transition for Hispanics. Thus there is a clear interaction effect of ethnicity and cohort on reproductive performance. Those effects are all significant at a level of $p < 0.0001$. Figures 6.5a, 6.5b, 6.6a and 6.6b show the effects of cohort and ethnicity on age at first birth and total years of reproduction. These figures mirror the results on completed fertility.

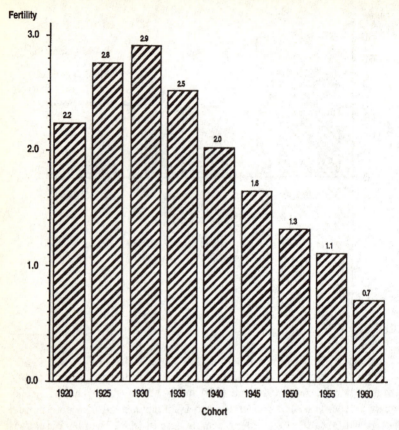

Figure 6.4a   Completed fertility by 5-year cohort, Anglo sample

Cohort/ethnicity classes with high completed fertility reproduce earlier and have a longer span between first and last births than those with lower completed fertility.

Figures 6.7a–c and 6.8a–c show the frequency distribution of completed fertility among different cohort/ethnicity cells. For Anglo men, there is a clear peak in the frequency distribution at two children, especially for men born before 1920 and men born between 1940 and 1945 (men born after 1945 are omitted because many may not yet have completed their fertility). For men born between 1920 and 1939 (those who reproduced during the Baby Boom), we see a much greater frequency of men with three children. Hispanics show a peak frequency of three, with a greater variance for men born before 1920.

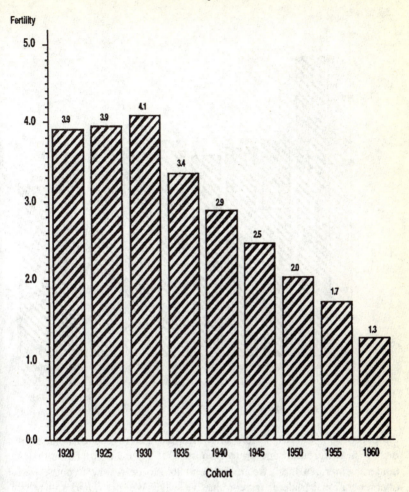

Figure 6.4b Completed fertility by 5-year cohort, Hispanic sample

Thus for the model we presented above to be applicable, we should find that optimum fertility for maximising number of grandchildren should be close to two for Anglos and between three and four for Hispanics. However, caution should be exercised here because of the possibility of phenotypic correlations. It is possible that there is variation among men in the optimum level. For example, men with greater access to resources may be able to produce more children and therefore should have a higher optimum than those with fewer resources. This possibility is illustrated in Figures 6.9a and 6.9b. Figure 6.9a illustrates a single global optimum for

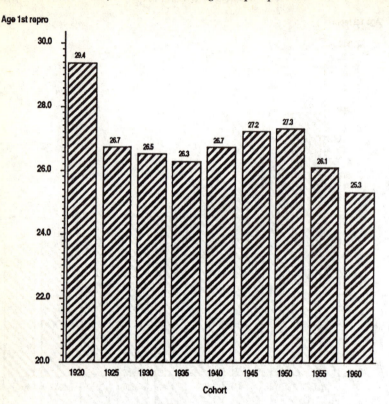

Figure 6.5a   Age at first birth by 5-year cohort, Anglo sample

the population, whereas Figure 6.9b illustrates heterogeneous optima for men with differential access to resources. If Figure 6.9b characterises modern American men, we might be unable to detect the hypothesised intergenerational tradeoff in reproductive value. We might find a positive correlation between fertility in the first and second generations because men with more resources or men from ethnicity/cohort classes that could support more children would both have higher own fertility and higher offspring fertility. Therefore, we must disaggregate the data by income, cohort, and ethnicity to test for such a possibility.

Tests of the Applicability of the Model

The association between children and grandchildren.
To determine if there was a level of first generation fertility that maximised number of grandchildren, polynomial regressions of number

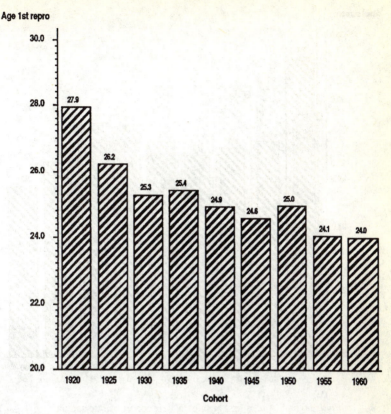

Figure 6.5b   Age at first birth by 5-year cohort, Hispanic sample

of grandchildren on number of children were run for the whole sample and by ethnicity, cohort and income quartile. If number of grandchildren peaks at some intermediate level of fertility as depicted in Figures 6.9a or 6.9b, a second-order polynomial regression should yield a positive linear term and a negative squared term. The full model we tested included the respondent's father's number of grandchildren as the dependent variable and father's number of children, father's number of children squared, ethnicity, cohort, father's income and all two-way interaction terms as predictor variables. This model was then reduced to include only significant effects. This analysis included all men for whom all siblings were at least 45 years of age (or who would have been 45 but had died earlier than 45) with known reproductive histories. This yielded a sample of 4066 men (respondent's fathers) with complete sets of grandchildren.

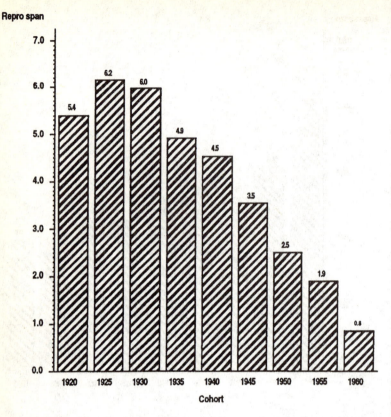

Figure 6.6a   Reproductive lifespan by 5-year cohort, Anglo sample

The analysis shows that number of children is, by far, the strongest predictor of variance in number of grandchildren. It alone accounts for 57 per cent of the total variance in number of grandchildren. Although, in a polynomial regression, the partial *p*-value of number of children squared is significant at the 0.0001 level, adding it to the model only changes the percentage of variance explained by 0.5 per cent and reduces the *F*-value from 5338 to 2714 (see Table 6.2). Moreover, the parameter estimate is just barely positive at 0.07. Adding cohort, ethnicity and parental wealth along with interaction effects only increases the variance explained to 61 per cent. The linearity of the relationship of children to grandchildren is striking (see Figures 6.10a and 6.10b). Even though the relationship is fit with a polynomial equation, the line is virtually straight

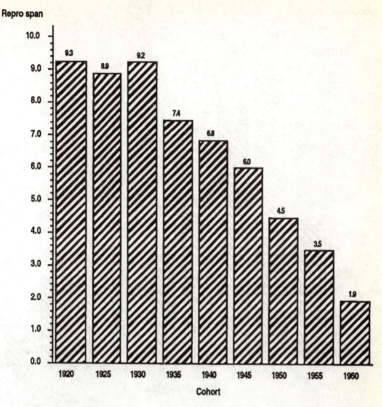

Figure 6.6b   Reproductive lifespan by 5-year cohort, Hispanic sample

for both Anglos and Hispanics. If anything, the lines bend slightly upward at high levels of fertility, due to a slight tendency for the children of men who had large families to have large families themselves.

A simplified model was also run for each ethnicity cohort cell and for each quartile of father's income, stratified by ethnicity. There was no evidence of a negative squared term in the data sets disaggregated by ethnicity and income. In fact, the second order polynomial term of parental fertility was either non-significant or just marginally positive. Again, within each of the eight ethnicity and income cells, number of children accounts for about 50 per cent of the variance in number of grandchildren. In no case was there evidence of an optimum at an

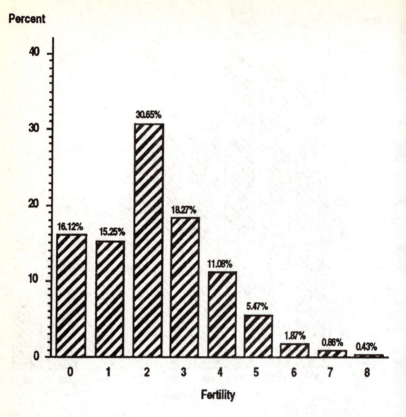

Figure 6.7a   Frequency distribution of completed fertility, Anglo men born before
           1920

intermediate level of first generation fertility. In all cases maximum
fertility was associated with maximum number of grandchildren.

   Another way to examine this relationship is with regression of the
respondent's number of children on his father's number of children (see
Figures 6.11a and 6.11b). Here we again find no evidence of a tradeoff
when only males are considered. In no case and in no region of the domain
of father's number of children do we find a negative relationship between
father's children and respondent's children. The slope of the relationship
is not significantly different from zero for all cohort, ethnicity and income
cells. As stated above in the presentation of the model, this means that
maximal fertility is favoured and there is no maximum to the function that
relates first generation fertility to fitness.

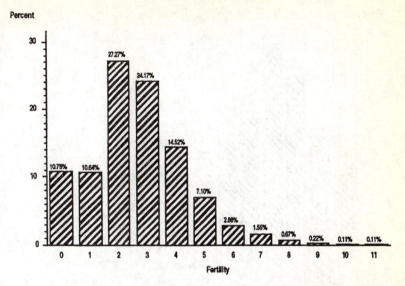

Figure 6.7b Frequency distribution of completed fertility, Anglo men born 1920–1939

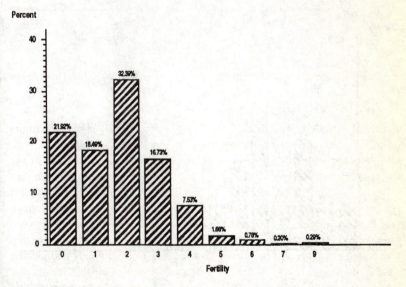

Figure 6.7c Frequency distribution of completed fertility, Anglo men born 1940–1949

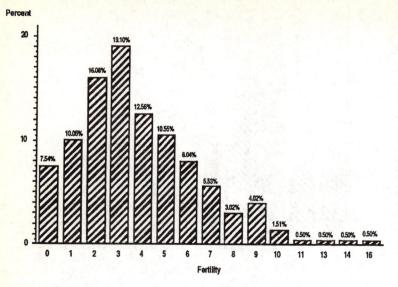

Figure 6.8a   Frequency distribution of completed fertility, Hispanic men born
before 1920

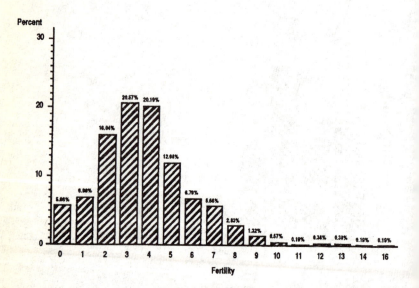

Figure 6.8b   Frequency distribution of completed fertility, Hispanic men born
1920–1939

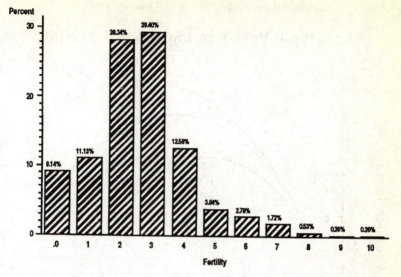

Figure 6.8c   Frequency distribution of completed fertility, Hispanic men born 1940–1949

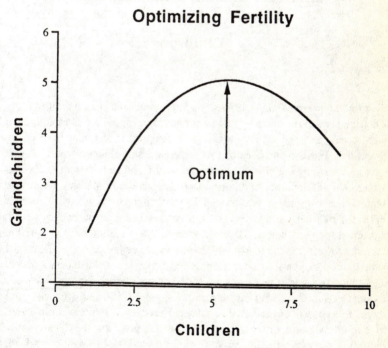

Figure 6.9a   Phenotypic variation in optimum fertility

Phenotypic Variation in Optimum Fertility

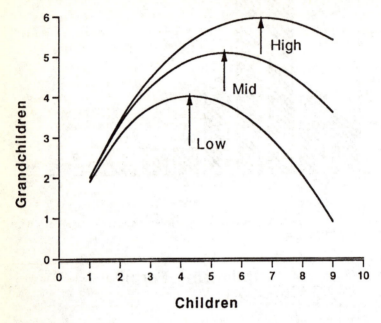

Figure 6.9b

Testing the intermediate relationships in the proposed causal pathway
The first step in the causal pathway proposed in Figure 6.2 is that parental wealth and parental fertility affect total parental investment in opposite directions. For the purposes of this paper, we skip directly to the second step to determine the effects of parental wealth and fertility on educational attainment and income. In addition to those predictor variables, the age to which the respondent was raised by both parents is used as another indicator of total parental investment received (e.g. if parents divorced, separated, or died before the respondent reached adulthood, the variable 'age raised' reflects the age at which biparental rearing ceased). The model tested includes years of education as the dependent or criterion variable and ethnicity, year of birth, year of birth squared, father's income, father's income squared, age raised, age raised squared, total sibship size and interaction effects as predictor variables. The squared terms were included to capture second order effects. Table 6.2 presents the final model including only significant effects. As predicted by the path model, all

Table 6.2   Regression models of number of grandchildren on predictor variables

Simple linear model			
N = 4066	F = 5338	p < 0.0001	R-square = 0.568
Variables in model	*F value*	*Partial p <*	*Parameter estimate*
Number of children	5338	0.0001	2.55 (0.03)
Reduced polynomial model			
N = 4066,	F = 2714	p < 0.0001	R-square = 0.572
Variables in model	*F value*	*Partial p<*	*Parameter estimate*
Number of children	5338 [186]	0.0001	1.77 (0.13)
Number of children ^2	40 [40]	0.0001	0.07 (0.01)
Full polynomial model without interaction terms			
N = 3673	F = 489	p < 0.0001	R-square = 0.616
Variables in model	*F value*	*Partial p <*	*Parameter estimate*
Number of children	5445 [157]	0.0001	1.64 (0.13)
Number of children ^2	35 [35]	0.0001	0.064 (0.01)
Ethnicity	43 [46]	0.0001	+
Father's cohort	43 [42]	0.0001	+
Father's income	7 [7]	0.01	−0.00003 (.00001)

Note: Ethnicity and Father's cohort were treated as indicator or class variables. Ethnicity was coded as Anglo, Hispanic and Other and Father's cohorts were 10-year birth cohorts from 1850 to 1929. Father's income is estimated on the basis of the average income for his profession in 1980 dollars, based on data from the US Census. Two numbers are given for the F-values in the multivariate model, the first is the F-value for the variables added in sequence they appear in the table and the second (in brackets) is the F-value for all variables added simultaneously, corresponding to SAS's Type I and Type III sum of squares procedures, respectively. The numbers in parentheses next to the parameter estimates are the standard errors of the estimate. Parameter estimates for each ethnicity and cohort are ommited for the sake of brevity.

measures of parental investment affect years of education in the predicted direction. Father's income and the age at which biparental care ended both positively affect years of education. The size of the respondent's sibship negatively affects years of education.[4] This result clearly shows that controlling for the effects of other factors such as cohort, ethnicity and income, first generation fertility is negatively associated with educational attainment.

The next model tested used the same predictor variables but substituted the respondent's income as the criterion variable. Again we found the

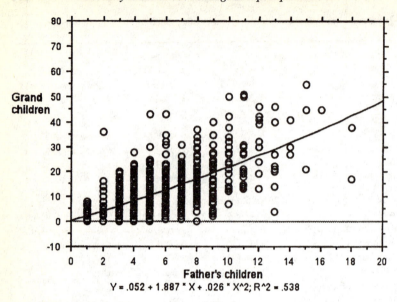

$$Y = .052 + 1.887 \text{ * } X + .026 \text{ * } X^2; R^2 = .538$$

Figure 6.10a   Children versus grandchildren, Anglos

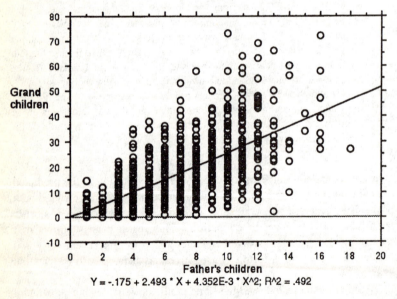

$$Y = -.175 + 2.493 \text{ * } X + 4.352E\text{-}3 \text{ * } X^2; R^2 = .492$$

Figure 6.10b   Children versus grandchildren, Hispanics

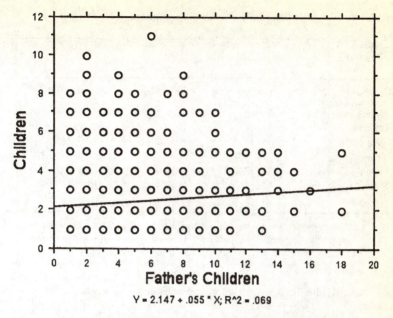

$$Y = 2.147 + .055 * X; R^2 = .069$$

Figure 6.11a   Father's children versus ego's children, Anglos

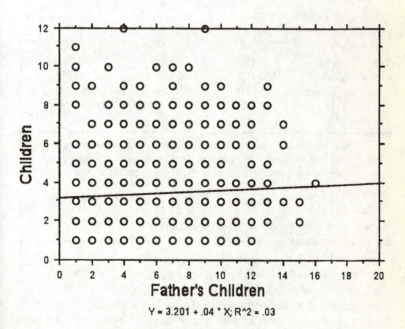

$$Y = 3.201 + .04 * X; R^2 = .03$$

Figure 6.11b   Father's children versus ego's children, Hispanics

Table 6.3A   Reduced regression model of effects of parental investment on years of education

N = 5087	F = 248	p<0.0001	R-square = 0.23
Variables in model	*F value*	*Partial p<*	*Parameter estimate*
Ethnicity	851 [345]	0.0001	+
Year of birth	57 [110]	0.0001	0.17 (0.16)
Year of birth ^2	89 (95)	0.0001	−0.002 (0.0002)
Father's income	291 [248]	0.0001	0.00009 (0.000005)
Size of ego's sibship	148 [143]	0.0001	−0.22 (0.02)
Age raised	52 [52]	0.0001	0.06 (0.009)

Note: Ethnicity is treated as an indicator or class variable. Ethnicity was coded as Anglo and Hispanic. See note on Table 6.2 above for further details on variable measurements, *F*-values and parameter estimates.

Table 6.3B   Reduced regression model of effects of parental investment on income

N = 5315	F = 97	p<0.0001	R-square = 0.13
Variables in model	*F value*	*Partial p<*	*Parameter estimate*
Ethnicity	330 [100]	0.0001	+
Year of birth	132 [44]	0.0001	718 (108)
Year of birth ^2	93 [92]	0.0001	−14 (1.4)
Father's income	84 [74]	0.0001	0.31 (0.03)
Size of ego's sibship	26 [27]	0.0001	−646 (124)
Age raised	3 [52]	0.002	446 (144)
Age raised ^2	8 [8]	0.007	−11 (4.1)

Note: Ethnicity is treated as an indicator or class variable. Ethnicity was coded as Anglo and Hispanic. See note on Table 6.2 above for further details on variable measurements, *F*-values and parameter estimates.

predicted effects. Age raised and father's income both affect respondent's income positively whereas parental fertility affects it negatively. These results are presented in Table 6.3.

The next steps in the proposed causal pathway are that income and education affect attractiveness to mates, and that attractiveness to mates and income both affect fertility. While we do not test for the effects of attractiveness to mates here, we do conduct the ultimate test concerning the relationship between income and fertility. It is here that the model breaks down.

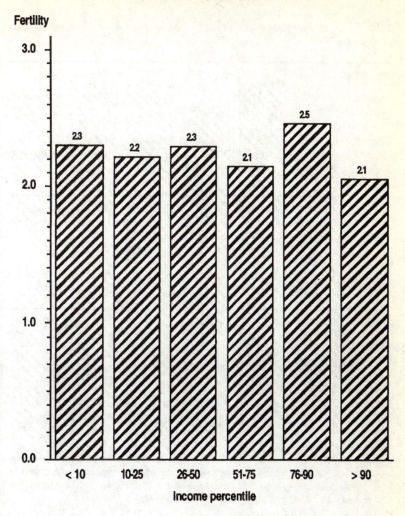

Figure 6.12a Completed fertility by income, Anglo men born before 1920

In Figures 6.12a–c and 6.13a–c completed fertility as a function of income is presented for three different age groups and for Anglos and Hispanics, respectively. Income is divided into cohort and ethnically-adjusted percentile scores. The first class represents the lowest 10 per cent of earners, the second includes the 10th to 25th percentiles, the third the 26th to 50th percentiles, the fourth the 51st to 75th percentiles, the fifth the 76th to 90th percentiles, and the sixth those earning above the

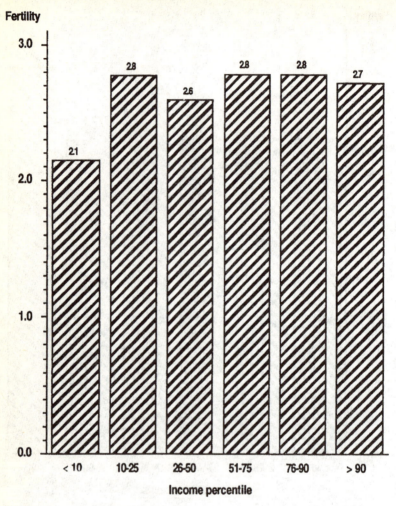

Figure 6.12b   Completed fertility by income, Anglo men born 1920–1939

90th percentile. The results show virtually no effect of income on fertility, either positive or negative. Among Anglos, there is a tendency for income to positively affect fertility for the group of men born between 1940 and 1949. This result may be due to the fact that age, income growth and fertility are confounded for men in their forties. Another possibility, of course, is that income does positively affect fertility for this group.

Fertility

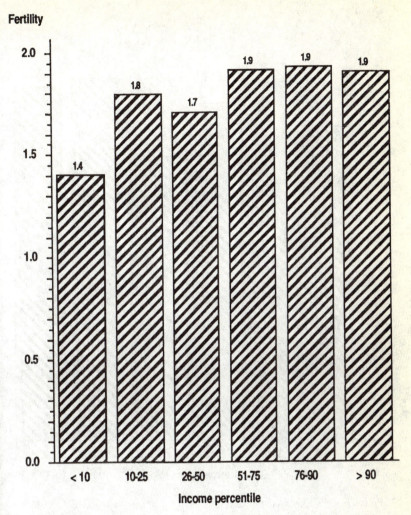

Figure 6.12c   Completed fertility by income, Anglo men born 1940–1949

Among Hispanics, there is a small negative effect of income on fertility in the earlier cohorts and no effect in the 1940–49 group. The negative effect in the men born earlier in this century may reflect a later demographic transition among Hispanics than among Anglos. It is often reported that wealthier and more educated individuals are the first to reduce fertility in response to modern conditions, and they are followed

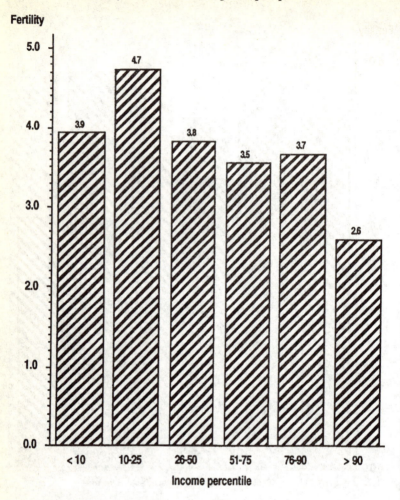

Figure 6.13a   Completed fertility by income, Hispanic men born before 1920

by poorer and less educated individuals in subsequent years. If Anglos completed the demographic transition prior to the years sampled in this study, we would not detect this timing. If Hispanics were in the process of passing through the demographic transition during this century, we may be seeing this effect in the earlier cohorts. In any case, there is no evidence of the strong positive effect of income on fertility required by the tradeoff model.

Fertility

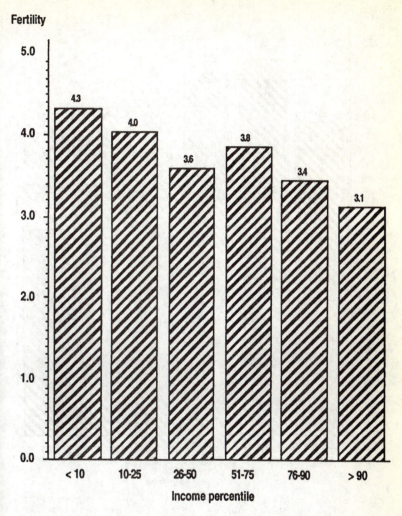

Figure 6.13b   Completed fertility by income, Hispanic men born 1920–1939

DISCUSSION

Implications of the Results for a General Theory of Human Fertility

Taken together, these results present a clear picture. A tradeoff model in which parents regulate fertility to maximise grandchildren produced does not characterise the behaviour of modern fertility. The data show that first

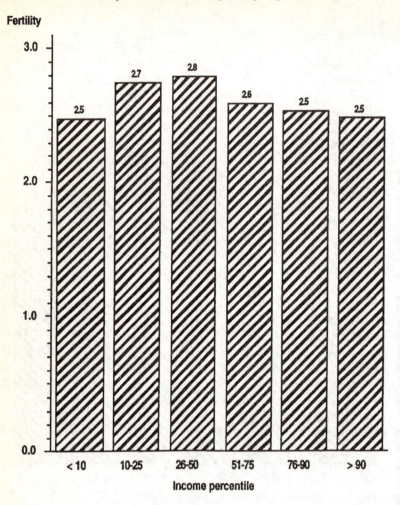

Fertility

Figure 6.13c   Completed fertility by income, Hispanic men born 1940–1949

generation fertility has no negative effect on second generation fertility and that in the absence of such a tradeoff, number of grandchildren would be maximised by maximising first generation fertility (at least in the domain of zero to twelve children). Most people, however, have two children. Moreover, there was little or no effect of income on completed fertility, especially among Anglos. Ethnicity and cohort effects were powerful. Cohort/ethnicity cells with high average fertility tended to show high fertility across all income classes and vice versa for cells with low fertility.

It is unlikely that long-term fitness could be maximised by such behaviour. It might be argued that grandchildren are a poor measure of fitness because longer-term multigenerational effects are ignored. The idea is that low fertility in times of relative prosperity assures the ability of descendants to weather population 'bottlenecks' that might occur under very unfavourable economic conditions. The empirical evidence we present here casts some doubt on the applicability of such a model. Men in our sample born before 1920 accomplished much of their reproduction during the years of the Great Depression. Yet, even during the most serious economic hardship experienced this century, we see no effect of income on fertility. For population bottlenecks to render such behaviour fitness-maximising, they must be more extreme than that experienced during the Great Depression and fertility decisions made many generations previous would have to effect the outcomes of those bottlenecks. We find this unlikely.

In addition to explaining these facts about fertility in modern industrial nations, any satisfactory theory of human fertility must also be capable of explaining other facts. It must generate empirically robust predictions about the pattern of variability in fertility among traditional small-scale societies. For example, it must be able to account for the fact that prior to contact with whites, Ache hunter-gatherers exhibited total fertility rates of about eight throughout this century, and !Kung hunter-gatherers only achieved rates of about four-and-a-half. The theory would also have to explain the pattern and pace of fertility reduction and non-reduction in response to modernization. It would have to generate predictions about the timing of fertility change and the demographic composition of groups reducing fertility in historic European populations. It must also explain current fertility patterns in the developing world. It must make predictions about those sectors of the population that are not lowering fertility, as well as those that are. All of these patterns must be accounted for in the development and testing of a model of human reproductive decision making.

To be adequate, the theory must specify both the factors people take into account in 'deciding' how many children to have and the specific socioecological and personal factors that interact with those psychological and physiological processes to generate variable fertility outcomes. In our view, a satisfactory theory would also have to explain how those decision-making processes could have evolved by natural selection. The theory must specify the evolutionary historical conditions that could have selected for the characteristics of those processes. It is not sufficient to 'explain' low modern fertility with the argument that humans are experiencing novel conditions to which their evolved psychological mechanisms respond non-adaptively. An explanatory theory must specify exactly what has changed, why those changes result in low fertility and what kinds of selection would have produced the suite of proximate mechanisms governing human fertility decisions.

Directions for Theory Development: Human Capital Investment in Competitive Labour Markets

In Figure 6.14 we present a qualitative model of the tradeoff between fertility and parental investment that generalises Figure 6.2. The model focuses on alternative uses of adult income. By income, we mean all time, physical and social resources that adults have at their disposal. It can be thought of as either a flow or rate that varies through time or as the sum (integral) of that flow throughout adulthood. This forms the budget that can be used in alternative ways that will be associated with alternative outcomes with respect to numbers of descendants in future generations. The fundamental tradeoff with respect to parental investment is between own reproduction and offsprings' reproduction, with the primary assumption being that income invested in own reproduction diminishes income that could be invested in offspring reproduction.

The model also specifies what we considered to be primary ways in which parental investment can be used to enhance offspring reproduction. First, and most obvious, is through impacts on mortality rates, particularly during the juvenile period. Other things being equal, expected lifetime reproduction per offspring will increase directly with increases in survival rates. Second, income can be invested in the embodied or 'living' capital[5] of offspring. By investing in living capital, adults can increase the body size and skills of offspring. Changes in living capital can affects the survival,[6] future income and social status of offspring. The latter two, in

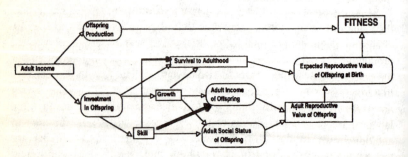

Figure 6.14   The determinants of fitness

turn, form the budget for offsprings' investment in own and next generation reproduction in a recursive process.

This set of causal pathways offers a guide for the investigation of the ecological and individual factors that should affect the investment tradeoff between own and offspring reproduction. Specifically, it focuses on the marginal impacts of physical size and strength and of skill on survival, income and social status. We have three major steps in the causal pathway. First, there are the functions that determine the marginal effects of investment of adult income on the survival, size, strength and skill of offspring. Second is the set of functions that determine the marginal effects of size, strength and skill on survival, future income and social status of offspring. Third, there are the differential impacts of adult income and social status of offspring on their reproduction. The total marginal effect of investments therefore will depend not only on their impacts on the first step but also on the marginal effects of those effects on income and social status and then ultimately on reproduction in the next generation.

We have placed a bold arrow on the link between skill and adult income because we believe that it is a critical defining feature of human parental investment, in general, and because we propose that it accounts for the secular changes in fertility and parental investment in modern industrial societies. Humans are extreme among mammals because of the long period of juvenile provisioning following weaning, that lasts some 14–18 years (see Kaplan (1994) for quantitative data on provisioning children in three foraging and small-scale horticultural societies). We propose that human adults in all societies are able to achieve high incomes because, as children, they are largely freed from self-provisioning and can invest their time in the building of human capital in the form of strength, skill and knowledge. This leads to the prediction that the length and intensity of parental provisioning will be determined, in large part, by the marginal impacts of human capital on incomes.

Several factors appear to have worked together to dramatically increase the value of investment in human capital in modern industrial society. First, changing technologies of production increased the impact of skill on productivity. Lindert (1986) estimates that in the period from 1867 to 1972 the percentage of national income attributable to human skills rose from 15 to 52 per cent. This suggests that diminishing returns to parental investment are likely to begin at much higher levels of investment in the competitive labour markets of large societies because there is so much room for upward and downward mobility. There is both qualitative and quantitative evidence that recognition of the importance of education as a determinant of income was directly involved in decisions to limit fertility in the late nineteenth and early twentieth centuries. Lesthaeghe and Wilson (1986), for example, present evidence of a very strong relationship between proportion of the population involved in agriculture and cottage production (and hence the proportion involved in the commercial wage labour and entrepreneurial market) and fertility among communities in western Europe at that time.

Second, secular changes in medicine and public health led to dramatic changes in child mortality rates. Becker (1975) shows analytically that, other things being equal, the value of investment in human capital increases with expected length of time over which the investment yields its return. Increases in survival rates increased expected lifespan and hence the expected period over which adult incomes would yield a return on investment in education.

These two factors together might be sufficient to account for increased parental investment and fertility reduction accompanying industrialisation. However, the two central findings of this study, i.e. (1) no association between income and fertility and (2) fertility levels much lower than the optimum for maximising genetic descendants) require additional theory development for their explanation. If optimal levels of investment in human capital increase as a result of changes in health and the technology of production, we should still find that income is positively related to fertility because larger budgets can support more children.[7] If people are adjusting fertility in relation to the amount they expect to invest in their children's human capital, current fertility patterns suggest that expected levels of investment are so well correlated with income that increases in wage rates do not result in more children. We propose that two characteristics of modern economies are responsible for these results: (1) the cumulative nature of the accrual of human capital related to economic performance[8] and (2) competitive equilibria in wage markets.

The acquisition of many skills that bring economic returns is dependent upon the base of precedent skills upon which they are built. This is especially true of mathematics, but also seems to be true of skills associated with reading and writing. Thus, for many skills, time and resources invested in their acquisition will produce returns that are positively associated with the stock of skills already in place. This is especially evident in university education in which success and drop-out rates appear to be well predicted by the base of skills established in high school.

This observation has several implications. First, skills parents have may form part of the base from which children draw their skills. Therefore, the value of investing monetary resources in children's education may depend directly on time parents dedicate to their children, if success at school, particularly at higher levels, depends upon the base children receive from parents. Although individuals who earn more per time spent working will have more money to invest in children, they will not necessarily have more time to invest in children.

Second, it means that the payoffs to investments in the higher education of children may be greater for parents who themselves are more educated. The strength of this effect should depend on the degree of complementarity between parental time and money investments in children's educational and occupational outcomes.

Third, because of the positive association between human capital and earnings, richer parents tend to possess more human capital. If, consonant with the above logic, the marginal returns from parental time and resources invested in children decrease more slowly with increases in the human capital of parents, the optimal level of parental investment may increase with capital embodied in parents. Thus, the extra income of richer parents may be balanced by increased optimal levels of investment in offspring to yield no net fertility effect. This may explain the lack of income effects on fertility rates in developed nations and the stronger income effects under traditional productive technologies that are not based upon skills requiring formal schooling.

The second feature of modern economies is that labour markets are competitive. A fundamental theoretical result of general equilibrium theory in competitive economies is that workers are paid according to their marginal product (that is, the increase in revenues they provide to the firm; see, however, Frank (1985) for a critique of this result). The theory of investment in human capital (e.g. Becker, 1975) predicts that people will invest in training to the point when the marginal returns on lifetime income from additional investment equal the marginal cost.[9] Those costs are expected to rise with age because of reduced years in the work-force to reap the advantages of higher wages and because of increasing opportunity costs in terms of lost wages as skill increases (Becker, 1975). This means that the equilibrium amounts of investment in human capital and wage rates will be directly linked through supply and demand in the labour market.

To understand this, imagine a situation of disequilibrium in which some skills that few possessed were critical to a new technology of production so that employing individuals with those skills greatly increased the firm's profits. The demand for those skills in combination with the short supply will produce high wage rates. If the present value of the costs to individuals of acquiring those skills were low compared to the present value of the higher expected wage rates, many individuals would invest in their acquisition. This would increase the supply of skills yielding lower equilibrium wage rates for those occupations, a lower marginal product (because of diminishing returns to numbers of workers with those skills) and a higher equilibrium proportion of individuals with skill. This process should continue to the point at which the present value of the cost of acquiring those skills should exactly equal the present value of increased earnings. Therefore, individuals with equal levels of human capital may be indifferent to some alternative skill–income combinations at equilibrium (i.e. the equilibrium will be a mixed probability distribution of skill and income) (see, for example, Behrman *et al.*, 1982, who calculate the present value of additional earnings from schooling using a sample of identical twins; those estimates appear to be close to its costs).

This places parents in the unenviable situation of having to adjust investment in children on the basis of the wage structure and costs of human capital that their children will face as adults when they must make their own human capital investment decisions. This, in turn, will depend heavily on the technology of production and the demand for commodities with differing factors and technologies of production.

Comparison of these two characteristics of modern economies (cumulative nature of skill acquisition and competitive equilibria in labour markets) with those of traditional human economies may help us understand the psychology underlying modern fertility and parental investment; that is, if the fundamental characteristics of the psychology and physiology of human fertility regulation and parental investment evolved in the context of a foraging lifeway (perhaps with some modification in the last 10 000 years of domesticated production). In traditional hunting and gathering economies, skills appear to be learned through play, practice and apprenticeship. Didactic instruction is very rare and children often learn by helping adults other than their parents. Thus, it is much less likely that more skilled parents would benefit more from investing in their children's skill than less skilled parents. Greater overall incomes due to higher levels of human capital (including strength and health as well as skill) should be associated with higher fertility as is empirically the case (Hill and Hurtado, 1994). In addition, economic returns from labour are not characterised by a competitive equilibrium and are unaffected by the skills held by other workers, except in the case of cooperative endeavours. Hunting and gathering are, for the most part, competitions against nature and the value of skill acquisition may not be a frequency-dependent function of the skill held by others.

This means that if cost functions are linear,[10] fertility would be proportional to income, both for parents and for children. Therefore maximising the sum of the incomes of all children produced would maximise genetic representation in future generations. If adult income linearly predicts adult reproductive value, psychological mechanisms that adjust fertility and parental investment to the adult income of offspring (rather than to reproductive value *per se*) could maximise fitness and evolve through natural selection.

The logic here is that optimising fertility in relation to the impacts of parental investment on next generation reproductive outcomes is a difficult problem to solve. The assumption that people will be able to make all the calculations required by the causal model depicted in Figure 6.14 may not be tenable. Psychological mechanisms or 'rules of thumb' that are simpler but approximate the results of those calculations well may be more likely to evolve. If adult income linearly predicted fertility in our evolutionary past (and, more generally, for most organisms), human psychology may be designed to maximise the sum of the energetic resources garnered (or, more generally, total income) by their descendants, and people may be insensitive to *actual* impacts of income on adult fertility[11].

Given that in the Albuquerque men sample modal lifetime fertility is two or three children for most cohorts, this view would predict that those values should be the modal optimum for maximising total income of descendants. It would also predict that variation in fertility within classes of similar wage earners will reflect the differential contributions of luck and human capital to the determination of individual wages and, hence, differential optimum for maximising the sum of offspring incomes. This will be a future focus of data analysis.

If this hypothesis is correct, it suggests that the critical novel elements in modern society are the increased importance of human capital in determining income and a positive relationship between parent's human capital and optimal investment in offspring to maximise the sum of their incomes. If this is correct, parents may be accurately adjusting investment in relation to cues (i.e. impacts on adult income of offspring) that no longer predict offspring reproductive value.

There are reasons to believe, however, that income is not the only determinant of offspring reproductive value affected by parental investment, even in foraging societies. For example, parental investment in offspring social status may affect mating success, especially for males. Moreover, intrasexual selection could be frequency dependent if: (1) the opposite sex chooses partners on the basis of their phenotypic characteristics relative to competitors or (2) physical conflicts determine the outcomes of mating competition. A second path through which the effects of parental investment in social status could be frequency dependent is through resource sharing. While return rates from foraging are less likely to depend upon human capital held by others, the final distribution of food in a foraging band may be significantly affected by relative social status. In spite of considerable attention to food sharing among foragers (Kaplan and Hill, 1985; Kaplan *et al.*, 1990; Hawkes, 1993; Hill *et al.* 1993), we know very little about the determinants of food access except that larger families tend to get larger shares of food. The fact that foragers tend to live in small groups and that the number of potential mates and competitors for mates at any one time is often low, parental investment could be a game with parents making decisions about their children's human capital as it impacts *relative* social status. While the shape of the function that translates differential competitive ability into differential reproductive success will determine the outcomes associated with alternative levels of parental investment, perhaps the benefits of being just a little better than competitors would drive parental investment upward and fertility downward. This might imply that the mechanisms underlying fertility decisions should be sensitive to both the intensity of competition under prevailing conditions and to the level of parental investment that the offspring of competitors are receiving.

If the psychology of parental investment is evolved to adjust to both income and relative status of children within local groups, a different set of models will be necessary to understand fertility and parental investment in the context of competitive labour markets, modern consumption possibilities and the status effects of different kinds of human capital.

CONCLUSIONS

The data presented here demonstrate that optimality models of fertility that maximise number of third generation descendants are not likely candidates for explaining modern human fertility behaviour. We offer the beginnings of a new theoretical approach to fertility reduction that is grounded in an attempt to build a general theory of human reproductive decisions. A focus on the relationships between investment in human capital, technologies of production, resource redistribution and status effects on mating offers new directions for theory building and empirical research. We clearly need to develop quantitative models that specify budgets for parental investment and the routes through which parental investment affects adult outcomes.

The proposition that competitive labour markets drive fertility reduction through a change in the value of investment in human capital generates a number of simple predictions. For example, it predicts that variation in the costs of human capital acquisition, the marginal product of individuals with different skill levels on productive output and the demand for commodities with different production technologies should determine variation in cohort-specific fertility rates. Cohorts for whom small differences in ability have large effects on economic outcomes are expected to demonstrate lower fertility than cohorts who reproduce when the wage premium for skill is low. In the developing world, analogous effects should be observable. The timing and patterning of labour market competition should predict when and who reduces fertility in the developing world. Sectors of developing nations where economic success does not depend upon human capital acquired through education should continue to have high fertility. Individuals who do not have the means to educate children and for whom high fertility will not lessen the economic outcomes for children should also exhibit high fertility. Fertility reduction should only occur when (1) competitive labour markets exist, (2) parents have the means to invest in human capital through education and (3) increased fertility lowers achieved income of children.

Fertility reduction in the former Soviet Union and its satellite countries is also a test case for this theory. With free education and alleged equal economic opportunity, fertility reduction would be unlikely according to this theory. Since we know fertility was especially low in those nations (Van de Kaa, 1987), it must be that either the theory is incorrect, or educational attainment and hence economic success were highly competitive and did depend on parental fertility.

The theoretical approach we propose here requires further development. The data show, however, that a new theory is required. The demonstration of the inapplicability of the fitness-maximising model provides us with new opportunities and directions.

ACKNOWLEDGEMENTS

We dedicate this paper to Daniel R. Vining Jr who first identified social versus reproductive success as the central problem of human sociobiology. His challenge inspired this research and our formulation of the competitive labour market theory.

Support for the research project, 'Male Fertility and Parenting in New Mexico', began with two seed grants from the University of New Mexico Biomedical Research Grants, 1988 and 1989, and one from the University of New Mexico Research Allocations Committee, 1988. Further seed money as well as interim funding came from the William T. Grant

Foundation (nos 89130589 and 91130501). The major support for the project came from the National Science Foundation 1990–1993 (nos BNS-9011723 and DBS-911552). Both National Science Foundation grants included Research Experience for Undergraduates supplements.

The authors would like to thank Robin Dunbar, Kim Hill, Alan Rogers and Phil Szydlowski for helpful comments on drafts of this paper as well as the many undergraduate and graduate students at the University of New Mexico who worked on the Albuquerque Men project in interviewing, coding, data entry, office management and data management and analysis.

NOTES

1. In most biological and demographic models, fertility is generally defined as a rate, often as daughters produced per unit time (e.g. Charnov, 1993; Stearns, 1993; Rogers, 1993). In the case of modern industrial societies with 'parity-dependent' fertility and very low adult mortality rates prior to the end of the reproductive period (Henry, 1961), completed lifetime fertility is probably a more useful measure.

2. Reproductive value at birth is defined as:

$$V_0 = \int_{x=0}^{x=v} l_x m_x e^{-rx}$$

   where l_x is the probability of surviving to age x, m_x is the instantaneous fertility rate at age x and r is the instantaneous population growth rate.

3. The second derivative test shows exactly this.

4. The variable 'years of education' is measured in terms of the highest degree the respondent achieved rather than in terms of the true number of years he spent in school. For example, high school graduates were assigned 12 years of schooling, recipients of bachelor's degrees 16 years, etc.

5. This generalises the economic concept of human capital to nonhumans as well.

6. For the purpose of simplicity, this pathway is not shown in Figure 6.14.

7. We have modelled this tradeoff between fertility and investment in the human capital of offspring quantitatively. Our simple model shows that fertility increases linearly with income.

8. See Becker and Tomes (1986), Becker and Barro (1988) and Becker *et al.* (1990) for a very similar discussion. We only discovered their papers after having written this section.

9. This conclusion is, of course, subject to many caveats. It defines lifetime income in terms of present values so that future income is devalued in relation to the time pattern of interest rates. It also assumes that individuals can borrow freely at the current market interest rate to finance consumption in any time pattern as long as the present value of total expenditures do not

exceed the present value of total income. It also assumes that individuals are indifferent to risk. Market imperfections and risk modify the details of this conclusion, but the fundamental insight remains the same.

10. If some costs of rearing children are shared among all children (such as investments in housing) or if there were diminishing returns to income, then cost might not be a linear function of the number of children (see Becker, 1981, ch. 5 for a discussion).

11. This view is rather unappealing because of its *ad hoc* nature. Moreover, people seem to be concerned about the mating prospects for their children as well as their adult incomes. Nevertheless, while Albuquerque men consistently mentioned the education and income of their children as factors in fertility decisions during focus group discussions, none mentioned fertility or referred to anything resembling lifetime reproductive success.

REFERENCES

Becker, G. S. (1975), *Human Capital* (New York: Columbia University Press) 2nd edition.

Becker, G. S. (1981), *A Treatise on the Family* (Cambridge, MA: Harvard University Press).

Becker, G. S. and Tomes, N. (1986), 'Human capital and the rise and fall of families', *Journal of Labour Economics*, vol. 4, pp. s1–s39.

Becker, G. S. and Barro, R. J. (1988), 'A reformulation of the economic theory of fertility', *Quarterly Journal of Economics*, vol. 103, pp. 1–25.

Becker, G. S., Murphy, K. M. and Tamura, R. (1990), 'Human capital, fertility and economic growth', *Journal of Political Economy*, vol. 98, pp. s12–s37.

Behrman, J. R., Pollack, R. A. and Taubman, P. (1982), 'Parental preferences and provision for progeny', *Journal of Political Economy*, vol. 90, pp. 52–73.

Charnov, E. (1993), *Life History Invariants: Some Explorations of Symmetry in Evolutionary Ecology* (New York: Oxford University Press).

Easterlin, R. A. (1987), *Birth and Fortune: The Impact of Numbers on Personal Welfare* (Chicago: University of Chicago Press) 2nd Edition.

Frank, R. H. (1985), *Choosing the Right Pond: Human Behaviour and the Quest for Status* (New York, Oxford University Press).

Hawkes, K. (1993), 'Why hunter-gatherer work: an ancient version of the problem of public goods', *Current Anthropology*, vol. 34, pp. 341–61.

Henry, L. (1961), 'Some data on natural fertility', *Eugenics Quarterly*, vol. 8, pp. 81–91.

Hill, K. and Hurtado, A. M. (1994) *Ache Life History: The Ecology and Demography of a Foraging People* (Albuquerque: Department of Anthropology, University of New Mexico).

Hill, K., Kaplan, H. and Hawkes, K. (1993), 'Why do male foragers hunt and share food?', *Current Anthropology*, vol. 34, pp. 701–10.

Kaplan, H. (1994), 'Evolutionary and wealth-flows theories of fertility: empirical tests and new models', *Population and Development Review*, in press.

Kaplan, H. and Hill, K. (1985), 'Food sharing among Ache foragers', *Current Anthropology*, vol. 26, pp. 223–45.

Kaplan, H., Hill, K. and Hurtado, A.M. (1990), 'Risk, Foraging and Food Sharing among the Ache', in E. Cashdan (ed.), *Risk and Uncertainty in Tribal and Peasant Economies* (Boulder, CO: Westview Press) pp. 107–44.

Lack, D. (1968), *Ecological Adaptations for Breeding in Birds* (London: Methuen).

Lesthaeghe, R. and Wilson, C. (1986), 'Modes of production, secularization, and the pace of fertility decline in western Europe, 1870–1930', in A. J. Coale and S. C. Watkins (eds), *The Decline of Fertility in Europe* (Princeton, NJ: Princeton University Press) pp. 261–92.

Lindert, P. H. (1986), 'Unequal English wealth since 1670', *Journal of Political Economy*, vol. 94, pp. 1127–62.

Rogers, A. R. (1990), 'The evolutionary economics of human reproduction', *Ethology and Sociobiology*, vol. 11, pp. 479–95.

Rogers, A. R. (1993), 'Why menopause?', *Evolutionary Ecology*, vol. 7, pp. 406–20.

Smith, C. C. and Fretwell, S. D. (1974), 'The optimal balance between size and number of offspring', *American Naturalist*, vol. 108, pp. 499–506.

Stearns, S. C. (1993), *The Evolution of Life Histories* (New York: Oxford University Press).

US Department of Commerce, Bureau of the Census (1980), *General Population Characteristics: New Mexico 1980* (Washington, DC: US Goverment Printing Office).

US Department of Transportation, Federal Highway Administration (1987), *Highway Statistics 1985,* TD2.22:985 (Washington, DC: US Government Printing Office).

Vining, D. R. (1986), 'Social versus reproductive success – the central theoretical problem of human sociobiology', *Behavioural and Brain Sciences*, vol. 9, pp. 167–260.

7 Reproductive Decisions Viewed from an Evolutionarily Informed Historical Demography

Eckart Voland

INTRODUCTION

The double determination of human behaviour and reproduction by biologically evolved reproductive interests on the one hand and socio-ecologically constrained opportunities for living and breeding on the other has become the focus of both the sister disciplines of sociobiology and behavioural ecology in recent years. Human sociobiological research aims at uncovering the genetic aspects of human behavioural patterns by investigating the ultimate causes, mechanisms and adaptive consequences of kin selection, social reciprocity, differential parental investment, sexual selection and other basic elements of social evolution (Trivers, 1985). By focusing on genetical concepts, sociobiological approaches achieve a high degree of generalisability when explaining human social performance (Winterhalder and Smith, 1992); however, only rarely do they achieve a satisfactory specificity when the concern is the explanation of the contextual variability of human social behaviour. For example, the evolved preferences in male and female mate choice and reproductive strategies are well-known and easily explained as an outcome of sexual selection; but the causes of their phenotypic plasticity remain obscure, Under what circumstances do male and female interests converge in monogamous mating systems as opposed to polygamous ones? Questions of this kind fuel behavioural ecology.

Human behavioural ecology investigates the differing manifestations of the biologically evolved interests of self-preservation and reproduction within specific ethno-historical and ecological contexts in order to discern the adaptive design of the behaviour-regulating mechanisms involved. This is tantamount to asking questions about the biological function of behaviour and the behavioural differences in contrasting social, cultural, historical and ecological milieux.

That environmental variation influences human behavioural tendencies has, of course, been known for a long time. Social and cultural anthropologists have done a lot of work demonstrating that differences in social structure, technology and/or patterns of resource exploitation shape differences in human social and reproductive behaviour within and between populations. However, the specific achievement of behavioural ecology has been to make explicit the assumption that correlations between environment and behaviour of this kind are brought about and maintained by evolutionary processes.

Behavioural ecologists view the life performance of an individual in terms of his/her biological effort to maintain and eventually increase his or her genetic material (Williams, 1966; Alexander, 1987). Accordingly, a central interest has been to investigate how humans organise their reproductive effort over the course of a lifetime and whether their actual 'life-styles' represent optimal solutions to the basic biological problem of reproduction, taking the prevailing living conditions into account. One of the basic trade-offs concerns the balance between growth, development (or maintenance) and reproduction (Stearns, 1992). For example, interpreting variance in the age at menarche (which in traditional populations is often strongly correlated with the beginning of reproduction) as an outcome of different solutions to the development/reproduction trade-off problem seems to be promising (Borgerhoff Mulder, 1992).

Decisions on the patterning of reproduction hinge in the first place on the question of how much an organism should invest in its own reproduction and how much in the reproduction of relatives. Female celibacy in western European social history is a rewarding focus of research in this respect, since it has been shown that the upper class daughters' renunciation of a family of her own probably was beneficial for lineage survival on average (Hager, 1992). In the second place, reproductive decisions must deal with the problem of how much to invest in mating effort (i.e. in courting and controlling attractive partners). Dowry competition (Gaulin and Boster, 1990; Rao, submitted) and bride-price competition (Borgerhoff Mulder, 1988) are common outcomes of this kind of reproductive decision making. And finally, of course more direct decisions are to be made (cf. Borgerhoff Mulder, 1992): How many offspring should an organism conceive? How long should the intervals between successive reproductive phases be? Should the offspring be cared for as long as possible or should they be encouraged to become independent as soon as possible? What should the personal expenditure of the parents consist of? Should they 'give everything' and reproduce less often or should they invest less in each offspring and thus have offspring more frequently or in larger clutches? Should they invest in all offspring equally or is it more advantageous to make distinctions between individual offspring?

A specific reproductive history results from the sum of all these decisions. The adaptive value of such a strategy set is evaluated by natural selection against the circumstantial opportunities in which the individuals concerned find themselves. Since the individuals in a population will often differ in their circumstances, the reproductive decisions that individuals make can be expected to be different. Individuals may differ, for example, in the availability of kin to act as helpers (Turke, 1989) or in their availability of resources (Low and Clarke, 1991), as well as in their physical condition (Winkler and Kirchengast, 1994), which might lead to differentials in reproductive performance. The factors that determine an individual's personal circumstances can be genetic, ecological, sociocultural or even accidents of history.

Some of the allocation 'decisions' will have been more or less genetically fixed during phylogeny and are beyond the control of the individual; others permit or even require spontaneous phenotypic adjustment to the prevailing circumstances. Natural selection, therefore, will not simply promote the best of all theoretically conceivable strategies for the allocation of reproductive effort, but the best of those actually available to an individual at the time (for examples see Cheney, 1983; Dunbar, 1991). Since there may be different optima within a population, this is a strong argument for studying reproductive performance not only at the population level, but also at finer levels of analysis (cf. Low, 1993).

Our current knowledge of human behavioural ecology suggests, that, at least in traditional and historical populations, people by and large do everything to achieve a maximum possible personal share of the genetic reproduction of their population (Borgerhoff Mulder, 1991; Cronk, 1991; Smith, 1992a, b; Smith and Winterhalder, 1992). Thus they follow the biological imperative of fitness maximisation with the consequence of being automatically involved in interpersonal reproductive competition.

HISTORICAL DEMOGRAPHY AND DARWINIAN APPROACHES TO HUMAN REPRODUCTIVE DECISION MAKING

It has now become clear that an adequate understanding of evolutionary processes in large and long-lived organisms such as human depends on a fine-grained analysis of the reproductive decisions at the individual level, combined with detailed knowledge of each individual's personal circumstances and the way these change over its lifetime (Dunbar, 1993). In contrast to long-lived mammals and birds, for which it is seldom possible to combine both detailed information on circumstances with long-term data on the fitness consequences of reproductive decisions, there does exist one source of data that overcomes this problem for humans. This is the detailed demographic records contained in the parish registers of births, marriages and deaths that were kept in Europe mostly from the seventeenth century onwards. Depending on local circumstances, these data reliably document 150–200 years of pre-modern population history. On the basis of church records and other historical sources, numerous vital and social statistical data can be linked to individual lives and to the histories of whole families and lineages, as well as to village genealogies and even the genealogical networks of entire regions.

Recently, a vigorous discussion has started on the proper way to study human adaptation (see Borgerhoff Mulder *et al.*, in preparation for an overview). To put it simply, the starting point for much of the fuss is a disagreement about what constitutes an adaptation: is it a trait that maximises genetic fitness (irrespective of the origin of that trait) or is it a trait that was shaped by natural selection (irrespective of its current contribution to genetic fitness). While proponents of the former point of view (often labelled Darwinian anthropologists) lay their main emphasis on studying differential reproductive success, proponents of the latter view (often called Darwinian psychologists) are mainly interested in the design of the behaviour-regulating mechanisms while ignoring fitness differentials in current human environments on the grounds that these are not identical with the Pleistocene milieu in which these mechanisms evolved.

Irrespective of the heuristic approach preferred, the methods, results and insights of historical demography have something to offer us. Demographic variations allow conclusions to be drawn about the tendencies and inclinations that characterise the human psyche, including those with reproductive implications. Imhof (1984) gives an example of how aggregate data on infant and child mortality reflect parental attitudes towards child welfare; this can become the focus of a Darwinian approach even if the reproductive consequences of differing parental rearing styles remain unknown (Voland, 1989). The same holds true for family reconstitution studies. It might well be worth while testing predictions from evolutionary theory on, say, differential predictions from evolutionary theory on, say, different parental investment even if the fitness consequences cannot be measured (Voland, 1989; Low, 1993).

As mentioned before, historical demography, and especially family reconstitution studies, provides a valuable opportunity for determining fitness differentials because the reproductive consequences of human behaviour – in favourable cases – can be read off directly from the data. Thus, various measures of reproductive success can enter an evolutionary analysis as dependent variables, the variances of which then have to be explained with regard to their causes and biological function. To provide more specific examples of how we might do this, I will give a short overview on some results of the Krummhörn study that I and my colleagues have undertaken over the past decade or so.

THE KRUMMHÖRN STUDY

General Background

The Krummhörn region is situated in the northwest of Ostfriesland, Germany, and comprises an area of 153 km^2 with a nearly stable cross-sectional population size during the eighteenth and nineteenth centuries of approximately 14 000 individuals distributed over 32 parishes. Its soil ('younger marsh') is extremely fertile, allowing for a very productive agriculture as well as dairy farming. At the end of the nineteenth century, the marsh regions covered only 7.3 per cent of the total area of Hannover province, but they produced 22.2 per cent of its agroeconomic profit (Meitzen, 1894).

In contrast to the Geest and moor regions of Ostfriesland, large and medium-sized businesses dominated the farming economy of the Krummhörn. A capital and market oriented agriculture was able to develop successfully and replace a purely subsistence economy earlier than elsewhere in Germany. Accumulation of proceeds was possible and, indeed, led to remarkable wealth concentration in some lineages. Unogeniture prevailed, with (as a normative rule) the youngest son inheriting the undivided property. The non-inheriting siblings had to be compensated by cash or other movable wealth.

Because the Krummhörn was surrounded by the North Sea on three sides and by inaccessible moorlands on the fourth side, neither a geographic expansion nor a substantial growth of the population was possible. In addition, the very early and complete colonisation of the area prevented any significant population increase, since there were no commons or wasteland available. In terms of classical animal ecology the

Krummhörn region could be regarded as a saturated habitat that had only a limited amount of breeding places available.

It was the ownership of land that imposed the social structure of the Krummhörn population. It defined social prestige, political influence and rights, and, most importantly, the everyday transactions of the people. The social class contrast between farmers and labourers was extremely marked in nearly every material and immaterial aspect of their life-styles. Social attitudes and behaviour reflecting these differences were underlined by the prevailing Calvinistic religion that tended to promote attitudes of social inequality. The extreme gap between farmer's and labourers' socioeconomic opportunities was recognised by everybody and ultimately led to some social dissatisfaction during the course of the nineteenth century on the part of the working class.

This population underwent a family reconstitution study using church records as well as tax lists, using the standard methodology of historical demography. The tax lists contain entries on land ownership, thereby making it possible to reconstruct the social structure of the population using objective criteria. All households with more than 75 'Grasen' of land (1 'Gras' ≈ 0.37 ha) were considered to belong to the upper class of relatively wealthy farmers. Although the 75-Grasen threshold was somewhat arbitrary, it seems to have been quite useful none the less. By and large, registrations were fairly complete and reliable from 1720 onwards, although up to 1750 it is likely that stillbirths were incompletely registered. The data were organised with the KLEIO databank system and analysed by SPSS-x routines (cf. Engel, 1990 for more details and further references).

Differential Reproductive Success

The chance preservation of a Napoleanic tax list allows us to identify the 300 absolutely wealthiest men of Ostfriesland, including those from the Krummhörn region, for the year 1812. Table 7.1 summarises their reproductive performance and compares it with the contemporary population mean. On average, the elite men got roughly two more children than ordinary men. Even if an increased infant and child mortality (including striking sex differentials, see below) tended to reduce the rich group's initial reproductive 'advantage', nevertheless they were each able to raise one child more to adulthood than the average man. Moreover, children from the elite group had markedly better local marriage (and thus reproductive) prospects than the offspring of ordinary families. Whereas an average man could expect to get two of his children married (and thus,

Table 7.1   Measures of average lifetime reproductive success of the 60 wealthiest men of the Krummhörn in 1812 and of the contemporary population mean (n = 966) (adapted from Klindworth and Voland, 1954)

	1812 elite	*Population mean*	*p<*
Children	6.58	4.59	0.001
Stillbirths	0.015	0.037	0.05
Liveborn	6.48	4.42	0.001
Infant mortality	0.195	0.134	0.01
1-year-olds	5.22	3.83	0.001
Child mortality	0.201	0.185	n.s.*
15-year-olds	4.17	3.12	0.001
Celibates	0.112	0.120	n.s.*
'Emigrants'	0.156	0.272	0.001
Married children	3.05	1.90	0.001

*n.s. = Not significant.

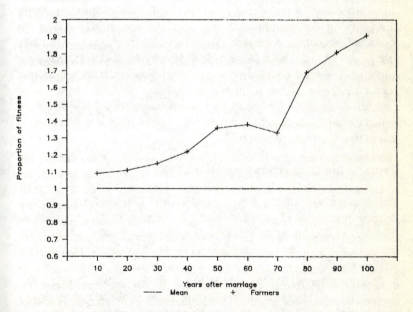

Figure 7.1   Ratio of farmers' fitness to the overall population mean (Krummhörn, marriage cohort 1720–1750) (from Voland, 1990)

only just replace himself in genetic terms), a rich farmer, who ended up with three married children on average, succeeded in contributing 50 per cent more to the local gene pool.

All of these effects accumulated to yield pronounced social status differences in Darwinian fitness. This can be shown, for example, by comparing the long-term reproductive success of an upper-class farmer family with the population mean by adding together all age- and sex-specific 'reproductive values' (Fisher, 1930) of all the living descendants at defined time intervals (Figure 7.1). In short, a prosperous farming couple of the eighteenth century had almost twice as many gene replicates in the local population 100 years after wedding than an average family. Hence, as is also known to be the case in pre-modern Swedish (Low and Clarke, 1991) and Norwegian (Røskaft *et al.*, 1992) samples (as well as traditional non-western populations: see Irons, 1991), wealth was correlated with lifetime reproductive success within the Krummhörn population.

Not all of the Krummhörn people had the same opportunities of spreading their genetic material in the evolutionary game, because the ownership of land was a component of natural selection. This, in turn, was associated with an important consequence: striving to maintain or even increase the size of the property and striving for social upward mobility (i.e. striving for cultural success) was tantamount to striving for reproductive success, regardless of whether this correlation was actually recognised or not. The surmise, first voiced by Irons (1979), that there might be a positive correlation between social and reproductive success seems to apply to the Krummhörn case too. In this sense, social competition for privileged positions in the Krummhörn social system is to be understood as a cultural reflex of a basic biological process, namely that of reproductive competition.

Reproductive Decision-making: Mate Choice

The average age among Krummhörn men (1720–1874) at their first marriage was about 30 years and there were virtually no social differences (Figure 7.2). The brides of farmers with large holdings were 24.9 years old on average and thus 2.3 years younger than those of the propertyless workers.

These widespread (cf. Voland and Engel, 1990; Low and Clarke, 1991; Røskaft *et al.*, 1992) social status differences in the marriage age of women could possibly be the result of a conditional female partner choice strategy. The maxim of mate selection would then read: 'If you are young,

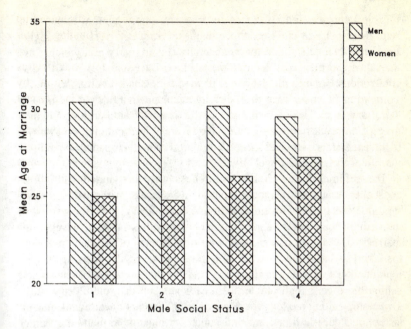

Figure 7.2   Mean age for men and women (first marriages only) by ownership of the men (Krummhörn 1720–1874). Male social status: 1 = farmers, 2 and 3 = smallholders, 4 = landless (from Voland and Engel, 1990)

be demanding and only marry a man who promises to provide you with above-average reproductive success. The older you become, the more you should give up your choosiness!' And in fact the Krummhörn data suggest that women of different ages did show striking differences in their choice of husbands: the younger the women were when they married, the more likely it was to be to a well-off man. Almost one-third of the women under 20 years of age (compared to less than 10 per cent of the women over 30 years of age) married a farmer; conversely, one in five of the farmers, but only one in every 25 of the landless men married a women under 20 (Voland and Engel, 1990).

If one assumes that young women were equally attractive as marriage partners for men from all social groups, then the variation in the marriage age of women can only be seen as the outcome of systematic mate choice on the part of the women's preference for socially successful men. Incidentally, the social status of a bride's natal family had no significant influence on her marriage age, despite pronounced social endogamy.

This interpretation allows us to propose a more general hypothesis: hypergamous women (i.e. those who successfully pursued a higher standard when selecting a mate) generally should marry at a younger age than those women who married within their own social class. Our data confirm this. Among the daughters of the landless, social climbers are 2.3 years younger on average than socially endogamous brides at the time of their marriage. The converse is true for upper-class daughters: if they married beneath their social status, they were 1.3 years older, on average, than their sisters, who had succeeded in preserving their social standing by marriage (Voland and Engel, 1990).

These female mate-choice preferences were associated with direct consequences for the personal reproductive success of the women, since reproductive success declined with a rising marriage age and rose with increasing social status (Table 7.2). The upper-class farmers' wives in all marriage age classes had an advantage over women of the same age from the other social groups. At the same time, however, the costs of delayed reproduction rose with marriage age, since younger women, of course, left behind more gene replicates in the next generation than did older women. Therefore, waiting too long for a 'good match' was not a worthwhile pursuit in terms of genetic fitness maximisation. A woman who married a farmer while she was under the age of 20 years contributed 1.2 more adult children

Table 7.2 Mean number of adult children in the local population by female age at marriage and male land ownership (Krummhörn, 1720–1874). Number of women in parentheses (from Voland and Engel, 1990)

Female age at marriage	Male social status* 1	2	3	4	Mean
<20	3.4 (14)	4.0 (5)	2.1 (9)	2.2 (13)	2.8 (41)
20–25	3.0 (26)	2.8 (20)	3.1 (56)	2.5 (80)	2.8 (182)
25–30	4.4 (17)	2.8 (10)	1.7 (39)	2.2 (87)	2.1 (153)
>30	2.9 (9)	1.2 (7)	1.1 (29)	1.4 (58)	1.5 (103)
Mean	2.9 (66)	2.7 (42)	2.2 (133)	2.1 (238)	2.3 (479)

*Social status defined as: (1) farmers, (2) and (3) smallholders, (4) landless.

to the next generation, on average, than a same-aged woman who was married to a labourer, and among those marrying between the ages of 20 and 25 years, these differences still amounted to a 'half child' on average.

Regardless of what proximate factors led the Krummhörn women to select their husbands as they did, their differentiated mate-choice behaviour resulted in systematic consequences for their personal reproductive success. Thus, the psychosocial reward for 'good' mate choice generally went hand in hand with a genetic 'reward' through above-average reproduction. And, therefore, it would be absolutely misleading to see a contradiction between the proximate causes for mate selection (factors such as the emotions, material expectations and normative rules) and their ultimate causes (namely the striving for the best possible reproductive partnership).

Reproductive Decision-making: Differential Parental Investment

The community of Reepsholt (next door to the Krummhörn), has an almost complete register of godparents for the second half of the eighteenth century. We have used the existence of this source as an opportunity to test the old local proverb that 'dear children have many names'. What this traditional saying means is that children who are loved have many godparents.

Figure 7.3 shows the average number of godparents of these Reepsholt children, differentiated according to whether or not they survived their first birthdays. The numbers reveal a curious trend (even if this is not quite statistically significant at the 5 per cent level): those children that survived in the families of farmers and smallholders had more godparents on average than those that died.

Of course, the fate of a newborn child did not directly depend on the number of his or her godparents, but both quality and quantity of parental care and the number of godparents probably reflect the parents' willingness to invest in a given child, and hence the parents' reproductive interest in this specific child. Parents quite obviously knew at the birth of a child whether it would be a 'dear' (i.e. 'loved') one or not. Thus, it seems that parental manipulation could have played a role here. It does not take much imagination to see how different assessments of a child's 'reproductive value' might result in differences in breastfeeding, in parental responsiveness and care, in the provision of medical and caloric resources, in workloads, in the strictness of physical and psychological punishment and in numerous other intrafamilial transactions. Such

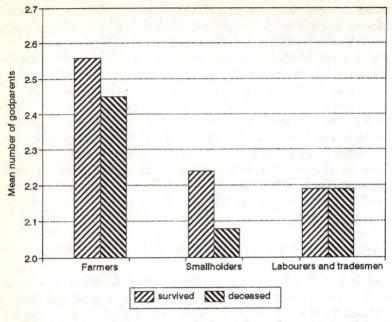

Figure 7.3   Mean number of godparents for children surviving or not surviving
their first year of life (adapted from Voland, 1989)

differences can be expected to have a direct influence on the probability of
dying under the life-threatening conditions of former times.

This evidence for the coexistence, even within the same families, of
sincere parental love and the mental and physical rejection and/or neglect
of one's children point to a latent ambivalence in the human brood care
system. Parental love is optional and is given or withheld in the light of
specific parental interests. Evolutionary theory states that these parental
interests ultimately are reproductive interests.

Evolutionary theory predicts that parents should allocate their
reproductive investment according to, among other considerations, the
reproductive value of their children (i.e. according to their expected future
reproductive chances and opportunities). This is influenced to a very
decisive degree by the child's gender. Even in the earliest phases of
sociobiological theory formulation, it was recognised that the differing
roles of the sexes in the Darwinian process meant that parents could
achieve fitness advantages under certain circumstances by not investing
equally in girls and boys, but by preferring that sex which could be
considered to be the more hopeful candidate for future reproduction. This

idea has entered the literature as the so-called Trivers/Willard hypothesis (Trivers and Willard, 1973).

Interestingly, in the Krummhörn, infant mortality of upper-class farmers' sons was highest among all social groups (Fig. 7.4). Within the wealthiest families, it amounted to 23.0 per cent of all live-born boys, a value that is approximately twice that of the population as a whole (Klindworth and Voland, in preparation). Moreover, their increased mortality risk was influenced by the number of previously born (and still) living brothers. In contrast, farmers' daughters' survived chances were much better on the whole with an increased mortality risk only when there were three or more sisters living (Fig. 7.5). In other words, farmers invested more in the lives of their daughters than in the lives of their sons (Voland *et al.*, 1991; Voland and Dunbar, submitted).

What could have been the functional background for these patterns of sex-discriminating parental care? Was it related – as evolutionary theory suggests – to the differing reproductive prospects of the children? This can not be ruled out, because in fact the farmers' sons frequently remained

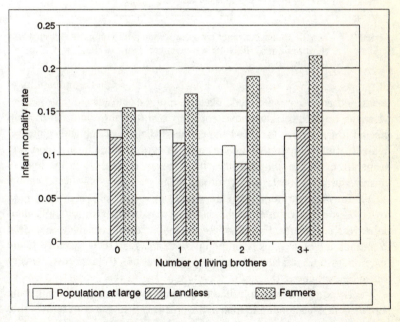

Figure 7.4   Male infant mortality by social group and number of living brothers (Krummhörn, 1720–1874) (adapted from Voland and Dunbar, submitted).

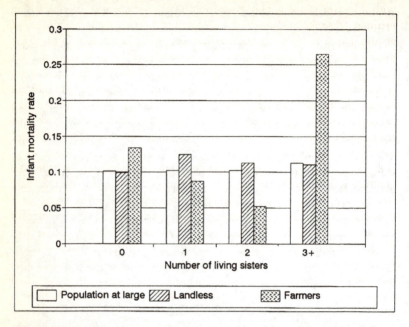

Figure 7.5   Female infant mortality by social group and number of living sisters (Krummhörn, 1720–1874) (adapted from Voland and Dunbar, submitted).

unmarried and they were more likely to emigrate than were their sisters. Marriage opportunities were not equitably distributed in the Krummhörn; instead, they clearly favoured the farmers' daughters and discriminated against their sons (Voland *et al.*, 1991). The differing survival probabilities of the children from the three social classes correlate very closely with their local marriage probabilities.

Whereas the farmers' daughters were able to displace their female lower-class competitors from the marriage market, the farmers' sons were rather less successful. Even though a farmers' son should have been able to outrank a labourer easily in the marriage market, the probability of his remaining single was about twice as high as that of a workers' son. How is this to be explained?

The Krummhörn people tended to have the same social status that their parents had. This applied to men and women equally and corresponds to a widespread structural feature of pre-modern rural populations (for example cf. Low, 1989 for the Swedish case). Moreover, in the Krummhörn there were, on the whole, more social descents than climbs, with a loss of status having been more likely for married daughters than for married sons, both among the children of farmers and among those of smallholders. Half of the married farmers' sons, but only a third of the married farmers' daughters had the same social status as their parents (Voland *et al.*, 1991). Among farmers, marriage and economic independence from one's parents were linked to expectations of high status, particularly in the case of sons. It seems that the men often preferred to remain single rather than accept a reduction in status, whereas their sisters were more willing to tolerate a loss of social prestige in order to marry.

It seems that the underinvestment in farmers' sons results from the contradiction between reproductive role expectations on the one hand and the lack of socioeconomic opportunities for translating these role expectations into reality on the other. During the course of the eighteenth century, the number of major agricultural holdings decreased slightly in the Krummhörn. The ongoing concentration of property set narrow limits to the reproductive possibilities of the farming population. In this constrained setting, the farmers' underinvestment in their sons is explained by the lack of opportunities that society had available for them to make a living. Every son that survived in addition to the heir was, to a certain degree, 'useless' from the viewpoint of reproduction, because he was barely able to contribute to the primary goal of the family, namely fitness maximisation through the preservation of social status.

In order to fully understand the gender-related differences in survival, one more fact is needed: under the Frisian inheritance system, which dated back to medieval times, a daughter's share of an inheritance comprised only half that of a son. In the light of this, differences in infant and child mortality reflect the differing 'production costs' of the children in precisely the way predicted by the 'local resource competition model' of sex-ratio adjustment (Clark, 1978; Silk, 1983). The overproduction of sons, but not of daughters, is expensive for high-ranking families, because these sons depend on the same parental resources and, therefore, seriously compete with one another for these resources. The figures on the probability of marriage reflect this competition: while the chances of marriage seem not to depend on the number of siblings of the same sex for either the sons or the daughters in labourers' families, the situation is very different for farmers. The chances of marriage drop dramatically for their sons if there are three or more brothers who attain adulthood (Voland and Dunbar, submitted).

Differential parental investment can, therefore, be understood in both senses of the term as being cost/benefit oriented. From the economic viewpoint, it is cost/benefit oriented because the costs of the later transfer of property from one generation to the next had already been considered in family planning. In order to maintain the economic profitability of their farms, the farmers deliberately tried to ensure that as little capital as possible flowed out of the business in the course of transfer of ownership after their death. The primary objective was the concentration of property. This strategy proved to be the undoing of some of the 'surplus sons'. The much lower costs for a daughter were more readily absorbed so that their survival did not represent any extreme economic hardship.

On the other hand, the differential parental investment of the Krummhörn farmers seems to have been cost/benefit oriented in terms of genetic fitness maximisation too. By striving for the economic profitability of their businesses, they automatically took care of lineage survival (i.e. for the long-term preservation of their genes in the population). Every short-term increase in reproductive fitness, such as could theoretically have been achieved by a more efficient upbringing of one's sons and an equal distribution of property, would have meant an economic (and, at the same time, a genetic) loss in the long term.

Population Differences in Reproductive Decision-making: What Plays a Role Here?

The Krummhörn scenario does not apply everywhere, however: other pre-modern farming societies show different investment differentials (Voland *et al.*, in preparation). An example is provided by the population of Leezen, another north German community (Fig. 7.6). Differential infant mortality for boys and girls based on social group was found here too, especially for firstborn children. However, in contrast to the Krummhörn situation, these differentials reveal the opposite trend. The lowest rate of male infant mortality and the highest rate of female infant mortality occurred among the highest social class, the land-owning farmers. Thus, they formed the only social group in which girls were exposed to a higher risk of infant death than boys.

The geographic distance between the two regions is only a little more than 100 miles. Their political, economic and cultural experiences were roughly the same. However, there must be some point which was different in the socioecological setting. and to which each group reacted in a different manner. And indeed, there is one essential difference: it can be found in the demographic patterns of the two populations.

Whereas almost no population growth occurred in the Krummhörn (Engel, 1990), the Leezen population expanded (albeit at a moderate rate)

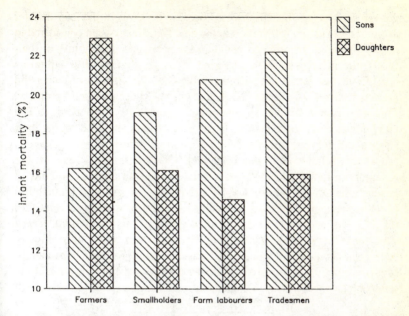

Figure 7.6   Infant mortality (firstborns only) by sex and social group (Leezen 1720–1869) (adapted from Gehrmann, 1984; Voland, 1984)

and participated to some extent in the demographic 'take off' of the nineteenth century. Hence, it seems possible that population growth could correlate with differential parental investment.

By chance, a group of historians selected some other Ostfrisian parishes as the target of an historical demography study on differential life expectancy in pre-modern Germany (Imhof, 1990). Due to this fortunate circumstance, we are in a position to make an analysis of the relationship between social group differences in sex-typical infant mortality and population increase in five north German populations (Voland *et al.*, in preparation).

Figure 7.7 shows sex-related infant mortality, presented as a ratio of female mortality to male mortality, in the upper-class farmers and the landless workers. While the figures for the farmers tend to increase together with the growth in population, parental investment by the workers, on the other hand, does not appear to be influenced by this parameter. Dividing the infant mortality index for the farmers by that for the workers gives us a quantity ('*T/W*') that can be used as an index of the Trivers/Willard effect of differences in parental investment allocation in

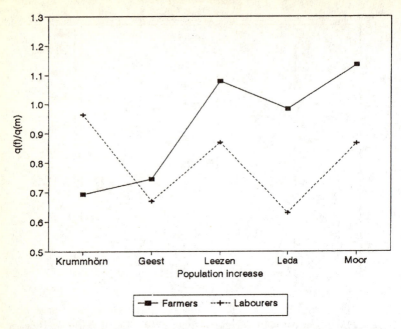

Figure 7.7   Ratio of sex-typical infant mortality (q_f/q_m) in the upper and lower
classes of five north German populations, arranged according to their
mean population increase (from Voland *et al.*, in preparation)

the two sexes by the two social groups. If there were no class effects in
terms of differential parental investment, then *T/W* would lie at the
expected value of one, whatever population growth rates may prevail.
Figure 7.8 shows that this is not in fact the case.

The results thus suggest that different patterns of population increase
define different reproductive scenarios. Population growth implies that the
Darwinian fitness race predominantly takes the form of expansion
competition. In contrast, demographic stagnation necessarily causes
genetic displacement with a high level of local resource competition. That
the degree of local resource competition influences parental sex allocation
decisions is widely known to be the case in birds (Gowaty, 1993) as well
as mammals (Clutton-Brock and Iason, 1986), and especially non-human
primates (Johnson, 1988; Van Schaik and Hardy, 1991). Historical
demography indicates that humans too are capable of responding
adaptively to the level of local resource competition in that rank effects
sex-biased parental investment as a function of the prevailing population
dynamics.

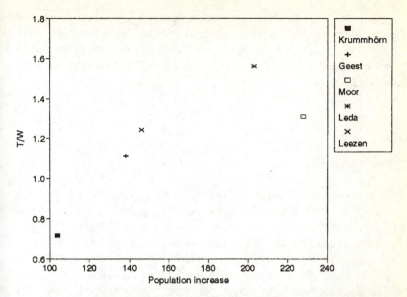

Figure 7.8   Trivers/Willard effect (T/W) in five north German populations. See
text for explanation (adapted from Voland *et al.*, in preparation)

The proximate mechanism no doubt involves some kind of economic
rational decison-making, since sex-biased infant and child mortality is
known to depend on sex-biased opportunities in the local agricultural
economy (Hammel *et al.*, 1983; Ginsberg and Swedlund, 1986; but see
Fridlizius, 1988). Such findings are compatible with behavioural ecology
models of differential parental investment, since the abundance or absence
of economic opportunities constitute different opportunities for natural
selection. Economic, rational-choice models of human reproductive
decision-making are thus complementary, and not contradictory, to
behavioural ecology models (Cronk, 1991).

Other things being equal, sons appear to fulfil the reproductive
expectations of high-ranking parents more often in expanding systems
than daughters do, whereas in stagnating populations an over-production
of sons soon becomes too costly. Demographically expanding groups are
those in which resources can be exploited in an increasingly efficient
manner. In traditional Western farming societies, this was mainly the
business of men. Their competence and their opportunities determined,
to a significant degree, what a family's reproductive success would be.
In stagnating populations, men were denied this opportunity. The limits
of growth had been attained and, as a result, intrafamilial resource

competition increased. Sons, therefore, had few chances to contribute to the reproduction of their natal families. They were lacking – so to speak – the traditional field of activity assigned to them by evolution (and/or social history) and, thus, could not adequately fill their reproductive roles.

CONCLUSIONS

The existence of differences in reproductive decision-making within and between populations, and the fact that they are dependent on the social and demographic context, emphasises an important characteristic of behavioural ecology. It is clear that those who want to uncover biological adaptations in human behaviour by searching for behavioural universals will inevitably be disappointed in the long run (Dunbar, 1988). The biological adaptiveness of human behaviour is not expected to manifest itself in invariance and complete independence from environmental influences. On the contrary, most of the evolved behaviour-regulating mechanisms are conditional. This means that in situation A they may motivate towards a specific behaviour, while in situation B they may motivate towards another (possibly completely different) behaviour. For example, sincere parental love and care on the one hand and physical or psychological neglect, abortion and infanticide on the other, are different outcomes of the same parental brood-care system, the biological adaptiveness of which is demonstrated by its strategic flexibility and not by its phenotypic rigidity. As I have tried to show, historical demography can help in determining the switch points for these kinds of conditional reproductive strategies and it thus offers us a valuable tool for the study of human behavioural ecology.

ACKNOWLEDGEMENTS

Sincere thanks to Robin Dunbar for his substantial support and help in uncountable things. Financial support was from the Deutsche Forschungsgemeinschaft (DFG) and the Science Engineering and Research Council (SERC).

REFERENCES

Alexander, R. D. (1987), *The Biology of Moral Systems* (Hawthorne: Aldine De Gruyter).
Borgerhoff Mulder, M. (1988), 'Kipsigis bridewealth payments', in L. Betzig, M. Borgerhoff Mulder and P. Turke (eds) *Human Reproductive Behaviour – A Darwinian Perspective* (Cambridge: Cambridge University Press).
Borgerhoff Mulder, M. (1991), 'Human behavioural ecology', in J. R. Krebs and N. Davies (eds), *Behavioural Ecology – An Evolutionary Approach* (Oxford: Blackwell).
Borgerhoff Mulder, M. (1992), 'Reproductive decisions', in E. A. Smith and B. Winterhalder (eds), *Evolutionary Ecology and Human Behaviour* (Hawthorne: Aldine De Gruyter).
Borgerhoff Mulder, M., Thornhill, N. W., Voland, E. and Richerson, P. (in preparation), 'The place of behavioural ecological anthropology in evolutionary social science', in P. Weingart, S. Mitchell and S. Maasen (eds), *Human by Nature*.
Cheney, D. L. (1983), 'Extrafamilial alliances among vervet monkeys', in R. Hinde (ed.), *Primate Social Relationships* (Oxford: Blackwell).
Clark, A. (1978), 'Sex ratio and local resource competition in a prosimian primate', *Science*, vol. 201, pp. 163–5.
Clutton-Brock, T. H. and Iason, G. R. (1986), 'Sex ratio variation in mammals', *Quarterly Review of Biology*, vol. 61, pp. 339–74.
Cronk, L. (1991), 'Human behavioural ecology', *Annual Review of Anthropology*, vol. 20, pp. 25–53.
Dunbar, R. I. M. (1988), 'Darwinizing man: A commentary', in L. Betzig, M. Borgerhoff Mulder and P. Turke (eds), *Human Reproductive Behaviour – A Darwinian Perspective* (Cambridge: Cambridge University Press).
Dunbar, R. I. M. (1991), 'On sociobiological theory and the Cheyenne case', *Current Anthropology*, vol. 32, pp. 423–34.
Dunbar, R. I. M. (1993), 'Behavioural adaptation', in G. A. Harrison (ed.), *Human Adaptation* (Oxford: Oxford University Press).
Engel, C. (1990), 'Reproduktionsstrategien im sozio-ökologischen Kontext – Eine evolutionsbiologische Interpretation sozialgruppenspezifischer demographischer Muster in einer historischen Population (Krummhörn, Ostfriesland im 18. und 19. Jahrhundert)', dissertation, University of Göttingen.
Fisher, R. A. (1930), *The Genetical Theory of Natural Selection* (Oxford: Clarendon Press).
Fridlizius, G. (1988), 'Sex-differential mortality and socio economic change, Sweden 1750–1910', in A. Brändström and L. G. Tedebrand (eds), *Society, Health and Population during the Demographic Transition* (Stockholm: Almqvist & Wiksell).
Gaulin, S. J. and Boster, J. S. (1990), 'Dowry as female competition', *American Anthropologist*, vol. 92, pp. 994–1005.
Gehrmann, R. (1984), *Leezen 1720–1870 – ein historischdemographischer Beitrag zur Sozialgeschichte des ländlichen Schlewiq-Holstein* (Neumünster: Wachholtz).
Ginsburg, C. A. and Swedlund, A. C. (1986), 'Sex-specific mortality and economic opportunities: Massachusetts, 1860–1899', *Continuity and Change* vol. 1, pp. 415–445.

Gowaty, P. A. (1993), 'Differential dispersal, local resource competition, and sex ratio variation in birds', *American Naturalist*, vol. 141, pp. 263–80.

Hager, B. J. (1992), 'Get thee to a nunnery: female religious claustration in medieval Europe', *Ethology and Sociobiology*, vol. 13, pp. 385–407.

Hammel, E. A., Johansson, S. R. and Ginsberg, C. A. (1983), 'The value of children during industrialization: sex ratios in childhood in nineteenth-century America', *Journal of Family History*, vol. 8, pp. 346–66.

Imhof, A. E. (1984), 'The amazing simultaneousness of big differences and the boom in the 19th century – some facts and hypotheses and infant and maternal mortality in Germany, 18th to 20th century', in T. Bengtsson, G. Fridlizius and R. Ohlsson (eds), *Pre-industrial Population Change – The Mortality Decline and Short-term Population Movements* (Stockholm: Almquist & Wiksell).

Imhof, A. E. (1990), *Lebenserwartungen in Deutschland vom 17. bis 19. Jahrhundert* (Weinheim: VCH).

Irons, W. (1979), 'Cultural and biological success', in N. A. Chagnon and W. Irons (eds), *Evolutionary Biology and Human Social Behaviour: An Anthropological Perspective* (North Scituate: Duxbury).

Irons, W. (1991), 'Anthropology', in M. Maxwell (ed.), *The Sociobiological Imagination* (Albany: SUNY Press).

Johnson, C. N. (1988), 'Dispersal and the sex ratio at birth in primates', *Nature*, vol. 332, pp. 726–8.

Klindworth, H. and Voland E. (in preparation), *How did the Krummhörn Wealthy Elite Achieve an Above Average Reproductive Success?*

Low, B. S. (1989), 'Occupational status and reproductive behaviour in nineteenth-century Sweden: Locknevi parish', *Social Biology*, vol. 36, pp. 82–101.

Low, B. S. (1993), 'Ecological demography: a synthetic focus in evolutionary anthropology', *Evolutionary Anthropology*, vol. 1, pp. 177–87.

Low, B. S. and Clarke, A. L. (1991), 'Resources and the life course: patterns through the demographic transition', *Ethology and Sociobiology*, vol. 13, pp. 463–94.

Meitzen, A. (1894), *Der Boden und die landwirtschaftlichen Verhältnisse des Preussischen Staates* (Berlin: Parey).

Rao, A. (submitted), 'The fittest families: parental investment and marriage transactions'.

Røskaft, E., Wara, A. and Viken, A. (1992), 'Reproductive success in relation to resource-access and parental age in a small Norwegian farming parish during the period 1700–1900', *Ethology and Sociobiology*, vol. 13, pp. 443–61.

Silk, J. (1983), 'Local resource competition and facultative adjustment of sex ratios in relation to competitive abilities', *American Naturalist*, vol. 121, pp. 56–66.

Smith, E. A. (1992a), 'Human behavioural ecology: I', *Evolutionary Anthropology*, vol. 1, pp. 20–5.

Smith, E. A. (1992b), 'Human behavioural ecology: II', *Evolutionary Anthropology*, vol. 1, pp. 50–5.

Smith, E. A. and Winterhalder, B. (eds) (1992), *Evolutionary Ecology and Human Behaviour* (Hawthorne: Aldine De Gruyter).

Stearns, S. C. (1992), *The Evolution of Life Histories* (Oxford: Oxford University Press).

Trivers, R. (1985), *Social Evolution* (Menlo Park: Benjamin/Cummings).

Trivers, R. L. and Willard, D. E. (1973), 'Natural selection of parental ability to vary the sex ratio of offspring', *Science*, vol. 179, pp. 90–2.

Turke, P. W. (1989), 'Evolution and the demand for children', *Population and Development Review*, vol, 15, pp. 61–90.

Van Schaik, C. P. and Hardy, S. B. (1991), 'Intensity of local resource competition shapes the relationship between maternal rank and sex ratios at birth in cercopithecine primates', *American Naturalist*, vol. 138, pp. 1555–62.

Voland, E. (1984), 'Human sex-ratio manipulation: historical data from a German parish', *Journal of Human Evolution*, vol. 13, pp. 99–107.

Voland, E. (1989), 'Differential parental investment: some ideas on the contact area of European social history and evolutionary biology', in V. Standen and R. A. Foley (eds), *Comparative Socioecology – The Behavioural Ecology of Humans and Other Mammals* (Oxford: Blackwell).

Voland, E. (1990), 'Differential reproductive success within the Krummhörn population (Germany, 18th and 19th centuries)', *Behavioural Ecology and Sociobiology*, vol. 26, pp. 65–72.

Voland, E. and Dunbar, R. (submitted), 'Resource competition and reproduction – The relationship of economic and parental strategies in the Krummhörn population (1720–1874)'.

Voland, E. and Engel, C. (1990), 'Female choice in humans: a conditional mate choice strategy of the Krummhörn women (Germany 1720–1874)', *Ethology*, vol. 84, pp. 144–54.

Voland, E., Siegelkow, E. and Engel, C. (1991), 'Cost/benefit oriented parental investment by high status family – the Krummhörn case', *Ethology and Sociobiology*, vol. 12, pp. 105–18.

Voland, E., Dunbar, R. I. M., Engel, C. and Stephan, P. (in preparation), 'Population increase and sex-biased parental investment in humans: Evidence from 18th and 19th century Germany'.

Williams, G. C. (1966), *Adaptation and Natural Selection* (Princeton: Princeton University Press).

Winkler, E.-M. and Kirchengast, S. (1994), 'Body dimensions and differential fertility in !Kung San males from Namibia', *American Journal of Human Biology*, vol. 6, pp. 203–13.

Winterhalder, B. and Smith, E. A. (1992), 'Evolutionary ecology and the social sciences', in E. A. Smith and B. Winterhalder (eds), *Evolutionary Ecology and Human Behaviour* (Hawthorne: Aldine De Gruyter)

8 English Fertility, 1600–1900: Is an Economic Analysis Tenable?

P. R. Andrew Hinde

INTRODUCTION

There is a current debate in the demographic literature about the adequacy of explanations of the demographic transition that see the fertility decline as a consequence of people (by which is usually meant married couples) adjusting their reproduction in the light of changing social and economic circumstances. These explanations, termed by Carlsson (1966) *adjustment hypotheses,* were characteristic of the original versions of the theory of the demographic transition (Notestein, 1945; Davis, 1963), in which it was held that social and economic development (termed 'modernisation' by Notestein, 1945) were ultimately responsible for the fertility decline. Davis's account was particularly clear. He maintained that fertility decline was one of several possible responses that a population could make to increasing economic strain. This strain was, in turn, caused by rapid population growth consequent upon the decline in mortality, which resulted from economic development.

The original theories of the demographic transition were formulated at the aggregate level, in the sense that they were concerned with explaining macro-scale changes. The details of the countless individual actions which led to reduced fertility were rarely explicitly incorporated into the analysis. During the 1960s and 1970s, however, economists turned their attention to the analysis of fertility behaviour at the individual level (Becker, 1960; 1981; Easterlin *et al.*, 1980). Reproductive decisions are seen as being made by individual couples, and as being economically rational. The economic theory of fertility has been elaborated in a large and complex body of literature (see Cigno, 1991, for a recent summary), but its central assumption 'is that the changing balance between the costs and benefits of childbearing, resulting in reduced parental demand for children, is the fundamental force behind fertility decline' (Cleland and Wilson, 1987, p. 5). Prior to the fertility transition, the demand for children was high

160

because children were an economic asset to their parents. However, with social and economic development and industrialisation, children increasingly became an economic burden. Partly this occurred because, as incomes rose, it became necessary for parents to devote more resources to each child. The result was that it became economically rational for parents to have fewer children, but to spend more money on each.

In the last 15 years, however, these explanations of fertility decline have been challenged by demographers. An alternative interpretation of the fertility transition, which places much more weight on cultural and ideational factors than on economic ones has appeared (Cleland and Wilson, 1987; see also Cleland, 1993). Put very simply, the argument runs that in pre-industrial times fertility was high not because the demand for children was high, but because societal and cultural attitudes were hostile to birth control. Indeed, in some pre-transitional populations, children may have been an economic burden on their parents, but the prevailing ideational climate prevented parents from translating their desire (for fewer children) into reality. Only towards the end of the nineteenth century in most of western Europe was this situation altered as new ideas about the acceptability of birth control diffused rapidly through societies, aided by mass education. The idea of birth control, therefore, was an innovation, and it was the timing of this innovation which was the chief determinant of the timing of the fertility transition, rather than any form of adjustment to new social and economic circumstances. The appearance of other relevant innovations, such as new birth control devices, can even be seen as a consequence of the new demand for fertility control. It is probably fair to state that this *innovation hypothesis* is now in the ascendant amongst demographers.

In this paper, I wish to discuss these two accounts of fertility behaviour in the light of the English experience between 1600 and 1900. This period covers the last 250 years of the pre-transitional era and at least the first half of the fertility transition. The English experience is of particular relevance to the debate, since it has been cited specifically in support of the innovation hypothesis (Cleland and Wilson, 1987).

THE EMPIRICAL BACKGROUND TO THE INNOVATION HYPOTHESIS

Why has the innovation hypothesis come to be preferred to the explanation in terms of adjustments to new social and economic circumstances? The answer lies partly in the results of recent empirical analyses of European fertility in the past, and especially of English fertility.

Long-term trends in overall fertility in England at the national level have been documented by Wrigley and Schofield (1981) and by Wilson and Woods (1991). These authors have shown that overall fertility fluctuated over time. Taking the gross reproduction rate (GRR) as a measure of fertility (the GRR is the average number of daughters a woman would have during her lifetime), Wrigley and Schofield showed that the GRR fell from 2.25 in 1600 to about 1.9 in the 1660s, before rising to almost 3.0 in the decade 1811–20. It then declined to about 2.5 by the middle of the nineteenth century, levelling off for a short period before beginning a sustained decline to below 1.0 in the 1930s.

Overall fertility, however, responds both to changes in the fertility of married couples and to changes in the intensity of marriage, as measured by the mean age at marriage and the proportions marrying. (It is also affected by illegitimate fertility, but this formed a very small proportion of births in England between 1600 and 1900.) It was shown conclusively by Wrigley and Schofield (1981) that fluctuations in the GRR were caused largely by changes in the intensity of marriage, rather than marital fertility. This conclusion has since been reinforced by family reconstitution studies, which have shown that fertility within marriage was almost constant in England from 1600 until the second half of the nineteenth century (Wrigley and Schofield, 1983; Wilson and Woods, 1991). Only during the final quarter of the nineteenth century is there convincing evidence of a decline.

Family reconstitution studies have also revealed two further crucial points about fertility within marriage between 1600 and 1800. First, it seems not only to have been constant over time, but over space as well. Wilson (1984), using data from fourteen parishes from various parts of England, showed that the total marital fertility rate (the average number of children a woman would bear between the ages of 20 and 49 years assuming she was married throughout and bore children at the prevailing age-specific marital fertility rates) varied only from 6.45 to 7.78. This degree of variation is small compared with that found in other countries during the same period (see, for example, the analysis of fourteen German villages in Knodel (1988)). Wilson concludes (1984, p. 240) 'it seems that homogeneity with respect to marital fertility can be regarded as a general English characteristic'.

Second, by using a variety of ingenious techniques, it has been demonstrated that the use of birth control was almost entirely absent in England between 1600 and 1800 (Wilson, 1984). In fact, by 'birth control' here is meant *family limitation*, the use of birth control by married couples to stop having children once a given number have been achieved. This is a critical point to which we shall return.

Thus we have a picture of fertility within marriage in England varying little over time or space prior to 1850 and being uncontrolled, in the sense that deliberate family limitation behaviour was absent. What of the period after 1850?

At a national level, a sustained decline in overall fertility began during the 1870s and it is fairly clear that this decline was almost entirely due to a decline in fertility within marriage (Teitelbaum, 1984). Using census and vital registration data, it has proved possible to analyse the course of the fertility decline on a regional basis and on the basis of occupational groups (Woods, 1987). The results of these analyses seem to show that the decline of fertility in England was remarkably homogeneous, occurring in all areas of the country within a short space of time. If we take a decline of marital fertility to a level of 10 per cent below the level of 1871 as an indicator of the onset of the fertility transition, every county in England achieved this between 1886 and 1901 (Teitelbaum, 1984, p. 135). Indeed 'even when registration districts are used to analyse marital fertility patterns ... the speed with which [marital fertility] declined and the extent to which the decline was a national phenomenon are the most striking features of the patterns of change' (Woods, 1987, p. 300). (Registration districts were much smaller units than counties: there were some 600 of them in nineteenth-century England.)

It is, however, the case that there were occupational differentials in fertility levels during the second half of the nineteenth century. In general, the middle classes had lower marital fertility than the working classes. In addition, certain occupations stand out as having distinctive fertility patterns. Textile workers, for example, manifested lower fertility than other manual workers; coal miners, by contrast, were particularly fertile. Indeed, many of the geographical differentials which do emerge at this period can be put down to the different occupational structures of the regions. Nevertheless, Woods (1987) points out that when successive marriage cohorts from the 1860s through to the 1890s are examined for several occupational groups drawn from all classes, marital fertility was declining in all of them. Although the pace of the decline, and the levels of marital fertility at which it was occurring, did vary with occupation, the timing of the decline appears not to have done.

The picture which has emerged from this brief and generalised description of English fertility between 1600 and 1900 appears disarmingly simple. Fertility within marriage prior to the middle of the nineteenth century was constant over time and space and was characterised by an absence of family limitation. Sometime during the second half of that century, however, a roughly simultaneous decline set in in all sections of the population and in all regions.

The conclusion which many demographers have drawn from this is that whatever caused the decline of fertility within marriage appeared relatively suddenly and spread very rapidly through the English population. Woods (1987) contends that changes in ideas and attitudes towards birth control are, therefore, much more plausible candidates than economic changes, for example, those in the demand for children. Critical here is the appearance of the idea that fertility was an issue over which parents might exert 'conscious choice' (Coale, 1973). In pre-transition England, he writes '[c]hildren were the gifts of God, and God could only be thwarted by postponing marriage ... or practising a degree of celibacy in marriage. ... By the last quarter of the nineteenth century these aspects of the dominant moral code had probably lost their force' (Woods, 1992, p. 53). Thus we now have what Crafts (1989, p. 335) has described as a 'general stress on cultural factors and improved knowledge/availability of birth control as dominating the ... fertility transition' and a primacy accorded to ideational changes, particularly the novelty of the idea of fertility control being part of the 'calculus of conscious choice'.

This account of the fertility transition has also received empirical support from the results of the European Fertility Project, a major study of the chronology and geography of the decline across more than 700 European provinces by a team based at Princeton University. These showed that differentials in the timing of the fertility decline were not associated at all closely with conventional indicators of social and economic development (Coale and Watkins, 1986). There was, however, strong evidence that in certain areas (for example Belgium), fertility patterns during the transition were closely associated with cultural and linguistic boundaries (Lesthaeghe, 1977) and with levels of secularisation (Lesthaeghe, 1983).

REPRODUCTIVE DECISIONS IN PRE-TRANSITIONAL ENGLAND

This volume is about reproductive decisions and in this section I wish to look in more detail at the decision-making process implied by the two explanations of fertility change outlined in the introduction.

Before doing so, however, it is necessary briefly to ask who the agents are who make decisions about fertility. Ultimately, of course, decisions can only be made by parents. Yet individual couples are set within communities of varying scales: families, villages, regions and nations, and it is possible (indeed likely) that individual couples' decisions are, to a greater or lesser extent, influenced by the community in which they live (Lesthaeghe, 1980). One can think about community-level influences either by viewing them as constraints (possibly very strong constraints) on individual-level choice or by imagining that these larger units effectively make decisions themselves, which are binding on their members. The second of these might, of course, be couched in terms of decisions made by powerful individuals within these communities, who hold sway over more junior members. One possible example of such community-level decision-making will be discussed later.

It is clear that the innovation and adjustment hypotheses imply very different scenarios with respect to fertility decisions. The adjustment hypothesis implies that decisions about how many children to have are made in all societies and the economic analysis of fertility change implies that these decisions are largely made on economic grounds, as a result of a cost–benefit analysis. The microeconomic theory of fertility takes a more extreme position and makes explicit the fact that the decisions are made by individual couples, by maximising a quantifiable utility function.

By contrast, the innovation hypothesis, especially in the form now most prevalent amongst demographers, implies that couples in pre-transition times did not make intentional reproductive decisions at all. If fertility was not within the 'calculus of conscious choice', then it is hard to see how deliberate decisions about it could be made.

Viewed in this light, in order to find out whether an economic analysis of fertility in England between 1600 and 1900 is tenable, we need to answer two questions. First, is there any evidence that couples, or, indeed, communities or other institutions, did take decisions about fertility prior to the fertility transition? If the answer to this question is 'no', then it will be difficult to sustain the adjustment hypothesis. On the other hand, if the answer is 'yes' (even 'yes, possibly'), we can go on to tackle the issue raised in the title of this paper by asking the second question: to what extent were these decisions made on economic grounds?

The demographers' approach to the first question rests critically upon the idea of what is called *natural fertility*. According to the definition of Henry (1961), natural fertility is that which exists in the absence of deliberate birth control. Deliberate birth control is held to occur when the fertility behaviour of the couple is influenced by the number of children already born. In other words, natural fertility is fertility that is not controlled within marriage in a parity-specific way. This means, above all, that family limitation behaviour is absent: that parents do not stop having children once they have reached some desired number. Natural fertility is compatible with various practices, such as breastfeeding for lengthy periods, which have the effect of reducing the level of fertility, provided that the practice of these by married couples is independent of the number of children they already have.

As we have seen, the evidence to date suggests that fertility within marriage in pre-transitional England was natural. There are two possible interpretations of this. First, this fertility régime was the result of rational reproductive choices. This implies that the demand for children equalled or exceeded the supply which could be obtained even under natural fertility, since if it did not, we should expect family limitation to have been practised. Second, fertility was natural because birth control was proscribed for cultural reasons: it was not an option. (It is also possible that both these interpretation are true). The adjustment hypothesis is consistent with the first of these, the innovation hypothesis with the second.

Put in this way, establishing that the innovation hypothesis was dominant can be done by demonstrating that the demand for children was less than the supply. Cleland and Wilson (1987), who advocate the innovation hypothesis, thus back up their view by stating that, in pre-transitional England, there is 'overwhelming evidence that children represented a net economic loss to their parents' (Cleland and Wilson, 1987, p. 15). The fact that we do not observe family limitations, therefore, suggests that other factors, for example attitudes to birth control, prohibited what would have been rational fertility behaviour, so that parents carried on having children despite their cost.

In the next section I shall consider the demand for children in pre-transitional England in more detail. Before doing so, however, it is necessary to raise a difficulty with the foregoing argument. This difficulty arises from the way in which the dichotomy between natural and controlled fertility is defined. Put simply, the concept of natural fertility itself is ambiguous (Knodel, 1983; Hinde and Woods, 1984; Landers, 1990). For it is possible to imagine scenarios where fertility is controlled, as a result of conscious, deliberate decisions, by the spacing of births rather than by the 'stopping' behaviour implied by the idea of family limitation. Provided that this behaviour was not parity-specific, such a situation could be compatible with natural fertility, if Henry's definition is adhered to. Moreover, if this behaviour was not parity-specific, it could not be easily identified from family reconstitution data by the methods conventionally employed by demographers, since these methods assume that the control of fertility was exercised by family limitation.

Spacing behaviour, of course, might be identified by analysing the intervals between births. This has been done for the English family reconstitution data by Wilson (1986). Unfortunately, Wilson's analysis is of little help, for it ruled out the use of deliberate birth control *a priori* on the grounds that fertility was 'natural'. Thus, although Wilson did find variations in the length of birth intervals amongst the English communities he examined, he attributed these to variations in breastfeeding practices or other determinants which were compatible with the definition of natural fertility.

In sum, then, the available demographic evidence does not permit us to rule out the possibility of fertility control being exercised through spacing behaviour and hence the possibility of conscious choice over fertility being exercised in pre-industrial England.

THE DEMAND FOR CHILDREN IN ENGLAND BETWEEN 1600 AND 1900

Let me now turn to the demand for children in England between 1600 and 1900. Measuring the demand for children is a complex task, because the costs of and benefits from children to their parents derive from several sources. To simplify matters I am going to restrict attention to three areas: psychic benefits, the economics of bringing up children within the parental household and the potential importance of children as a form of old-age security.

Psychic Benefits

The psychic benefits of children to the parents derive in part from the satisfaction parents obtain from knowing that they have ensured the survival of their genetic material for at least one generation. They also arise from the fact that watching children grow up is an immensely satisfying experience for most parents. Children provide company and relief from boredom. There is no doubt that, in pre-industrial England, these benefits were considered important. As Macfarlane (1985, p. 51) writes: '[c]hildren were a psychological gratification to their parents, fulfilling their needs in various ways: the biological craving of women to reproduce, the desire of all humans to see mirrors of themselves, the desire for companions, the desire for objects to love and care for'.

These psychic benefits, however, are unlikely to play a great role in an account of fertility changes, since it is probable that they operate in all societies, both pre- and post-transitional. It seems to me that Macfarlane's statement could just as well refer to England in the late nineteenth century or even the twentieth century. I admit that this is rather a sweeping generalisation and would bear further scrutiny; unfortunately, there is not space in this paper to discuss it further.

The Costs of Bringing Up Children

What, then, of the costs to parents of bringing up these desirable creatures in England between 1600 and 1900? In the pre-industrial era, there seems to be general agreement that children were costly to raise. To understand why this was so we need to consider the household formation system which operated (Hajnal, 1982). Broadly speaking, this system entailed late and non-universal marriage. Most offspring left the parental household during their teens to enter neighbouring households as servants; they remained as servants until they married. Once married, they set up their own household. It was almost unknown for married offspring to remain within the household of their parents. Moreover, once children had left home to go into service, they 'did not remit significant amounts of money back to their parents' (Cleland and Wilson, 1987, p. 15). Although it is possible that children did provide some wage income whilst living with their parents, because of the early age at leaving home (Wall, 1978), it seems probable that this income did not compensate parents fully for the costs of caring for and feeding children from birth.

Towards the end of the eighteenth century, however, there is evidence that things were changing. With industrialisation, jobs for children became available in factories and they were sent out to work, even at quite an early age. There are stories of children as young as 3 and 4 years of age working in coal mines and textile factories. Certainly, it seems that Macfarlane's observation that, in this period, '[b]y the age of 10 [children] might have produced a surplus and by 14 have accumulated a good deal' (1985, p. 76) commands empirical support. In sum, then, we can suggest that around 1800, children's economic value to their parents was probably quite a lot higher than it had been 100 years earlier. The timing of this change is important, because the family reconstitution evidence comes almost entirely from the period *before* 1800.

The conditions of employment of young children were very hard and this eventually provoked national concern. During the middle years of the nineteenth century, laws were enacted forbidding the employment of children below certain ages in many occupations (Keeling, 1914). By the last quarter of the century these restrictions were widespread. Moreover, the education of children up to the age of 14 years became compulsory during the 1870s (Barnard, 1961). Thus the economic value of children's labour income to the parents is almost certain to have fallen during the century.

Children as a Form of Old-Age Security

Finally, let me examine the situation with respect to the financial and psychological benefits children might have conferred on their parents when the latter were ill or old. This seems to be the most difficult of the three areas about which to reach conclusions. Indeed, Cleland and Wilson (1987) do not mention it directly, leaving the costs of bringing up children to bear the burden of the case that children represented a net economic loss to their parents.

It certainly seems likely that elderly people in England throughout the period 1600–1900 had to rely on transfer payments in order to live. In family life-cycle simulations conducted by the Cambridge Group for the History of Population and Social Structure, and described by Smith (1986), the households of the elderly suffered a current account deficit. Although it is possible that some elderly people would be able to live off their savings, the Cambridge Group simulations suggest that only parents whose children all left home at ages considerably below the usual age of leaving home would be able to do so. Most couples, therefore, would require transfer payments in their old age. The same may well have been true of a number of those who never married, and these may have comprised around 10 per cent of the total (Wrigley and Schofield, 1981).

Having dealt with the demand for transfer payments, we must address the question of whether or not children were an important potential source. Macfarlane (1985, p. 116) states that, at least in the pre-industrial period, 'children were only one of the mechanisms by which people in England dealt with risk'. Yet there is considerable evidence to support the view that children made an important contribution to their parents' welfare in the latter's old age. For example, in the community of Ardleigh in Essex in 1795–96, 'there were no pauper widows whatsoever living alone ... for they were to be found in the households of their married children' (Smith, 1986, p. 202).

According to Smith (1986), however, it is important to distinguish between transfer payments made from children to their own parents and transfer payments made in general from children to the elderly in the same community. He argues that care for the elderly in pre-industrial England was organised at a community level. If this is the case, then what matters for the security of the elderly is the overall number of children within a community compared with the number of elderly dependents. Although the existence of these wider networks of social support might, to a particular couple, appear to reduce the perceived economic benefits from children, attempts by a large proportion of couples to reduce fertility could pose a threat to the future well-being of their generation.

During the nineteenth century, children continued to play an important role in the care of their elderly parents. In a study of a Devonshire parish between 1851 and 1871, Robin (1984) found that more than half of parents in their seventies were living with one of their offspring.

Thus it seems that the evidence that the demand for children was low in England prior to the fertility transition in England is not, perhaps, so clear cut as Cleland and Wilson (1987) would have us believe. Although they are almost certainly right about children's labour income for the pre-industrial period, the net costs of bringing up children may well have fallen during industrialisation. Moreover, throughout the period between 1600 and 1900, there is clear evidence that children were an important source of support for aged parents, whether directly or indirectly through community-level welfare schemes.

This brief summary suggests that the argument that economic considerations played a part in fertility decisions in pre-industrial England may not be so easy to dismiss. For, even accepting the fact that children were costly to raise, parents may have felt obliged to bear that cost in order to make sure that enough children survived to make their old age secure. Further, if welfare was organised at the community level, then even if fertility behaviour was socially controlled (for example by élites) the motivation for that social control might have been a concern to ensure that fertility 'did not fall in such a way as to endanger the adequacy of future local labour supplies' (Smith, 1986; see also Potter, 1983). Therefore, the fact that we do not observe attempts to control fertility in pre-industrial England, despite the fact that children were costly to raise, does not *necessarily* mean that demand theories of fertility are inapplicable.

ECONOMIC FACTORS AND REPRODUCTIVE DECISIONS

We can now turn to the second question. Is there any evidence that economic factors were influential in the reproductive decisions that were made? To answer this question, it is necessary to link together people's motivations and fertility outcomes. Specifically, we wish to know if economic motivations led to particular decisions being made which then affected fertility.

Here we reach perhaps the most critical limitation of the existing analyses of fertility in historical England. This link is simply not made. The family reconstitution evidence produces accurate measurements of the fertility outcome, but conclusions about the decision-making process which led to that outcome are inferred by making use of ambiguous concepts like natural fertility.

For the late nineteenth century the situation is little better. The fertility evidence is almost exclusively aggregative in nature, dealing either with regions, or occupational groups. It tells us about the fertility outcome (measured at the group level), not about the fertility decisions made at the individual level and reaching conclusions about individual decisions on the basis of aggregative data on outcomes is beset by logical difficulties. Yet if we are to understand the causes of the fertility transition and the factors which determine fertility behaviour, surely the decision-making process is central. Historical demographers have failed so far adequately to relate their statistical evidence to this process.

To be fair to them, however, this is partly (one might even say largely) because of the difficulty posed by the data they have to work with. For example, the family reconstitution evidence comes from a total of 25 small communities throughout the whole of England (not a large sample, comprising less than half of one per cent of the total population) and has been built up by the laborious process of linking together information from the Church of England baptism, marriage and burial registers. In order to gain reliable estimates of age-specific fertility rates, it has been necessary to take communities as wholes and to consider long periods of time. Thus the fertility statistics which have been produced typically relate to whole communities over long time periods (half a century). Disaggregating communities on the basis of social class or occupation is also made difficult by the paucity of occupational data. Church of England registers contain very little information about the social and economic circumstances of the couples they analyse.

For the nineteenth century, even analyses at the village level frequently become impossible, since the Church of England registers, especially those on baptisms (which form the source of data on births) are less reliable than for earlier periods. Although civil registration data are available from 1837, access to information about individuals has, so far, been denied by administrative action. Individual-level census data are available from 1841, and attempts have been made to analyse fertility at the individual level using these (Woods and Smith, 1983; Hinde, 1985; Garrett and Hinde, forthcoming), but such methods rely on a series of rather dubious assumptions and the resulting schedules are typically based on a rather small number of woman-years of exposure. Record-linkage of individual-level census and parish or civil register data can potentially yield more reliable estimates, but work on this subject is still at a very early stage (Hinde, 1987; Davies, 1991; Robin, 1992).

Given this situation, it seems that it is going to be extremely difficult to demonstrate convincingly an economic motivation (or, for that matter, any other motivation) behind reproductive decisions. However, I have found two studies which have tried to do this. These are worth describing in some detail.

The first is an analysis by Levine (1977) of family reconstitution data for the village of Shepshed in Leicestershire. He describes the demographic history of this village during the late eighteenth and early nineteenth centuries. He shows that, towards the end of the eighteenth century, there was a decline in the mean age at marriage for women. This led to a rise in overall fertility and a rise in the proportion of people below childbearing age. In the second quarter of the nineteenth century, however,

> the population of Shepshed was confronted with drastically changed economic prospects for which its new demographic profile was most unsuitable. Many young people left the village after 1825, but those who stayed were ill-equipped to reduce the number of children they would inevitably bring into the world. ... Because both men and women reached their maximum earning capacities at an early age, it was unlikely that a reduction in income would call forth a significant rise in their age at marriage. ... Thus, the only option to those who were to reduce their family size was a limitation on fertility. (Levine, 1977, pp. 65–66)

Levine goes on to explain how one particular group within the village, the framework knitters, developed a reproductive strategy which attempted to reconcile two, partially conflicting, economic demands. The first arose from the fact that it was 'economically most sensible to hurry over the stage during which the dependency ratio within the family was most disadvantageous – the first years of a marriage when children contributed nothing to production, consumed the cost of their own support, and, in addition, distracted the wife/mother so that her contribution was reduced' (Levine, 1977, pp. 80–81). The second arose from the need to ensure that at least one child survived to provide for the parents' old age. He says that 'this contradiction was resolved by maintaining high fertility until at least one child was old enough to contribute his or her labour to the family economy. Only at this point could family limitation commence' (Levine, 1977, p. 82). These economic considerations applied only to the framework knitters. When the marital fertility of this group was compared with that of the rest of the population (something which Levine was able to do, exceptionally, with the Shepshed data) he found that family limitation behaviour, also, was confined to the framework knitters.

Levine's analysis is particularly interesting in the context of the preceding discussion of the demand for children, in that he maintains that the demand for children arose from parents' need for old-age security, and not because children provided labour income – indeed, they were costly to raise.

The second study is that carried out by Landers (1990), who used family reconstitution to examine the fertility on London Quakers between 1650 and 1849. His analysis suggests that both family limitation and birth spacing were practised by various sub-groups of Quaker women during the eighteenth century, and that 'the age-specific character of the spacing behaviour, together with its rapid appearance from one cohort to the next, leaves little room for doubt that it was volitional in nature' (Landers, 1990, p. 106). Landers accounts for this behaviour in economic terms, arguing that it falls within the bounds of what can be considered economically 'rational'. Specifically, he maintains that it was the result of a desire to minimise the 'current cost' of children: 'a rational fertility strategy, on this criterion, is one which minimises the maximum number of dependents, or alternatively which minimises the period during which large numbers are present' (Landers, 1990, p. 107).

These two examples are the only ones I have found for the period before the middle of the nineteenth century which have tried explicitly to link fertility outcomes to the decisions which produced them (there are one or two dealing with a later period, for example Friedlander (1973), which explain fertility decisions in a similar vein). It is, therefore, of considerable significance that they both attribute an economic motivation to these decisions. It seems that a plausible case can be made for supposing that economic factors did play some part in reproductive decisions in England between 1600 and 1900. Levine's analysis, especially, is of great importance because not only does it seem to demonstrate the existence of economically motivated reproductive decision-making in pre-transitional England, but it suggests that there may well have been differences in fertility behaviour within communities. The majority of existing family reconstitution studies are silent about such differences. It would seem that an extreme position that fertility prior to the transition was not a matter of conscious choice and that the idea of birth control was a new innovation is difficult to maintain.

This may seem like a vindication of the economic analysis, but to draw this conclusion would be premature. First, the direct evidence of economic motivations for fertility behaviour is drawn from two rather special groups. The framework knitters of Shepshed in the second quarter of the nineteenth century were subject to adverse economic circumstances which were, even by historical standards, extreme (after 1815, their real wages fell by 40 per cent (Levine, 1987). London's Quakers, too, as Landers points out, differed 'theologically' from other groups in their attitude to young children and in particular in stressing the 'nurture' of children. This led 'to a desire for smaller families so that parents could concentrate more attention on each child' (Landers, 1990, p. 94).

This leads to a second point and a vital one. The Quakers' desire to devote great attention to 'nurture' seems to have been heavily influenced by their distinctive culture and belief-system. The 'rationality' of birth control for the Quakers was, therefore, inseparable from their distinctive culture and beliefs, and the attitudes which stemmed from them. One cannot understand their fertility behaviour, therefore, without reference to *both* economic *and* cultural factors. The two are interlinked. This suggests that explanations of English fertility change which view one particular set of factors, whether economic or cultural, as dominant, are likely to be partial. Third, it seems that even when economic factors did play a part in reproductive decisions, the basis on which couples made their decisions sits rather uneasily with the microeconomic analysis of fertility. Rather than maximising utility, as the economic theory of fertility suggests, couples seem to have been minimising risk.

CONCLUSION

We have seen that during the last 15 years or so, many demographers have abandoned the notion that fertility decline was related to economic development in a straightforward way at the aggregate level. They have also argued strongly against microeconomic theories of the fertility decline based on changes in the demand for children and, more generally, against the idea that fertility decline was an adjustment process. Their alternative hypothesis is that cultural and ideational shifts, especially in attitudes towards the acceptability of birth control, were the fundamental determinants of the timing of the fertility transition.

In this paper, I have tried to challenge their denial of economic motivations for reproductive decisions in the English past. The question asked in the title of the paper was 'is an economic analysis of English fertility between 1600 and 1900 tenable?' If by an 'economic analysis' is meant a *purely* economic analysis, on the lines of certain variants of the original demographic transition theory, or the microeconomic theory of fertility, which neglects cultural and attitudinal factors (or, as some of the original proponents of the demographic transition theory did, treats them as one of the things to be explained, rather than as part of the explanation) then the answer must be no. If, on the other hand, is meant an analysis which recognises that couples, or even communities, may make decisions about reproduction for economic reasons, although their decisions will also be influenced by the cultural context in which they are (and the cultural influence may, in some places and at certain times, be dominant), then I think it perfectly tenable: indeed, it seems to me, in the light of our lack of detailed knowledge of the reproductive decisions of our ancestors, to be the most reasonable position to hold.

There are, perhaps, some lessons to be learned from the history of demographers' attempts to account for fertility change. Most of the empirical work has been carried out at the aggregate level. As I have already mentioned, data limitations are an important reason for this. But they are not the only one. Another is the rigorously social scientific approach adopted by demographers to the subject of fertility. According to the editors of a recent collection of papers on the European fertility decline, '[w]hen demographers study fertility at aggregated levels (the nation, or even the province) they seek causes in large structural changes. When the same events are studied at the village or household level, however, it is not uniformity but diversity, not one cause but many, which emerge' (Gillis *et al.*, 1992, p. 3). By using an aggregate level of analysis, demographers have 'chosen to privilege large-group behaviour at the expense of familial experience. One is bound to ask whether couples or regions, as it were, had babies' (Levine, 1992, p. 327).

As a result, existing studies have given insufficient emphasis to placing their actors in a historical context; they have not fully acknowledged the extent to which people act on the basis of where they find themselves, that behaviour is historically contingent (Levine, 1987; 1992). This historical contingency is, for example, fundamental to Levine's account of the fertility of Shepshed's framework knitters. They reacted to the specific economic and demographic situation which confronted them in the second quarter of the nineteenth century. It seems reasonable to suppose that they were not unique. Thus, for particular groups, at particular times, it may have been rational to adopt specific patterns of reproduction to achieve specific ends. Sometimes these involved parity-specific control, sometimes these involved spacing behaviour.

What are the implications of this for future research on English fertility between 1600 and 1900? One implication is that we need to move beyond the aggregative kind of analyses exemplified by the European Fertility Project and even by family reconstitution studies which treat communities as wholes. There is a need to place the individual at the focus of our efforts to understand human behaviour and to recognise that reproductive decisions are located firmly in historical time. In short, we need to put the history back into historical demography (Gillis *et al.*, 1992).

However, this is easy to say but hard to do. There is a danger that in the act of putting the history back, the demography will get taken out. The merits of the demographers' approach (especially its quantitative rigour) should not be underestimated. The most profound and elegant historically rooted accounts of historical fertility trends will not convince if they are at odds with the facts and figures. It is also important to remember that individuals are located also within communities and that these communities may heavily influence their decisions – but that they too are at the mercy of historical events.

Finally, there are very real difficulties with data. The analysis of individual-level historical demographic data is a tremendously time-consuming process. Fertility statistics which span 50-year time periods are bound to remove historical content, but even obtaining these has taken years of painstaking effort. Given this difficulty, it seems to be that we should admit that at present we know rather little about the factors which influenced reproductive decisions in the English past, acknowledge that discovering more about these factors is going to be a long and arduous process, and exercise caution in constructing wide-ranging explanations.

REFERENCES

Barnard, H. C. (1961), *A History of English Education from 1760* (London: University of London Press) 2nd edition.

Becker, G. S. (1960), 'An economic analysis of fertility', in National Bureau of Economic Research (ed.), *Demographic and Economic Change in Developed Countries* (Princeton, NJ: Princeton University Press).

Becker, G. S. (1981), *A Treatise on the Family* (London: Harvard University Press).

Carlsson, G. (1966), 'The decline of fertility: innovation or adjustment process?', *Population Studies*, vol. 20, pp. 149–74.

Cigno, A. (1991), *Economics of the Family* (Oxford: Clarendon Press).

Cleland, J. (1993), 'Equity, security, and fertility: a reaction to Thomas', *Population Studies,* vol. 47, pp. 345–52.

Cleland, J. and Wilson, C. (1987), 'Demand theories of the fertility transition: an iconoclastic view', *Population Studies*, vol. 41, pp. 5–30.

Coale, A. J. (1973), 'The demographic transition', in IUSSP (ed.), *International Population Conference, Liège* (Liège, Belgium: International Union for the Scientific Study of Population) vol. 1.

Coale, A. J. and Watkins, S. C. (eds) (1986), *The Decline of Fertility in Europe* (Princeton, NJ: Princeton University Press).

Crafts, N. F. R. (1989), 'Duration of marriage, fertility and women's employment opportunities in England and Wales in 1911', *Population Studies*, vol. 43, pp. 325–35.

Davies, H. R. (1991), 'Automated record linkage of census enumerators' books and registration data: obstacles, challenges and solutions', *History and Computing*, vol. 4, pp. 16–26.

Davis, K. (1963), 'The theory of change and response in demographic history', *Population Index*, vol. 29, pp. 345–66.

Easterlin, R. A., Pollack, R. A. and Wachter, M. L. (1980), 'Towards a more general model of fertility determination: endogenous preferences and natural fertility', in R. A. Easterlin (ed.), *Population and Economic Change in Developing Countries* (Chicago, IL: Chicago University Press).

Friedlander, D. (1973), 'Demographic patterns and socioeconomic characteristics of the coal mining population in England and Wales in the nineteenth century', *Economic Development and Cultural Change*, vol. 22, pp. 39–51.

Garrett, E. M. and Hinde, P. R. A. (forthcoming), 'Work patterns, marriage and fertility in late-nineteenth century England', in R. M. Smith (ed.), *Regional and Spatial Demographic Patterns in the Past* (Oxford: Blackwell).

Gillis, J. R., Tilly, L. A. and Levine, D. (1992), 'Introduction: the quiet revolution', in J. R. Gillis, L. A. Tilly and D. Levine (eds), *The European Experience of Declining Fertility: a Quiet Revolution 1850–1970* (Oxford: Blackwell).

Hajnal, J. (1982), 'Two kinds of preindustrial household formation system', *Population and Development Review*, vol. 8, pp. 449–94. Reprinted in R. Wall, J. Robins and P. Laslett (eds), *Family Forms in Historic Europe* (Cambridge: Cambridge University Press).

Henry, L. (1961), 'Some data on natural fertility', *Eugenics Quarterly*, vol. 8, pp. 81–91.

Hinde, P. R. A. (1985), 'The fertility transition in rural England', unpublished Ph D thesis, University of Sheffield.

Hinde, P. R. A. (1987), 'The population of a Wiltshire village in the nineteenth century: a reconstitution study of Berwick St James, 1841–71', *Annals of Human Biology*, vol. 14, pp. 475–85.

Hinde, P. R. A. and Woods, R. I. (1984), 'Variations in historical natural fertility patterns and the measurement of fertility control', *Journal of Biosocial Science*, vol. 16, pp. 309–21.

Kneeling, F. (1914), *Child Labour in the United Kingdom: a Study of the Development and Administration of the Law Relating to the Employment of Children* (London: King).

Knodel, J. E. (1983), 'Natural fertility: age patterns, levels and trends', in R. A. Bulatao and R. D. Lee (eds), *Determinants of Fertility in Developing Countries* (London: Academic Press) vol. 1.

Knodel, J. E. (1988), *Demographic Behaviour in the Past: a Study of Fourteen German Village Populations in the Eighteenth and Nineteenth Centuries* (Cambridge: Cambridge University Press).

Landers, J. (1990), 'Fertility decline and birth spacing among London Quakers', in J. Landers and V. Reynolds (eds), in *Fertility and Resources* (Cambridge: Cambridge University Press) (Society for the Study of Human Biology Symposium 31).

Lesthaeghe, R. (1977), *The Decline of Belgian Fertility, 1800–1970* (Princeton, NJ: Princeton University Press).

Lesthaeghe, R. (1980), 'On the social control of human reproduction', *Population and Development Review*, vol. 6, pp. 527–48.

Lesthaeghe, R. (1983), 'A century of demographic and cultural change in Western Europe: an exploration of the underlying dimensions', *Population and Development Review*, vol. 9, pp. 411–35.

Levine, D. (1977), *Family Formation in an Age of Nascent Capitalism* (London: Academic Press).

Levine, D. (1987), *Reproducing Families: the Political Economy of English Population History* (Cambridge: Cambridge University Press).

Levine, D. (1992), 'Moments in time: a historian's context of declining fertility', in J. R. Gillis, L. A. Tilly and D. Levine (eds), *The European Experience of Declining Fertility: a Quiet Revolution 1850–1970* (Oxford: Blackwell).

Macfarlane, A. (1985), *Marriage and Love in England 1300–1840* (Oxford: Blackwell).

Notestein, F. W. (1945), 'Population – the long view', in T. W. Schultz (ed.), *Food for the World* (Chicago, IL: Chicago University Press).

Potter, J. E. (1983), 'Effects of societal and community institutions in fertility', in R. A. Bulatao and R. D. Lee (eds), *Determinants of Fertility in Developing Countries* (London: Academic Press) vol. II.

Robin, J. (1984), 'Family care of the elderly in a nineteenth-century Devonshire parish', *Ageing and Society*, vol. 4, pp. 505–16.

Robin, J. (1992), 'The census and multi-record linkage: Colyton 1851–1881', paper presented at the meeting of the British Society for Population Studies on Development in Analysis Using Historical Censuses.

Smith, R. M. (1986), 'Transfer incomes, risk and security: the roles of the family and the collectivity in recent theories of fertility change', in D. Coleman and R. Schofield (eds), *The State of Population Theory: Forward from Malthus* (Oxford: Blackwell).

Teitelbaum, M. S. (1984), *The British Fertility Decline: Demographic Transition in the Crucible of the Industrial Revolution* (Princeton, NJ: Princeton University Press).

Wall, R. (1978), 'The age at leaving home', *Journal of Family History*, vol. 3, pp. 181–202.

Wilson, C. (1984), 'Natural fertility in pre-industrial England', *Population Studies*, vol. 38, pp. 225–40.

Wilson, C. (1986), 'The proximate determinants of marital fertility in England 1600–1799', in L. Bonfield, R. M. Smith and K. Wrightson (eds), *The World*

We Have Gained: Histories of Population and Social Structure (Oxford: Blackwell).

Wilson, C. and Woods, R. (1991), 'Fertility in England: a long-term perspective', *Population Studies*, vol. 45, pp. 399–415.

Woods, R. (1987), 'Approaches to the fertility transition in Victorian England', *Population Studies*, vol. 41, pp. 283–311.

Woods, R. (1992), *The Population of Britain in the Nineteenth Century* (London: Macmillan).

Woods, R. and Smith, C. W. (1983), 'The decline of marital fertility in the late nineteenth century: the case of England and Wales', *Population Studies*, vol. 37, pp. 207–25.

Wrigley, E. A. and Schofield, R. S.(1981), *The Population History of England 1541–1871: a Reconstruction* (London: Edward Arnold).

Wrigley, E. A. and Schofield, R. S. (1983), 'English population history from family reconstitution: summary results 1600–1799', *Population Studies*, vol. 37, pp. 157–184.

9 Stopping, Starting and Spacing: the Regulation of Fertility in Historical Populations

John Landers

Fertility variations and their causes are of central importance to the comparative demography of historical populations since it appears, both empirically and theoretically, that mortality and fertility levels co-varied, and that much mortality variation can be understood in terms of fertility. Empirically, population growth rates seem to have varied much less than those of fertility (Wrigley, 1987), whilst theoretically it is generally assumed that population growth, as Malthus famously argued, was strongly constrained by the biological and physical environment. Proximate mechanisms vary – in hunter-gatherer societies the concept of ecological 'carrying capacity' may be relevant, whereas in early-modern Europe we are more concerned with supply inelasticities in agriculture – but the results are much the same: beyond a certain point, as pre-industrial populations expanded, material living standards fell and mortality tended to increase.

The relevance of fertility variations to this process is evident from a comparison of two hypothetical populations (H) and (L), with fertility high and low respectively, but in each case above their common level of mortality. Both populations expand, leading in turn to falling living standards and increasing mortality, a process which can end only when birth and death rates equal each other. Evidently this will occur earlier in L than in H, and L will thus have correspondingly lower mortality and higher living standards. Still better results ensue in a third case, L^0, where fertility is also responsive to changes in living standards. Here the initially low birth rates fall further as conditions deteriorate, arresting population growth after only moderate increases in mortality. Historical demographers use the term 'low-pressure demographic regime' to characterise the dynamics of 'L' type populations, 'high-pressure' regimes being those in which it is mortality which brings population and resources back into balance.

The importance of fertility variation, however, goes beyond population pressure on resources for, counter-intuitively perhaps, population age-structure has historically been determined largely by fertility, and the higher the Total Fertility Rate (TFR: the average number of children that a woman would have she survived to age 50) the larger the proportion of children and young people the population will contain. At an e_0 of 30, a population with a TFR around five will, without migration, have 34 per cent of its members below the age of 15, rising to 45 per cent with a TFR of eight: corresponding percentages for an of e_0 of 40 are 38 per cent and 48 per cent.[1] This variation has considerable economic implications. As the proportion of young children rises, so does the dependency burden on the economically active and hence, the pressure to enrol children in the labour force as early as possible (to the detriment of education and training). The association of high mortality with high fertility exacerbates the problem. As e_0 declines from 40 to the 30, so the proportion of live-born who survive to the age of fifteen falls from 0.662 to 0.537. Hence, high-pressure regimes are inherently 'wasteful', in terms of economic demography, since a large proportion of young dependants will never survive to become economically productive – a further disincentive to the investment of resources in the young.

Lower and more variable levels of fertility, and thus more effective fertility regulation, could evidently yield appreciable benefits. Fertility regulation as a concept, however, can be interpreted in two senses: a general sense, of mechanisms – ecological, physiological, socioeconomic, or other – capable of explaining observed variations in fertility; and the more restricted, and generally more interesting, sense, of conscious control of fertility, whether individual or collective. Our understanding of regulation in the first sense has benefited greatly from the distinction between ultimate determinants of fertility and the proximate determinants, or intermediate fertility variables, and from the development of a quantitative framework for analysing the impact of the latter (Bongaarts, 1978).

In historical studies, we generally lack the information required to fit the model in its entirety, but we can still identify the effects of a number of proximate determinants as a preliminary to understanding why these themselves should vary as they do. As a first step, it is useful to identify three sources of variation in the structure of women's reproductive careers:

(i) 'Starting' – the proportion of women who reproduce and the age at which they begin their reproductive careers.

(ii)   'Stopping' – the age at which reproduction ceases.
(iii) 'Spacing' – the temporal distribution of births within the reproductive career.

In most historical populations, fertility was largely confined to marriage and so variations in (i) reflect marriage patterns – and thus the demographic variable termed 'nuptiality' – whereas (ii) and (iii) relate to differences in the structure of marital fertility. We shall examine marital fertility and nuptiality in turn, but first it is necessary to consider the scope and limitations of our survey.

SOURCES AND METHODS

When does history stop? In one sense all population dynamics are historical by definition since the events which constitute them are inscribed in time and a population's demographic structure is a product of its past experience. For practical purposes, however, we need some cut-off point, and a natural watershed is provided by the so-called 'demographic transition' from high to low fertility and mortality which began in Europe during the later nineteenth century. At the other extreme, the starting point of our survey, like its geographical scope, is constrained by the sources. Ideally, fertility analysis requires, at a minimum, the calculation of fertility rates by age ('age-specific fertility rates' or ASFRs) which in turn yield the 'total fertility rate' (TFR, i.e. the number of children produced in a full reproductive life span). In contemporary developed countries, the necessary data can be obtained from civil censuses and vital registration, but in most of Europe these become available only during the nineteenth century (the opening of the 'statistical era'), and not till some time after 1900 do they allow ASFRs to be calculated. Elsewhere in the world they become available only in the present century, if at all.

The nineteenth century European material does, however, permit the use of a form of indirect standardisation devised by Coale for the Princeton European Fertility Study (Coale and Watkins, 1986). Coale has derived four fertility indices: I_i, I_g, I_h, and I_m, which can be calculated from birth totals and census age-distributions of women by marital status. They are defined as follows:

$$I_f = \frac{B}{\text{S}(f(i) \cdot w(i))}$$

$$I_g = \frac{B_m}{\text{S}(f(i) \cdot m(i))}$$

$$I_h = \frac{B_h}{\text{S}(f(i) \cdot u(i))}$$

$$I_m = \frac{\text{S}(f(i) \cdot m(i))}{\text{S}(f(i) \cdot w(i))}$$

where B, B_m, and B_h are the total number of births, the total births to married women and the total births to unmarried women, respectively; $w(i)$ is the number of women, $m(i)$ the number of married women, and $u(i)$ the number of unmarried women in the (i)th age-group and $f(i)$ is the corresponding age-specific marital fertility rate (ASMFR) for Hutterite women. The indices are thus effectively weighted averages of age-specific total, marital and non-marital fertility, and of proportions married, with the Hutterite fertility rates as weights. The latter were chosen since they represent the maximum observed in a well-documented population.

In much of north-western Europe, ecclesiastical parish registers of baptisms, marriages and burials allow us to chart variations in fertility for up to two or three centuries before the onset of the statistical era. The technique of family reconstitution (Wrigley, 1966a), a form of nominal record linkage developed to exploit such materials, yields ASMFRs and ages at marriage as well as rates for mortality in infancy and childhood. It is, however, extremely demanding, both of the researcher's time and the quality of the sources and so the number of reconstituted communities is very small relatively speaking. In England, however, the technique of 'aggregative back projection' has enabled Wrigley and Schofield (1981) to reconstruct national population trends for the period 1541–1871 using a sample of 404 parish registers. Wrigley and Schofield's study has provided us with crude vital rates, population size and age-structure estimates, and series for the average life-expectation at birth (e_0) and TFR. Furthermore, by combining these results with material from family reconstitution studies, it has proved possible to decompose movements in female marriage rates into components due to age at marriage and proportions marrying.

MARITAL FERTILITY

Marital fertility levels, for a given age at marriage, depend on the age at which reproduction ceases and the average interval between successive births. Hence the regulation of marital fertility may operate through variations in either spacing or stopping, a crucial distinction for demographers, relating as it does to a conceptual opposition introduced by Louis Henry (1961) who distinguished between two patterns of marital fertility which he termed 'natural fertility' and 'family limitation'. Since natural fertility was defined as marital fertility in the absence of family limitation, the distinction turns on the definition of the latter.

Stopping

Henry defined family limitation as parity-dependent fertility-restricting behaviour (i.e. behaviour which is bound to the number of children already born and is practiced more intensively as the couple reach a desired family size which they do not wish to exceed). It is thus a form of fertility regulation based on 'stopping', the premature cessation of reproduction and Knodel (1977, 1988), in particular, has subsequently developed Henry's argument that the secular decline of fertility involved a transition from natural fertility to family limitation. This proposition is, to a degree, testable since natural fertility leads to a characteristic pattern of ASMFRs with a convex curve when plotted against age. Under family limitation this curve becomes concave, a finding which Coale and Trussel (1978) have used to develop a model of age-specific fertility depending on two parameters one of which, m, measures the deviation from the curve of natural fertility.

ASMFRs are readily obtainable from family reconstitution studies which also provide some additional means of detecting family limitation. Thus, under natural fertility, the women's median age at last birth is generally around 40. Hence a significantly lower figure suggests family limitations, as do final birth intervals which are very long relative to penultimate intervals (probably reflecting accidental conceptions or the deliberate 'replacement' of an earlier child who has died). The results generally bear out the Henry–Knodel argument in that family limitation does seem to have been absent from pre-transitional populations and its adoption to have reflected a 'once for all' transformation, so that once natural fertility is displaced it does not reappear.[2] Before the late nineteenth century this type of stopping regulation was mostly confined to a small number of so-called 'forerunner' groups, generally urban and clearly marked out from the surrounding population by their elite status or adherence to a minority religious faith (Livi-Bacci, 1986). Family limitation also seems to have been the rule among peasant communities in parts of Hungary at least by the 1840s (Vasary, 1989), but its most striking manifestation was in rural France where it began to be practised on the level of the Revolution and was evidently widespread in a number of regions by the 1830s (Wrigley, 1985).

Spacing

The importance of birth spacing as a form of fertility regulation can be seen from Figure 9.1 which maps I_g for European provinces in 1870. With the exception of the previously mentioned areas in France and Hungary, we can assume natural fertility prevailed among the population at large and thus that I_g variations reflected those in birth spacing. The results of a number of family reconstitution studies, given in Table 9.1, reveal that such variations considerably pre-dated the statistical era and were

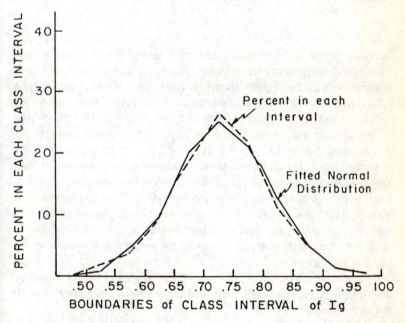

Figure 9.1   Percentage distribution of provinces of Europe by the pre-decline plateau of I_g
Source: Coale and Treadway (1986)

Table 9.1   Cumulative age-specific marital fertility per woman (ages 20–44 years)

France (–1769)	
North-west	7.46*
North-east	8.75*
South-east	7.20*
South-west	6.43*
England (1600–1799)	
13 parishes	6.14*
German villages (1740–1790)	
Bavaria (3)	10.40[†]
Waldeck (4)	8.31[†]
Scandinavia	
Alskog (1770–1794)	6.61[†]
Sejerø (1780–1799)	7.41[†]
Irish Quakers (1750–99)	11.00[‡]

Sources: *Wrigley and Schofield (1983); [†]Flinn (1981); [‡]Vann and Eversley (1992).

historically quite stable. The meaning of this phenomenon is of great theoretical importance to demographers, affecting as it does our interpretation of the fertility transition itself. This, broadly speaking, has taken one of two forms, labelled, respectively, 'innovation' and 'adjustment process' (Carlsson, 1966).

The former links fertility decline to an underlying discontinuity in demographic behaviour, arguing that conscious fertility regulation within marriage was absent from pre-transitional populations and that its appearance must be explained, at least proximately, in terms of cultural changes and the development of a 'rational' approach to family formation. By contrast, the adjustment process view sees conscious fertility regulation as a general feature of human populations and attributes the decline to changing economic and social circumstances which made large families less desirable.

There is very little direct evidence with which to resolve this issue, but demographers have generally accepted the innovation perspective on the following grounds:[3]

(i)   Contemporary writings condemned contraception and related practices but appeared to assume that these are restricted to illicit sexual relations. References to deliberate fertility control within marriage are absent prior to the appearance of parity-specific family limitation.

(ii) The high rate of infant and child mortality, together with abandonment in some circumstances, suggests a considerable number of unwanted births.

(iii) Family reconstitution studies provide no evidence for a 'replacement effect' (i.e. a tendency for conception to follow more rapidly should a previous child die) under natural fertility beyond that expected from the effect of interrupted lactation. Replacement effects do occur, however, among populations practising family limitation.

(iv) The spread of family limitation in time and space, and its apparent irreversibility, is consistent with the diffusion of an innovative practice from a limited number of 'vanguard' groups.

(v) Where, as in England, pre-transitional marital fertility series are available for lengthy periods their levels are remarkably constant compared to the fertility swings seen among populations practising family limitation.

These arguments may have been generally persuasive, but they are not incontestable. Thus (i) is an argument from a silence which may only reflect contemporary views of fit matters for discussion in public print or private correspondence. The implicit assumption in (ii), that much infant mortality was volitional, is at least debatable, and child abandonment may have resulted from unforeseen changes to the mother's circumstances post-conception – particularly her own abandonment by the child's father – as often as from an *a priori* unwanted conception (Wilson, 1989).

Arguments (iii) and (iv) are forceful in their own terms but are circular in equating parity-specific family limitation with the conscious control of fertility *in toto*. Knodel has provided a number of reasons for doing this (Knodel, 1977), but Landers (1990) has suggested that, under certain circumstances, a desire to minimise the burden of current dependency would be best served by parity-independent spacing, a form of regulation which need not yield strong replacement effects. Hence family limitation itself might be an innovation without this implying that conscious control as such was absent from natural fertility populations. The findings referred to in (v), however, do imply that the determinants of any such control must have remained constant over very long periods.

If the assumption that conscious control was absent from natural fertility regimes should be treated with some reserve, it does none the less underlie much of the empirical work done on the topic. This is partly because such an assumption allows the effects of the remaining proximate determinants of fertility to be quantified using birth interval distributions of the kind obtainable from family reconstitution studies. Such intervals are of two kinds: 'protogenesic' intervals, from marriage to the first birth and 'intergenesic' intervals between successive births. Both can be subdivided into a number of components:

(i)   The 'non-susceptible period' (NSP), lasting from the birth which opens the interval to the resumption of ovulation, and largely determined by the duration of lactation together with the frequency and intensity of suckling during lactation. This component is absent from the protogenesic interval.

(ii) The 'waiting time to conception' (WTC) lasting from the resumption of ovulation to the occurrence of conception. In the absence of attempts to prevent conception, the duration of the WTC is determined by a quantity termed 'fecundability' – essentially the probability of conception occurring in a given menstrual cycle – which varies with age and coital frequency (Wood and Weinstein, 1988).

(iii) Gestation, assumed to last for 9 months. Mean gestation appears to vary little between populations in spite of considerable inter-individual variations.

(iv) A statistical allowance for pregnancy wastage which has the effect of extending mean birth intervals. This cannot be calculated for historical populations, due to the lack of data, but it is assumed to be too small and insufficiently variable to distort estimates of components (i)–(iii).

The protogenesic interval minus 9 months – discarding intervals due to pre-nuptial conceptions[4] – gives us an approximation to the WTC and allows us to estimate mean fecundability at marriage (Wilson, 1986). Similarly, assuming that fecundability changes very little in the early years of marriage, the NSP is given by the difference between the protogenesic and first intergenesic intervals.[5] The results of a number of studies are given in Tables 9.2 and 9.3 and bear out the assumption generally held by demographers that it is NSP differences which are responsible for most of the overall variation in birth intervals (Leridon and Menken, 1979; Santow, 1987; Goldman *et al.*, 1987). We should note, however, that mean fecundabilities do vary appreciable between populations, although the underlying reasons for this are obscure. Work patterns doubtless play

Table 9.2   Estimates of mean fecundability in historical populations

German villages (–1849)	
Bavaria (3)	0.25
Waldeck (4)	0.19
Ostfriesland (2)	0.19
Crulai, France	0.18
Tourouvre, France	0.21
Genevan bourgeoisie	0.23
French Canada	0.31
Blankenberghe, Belgium	0.28
Rural Flanders	0.29

Source: Wilson (1986).

Table 9.3   Estimates of non-susceptible period (months)

England	
1600–49	12.2
1650–99	13.3
1700–49	11.5
1750–99	12.1
France	
Crulai (1674–1742)	10.2
Ile de France (18th century)	8.6
German village (1800–49)	
Bavarian (3)	4.1*
Waldeck (4)	14.8*
Ostfriesland (2)	15.5*
French Canada (1700–30)	5.2
Blankenberghe, Belgium (1650–1849)	5.2

*Calculated from infant survival method.[5]
Source: Wilson (1986).

some part (through their effects on temporary migration and spousal separation), but the bulk of this variation must be due to differences in coital frequency requiring to be explained in terms of the effective content of marriage and a broad range of factors relating to gender relations and ideologies.

The physiological basis of the relationship between lactation and the NSP is well understood (Habicht *et al.*, 1985) and, where external evidence is available, it confirms the expectation that populations practising extended breastfeeding should have long birth intervals and vice versa. Why methods of infant feeding should have been so variable, however, has yet to be fully understood. Once more, work patterns were probably important in some contexts. The very short intervals found in some early-modern cities may have reflected mothers' need to return to work alongside their husbands and thus wean their infants early, whilst in other cases short durations of NSP were due to infants being wet-nursed, whether from fashion or to free mothers for other work (Flinn, 1981).

Conversely the large, complex, households found in south-western France may have enabled women to share domestic tasks, allowing mothers to breastfeed for longer periods and thus producing the extended birth intervals observed in the region (Goubert, 1977; Flandrin, 1979). A related explanation has been proposed to explain England's relatively low marital fertility. In this instance, the Elizabethan Poor Law generated transfer payments between households at different stages of the developmental cycle which, it is suggested, permitted mothers to undertake extended nursing (Smith, 1981a, 1986). In other cases, however, where breastfeeding durations were short or non-existent, the proximate explanation, at least, was evidently a cultural preference for artificial feeding. Such preferences prevailed in parts of Scandinavia (Lithell, 1981; Bräandström, 1988) but were most strikingly evident in parts of southern Germany where they amounted to a virtual taboo on breastfeeding (Knodel, 1968, 1988).

NUPTIALITY AND MARRIAGE

The effect of marriage patterns on birth rates is easy to overlook, but its potential impact on fertility is considerable (Lesthaeghe, 1971). In the absence of illegitimate fertility, nuptiality determines both the proportion of women ever 'exposed to the risk' of fertility and the duration of such exposure and thus operates as a 'starting' pattern of fertility regulation. Evidently, the time of marriage affects the duration of the reproductive career and thus the only fertility achieved for a given birth interval. For an interval of around 2 years for women in their twenties and early thirties, delaying marriage from 20 to 24 could lower cohort fertility from around eight to six, a reduction of about 25 per cent.

Nuptiality also affects birth rates through its influence on generation length, which can be thought of as the interval between the 'mid-points' of successive cohorts' reproductive careers and is approximated by the mean age of maternity. The effect is expressed by the formula:

$$r = \sqrt[t]{R_0}$$

where t is the female generation length, R_0 the net reproduction ratio (the number of same-sex offspring per individual under the prevailing mortality and fertility) and r the intrinsic rate of natural increase, or 'Lotka rate' (equal to the asymptotic growth rate of a population with given fertility and mortality). These quantities are defined separately for males and females and, although r will be the same in each case, R_0 and t will generally differ.

The proportion of women at risk to legitimate fertility, in turn, reflects both the proportion ever-married and the joint influence of adult mortality and re-marriage propensities. Where mortality is high, the effects of the latter may be considerable. Thus with a female e_0 of 30 years, male and female ages at marriage equal at 25, and uncorrelated spousal mortality, over 17 per cent of wives will be widowed before 40, the proportion rising to more than 19 per cent as female e_0 falls to 25 years.[6] Female re-marriage propensities were clearly very important in such circumstances, but those of males might also have an indirect effect. Where widowers disproportionately married younger spinsters, widows' re-marriage chances were reduced, and the fertility-reducing effects of large spousal age-differences would lower the wives' fertility below that of women marrying age-mates.[7]

For nuptiality to have these effects, of course, requires that fertility outside marriage be kept low and this moves us from nuptiality as a demographic variable to marriage as a social and cultural fact. It is this transition which both complicates nuptiality analysis and underlies the prospect if offers of linking population studies to the broader study of human societies. Defining marriage, or even specifying its functions, cross-culturally is notoriously difficult, but such functions evidently include the allocation of rights and responsibilities towards children, as well as rights to the sexual and labour services of women and to their reproductive capacity.

Marriage, however, cannot be understood in isolation and from other institutions. Most immediately, through its role in establishing alliances and legitimating descent, marriage is integral to the wider structure of kinship systems. Furthermore, formal or 'full' marriage may coexist in a given society with more or less formally recognised concubinage, cohabitation or morganatic unions. At the same time, and of considerable importance in the study of historical European populations, there is an important relationship between marriage and the general structure of social control. This arises most visibly where marriage is delayed: in the case of males institutions are required, ranging from age-set systems to monastic institutions, in order to 'ration' access to women and cope with the potentially disruptive presence of unmarried young men. Delayed marriage for women raises other problems, particularly the possibility of 'bastard' births and thus requires some means of social control of the sexuality of unmarried women. Simultaneously, on the cultural or ideological level, these institutional networks create systems of definitions of what it is to be male or female, old or young.

Thus, in considering marriage we find ourselves confronting a network of institutions ramifying into what Mauss (1970) referred to as the 'total social fact'. Hence, in analysing nuptiality we encounter considerable complexity at the level of explanation since the demographic implications of a given marriage pattern – whether 'homeostatic' or not – may be a fortuitous consequence of social arrangements whose governing rationale lies elsewhere (Lesthaeghe, 1980). Conversely, it is of course possible that the patterning of institutions underpinning a given nuptiality regime is to be explained in terms of the latter's beneficial demographic consequences, whether for society as a whole or for dominant elements within it.

European Marriage Patterns

The above considerations apply with especial force to the characteristic marriage pattern first described by Hajnal (1965) using census data from around 1900. Hajnal argued that an imaginary line across Europe, from Trieste to St Petersburg, separated two regions: the 'east' in which female marriage occurred close to puberty and was effectively universal, and the 'west' in which marriage was delayed and an appreciable proportion of the population remained permanently unmarried ('celibate'). Two 'typical' configurations of age-specific proportions married are given in Table 9.4, but a more convincing demonstration can be found in the provincial I_ms mapped in Figure 9.2.

The reality of the 'Hajnal line' emerges forcefully, although there are two exceptions to the rule of low western I_ms. The first, covering central and south-western France, is more apparent than real and reflects relatively recent changes in marriage behaviour following the adoption of family limitation. The second exception, however, covering the northern shores of

Table 9.4   Percentage single by age-group in selected countries around 1900

	Males			Females		
Country	20–24	25–29	45–49	20–24	25–29	45–49
Belgium	85	50	16	71	41	17
Serbia	50	18	3	16	2	1

Source: Hajnal (1965).

the Mediterranean and their hinterlands, cannot be explained in this way and is now thought to represent a distinct 'Mediterranean' pattern or patterns (Smith, 1981b; Benigno, 1989), as opposed to the 'North-Western European Marriage Pattern' (NWEMP) found in Britain, the German speaking countries, Scandinavia, the Low Countries and Northern France.

The central characteristic of NWEMP was the late age of marriage for women, combined with an appreciable incidence of permanent celibacy. It was also distinguished by a high frequency of widow remarriage, in which it differed sharply from the pattern prevailing in at least some of the Mediterranean region (Laslett, 1977; MacFarlane, 1978). Male marriage was also delayed substantially beyond puberty, but this is not so unusual and in some Mediterranean areas mean male marriage ages might be in the mid to late twenties whilst women married in their teens. Although Hajnal has subsequently (Hajnal, 1983) suggested 23 as a minimum female age at marriage consistent with NWEMP, it would be a mistake to attach too much significance to any given 'threshold'. Ages at marriage varied appreciably in time and space within this regions, and such variability was integral to what Wrigley (1981) has aptly termed a 'repertoire of adaptive responses' rather than a fixed set of relationships. Indeed, the crucial feature is probably not even the existence of an extended interval between puberty and marriage, but rather that marriage was tied to social and economic, rather than to biological, contingencies.

Explaining the North-Western European Pattern

The role of NWEMP in reducing overall levels of fertility in the region is clear; birth rates in the region were rarely in excess of 40 per thousand and might fall below 30. Why, however, did it exist? In principle such a question can be answered in either of two ways: historically, in terms of when and how it came into existence, or structurally, in terms of its relationship to other social and economic institutions of early-modern

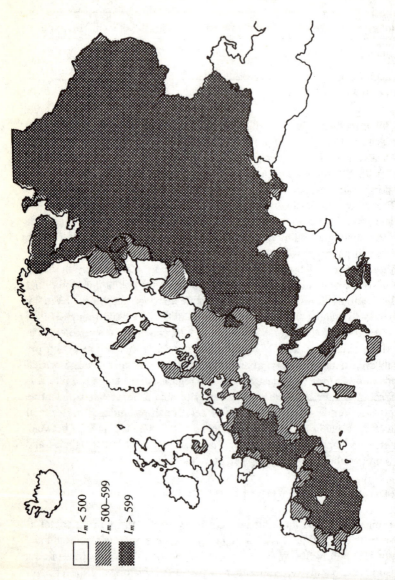

Figure 9.2 Index of proportions married (I_m) in European provinces in 1990
Source: Coale (1970); redrawn by Daisy Williamson.

Europe and to the life-cycle of individuals within its population. Historically, in spite of some stimulating conjectures (Goody, 1983; Smith 1990; Seccombe, 1992), little is known. The pattern was evidently well-established in the region by the early sixteenth century and is attested for some areas as early as the fourteenth century, but beyond this the picture becomes very cloudy.

The structural position of the NWEMP is, however, much clearer, and has been depicted in two general models (Schofield, 1976, 1989), both of them founded on the relationship between marriage and the region's equally distinctive pattern of household structure and formation. Work on the latter was initiated by Peter Laslett and colleagues at the Cambridge Group for the History of Population and Social Structure during the 1960s and focused initially on the question of average household size (Laslett and Wall, 1972). Laslett showed that this had remained remarkably constant over a period of several centuries effectively refuting the earlier view which associated the industrial revolution with the advent of the nuclear family in western Europe.

More recently attention has shifted to questions of household membership and the development cycle of households, for it is here that north-western Europe stands out most clearly from other regions of the world. Two features emerge from comparisons of the kind carried out in Table 9.5: firstly, the near absence of non-nuclear kin, and the low incidence of households with more than one married couple and, secondly, the presence in many households of individuals unrelated to the household

Table 9.5 Persons per 100 households by relationship to head – rural Denmark (average for 1787 and 1801) and rural India (1951)

	Rural Denmark			*Rural India*		
	Males	*Females*	*Total*	*Males*	*Females*	*Total*
Married heads and wives	88	88	176	71	71	142
Other heads	5	7	12	19	10	29
Children	99	96	195	110	81	191
Other relatives	8	15	23	48	74	122
Servants	50	40	90	–	–	–
Others	5	9	14	3	3	6
Total	255	255	510	251	239	490

Source: Hajnal (1983).

head. These individuals – known generically as 'servants', or more specifically 'life-cycle servants' – lived as members of the household, participating in its productive tasks and were apparently unique to north-western European society (Kussmaul, 1981).

Generally young, almost always unmarried (Table 9.6), they contracted themselves to work for fixed periods – often a year – receiving much of their remuneration in kind. Such employment occupied the life-cycle stage between leaving home, often at a remarkably early age by present day standards, and becoming a household head, providing as it did the means of accumulating the petty capital and skills required to provide for and manage an independent domestic unit. Hajnal has linked these findings to his earlier work on marriage patterns and proposed two models of household formation: (i) the north-west European 'simple' household system and (ii) the joint family system.

From our point of view the key distinction between the two lines is the stipulation that under (i) young couples assume charge of their own household at marriage with the husband as household head, whereas under

Table 9.6   Servants as a percentage of total population by age

Age-group	Nine Flemish villages 1814		Six English communities 1599–1796	
	Male	Female	Male	Female
10–14	14	5	5	4
15–19	38	31	35	27
20–21	48	36	30	40
25–29	35	25	15	15
30–39	23	6	6	7
40–49	8	2	2	2

Age-group	Iceland (3 Co.s) 1729		Norway 1801
	Male	Female	Combined
10–14	21	20	10
15–19	33	34	32
20–24	39	44	33
25–29	34	32	19
30–39	12	24	8
40–49	9	17	3

Source: Hajnal (1983).

(ii) they 'often start life together in a household of which the older couple are in charge (usually the household in which the young husband has been a member)' (Hajnal, 1983, p. 69). It is this requirement that each marriage be associated with a structurally independent nuclear family household which imposed the socioeconomic 'hurdle' to be surmounted before legitimate reproduction could commence and underlies the two structural models of the NWEMP.

The difference between the two lies in the way the hurdle was surmounted and the 'means to marry' acquired. The first, sometimes known as the 'hearth' model, assumes that each household was associated with a small-scale productive unit, a farm or craft workshop (generically a 'hearth') whose supply was sufficiently inelastic as to be considered fixed in the medium term. Thus for a new marriage to take place a hearth must be transferred between generations and this is assumed to have occurred by inheritance. The system envisaged is akin to one of ecological niches associated with a relatively inflexible form of demographic homeostasis. Should, for some exogenous reason, adult mortality rise, younger people would gain their inheritance earlier, leading to fall in marriage ages and an increased birth rate. Conversely, declining adult mortality would eventually lead to an offsetting decline in fertility.

The alternative is to assume that couples accumulate the wherewithal for marriage by savings or other *inter vivos* transfers. This 'real wage' (or 'nest egg') model also gives rise to a form of demographic homeostasis but one which is delayed and has different economic implications. In this case, 'Malthusian' rigidities mean that population growth pushes up prices faster than nominal wages and so real wages fall, enforcing a longer period of saving before the necessary 'nest egg' can be amassed. Age at marriage thus rises, whilst some people may never be able to marry, and the birth rate eventually declines. This system is more flexible than the other, since it is capable of responding to exogenous changes in the demand for labour or the supply of subsistence commodities, but the response of nuptiality to population growth is indirect and delayed.

As Schofield (1989) has pointed out, the two models make very different assumptions about the prevailing economic and social milieu. The first implies what he terms a 'familistic' dependence of individuals' economic welfare on their kin – even in the absence of actual co-residence – together with a weakly developed labour market. Conversely the second assumes highly-developed labour markets in which individuals seek their own fortunes, having only secondary assistance from relatives. None the less, this is an 'individualist – collectivist', rather than simply an 'individualist', model, because of the structurally-determined inability of nuclear families to cope alone with the contingencies of the life-cycle and the hazards of illness and bereavement. Hence, in the absence of kin support, some system of resource transfers is required – as much between households at different stages of the life-cycle as between social strata – and thus a form of risk-sharing at the community level.

England and France

If we are to examine the fertility-regulating function of the NWEMP, along the lines suggested in the preceding section, it is necessary to follow the evolution of nuptiality and the related variables over an extended period. Two European countries, England and France, provide sufficient data to make this possible, although only in England is a really long run of data available. France is, none the less, of particular interest because of its early adoption of family limitation and corresponding failure to experience substantial population growth in the century after 1750.[8]

At the latter date, French mortality was very high, with e_0 in the mid-twenties, and marital fertility, though varying regionally, was at about three-quarters of the Hutterite level nationality. Combined with a mean age at marriage also in the mid-twenties and permanent celibacy at about 5 per cent, this yielded a TFR around five. Like many European countries, France experienced declining mortality in the later eighteenth century but on an unusual scale. By the 1830s, e_0 had risen to around 40, comparable to that in England and Sweden, which had previously enjoyed much lower mortality than France.

The evolution of French nuptiality and fertility, however, was qualitatively distinct. Female age at marriage had risen to 26.5 years by 1780, whilst the proportion never marrying rose to more than 10 per cent for women born in the first quarter of the nineteenth century. This phenomenon is interpreted by Wrigley (1985) in terms of a squeeze on nuptiality imposed by mortality decline within a 'niche' system of population regulation. If this interpretation is correct, however, the consequences were far-reaching – nothing less than the transformation of the entire system.

The first sign of this was evidence of a growing strain on the system as illegitimate fertility rose from around 1 per cent of all baptisms in the early eighteenth century to more than 5 per cent by 1820. More profoundly, marital fertility began to fall after 1780 and, when it stabilised for a generation in the mid-nineteenth century, it was at a level around half that of the Hutterites. Wrigley's suggestion is that a 'stopping' system of fertility control within marriage was adopted in preference to nuptiality-based 'starting' as mortality decline made the constraints of the latter unacceptably restrictive, a suggestion reinforced by a reversal in the trend of female nuptiality in the second quarter of the nineteenth century.

The English series presents a very different picture and allow us to follow the country's demographic regime over three centuries during which it went through two cycles of population growth. Population grew rapidly in the century 1540–1640 and again after 1770. In each case an important role – the dominant role in the second cycle – was played by fertility, which was high relative to the intervening period of stagnation; the apparent stability of marital fertility over the whole period implies that nuptiality change was responsible for this (Wrigley and Schofield, 1981). The relationship between nuptiality and mortality, however, was quite different from that predicted by the niche model and observed in France, since both the crude first marriage rate (CMFR) and e_0 rose during the rapid growth of the later eighteenth century.

At first sight, the real wage model performs much better with the CMFR tracking movements in real wages with a lag of some 20 years. But a decomposition of movement in the crude rate into components due to age at marriage and proportions marrying reveals a more complex picture (Weir 1984; Schofield, 1985, 1989). The later seventeenth century decline in fertility was due to a fall in proportions ever marrying (to below 80 per cent for women born in the second quarter of the seventeenth century), whilst age at marriage also fell slightly. The proportion marrying rose to more than 90 per cent for women born in the 1690s and the surge in fertility later in the century reflected lower ages at marriage. However, as Goldstone has demonstrated with an improved real-wage series, of the two components of nuptiality only proportions marrying responded in the manner predicted (Goldstone, 1986).

Goldstone has proposed a model in which the population is divided into three categories:

(1) A 'traditional' sector (*T*) composed of farmers, artisans, craftsmen etc.
(2) A 'non-traditional' sector composed of individuals unable to obtain employment in (1) and sub-divided into:
    (2a) 'proletarians' (*P*), who manage to obtain enough waged labour to marry and raise a family;
    (2b) the 'unemployed' (*U*) unable to obtain sufficient income to marry.

Traditional workers become servants or apprentices for an extended period whose duration is largely governed by convention and so marry late, whilst proletarians marry as early as they can. The population mean age at marriage thus depends on the ratio $P : T$ and the proportion marrying on $(P + T) : U$. Employment in the traditional sector clearly failed to keep pace with population in either of the two episodes of expansion, but there was a crucial difference in the response of the non-traditional sector. In the sixteenth and seventeenth centuries, opportunities for waged labour lagged behind the supply of potential labourers. $(P + T) : U$ thus fell and with it the proportion marrying, although there was sufficient growth in (P) for some fall in mean age at marriage to occur. The later eighteenth century, by contrast, saw the demand for waged labourers expand sufficiently to absorb most of the growth in population and mean age at marriage thus declines.

CONCLUSIONS

Variations in the overall fertility levels of historical European populations were due to differences in patterns of 'starting' and 'spacing' reproductive behaviour. Parity-specific 'stopping', the hallmark of post-transitional fertility regimes, was generally confined to small, clearly defined, sub-populations which are usually seen as a kind of reproductive *avant-garde*, entering precociously into the modern demographic world. In both France and Hungary, however, family limitation spread widely among regional peasant populations and although, in France at least, the effects of cultural modernisation have been postulated as an explanation, it is clear that the social and economic matrix remained pre-industrial and agrarian. In these cases, pressure on the land due to falling mortality (in France) or legislative reforms (regarding inheritance in France and tenure in Hungary) may have been responsible, but if this was so then the limited information at our disposal suggests that it was a very unusual phenomenon in early-modern Europe, for natural fertility appears to have been ubiquitous.

Marital fertility was none the less very variable geographically, reflecting variations in birth spacing, although there is little evidence for substantial secular change prior to the adoption of family limitation. It remains unclear whether, and if so how far, birth intervals were deliberately prolonged, but even if this was the case, their temporal stability suggests that the pressure of social norms, or powerful and enduring circumstantial constraints on behaviour, were responsible;[9] there is little evidence that marital fertility was governed by the kind of conscious, individual-level, regulation which we associate with regimes of family limitation.

Where individual, strategic, decision-making evidently was of the greatest importance was at the level of marriage patterns. The effect of the nuclear family household system in north-western Europe was to separate female marriage from biological maturation and constitute it as a socioeconomic fact. Women might thus acquire a power of reproductive decision-making rare in pre-industrial societies, but it was a power tightly constrained by the rules of household and family formation[10] and the productive limits of a pre-industrial economy. The effects of the former on nuptiality – and thus on birth rates – in the region were profound, and it is likely that mass living standards, particularly in England, were thereby raised significantly above those prevailing elsewhere in the world at the time (Wrigley, 1987).

It would none the less be a mistake to see the NWEMP simply, or even primarily, as a system of population regulation. As Lesthaeghe (1981) has argued, it is equally probable that the benign macro-demographic effects were an unintended consequence of restrictions imposed for much more circumscribed and self-interested motives. In Lesthaeghe's view, these are to be found in the attempts of local elites to prevent the formation of a 'lumpenproletariat' capable of challenging the former's control over resources.[11] Interestingly, Lesthaeghe exempts England – which he sees as characterised by greater social integration – from the scope of this explanation, and here a 'culturally determined moral economy' (Smith, 1981a) has been invoked to explain popular reluctance to marry before a certain standard of living had been assured. Even if this is so – and pressure from social superiors may have played an important role here too – it remains the case that the scope of decision making was essentially short-term and particularistic. There is little evidence of a concern for the broader issue of demographic homeostasis

NOTES

1. These results were obtained using the Princeton Regional Model North family of female life tables and stable populations (Coale and Demeny, 1983). The TFRs given are approximate as the stable populations are tabulated according to growth rate rather than fertility level (the actual TFR

values in the four cases are 5.16, 7.82, 5.29 and 8.00). The burden of childhood dependency is not offset by the slightly lower proportions of the elderly found at higher TFRs: the full dependency ratios (the ratio of individual aged 0–14 years, plus those over 60, to those in the intervening age-groups) are 0.720, 0.949, 0.804, and 1.065 in the four cases cited.

2. The case of Colyton in Devon, studied by Wrigley, may be an exception to this rule, but, if so, it appears to be an isolated one (Wrigley, 1966b, 1978; Wilson, 1984).

3. Prominent proponents of the innovation perspective include, in particular, John Cleland (Cleland and Wilson, 1987) and John Knodel (1977). The summary set out in the following paragraphs is based primarily on the arguments of Knodel and Van de Walle (1979).

4. It is also necessary to 'trim' the right-hand tail of the birth interval distribution to eliminate spurious long intervals arising from an intervening birth's having escaped registration (see Wilson, 1982).

5. Deliberate attempts to delay births may have a number of effects on these measurements. If the protogenesic interval is deliberately prolonged, this will result in an underestimate of 'true' fecundability since the latter is defined as the probability of conception for couples making no attempt to prevent it. Estimates of NSP will be unaffected if the protogenesic and first intergenesic intervals are extended by equal amounts, but will be inflated if the former are extended disproportionately. (For evidence that the latter may have occurred in the initial stage of at least one instance of fertility decline, see Garrett (1990). It is, however, also possible to estimate NSP by measuring the impact of an early infant death on the length of the subsequent birth interval. Although the assumptions here may be somewhat less secure than those of the interval comparison method the results are, in general, reassuringly similar (Wilson, 1986).

6. These calculations are based on the Princeton Regional Model Life Tables, North model.

7. The marriage chances of the younger generation could also, of course, be much reduced where their parents' property passed to younger step-parents in what has been termed 'diagonal inheritance' (Flandrin, 1979).

8. The analysis put forward here is that of Wrigley (1985) and is one of a number which have been essayed since the middle of last century. Factors invoked in the latter include the Napoleonic reforms of inheritance law, and the social and cultural changes associated with the Revolution, but none of these appears sufficient, on its own, to explain the phenomenon; for a recent review see Chesnais (1992, ch. 11). Dûpaquier (1988), provides a general discussion of population regulation in France before the nineteenth century, stressing the role of marriage and the niche model.

9. The social and cultural determination of birth spacing has been little studied among European population, but the process has received considerable attention in the African case: see Page and Lesthaeghe (1981).

10. It has been suggested that these constraints may partially have broken down in the eighteenth century due to the process sometimes termed 'proto-industrialisation'; for contrasting views see, Levine (1987), Houston and Snell (1984) and Schofield (1989).

11. A variant of this argument is developed by Dûpaquier (1972) who suggests that the 'niche' system of marriage regulation reflected land-owners' desire to avoid the proliferation of small tenements with the associated difficulties of management, rent-collection, etc. By contrast economic historians of the 'proto-industrial' school have argued that in parts of central Europe the autonomous peasant communities which arose from the ashes of feudalism did regulate marriage in order to limit population pressure on common resources; see especially Kriedte *et al.* (1981).

REFERENCES

Benigno, F. (1989), 'The southern Italian family in the early modern period: a discussion of co-residence patterns', *Continuity and Change*, vol. 4, pp. 165–94.

Bongaarts, J. (1978), 'A framework for analyzing the proximate determinants of fertility', *Population and Development Review*, vol. 4, pp. 105–32.

Brändström, A. (1988), 'The impact of female labour conditions on infant mortality: a case study of Nedertorneå and Jokkmokk, 1800–96', *Social History of Medicine*, vol. 1, pp. 329–58.

Carlsson, G. (1966), 'The decline of fertility: innovation or adjustment process?', *Population Studies*, vol. 20, pp. 149–74.

Chesnais, J. C. (1992), *The Demographic Transition: Stages, Patterns and Economic Implications* (Oxford: Oxford University Press).

Cleland, J. and Wilson, C. (1987), 'Demand theories of fertility and the fertility transition: an iconoclastic view', *Population Studies*, vol. 41, pp. 5–30.

Coale, A. J. (1970), 'The decline of fertility in Europe from the French Revolution to World War II', in S. J. Behrman, L. Corsa and R. Freedma (eds), *Fertility and Family Planning: A World View* (Ann Arbor: University of Michigan Press).

Coale, A. J. and Demeny, P. (1983), *Regional Model Life Tables and Stable Populations* (London: Academic Press) 2nd edition.

Coale, A. J. and Treadway, R. (1986), 'A summary of the changing distribution of overall fertility, marital fertility, and the proportion married in the provinces of Europe', in A. J. Coale and S. C. Watkins (eds), *The Decline of Fertility in Europe* (Princeton: Princeton University Press).

Coale, A. J. and Trussel, T. J. (1979), 'A technical note: finding the two parameters that specify a model schedule of marital fertility', *Population Index*, vol. 44, pp. 203–13.

Coale, A. J. and Watkins, S. C. (eds) (1986), *The Decline of Fertility in Europe* (Princeton, NJ: Princeton University Press).

Dûpaquier, J. (1972), 'De l'animal à l'homme: le mécanisme autorégulateur des populations traditionalles', *Revue de l'Institut de Sociologie*, vol. 45, pp. 177–211.

Dupâquier, J. (1988), 'L'autorégulation de la population Française (XVIᵉ–XVIIIᵉ siècle)', in J. Dûpaquier, G. Cabourdin, B. LePetit *et al.* (eds), *Histoire de la Population Française: vol. 2, De La Renaissance à 1789*, pp. 413–36.

Flandrin, J. (1979), *Families in Former Times* (Cambridge: Cambridge University Press).

Flinn, M. W. (1981), *The European Demographic System, 1500–1820* (Brighton: Harvester).

Garrett, E. M. (1990), 'The trials of labour: motherhood versus employment in a nineteenth-century textile centre', *Continuity and Change*, vol. 5, pp. 121–54.

Goldman, N., Westoff, C. F. and Paul, L. E. (1987), 'Variations in natural fertility: the effect of lactation and other determinants', *Population Studies*, vol. 41, pp. 127–46.

Goldstone, J. (1986), 'The demographic revolution in England: a re-examination', *Population Studies*, vol. 40, pp. 5–33.

Goody, J. (1983), *The Development of the Family and Marriage in Europe* (Cambridge: Cambridge University Press).

Goubert, P. (1977), 'Family and province, a contribution to the knowledge of family structure in early-modern France', *Journal of Family History*, vol. 2, pp. 179.

Habicht, J.-P., Davanzo, J., Butz, W. P. and Meyers, L. (1985), 'The contraceptive role of breastfeeding', *Population Studies*, vol. 9, pp. 213–32.

Hajnal, J. (1965), 'European marriage patterns in perspective', in D. V. Glass and D. E. C. Eversley (eds), *Population in History: Essays in Historical Demography* (London: Edward Arnold).

Hajnal, J. (1983), 'Two kinds of pre-industrial household formation system', in R. Wall (ed.), *Family Forms in Historic Europe* (Cambridge: Cambridge University Press) pp. 65–104.

Henry, L. (1961), 'Some data on natural fertility', *Eugenics Quarterly*, vol. 8, pp. 81–91.

Houston, R. A. and Snell, K. (1984), 'Proto-industrialization? Cottage industry, social change and industrial revolution', *Historical Journal*, vol. 27, pp. 473–92.

Knodel, J. (1968), 'Infant mortality and fertility in three Bavarian villages: an analysis of family histories from the 19th century', *Population Studies*, vol. 22, pp. 297–318.

Knodel, J. (1977), 'Age patterns of fertility and the fertility transition: evidence from Europe and Asia', *Population Studies*, vol. 31, pp. 219–49.

Knodel, J. (1988), *Demographic Behavior in the Past* (Cambridge: Cambridge University Press).

Knodel, J. and Van de Walle, E. (1979), 'Lessons from the past. Policy implications of historical fertility studies', *Population and Development Review*, vol. 5, pp. 217–45.

Kriedtde, P., Medick, H. and Schlumbohm, J. (1981), *Industrialisation Before Industrialisation* (Cambridge: Cambridge University Press).

Kussmaul, A. (1981), *Servants in Husbandry in Early-Modern England* (Cambridge: Cambridge University Press).

Landers, J. (1990), 'Fertility decline and birth spacing among London Quakers', in J. Landers and V. R. Reynolds (eds), *Fertility and Resources* (Cambridge: Cambridge University Press) pp. 92–117.

Laslett, P. (1977), 'Characteristics of the Western family considered over time', in *Family Life and Illicit Love in Earlier Generations* (Cambridge: Cambridge University Press), pp. 12–49.

Laslett, P. and Wall, P. (eds) (1972), *Household and Family in Past Time* (Cambridge: Cambridge University Press).

Leridon, H. and Menken, J. (1979), *Natural Fertility* (Liège: Ordina).

Lesthaeghe, R. (1971), 'Nuptiality and population growth', *Population Studies*, vol. 25, pp. 415–32.

Lesthaeghe, R. (1980), 'On the social control of reproduction', *Population and Development Review*, vol. 6, pp. 527–48.

Levine, D. (1987), *Reproducing Families: The Political Economy of English Population History* (Cambridge: Cambridge University Press).

Lithell, U.-B. (1981), 'Breast feeding, infant mortality and fertility', *Journal of Family History*, vol. 6, pp. 182–94.

Livi-Bacci, M. (1986). 'Social-group forerunners of fertility control in Europe', in A. J. Coale and S. C. Watkins (eds), *The Decline of Fertility in Europe* (Princeton: Princeton University Press).

MacFarlane, A. (1978), 'Modes of reproduction', in G. Hawthorn (eds), *Population and Development*.

Mauss, M. (1970), *The Gift: Forms and Functions of Exchange in Archaic Societies* (London: Cohen and West).

Page, H. J. and Lesthaeghe, R. (1981), *Child-Spacing in Tropical Africa: Traditions and Change* (London: Academic Press).

Santow, S. (1987), 'Reassessing the contraceptive effect of breastfeeding', *Population Studies*, vol. 41, pp. 147–60.

Schofield, R. S. (1976), 'The relationship between demographic structure and environment in pre-industrial Europe', in W. Conze (ed.), *Sozialgeschichte der Familie in der Neuzeit Europas* (Stuttgart) pp. 147–60.

Schofield, R. S. (1985), 'English marriage patterns revisited', *Journal of Family History*, vol. 10, pp. 2–20.

Schofield, R. S. (1989), 'Family structure, demographic behaviour and economic growth', in J. Walter and R. S. Schofield (eds), *Famine, Disease and the Social Order in Early Modern Society* (Cambridge: Cambridge University Press).

Seccombe, W. (1992), *A Millenium of Family Change: Feudalism to Capitalism in North-western Europe* (London: Verso).

Smith, R. M. (1981a), 'Fertility, economy and household formation in England over three centuries', *Population and Development Review*, vol. 7, pp. 595–622.

Smith, R. M. (1981), 'The people of Tuscany and their families in the fifteenth century: medieval or mediterranean?', *Journal of Family History*, vol. 6, pp. 125.

Smith, R. M. (1986), 'Transfer incomes, risk and security: the roles of the family and the collectivity in recent theories of fertility change', in D. Coleman and R. S. Schofield (eds), *The State of Population Theory* (Oxford: Blackwell).

Smith, R. M. (1990), 'Monogamy, landed property and demographic regimes in pre-industrial Europe: regional contrasts and temporal stabilities', in J. Landers and V. R. Reynolds (eds), *Fertility and Resources* (Cambridge: Cambridge University Press) pp. 164–88.

Vann, R. T. and Eversley, D. (1992), *Friends in Life and Death: The British and Irish Quakers in the Demographic Transition* (Cambridge: Cambridge University Press).

Vasary, I. (1989), 'The sin of Transdanubia': the one-child system in rural Hungary', *Continuity and Change*, vol. 4, pp. 429–68.

Weir, D. R. (1984), 'Rather never than late: celibacy and age at marriage in English cohort fertility, 1541–1871', *Journal of Family History*, vol. 9, pp. 340–54.

Wilson, A. F. (1989), 'Illegitimacy and its implications in mid-eighteenth century London: the evidence of the Foundling Hospital', *Continuity and Change*, vol. 4, pp. 103–64.

Wilson, C. (1982), 'Marital fertility in pre-industrial England 1550–1849', unpublished PhD thesis, University of Cambridge.

Wilson, C. (1984), 'Natural Fertility in Pre-Industrial England, 1600–1799', *Population Studies*, vol. 38, pp. 225–41.

Wilson, C. (1986), 'The proximate determinants of marital fertility in England 1600–1799', in L. Bonfield, R. Smith and K. Wrightson (eds), *The World We Have Gained* (Oxford: Blackwell).

Wood, J. W. and Weinstein, M. (1988), 'A model of age-specific fecundability', *Population Studies*, vol. 42, pp. 85–114.

Wrigley, E. A. (1966a), 'Family limitation in pre-industrial England', *Economic History Review*, vol. 19, pp. 82–109.

Wrigley, E. A. (1966b), 'Family reconstitution', in E. A. Wrigley (eds), *Introduction to English Historical Demography* (London: Weidenfeld and Nicolson) pp. 96–159.

Wrigley, E. A. (1978), 'Marital fertility in seventeenth century Colyton: a note', *Economic History Review (2nd ser.)*, vol. 31, pp. 429–36.

Wrigley, E. A. (1981), 'The prospects for population history', *Journal of Interdisciplinary History*, vol. 12, pp. 207–26.

Wrigley, E. A. (1985), 'The fall of marital fertility in nineteenth-century France: exemplar or exception?', *European Journal of Population*, vol. 1, pp. 31–60, 141–77.

Wrigley, E. A. (1987), 'No death without birth: the implications of English mortality in the early modern period', in R. Porter and A. Wear (eds), *Problems and Methods in the History of Medicine* (London: Croom Helm) pp. 133–50.

Wrigley, E. A. and Schofield, R. S. (1981), *The Population History of England 1541–1871: A Reconstruction* (London: Edward Arnold).

Wrigley, E. A. and Schofield, R. S. (1983), 'English population history from family reconstitution: summary results', *Population Studies*, vol. 37, pp. 157–84.

10 Obstacles to Fertility Decline in Developing Countries

John Cleland

INTRODUCTION

Between 1950 and 1970, the annual percentage growth of the world's population rose from about 1.8 to just under 2.1 per cent, largely in response to improving mortality conditions in developing countries. During the 1970s, this accelerating trend was reversed and, by the end of that decade, the annual growth rate had dropped to 1.7 per cent, just below the rate in 1950. The reason for this change, of course, has little to do with mortality; life expectancies continued to rise, albeit at a slower pace than in previous decades. The slowing down in the rate of growth was caused primarily by appreciable reductions in fertility, particularly in some of the huge populations of Asia.

While it was clear that global population growth would never again reach the peak of the late 1960s, the last decade has seen no further deceleration; the growth rate has remained steady at about 1.7 per cent per annum. This stagnation has caused concern about the apparent failure of birth control programmes among individuals and agencies who see rapid population growth as a threat to social and economic development or to a sustainable environment. More careful demographic analysis, however, shows that much of this concern is misplaced. The stabilisation of rates of population growth reflects, in part, technical factors, from which there was no escape. Horiuchi (1992) and Horiuchi and Kandiah (1993) identify three main factors that have acted to sustain constant rates of growth in the 1980s. The first of these concerns the effects of age structure. During the 1980s, the proportion of total population in the reproductive age span rose, as a consequence of the high fertility that prevailed 20–30 years earlier. The crude birth rate, and hence the population growth rate, is sensitive not only to rates of childbearing but also to the size of the denominator to which these rates apply and thus the large cohorts in the age span 20–40 years buttressed natality.

The second factor relates to events in China and, to a lesser extent, India. Together these two countries comprise over one-third of the world's population and their contribution to global trends is correspondingly large. In the 1970s, China experienced a massive fertility decline from about 6.0 births per woman to under 2.5 births. This shift in reproductive behaviour constitutes by far the single most important fertility change of the last 40 years. Since 1980, however, there has been little further decline as rural couples rejected government attempts to impose its one-child policy. In India, the story is more complex. Fertility decline started earlier than in China but proceeded at a more gentle pace. As in China, efforts to promote family planning encountered strong resistance because of the excesses associated with the emergency period of Prime Minister Gandhi's regime. When she fell from power in 1977, the family planning programme also lost much of its credibility and, partly as a consequence, the fertility decline stalled until the mid-1980s. Thus in both countries, steep fertility decline in the 1970s gave way to very modest declines in the 1980s. In the case of China, this shift was inevitable, because fertility was already approaching replacement level by 1980. In India, on the other hand, total fertility was still high (about 4.8 births per woman) in 1980 and the lack of further decline for the next 5 years was more the result of political miscalculation than an unavoidable consequence of past success.

The third factor identified by Horiuchi and Kandiah concerns the temporal phasing of the onset of fertility decline. Between 1965 and 1975, a total of 39 countries showed the first unmistakable signs of fertility decline. This number is not only large but it also includes some of the most populous states in the world. China and India have already been singled out for comment but Brazil, Turkey, Thailand, Egypt, Mexico and Indonesia also belong to this group. By contrast, the number of countries initiating fertility transition between 1975 and 1985 fell to 18. This group includes one very populous country (Bangladesh), but the other very large populations (Nigeria, Ethiopia, Iran and Pakistan), which had maintained constant high fertility up until 1975, still showed little convincing sign of decline throughout the 1980s. Future global fertility trends and thus population increase in the next century now depend to an appreciable extent on what happens in countries where fertility is yet to decline. The main objective of this chapter is to identify the remaining areas of high fertility and to examine the possible obstacles to future fertility decline, drawing upon the mass of empirical evidence that has accumulated over the last 20 years. The chapter starts with a descriptive account of fertility trends in major developing regions. Within this broad perspective, selected obstacles to decline are then analysed.

FERTILITY TRENDS IN DEVELOPING COUNTRIES, 1960–1990

Figure 10.1 summarises trends in fertility over the period 1960–1990 for major developing regions. The chosen indicator of fertility is the total fertility rate, a conversion of period age-specific rates into implied lifetime numbers of births per woman. The data source is the United Nations Population Division, specifically its 1992 Revision of World Population Prospects. Many of the fertility estimates published by the United Nations are based on defective data and, in other cases, amount to little more than informed guesswork. However, there exists no superior international compilation of relevant information and the broad picture is undoubtedly valid.

The early 1960s is an appropriate starting point for a review of fertility trends in developing countries. Prior to 1960, falls in fertility were very uncommon. Indeed, there is evidence, particularly for some Latin America and African countries that fertility increased prior to that date (e.g. Dyson and Murphy, 1985; Feeney,1988). In some instances, falling marriage ages were responsible; in others, attenuation of traditional fertility constraints, such as prolonged breastfeeding and post-natal sexual abstinence, provide the most plausible explanation.

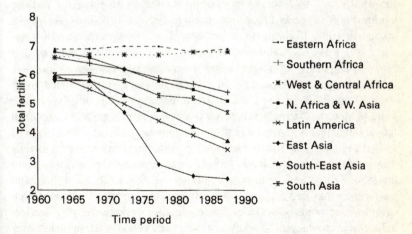

Figure 10.1   Trends in total fertility: major developing regions, 1960–1990

In 1960, total fertility in all eight regions considered here were contained within a rather narrow span of 5.8–7.0 births per woman. Fertility levels were highest in East Africa and the Arab states of North Africa and Western Asia, and lowest in East and South-east Asia, primarily because of late marriage ages. Fertility declined first in Latin America. Leaving aside Argentina and Uruguay, which rightly belong to the earlier European fertility transition, Guzman (1993) dates the onset of decline to be in the 1960s for all countries of continental Central and South America, except Bolivia and Mexico, where it occurred in the early 1970s. Despite this remarkable synchronicity, the pace of decline varied considerably and, by the quinquennium 1985–1990, total fertility ranged from over 5.5 births in three Central American countries (Guatemala, Honduras and Nicaragua) to less than 3.0 in Argentina, Colombia, Chile and Uruguay. No state in Latin America has yet approached replacement level fertility. Total fertility in Argentina, for instance, has fluctuated around 3.0 births for the last 30 years. However, it is worth noting that Spain and Italy, the origin of much of Latin America's population, are both amongst the lowest-fertility countries in the world. It is difficult, therefore, to argue that any cultural features of Latin American society will continue to sustain moderate fertility level indefinitely into the future.

The immense diversity of Asia precludes any simple generalisation about fertility transition in that region. However, analysis in terms of three sub-regions, East, Southeast and South, mitigates the problem. East Asian trends (excluding Japan) are dominated by China and Figure 10.1 clearly shows the steep decline of the 1970s, followed by the relative stability of the 1980s. A 1992 survey conducted by the State Family Planning Commission suggests that a further sharp decline in fertility may have started in 1989. Contrary to the expectations of most experts on China, there was a further tightening of population policy at this time with a renewed emphasis in rural areas on a 4-year gap between first and second births, followed by sterilisation. In Sechuan province, with a population of over 100 millions, a one-child policy is being strongly enforced in the more prosperous, densely settled rural areas. It is now possible that total fertility in China is about 2.0 births or even lower.

Fertility in South Korea has fallen even further than in China and is now below replacement level, giving rise to concerns about shrinkage of the labour force and rapid population ageing. Since the late 1960s, the government has had a strong population control policy. It developed an extensive network of services and made considerable use of financial inducements to couples to adopt contraception. By contrast, the regime in North Korea, a more prosperous and heavily industrialised state at the time of partition, has been hostile or indifferent to family planning. As shown in Figure 10.1, the onset of decline in North Korea occurred about a decade later than in the South, but over the last 20 years, the speed of decline has been slightly greater in the North, leading to a convergence at low levels. Government policies, it appears, have in this instance influenced the timing of transition but not its medium-term outcome.

In South-east Asia, the onset of fertility of decline coincides with that in East Asia but the pace of change has been more modest and total fertility was around 3.7 births in the period 1985–1990. This regional average masks considerable inter-country variability. Not surprisingly perhaps, period fertility is below replacement level in Singapore and is fast approaching this level in Thailand. The Indonesian regime has shared with the Thai government a strong commitment to reducing population growth and now records a fertility that is not much above 3.0 births.

There follows a group of countries – the Philippines, Vietnam, Malaysia, Myanmar and Cambodia – where the current level of childbearing lies in the range of 4.0 to 4.5 births. This group encompasses a huge diversity in standards of living and variations in population policies. Fertility declines began early in the Philippines and Malaysia,

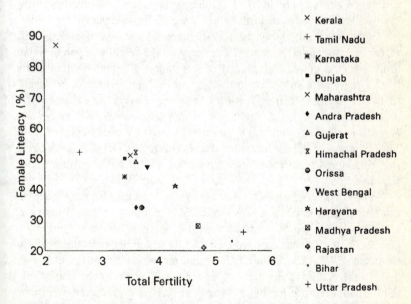

Figure 10.2   Scatterplot of Indian states, by level of female literacy and total fertility

both rather advanced socially and economically in the 1960s compared to other countries in the region; but levels of childbearing have almost plateaued over the last decade or so. In the Philippines, the strong opposition of the Roman Catholic church to 'artificial' means of birth control has prevented successive governments from creating comprehensive family planning services while, in Malaysia, policies of population containment were reversed in the mid-1980s towards a much more expansionist vision of population growth. Fertility among the Malays actually rose in the 1980s though that of the Chinese and Indian communities continued to decline. In Vietnam, the government has an unambivalent policy to promote family planning, while in Cambodia and Myanmar there is evidence of fertility decline against a background of official hostility or indifference.

Demographic analysis of South-East Asia thus demonstrates vividly that simple generalisations about the socioeconomic determinants of fertility are unwarranted. For instance, high material and educational standards in Malaysia and the Philippines have not been translated into small family sizes. In 1960, adult literacy in the Philippines was 72 per cent in contrast to 39 per cent in Indonesia, and income per head estimated to be US$230 compared to $121 in Indonesia. There was also a large difference in life expectancy: 51 compared to 41 years. Yet fertility in the late 1980s was nearly one birth higher in the Philippines than in Indonesia.

South Asia, comprising the Indian sub-continent and extending west as far as Iran, contains about 20 per cent of the world's population and represents the greatest numerical concentration of poverty. Many parts of this region are still characterised by stable high fertility or by small, tentative declines. In Iran, for instance, there is as yet no evidence of a drop in fertility (though, admittedly, evidence is sparse). In Pakistan and Nepal, recent surveys show modest levels of contraceptive use. Interpretation of the demographic data is controversial, but it is probable that total fertility in Pakistan is about 6.5 and in Nepal a little under 6.0 births.

No discussion of India's fertility can ignore variations between states. In the four largest northern states – Madhya Pradesh, Rajastan, Bihar and Uttar Pradesh – which together comprise nearly 40 per cent of India's population, fertility has declined only slightly with births per woman still in the range of 4.7–15.5. At the other extreme are the southern states of Kerala and Tamil Nadu, where fertility is almost at replacement level. This north–south divide in fertility has been attributed to a gradient in the status of women (Dyson and Moore,1983). Certainly, there is a strong relationship between female literacy and fertility at the state level (Figure 10.2).

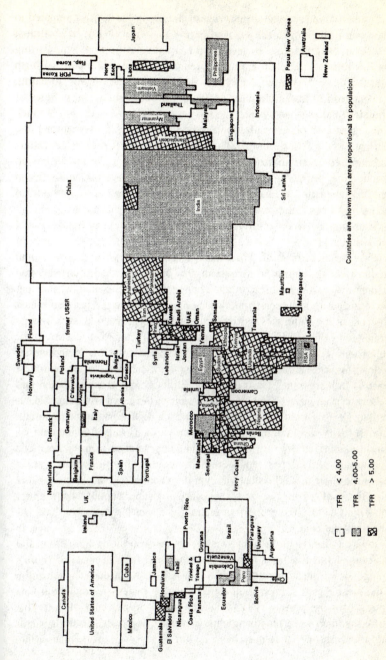

Figure 10.3 Total fertility rate (TFR) by country, 1990

Countries are shown with area proportional to population

TFR < 4.00

TFR 4.00-5.00

TFR > 5.00

The most unexpected demographic development in South Asia has taken place in Bangladesh. This country possesses none of the features thought to be conducive to fertility transition. It is predominantly rural, has low levels of adult literacy and school enrolment and still has high child mortality. Nevertheless, fertility declined in the 1980s by at least 30 per cent from traditional levels of about 7.0 births per woman. The UN estimates for 1985–1990 is 5.1; the most recent survey, conducted in 1991, indicates that 40 per cent of couples are practising contraception and that fertility may be low as 4.5. This steep decline represents a serious challenge to most theories of transition. Indeed, a poverty-induced reproductive change appears more plausible than a development-induced one. Yet even this thesis can muster little empirical support. Fertility decline has been rather even across economic strata and there is thus no obvious link between reproductive behaviour and extreme poverty of landlessness.

UN estimates for East, West and Central Africa show constant high fertility over the entire 30 year span. For West and Central Africa, this picture is almost certainly correct. Though there is evidence of incipient declines among younger women in Senegal, south-west and south-east Nigeria, other countries with recent relevant evidence still record unchanged levels. The latter include Ghana, Togo, Mali, Liberia and Cameroon. The UN portrayal of East Africa, however, is somewhat misleading; the impression of constant high fertility is the result of upwards adjustments of estimates for Ethiopia and Uganda that offset declines in Kenya and Zimbabwe. The change in Kenya is remarkable. In the late 1970s, surveys in Kenya depicted a highly pronatalist society. Total fertility was about 8.0 births per women, only 16 per cent of currently married women reported that they wanted to have no more children and only 7 per cent were using contraception. Only ten years later, little short of a reproductive revolution had taken place. Fertility had fallen to about 6.5, 27 per cent were practising contraception and, perhaps most significantly, the proportion claiming to want no more children had risen to 49 per cent.

However, Kenya and Zimbabwe are not, as so often is claimed, in the forefront of fertility transition in sub-Saharan Africa. That label rightly belongs to the black population of South Africa. According to the results of the most recent survey, total fertility among the black population was about 4.6 in the period 1987–1989 and about 50 per cent of currently married women were practising contraception. Moreover, the decline is a long-standing one, that may have begun as early as the 1960s. Other countries in Southern Africa – Botswana, Swaziland, and Namibia – have also experienced decline, though not on the scale of South Africa.

Until recently, many population experts were profoundly pessimistic about the prospects of fertility decline in sub-Saharan Africa and maintained that uniquely pronatalist features of culture and social organisation in the region might buttress high fertility regimes until a relatively late stage of socioeconomic development. Events of the 1980s have demonstrated that reproductive behaviour is not as immutable as previously thought. Indeed it appears likely that much more widespread decline will take place in the near future in East and Southern Africa. The prospects for change in Central and West Africa are less certain.

The final developing region to be considered is North Africa and Western Asia, comprising most of the Arab states, plus Israel and Turkey. The range of living standards is very wide. At one extreme are the United Arab Emirates, Kuwait and Saudi Arabia – classified as high income countries. At the other end are Sudan and Yemen with annual incomes per head of less than US$500. In the region as a whole, fertility has fallen by 25 per cent over the last 30 years, from 6.8 to 5.1 births. The onset and depth of decline, however, has little obvious connection with wealth or degree of urbanisation. Recent results from the Gulf Child Health Survey programme confirm that total fertility remains high in Saudi Arabia (6.5), among the indigenous population of Kuwait (6.5) and in the United Arab Emirates (5.9) (Farid, 1993). Conversely, fertility decline started earlier and has advanced further in countries with modest standards of living such as Egypt, Tunisia and Morocco, where total fertility lies within the range of 4.0–5.0. In the Arab world, the imprint of divergent population policies is clearly evident. Egypt, Tunisia and Morocco are among the few Arab countries where support for family planning has been unequivocal. Many other governments have welcomed the prospect of expanding populations – in some cases, because it implies a lessening dependence on imported labour – and have been hostile to the promotion of family planning. This factor goes some way to explaining the persistence of high fertility in affluent, highly urbanised and increasingly educated countries.

Figure 10.3 summarises the geographical distribution of three broad fertility bands: high (5.0 or more birth per woman), medium (4.0–4.9 births) and low (<4.0 births per woman). The map reinforces the point that the persistence of high fertility is largely confined to sub-Saharan Africa, South Asia and some of the Arab states of North Africa and Western Asia. Fertility at this level has almost disappeared elsewhere in Asia and in Latin America.

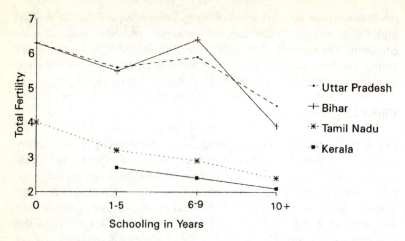

Figure 10.4   Rural total fertility rates by educational level of women, selected
                 states of India, 1984
Source: Office of the Registrar General (1990)
Note: Kerala estimate for 0 years not shown, because too few cases

This descriptive review of fertility trends in the last 30 years has also
served to emphasise that simple mono-casual explanations of fertility
transition crumble in the face of even cursory examination of the evidence.
There are, for instance, examples of fertility at very low levels of
economic and social development and lack of decline in settings of
relatively high development. In some countries there is strong
circumstantial evidence that government policies and programmes to
promote birth control have played an important role, but others where
fertility has declined in a context of government hostility or ambivalence.

This empirical complexity is paralleled by a total lack of agreement
among population scientists on a general theory of fertility. In the section that
follows on obstacles to fertility decline, it is therefore inappropriate to seek to
identify single dominant factors that apply across time and space. A more
modest and realistic aim is to assess factors that may impede or facilitate
decline, but are by themselves neither necessary nor sufficient determinants.

OBSTACLES TO FERTILITY DECLINE

No attempt is made in the following pages to undertake a comprehensive
assessment of factors that impede the onset or speed of fertility decline in

developing countries. Rather three factors have been identified for review: high child mortality, low status of women, and low level of adult education. The reason for this selection is that all three figure prominently in the current international debate on population. Analysis of their relationships to fertility is thus of great practical significance.

High Child Mortality

One of the central ideas in demographic transition theory is that fertility decline is an adaptive response to improved survival chances. Under conditions of very high mortality with expectations of life of 20–30 years, five or so births per woman were necessary to ensure continuation of the species. Once mortality falls, this reproductive imperative is undermined and, sooner or later, the cultural props that supported it lose their force and behaviour itself is modified. Parents no longer have to replace dead children with new births and, perhaps more importantly, no longer have to bear many children as an insurance against future possible losses.

This direct stimulus–response relationship between mortality and fertility lost much of its appeal when details of the European transition were established through the Princeton European Fertility Project (Coale and Watkins,1986). Contrary to expectations, they found that fertility decline did not necessarily follow mortality decline. In some regions of Europe, there was a parallel transition; in others, large improvements in child survival followed the decline in fertility. Whatever triggered fertility transition in Europe, it appears that societal or parental perceptions about survival of children could not have been a uniform, underlying factor.

The situation with regard to contemporary developing societies is very different. Large improvements in mortality were almost universal, particularly in the 20 years following the Second World War. Without exception, then, substantial mortality decline preceded fertility decline in the demographic transitions of Asia, Latin America and elsewhere. Thus the thesis that reproductive behaviour may respond in a rather direct way to changing morality is at least superficially plausible in the case of developing countries and should not be rejected, just because it clearly played a less important role in the European transition.

In the context of this chapter, the relevant question is as follows: To what extent might high mortality contribute to the persistence of high fertility in sub-Saharan Africa, South Asia and elsewhere? The answer is of considerable practical importance because it is likely to influence allocation of resources by large aid organisations. To the extent that high mortality represents an obstacle to fertility decline, it may be more effective to press ahead with child survival programmes, leaving aside for the time being major investments in family planning.

At the outset, it should be acknowledged that there is a crucial gap in the evidence. As already mentioned, the most obvious direct pathway of influence concerns parental perceptions of child survival chances. Unfortunately, there has been no serious study of this topic. We know very little about the extent to which declines in child mortality impinge upon the consciousness and decision-making of reproductive actors. The relevant evidence is sparse and oblique but it does suggest that perceived changes in mortality have not been a major influence on fertility attitudes and behaviour. For instance, fears of losing children do not figure greatly in self-reported reasons for wanting large families or for non-use of birth control. Nor are reductions in mortality commonly offered as a reason for wanting a family of modest size.

The largest body of evidence on the mortality–fertility relationship consists of comparative analyses of national demographic trends using aggregate data on literacy, income and so on. There is, not surprisingly, a statistical association between levels and trends in mortality and fertility. Most analyses of demographic indicators in developing countries have found child mortality and life expectancy to be strongly predictive of fertility levels and trends, even after controls for obvious confounding factors such as income per head and literacy (e.g. Mauldin and Berelson,1978; Cutright,1983). Of the major regions considered in this chapter, sub-Saharan Africa (except the southern part of the continent) and South Asia record the highest levels of infant mortality and the lowest life expectancies. Thus infant mortality is estimated by the UN to be about 100 deaths per 1000 births for South Asia in the period 1985–1990, compared to 31 for East Asia, 63 for South-East Asia and 53 for Latin America. Infant mortality is higher still in East, West and Central Africa, ranging from 108 to 115 deaths per 1000 births. However, these statistical associations do not constitute strong evidence of a causal link because of the impossibility of taking into account political, cultural and other antecedent factors that might determine both mortality and fertility.

An alternative form of enquiry is to assess mortality conditions at the onset of fertility transition for those countries that have entered transition. Table 10.1 shows the results derived from recent work by Casterline (1993) and Guzman (1993). It is immediately apparent that changes in reproductive behaviour have started under very variable mortality levels. Within Asia, the range is from 81 to 145 in terms of infant mortality and 60–45 in terms of life expectancy. The corresponding figures for Latin America are 62–151 and from 67 to 46. Indeed in this region, infant

Table 10.1 Life expectancy at birth and infant mortality at onset of fertility decline

	Year of onset of fertility decline	Life expectancy	Infant mortality
Asia			
China	1970	59.6	81
Taiwan	1955	58.6	NA*
Sri Lanka	1955	56.6	91
Thailand	1965	56.1	95
Philippines	1965	54.5	76
Korean Republic	1960	52.6	100
Malaysia	1960	52.1	82
India	1970	48.0	145
Indonesia	1970	46.0	124
Bangladesh	1975	44.9	140
Latin America			
Costa Rica	1961	67.2	83
Paraguay	1963	64.4	62
Panama	1962	61.7	64
Mexico	1972	62.6	72
Venezuela	1960	59.5	81
Colombia	1962	57.9	92
Chile	1962	57.9	110
Ecuador	1965	55.7	113
Brazil	1960	54.7	116
Dominican Republic	1962	53.6	118
El Salvador	1962	52.3	123
Peru	1965	50.3	131
Honduras	1966	50.0	131
Nicaragua	1962	48.5	131
Bolivia	1972	46.7	151
Guatemala	1960	45.6	125

*NA, not available.
Source: Adapted from Casterline (1993) and Guzman (1993).

mortality was well over 100 deaths per 1000 births at the onset of fertility decline for 10 of the 16 countries examined by Guzman.

The contents of Table 10.1 carry the important message that any link between mortality and fertility transition must be tenuous, or indirect, or heavily conditioned by other fertility determinants. There is clearly no threshold below which mortality must decline before fertility responds. A second important point is that levels of morality in Africa or in pre-transitional societies elsewhere (e.g. Pakistan and Nepal) are not incompatible with falling fertility, judged by the experiences of other regions.

This rather negative conclusion immediately should be balanced by a recognition that mortality decline should be regarded as a chronologically remote and possible indirect, but nevertheless fundamental cause of fertility decline. The combination of high fertility and high child survival is best viewed as a deviation from an historic norm that can last no more than a few generations. The adverse effects of rapid rate of population growth that results from this combination sooner or later evoke a response among governments or citizens, or both. For example, government-sponsored family planning programmes should be viewed as an indirect consequence of mortality decline.

One other potential link deserves consideration: a synergy between use of health and family planning services. The existence of effective and high quality maternal and child health services may greatly facilitate the development and acceptability of family planning services. The link may stem in part from simple considerations of access to modern contraceptives and counselling. Ante-natal visits offer opportunities for counselling. Post-natal checks and child immunisation services provide more direct occasions for contraceptive adoption. Perhaps as important is the potential for health service workers to dispel fears about modern contraception. Worries about side-effects and adverse health consequences are the most common reasons proffered by women for non-use and discontinued use of modern contraception. When motivation to control family size is itself ambivalent, such considerations may act as serious barriers to fertility regulation. Trusted health workers are uniquely well-placed to address and overcome these fears. Similarly, successful experience with allopathic procedures and drugs in the context of health may be conducive to adoption of modern contraceptives.

The relationship between access and utilisation of health and family planning services has received surprisingly little research attention. The few strands of evidence, however, are positive. In rural Mexico, contraceptive uptake was nearly six times higher in communities where most women received ante-natal care from state health services than in communities where traditional birth attendants provided such care (Potter, *et al.*, 1987). And in rural Morocco, receipt of ante-natal care and child immunisation were also strongly predictive of contraceptive use, net of education and other obvious confounders (Norton, 1993).

The practical implications of these highly suggestive, but far from conclusive, findings are perhaps diminished by the fact that primary health care systems in many developing countries deteriorated in the 1980s as a result of economic recession and structural readjustment policies. There is also a growing tendency for contraceptive services to gain independence from health care systems. Many community-based contraceptive distribution schemes, for instance, make little effort to provide even rudimentary health advice or services.

The most important practical conclusion to be drawn from this brief review of the mortality–fertility relationship is a negative one. There is little scientific justification for the view that high mortality acts as an important barrier to fertility transition in countries where the level of reproduction remains high. Even if exceptional efforts were made to achieve a rapid reduction in child mortality by, say, 20 per cent in Northern India or West Africa, for example, it is uncertain whether this improvement would be perceived by parents. This conclusion, of course does not imply child survival improvements should be lower priority than at present; rather, they should be justified in their own right and not as an indirect means to achieve other objectives.

The Position of Women

It has long been argued that low status of women – in terms of limited access to resources and subordination to male control – might be an important obstacle to demographic modernisation. In the rhetoric of the international family planning movement and in conference recommendations, improvement in the position of women is increasingly portrayed as a precondition for the achievement of low mortality and fertility.

Underlying the rhetoric are several plausible pathways of influence. The most obvious one rests on an assumption that men are inherently more pronatalist than women, if only because they do not experience the demands of pregnancy and childbirth nor do they bear the main burden of childrearing. For Africa, the thesis has been argued in more specific terms. The advantages of high fertility accrue mainly to men because, typically, children belong to the male lineage and contributions can be extracted from them when they reach adulthood. Conversely, the costs of children, in terms of expenditures on food, clothing and education, fall disproportionately on women (Frank and McNicoll, 1987). To the extent that men, for whatever reason, are typically more pronatalist than women, the decision-making power of wives could act as a crucial fertility determinant.

The key element in these arguments is whether or not men in certain cultures are indeed more pronatalist than women. There is much anecdotal evidence in favour of this proposition, but surprisingly little confirmation from surveys that have interviewed both wives and husbands. A review by Mason and Taj (1987) found no consistent difference between the sexes in terms of reproductive goals. Indeed, in high fertility societies, women were often more pronatalist than men. More recent evidence from Demographic and Health Surveys in Africa also serves to undermine the thesis of men's pronatalism.

A related pathway of influence is that, in male-dominated societies, with arranged marriages and large inter-spousal age differences, there is little husband-wife communication, particularly on potentially embarrassing matters that concern sex and procreation. Some of the earliest detailed research on fertility regulation strongly supports the view that inter-spousal communication is an important influence on the effectiveness of reproductive control (e.g. Hill *et al.*, 1959; Poffenberger,1968). The concept is obviously difficult to measure in large scale, standardised surveys and few recent studied can match the depth and detail that characterised some of the early pioneering enquiries. Accordingly, no firm conclusions are warranted though it seems inherently unlikely that lack of communication could stand for long in the way of strong motivations to reduce fertility.

A third possible link concerns the economic dependency of women on men. The arguments have been expressed most powerfully by Cain *et al.*, (1979) in the context of Bangladesh. In a patriarchal society, a women's life is marked by a succession of dependencies on men: father, husband, son. Unable to seek employment and with no independent asset base, women have a strong vested interest in producing sons because, in their absence, widowhood or divorce may imply economic disaster. Such sentiments, it is argued, act to sustain moderate to high fertility.

There can be no doubt of the strong preference for bearing sons rather than daughters in East and South Asia and to a lesser extent in the Arab States. Elsewhere, however, equal numbers of sons and daughters are the dominant aspiration. Thus son-preference can have little relevance to the persistence of high fertility in Africa. In South Asia, on the other hand, the possible importance of the topic cannot be dismissed cursorily. However, it should be noted that China, Taiwan and Korea, all societies with historically very strong son-preferences, now have very low fertility. This apparent inconsistency between preference and behaviour cannot be explained solely by the benign impact of socioeconomic development on gender values. Rather it is attributable to the fact that East Asian couples are now generally content with one son only, a desire that is compatible with low fertility. Indeed, with the growing practice of sex-selective abortion, fertility can fall to very low levels even in the presence of a widespread cultural desire for a son.

In high fertility South Asia, the most commonly desired family size is two sons and a daughter, just as it was in Korea and Taiwan a few decades ago. Some have argued that, in the absence of non-familial institutions to guarantee welfare in old age or times of adversity, a woman's best strategy is to have at least two sons (e.g. Cain, 1983). Others have adduced evidence that Indian women value sons more for emotional than for economic security, with the implication that one may suffice (e.g. Vlassof, 1990). This interpretive contrast has not been resolved though it appears likely that South Asia will follow the course of East Asia and that gender bias will not prevent declines in fertility down to low levels.

The final feature of women's position that may be relevant to fertility transition is the institution of purdah, or seclusion. This is associated particularly with Islam but is also prevalent in Hindu North India. Seclusion carries two implications that are relevant to the present discussion. First, it acts as a barrier to non-domestic employment by women. In economic explanations of fertility transition, the value of women's time and the opportunity costs of childbearing have played a central part. The arguments are both familiar and persuasive. As economies modernise, new job opportunities for women arise and they progress from unpaid work on the family farm, for instance, to cash employment in factories or businesses. This shift represents a huge increase in the opportunity costs of childbearing, which takes the highly visible form of forgone wages. Demand for children falls and the level of childbearing itself responds to the new situation.

A huge amount of effort has been devoted to empirical examination of this employment–fertility relationship, but the results have been generally negative. Neither at an aggregate level nor at an individual level has a decisive impact of employment on childbearing preferences or behaviour been established (UN, 1987). Rising employment for women has not emerged as a common precursor of fertility transition. More frequently, large-scale entry of women into the labour force has followed the decline in family sizes.

The second relevant aspect of female seclusion is less narrowly economic in nature. To the extent that women are largely confined to their homesteads and immediate vicinity, their exposure to new ideas and models of behaviour is limited, and their access to both health and family planning services is reduced. In view of the fact that most family planning services and methods are designed for use by women, these restrictions may represent a serious barrier to effective fertility regulation that can best be overcome by services at community and household level.

Do these sociological and geographical dimensions of women's seclusion represent an obstacle to fertility decline? For sub-Saharan Africa, once again, the case is implausible. In most African societies, there are few restrictions on mobility. Moreover, powerful women's organisations exist, organised on religious, economic or other grounds, that provide ample opportunity for diffusion of new ideas and values, including those that might legitimise the concepts of smaller families and fertility regulation. Similarly, access to static services is not especially problematic in Africa. In the Arab States and South Asia, the arguments are more compelling because of the existence of undeniable restrictions on the lives of women.

There is rather little evidence by which the effects of this dimension of seclusion can be assessed. It can be argued that the appropriate level of analysis is the entire society rather than the family or the individual. Such national-level analyses are rarely convincing because the units of study are small in number and appropriate indicators unavailable for many of them. Furthermore, demographic surveys have been unimaginative in their measurement of the status of women, relying in the main on time-honoured but inadequate variables such as education, employment, age at marriage and inter-spousal age differences.

One recent exception is the 1989 Bangladesh Fertility Survey, in which self-reported measures of mobility and domestic autonomy were collected. Subsequent analysis indicates that both factors are highly predictive of contraceptive use and fertility, net of controls for socioeconomic status, residence and other controls (Cleland *et al.*, 1993). This result accords with other evidence that the success of the family planning programme in Bangladesh is largely attributable to the activities of literate female workers who provide contraceptive counselling and supplies at the doorstep, thereby overcoming problems of access to static services (Phillips *et al.*, 1988). Whether or not similar findings would be obtained in North India or the Arab States of course is uncertain but, at least in Bangladesh, there is strong evidence that the seclusion of women acts as an obstacle to effective regulation of births.

To sum up, this brief review of the links between the status of women and fertility decline has yielded a complex and mixed set of tentative conclusions. The strongest negative result concerns the participation of women in public life, including the formal labour force. Improvements in this dimension of women's status appears to be more often a consequence than a cause of declining fertility, Similarly, there is little empirical support for the widely held view that husbands typically want more children than their wives, thus undermining the assertion that male hegemony in domestic decisions, including reproductive ones, buttresses large family sizes. In terms of effective implementation of reproductive choices, however, the evidence is more positive. Low levels of inter-spousal communication are likely to be more characteristic of patriarchal than egalitarian societies and may impede the translation of reproductive wishes into appropriate actions for obvious reasons. The relevant research evidence is regrettably rather meagre in this regard. Finally, the physical seclusion of women may act as a severe obstacle to contraceptive access, that requires a major and expensive commitment in terms of domiciliary services to overcome.

Adult Education

Of all the indicators of socioeconomic status, education has been the most widely used by demographers and has proved to be the most powerful predictor of demographic outcomes. In cross-national comparisons, the level of adult education – or its surrogate the per cent literate – typically emerges as a stronger correlate of fertility level or fertility decline than alternative indicators of development, such as per cent urban, income per head and so on. Of course, the combination of high literacy and low living standards, or vice versa, are not common but, when they do appear in conjunction, education is clearly the more decisive demographic determinant. South India and Sri Lanka are among the better-known examples of societies where educational advance has proceeded faster than improvements in material living standards and both experienced early transition to low fertility. Conversely, countries where incomes have outstripped education progress, tend to have high mortality and fertility. The most vivid examples are the oil-rich Arab states whose recent great wealth is only now starting to be reflected in rising educational standards among the adult population. As we have already seen, fertility remains extremely high in most of the more affluent of these countries.

Even more intensively studied by demographers have been cross-sectional differentials of fertility and contraceptive use at the individual level. In broad terms, the level of fertility falls monotonically with increasing parental education in East Asia, Latin America and the Arab states. In South Asia and Africa, the association is more likely to be curvilinear; the highest level of fertility is often found among families where the mother has received a few years of schooling. A negative impact of educational attainment is not found until completed primary or even school levels (Cochrane, 1983). Other studies have shown that the association between parental schooling and fertility is reduced but nevertheless remains strong when economic and other factors, themselves related to education, are taken into account and that the effect on fertility of maternal education is slightly greater than that of paternal education (Cleland and Rodriguez, 1986).

The obsession with cross-sectional differentials in fertility within specific societies tends to obscure huge inter-country variations in the fertility of specific educational strata. The point is well illustrated by referring again to the demography of Indian states. Figure 10.4 shows the level of rural fertility for different categories for the two lowest and the two highest fertility states. At each level of education (here defined in terms of women's schooling), there is a very large difference between Kerala and Tamil Nadu, on the one hand, and Uttar Pradesh and Bihar on the other. For instance, women with a few years of schooling bear about three births in the southern but about 5.5 births in the northern states. These results testify to a powerful contextual effect of education. In a well-educated society, even those at the lowest levels of educational attainment are likely to have few children. The policy lesson usually drawn – namely that girls in Northern India need to be educated for 10 or more years to achieve a predictable fertility reduction – is wrong. It is more justifiable to deduce that when Uttar Pradesh and Bihar achieve the same generally high standards of adult education that have already been achieved in southern India, the level of childbearing in *all* educational strata would be much lower than at present.

There is further abundant evidence that lack of formal schooling cannot be regarded as an absolute barrier to fertility reduction. What typically happens in the course of fertility transition is that educated urban couples are the first to adopt birth control and reduce their family size. This new form of behaviour spreads with varying speeds to lower educational strata and finally to be least educated. At the start of transition, educational differentials area usually modest; in the midst of transition, they are very wide; and in the final stages they narrow again. The most elegant demonstration of these phases is an analysis of 15 countries for which high quality survey data were available for two time points (Rodriguez and Aravena, 1991). Their results strongly suggests that once transition gets underway, it typically spreads to the less advantaged strata, in a self-sustaining process of diffusion.

Finally, we may note that a few countries have achieved almost simultaneous fertility reduction among all education strata, when the overall levels of adult literacy were still low. Indonesia in the mid-1970s and Bangladesh in the early 1980s are the most clear-cut examples. In both cases, fertility fell in the context of very strong government commitments to reduce the birth rate. In Indonesia, couples were subjected to considerable social pressure (Warwick, 1986). In Bangladesh, the main expressions of government policy were extensive use of the mass media, generous financial compensation for those willing to undergo sterilisation and widespread deployment of fieldworkers.

CONCLUDING COMMENTS

The main lesson from this review of fertility trends in the period 1960–1990 is that there exists no single overriding determinant of, or obstacle to, fertility decline. Any simple generalisation encounters sufficiently numerous and important exceptions as to undermine its validity. The interplay of economic, social, cultural and political factors is so complex that any claims to understand the causes of fertility transition, or to predict future trends, are fraudulent.

Of the particular obstacles to decline that have been examined, low levels of adult education emerge as the most important influence. High levels of adult literacy are typically associated with fertility decline though clearly the link can be broken or weakened by opposition, based on religion (for example, the Philippines) or political considerations (for example, some of the Arab States). Among populations where the bulk of the adult population has received little or no formal schooling, fertility transition is rare and the few exceptions are most readily explained in terms of very strong government policies and programmes to achieve fertility reduction.

Why then is the influence of education so pervasive? Almost certainly it has little connection with the content of what is taught in schools. Perhaps the crucial attribute of better-educated societies is that they have achieved at least partial break with the past and are exposed, and receptive, to new ideas, aspirations and models of behaviour. Birth control within marriage is far more likely to take root and flourish in such settings than in largely illiterate societies where adherence to traditional values is liable to be stronger.

If this interpretation of the education–fertility relationship in terms of an ideational theory of social change is correct, the prospects are bright for further widespread fertility decline in developing countries. In most countries there have been dramatic improvements in educational enrolments over the last 30 years and the educational compositions of adult populations are changing accordingly. Moreover, the world is increasingly interlinked by electronic media, with their compelling messages of different life-styles, by motorised transport and by migration.

REFERENCES

Cain, M. (1983), 'Fertility as an adjustment to risk', *Population and Development Review*, vol. 9, pp. 688–702.

Cain, M., Khanam, S. R. and Nahar, S. (1979), 'Class, patriarchy and women's work in Bangladesh', *Population and Development Review*, vol. 5, pp. 405–38.

Casterline, J. (1993), 'Fertility transition in Asia', in T. Locoh and V. Hertrich (eds), *The Onset of Fertility Transition in Sub-Saharan Africa* (Liège: Ordina).

Cleland, J. and Rodriguez, G. (1986), 'The effect of parental education on marital fertility in developing countries', *Population Studies*, vol. 42, pp. 419–42.

Cleland, J., Kamal, N. and Slogget, A. (1993), 'Links between fertility regulation and the education and automony of women in Bangladesh', unpublished paper, London School of Hygiene and Tropical Medicine, Centre for Population Studies.

Coale, A. J. and Watkins, S. C. (eds) (1986), *The Decline of Fertility in Europe* (Princeton, NJ: Princton University Press).

Cochrane, S. (1983), *Fertility and Education: What Do We Really Know?* (Baltimore, MD: Johns Hopkins University Press).

Cutright, P. (1983), 'The ingredients of recent fertility decline in developing countries', *International Family Planning Perspectives*, vol. 9, pp. 101–9.

Dyson, T. and Moore, M. (1983), 'Kinship structure, female automony and demographic behaviour', *Population and Development Review*, vol. 9, pp. 35–60.

Dyson, T. and Murphy, M. (1985), 'The onset of the fertility transition', *Population and Development Review*, vol. 11, pp. 399–440.

Farid, S. (1993), 'Family planning, health and family well-being in the Arab world', paper presented at Arab Population Conference, Amman, 1993.

Feeney, G. (1988), 'The use of parity progression ratios in evaluating family planning programs', in *Proceedings of African Population Conference, Dakar, 1988* (Liège: IUSSP) 7.1.17–7.1.30.

Frank, O. and McNicoll, G. (1987), 'An interpretation of fertility and population policy in Kenya', *Population and Development Review*, vol. 13, pp. 209–43.

Guzman, J. M. (1993), 'The onset of fertility decline in Latin America', in T. Locoh and V. Hertrich (eds), *The Onset of Fertility Transition in Sub-Saharan Africa* (Liège: Ordina).

Hill, R. J., Stycos, M. and Back, K. (1959), *The Family and Population Control* (Chapel Hill: University of North Carolina Press).

Horiuchi, S. (1992), 'Stagnation in the decline of the world population growth rate during the 1980s', *Science*, vol. 257, pp. 761–65.

Horiuchi, S. and Kandiah, V. (1993), 'Recent trends and prospects in world population growth', paper presented at IUSSP XXII General Conference, Montreal, 1993.

Mason, K. O. and Taj, A. M. (1987), 'Differences between women's and men's reproductive goals in developing countries', *Population and Development Review*, vol. 13, pp. 611–38.

Mauldin, W. P. and Berelson, B. (1978), 'Conditions of fertility decline in developing countries, 1965–75', *Studies in Family Planning*, vol. 9, pp. 90–146.

Norton, J. (1993), 'Health behaviour and the use of modern contraception in urban and rural Morocco', unpublish MSc thesis, London School of Hygiene and Tropical Medicine.

Office of the Registrar General (1990), *Fertility Differentials in India, 1984* (New Delhi: Vital Statistics Division, Office of the Registrar General, India).

Phillips, J., Simmons, R. Koening, M. A. and Chakraborty, J. (1988), 'The determinants of reproductive change in a traditional society: evidence from Matlab, Bangladesh', *Studies in Family Planning*, vol. 19, pp. 313–34.

Poffenberger, T. (1968), 'Motivational aspects of resistance to family planning in an Indian village', *Demography*, vol. 5, pp. 757–66.

Potter, J., Mojarro, O. and Nunex, L. (1987), 'The influence of health care on contraceptive acceptance in rural Mexico', *Studies in Family Planning*, vol.18, pp. 144–56.

Rodrigues, G. and Avavena, R. (1991), 'Socio-economic factors and the transition to low fertility in less developed countries', in *Proceedings of the Demographic and Health Surveys World Conference* (Maryland, Columbia: IRD Macro International Inc) vol.1, pp. 39–72.

United Nations (1987), *Fertility Behaviour in the Context of Development* (New York: Department of International Economic and Social Affairs) Population Studies no. 100.

Vlassof, C. (1990), 'The value of sons in an Indian village: how widows see it', *Population Studies*, vol. 36, pp. 45–9.

Warwick, D. P. (1986), 'The Indonesian Family Planning Programme: Government influence and client choice', *Population and Development Review*, vol. 12, pp. 453–90.

11 Imperatives to Reproduce: Views from North-west England on Fertility in the Light of Infertility

Jeanette Edwards

In terms of the real world in which we live and where we try to cherish our dear ones, Oedipus *does* escape his fate. he does not murder the man who saved him from death, nurtured him, gave him a bicycle, had his teeth straightened, paid for driving lessons, etc. Nor does he impregnate the woman who wiped his bum, taught him to sneeze, and catered to all the indignities of childhood that effectively de-eroticise the relationship between mothers and sprogs. Oedipus's genuine filial feeling are not outraged. His biological parents are perfect strangers.

(Carter, 1992)

Biology cannot tell us how to behave in the modern world. It can often explain why we do certain things. Baroness Warnock states 'My argument will be that, though the philosopher will not produce proof or certainty, yet analysis itself may be, in a modest way, useful. It may lead, though slowly, both to better decisions and to the possibility of explaining a decision once it is made'. The word biologist could just as easily be substituted for philosopher. (Potts, 1992)

The two quotations cited above, from quite different writers, writing from different vantage points and for different purposes, exemplify interlinked strands of what, from an anthropological perspective, might be termed 'Western' concepts of reproducing persons.[1] On the one hand, an emphasis on the nurturing and social aspects of parenting and, on the other, the primacy of biology in the activities of humans. These two strands can also be discerned in more specific English kinship ideas which emphasise both the reproduction of individuals and the creation of relationships. As Marilyn Strathern notes:

230

English kinship constructs ... are as much about reproducing the essentialism of individuality as they are about relational definitions of personal identity. That is precisely their contemporary power.

(Strathern, 1993)

This chapter focuses on the ways in which residents of 'Alltown', in the last decade of the twentieth century, draw on notions of biology, personal fulfilment and social relationships to explore fertility and parenting.[2] The people whose views are presented here do not explore factors they perceive as influential in having or not having children in bounded and discrete forms as if they were decisions, but rather as interrelated elements of an incomplete picture. Of particular interest, is the way in which those with whom I spoke both empathise with what they identify as 'the heartache' of infertility and 'the desperation' of those who cannot conceive a child, and relate their own experiences of parenting in terms which highlight poignantly its difficulties and traumas. The influences and pressures described as formative in having children are also those which act to stigmatise childlessness and by association infertility.[3]

AN ANTHROPOLOGICAL PERSPECTIVE

In Britain, as in other European countries and the United States, the technological or medical assistance of conception has been the focus of much public concern and has attracted a great deal of media attention. It raises ethical and practical issues which have been addressed by, amongst others, clinicians, parliamentarians, philosophers and feminists. Medical intervention in human conception serves to make explicit cultural understandings of, for example, the reproduction of persons, what constitutes a parent and how individuals are related. Such concepts fall under the rubric of kinship and raise questions of interest to social anthropologists.[4] It is clear, from an anthropological perspective, that human reproduction not only reproduces individuals but also creates kinship: children are born, in English terms (see also, for example, Firth *et al.*, 1969; Schneider, 1980; Robertson, 1991), as sons, daughters, grandchildren, nieces and nephews. Furthermore, children create parents.

As well as an interest in kinship, social anthropology also has an interest in perspectives, both in the way in which a particular social practice may be viewed differently from the vantage point of different interest groups and also in the way in which a person's view of a particular social phenomenon shifts depending on the question they are, at that moment, addressing. The limits to, or possibilities presented by, conceptive technologies look different from the perspective of those requiring fertility services and those who do not; or from the viewpoint of those responsible for debating and forming legislative guidelines (Franklin, 1993) and clinicians pushing for more effective and successful treatments in terms of babies born and satisfied 'patients' (Price, 1992). While each may draw on similar conceptualisations of what constitutes persons and their reproduction, particular strands of that understanding get emphasised and others screened out according to the vantage point of each.

At the same time, people make sense of medically assisted conception in the context of specific dilemmas. For example, in exploring possibilities presented by new reproductive technologies (NRT),[5] people may, on the one hand, empathise with the difficulties presented by infertility and argue that 'couples' should be helped to conceive by whatever means are available and, on the other, argue that there are limits to human intervention in reproduction and 'interfering with nature' is dangerous.

As I have suggested elsewhere (Edwards, 1993), such seemingly opposing views do not imply a lack of logic or a fickleness on the part of those presenting them, be they 'lay' or 'expert', but are views which address the complexity of social life, from a variety of shifting perspectives. It is the complexity and seeming ambivalence mentioned above that I address here with reference to reproductive decisions.[6]

AN ALLTOWN PERSPECTIVE

Alltown is just north of the Greater Manchester conurbation. It grew up with the textile industry, attracting during the early and middle part of the nineteenth century labouring families from rural areas of England and Ireland. With the demise of the textile industry, the large mills were replaced by small manufacturing units as the main places of employment in the town. These are equally as bedevilled by short-time and redundancy at the end of the twentieth century as the cotton mills were by the end of the nineteenth century. Since the 1970s there has been a small but steady influx of middle-class households, wage earners of which commute to the nearby conurbation to work. The present-day population is about 15 000. The views and comments from Alltown which I record here are taken from both those who consider themselves to be Alltown 'born and bred' and from those who consider themselves to be 'incomers' (both recent and more established) and from both men and women (although it is predominantly women's views that are drawn upon in this chapter) from a range of social backgrounds.

The comments from residents of Alltown presented below are from discussions and conversations I had with them about NRT during the winter of 1990–1991. The project was one of five exploratory studies which aimed to show how the social and cultural implications of NRT might be discerned. My work in Alltown followed and built upon previous research which had entailed 12 months residential fieldwork (Edwards, 1990). The conversations I had were with adults between 19 and 90 years of age, many of whom I had worked with previously. They also built upon what they knew of me and their own understandings of the kind of 'work' I do (Edwards *et al.*, 1993). The people whose views are presented here were not, themselves, directly involved in fertility services. They do not represent a particular 'lay' perspective nor are they representative of the range of views in the locality, rather they exemplify responses to questions of fertility and infertility, to the appropriate reproduction of persons and to what is entailed in becoming and being a parent. My explicit interest in NRT provoked people to discuss what they understood to be pertinent issues; they drew on what they knew from personal experience, from social networks which they create and in which they are active, from their knowledge of Alltown and from mass media, such as magazines, television and newspapers.

In a review of feminist writings on motherhood and in the light of her own treatment for infertility, Ann Snitow (1992) concludes that there has been a shift since the 1970s from a critique of motherhood and support of the choice not to become a parent to a present-day pronatalism both within feminist debate and in a wider society. While presenting her work in 1992 to students and colleagues, she was struck by the way in which younger women present identified and described the enormous pressure they felt under to have children. The young women argued that they were receiving messages from many directions, notably the medical profession, media and other women, that if they did not have children – and furthermore have children soon – they were exposing themselves to the risk of, amongst other things, endometriosis, cancer and infertility. Snitow, while not denying that pregnancy in older women may entail particular risks from a medical perspective (cf. Berryman, 1991), is nevertheless reminded of the threat to women, in currency during the nineteenth century, that if they continued in higher education their uteruses would shrivel up.

The women with whom I spoke in Alltown did not, for the most part, identify a medical necessity to become pregnant either at all, or sooner rather than later. However, many did imply that the availability of, and possibilities presented by, NRT intensified the pressure on women to have children; infertility, in other words, may no longer be evoked as a valid reason for remaining childless (see also Bartholet, 1993). In discussions which touched on the possibility of post-menopausal women using fertility services to become pregnant, concern more often than not focused on children born through such intervention. They talked of the greater likelihood of their being orphaned before adulthood and, with reference to their knowledge of Alltown, they spoke of the stigma which children born of older parents would suffer. Generally, however, people assume that, in Alltown at least, most women reaching a certain age would have had or be planning to have a child[7] (see also Woollett, 1991). And it is this assumption which informs an empathy and understanding of the traumas and stigma of infertility.

My aim in what follows is to show how interrelated aspects of reproductive decisions may be discerned through people's understandings of NRT, in particular the ways in which they make sense of maternal surrogacy and access to *in vitro* fertilisation (IVF). The practicalities and implications of surrogacy arrangements lead people to explore motives of surrogate and commissioning parents. While the controversy engendered by women not in heterosexual relationships but requiring IVF lead people to consider reasons people have for wanting children. Thus the NRT act as an ethnographic window through which taken-for-granted notions of procreation can be glimpsed.

VIRGINS AND SURROGATES

Recent research by Helena Ragone (1994) on surrogate motherhood in the United States, elicits the views of women who act as surrogates[8] and shows how motivations imputed to them by a wider society and avidly reported and commented on by the media, do not fully fit with the way they define themselves and their role. Many of the women she interviewed described their role as a vocation – as 'a calling'. They also emphasised the specialist and unique nature of it, pointing out that it is something *they* do well and not something *anybody* could do. Ragone's analysis points to the status acquired by surrogates in childbearing, an activity which is usually accorded little status or prestige in American society. She suggests that surrogate mothers are able to transcend the role of mother and wife, at the same time as reaffirming it. Thus, the woman acting as a surrogate acquires status, attention and respect for practices which usually attract little status or respect; practices which, in a different context, are thought of as 'natural'.

The Alltown people with whom I spoke, oscillated between a view of surrogacy which emphasised the altruism and kindness of women who act as surrogates and a view which stresses the commercial connotations of 'trading' in babies. While no one I spoke with in Alltown criticised the financial aspect of the transaction from the perspective of women acting as surrogates (it was generally thought that women ought to be compensated financially for giving up a year of their lives[9]), people did express a more diffuse disquiet at what brings to mind the commercialisation of, and 'trafficking' in, babies. To relate surrogacy, however, to wider social practices which are negatively evaluated does not necessarily imply a criticism of individual surrogate mothers.

During the early part of 1991, towards the ends of my fieldwork in Alltown, the so-called 'virgin birth' controversy caught the media imagination.[10] Media attention focused on advisory services said to be assisting 'single women' in their quest to conceive through donor insemination (see, for example, Shore, 1992 and ensuing discussion), but it was the 'selfishness' of women who chose to conceive without a male partner that became a central theme in this reportage. To me, at the time, Alltown people seemed much less concerned with the implications of single women or lesbians making use of fertility services than they were for example with the implications of surrogacy or the potential of transferring gametes between kin. Those who did offer a view on the controversy were of the opinion that it would affect very few people and, moreover, people who were not connected to them in terms of geography or economics; it was assumed that one would need money to engage in IVF as a single person and that it was the kind of thing that might go on in London, but not Alltown. One woman expressed a concern that if lesbians took up the option they might instil in their children a hatred of men and another expressed disbelief that many women would want a child before 'you know, doing it'. But such views were counterbalanced with a 'why not?' and comments were often made about the fact that many children, if not most, were brought up adequately without much input from fathers anyway.

Discussion of 'virgin births' and surrogacy arrangements were also located in, and understood through, the social relationships which they create and in which they are embedded. Hence, Mary Greenwood, an Alltown woman in her mid-fifties, talking in this instance about single women conceiving through IVF, commented that 'those who oppose it – if it happened in their families they'd understand'; in other words, if it were an experience relevant to those they loved and cared for, they would hold a different and less censorial view.

Selfish Desires

Sandra Lee and Lucy Davis are friends, neighbours and work partners, both in their early thirties and each married with two children. During an interview with them, I was asked whether I had seen 'Kilroy' (a British daytime, audience-participation 'chat show') on the television the day before. They described the show, in which guests and audience had discussed the 'news' that single women, not in heterosexual relationships, were being offered IVF. Lucy summarised the main arguments for me thus:

> The men were saying 'you're taking our role from us'. And the women were saying 'its a free choice – better than a one night stand with somebody who might have Aids'.

Lucy pointed out that the presenter and host of the show, Kilroy Silk, 'as nice and unbiased as he is', seemed to be suggesting to women in the audience that they were 'man haters' and 'selfish'. 'But why then', commented Sandra, 'does *anybody* have a child?

LD   Men have children to please their wife; to carry on their name ...
SL   and some just want a child to bully.
LD   *Everybody* has a child for selfish reasons – you don't say I'm going to have a child to perpetuate the species, or because the bible says go forth and multiply – but because you *want* children. And all your own dreams and aspirations are put on to that child.
SL   You don't have a child for company ... because, in that respect, it's a hindrance. It isn't selfish because you wouldn't have any if you were selfish.

The women argue, on the one hand, that everybody has children for selfish reasons and, on the other, that nobody does. These views are not mutually exclusive; one may *want* children but nevertheless acknowledge the duress entailed in caring for them. Alltown women may argue that infertile couples should be helped in whatever way possible *and* acknowledge that being a mother is not only difficult but 'terrible'. In the words of another Alltown woman, Nancy Miller:

It's a terrible thing, isn't it, motherhood. You want it so desperately and if you can't have it, they don't feel complete without it and yet they'll do *anything* to get it, you know, won't they? Yeah, you stand back and look at it when you've got your own and you think, 'oh my god, I must need my head tested'.

While people are awed by the 'truly wonderful thing' a surrogate does in having a baby for somebody else, they are, in a different context, sceptical of the motives and speculate about the character of women who are able to 'hand over babies' they gestate. Some people implied that they must be 'hard', able to 'switch off' their emotions and consequently not become attached to the fetus. One woman speculated it would probably be 'professor types' like me who would embark on surrogacy as an experiment – to see what it was like. Another elaborated: 'Lady scientists, who want to know it can be done. [They] use themselves to prove it'. Another view was that women may do it because they crave attention or are chasing fame. These comments all address the dilemma of separating the gestational and nurturing role of 'mother'. They draw on the cultural value attached to creating and maintaining a relationship between gestational mother and fetus which, ideally, should be sustained after birth. Again, such views are not categorical criticisms of individual women who act as surrogates, nor do they serve as a rejection of the practice. As mentioned above, people present seemingly contradictory views according to the perspective taken. They understand the needs of infertile couples and the altruism of surrogates in the light of cultural ideas about parenting, and connections constantly made between social and biological relations are of a cultural order and culturally specific (see also Strathern, 1993).

Family Claims

One of the first things that struck me when I began talking to Alltown people about NRT was the way in which kin were perceived to 'want' children; to be keen to claim their ties. A consideration in NRT which came up again and again is the claim of grandparents on children born through the 'donation' of gametes. One woman, in her early twenties with two young children, outlined different scenarios in which the gametes of siblings are substituted. She predicted the responses of kin and used such responses as criteria for considering the merits of different possibilities. Thus, she conjectured, a single man donating sperm to his infertile brother would cause no conflict because: 'for the man's family ... the baby is theirs' and, because the donor is unmarried, there is 'no other family to get annoyed'; furthermore, the woman's 'family is not bothered because it's her egg, and she gave birth, and the baby looks like her husband'. She also argued that substituting the eggs of sisters would also lead to happy families: their 'family is not bothered ... whichever egg it is, it's still their grandchild' and the father's 'family is not bothered because it is his sperm and it looks like him'.

The perceived claims of kin are one aspect of what I propose are complex and interrelated elements within the social practices and understandings of reproduction and kinship; understandings which influence and inform ideas about fertility and the implications of infertility. In these examples, the genetic connection between family members is brought to the fore, but the risk that is identified is to relationships.

The 'Urge' to Have Children

Alltown residents with whom I spoke about NRT talked of what they perceive to be the frustration of infertility, namely, a sense of personal inadequacy it engenders and resulting pressures on the relationship between spouses. One man, in his mid twenties and father of two children, guessed that it would have caused a great deal of conflict between him and his wife if they had not been able to have children. 'There would be rows', he said, 'arguments – "shall we do this, shall we do that?" '

I asked Sandra Lee and Lucy Davis why they felt there was such an 'urge' to have children. 'It is God's way of perpetuating the species', replied Sandra. 'An inbuilt drive', added Lucy, 'even in their 50s and 60s women can be broody ... it's inbuilt in us'. They stressed further the innateness and inevitability of reproduction through the example of insects: 'Insects die having babies – but they still do it'.

From this affirmation of biological inevitability, Sandra went on to talk of her step-sister who, she explained, is married and does not *want* children. In fact, Sandra pointed out they 'don't *need* children; she has got a fantastic career and her needs are met from her job' (original emphasis). She also explained that her step-sister had had a 'bad upbringing' – her father having 'left her for another two little girls' (Sandra and her sister); such an experience of rejection, she implied, has inevitably diminished her urge to have children. Consider the way in which this conversation continued. We join it at a point when Sandra remarks on the sense of 'purpose' entailed in having children:

SL [With children you] feel to be needed; with children you've got a purpose.

LD You see young girls, they've got nothing but it is expected of them. As soon as they get old enough they have kids – you see them around Alltown – 16, 17, 18-year-olds pushing prams.

SL Pressure comes from work friends after marriage – 'when you starting a family?' Pressure [comes] from other women.

JE Why?

LD Because *they* have ... If you're not married by late 20s [they] think you're a lesbian. Yet if you've got a good career or if very well off, then excuses are given like '[it's] because she's not found somebody suitable'. If it's ordinary people, they get gypped about it.

SL If [you're] 30 and haven't had children, they can't believe you don't want any – it's your duty and your job – and [they] ask 'is it because you can't?'.

The words of Sandra and Lucy exemplify the complexity entailed in understanding 'the urge' to have children. They shift from ideas about 'inbuilt drives' to making explicit what they know of the persuasion and pressure from external sources; they identify distinctions between social and economic classes and move from ideas about personal fulfilment and achievement to determining influences of history and background.

The 'urge' then to have children may be located in one's biology, as it is in one's past experience and present needs. The following excerpt, taken from a discussion which took place between members of a creative writing class in Alltown, shows how 'biological desires' are not perceived as fixed endowments; they are not evenly allocated and may be more or less diluted. Class members are all women between the ages of 40 and 70.

MB But in our family, we borrow ...

PE ... women who can't have children ...

MB borrow children, you know?

SM And there are men who want to produce their own offspring.

MB/SE Yes

SE So it *is* biological in some people, but in others, they're not interested in any children.

JE Well if it's biological, does that not mean it's in us all?

SE Well, no, because different things come in different strengths, you know? Human desires come in different strengths, don't they, in different people?

PE I think perhaps in some your ambition is stronger than your need for children.

It is the complexity of people's ideas about having or not having children, and the fact that such ideas are not couched in terms of discrete and bounded 'decisions' but in terms of needs and imperatives which emerge from and are embedded in social relationships, that I wish to underline here.

Reproduction by Proxy

Women in Alltown talk of the need to compensate for men as fathers. One woman argued that the reason women are so *attached* to their children is because 'men are not on the scene'; women, she went on, are forced in many cases, and much of the time, to 'make up' for men's lack of involvement with their children. One woman, Mary Greenwood, spoke of why she had been very protective of her children:

> I used to have a bad name around home for sticking up for my kids. I'd get them in and I'd give them a right good telling off, but outside I'd stick up for them ... I don't think I'd have been as protective to mine if *he* had been more of a father. I felt as if I were doing it for the two of us.

As well as making up for men, women also speak of having children on behalf of them. Nancy Miller, quoted earlier, had a difficult and traumatic first marriage in which she suffered domestic violence and poverty. Accompanied by her three children, at the time aged 2, 4 and 6, she left her husband and returned to Alltown. She obtained a divorce, remarried and, after setting up home with her own and her second husband's three children, she and her husband had a child. Her husband died 12 years later. Mrs Miller points out that she is a mother of seven children, all of whom she has successfully and happily brought up. Now in her mid fifties and remarried, she talked with me about NRT and related it to how much she had wanted children:

> ... if I thought, when I was a young woman, if *I* couldn't bear any children, I would have done anything, anything at all to have children ... I always wanted children. I wanted to be a nursery nurse and as I couldn't be, I thought I'd have as many as I could. Have my own nursery. No, children are ... even now ... five days a week I look after two of my daughter's children and we have a baby that lives here as well.

Mrs Miller married her present husband, who had no children of his own, when she was in her early forties:

NM   [when I] got married, I was too old to have any.
JE   ... would you have fancied one?
NM   I think I might have had one for him.
JE   You think he would have liked to?
NM   I think so. We were engaged for a while and I thought at one stage I was pregnant but it was to be an early change. And now he, he never for a minute said that it mattered. He said no, no, it's alright, it doesn't matter, you know. But I was all for packing it in and letting him find somebody younger, you know, because I really felt he did want a child.

Mrs Miller went on to talk of surrogacy and thought she would have acted as a host mother for any of her sisters had they not been able to carry a baby. This reminded her of one of her daughters-in-law who 'was one of those', that is, somebody who had had great difficulty bearing children. Mrs Miller's daughter-in-law had painfully and traumatically experienced the cot death of her first child and several subsequent miscarriages. Eventually she carried a baby to full term by staying in bed 'all day, every day'.

Alltown women who spoke about surrogacy all said how difficult it would be for *them* to 'hand over' a baby, but many added the caveat that they could have done it for someone they knew, that is, in the context of a pre-existing and 'close' relationship. One woman reflected that she would have considered acting as a surrogate for her sister had the need arisen but, she added, she could not do it for someone she did not care for. It was also thought that a woman acting as a surrogate would be less likely to change her mind about relinquishing a baby if she were doing it for someone she knew.[11] The decision to have a child on behalf of a partner or on behalf of kin, cannot be divorced from the social relationships of which it is a part, as a social event isolated from the relationships which it creates and in which it is embedded.

THE SHIFTING GROUND OF THE 'NATURAL'

NRT not only makes explicit what has thus far been taken for granted in English notions of relatedness but it also displaces and redefines what has been thought of as 'natural' (see also Strathern, 1992a). When Alltown people dwell on possibilities presented through surrogacy, the substitution of gametes (practices which might have otherwise been thought problematic) now become possible and are perceived to be more 'natural'. It is as if intervention in reproduction at a gamete level becomes more acceptable when placed alongside intervention at the level of babies. One Alltown man pointed out that surrogacy was 'not a good idea – it is not natural'. He had, earlier in the conversation, argued against donor insemination (DI) but now commented that at least sperm donation was 'keeping things simple' whereas surrogacy was 'like messing with a human body' (the baby). The substitution of human gametes, in the light of surrogacy, is thought to be, if not desirable, at least less problematic and certainly 'more natural'.

Understandings of intervention in reproduction are often couched in terms which elaborate on the theme that 'nature' has failed and that technology can now give 'nature' a helping hand (see also Hirsch, 1993; Franklin, 1993; Strathern, 1992b). Possibilities presented by NRT, which allow for a distinction to be made between, for example, gestational and social maternity, evoke ambiguity over what is to be defined as natural. The desperation to have children, the need to trace ancestors, to find 'fathers' and the perception that children will feel strange if not conceived in a 'natural' way, are all culturally specific ideas represented as 'natural'.

One young woman in Alltown, drawing an ironic analogy with 'natural' foods (and their class connotations), predicted that prestige currently attached to 'natural' childbirth would, in the future, be found in 'organically grown babies'. Another woman, when exploring the possibilities presented through NRT, remarked that she wished 'natural births' for her family. This led her to think of medical intervention at the time of death, and she concluded, 'if you want a natural death, you're going to have to decide that you want it: it's not just going to come'. Possibilities presented through medical assistance render visible (as socially contrived) events such as birth and death previously thought to be inevitable and 'natural'. The concept of 'natural' is not in this process rejected but to achieve it now requires human activity.

Attachments and Responsibility

While sometimes couched in idioms of 'bonding', the attachment between mothers and their offspring, is not necessarily considered a 'natural' or inevitable thing. Paula Seddon, twice married with four children, wondered whether attachment was the same as responsibility. 'Do you get to care for children through doing for them?', she asked and continued:

'parenting is not genetics, it's what you do'. She spoke of the difficulties of caring for her teenage son:

> The more I've thought about it the more confused I've become, the more I've questioned how I do actually feel related. This attachment – is it actually there? Thinking about B. and the problems we've had with him: do I really feel attached to him? or do I feel responsible for him or because I feel I ought to be? The more shitty he is, the less responsible I feel.

Such relationships are also viewed as devices allowing for the smooth running of society; if, of course, women did not take their role as seriously as most do, then chaos would reign.

Comments such as 'motherhood is not something that comes naturally' and 'maternal instinct grows as a child grows' question what is elsewhere construed as the inevitability of 'natural' feelings towards children. Thinking of surrogacy leads people to explore the relationship between a woman and the fetus she is carrying, sometimes in fairly pragmatic terms:

> ... only way you can cope with pregnancy is if you've got feelings about the baby who is kicking you in the ribs, making you pee every two seconds etcetera, etcetera. You'd go stark staring bonkers if you couldn't feel attached to it – you know, couldn't feel some sort of affection for it when it kicks you awake.

A similar pragmatism is apparent when women talk of their responsibilities as mothers towards children. Alltown women suggest that mother's attachments to babies and children serve society well. As one woman remarked:

> ... society couldn't really function if it wasn't there, because we're all expected to take responsibility for our own. It would be a shitty mess if we didn't.

Thinking of the possibility of mothers donating eggs to their daughters provoked Karen Keats to reflect on social 'rules' implicitly understood and rarely brought to mind:

> I think all these things are actually worked out by, y'know, by rules which we understand even if we don't articulate them. And that we accept that this is my child and the ultimate responsibility for deciding is mine, [or] this is my grandchild and my responsibility is to support

the mother … they are not the same kind of responsibilities and we don't feel the same duties. And even though we might not say all these things, nevertheless when we are making decisions and relating between the different people we are actually following rules that we all understand and which we all accept. … I don't know what the effect will be, y'know, for example, of our Dawn saying 'this is my child' and me saying 'this is my child'. … The same as [if] you go into your neighbours – say your neighbour's poorly and she's got a baby and you go in and look after the baby, you do so with well-understood terms. Everybody understands exactly the terms on which you are looking after this baby. Without articulating it … because it has been understood for so long that nobody, you know, even kind of questions it, do they? But, I mean, what happens when you smash it all up? I don't know.

Alongside ideas about unwritten and unspoken rules, which order social relationships and delimit expectations, is a discourse of maternal 'bonding'. But, it is argued, such a process does not come naturally and is not automatic. It took Sandra Lee a while to love her first child and Lucy Davis wanted a girl the second time around, hence she did not 'like' her son for a long time. Another woman, Susan Clarke, explains that she would die for her children and if they were hurt she would prefer it to be her, but she does not love them with the same affection she feels for her partner.

These are not unusual experiences and are feelings which women do not discuss lightly. Such experiences evoke guilt, feelings of inadequacy and, as one woman said, she wonders daily if she is 'normal'. The knowledge that these women have of motherhood poses dilemmas in a world which has high, as well as unreal, expectations of the altruism, dedication and devotion of mothers towards their children.

My intention in this chapter has been to present views of people from Alltown in a way which indicates the complexity of their ideas about having children and being a parent. People make sense of fertility in ways which belie simplistic or single notions of either biological needs or social imperatives, although they continually make connections between the two. They talk of numerous reasons and rationales for having children and describe clearly and evocatively biological, social and personal imperatives to reproduce. In so doing they explore wider contexts of, for example, class, gender, kinship and community within which reproductive decisions are embedded and which, in turn, are reproduced through human procreation. However, factors which are perceived to influence reproduction are not presented as discrete containable 'decisions' but as a myriad of interconnected perspectives. The people whose views are presented here do not describe the making of a decision to have a child as a self-contained event, rather they introduce and explore, retrospectively, factors which fed in to their own experiences and the experiences of those they know; this they do through what they know about Alltown and what they know about creating and sustaining social relationships.

ACKNOWLEDGEMENTS

My debt to friends and associates in Alltown remains. I am grateful to Robin Dunbar and Patrick Crozier for their comments and advice.

NOTES

1. The term 'Western' is problematic in the sense that there is no such thing as a typically 'Western' person. Furthermore neither is there a Euro-American (Strathern, 1993), nor a person who typifies 'the English'. However I use 'English' below as I use 'Western' here to refer to a particular discourse which spans different countries and is disseminated (some would say privileged) through mass media and communications.
2. The name of the town has been changed for conventional reasons of privacy. However, in using a fictitious name I hope also to convey the notion that my interest is in cultural understandings which are not particular to Alltown. I do not consider Alltown, in this respect, to be idiosyncratic; similar ideas will be found in other localities in Britain and amongst different interest groups, such as politicians and clinicians (Edwards, 1992; Edwards *et al.*, 1993).
3. Naomi Pfeffer (1987) remarks that physical infertility is not synonymous with involuntary childlessness and that some people are impeded socially rather than physically from having children. Alltown people refer to the stigma attached to childlessness, through both infertility and not having children within marriage and before a certain age.
4. Selected findings from a recently completed study 'The representation of kinship in the context of the new reproductive technologies' funded by the ESRC (R000 23 2537) can be found in Edwards *et al.* (1993). This chapter draws extensively on that research.
5. I use the term loosely here to refer to the medical and technological assistance of conception. Colloquially, IVF is often used as a generic term covering new reproductive technologies. It should be noted, however, that some practices can hardly be thought new (see, for example, Smart, 1987; Haimes, 1992) and some require little in the way of technology (Pfeffer,

1987) nor indeed, theoretically, the intervention of clinicians (see, for example, Hornstein, 1984).

6. I am not using the term 'reproductive decision' in a strict sense as a biologist might to denote a point at which an organism 'chooses', at either a genetic, subconscious or conscious level, a particular trajectory in order to maximise its fitness (I am grateful to Robin Dunbar's comments on this point). But rather, as a short hand term to refer to the way in which people make sense of having or not having children.

7. Such assumptions are made by men as well as by women. One man, who would define himself as Alltown born and bred, in his mid-thirties and father of two children, in response to a question about whether he had always wanted children, replied: 'you don't really think about it, (you) just assume you'll get married and have kids'.

8. The terms 'surrogate' and 'surrogate mother' are problematic. Women acting as surrogates reason that the term 'mother' should be reserved for the woman who is going to raise the child (Ragone, 1994; see also Zipper and Sevenhuijsen, 1987). Some writers question the term 'surrogate', asking why women who bear and give birth to a child should be called a 'surrogate'; some consider 'birth mother' (Ragone, 1994), 'contract parent' (Bartholet, 1993) or 'gestational mother' to be more accurate terms.

9. Nor does the financial aspect of surrogacy contracts feature prominently in surrogates own descriptions of their role and motivations (Ragone, 1994).

10. The term 'virgin' birth is in itself interesting, particularly when used to refer to lesbians who conceive through donor insemination. It suggests that women are and remain virgins until they indulge in heterosexual sex, which begs the question of what status homosexual sex has in such social constructions. I am reminded of a health promotion worker, in a completely different context, talking to a group of women about HIV/AIDS, who pointed out that her second child had been a 'virgin birth': insemination had taken place digitally and by accident.

11. Ragone's (1994) work indicates that licensed surrogacy programmes in the United States which encourage a relationship between maternal surrogate and commissioning couple experience fewer 'problems' than those where a relationship is actively discouraged and the surrogate and adoptive parents are unknown to each other.

REFERENCES

Bartholet, E. (1993), *Family Bonds: Adoption and the Politics of Parenting* (New York: Houghton Mifflin).

Berryman, J. C. (1991), 'Perspectives on later motherhood', in A. Phoenix, A. Woollett and E. Lloyd (eds), *Motherhood: Meanings, Practices and Ideologies* (London: Sage).

Carter, A. (1992), *Expletives Deleted* (London: Vintage).

Edwards, J. (1990), 'Ordinary people: a study of factors affecting communication in the provision of services', unpublished PhD thesis, Manchester University.

Edwards, J. (1992), 'Shifting perspectives on new reproductive technologies', *Anthropology in Action*, vol. 11, pp. 8–9.

Edwards, J., Hirsch, E., Franklin, S., Price, F. and Strathern, M. (eds) (1993), *Technologies of Procreation: Kinship in the Age of Assisted Conception* (Manchester: Manchester University Press).

Firth, R., Hubert, J. and Forge, A. (1969), *Families and their Relatives. Kinship in a Middle-class Sector of London* (London: Routledge & Kegan Paul).

Franklin, S. (1993), 'Making representations: the parliamentary debate on the Human Fertilisation and Embryology Act', in J. Edwards, E. Hirsch, S. Franklin, F. Price and M. Strathern (eds), *Technologies of Procreation: Kinship in the Age of Assisted Conception* (Manchester: Manchester University Press).

Haimes, E. (1992), 'Gamete donation and the social management of genetic origins', in M. Stacey (ed.), *Changing Human Reproduction: Social Science Perspectives* (London: Sage).

Hirsch, E. (1993), 'Negotiated limits: interviews in south-east England', in J. Edwards, E. Hirsch, S. Franklin, F. Price and M. Strathern (eds), *Technologies of Procreation: Kinship in the Age of Assisted Conception* (Manchester: Manchester University Press).

Hornstein, F. (1984), 'Children by donor insemination: a new choice for lesbians', in R. Arditti, R. Dueli Klein and S. Minden (eds), *Test-tube Women: What Future for Motherhood* (London: Pandora).

Pfeffer, N. (1987), 'Artificial insemination, *in-vitro* fertilisation and the stigma of infertility', in M. Stanworth (ed.), *Reproductive Technologies: Gender, Motherhood and Medicine* (Cambridge: Polity).

Potts, M. (1992), 'The nature of love', in D. Bromham *et al.* (eds), *Ethics in Reproductive Medicine* (London: Springer).

Price, F. (1992), 'Having triplets, quads or quins: who bears the responsibility', in M. Stacey (ed.), *Changing Human Reproduction: Social Science Perspectives* (London: Sage).

Ragone, H. (1994), *Surrogate Motherhood: Conception in the Heart* (Boulder, CO: Westview Press).

Robertson, A. F. (1991), *Beyond the Family: the Social Organisation of Human Reproduction* (Cambridge: Polity).

Schneider, D. M. (1980), *American Kinship: a Cultural Account* (Chicago: University of Chicago Press) 2nd edition.

Shore, C. (1992), 'Virgin births and sterile debates: anthropology and the new reproductive technologies', *Current Anthropology*, vol. 33, pp. 295–314.

Smart, C. (1987), 'Law and the problem of paternity', in M. Stanworth (ed.), *Reproductive Technologies: Gender, Motherhood and Medicine* (Cambridge: Polity).

Snitow, A. (1992), 'Feminism and motherhood: an American reading', *Feminist Review*, vol. 40, pp. 32–52.

Strathern, M. (1992a), '*After Nature: English Kinship in the Late Twentieth Century* (Cambridge: Cambridge University Press).

Strathern, M. (1992b), *Reproducing the Future: Anthropology, Kinship and the new Reproductive Technologies* (Manchester: Manchester University Press).

Strathern, M. (1993), 'Nostalgia and the new genetics', in D. Battaglia (ed.), *The Rhetoric of Self Making* (Berkeley: University of California Press).

Woollett, A. (1991), 'Having children: accounts of childless women and women with reproductive problems', in A. Phoenix, A. Woollett and E. Lloyd (eds), *Motherhood: Meanings, Practices and Ideologies* (London: Sage).

Zipper, J. and Sevenhuijsen, S. (1987), 'Surrogacy: feminist notions of motherhood reconsidered', in M. Stanworth (ed.), *Reproductive Technologies: Gender, Motherhood and Medicine* (Cambridge: Polity).

12 The Timing of Childbearing in Developed Countries

Máire Ní Bhrolcháin

INTRODUCTION

It is now well-recognised that the large shifts that have occurred in the fertility of the developed world during the post-war period have had as a major component changes in the timing of childbearing. We now know that the post-war Baby Boom was not primarily due to an increase in the number of large families, but is attributable principally to rises in the level of marriage and of low-order births, and acceleration in the tempo of marriage and the low orders of birth (Ryder, 1980; Ní Bhrolcháin, 1987). The substantial declines in fertility seen throughout the developed world in the last two decades also have, as a central component, a deceleration in the pace of fertility; the 'baby bust' has been due both to a reduced level of childbearing and to a move to a later pattern of childbearing. Ryder (1980) has estimated that 58 per cent of the change in period total fertility between the 1930s trough and its peak in the US in the late 1950s was attributable to the accelerated tempo of fertility, and that 55 per cent of the subsequent decline in period fertility to the late 1970s was due to tempo effects. Nevertheless, studies of the timing of fertility still appear to be less common than investigations of the overall level of fertility. The present paper examines a number of facets of fertility tempo, with a view to identifying and documenting central trends and discussing possible interpretations. Attention is focused initially on a selection of European countries for which key indicators are available, and subsequently on England and Wales, for which more detailed information has been compiled.

AGE AT CHILDBEARING

Information on European developments in the mean age at first birth is provided by Sardon (1990) up to the mid 1980s and has been supplemented

249

by more recent figures for England and Wales from the Office of Population Censuses and Surveys (OPCS, 1992). Data from Sardon's compilation are plotted in Figures 12.1a and 12.1b for those 11 countries for which information is available from 1951 onwards[1]. Sardon's data are presented in preference to other sources since he has compiled time-series of the standardised rather than the crude period mean age at childbearing[2]. The standardised mean, though regrettably used less widely than the crude period mean age, is to be preferred to the crude mean since it is uninfluenced by the age structure of women at risk of having a birth in a particular year.

Trends in the period mean age at childbearing are very similar in all 11 countries, with a steady decline from 1951 onwards in all of them. Having reached low values of between 26.2 and 27.5 years, this trend is reversed in the 1970s and since then the mean age at childbirth has been increasing. There is a remarkable similarity between countries in the timing of the reversal in the trend in the mean age of childbearing. Ten of the 11 countries examined here reached the turning point in their standardised mean age at childbearing between 1974 and 1976 with, in Austria, a

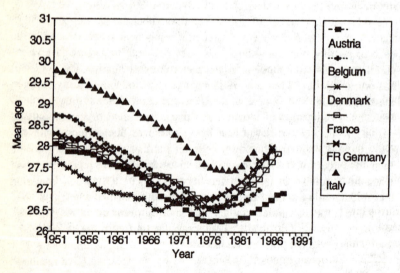

Figure 12.1a   Period mean age at maternity, standardised. European countries, 1951–1991

Source: Sardon (1990).

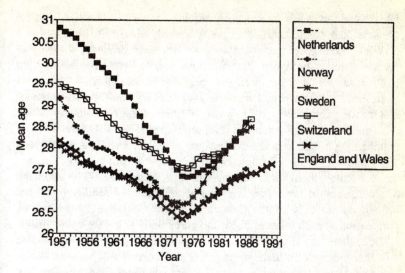

Figure 12.1b Period mean age at maternity, standardised. European countries, 1951–1991

Source: Sardon (1990) and author's calculations based on data supplied by OPCS

double dip. The exception is Italy where the turnaround was somewhat later – in 1979. In Austria, the shift back to later childbearing was not fully under way until 1981. We see, therefore, that cross-national trends in the mean age at childbearing have moved in even more concerted fashion than has the Total Fertility Rate (TFR: the number of births that a woman would have if she experienced through her lifetime the age-specific birth rates obtaining in a given year). Recent lows in TFR were reached across these countries over the whole 16 year period since 1977, when England and Wales reached its post-war low of 1.66 children per woman. Some European countries, such as Italy and Spain, continue to experience declines in the TFR up to the present, contrasting with the remarkable coordination between the countries examined here in timing trends.

Recent European trends in the mean age of childbearing have resulted in greater homogeneity among European countries than was present in the past. In 1951 there was a range, among the 11 countries studies here, of 3.1 years between the earliest and latest mean age at childbearing (Denmark 27.7, Netherlands 30.8); by contrast, the range in 1983, the latest year for which figures are available for all 11 countries, was 1.6 (Austria 26.5, Netherlands 28.1), just about half of the 1951 spread.

While the average age at childbearing has been increasing for the past decade or more, European women are not yet, on the whole, having their children as late as in the immediate post-war period. Of the 11 countries examined here, only in Denmark and Sweden has the mean age of childbearing returned to 1951 levels. In none of the countries for which the time-series in Sardon's monograph extend back before 1951 is childbearing as late as at the earliest date available, dates ranging between 1990 and the 1930s. By and large, it seems, recent patterns are not unprecedented, though this statement needs to be qualified. The mean age of childbearing is not a pure measure of the timing of fertility since it is influenced not only by the timetable of births but also by the rate of progression to each order of birth, and particularly to higher orders (births of order three and above). Where there is a greater propensity to proceed to higher orders of birth, the mean age of childbearing will be, other things being equal, correspondingly later. The very late mean age of childbearing

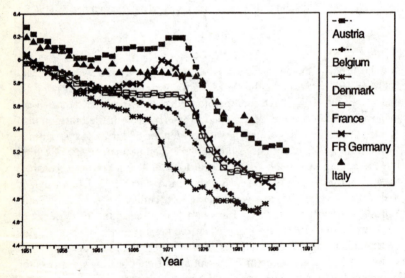

Figure 12.2a Standard deviation of age at maternity, European countries, 1951–1991

Source: Sardon (1990)

characteristic of European countries in the earlier part of the century will therefore have been due, in part, to larger family sizes.

A further perspective on the timing of childbearing overall can be obtained by examining the spread of each country's period age-specific fertility schedule, represented by its standard deviation[3]. Trends in this quantity are given in Figure 12.2a and 12.2b, again for the 11 countries in Sardon's tables. The picture here is also one of decline – that is, there is a common tendency, beginning in the mid-1960s to mid-1970s, for a reduction in the standard deviation of the age of childbearing. Into the 1970s in Europe, childbearing became not only earlier but also more compactly distributed by age. For the most part, there are no signs of a reversal in this European tendency before about the mid-1980s, when the available series end; but the series for England and Wales, which extends to 1991, displays a renewed increase in the dispersion of fertility rates from the early 1980s to 1991. Possible reasons for this development are considered further in the next section, in conjunction with comparable evidence for the age at first birth.

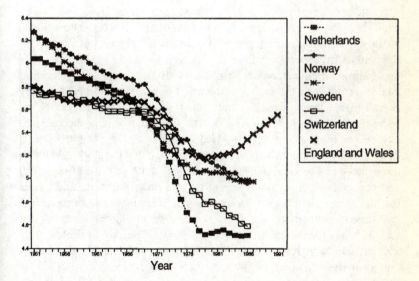

Figure 12.2b Standard deviation of age at maternity, European countries, 1951–1991

Source: Sardon (1990) and author's calculations based on data supplied by OPCS

THE START OF CHILDBEARING

Both temporal change and inter-country variation in the mean age of childbearing reflect, as we saw above, not only tempo but quantum components also. Ideally, the comparative study of fertility timing requires indices representing the speed of completion of each stage of the fertility process: the average (mean or median) age at first birth together with the duration of subsequent birth intervals. Also of potential interest is information on the span of childbearing together with the age at final birth. Variation in the start of childbearing has been, by Ryder's (1980) estimates, the major component of the total variation in the timing of childbearing in the post-war period in the US.

This section therefore begins by considering trends in the average age at the start of childbearing. The preferred indicator is, again, the standardised[4] rather than crude period mean age at first birth, because it is uninfluenced by the age structure of the population at risk of first birth. While comparative figures on the crude period mean age at first birth are not uncommon, standardised period indices tend not to be available on a comparative basis. This section therefore presents figures for England and Wales only.

Trends in the period mean age at first birth for England and Wales, 1938–1991, are given in Figure 12.3 and contrasted with the figures for the mean age at childbearing overall, a somewhat longer time-series for England and Wales being shown here than in Figure 12.1b. The timing of first birth is, of course, earlier than that of all births, with a difference of 2–3 years between the two series across the period examined. Like the overall figure, the mean age at entry into motherhood declined during the two-and-a-half decades following the war. In 1970, when the pace of entry into childbearing was at its most rapid, the mean age at first birth was, at 23.7, over 2 years below its value of 26.2 in 1946. By 1991, entry into motherhood had become later and women were starting childbearing at 25.5 years on average, close to the pace of the immediate post-war period. Note that the phasing of the post-war decline and subsequent rise in the period mean age at motherhood was fairly symmetrical in England and Wales: it took 22 years for the mean age at entry into childbearing to decline from 25.5 in 1948 to its low point in 1970 and it was a further 21 years before this level was regained, in 1991. As is true of the overall mean age of childbearing, entry into motherhood is not yet as late as in the immediate pre-war period, with a period mean age at first birth of 26 in 1938.

While the trends in the mean age at first and at all births are very similar, with both displaying a continuous decline from the late 1940s to the early 1970s followed by a substantial rise, it is noteworthy that the two

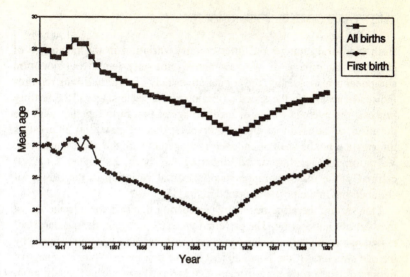

Figure 12.3   Period mean age: all and first births, England and Wales, standardised

Source: Author's calculations based on OPCS (1987a, 1987b) and data supplied by OPCS

series do not turn around at the same time. The steady fall in the mean age at the start of childbearing was reversed in 1971, 4 years before the overall mean age started rising again in 1975. The likely reason is that mentioned earlier – while the mean age at all births is heavily influenced by the mean age at first birth, progression to higher-order births is also an influential component of the overall mean age; the continuation into the 1970s of the sharp reduction, begun in 1964, in progression to births of order three and above (Ní Bhrolcháin, 1987; Murphy and Berrington, 1993) had an impact in further lowering the overall mean age at childbearing after the mean age at first birth had started to turn around.

The variability in the age at entry into motherhood, using the standard deviation of the age-specific first birth schedule, is plotted in Figure 12.4 together with the standard deviation of the overall age-specific fertility distribution, for England and Wales 1938–1991. The dispersion of age at birth overall displays a slow decline from 1945 to 1964 followed by a rapid downward shift to the late 1970s and then a subsequent recovery, still under way in 1991. By contrast, the dispersion in age at first birth,

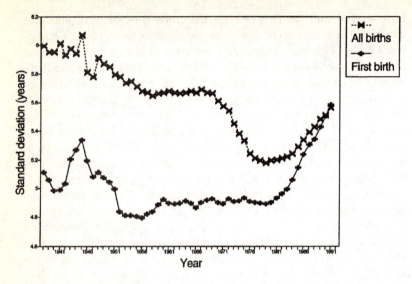

Figure 12.4   Standard deviation of age at all and at first births, England and
Wales, standardised

Source: as Figure 12.3

having declined rapidly during the immediate post-war years, is fairly
stable from the early 1950s to the late 1970s, when it begins a rapid
ascent, also continuing to 1991. An increase in the dispersion in age at
entry into motherhood has also been reported for the US by Bloom and
Trussell (1984) and for Spain by Castro Martin (1992). We can make a
number of inferences from these patterns. First, the decline to the late
1970s in the standard deviation in the age at childbearing was not due to
any change in the dispersion in age at entry into motherhood, which was
fairly constant during this period. The move to an earlier age at first birth
was, in other words, achieved by a general shift in the age-specific first
birth schedule, rather than a change in its shape; this remained true until
the late 1970s, even after the mean age at first birth had begun to rise
again. By contrast, the reduction in the overall age of childbearing was
accompanied by a change in the character of the age-specific fertility
schedule, with fertility becoming, up to the late 1970s, more concentrated
by age, before then increasing in dispersion once again. There are two
possible contributory factors to the decline in the variability in the age at

birth overall into the late 1970s – the contraction of birth intervals, considered in a later section, and the reduction in progression to higher-order births, with the corresponding reduction in birth rates at older ages (35+). The stability in the dispersion of first birth rates up to the late 1970s means that changes in the schedule of first birth rates did not influence the overall dispersion up to then. It seems likely, however, that the increase in the standard deviation of the age at birth overall during the 1980s is attributable, in whole or in part, to the very steep rise in the variability of the age at first birth; the standard deviation of the period age at motherhood exceeded that of the overall age-specific fertility schedule by 1991, having been well below it throughout the entire period since 1938.

There is currently greater diversity in the age at which women enter motherhood than there has been at any time since annual age-specific records began in 1938. One reason may lie in the greater control over fertility afforded by the contraceptive pill, allowing women to initiate their childbearing career precisely when they wish and facilitating also a dissociation between decisions about union formation and decisions about the start of family formation. A further possible reason for this development is that the vast majority of married women can now expect to combine childbearing and rearing with labour-force involvement. Greater variability in the age at entry into motherhood may reflect differing solutions to the problem of how to co-ordinate the two activities through the life-cycle – that is, greater diversity in the life-cycle patterns or strategies through which motherhood and work are combined.

THE END OF CHILDBEARING

The age at which women have their last child has been examined frequently in historical studies of fertility, primarily in an attempt to identify the use of birth control. But hardly any attention has been given to this feature of the childbearing career in contemporary developed countries, for reasons that are not at all clear. That this neglect may be unwarranted is suggested by the data plotted in Figure 12.5 which show, by the right-hand scale, the median age at last birth among women born between 1911 and 1948,[5] along with the median age at first birth in these same cohorts (left-hand scale).[6] The figures are given in Tables 12.1 and 12.2. Both right- and left-hand axes of the graph being to the same scale, it is clear that there has been a more substantial change in the median age at which women finish childbearing than in the median age at which they

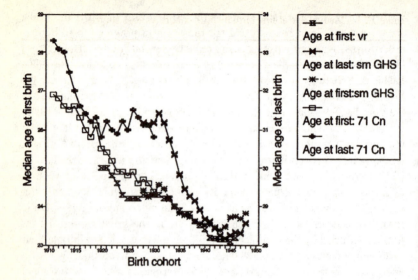

Figure 12.5   Median age at first and at last birth, birth cohorts, 1911–1948

Source: see Tables 12.1 and 12.2

start. The median woman born in 1945 had her first birth at age 23.1 years (vital registration figure), 3.8 years earlier than her counterpart born in 1911, for whom the figure was 26.9. The change in the age at last birth across these cohorts has been larger, with the cohort of 1911 having had their last child at a median age of 33.3 years, falling to 28.2 among women born in 1945, a decline of 5.1 years. The decline across these cohorts in the median age at last birth is over a year more than in the median age at first birth. Much has been made of fluctuations in the timing of fertility resulting from variation in the onset of childbearing. It is clear that the end of childbearing has been subject to greater change. That this is likely to be true more generally is suggested by similar results for Finland evident in Figure 12.1 of El-Khorazaty (1992). The finding has several implications.

First, trends in the age at last birth cannot be accounted for simply as a shift in the overall schedule of fertility rates. In fact the average age at last birth is affected by the level of progression to higher orders of birth as well as by timing factors, since the mean age at last birth can be written as:

$$a_L = a_1 + p_1 i_2 + p_1 p_2 i_3 + p_1 p_2 p_3 i_4 + \ldots + p_1 p_2 \ldots p_{m-1} i_m$$

Table 12.1   Median age at first birth by birth cohort: various sources

	1971 Census	Vital registration	GHS 1986–89	GHS smoothed
1911	26.9			
1912	26.8			
1913	26.6			
1914	26.5			
1915	26.6			
1916	26.3			
1917	26.0			
1918	25.8			
1919	26.1			
1920	25.5	25.0		
1921	25.4	25.0		
1922	25.2	24.8		
1923	24.9	24.6		
1924	24.9	24.3		
1925	24.8	24.2		
1926	24.9	24.2		
1927	24.6	24.2	24.3	
1928	24.7	24.3	24.7	24.4
1929	24.6	24.3	24.0	24.3
1930	24.4	24.3	24.3	24.3
1931		24.3	24.7	24.6
1932		24.2	24.6	24.5
1933		24.2	24.0	24.2
1934		24.0	24.1	24.0
1935		23.9	23.7	23.8
1936		23.8	23.8	23.8
1937		23.8	23.8	23.7
1938		23.6	23.5	23.6
1939		23.5	23.7	23.6
1940		23.4	23.4	23.5
1941		23.2	23.6	23.5
1942		23.2	23.5	23.5
1943		23.2	23.3	23.4
1944		23.1	23.4	23.5
1945		23.1	23.8	23.7
1946		23.2	23.9	23.8
1947			23.4	23.7
1948			24.1	23.8

Sources: Longitudinal Study tabulations; OPCS (1987b) and unpublished updated figures supplied by OPCS; GHS tabulations by author.

Table 12.2   Median age at last birth by birth cohort: various sources

Birth cohort	1971 Census	1986–89 GHS	GHS smoothed	GHS age at last <40
1911	33.3			
1912	33.1			
1913	33.0			
1914	32.5			
1915	32.0			
1916	31.6			
1917	31.4			
1918	31.2			
1919	31.3			
1920	30.8			
1921	31.2			
1922	31.0			
1923	30.9			
1924	31.2			
1925	31.0			
1926	31.5			
1927	31.3	31.2		30.8
1928	31.1	31.1	31.2	30.9
1929	31.1	31.3	31.1	31.1
1930	30.8	30.8	31.2	30.3
1931		31.8	31.4	31.3
1932		31.2	31.2	31.0
1933		30.5	30.7	30.5
1934		30.7	30.4	30.6
1935		29.5	29.8	29.5
1936		29.6	29.5	29.5
1937		29.1	29.3	29.0
1938		29.3	29.2	29.3
1939		28.9	28.9	28.8
1940		28.5	28.7	28.3
1941		28.8	28.6	28.7
1942		28.3	28.4	28.2
1943		28.3	28.3	28.2
1944		28.1	28.2	28.1
1945		28.2	28.3	28.1
1946		28.5	28.3	28.3
1947		28.1	28.3	28.0
1948		28.5	28.6	28.3
1949		29.2		

Sources: Longitudinal Study tabulations; GHS tabulations by author.

where a_L is the mean age at last birth, a_1 is the mean age at first birth, p_x is the proportion of women reaching parity x who proceed to a further birth, i_x is the mean birth interval of order x and m is the maximum number of births to any woman. From this expression, it is seen that the age at last birth is influenced by three sets of factors: the age at first birth, the length of interbirth intervals, and the parity progression ratios (the proportion of women reaching a given parity who have at least one further birth). The very substantial declines in the higher order parity progression ratios (progression to births of order three and above) across these cohorts (see Table 12.3) are therefore likely to have been an important contributor to the decline in the average age at last birth. However, as is seen in the next section, there have been declines also in interbirth intervals that have contributed to making the childbearing span more compact.

We need also to consider how far the shift to an earlier age at completing childbearing has itself been an objective of changing behavioural patterns and has been influenced directly by social and economic factors and how far it has merely been the incidental outcome of decisions taken on other grounds. Our explanatory efforts tend to be directed to exploring the reasons for changes in the number of births or in the timing of first birth and, to a lesser extent, that of subsequent births, but little attention has been given to the determinants of the timing of the final birth. Of mothers born in 1911, nearly two-fifths (38 per cent) had their last child at age 35 and above, compared with 29 per cent of mothers born in 1926 and 12 per cent of those born in 1941–5. This change is not purely attributable to the reduction in family size: among women with two children, the figures are 35, 17 and 8 per cent, respectively. In view of such major changes across the century in the age at family completion, we should surely consider whether the age at last birth has been an element of decision-making by couples. It could, however, be difficult to disentangle

Table 12.3   Parity progression ratios by birth cohort*

	Birth cohort	a_1	a_2	a_3
LS-based				
	1911	0.67	0.51	0.43
	1930	0.80	0.53	0.50
GHS-based				
	1945–48	0.85	0.41	0.35

*a_1 is the proportion with one child who have at least two children, etc.
Sources: Longitudinal Study tabulations; GHS tabulations by author.

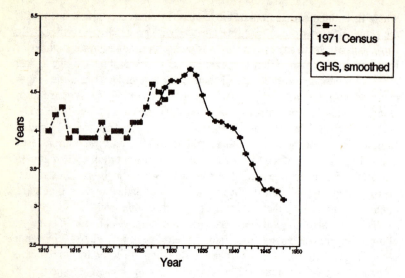

Figure 12.6   Median time between first and last birth, birth cohorts, 1911–1948

Source: Tabulations from Longitudinal Study and GHS, 1986–89

shorter intervals, reduction in completed parities and age at last birth from each other.

There are indications in the later part of the series that both the age at first birth and the age at last birth were rising in the cohorts of the late 1940s. The truncation in the cohort series does not allow us to reach a decisive conclusion about a turnaround in the age at last birth series. However, there appears a fairly definite reversal in this respect in the median age at first birth, on GHS evidence. The latter is, of course, consistent with the unambiguous indications from the period data seen earlier of a reversal since 1970 in the period mean age at first birth. One would expect, because of this, that the age at last birth has also been getting later in recent times.

THE SPAN OF CHILDBEARING AND BIRTH INTERVALS

The findings of the preceding section imply that, because of the more substantial change in the median age at last than at first birth the span of

Table 12.4 Median time from first to last birth by birth cohort, various sources

Birth cohort	1971 Census	1986–89 GHS	GHS smoothed
1911	4.0		
1912	4.2		
1913	4.3		
1914	3.9		
1915	4.0		
1916	3.9		
1917	3.9		
1918	3.9		
1919	4.1		
1920	3.9		
1921	4.0		
1922	4.0		
1923	3.9		
1924	4.1		
1925	4.1		
1926	4.3		
1927	4.6	4.3	
1928	4.5	4.3	4.4
1929	4.4	4.7	4.6
1930	4.5	4.7	4.6
1931		4.6	4.6
1932		4.8	4.7
1933		4.8	4.8
1934		4.8	4.7
1935		4.4	4.5
1936		4.3	4.2
1937		4.0	4.1
1938		4.3	4.1
1939		4.0	4.1
1940		4.1	4.0
1941		4.0	3.9
1942		3.6	3.7
1943		3.7	3.6
1944		3.3	3.4
1945		3.2	3.2
1946		3.3	3.3
1947		3.3	3.2
1948		2.9	3.1
1949		3.3	

Sources: Longitudinal Study tabulations; GHS tabulations by author.

childbearing has been getting narrower. That this is indeed so can be seen explicitly from Figure 12.6 and Table 12.4 which show the median time between first and last birth, by birth cohort of mother.[7] The span initially rose from a median of 4 years in the cohort of 1911 to nearly 5 years in the high fertility cohorts of the mid-1930s. There followed a substantial decline to a median of just over 3 years among women born in the late 1940s. The period given to forming a family among recent cohorts is shorter and more compact than it has been in the past. Women are, furthermore, more homogeneous in respect of the time taken to complete than was formerly the case: the standard deviation of the span of childbearing has declined steadily from the cohorts of the mid-1920s through to the late 1940s (Figure 12.7). The time taken to complete family formation has, thus, become both shorter and more narrowly distributed among women.

As mentioned earlier, these changes could be attributable in part to the decline in family size from the cohorts of the mid-1930s, rather than to the contraction of individual birth intervals. That the decline in family size is

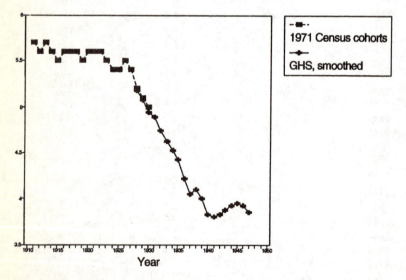

Figure 12.7   Standard deviation of the span of childbearing, birth cohorts, 1911–1948

Source: as Figure 6

Table 12.5   Estimates of birth intervals, various sources

	Family Census 1946	1971 Census period life table	1979–82 GHS period life table	Hospital Inpatient Enquiry (HIPE)[‡]
Interval from first to second birth (months)				
1910[*]	36.6			
1917	39.4			
1922	40.0			
1927	40.8			
1932	44.2			
1941		41.1		
1942		40.2		
1943		41.1		
1944		41.6		
1945		43.1		
1946		41.9		
1947		37.6		
1948		37.6		
1949		34.2		
1950		34.1		
1951		34.4		
1952		32.5		
1953		32.3		
1954		31.2		
1955		32.7		
1956		31.2		
1957		31.5		
1958		30.7		
1959		29.3		
1960		29.4		
1961		29.0		
1962		28.2		
1963		28.3		
1964		27.0		
1965		28.4		
1966		27.7		
1967		27.7		
1968		28.4		
1969		28.0		
1970		29.1[†]	28.3	
1971			28.2	
1972			31.8	31
1973			31.7	31
1974			30.5	32
1975			30.7	33
1976			30.7	33

Table 12.5   Continued

	Family Census 1946	1971 Census period life table	1979–82 GHS period life table	Hospital Inpatient Enquiry (HIPE)[‡]
1977			31.3	34
1978			29.9	34
1979			27.8	33
1980				32
1981				31
1982				31
1983				31
1984				31
1985				32
1986				32
1987				32
1988				32
1989				32
1990				33
1991				34
Interval from second to third birth (months)				
1910[*]	45.1			
1917	44.3			
1922	40.8			
1927	45.8			
1932				
1941				
1942				
1943				
1944				
1945				
1946				
1947				
1948				
1949				
1950		36.2		
1951		34.9		
1952		36.7		
1953		34.6		
1954		33.4		
1955		33.0		
1956		34.5		
1957		32.6		
1958		32.5		
1959		33.1		

Table 12.5   Continued

	Family Census 1946	1971 Census period life table	1979–82 GHS period life table	Hospital Inpatient Enquiry (HIPE)[‡]
1960		33.7		
1961		32.2		
1962		33.0		
1963		31.0		
1964		33.6		
1965		33.6		
1966		34.7		
1967		34.2		
1968		36.3		
1969		36.4		
1970		34.5[†]	38.7	
1971			36.5	
1972			33.2	39
1973			34.5	39
1974			39.8	39
1975			37.0	41
1976			37.0	42
1977			37.1	42
1978			34.8	43
1979			39.6	44
1980				41
1981				40
1982				40
1983				40
1984				40
1985				40
1986				39
1987				38
1988				38
1989				38
1990				37
1991				39

[*]The derivation of these Family Census intervals is described in Appendix 2. The original data relate to marriage cohorts. The estimates are located here 5 years after the year of marriage of the middle cohort of the group.

[†]The estimate covers 1970 and the early part of 1971.

[‡]The HIPE data refer to the duration of intervals of the specified order closed in the year in question.

Sources: Glass and Grebenik (1954); Ní Bhrolcháin (1987); unpublished analysis by the author of 1979–82 GHS data; *Birth Statistics*, various years.

not the whole explanation for the trend toward greater compactness is seen from Table 12.5 and Figures 12.8 and 12.9, which plot estimates of the second and third birth intervals from 1910 to the present. An attempt to produce such a long series necessarily relies on a variety of sources, not always completely comparable. The pre-war estimates are based on the Family Census of 1946 and are not true medians, but are presented here as a rough guide to the duration of these intervals prior to the war (see Appendix 2). The 1971 Census series are life-table medians among women having progressed to each order of birth within 10 years of the preceding birth, based on 1971 Census maternity histories (Ní Bhrolcháin, 1987). Analysis of the GHS rounds of 1979–82 provided further synthetic life-table estimates for the period 1970–79. Finally the Hospital Inpatient Enquiry figures (OPCS, 1992 and preceding years) are estimates of the median closed interval since the preceding birth among births of a given order occurring during the specified year; these medians are not directly comparable with the life-table estimates[8] but are presented here in an attempt to provide up to date information, since intervals based on a

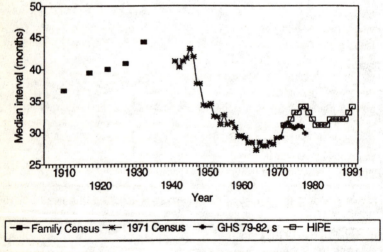

Figure 12.8   Estimated median second interval, for England and Wales and Great Britain, 1910–91

Source: see Table 12.5

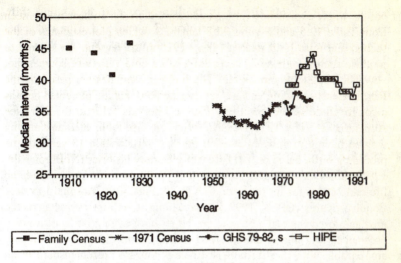

Figure 12.9   Estimated median third interval, England and Wales (1910–1925) and Great Britain, (1910–1991)

Source: see Table 12.5.

synthetic life-table are not yet available for more recent years. We see from these figures that the duration of interbirth intervals has not been constant throughout the period examined.

Three points are evident in relation to the second birth interval. First, there are fairly clear indications that the second birth interval was longer among marriage cohorts in the earlier part of the century than in the post-war period; the range of the estimates is between 36 and 44 months between about 1910 and the early 1930s compared with a range of 27–43 from 1941 onwards[9] or 27–34 from 1950 onwards – the 1940s are probably best omitted in this comparison as likely to have been influenced by the unusual conditions of the war and its aftermath. Second, there was a decided, if small, decline in the median interval from the early 1950s (a median of 32–34 months) to the mid to late 1960s (27–28 months). Finally, in the 1970s there is a slight recovery to a figure of 30–31 months median and the figure then remains steady in the 1980s at 31–32 months. The interval from second to third birth behaves in a similar way. Pre-war averages are in the range 40–45 months, during the 1950s and 1960s life-table medians lie between 31 and 36 months, with indications of a small decline into the 1960s; in the 1970s there appears to be a slight shift upwards in the life-table median to around 37 months and in the 1980s the figures are fairly steady at between 38 and 40 months. We see, therefore, that the span of childbearing has indeed become more compact and that this is in part due to the contraction of interbirth intervals which, while recovering slightly since the late 1960s, have remained fairly short, particularly the interval from first to second birth. The pace of childbearing, once it has started, appears to be remaining fairly rapid in the 1970s and 1980s, despite the slowing down in the speed of entry into motherhood. We proceed in the next section to consider the interpretation of these findings.

DISCUSSION

The underlying causes of the developments we have witnessed in the post-war period are best considered in relation first to trends in the age at entry into childbearing and then to acceleration in fertility after the first birth.

Up to 1970, entry into motherhood became earlier. The acceleration in first birth rates into the late 1960s is probably best considered as part of a joint process involving decisions about marriage, which also increased in volume and pace during this period. In the 1950s and up to the late 1960s, the first birth interval was very short, with 50 per cent of women having their first child within 16–19 months of marriage (Ní Bhrolcháin, 1987). Survey data for women aged 35–49 in 1976, who had their first birth in the 1950s and 1960s, show that over half of women were either pregnant at marriage or did not use any contraception between the time of marriage and the birth of their first child (Ní Bhrolcháin, 1988). It seems likely, therefore, that decisions about marriage and childbearing were made in combination, since the birth of the first child followed so closely on marriage. Explanations for these phenomena are, of course, still tentative. The prosperity of the post-war period is probably the major candidate explanation for the more frequent and more rapid entry into marriage and family formation through the 1950s and 1960s. With rises in real wages, an early start to marriage and family formation became feasible. A further possibility is that the achievement of low fertility through improved contraceptive methods may have played a role: couples could take the step of marrying and of marrying earlier with the knowledge that family size could be controlled. It was no longer necessary to delay marriage to reduce the time at risk of childbearing. This explanation is consistent with the view outlined below regarding what I have termed 'contraceptive confidence' (Ní Bhrolcháin, 1988).

What led to the turnaround, in 1971[10], in the trend to earlier childbearing is still hard to specify. A key contributory factor has probably been the availability since the early 1960s of the highly effective contraceptive pill, together with the legalisation of abortion in 1967. Together these gave women much greater control over the start of childbearing. As a concomitant, the proportion of first births within marriage that were premaritally conceived dropped sharply during the 1970s, probably resulting in a reduction in marriages, as Bourgeois Pichat (1987) has argued. While in the early 1970s the most likely outcome of a non-marital conception was that the couple married and had a legitimate birth, this is now the least likely outcome. Among those who do marry, efficient contraception has enabled couples to delay births within marriage, as is evident from the substantial increase in the median first birth interval from 19 months in 1970 to 31 months in 1977, with an easing to around 27 months in the 1980s (Hospital Inpatient Enquiry figures, published regularly by the OPCS). Beyond the capacity to control fertility, the availability of efficient contraception has probably been responsible for further developments that reinforce its direct effects (Van de Kaa, 1986; Preston 1987). Near-perfect contraception allows sexual experimentation outside marriage, free of the risk of pregnancy, and has facilitated the growth of informal cohabitation. Together, this provides young people with alternatives to marriage and family life, while nevertheless retaining the advantages formerly confined largely to marriage – sexual experience and companionate co-residence. Furthermore, cohabiters have lower fertility than married couples (Lelièvre, 1993). The pill can therefore be seen as having created a disjunction between marriage, childbearing, sexual relationships and co-residence, of which delayed childbearing is a natural outcome. It has also been suggested that through opening up these new options, the pill has had the effect of reducing the value placed on marriage and family life and that the normative pressure to marry and have children has weakened correspondingly.

Highly efficient contraception is, thus, a likely contributory cause of the trend to delayed parenthood through both a direct route – the technological effect of controlling births – and through indirect means – expanding the range of available and viable life-styles and altering norms and values. Other socioeconomic factors are also likely to have been at work. Since childbearing in the 1970s was still largely within marriage and since marriage is almost always accompanied by the setting up of an independent household, trends in the UK housing market in the 1970s –

the move to higher levels of home ownership together with substantial increases both in interest rates and in house prices – may well have had a delaying effect on entry into parenthood. The secular increases in women's education and in women's labour-force participation are also likely to have influenced the upward trend in the age at first birth. These two are related in that more highly qualified women will have had better earning opportunities and these, in turn, will have made work-force involvement more attractive. Since economic activity and childbearing and rearing are competing activities, motherhood will have been correspondingly postponed. Furthermore, the very substantial trend upward in the participation of married women in the labour force after childbearing is likely to have created an incentive for women, particularly those with qualifications, to gain experience and establish their earning potential before embarking on family formation, so as to facilitate the return to work after childbearing.

This brings us to the second aspect of fertility tempo in which changes have been observed in the post-war period – timing changes subsequent to first birth. Though these have contributed less than has variation in age at first birth to the variability in fertility timing over the period considered, they are nevertheless potentially very significant in giving clues to the underlying processes that may be operating. On the face of it, it seems paradoxical that during a period when contraception has been improving, birth intervals have been getting shorter. Nevertheless, this is what the data show into the late 1960s and I have developed a view, based in part on Keyfitz (1980), suggesting what the mechanism may be. The theory relates to the impact of women's employment on birth timing in conjunction with what I term 'contraceptive confidence'. The theory has several components.

Contraceptive Confidence

In a population with low family-size desires, women who do not have an effective means of contraception available have an incentive to space out their births more widely in order to leave as little time as possible at risk, after the last wanted birth, for a birth of an unwanted order. By contrast, women who have an efficient birth control method at their disposal can afford to space their births more closely because they can be sure that they have the means to stop childbearing as soon as they reach their desired family size. Furthermore, confidence about contraceptive success could have the effect of allowing an earlier start to childbearing for the same reason: there is no need to delay childbearing so as to ensure a smaller family size. Evidence in support of this view includes the longer intervals obtaining among pre-war marriage cohorts, an association between shorter birth interval length and efficiency of contraceptive method used after the end of childbearing, together with clear evidence of shorter birth intervals among better educated women, who would be expected to be most assured in relation to their birth control capabilities (Ní Bhrolcháin, 1988, 1993b). Increasing assurance about contraceptive success could, therefore, be responsible both for the shorter birth intervals prevalent during the post-war period and for the decline in interval length occurring during the 1950s and into the late 1960s.

Nevertheless, contraceptive confidence might be expected to have a more substantial effect if operating in association with other incentives to compress childbearing. I have suggested that the desire for labour-force involvement may provide such an incentive for the following reasons.

'Work Now' and 'Work Later' Effects

Women who wish to combine labour-force involvement and childbearing have a number of options. In order to increase their time in the labour force they can: (i) reduce their fertility in order to hasten the time when they can return to work; (ii) shorten their birth intervals for the same reason; (iii) work during interbirth intervals; or (iv) return to work sooner after the birth of their youngest child. They can, of course, also combine these possibilities in a variety of ways. My contention is that options (ii), (iii) and (iv) have been operating during the post-war period in Britain, it is possible that option (i) has also been in play, particularly more recently, but evidence on this is much harder to establish. I have suggested that there are two ways in which a desire for employment may affect fertility. Women may, on the one hand, wish to engage currently or very soon in the labour market, a desire that will result in the postponement, whether temporary or permanent, of the next birth: this is the 'work now' effect. On the other hand, a woman may plan forward to returning to the labour market in the future, and in doing so may shorten the time to the next birth, perhaps even having a birth that might not otherwise have occurred: this is the 'work later' effect. The two types of work effect may, in other words, have countervailing impacts on fertility: the desire for current work having a delaying and curtailing influence on childbearing and the prospect of future work having an accelerating and positive influence. Further details and evidence are presented in Ní Bhrolcháin (1986a, b). I have argued that during the first post-war phase, to the late 1960s, the 'work later' effect was predominant, since the principal increases in women's labour-force participation during the 1950s and 1960s were occurring among older women, those who had, by the large, completed their childbearing. The result was an acceleration of fertility – in the pace of second and later births and possibly also having an effect in speeding up the pace of the first birth. Beginning in the 1970s, however, the economic activity rates of younger married women began to increase more swiftly and mothers increasingly returned to work before they had completed childbearing. There was, in other words, an increase in the 'work now' effect, with a resulting deceleration in fertility, and especially in the pace of the first birth. Note that while there appears to have been a slight lengthening of the second birth interval during the 1970s, it has remained fairly compact, with a median of around 31 months. Not only has the average duration of the second interval become more compact but its spread has become narrower also[11]. I would argue that the reason for the continuing compactness of childbearing once it has started, and in spite of very substantial deceleration in first birth rates, is the likelihood that there is an interplay between the 'work now' and 'work later' effects, the one having the effect of delaying childbearing and the second keeping the span fairly short and tightly controlled.

In sum, we have seen a move from a pre-war régime in which there was a late start to childbearing and a slower pace once it had begun, to a pattern, most pronounced in the late 1960s, of early into motherhood together with more rapid pace of subsequent births and finally a return to a later age at first birth but with a retention of a fairly compact span of childbearing in the late 1980s. There is now greater diversity among women in the age at first birth but a continuing homogeneity in respect of the time taken to complete family building. Increasing contraceptive capability is likely to have been influential in these developments, as are socioeconomic trends in housing, education, labour-force involvement and changing cultural values, particularly relating to women's roles. However, these factors may not always have operated in the way we might expect, with both contraception and labour-force involvement having possibly played a role both in the acceleration and in the deceleration of fertility seen in the past five decades.

ACKNOWLEDGEMENTS

I thank the Office of Population Censuses and Surveys both for providing unpublished tabulations and for allowing use of the OPCS Longitudinal

Study (LS). My thanks also to members of the LS Support Programme at the Social Statistics Research Unit, City University for assistance with accessing the LS data and to Keith Spicer and Roma Chappell for setting up the GHS data files used in the paper. Material from the General Household Survey, made available through the Office of Population Censuses and Surveys and the ESRC Data Archive, is used by permission of the Controller of HM Stationery Office.

NOTES

1. Austria, Belgium, Denmark, France, Federal Republic of Germany, Italy, Netherlands, Norway, Sweden, Switzerland, and England and Wales.
2. The standardised period mean age at childbearing is $\Sigma af_a/\Sigma f_a$ where f_a is the fertility rate at age a, $a= 15, 49$.
3. That is, by $\sqrt{(\Sigma f_a(a-\overline{a})^2/\Sigma f_a)}$, where $\overline{a}$ is the mean of the age specific fertility schedule, defined in Note 2.
4. That is, $\Sigma af^1_a/\Sigma f^1 a$ where f^1_a is the first birth rate at age a, $a = 15, 49$.
5. The figure for first birth are derived from the 1971 Census, vital registration data (OPCS, 1987b, Table TC2 and updated figures supplied by OPCS) and the 1986–89 General Household Surveys (GHS); those for last birth are derived from the 1971 Census and the 1986–89 GHS. For the GHS cohorts, data are confined to women aged 40+ at survey; the 1971 Census cohorts of 1930 and before are, of course, also aged 40+ at census. Further details are given in Appendix 1.
6. I have argued extensively elsewhere that the period approach is to be preferred to the cohort approach in depicting fertility trends through time that represent fertility as *explanandum* (Ní Bhrolcháin, 1992). However, there may be some quantities of interest that are more easily or naturally represented in cohort mode. The age at the last birth and the span of childbearing seem to be such indicators. Though it might be possible to find a period analogue to these quantities, they are examined here in cohort mode because the data are available in this form.
7. Women with one child are included in the calculation of the median, having a span of zero months. For the most recent GHS cohorts there is the possibility of a downward bias resulting from truncation in the fertility history at ages before 45. Although this bias is no larger than in the case of age at last birth, it is relatively greater and so the GHS figures here are confined to women aged under 40 at last birth to provide a consistent and unbiased series from 1927 to 1948.
8. In particular, closed intervals of this kind may be biased by the structure by duration of the population at risk to have a birth of a particular order; see Ní Bhrolcháin (1993a).
9. Estimates of the second interval going back to 1941 are presented, when nearly all experience to exact age 30 will have been covered. This is somewhat young for the occurrence of the second birth but, as is shown in

Ní Bhrolcháin (1993b), the age at first birth is only weakly associated with the duration of closed second birth interval; the 1940s estimates are, therefore, unlikely to be much affected by age selectivity. They are more likely to be affected by the disruptions of war and its aftermath. Estimates of the third interval are presented only for 1950 onwards.

10.   It is worth noting that while the mean age at childbearing reached its lowest value in the post-war period in 1970, the timing of the first birth evaluated from the median first birth interval had begun to lengthen prior to 1970 – the period median first interval was getting longer from 1965 onwards (Ní Bhrolcháin, 1987, Table 3).

11.   The standard deviation of the interval from first to second birth was 3.49 months in the birth cohort of 1911, 2.61 in the cohort of 1930 and 2.18 among those born in 1945–48 who had reached age 40+ by the time of 1986–89 GHS interview.

REFERENCES

Bloom, D. E. and Trussell, J. (1984), 'What are the determinants of delayed childbearing and permanent childlessness in the United States?', *Demography*, vol. 21, pp. 591–611.

Bourgeois Pichat, J. (1987), 'The unprecedented shortage of births in Europe', in K. Davis, M. S. Bernstam and R. Ricardo-Campbell (eds), *Below-Replacement Fertility in Industrial Societies, Population and Development Review*, vol. 12 (suppl.), pp. 3–25.

Castro Martin, T. (1992), 'Delayed childbearing in contemporary Spain – trends and differentials', *European Journal of Population*, vol. 8, pp. 217–46.

El-Khorazaty, M. N. (1992), 'Time series analysis of three centuries of childbearing and fertility process in Finland', *Yearbook of Population Research in Finland*, vol. 30, pp. 44–67.

Glass, D. and Grebenik, E. (1954), *The Trend and Pattern of Fertility in Great Britain. Papers of the Royal Commission on Population*, vol. 6 (London: HMSO).

Keyfitz, N. (1980), 'Population appearances and demographic reality', *Population and Development Review*, vol. 6, pp. 47–64.

Lelièvre, E. (1993), 'Extra-marital births occurring in cohabiting unions', in M. Ní Bhrolcháin (ed.), *New Perspectives on Fertility in Britain* (London: HMSO).

Murphy, M. and Berrington, A. (1993), 'Constructing period parity progression ratios from household survey data', in M. Ní Bhrolcháin (ed.), *New Perspectives on Fertility in Britain* (London: HMSO).

Ní Bhrolcháin, M. (1985), 'Birth intervals and women's economic activity', *Journal of Biosocial Science*, vol. 17, pp. 31–46.

Ní Bhrolcháin, M. (1986a), 'Women's paid work and the timing of births: longitudinal evidence', *European Journal of Population*, vol. 2, pp. 43–70.

Ní Bhrolcháin, M. (1986b), 'The interpretation and role of work-associated accelerated childbearing in post-war Britain', *European Journal of Population*, vol. 2, pp. 135–54.

Ní Bhrolcháin, M. (1987), 'Period parity progression ratios and birth intervals in England and Wales, 1941–1971: a synthetic life table analysis', *Population Studies*, vol. 41, pp. 103–25.

Ní Bhrolcháin, M. (1988), 'The contraceptive confidence idea: an empirical investigation', *Population Studies*, vol. 42, pp. 205–25.

Ní Bhrolcháin, M. (1992), 'Period paramount? A critique of the cohort approach to fertility', *Population and Development Review*, vol. 18, pp. 599–629.

Ní Bhrolcháin, M. (1993a), 'Describing time trends in fertility using maternity history information', in M. Ní Bhrolcháin (ed.), *New Perspectives on Fertility in Britain* (London: HMSO).

OPCS (1987a), *Birth Statistics. Historical Series* (London: HMSO).

OPCS (1987b), *Period and Cohort Birth Order Statistics* (London: HMSO) Series FM1 no. 14.

OPCS (1992), *Birth Statistics 1991* (London: HMSO).

Preston, S. (1987), 'Changing values and falling birth rates', in K. Davis, M. S. Bernstam and R. Ricardo-Campbell (eds), *Below-Replacement Fertility in Industrial Societies, Population and Development Review*, vol. 12 (Suppl.), pp. 176–95.

Ryder, N. B. (1980), 'Components of temporal variations in American fertility', in R. W. Hiorns (ed.), *Demographic Patterns in Developed Societies* (London: Taylor and Francis).

Sardon, J.-P. (1990), *Cohort Fertility in Member States of the Council of Europe* (Strasbourg: Council of Europe) Population Studies no. 21.

Van de Kaa, D. (1986), 'Europe's second demographic transition', *Population Bulletin*, vol. 42(1).

APPENDIX 1

Cohort Data on Age at First Birth

The median age at first birth from the 1971 Census (1 per cent Longitudinal Study) is based on postmarital births only, while the estimates from vital registration are adjusted to take account of premarital births and GHS data are based on all births. GHS single year cohorts have been smoothed by a three-point moving average because of irregularities arising from smaller numbers than in the census cohorts. The decline observed between the 1971 cohorts and both vital registration and GHS figures will be slightly overstated by these figures, since premarital births are not taken account of in the 1971 Census cohorts. Censorship of the most recent cohort presented (1948), which had reached 40 by the data of interview (tables are confined to women aged 40+ at interview), will have had a negligible effect on the estimate of the median age at first birth both because it is a median, rather than a mean, and because the frequency of first births after age 40 is very small.

The vital registration series is systematically below the 1971 Census series, where they overlap; this is almost certainly because of the adjustment made by OPCS to the registration series to take account of premarital births. Estimates for the cohorts of 1939 onwards from the GHS and vital registration diverge somewhat, with GHS figures being systematically higher by about half a year. The origin of this discrepancy is not clear.

Cohort Data on Age at Last Birth

The data on age at last birth are from two sources: the 1971 Census (LS) maternity histories and the maternity histories from the GHS rounds of 1986–89. Figures presented are confined to those birth cohorts – 1930 and earlier – aged at least 40 at census. The GHS single year cohort estimates have been smoothed, using a three-point moving average; again the estimates are confined to those women in each cohort who had reached age 40 by the time of interview. The latest interview year being 1989–90 and the latest cohort presented being that of 1948. In the case of the age at last birth which is, of course, later than the age at first birth, there is the possibility of some bias in the figures with the later cohorts. However, analysis within the GHS sample shows that this is likely to be very minor. Among women aged 45+ at survey, the overall median age at last birth was 29.75, while the figure when confined to those aged 45+ who had their final birth at aged under 40 is 29.58, a difference of 0.17 years. It seems very unlikely therefore that the 1971 Census figures for the late 1920s cohorts are much affected by bias. This conclusion is reinforced by the close agreement between the 1971 Census estimates for the median age at last birth for the cohort of 1927–1930, who were aged 40–44 at 1971 Census, and those obtained for these same cohorts from the 1986–89 GHS, when they were aged 55+ and thus certainly not truncated in their fertility histories.

APPENDIX 2: BIRTH INTERVAL DATA

The 1946 Family Census birth interval data are discussed in Ní Bhrolcháin (1985). Glass and Grebenik (1954) presented, for women of parities 1–4 separately, the median duration of marriage at successive orders of birth, for marriage cohorts. These have been subtracted, within parity groups, to obtain approximate median durations from first to second and from second to third birth. Finally, for each marriage cohort, a weighted average has been obtained of these approximate parity-specific medians to provide estimates of 'median' intervals, over all parities, for each marriage cohort. The weights are the proportions having each completed family size of the order of the interval and above, within cohort, and it is assumed that the intervals of women with five or more births are the same as those of women with four births, since parity 4 is the highest parity distinguished. These are, of course, very approximate figures and should be considered merely a rough guide to the average interval duration in the pre-war period. Finally, in Figure 12.8 and 12.9 the intervals have been located in the calender year 5 years after the year of marriage of the middle cohort of the cohort group; thus the figure for the marriage cohort of 1900–9 is assigned to 1910, that for the 1910–14 cohort to 1917, and so on.

13 Low Fertility in a Pastoral Population: Constraints or Choice?

Sara Randall

INTRODUCTION

When considering the demography of pastoral populations, a frequently encountered theme is that of slow population growth, usually attributed to low fertility. The hypothesis that pastoralists have to control human numbers in order to keep them in line with animal resources is often invoked and some authors have investigated the mechanisms by which this balance might be achieved. These include migration, economic transformation, high mortality and low fertility (see Randall, in press, for a full review). There is no conclusive evidence which shows that all pastoralist populations have low fertility, but their demographic régime does tend to differ from groups practising different subsistence strategies and fertility appears to rise on sedentarisation and the adoption of agriculture (Henin, 1968, 1969).

How pastoralists achieve this lower fertility is clearly of interest. The mechanisms invoked range from the social control of fertility through restrictive marriage (Spencer, 1973; Randall, 1984; Randall and Winter, 1985; Fulton and Randall, 1988) to biological constraints of sterility (Henin, 1968, 1969; Swift, 1977), seasonality of fecundability and therefore births (Leslie and Fry, 1989) and patterns of breastfeeding and postpartum amenorrhea (Sindiga, 1987; Little, 1989).

Each of these mechanisms demands a different degree of potential decision-making and this leads to the question of whether pastoralists are consciously restraining fertility because of a perception of limited resources or whether they are subject to particular ecological circumstances which constrain reproduction against their will. Ecological constraints such as severe climatic conditions, nutrition or diseases which affect reproduction contrast with direct and conscious reproductive decisions of contraception, abortion and abstinence, or social constraints such as marriage which may include, but are not restricted to, reproductive decisions.

In this paper I want to compare the demographic evidence for constraints on fertility amongst Malian pastoral Kel Tamasheq with the population's own perception of their reproduction and fertility, highlighting conflicts between the theories of the desirability of constraining pastoralists' population growth, and the actual perception of these constraints.

Kel Tamasheq

Kel Tamasheq (Tuareg) are traditionally nomadic herders from the West African Sahel. Those studied here were all nomadic at the time of the surveys, herding sheep, goats, cattle and camels and never cultivating. Two areas were studied, the Inner Niger Delta, where Kel Tamasheq spend the dry season sharing the flood plain with sedentary cultivators, fishers and other pastoralists and agropastoralists. The Gourma is a much more isolated area south of the Niger bend, which, with the exception of communities directly adjacent to the river was a zone entirely dedicated to nomadic pastoralism.

The society is very hierarchical with a complex hereditary class system. Previous analysis of their demography has shown substantial mortality differences by social class both for children (Hill and Randall, 1984) and adults (Randall, 1984), but little variation in fertility. This is surprising given that household structure and economic behaviour was traditionally very different according to social class, with a large proportion of the *iklan* being slaves to some of the richer high status *illelan*[1] (free people). Since the 1950s more and more *iklan* have been liberated and have become economically independent, but in the early 1980s when these surveys were done, social class was still a fairly good indicator of relative wealth with some *iklan* continuing to live in virtual slavery. The lack of variation in fertility justifies the combined analysis of all Kel Tamasheq.

In order to demonstrate where Tamasheq fertility is lower than levels which can be achieved under similar climatic and lack of health infrastructure constraints, they will be compared with the Bambara, a sedentary agricultural population – also from rural Mali – with very high fertility and a marriage pattern which maximises reproduction.

FERTILITY AND MARRIAGE

Indirect estimates of fertility made from data obtained from birth histories estimated the Total Fertility Rate[2] to be 5.3 for Kel Tamasheq from the

Gourma, 5.9 for Kel Tamasheq from the Delta and 8.0 for the Bambara; most of this variation has been explained by the different marriage patterns. Bambara marriage institutions of polygamy and the levirate (compulsory marriage to a childless brother's widow) permit women to remain married for all their reproductive lives and therefore maximise their fertility compared to the Kel Tamasheq where monogamy, substantial spousal age differences combined with high adult mortality and the acceptability of divorce, all conspire to maintain a substantial proportion of women of reproductive age unmarried and therefore not exposed to childbearing. The social and economic aspects of these different marriage patterns have been discussed elsewhere (Randall, 1984; Randall and Winter, 1985; Fulton and Randall, 1988).

But is marriage the sole mechanism for controlling Tamasheq fertility? Such an interpretation contradicts the population's perception of their own fertility.

The Logic of Marriage as a Fertility Restraint

Controls or constraints on fertility operate at three points of women's reproductive careers: starting, spacing and stopping. This is a useful framework for identifying the logical consequences of an expected constraint.

Marriage for Kel Tamasheq is clearly related to reproduction, in that reproduction is perceived as the primary purpose of marriage and this is confirmed by the Koran. This does not prevent marriage from serving other ends too, nor does is prevent people from having expectations (rarely fulfilled) of love and harmony within marriage. In terms of a fertility – resources relationship, marriage as practised by the Kel Tamasheq contains a logical feedback system. A man cannot marry without paying bridewealth in the form of animals and the woman and her family have to provide the tent (essential for married life) and its contents. Theoretically, therefore, without resources there can be no marriage; without marriage, no reproduction. Thus, the requirements of resources to generate Tamasheq marriage would logically have most effect on starting fertility leading to a later age at first marriage than Bambara, a higher proportion of unmarried men and women, and an increase in age at first marriage during lean times and for poorer individuals.[3]

It is clear from Table 13.1 that Tamasheq men marry earlier than Bambara and that Tamasheq women marry on average only marginally later than Bambara women, although the variance in their age at first marriage is much greater.[4] A higher proportion of Kel Tamasheq remain

Table 13.1   Marriage indices for Kel Tamasheq and Bambara

	Men			Women		
Index	Bambara	Gourma Tamasheq	Delta Tamasheq	Bambara	Gourma Tamasheq	Delta Tamasheq
Median age first marriage[*]	28.9	24.7	27.2	17.5	17.9	18.2
Percentage never marrying	0	1.7	1.1	0	4.1	5.5
Marriage rate (years)[†]	7.4	7.4	7.7	2.5	3.7	5.9

[*]Estimated graphically using proportions ever-married and age in single years for women and 5-year age groups for men.
[†]Estimated graphically from single year distribution of proportions married, this index is the number of years for the percentage ever married to increase from 25 to 75 per cent of the population.

unmarried. For women, therefore, age at first marriage, and thus potential age for starting fertility, varies little thus undermining the economic constraints argument.

PERCEPTION OF FERTILITY

Deliberate control of Tamasheq fertility via marriage directly contradicts the population's perception of fertility issues. Discussions of population size, fertility, reproductive issues and health with many Tamasheq women from different social classes and areas reveal a preoccupation with perceived biological constraints on fertility which prevent them from realising their desired potential.

Tamasheq women's perceptions of fertility follow three themes. Firstly they believe that they (particularly the high status women) suffer a disproportionate amount of spontaneous abortions and that a syndrome of repeated miscarriages and no live births is common. Secondly, they think that after a period of no fertility problems, a disproportionate number of women then do not conceive again despite continuing to have sexual relations. The third theme is that many Tamasheq women have very long birth intervals (4 years or more) despite wanting to conceive and having intercourse.

Discussions about fertility never suggested that a woman could have too many children, never indicated that women felt that constrained resources could be relieved if they had less children. The persistent theme was that Kel Tamasheq did not have enough children and that sub-fertility was a problem both for individuals and the population as a whole (which was becoming smaller relative to other Malian populations). The almost unanimous response to descriptions of contraception was that women wanted more children, not less, and they wanted as many children as possible.[5]

This perception of themselves as a population with a slow growth rate compared to other Malian groups reflects reality. Thus, on the one hand, their marriage pattern causes a 30 per cent reduction in fertility compared to the Bambara (Hill, 1985, Table 2.9) and on the other there is a strong perception that fertility is too low at the individual level and that biological constraints are preventing women from achieving their desired potential.

PARITY PROGRESSION RATIOS

In order to examine this basic contradiction further it is necessary to see to what degree Kel Tamasheq women's perception of their fertility problems is borne out by the data.

Parity progression ratios (PPRs) calculate the probability that having reached parity x, a woman will progress onto parity $x + 1$. For younger women, PPRs do not reflect the final probabilities of progressing from one parity to the next but provided that exposure (here taken as marriage) starts at about the same age, the ratios for each cohort are comparable and it will be possible to identify whether one group is producing children faster than the other.

Breastfeeding and Postpartum Amenorrhoea

Significantly different patterns of breastfeeding and postpartum amenorrhoea would generate different PPRs by age because of their effect on birth intervals. The mean duration of breastfeeding (estimated from current status questions) is 21 months for the Gourma Tamasheq, 20 months for the Bambara and 18 months for the Delta Tamasheq. Using this to calculate the effect on reducing fertility gives $C_i = 0.63$[6] for the

Bambara, 0.61 for the Gourma Tamasheq and 0.65 for the Delta Tamasheq. The reported mean duration of postpartum amenorrhoea is 13 months for Bambara, 12 months for Delta Tamasheq and 14 months for Gourma Tamasheq (Hill, 1985, Table 2.8). These patterns are extremely similar, particularly when the two Tamasheq populations are combined.

Marriage Categories

Parity progression ratios have been calculated for three marital status groups and the two ethnic groups, the Bambara and the Kel Tamasheq (Delta and Gourma data have been combined because both are subject to the same economic (pastoralist) and cultural (Tamasheq) constraints). Three different marriage categories were defined:

(1) Women currently married and in their first marriage (maritally stable women).
(2) Women currently married and in their second plus marriage have had some disruption to their marital, and therefore childbearing, history (maritally mobile women).
(3) Women currently widowed or divorced. There are too few Bambara women in this category to calculate the PPRs.

The numbers of women in each grouping by ethnic group (Table 13.2) is itself extremely instructive about the different marriage patterns in each population.

Anticipated Results

Parity progression ratios were calculated for all women and then for each of the marriage categories.

It was expected that for all women, PPRs would be lower at each progression for Kel Tamasheq because of the fertility-reducing effect of their marriage pattern. However, by comparing Bambara and Tamasheq PPRs for the women who are currently married and in their first marriage, this marriage pattern is controlled for. If all fertility differentials are caused by the marriage disruption, there should be no difference between maritally stable Bambara and Tamasheq. If, on the other hand, the biological constraints identified by Tamasheq women are operating, then one would expect Tamasheq PPRs to be lower.

The three different fertility problems outlined would produce different patterns. Repeated miscarriages and no live births would lead to low pp0

Table 13.2   Numbers of Bambara and Tamasheq women by marriage category

Age	Current 1st marriage		Current 2nd+ marriage		widowed/divorced	
	Bambara	Tamasheq	Bambara	Tamasheq	Bambara	Tamasheq
15–19	113	223	0	8	0	24
20–24	357	438	10	44	3	60
25–29	311	279	20	85	1	67
30–34	200	177	39	106	3	60
35–39	161	119	30	89	3	82
40–44	142	74	49	64	8	88
>45*	103	66	50	61	14	93
Total	1387	1376	198	457	32	474

*For Bambara and Delta Tamasheq, women were interviewed up to and including age 50. For Gourma Tamasheq, women were interviewed up to and including age 54.

(pp0 = probability of having a first birth) and thus less women becoming mothers. Secondary sterility would cause a reduction in the middle PPRs with a possible increase for the high parities. Very long birth intervals would cause all the PPRs to be lower.

Current status marriage data and qualitative evidence all show that Bambara women remarry very quickly after divorce or widowhood, compared to Tamasheq women. Thus it was expected that for maritally mobile women, Tamasheq PPRs would be lower than those of the Bambara and for the latter to differ little from those of the maritally stable.

Parity Progression Ratios for All Women

These differ considerably between ethnic groups, as expected (Figure 13.1). A higher proportion of Bambara women become mothers, with only around 3 per cent failing to reproduce. The clustering of pp0 for all Bambara women over thirty reflects the universal and young age at marriage coupled with low levels of primary sterility. Lower pp0 for Kel Tamasheq could reflect either the fact that marriage is not universal and some women marry relatively late, or higher levels of primary sterility.

For all Kel Tamasheq age groups, pp2 (progression from the second to third birth) is less than 0.9 and falls thereafter for each parity. This is in contrast to the Bambara, for whom for each additional 5 years of age up to 45, about 95 per cent of women have another birth, confirming that the

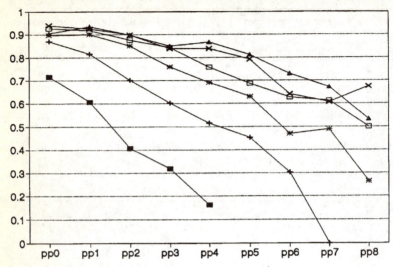

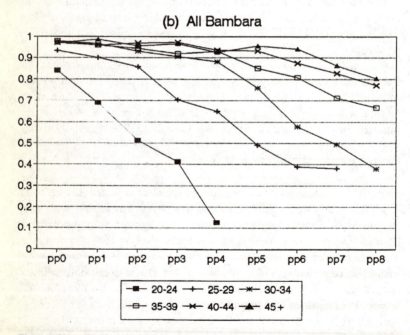

Figure 13.1 Parity progression ratios
(a) All Kel Tamasheq
(b) All Bambara

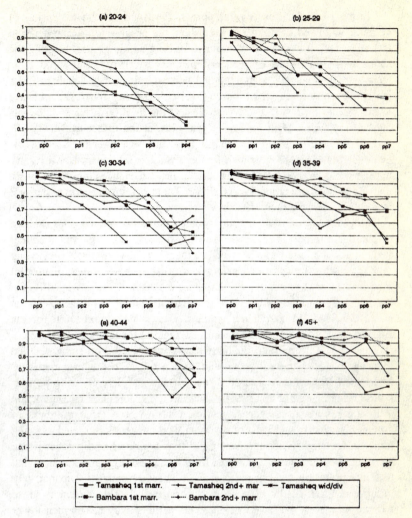

Figure 13.2   Parity progression ratios – by age, marital status and ethnicity

vast majority of women continue to reproduce throughout their potential reproductive period.

Parity Progressions by Marital Status

Contrary to expectations, Figure 13.2 demonstrates that maritally stable women (marked ■) differ by ethnic group, with Bambara PPRs consistently higher than the Tamasheq for each age group.

Figure 13.2 clarifies several points. Firstly, with the exception of younger widowed or divorced Tamasheq, the progression to motherhood is similar for all ever-married women for both ethnic groups, refuting the Tamasheq perception of frequent primary sterility within marriage. However, for maritally stable women, after the first birth, Bambara PPRs are consistently higher than those of Tamasheq women, diverging clearly at the second birth for 20–24-year-olds, at the third birth for 25–29-year-olds, at the fourth birth for 30–34-year-olds, at the fifth birth for 35–39- and 40–44-year-olds and at the sixth birth for those over 45. There is no evidence that Tamasheq women frequently suffer secondary sterility early in their reproductive careers. Thus the fertility differences for continuously married women are composed of slower Tamasheq progression to parity 2 at younger ages and thereafter slower reproduction.

The PPRs for maritally mobile women (marked +) are irregular because of smaller numbers. Progressions to motherhood are high and identical (except for the small numbers of Bambara 20–24-year-olds), suggesting that for both ethnic groups primary sterility is not a cause of marital mobility. In neither population is there a clear pattern of lower PPRs for the maritally mobile compared to the maritally stable, with the exception of 35–39-year-old Tamasheq women. This is not unexpected for the Bambara, where divorce is rare, and who practise the levirate.

For the Kel Tamasheq, qualitative data combined with some detailed marriage histories had suggested that, in general, women whose marriages had ended (for whatever reason) tended to wait relatively long periods before remarrying but that usually they did remarry. Taken in conjunction with the results of the cross-sectional survey, the large numbers of younger, currently widowed or divorced women were interpreted as being likely to remarry and be replaced by different widows or divorcees if one were to repeat the survey. It seems from these parity progression data that this interpretation was, in part, wrong. Currently married, but maritally mobile, women differ little from the maritally stable, whereas those women who were widowed or divorced at the survey have much lower fertility, suggesting much longer periods without being exposed to pregnancy.

Kel Tamasheq Social Classes

An examination of the PPRs by social class should be a clear indicator of whether economic constraints are a major determinant of fertility, since many *iklan* had no possessions at all and their children didn't work for them but for their masters. Economically independent *iklan* were generally poorer than most *illelan*, although there are poor *illelan* too.

From Figure 13.3 it is clear that there is virtually no difference between the PPRs for the two status groups. The only consistent pattern is that , within each age group, pp0 is lower for the *illelan* (see Table 13.3). Comparisons of women in different marriage categories showed no difference at all except for young women currently widowed or divorced (Figure 13.4). Here, *iklan* have much higher progression to motherhood and from first to second birth.

DISCUSSION

Two points emerge from this analysis of the parity progression ratios. Firstly, marriage instability has little effect on the fertility of Tamasheq women who remarry again, whereas those who were widowed or divorced at the time of the survey appear to be primarily long-term widows/divorcees rather than women between marriages.

Tamasheq women's perception of their fertility problems is partly borne out by the data – which shows general subfecundity manifested in slower reproduction than the Bambara, despite similar durations of breastfeeding and postpartum amenorrhoea. The idea that Tamasheq women have higher levels of primary sterility is not valid for the population as a whole, but does apply to *illelan* women.[7]

Decision-Making

Having established that fertility differences between Tamasheq and Bambara occur both because of the marriage pattern and within marriage categories, what evidence is there for reproductive decision-making versus biological constraints?

Tamasheq marriage incorporates a web of social, economic and reproductive decisions which are impossible to disentangle. Despite being theoretically premised on resource availability, in reality Tamasheq marriage occurs under all economic circumstances. Unlike Bambara, Tamasheq society can accommodate the unmarried, widowed and divorced. It has to, because monogamy, coupled with a young age structure, spousal age differences and high mortality, generates substantial numbers of currently unmarried women who are unmarriageable because of a shortage of men. Whether monogamy has evolved as a response to

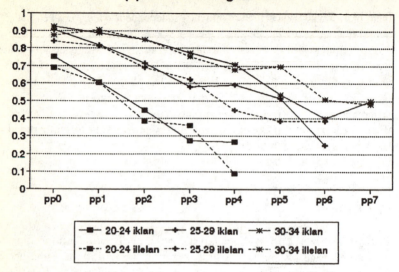

(a) all women aged 20-34

Legend:
- —■— 20-24 iklan
- —+— 25-29 iklan
- —✳— 30-34 iklan
- --■-- 20-24 illelan
- --+-- 25-29 illelan
- --✳-- 30-34 illelan

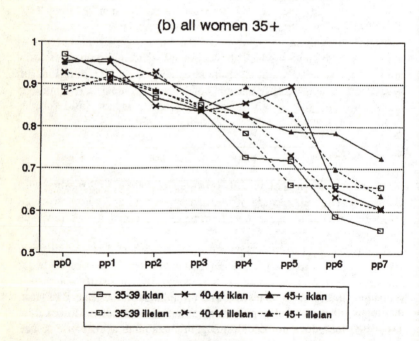

(b) all women 35+

Legend:
- —□— 35-39 iklan
- —✕— 40-44 iklan
- —▲— 45+ iklan
- --□-- 35-39 illelan
- --✕-- 40-44 illelan
- --▲-- 45+ illelan

Figure 13.3   Tamasheq social class PPRs
(a) All women aged 20–34
(b) All women 35+

Table 13.3   Progression to motherhood (pp0): *iklan* and *illelan*

	all women		widow/divorced	
Age	iklan	illelan	iklan	illelan
20–24	0.75	0.69	0.87	0.67
25–29	0.91	0.84	0.91	0.85
30–34	0.92	0.88	0.96	0.88
35–39	0.97	0.89	0.97	0.93
40–44	0.95	0.93	1.00	0.98
> 45	0.95	0.88	1.00	0.90

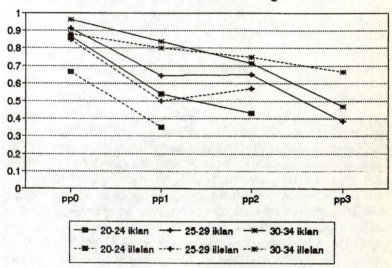

Figure 13.4   PPRs for *iklan* and *illelan*, widowed and divorced women aged 20–34

economic constraints is unanswerable, but unlikely in the face of the fact that many other pastoral populations are not monogamous. Moreover, a Tamasheq man does not decide to be monogamous in response to his economic situation: monogamy is a social constraint on behaviour, it is normal and does not involve a decision. On the other hand, slower Tamasheq childbearing within marriage is potentially a consequence of fertility decisions which can be examined through considering the proximate determinants of fertility.

Although women recognise the link between breastfeeding and postpartum amenorrhoea, and are aware of individual variation, they breastfeed to feed their children and to keep their children alive. Breastfeeding is not a fertility decision, it is behaviour with fertility consequences. Different levels of infant mortality affect the birth intervals through curtailed breastfeeding and postpartum amenorrhoea. Direct measures of the mortality rate over the first year of life, $_1q_0$, were 0.205 for the Bambara, and 0.125 and 0.155 for the Delta and Gourma Tamasheq, respectively, with most of the difference concentrated in the neonatal period. The mean duration of breastfeeding[8] controls for these differences and thus cannot explain the slower Tamasheq reproduction.

The remaining proximate determinants which involve decisions are coital frequency, abstinence, contraception and abortion. There is no evidence that, at the time of the surveys, Kel Tamasheq women used any form of modern contraception or abortion within marriage.

Data on coital frequency are not available, although it is possible to speculate on possible reasons for variation. For monogamous Tamasheq women, coital frequency is likely to be higher than for polygamous Bambara, although one might expect that a nomadic pastoral economy would engender substantial spousal separations. However, Kel Tamasheq tend to migrate in family groups with husbands and wives together, and thus minimise separation. Long-term labour migration of men to Ivory Coast and other urban areas became more common during the 1980s, particularly for the *iklan*, but at the time of the surveys it was still relatively infrequent for married men. Seasonal migration for younger Bambara men with absences of 4 or 5 months was very common. The overall effect of spousal separation is probably similar for the two populations. Under no circumstances can these separations be considered reproductive decisions – they are economic decisions with possible reproductive consequences.

Abstinence is slightly different. Only extremely long postpartum abstinence exceeding the period of postpartum amenorrhoea would generate the fertility differentials observed in the maritally stable women. Bambara women also practice postpartum abstinence, and 'in rural Mali, postpartum sex taboos are still widespread and strongly followed' (Dettwyler, 1987, p. 641). From the Demographic and Health Survey (DHS) (République du Mali, 1989, Table 2.6), mean duration of postpartum abstinence was 6.1 months whereas for 'other ethnic groups' which includes Kel Tamasheq, it was 5.2 months.

In these surveys, no quantitative data were collected on abstinence, but qualitative data indicate that some Tamasheq women abstain from intercourse for several months after birth. A very few say they abstain until the child is weaned at around age 2 years. The majority believe abstinence to be a good thing because it ensures that women do not get pregnant too soon and have to wean the breastfeeding child;[9] but for most women, abstinence of more than 2 months depends on the will of the husband and is very difficult:

'because when you get a man and a woman in the same tent, who love each other, they can't avoid having sex'

Thus monogamy, which for the population leads to lower fertility, for individual woman could generate shorter birth intervals because in the absence of co-wives, postpartum astinence is harder to achieve.

Abstinence is therefore a conscious fertility-related decision for a few Kel Tamasheq, but is motivated by a desire to maximise child survival rather than control family size. The DHS data suggest that mean durations of Tamasheq abstinence are unlikely to be longer than those of the Bambara and thus cannot explain the slower fertility.

Women are very concerned about '*tessumde*' (Randall, 1993), a gynaecological disease that they believe inhibits conception and can cause sterility. This disease has a well-defined set of symptoms: low back pain, various foul vaginal discharges, in severe cases developing into severe back pain, amenorrhoea and abdominal pain combined with fever. Advanced *tessumde* causes sterility although it is recognised that sterility can occur without *tessumde*. There are female specialist healers who treat only this disease; all women are aware of it and fear it, and take preventative measures to avoid developing it; if they experience preliminary symptoms, they take them very seriously. If, as seems likely, this disease indicates a relatively high incidence of gynaecological infections which impair fecundity, and sexually transmitted disease such as gonorrhea and chlamydia, these could explain the longer birth intervals and lower parity progression ratios at each age.[10]

Such biological constraints on reproduction are hardly evidence of fertility decisions. If defined as a conscious decision to behave in a certain way in order to modify ultimate family size, such decisions are effectively absent in this population. On the other hand, there is much behaviour adhering to cultural norms, engendering substantial fertility consequences. The marriage pattern, dominated by monogamy, reduces fertility by over 30 per cent, yet no Kel Tamasheq perceives marriage as an important constraint because unmarried women are just a fact of life. Nobody expects them to conceive (in fact there would be horror if they did) and their role in restricting population growth goes largely unperceived because, for Kel Tamasheq, they are not abnormal. Why monogamy should prevail in Kel Tamasheq society is a puzzle which cannot be answered here. As Muslims, the men are permitted to have more than one wife, and occasionally men do attempt polygamy; the wives always object.

The apparent lack of awareness of the effect of marriage on fertility contrasts strongly with their preoccupation with biological constraints. Tamasheq women spend much time bemoaning their low fertility and their fertility problems. Yet behaviour which could enable them to have higher fertility is available, religiously sanctioned and practised by most of the surrounding populations – namely, polygamy. Eradication of gynaecological disease might increase the fertility of women within marriage but it would have a far smaller effect than that of changing their whole marriage pattern. This combination and the essential contradiction of the two types of fertility constraint, clearly demonstrate that low Tamasheq fertility is not the consequence of cumulative individual decisions to consciously control fertility, whether from economic or any other rationale.

ACKNOWLEDGEMENTS

The Bambara and Kel Tamasheq demographic surveys were funded by ILCA as part of their socio-economic research programme. The qualitative Tamasheq research was funded by the Population Council, under their Determinants of Fertility Programme. Further Tamasheq work on health behaviour was part of a study commissioned by Norwegian Church Aid and undertaken by the author, NCA personnel and researchers from the Institut National de Recherche en Santé Publique, Bamako, Mali.

NOTES

1. All free (never enslaved) Tamasheq are *illelan*, but this term encompasses many groups ranging from the few powerful warrior nobles, religious groups, rich and poor vassals, low status *illelan*, to blacksmiths. Numbers are insufficient to do analysis by each social class separately.
2. Total Fertility Rate is the sum of the age-specific fertility rates at a given point in time. Therefore it is the number of children a woman would have if she were subject to these age-specific rates over her reproductive lifetime.

3. During the drought years of the 1970s, instead of marriages being postponed because less cattle were available, the quality of the bridewealth diminished. Whereas for older women bridewealth animals had been young milk cows, for the younger ones bridewealth was composed largely of less valuable calves. In cases of destitution one would expect postponement of marriage. But in a largely Tamasheq refugee camp in Mauritania in 1992, there was a boom in marriages partly (or possibly entirely) because people believed that newly married couples would be given precedence in future UNHCR tent distributions. The religious elders had suspended the requirements of bridewealth for marriage.

4. For Tamasheq men, age at first marriage does differ by social class. Noble men (who make up about half the *illelan* population) have a median age at first marriage of about 29.3 compared to 26 for *iklan*, and 23 and 23.5 for low status *illelan* and *iklan* respectively in the Gourma.

5. With three exceptions – two women who expressed an interest in contraception for themselves both framed their case as a desire to avoid the risk and pain of labour and birth, not in terms of wanting to control ultimate family size. A third woman, whilst describing Tamasheq premarital heavy petting, said that girls would be interested in a contraception so they could have premarital intercourse which at the moment was impossible because of the risk of pregnancy.

6. C_i is an index which quantifies the effect of breastfeeding in reducing fertility from the potential maximal biological total fertility of 15.2 (estimated from the Hutterites). In a population with no breastfeeding, $C_i = 1$.

7. Since high status *illelan* women do not acknowledge *iklan* to be Kel Tamasheq because they are black and therefore are potentially, if not actually, slaves, their statements that 'we (Kel Tamasheq women) suffer from high levels of primary sterility' is an accurate reflection of their perception of the women who are in their social universe.

8. Breastfeeding duration was estimated from current status data. If neonatal mortality has been declining, which seems to be the case for the Bambara, the current mean breastfeeding duration could slightly overestimate the duration in the past.

9. The milk of a pregnant woman is believed to cause a breastfeeding child to fall ill.

10. The incidence of these diseases might be high in relation to the Bambara, but not nearly as high as has been observed in some African populations (Retel-Laurentin, 1979)

REFERENCES

Dettwyler, K. A. (1987), 'Breastfeeding and weaning in Mali: cultural context and hard data', *Social Science and Medicine*, vol. 24, pp. 633–44.

Fulton, D. J. R. and Randall, S. C. (1988), 'Households, women's roles and prestige as factors determining nuptiality and fertility differentials in Mali', in J. C. Caldwell, A. G. Hill and V. J. Hull (eds), *Micro-Approaches to Demographic Research* (London: KPI).

Henin, R. A. (1968), 'Fertility Differences in the Sudan', *Population Studies*, vol. 22, 147–64.

Henin, R. A. (1969), 'The patterns and causes of fertility differences in the Sudan', *Population Studies*, vol. 23, pp. 171–98.

Hill, A. G. (1985), 'The recent demographic surveys in Mali and their main findings', in A. G. Hill (ed.), *Population, Health and Nutrition in the Sahel* (London: KPI).

Hill, A. G. and Randall, S. C. (1984), 'Différences géographiques et sociales dans la mortalité infantile et juvénile au Mali', *Population*, vol. 6, pp. 921–46.

Leslie, P. and Fry, P. (1989), 'Extreme seasonality of births among Nomadic Turkana Pastoralists', *American Journal of Physical Anthropology*, vol. 79, pp. 108–15.

Little, M. A. (1989), 'Human biology of African pastoralists', *Yearbook of Physical Anthropology*, vol. 32, pp. 215–47.

Randall, S. C. (1984), 'The demography of three Sahelian populations', unpublished PhD thesis, University of London.

Randall, S. C. (1993), 'Blood is hotter than water: popular use of hot and cold in kel Tamasheq illness management', *Social Science and Medicine*, vol. 36, pp. 673–81.

Randall, S. C. (in press), 'Are pastoralists demographically different from sedentary agriculturalists?', in B. Zabe and J. Clarke (eds), *Population and Environment Change* (Liege: ORDINA for IUSSP).

Randall, S. C. and Winter, M. M. (1985), 'The reluctant spouse and the illegitimate slave', in A. G. Hill (ed.), *Population, Health and Nutrition in the Sahel* (London: KPI).

République du Mali (1989), *Enquête Démographique au Mali*, 1987 (Bamako, Mali: CERPOD; Columbia, Maryland: IRD/Westinghouse).

Retel-Laurentin, A. (179), *Causes de l'infécondité dans la Volta Noire* (Paris: PUF) INED Travaux et Documents, Cahier no. 87.

Sindiga, I. (1987), 'Fertility control and population growth among Maasai', *Human Ecology*, vol. 15, pp. 53–66.

Spencer, P. (1973), *Nomads in Alliance* (Oxford: Oxford University Press).

Swift, J. J. (1977), 'Sahelian pastoralists: underdevelopment, desertification and famine', *Annual Review of Anthropology*, 6, pp. 457–78.

Index

Liberia, 214
life-cycle servants, 195–6
life expectancy, 207, 212, 218
　e₀, average life-expectation at birth,
　　181, 183, 199
　see also mortality
life-history theory, 34–5
local resource competition, 151, 154–6
　see also parental investment
luteal function, 29
luteal phase, 10, 52, 65–6
　length, 23
　deficiency, 29
luteal progesterone levels, 27, 30
　mid-luteal progesterone levels: in
　　Boston women, 27, 30;
　　comparisons across populations,
　　32
luteinising hormone (LH), 14–15, 57
　concentration, 57–8
　pulsatile release of, 14–17
　pulse frequency: in men, 57; in
　　rhesus monkeys, 56–7
　secretion of, 65
　surge: constancy with age, 31
　synthesis of, 15

Manchester, England, 232–45
Malaysia, 211–12
Mali, 214, 280–94
malnourished women, *see* nutrition
Malthus, Thomas, 180
　'principle of population', 24
marriage, 162, 249, 270–1
　see also age at first marriage
marriage patterns, 181–3, 190–8, 280–4
　European marriage patterns, 192–3
　in Kel Tamasheq, 281–9, 294
　'Mediterranean', 193
　north-west European, 193–201
marital fertility, 29, 162, 182–4
　non-marital fertility rates, 183
　see also fertility rates
mate choice, *see* sexual selection
maternal health services, 220–1, 223
maternal investment strategy, 34–5
maternal reproductive effort, 34, 43
maternal surrogacy, 234–5, 237, 241,
　242

see also new reproductive
　technologies
maternal survival, 34–5
mating effort, 138
mechanisms, 2–4
　proximate, 2–3, 5
　ultimate, 2–3
　see also functional explanations
menarcheal age, 66, 138
menopause, 34
menstruation, 9, 10, 13, 35
　menstrual cycles, 14, 52–66: in
　　athletes, 59; in Bostonian
　　women, 44; in Lese, 39; in
　　Zairean women, 44
N-methyl-d-aspartate (NMDA), 55
Mexico, 208, 210, 220
microeconomic theories of fertility,
　160, 170, 174–5
　see also economic theory of fertility
　　reduction; fertility decline
migration, 279, 292
milk
　composition, 66
　production, 11–13: inhibition of, 12;
　　initiation of (lactogenesis), 12;
　　reduced rate of, 13; speed of
　　delivery, 13
　see also breastfeeding; lactation
miscarriages, 282, 284
modernisation, 160, 168
monogamy, 282, 289, 291, 292–4
monastic institutions, 192
monkeys, *see* rhesus macaques
monoecious sexual reproduction, 79
morganatic unions, 192
Morocco, 215, 220
Moroccan women, *see* menarcheal age
mortality
　adult mortality, 191, 197, 280–1,
　　289
　child mortality, 217–21, 280, 293
　decline in, 160, 198–9
　infant mortality, 147–50, 152–5, 218,
　　292
　mortality rates, 126, 128, 180–1,
　　182–3, 187, 207, 214
motivations, 5
　material, 76–7, 90–4

Dark Eagle – Book II

The Hidden

by

K. M. Ashman

Also by K. M. Ashman

The Exploratores
Dark Eagle
The Hidden
Veteranus
Scarab
The Wraith
Silures
Panthera

Seeds of Empire
Seeds of Empire
Rise of the Eagle
Fields of Glory

The Brotherhood
Templar Steel
Templar Stone
Templar Blood
Templar Fury
Templar Glory
Templar Legacy
Templar Loyalty

The India Summers Mysteries
The Vestal Conspiracies
The Treasures of Suleiman
The Mummies of the Reich
The Tomb Builders

combination of espionage, reconnaissance, and covert operations, these groups ensured that the Roman legions were always one step ahead of their enemies, securing the empire's dominance in a volatile and ever-expanding world.

Definition – 'Occultum'

That which is hidden, concealed or secret.

Pertaining to things that are not visible or known to the senses.

Hidden aspects of knowledge or matters that are deliberately kept out of the public eye or away from general understanding.

Prologue

Germania – 42 AD

The autumn wind rustled through the dense canopy of the forest as Talorcan moved slowly along the narrow paths of the Germanic forest. The world around him was alive with the sounds of nature, the rustling of leaves, the distant call of a raven, the whisper of the wind. Yet, Talorcan's mind was elsewhere, lost in the still raw memories of battles fought and comrades lost.

It had been nearly two years since he had led the Occultum deep into the lands of the Cherusci and although the group had ultimately failed in its mission, the experience had changed him forever and he knew he could never again live a normal life within the constraints of village life.

With his part played, he had returned to his homeland, a hunter once more along the banks of the lower Rhine and deep into the Cherusci forests. His services as a scout were still valued by the local Roman forces, but he preferred the quiet of the forest to the bustle of the camps.

The annual horse fair was one of the few events that drew him out of his solitude. Held between the tribes that dwelled between the Rhine and Weser rivers, it was a time for trade, for strengthening alliances, and for the display of the finest horses in the region. As he approached, the air buzzed with the shouts of traders, the laughter of old friends reunited, and the high-pitched whinnies of restless horses.

Hundreds of animals milled about in makeshift pens, their powerful bodies jostling for space. The pungent scent of sweat, leather, and the earthy smell of horse manure mingled with the smoky aroma of roasting meat from nearby fires, a familiar and overwhelming assault on his senses. Talorcan

inhaled deeply. The mingled scents were like a key unlocking a flood of memories, days spent haggling over horseflesh, nights filled with stories and songs around the fire.

But those days were long gone, replaced by the solitary existence he had now chosen for himself. The noise and energy of the fair clashed with the quiet solitude he had come to cherish in the forest, and he felt a pang of discomfort at the intrusion.

Yet, beneath the unease, there was something else, a flicker

of excitement, a sense of belonging that he could not entirely dismiss. This was where he had grown up, among these tribes, these people. The voices that called out to him in greeting, the faces that turned to nod in recognition, were those of old friends, men he had known since childhood. Their presence was both a comfort and a reminder of all that he had left behind.

Talorcan continued, his senses assaulted on all sides. He noticed the slight differences in accents, the subtle shifts in dialects, all indicators of the diverse tribes gathered here. Each man wore the marks of his people, from the fur-cloaked men of the north to the lean, sun-browned riders from the southern plains. The colours of their cloaks, the cut of their tunics, even the way they braided their hair, spoke volumes about their origins and status. It was a fabulous, yet terrifying gathering of the best Germania could offer, and like it or not, he was part of it.

The fair was a spectacle of life and energy, a celebration of the horse, and a rare gathering of tribes from across the region, but gradually the mood shifted, and a silence rolled through the camp like an incoming tide as a column of mounted men emerged from the forest's edge, their presence commanding immediate attention.

There was no need for announcement or conversation for every man present knew who they were the instant they saw them, the men from beyond the Elbe River.
the place where no man went if they harboured ambitions to die of old age. They were the Vandals, and they had never attended the fair before.

There were about a dozen of them in total, mounted on horses as black as midnight, their hooves digging into the earth. Each warrior was an imposing sight, clad in black leather armour that gleamed in the waning light, practical, well-worn, and designed for battle rather than display. Strapped across their backs were lethal-looking broadswords with handles worn smooth from prolonged use while each had an unstrung bow resting across their saddles, able to be strung within a heartbeat should they needed.

Their unexpected arrival was enough to send a shiver through the crowd. The Vandals wore their jet-black hair long, cascading past their shoulders in thick, well-groomed waves.

Their faces were stern, their eyes sharp and piercing, the faces of men who had seen many battles and emerged victorious.

Each man exuded an air of confidence, a haughty pride in
their own strength and skill that bordered on arrogance. Yet it was a confidence that had been earned, not given.

The tribesmen watched in stunned silence as the Vandals rode into the camp, leading a magnificent procession of over a hundred horses behind them. These were no ordinary beasts; they were powerful, muscular creatures, bred for war and endurance. Their glossy coats shimmered in the sunlight, their eyes intelligent and alert, as if they too sensed the significance of the moment. The horses moved with a grace and power that left even the most seasoned traders and horsemen awestruck.

The Vandals, for their part, appeared completely at ease. They moved with a purposeful calm, their heads held high, their expressions unreadable. There was no need for them to assert their dominance; their very presence did that for them. As they dismounted, the leather of their armour creaked softly, a sound barely heard over the heavy silence that had fallen over the camp.One of the Vandals stepped forward, his gaze sweeping across the assembled tribesmen. His eyes were cold, calculating, as if weighing each man and finding them wanting.

'My name is Wulfstan of the Hargundi,' he called, his voice guttural and cruel. 'Who is in command here?'

No one moved. The aura of the Vandals was too intense, their reputation too well-known. Yet the allure of the magnificent horses was too strong to resist for long and eventually one man stepped forward.

'My name is Gutterad,' he said, 'and there is no overall leader. We trade as equals, all arguments put aside for the duration of the fair and each man swears to keep their weapons sheathed on pain of death. Your presence is welcome, Wulfstan but we ask that you observe the agreement that has stood for generations.'

'Our blades will not taste blood this day,' answered the warrior. 'We have horses to trade and invite inspection.'

Gutterad nodded and turned slowly to look at the rest of the gathering, each man still staring in silence.

'Well,' he said, eventually, 'anyone interested?'

Slowly, cautiously, some of the braver traders began to

inch forward, their greed and curiosity overcoming their fear. The Vandals watched them approach with detached interest, their hands never straying far from the hilts of their weapons.

The tension in the air was thick enough to cut with a blade
and Talorcan, standing at the edge of the crowd, could feel it as keenly as anyone. His hunter's instincts told him that the Vandals had brought more than just horses to this fair, they had brought a challenge, an unspoken test of wills and though the horses were magnificent, it was the men who had brought them that held the true power.

Talorcan moved through the herd with the practised ease of a man who had spent his life around horses. The animals milled about, their powerful bodies shifting and snorting as traders pressed close to inspect them.

Each horse was a marvel, sleek, muscular, and exuding raw power.

Their coats shone like polished obsidian in the waning light, and their eyes gleamed with intelligence and spirit.

Talorcan ran his hand along the flank of one horse, feeling the strength of the muscles beneath the skin. The horse turned its head slightly, as if acknowledging his touch, and Talorcan couldn't help but admire the animal's fine breeding.

Around him, other traders moved with a mix of caution and excitement. They inspected hooves, checked teeth, and whispered amongst themselves about the quality of the stock. The Vandals had brought some of the finest horses any of them had ever seen, and the potential profits from acquiring even one of these beasts were immense. Yet Talorcan knew, as did most of the other traders, that the price would be steep, far beyond what most could afford.

He lingered for a moment longer, running his fingers through the horse's mane, his mind working quickly. There was no way he could afford to buy one of these animals outright.

His years as a hunter and occasional scout for the Roman forces had not made him wealthy, and the prices the Vandals would demand would be astronomical. But the allure of the horses was too strong, pulling at something deep within him. He needed to find a way to obtain one, and the more he thought about it, the more a dangerous idea began to take shape.

It was risky, perhaps even foolish, but Talorcan had lived on the edge of danger for years and knew how to seize an opportunity when it presented itself. This was one such moment and the horses were worth the risk. Decision made, he released a slow breath, stepped away from the magnificent animal, and began to weave
his way back through the traders, his mind set on the course he had
chosen.

The noise and bustle of the fair faded into the background as he focused on the Vandals, now gathered in a circle a short distance away. Each warrior crouched low to the ground as they ate, tearing at chunks of meat pulled from their travel bags.

They spoke in low voices, their language harsh and guttural, with the occasional bark of laughter punctuating the quiet murmur of their conversation. They seemed entirely at ease, unconcerned by the eyes upon them, confident in their own power and the fear they inspired.

Talorcan approached cautiously and as he neared the group, the closest Vandal looked up, his eyes narrowing as he took in the sight of the approaching stranger. The laughter ceased, and the other warriors turned their attention to him, their expressions hardening.

Talorcan stopped a few paces from the circle, meeting the gaze of the warrior who had first noticed him. This was no place for weakness or hesitation. He squared his shoulders, offering a slight nod of respect.

'Greetings, Wulfstan,' he began, 'I am Talorcan, a hunter from the lands of the Belgae. I have seen the horses you brought. They are magnificent.'

The Vandals regarded him with silent scrutiny, their expressions unreadable. After a tense moment, the warrior who had first noticed him spoke.

'They are not for the likes of you, hunter,' he said, his voice laced with a hint of contempt. 'These beasts are for men of wealth and power, not for those who scrape a living eating bear shit from the woods.'

Talorcan kept his expression neutral, though his heart pounded in his chest.

'I have no wealth,' he admitted, 'but I offer something else. Something worth a dozen such horses.'

Wulfstan's eyes narrowed further, a flicker of interest sparking behind the disdain.

'What item of wealth can buy such a beast? A king's crown perhaps?' He laughed at his own joke, an unnatural sound coming from a man so used to dealing death.

Talorcan swallowed hard and reached beneath his cloak,
a movement that caused the laughter to stop as suddenly as it started,
and all the Vandals reached for the hilts of their swords.

Talorcan slowed his movements before withdrawing a sheathed knife and stepped forward, offering it to the Vandal leader. The Vandals exchanged glances, and Talorcan could see they were intrigued, though wary.

'You offer me a knife?' said Wulfstan, his voice laced with disdain. 'A mere blade for one of my horses? I should kill you now for the insult.'

'It is no ordinary knife,' said Talorcan quickly. 'Examine the blade and you will see for yourself.'

Wulfstan stared at Talorcan before taking the knife from his hands and withdrawing it slowly from its sheath. As the blade appeared, he looked down, his eyes narrowing at the reflected sunlight that filtered down through the trees above. The midnight-black hilt, deeply engraved with ancient Celtic markings, was expertly inlaid with gold and silver, the work of a great craftsman but it was the graceful, wavy watermark, seemingly flowing in the steel itself that told him exactly what it was, and he looked up with new-found respect.

'Damascus Steel,' he said. 'How did this come into your possession?'

'I was given it for services rendered,' answered Talorcan truthfully. 'It is a beautiful thing but belongs in the hands of a man such as you.'

'Why not yours?'

'I am a hunter and the knives I use are for separating flesh from bones. I only unsheathe this blade it to stare at it in awe. I swore I would never get rid of it but if it were to buy me one of those horses, it is yours to keep.'

The vandal leader grunted and passed it around the rest of his men before standing up.

'These knives are much sought after,' he said, 'and are hard to find.' He paused and stared at Talorcan, his gaze seemingly piercing deep into the hunter's soul.

'I accept,' he said, suddenly, 'choose you horse,' and, without another word, turned away to re-join his men.

The following morning, as he approached the paddock, Talorcan couldn't help but feel a surge of excitement. He had sold his own horse for a fair price and now he was about to walk away with one of the finest animals he had ever seen. The thought of the powerful black stallion as his own filled him with a mix of pride and anticipation.

The paddock was quiet, most of the traders and fairgoers still rousing themselves from the previous night's revelry. The horses milled about, their breath steaming in the cool morning air, and the scent of damp earth and fresh hay mingled in the air. Talorcan's gaze quickly found the horse he had purchased, sleek, strong, with muscles rippling beneath its glossy coat. The animal was a marvel, and even as Talorcan approached, the horse lifted its head, ears pricking forward as if recognising its new master.

He took a moment to savour the sight, then moving with purpose, he slid the saddle onto the horse's back, adjusting it with care, his hands moving with practised efficiency. The stallion shifted slightly beneath him, but remained calm, a testament to its fine breeding.

Just as he was about to tighten the girth, something caught his eye. Across the paddock, near the edge of the forest, a figure was moving among the horses. At first, Talorcan thought nothing of it, just another slave tending to the Vandals' prized stock.

But as he looked closer, a strange feeling crept over

him, a prickling at the back of his neck. The man was tall, rugged, his clothes plain and worn, and his movements were deliberate yet gentle, expertly working with the animal to achieve the results he required. Talorcan watched, impressed with the man's affinity with the horses, a kinship that seemed as natural as breathing. It was a rare skill, one that was delivered by the gods at birth, and not one that could be learned in a thousand years. Moments later, the man turned towards him and just as Talorcan was about to voice his approval, his breath caught in his throat and for a moment, the world seemed to stop.

The slave froze, his brush suspended in mid-air as his eyes locked onto Talorcan's. There was a flicker of recognition, a flash of shock that passed between them like a lightning strike. Talorcan's heart pounded in his chest, the saddle forgotten as he stared at the man across the paddock.

The slave's face was gaunt, his hair longer and more unkempt than Talorcan remembered, but there was no mistaking him. It was Brennus. The same Brennus who had fought alongside
him in the Occultum, and they had all believed had perished in the
raging waters of the Rhine over a year ago. But here he was, alive, and serving as a slave to the Vandals.

For what felt like an eternity, the two men stared at each other, both too stunned to move or speak. Talorcan's mind raced, a thousand questions flooding his thoughts. How had Brennus survived? How had he ended up here, amongst the Vandals? But before he could voice even a single word, Brennus's expression changed from shock to something far more desperate. He shook his head violently, his eyes pleading, warning Talorcan not to act, not to call out. Then, without another moment's hesitation, Brennus turned sharply and ducked into the forest, disappearing into the shadows.

Talorcan's hands trembled as he tightened the saddle's girth, his mind reeling. He felt as if the ground had shifted beneath him, the solid world he had known suddenly filled with uncertainties. Brennus was alive, but he was a fugitive, a ghost hiding among enemies. And Talorcan had no idea what it all meant, or what he should do next.

As he mounted the stallion, the thrill of acquiring the magnificent beast was overshadowed by the shock of what he had just witnessed. His thoughts were consumed by the image of Brennus's gaunt face, the fear in his eyes. The world had become a far more dangerous place than it had been just moments before, and Talorcan knew, with a sinking feeling, that he could not leave this discovery alone.

Chapter One

Gallia

Seneca and Marcus rode side by side up the ancient road that meandered its way through the surrounding hills like a sleepy winding snake. The landscape of southern Gallia stretched out before them, rolling hills dotted with olive groves and the distant outline of a village nestled against the horizon.

Seneca adjusted his grip on the reins, his eyes narrowing as he considered the challenges that lay ahead. The road behind them led back to Rome, where Seneca had just concluded another clandestine meeting with their handler, Senator Lepidus, one of Emperor's newest advisers, and their heads were filled with the many demands he had just placed upon them. The fact that they were now a recognised arm of Rome's military strength was both comforting and frustrating at the same time. The former, as they now had access to far more resources and the latter, because there was now far more interference from above, often by those who had no idea how they worked.

The new Emperor, Claudius, was eager to secure his legacy, and the planned invasion was to be his boldest stroke. But Claudius was not a man of the legions, and his understanding of what it took to form something like the Occultum was limited at best and his demands to form similar units was proving difficult to achieve, not least because of the high standards Seneca had himself imposed.

The two men rode on, their minds on the training camp they had established in southern Gallia. It had been running for months now, drawing men from across the Empire, veterans of the legions, local fighters, and even a few mercenaries from distant lands. But the reality of the standards expected was far harsher than most had anticipated.

'We've had to send more men home than we've kept,' said Marcus eventually as the conversation turned to the training camp. 'Some were too aggressive, always looking for a fight, but with no control. Others, no fire at all, as if they thought this would be a long parade through the provinces. Then there are those who can't keep up, who collapse after a few days' march with a full pack.'

Seneca nodded, understanding the difficulty of the task before them. The Occultum was more than just a fighting force; it was a brotherhood, a unit where each man had to be as strong mentally as he was physically.

It wasn't enough to be a good soldier, they had to be able to operate in the shadows, to take on tasks that seemed impossible, and to endure hardships that would break most men.

'We can't afford weakness,' said Seneca. 'Not with what's coming. Britannia will be like nothing the Empire has faced before. The tribes are fierce, united under powerful leaders and the land itself is a challenge, wild, untamed, with weather that can turn on you in an instant. It will be up to us to pave the way the best we can with what we have. We have a few who show promise, who are willing to learn and have the raw potential. But they need more training, more testing. We're still weeding out the weak ones, the ones who don't have the stomach for what lies ahead.'

'And what about the invasion?' asked Marcus. 'Do you think we'll be ready?'

'We have to be. Claudius won't delay the invasion, not for anything. We'll be the first to set foot on Britannia's soil, and the legions will rely on anything we can give them in the way of intelligence.'

The weight of their mission settled heavily over them, the enormity of what they were preparing for not lost on either man.

They had seen what war could do, how it could tear men apart and reshape the world around them. But this was something new, something far more challenging than anything they had faced before.
The two men rode on in silence, the road stretching out before them, leading them back to the camp where the next wave of recruits awaited.

Two days later, they rode into the small camp hidden away in the depths of the forest, and as they approached, they could hear the sharp clang of metal on metal, punctuated by grunts and the occasional shout. They dismounted, leaving their horses tied to a branch and made their way towards the Occultum's makeshift training ground.

In the clearing, a group of men stood in a rough circle, their eyes fixed on the figures within. Sica and Falco were at the
heart of it, each facing off against a different opponent, their movements a blur of precision and power. The recruits they faced
were of varying skill, some were fast and aggressive, others cautious and calculating, but all were clearly exhausted, their bodies slick with sweat, their breaths coming in ragged gasps.

Sica was the smaller of the two, but his speed was unmatched, and he danced around his opponent, his movements calculated, every strike designed to test his opponent's defences. The recruit was skilled, his reactions sharp, but it was clear he was being pushed to his limits. Sica's eyes were cold, his expression impassive as he pressed the attack, never allowing the man a moment's rest.

Across the circle, Falco was a stark contrast. The ex-gladiator's massive frame towered over his opponent, a burly recruit with the look of a seasoned fighter. Falco moved with brute strength, his strikes powerful and relentless, each blow designed to overpower rather than outmanoeuvre. The recruit fought back valiantly, but it was clear he was struggling, his arms trembling under the force of Falco's assaults. Falco's face was split into a fierce grin, his enjoyment of the fight obvious, though there was no malice in his eyes, just the ruthless joy of a warrior testing his mettle.

Seneca and Marcus stood at the edge of the circle, observing in silence, taking in every detail.

Finally, Sica ended his bout with a lightning-fast move, disarming his opponent with a flick of his wrist and sending the man sprawling to the ground. He stepped back, his blade held loosely at his side, as if the fight had been nothing more than a casual exercise. Falco ended his own bout moments later, his opponent collapsing to one knee, gasping for breath, his own knife clattering to the ground.

Raven, who had been watching from a distance, stepped forward, his gaze lingering on each man, weighing their worth. When he finally spoke, his voice was soft but carried an edge that cut through the silence.

'You've fought well,' he said, 'but not all of you are fit to continue.' He pointed to two men, a young recruit with a fresh wound on his arm, and an older veteran who had been slower to react, his movements sluggish from exhaustion. 'You two, you're done.'

The two men's faces fell, but they didn't protest. With

heads bowed, they stepped back, knowing they had tried their best but had failed to reach the standard. The following morning, they would ride out and return to whence they came. The remaining recruits, still catching their breath, looked on with a mix of relief and dread,

hoping they had done enough to avoid the same fate. For a brief moment, it seemed the trials were over, and the recruits allowed themselves to relax, some even daring to think that they had earned a rest. But their hope was short-lived as Falco reappeared from behind a stack of supplies.

His broad grin was back in place, but this time, it carried a hint of sadistic pleasure as he hefted four heavy sarcinae, the large, bulky packs that every Roman legionary knew too well, and dropped them with a loud thud at the feet of the remaining recruits.

The men stared at the packs in stunned disbelief, their exhaustion giving way to despair.

'What's the matter?' he asked, 'did you think you were done for the day? Pick them up. You've got a three-day march ahead of you.'

The recruits, though nearly spent, scrambled to obey. They lifted the heavy packs, the strain evident on their faces as they shouldered the weight. The sarcinae were loaded with supplies and Falco watched them with a critical eye, ensuring that no one tried to lighten their load.

Raven stepped forward once more, his gaze settling on each man in turn.

'You will follow me,' he said, as if the coming march was nothing more than a stroll through the countryside. 'Anyone who falls behind, anyone who cannot keep up, well, let's just say that there will be no more second chances. Make your packs as comfortable as you can and make sure you fill your water bottles.'

The recruits exchanged nervous glances but said nothing. They knew that this was another test, perhaps the hardest yet, and as Raven shouldered his own pack, the group began to move, the recruits struggling to find their footing under the crushing weight of the sarcinae.

Seneca and Marcus watched them go. The training was harsh, but it had to be. The men who survived these trials would be the ones standing with them on the shores of Britannia, and, as
Raven led the recruits into the forests, Falco and Sica turned to join Seneca and Marcus.

'Do you think any of them will make it?' Marcus asked.

'Possibly,' Falco replied. 'This lot are actually quite good, but time will tell.'

Seneca grunted in agreement.

'Better they break now than in the field. Get some rest and meet back here at dusk.'

'As you wish,' said Falco and both he and Sica headed for the nearby stream to wash the sweat and blood from their skin.

Later that evening, Seneca gathered his men around the wooden table inside his tent. Falco leaned back in a chair, his muscular arms crossed over his broad chest, while Sica stood with his back to the doorway, his dark eyes focused and unreadable. Marcus stood alongside him, straight-backed, his expression as stern as ever, a centurion's discipline etched into every line of his face.

Seneca remained silent for a moment, allowing the weight of the upcoming task to settle over the room. His hand rested on the edge of the table, fingers tracing the coastline of

Britannia marked on the worn parchment. Seneca began, looking each man in the eye.

'The invasion of Britannia is imminent,' he said, 'and the emperor has tasked us with a critical role. We are to infiltrate the tribes along the eastern coastline, those closest to the landing sites where the legions will strike first.' He paused, letting the gravity of the assignment sink in. 'Our primary objective is to support those tribes who are already allies, and disrupt any preparations being made by those that are not. Also, if we can sway their leaders, convince them that aligning with us is in their best interest, we may be able to secure the coastline without a prolonged conflict. It will give the legions the foothold they need to push further inland.'

Falco grunted, a wry smile tugging at the corner of his mouth.

'And if they don't see things our way?'

Seneca's gaze hardened.

'If persuasion fails, we have orders to remove any troublesome leaders. Quietly if possible with someone more amenable to Roman interests.'

'And how are we to do that?'

'By making life difficult for any incumbent who refuses to see things from our point of view. We disrupt their way of life, putting pressure on their people, their families. Let them feel the pang of hunger, fear the assassin's blade in the depths of the night.

If we do it correctly, the Celts will see their leaders as weak and unable to protect them and possibly be forced into replacing them.

I have no doubt that this will be difficult, and we may not succeed

in doing as much as we would like, but even the smallest of

changes could help save hundreds of Roman lives. Make no mistake, if the tribes of Britannia unite as one, then our legions could be driven back into the sea.'

'The Britons will likely be wary of outsiders,' said Marcus, 'especially in these uncertain times. How do we plan to gain their trust?'

'I envisage that Raven will be influential in all this,' replied Seneca, 'he knows the country well, the people, their ways and traditions. We will be guided by him in all things but first, we have to get there. We cannot go as traders as they are fully aware Rome is knocking at their door, and we will look too suspicious. We will be taken over by some fishermen under the cover of darkness and once there, we will go to ground until Raven comes up with a strategy to go where we have to go.'

'And where is that exactly?' asked Marcus.

'Final details will be given to us closer to the time,' said Seneca, 'but until then, we have to prepare for all eventualities.'

'We will be ready,' said Falco.

Sica nodded once, a subtle acknowledgment of the darker tasks that might lie ahead.

'One more thing,' Seneca continued. 'Do not fall into the trap of thinking these are just barbarians with little intelligence or ability in warfare. They are a typical Celtic people, fiercely proud of their culture and heritage, and willing to die to defend it, but we have one advantage, the ongoing conflict between many of their tribes.'

'It is that conflict that we have to feed and nurture if our legions are to make even the slightest of gains in that strange land.'

'What about Decimus,' asked Falco, 'why is he not here?'

'I will brief him when he returns,' said Seneca, 'but he

will not be joining us in Britannia. Instead, he will be returning to Aquae Tarbellicae before we leave. There is no doubt that his skills are unsurpassed and to have him help train the recruits was truly a gift from the gods, but he has served his time and will stay behind in the Hornless Bull as our link back to Rome.'

'Doesn't he have a woman in Aquae Tarbellicae?' asked Marcus.

'He does, but as I have said, he had seen more blood and
conflict than all of us combined and deserves his retirement.'

'Stationed in the best ale house in the empire with a woman to keep his bed warm,' mused Falco. 'It sounds like the perfect posting to me.'

'One day that could be you,' said Sica from behind Falco's chair, 'if you live that long of course.'

'Don't you worry about me,' replied Falco, 'I'll be here long after we've pissed on your grave my friend.'

'Just make sure you have drunk a whole jug of ale first,' said Sica.

'Oh, I will,' said Falco. 'One of many.'

'I know there will be many questions,' said Seneca, interrupting the banter, 'and we will work out the answers over the coming weeks but until we get the orders to go, stay on top of these recruits. The more men we take, the easier it will be. Now go and get some sleep.'

Out in the forests, Decimus made his way silently through the darkness. A group of recruits followed in silence, their faces taut with concentration. Decimus moved with the quiet confidence of one who had spent a lifetime in the wilderness, his steps barely making a sound as he navigated the uneven terrain. He was a grizzled veteran, his hair silvered by age, but his eyes were sharp and his movements precise. Decades as an exploratore had honed his instincts to a razor's edge, and there was little in the forest that could escape his notice.

The recruits, all of whom had survived the brutal initial training so far, knew they were in for another test tonight. They had been hardened by endless drills and trials that had broken weaker men. But tonight was different. Tonight was about the art of surviving and thriving in the wilderness, the very essence of what it meant to be a member of the Occultum.

As they reached a small clearing, Decimus raised a hand, signalling for the men to stop. The recruits halted immediately; their breaths held as they waited for him to speak. Decimus turned to face them, his gaze sweeping over the group, measuring each man in the dim light.

'The night is your ally,' he began, 'it conceals you, it protects you, if you know how to use it. But it can also betray you if you are careless. The first lesson you must learn is not just how to move
through the darkness, but how to become a part of it.'

He crouched low, picking up a handful of dirt and letting it sift through his fingers.

'This land is your friend, but only if you respect it. Every leaf, every branch, every shadow can give away your position if you are not careful. To survive out here, to be truly unseen, you must learn to become a part of the landscape. Not merely to hide within it, but to disappear into it.'

The recruits watched him intently, their eyes wide in the moonlight, absorbing every word. Decimus gestured for them to crouch as well, and they followed suit, forming a rough circle around him.

'Concealment isn't just about hiding,' Decimus continued. 'It's about blending in. The best cover is the one that doesn't look like cover at all. You need to learn to read the land, to understand where you can hide and where you can't. And when you can't hide, you must learn to move silently and quickly, like a shadow passing through the night.' He reached out and pointed to a thick patch of undergrowth nearby.

'There,' he said. 'What do you see?'

'Cover,' replied one of the men, 'a place to hide.'

'You would think so,' said Decimus, 'but if it's obvious to you then it is just as obvious to others. You need to hide in plain sight, amongst the hollows and thickets that do not stand out. Pursuers will pass by the hidden and seek the obvious. To become one with your surroundings. To let the night hide you, to protect you. It is a skill in itself but will come with practice'

He motioned for the men to follow him again, leading them deeper into the forest. As they walked, he continued to teach, pointing out subtle signs that could give away their presence, a broken twig, a disturbed patch of dirt, the faintest rustle of leaves. Every detail mattered, and Decimus made sure they understood just how unforgiving the wilderness could be.

Eventually, they came to a narrow stream, its waters glinting faintly in the moonlight. Decimus crouched beside it, dipping his fingers into the cool water.

'Living off the land isn't just about food,' he said, 'though that's part of it, it's about understanding your environment, where to set traps, how to avoid leaving a trail that can be followed.' He stood up, motioning towards the trees.

'In a few days, Raven will teach you how to hunt, how to track game and set snares. But you must also learn how to move through the land without leaving a trace, how to navigate by the stars, and how to read the wind and the weather. These skills are what will keep you alive when the enemy is hunting you. They are what will allow you to strike from the shadows and disappear before your foe even knows you were there.'

The recruits nodded, the weight of his words sinking in. This was more than just another training exercise. This was about survival, about mastering the skills that would make them true members of the Occultum.

'Tonight,' Decimus said, his eyes narrowing, 'you will practice what I've shown you. We will separate into pairs, and each of you will have a task. But remember this: the night has eyes, and it sees everything. Use it to your advantage, or it will betray you.'

The recruits paired off; their earlier exhaustion forgotten in the face of this new challenge. As they moved off into the shadows, Decimus watched them go, his experienced eyes tracking their progress. He knew that some would excel, while others would struggle, but that was the point. This was where the true strength of the Occultum would be forged, in the darkness, in the silence, where only the fittest would survive.

Chapter Two

Isla Mona – Britannia

King Cunobeline, leader of the Catuvellauni, headed the procession of powerful warrior kings walking through the sacred forests of Isla Mona. The island was a place of power, a revered sanctuary where the land itself seemed to breathe with the spirits of the old gods. Here, amidst the towering trees and the whispers of the wind, the druids made their home, guarding the ancient wisdom passed down through countless generations.

As the tribal leaders approached the heart of the island, the air grew thick with the scent of burning herbs. The druids, robed in flowing garments of earth-toned wool, moved amongst them, their faces hidden beneath hoods adorned with mistletoe and oak leaves. Their voices, low and melodic, chanted in a language older than the stones beneath their feet, invoking the spirits of the land, the beasts, and the waters. The words, though incomprehensible to many, resonated with a deep, primal power that sent shivers down the spines of all who heard.

In the centre of the grove, an ancient stone circle stood against the ravages of time, its weathered surfaces etched with symbols that spoke of forgotten gods and the mysteries of the earth. A great fire burned within the circle, its flames dancing and crackling as the druids circled it, their chants rising and falling like the rhythm of the sea. The tribal leaders, warriors and chieftains from every corner of Britannia, watched in solemn reverence, their faces lit by the fire's glow.

One of the druids, an elder with a long white beard and eyes as piercing as a hawk, stepped forward, raising his arms to the sky. The others fell silent, their chants fading into the night as the elder's voice rang out clear and strong.

'Spirits of the earth, we call upon you,' he intoned, his voice carrying through the grove like a wind through the trees. 'Ancient ones, hear our plea. We honour you, guardians of the land, of the forests, and the rivers. We give thanks for your bounty, for the strength you lend us in our time of need.'

As his words echoed into the night, the other druids began to chant again, this time in a lower, more resonant tone, in time with distant drumbeats throbbing from the heart of the nearby forests.

The fire flared brighter, casting eerie shadows on the trees, and it seemed as though the very earth trembled in response to their call. The elder continued, his voice filled with a deep, unwavering faith.

'We ask for your blessing, great spirits. Bless our warriors with courage, our leaders with wisdom, and our people with peace. As we stand upon this sacred ground, let us be as one with the land, as it has been since the time before time.'

The chants grew louder, a powerful chorus that seemed to resonate with the heartbeat of the island itself. The leaders stood in silent awe, each feeling the connection deep within their souls. It was as if the spirits themselves had gathered to witness this moment, to lend their strength to the tribes that had long called this land home. Finally, the chants reached a crescendo, then slowly began to fade, leaving only the crackling of the fire and the rustle of leaves in the breeze.

The leaders remained still, absorbing the energy that still lingered in the air, before slowly making their way from the grove. The ceremony had been spiritual, and stirred the blood of all who witnessed it, united in their bond to the land, their gods and each other. But it was only a prelude to what would come next. First, a feast to celebrate the great coming together, but once done, the important reason why so many had travelled so many leagues to be there, to discuss a war that was threatening the shores of the place they had called home since time began. They emerged into a clearing, filled with rough tables filled with food and jugs of mead, and as the night wore on, the leaders of Britannia's tribes found themselves bound together not just by blood and land, but by the ancient rituals that had connected them to the gods and to each other since time immemorial.

All too soon, it came to an end and as a line of maidens carried away the remnants of the feast, all eyes turned to towards the huge slab of stone that lay to one end of the clearing. A silence fell upon them and as they watched, the man they had come so far to hear emerged from the forest and climbed up to stand upon the monolith. It was Mordred, the leader of the warrior caste who defended the druids of Isla Mona.

His entrance was deliberately dramatic, his every movement calculated to seize the focus of the gathered chieftains. His face was painted in intricate designs of woad, the deep blue patterns spiralling and intersecting in ways that seemed almost
otherworldly, giving him the look of a spirit from another realm. A cloak made from the feathers of a thousand starlings hung from his shoulders, the black and iridescent plumage catching the firelight in flashes of green and purple. The cloak rustled as he moved, mimicking the sound of wings in flight, adding an unearthly quality to his already imposing figure.
Atop his head sat a crown of antlers, curled and twisted like the branches of an ancient oak, a living embodiment of the old

gods.

Mordred stood still for a moment, allowing the weight of his presence to settle over the men before him. He needed no words to command their attention, his appearance alone was enough to hold them in thrall.

'Men of Britannia,' he began, 'you who are the keepers of this land, the protectors of its people, hear me now, for the spirits of our ancestors speak through me.' He raised his staff high, the skull at its tip gleaming white against the dark sky.

'This land is ancient, as are we, bound to it by blood and by spirit. The gods who dwell in the forests, the rivers, and the mountains look upon you tonight, watching, waiting. They pursue enlightenment, to know if you are still worthy of their favour, if you will stand against those who would seek to conquer what is ours.'

The men listened, captivated, as Mordred continued, his words weaving a spell over them.

'There are forces beyond these shores who would seek to take from us what is sacred. They come with iron and fire, with lies of peace and promises of gold. But we know the truth, these invaders come not as friends, but as conquerors, as destroyers of all we hold dear.'

His voice rose, his eyes blazing with fervour.

'We are the children of this land, born of its soil, and its power flows through our veins. The spirits of the earth, the beasts, and the water, these are our allies, our kin. They will fight with us, but only if we are true to them, if we are true to ourselves.'

Mordred paused, allowing his words to sink in. The men before him, warriors all, felt the gravity of his words, the truth in them resonating deep within their hearts.

'Tonight,' he continued, 'we have feasted as brothers,

as one people. But tomorrow, we must prepare for war. We must be as the beasts of the forest, cunning, relentless, and united. The invaders will show no mercy, and we must be prepared to do the same.'

Many of the chieftains nodded. The time for feasting was over, the time for battle approaching, and they knew that they would need all the strength and unity they could muster to face the storm that was coming.

Mordred stepped down from the plinth, the feathers of his cloak rustling like the wings of a thousand birds taking flight. He moved amongst them, slowly, each step considered as he regaled them with the stories older than the surrounding trees, of great gods, and greater warriors. Of battles and pain and slaughter, and of sacrifice and hope and fear, and above all, the one combining factor that tied them all together as one. The love of the people for the land.

As he passed, many bowed their heads in respect, acknowledging the druid's authority and the power of the gods he represented. The druid had spoken, and now many of the warrior kings of Britannia knew what they had to do. They would stand together, as one people, as one land, and they would fight with the strength of the gods at their side. The invaders would come, but they would find not a land to conquer, but a land ready to defend itself with the fury of the earth itself. Many were united for the first time in generations, each determined to fight to the last man to deny the oncoming storm, and as the night dragged inexorably to the first rays of the morning sun, most had sworn oaths of blood to protect their lands to the death. Most…but not all.

The morning sun hid behind a mountain of rolling clouds as Cunobeline and his men rode away from Isla Mona, the echoes of the druid's words still fresh in their minds.

Cunobeline rode at the front, his posture straight and regal despite the weight on his shoulders. His sons, Caratacus and Togodumnus flanked him on either side, their expressions as stormy as the sky above them. The silence between them was thick with tension, each man lost in his own thoughts, the camaraderie of the previous night now replaced by a palpable strain.

'So,' said Togodumnus, 'are you going to explain, or will we share this silence all the way back to Camulodunum?'

'I am a king,' replied Cunobeline, 'and have no need to explain myself to any man.'

'You are also our father,' said Togodumnus, 'and as your sons, we deserve to know why you embarrassed us last night.'

'Your embarrassment was not caused by me,' replied the old man, his gaze fixed on the path ahead, 'look instead to the theatrics of the madman dressed as a bird. It was he who boiled the blood with his clever words and so-called ancient incarnations, and it was he that demanded the pledges that will only end with the death of us all.'

Togodumnus looked across in horror. To refuse to commit to a united effort was one thing but to insult the holiest man in Britannia risked invoking the wrath of the gods themselves.

'Listen to you,' he hissed. 'Your words could not be more traitorous if they were uttered by Claudius himself. Mordred spoke true, this is our land, and the Romans have no right to it. We should be uniting the tribes, not dividing them with talk of peace. Why do you keep proclaiming the flight of the dove instead of the attack of the hawk?'

Cunobeline kept his gaze forward. He had anticipated

this confrontation, knowing his youngest son's fiery temperament and deep sense of duty to their people. But he also knew the harsh realities that Togodumnus refused to see.

'Because, my son,' he said eventually, 'we cannot win a war against Rome. The might of their legions is beyond anything we have ever faced. To unite the tribes in open defiance would be to send our young men to their deaths needlessly.'

Togodumnus bristled, his hands tightening on the reins.

'So, are we to do nothing? To stand by and let them take our land, our people? Where is the honour in that?'

'Honour,' Cunobeline said quietly, 'is not always found in battle. Sometimes, it is found in the decisions we make to protect our people, even if those decisions are difficult to bear.'

Caratacus glanced between his father and Togodumnus, his brow furrowed in thought. He had always been more pragmatic than his brother, but even he found it difficult to accept the path his father was suggesting.

'But how can we trust them?' he said, 'the Romans are conquerors. They come with words of peace but carry weapons of war. Their intentions are clear, they want to rule, not to trade.'

'I do not trust them, Caratacus,' replied his father, 'not fully. But I know that to fight them head-on would court destruction.

We are not so different from the tribes they have already conquered, the Gauls, the Iberians, the Germanic tribes. We cannot
win by force, but we can win by wisdom, by using their own desires against them.'

Togodumnus shook his head, his frustration boiling

over.

'Do you think they will leave us in peace if we bow to them? They will take and take until there is nothing left, until we are nothing more than another starving province in their gluttonous empire.'

Cunobeline turned to face his son, his expression stern, yet softened by the love he bore for him.

'If we resist, they will bring more of their legions, countless men trained in the ways of war and the land will be soaked with the blood of our people. But if we can give them what they want, trade, alliances, stability, then perhaps we can avoid that fate. Perhaps one day they will leave with their soldiers, and all that will remain are merchants and politicians. Men we can negotiate with, men who will not burn our fields and slaughter our warriors.'

Togodumnus' eyes blazed with anger, but also with the pain of seeing his father's resolve.

'And if you are wrong? If they take advantage of our weakness?'

'Then we will fight,' said Cunobeline, 'when the time is right, and on our terms. But until then, we must be patient. We must be clever. A king does not lead his people into a battle he knows they cannot win. He leads them to a future where they can thrive, even if that future is not the one he would choose for himself.'

The silence returned, and, as they rode on, the mist began to lift, revealing the rugged beauty of Britannia, a land worth fighting for, worth protecting. Cunobeline looked out over the hills, his heart aching with the knowledge of the difficult road ahead. He prayed that his choice would bring peace, that it would spare his people the horrors of war.

But deep down, he knew that nothing was certain, that

the future was as unpredictable as the winds that blew across these ancient lands.

Chapter Three

Aquae Tarbellicae

Weeks later, in a small house in a back street of Aquae Tarbellicae, Decimus lay in his bed, his arm draped protectively over Julia, sleeping peacefully in the crook of his shoulder. His role as instructor to the new members of the Occultum was complete, the gruelling sessions of training and endless drills finally at an end. He had honed the raw recruits into a formidable unit, ready for the challenges that awaited them in Britannia. But now, with the largest military campaign in recent memory on the horizon, his part in the Occultum's mission was changing. Lepidus had sent him to Aquae Tarbellicae, to serve as a link between the Occultum and Rome. It was an essential yet quieter role, one that would keep him out of the direct line of danger and a far cry from the life he had known as a veteranus of countless campaigns.

Since returning to Julia, he had finally allowed himself to relax, to let down his guard, something he hadn't done in years. His eyes closed again as he drifted in and out of sleep, still struggling to adjust to the comfort of a soft mattress and clean sheets, but as he finally drifted off, a gentle knock forced his eyes open, his instincts honed from years of danger bringing him immediately to full alertness.

He slipped out of bed as quietly as he could, careful not to wake Julia, grabbed a tunic from the chair, throwing it over his broad shoulders, and moved swiftly to the door. He hesitated for a moment before opening it, his hand hovering over the hilt of the dagger he always kept within reach. When he finally opened the door, he found a young man standing there, panting slightly as though he had run a fair distance.

'What is it?' Decimus asked.

'My lord, Hannibal needs to see you, now.'

Decimus's frown deepened. The last thing he wanted was to be dragged out of bed in the middle of the night for some tavern keeper's message, even if that tavern keeper was as trusted and resourceful as Marcia.

'Could this not have waited until morning?'

The messenger shook his head.

'No, my lord. She said it was urgent, something about the Occultum, whatever that is.'

At the mention of the Occultum, Decimus's irritation was replaced by a cold knot of concern. Hannibal wasn't one to overstate a situation and if she had sent for him at this hour, it meant something had happened. He glanced back over his shoulder towards the bedroom where Julia still slept, the idea of leaving her so suddenly gnawing at him. But duty called, and he knew better than to ignore it.

'Tell her I'll be there as soon as I can,' he said and closed the door gently before turning back to the house.

Julia was awake now, sitting up in bed, her eyes bleary with sleep.

'What is it?' she asked softly, sensing the change in his mood.

Decimus walked over to her, sitting on the edge of the bed and brushing a hand through her hair.

'It's nothing,' he said, 'just some business that can't wait.'

'At this hour?
' she replied, 'what could be so urgent?'

He sighed, squeezing her hand gently.

'I don't know, but I can't ignore it. I won't be long.'

Julia searched his face for a moment, then nodded,

trusting his judgment as she always did.

'Be careful,' she whispered.

He stood and quickly pulled on his boots and cloak, fastening the simple clasp at his shoulder. He could feel Julia's eyes on him as he moved to the door, her silent concern hanging in the air between them. As he reached the door, he looked back at her, offering a small, reassuring smile.

'Get some rest, Julia. I'll be back before you know it.' With one last look, he turned and stepped out into the cool night air, closing the door quietly behind him.

The messenger was gone, and he hurried through the quiet streets of Aquae Tarbellicae, alone, with only the occasional flicker of light from a window or the distant bark of a dog breaking the stillness. Decimus's mind raced with possibilities. What could be so urgent that Hannibal would send for him in the dead of night? The Occultum was supposed to be laying low, preparing for the coming campaign. Had something gone wrong already? Had their plans been discovered?

When he finally reached the Hornless Bull, the familiar,
sturdy structure that had played such an important role in the lives of so many like him, he paused and stared up at the unassuming façade. The tavern was a place like no other, a den of inequity, a place or robbers and thugs, of traders and generals. A building where the rich and poor could mingle without discrimination and you could buy anything from a woman to a weapon, and everything in-between.

Now, in the hours before dawn, it stood quiet and unassuming, yet a place where unexpected news usually meant something bad had happened. With a deep sigh, he pushed open the door and walked inside. The main room of the tavern was dimly lit by a few sputtering lamps, the tables and chairs deserted at this hour. Marcia was waiting near the back, standing behind the bar with a look of grim determination on her face. She looked up as Decimus entered, her eyes narrowing slightly as she sized him up.

'Took you long enough,' she said.

'It's the middle of the night, Marcia,' Decimus replied, 'this had better be good.'

'I'm not sure if it is good or bad,' replied Marcia.

'Spit it out, Marcia, I have a warm bed to go back to.'

Marcia glanced around the empty tavern one more time before stepping closer, her voice lowering to just above a whisper.

'It's Brennus,' she began, her tone serious. 'Talorcan saw him.'

'You mean his body?' asked Decimus, his brow creasing as he tried to absorb the information.

'No, Decimus, he is alive and apparently, a slave of the Vandals.'

Decimus felt a jolt of shock, quickly followed by a surge of scepticism.

'That's impossible,' he said, shaking his head. 'Brennus is dead. Falco saw him go under in the Rhine. No one could have survived that, especially not in those waters.'

'That may be true,' she said, 'and yet Talorcan saw him just a month ago in Cherusci territory. He recognised him immediately, and from the look on Brennus's face, he recognised Talorcan too but went out of his way to avoid talking to him.'

Decimus frowned, a sense of unease creeping over him.

'Why would he do that?'

'I have no idea.'

'Where is Talorcan now?'

'He went back to Germania a few days ago to see if he can find out anything more but he came all this way to let us know first.'

'I don't understand,' said Decimus, 'if Brennus is alive and he recognised Talorcan, why wouldn't he reach out? What reason would he have to stay silent?'

Marcia sighed, running a hand through her hair, the tension in her shoulders betraying her own doubts.

'All I know is Talorcan said Brennus went out of his way to avoid him and when he tried to approach, Brennus just shook his head and disappeared into the forest. Talorcan had no choice but to leave without speaking to him. Think about it. If Brennus is alive and working for the Vandals, they must be holding something over him, something so terrible that he doesn't dare reach out, even to one of us. We need to come up with a plan to get him out.'

Decimus shook his head.

'No,' he said, 'If there's one thing we can't afford right now, it's a distraction or a mistake. We need to think this through carefully.'

'Then we must tell Seneca,' she said, a hint of urgency in her voice. 'He's the only one who can decide how we handle this. You have to go back.'

'You know I can't.'

'Why not.'

'Because Seneca and the rest need me here. The invasion is imminent, and it could be disastrous if the Occultum lost the one link they have with Rome. Believe me, in different circumstances I would go in an instant, but my priority has to be the support of those about to put their lives on the line, not on someone who may already be lost.'

'Seneca needs to know.' replied Marcia. 'He was a close friend of Brennus. What if I go in your stead?'

Decimus stared at the woman. He had known her for years and she could certainly look after herself, but to ride across country alone was something different altogether. Marcia leaned forward, her face drawn but determined.

'Decimus, let me take the message to Seneca,' she said, breaking the silence. 'I can be on the road by dawn, and you can stay here to coordinate whatever it is you have to do.'

He shook his head, his instincts rebelling against the idea.

'No. It's too dangerous.'

'It's a risk I'm willing to take,' Marcia interrupted, 'Brennus was also a good friend of mine and besides, I will take some of my workers to protect me. I'll travel light and avoid any unnecessary stops.'

Decimus stared at her, his mind wrestling with the logic of her words. She was right, of course. He couldn't afford to leave Aquae Tarbellicae with no contact back to Rome, not when there was so much at stake, but a comrade needed help, and they never left a man behind. She met his gaze evenly, her eyes unwavering.

'I'm not asking, Decimus,' she continued. 'I'm telling you what needs to be done. You know I can do this. Let me help.'

'So be it,' he said eventually. 'You take the message to Seneca. But you need to be careful, if anything happens to you out there...'

'I'll be fine,' Marcia assured him. 'I've travelled these roads before, and I know how to avoid trouble. You don't need to worry about me.'

Decimus nodded.

'I know, he said, 'but don't do anything stupid, and tell Seneca… tell him I'm trusting him to make the right call.'

'I will,' she promised. She reached out and clasped his arm briefly, a gesture of reassurance and solidarity. Then, without another word, she turned and left the tavern, the door closing quietly behind her.

Decimus stood there for a moment, the weight of responsibility heavy on his shoulders. He had done what was necessary, but that didn't make it any easier and as Marcia's footsteps faded into the morning, he knew that all he could do now was wait, and hope that Seneca would find a way to save Brennus without jeopardising everything they had worked so hard for.

Chapter Four

Britannia

Cunobeline and Caratacus rode side by side through the dense forests of Camulodunum. Cunobeline's white hair fluttered in the cool breeze, his posture slightly stooped in the saddle. He squinted ahead, where the trees gave way to the open plain where Togodumnus was waiting, having sent a message for them to meet him there at noon.

'Your brother is impatient,' Cunobeline muttered, glancing at Caratacus. 'Always too quick to move to the sword.'

'The times suit him,' said Caratacus, 'for many of the tribes crave blood. The Iceni speak of broken treaties, while the Trinovantes mutter about Roman merchants. They claim the Romans already bleed us dry without needing to lift a spear.'

'Trade is not conquest,' Cunobeline replied firmly. 'They send merchants, yes. But it is not an army.'

'True,' replied Caratacus, 'but some say the merchants are merely the scouts, and ships filled with soldiers will soon follow.'

Cunobeline sighed, the deep lines on his weathered face revealing his weariness.

'Rumours, always rumours. Rome is a beast of many parts, but even it must have limits. What reason would they have to throw their legions across the sea, just to claim a mist-covered island with so little gold?'

Caratacus's eyes darkened, and he tightened his grip on the reins.

'The same reason they always do, land, control and the

riches of conquest. Our lands may not glimmer with gold, but we have warriors, timber, and iron. The Roman eagle casts its shadow long and far and they have already broken the tribes of Gaul, Hispania and Germania. Britannia is one of the last free lands on the western edge of their empire.'

Cunobeline remained silent for a moment, considering his son's words as they passed through a narrow gap in the trees, the sunlight growing stronger as they neared the edge of the forest. The Romans were relentless in their pursuit of new territories, yet, he had always hoped to preserve Britannia's independence through negotiation and peace, not through bloodshed.

'The Romans will come,' Caratacus continued. 'Whether it is now or in the years to come, they will come. The question is, will we face them divided as we are, or will we stand together, a united force?'

Cunobeline glanced at his son. Caratacus, despite his youth, had wisdom and fire. He had the respect of many tribes, even those beyond the Catuvellauni.

'And what of your brother?' he asked quietly. 'Togodumnus craves power, but it is a power born of chaos. He seeks unity through war, not peace.'

Caratacus frowned, a shadow crossing his face.

'I have no doubt that Togodumnus has the safety of our people at heart, but he is increasingly influenced by the words of the druids. He needs to just take a step back and look at the needs of our island as a whole, not just our tribe. But I will say this. If it comes to a fight, which deep in my heart I believe it will, then I would want no other man at my side.'

'And now we ride to meet him on his terms,' Cunobeline said with a small, bitter smile. 'What does that say about us?'

As they emerged from the forest, a lone rider detached from the waiting group and began to approach. His figure was as stark as his ambition, the freshly shaved sides of his head and tattooed face giving him a sinister air that contrasted sharply with the more regal presence of his father and brother.

Cunobeline slowed his horse, his eyes narrowing as Togodumnus drew closer. Caratacus, ever alert, kept a steady gaze on his brother, knowing full well that the meeting, though framed as familial, could be anything but. When they were close enough to speak, Togodumnus pulled his horse to a halt, a wry smile creeping across his face.

'Father, brother,' he greeted them with a nod. 'I see you've answered my call. It's good to know that the bond of family still holds some sway.'

'We are here as you requested, Togodumnus,' said Cunobeline, 'what is it that could not wait until we met again at Camulodunum?'

Togodumnus looked between them, his eyes lingering on Caratacus for a moment longer.

'Unity, father. That is what could not wait. While we sit in the halls, discussing peace and treaties, the world around us prepares
for war. The Romans draw closer with each passing moon and the tribes grow restless, divided, uncertain of what is to come.'

'We have discussed this, Togodumnus,' said Cunobeline, 'on many occasions yet still you speak as though we have done nothing. There are good communications coming from Rome via their traders and messengers and while there is dialogue, there is hope.'

'Hope? Is that what you offer, father? The Romans will not be stopped by hope. They will not be turned away by words of peace. They will come with iron and fire, and they will crush us under their sandals unless we stand ready to meet them with strength.'

Cunobeline's grip on the reins tightened.

'You speak of strength, but at what cost? The tribes are not yet united, despite the war cries of Mordred. If you continue on this path, it will only bring more division and more bloodshed before any Roman soldier even touches the soil of these lands.'

Togodumnus's eyes flashed.

'The tribes are not united because you and others like you have made them weak with promises of peace. But I have seen the truth. I have spoken with the chiefs, the warriors, they want a leader who will fight. They want someone who will give them victory, not empty words.'

Cunobeline leaned forward in his saddle, his tone growing sharper.

'And what of the cost of your 'victory'? Do you think the tribes will follow you blindly into war? What happens when your fire burns too hot and they turn against you?'

Togodumnus smirked, as though he had anticipated the question.

'You think the people will turn against me? You think they do not see what must be done?' He straightened, his eyes gleaming with a fierce determination. 'I'll show you what they want.'

With a subtle wave of his hand, Togodumnus gave a signal. At first, there was only silence. Then, from the surrounding trees, the rustle of movement, faint at first but growing louder by the second.

Cunobeline turned in his saddle, his eyes widening as the tree line to the west began to shift and break. From the forest's edge, hundreds of men began to emerge, stepping into the open plain. They carried spears, shields, and swords, their faces hardened by battle and their clothes marked by the colours of their various tribes. Iceni, Trinovantes, Catuvellauni, and others stood side by side, a mixture of warriors, their loyalty now united under one banner. Caratacus, too, stared in disbelief. The sheer number of men, the variety of tribes represented, this was not a mere gathering of warriors; this was an army.

Togodumnus smiled, clearly relishing the shock on his father's and brother's faces.

'You see?' he said, gesturing to the sea of warriors before them. 'This is what strength looks like. This is what the people want. Not peace. Not negotiations. They want a leader who will defend them. They want an army that will strike fear into the hearts of our enemies.'

Cunobeline's face darkened, a deep sadness settling in his eyes as he looked at his son.

'And you believe this...' he gestured to the assembled force, 'this assembly of outcasts and warmongers, with not a recognised chieftain amongst them, is the only way? That this will save our people?'

Togodumnus's smile faded, replaced by an intensity that bordered on desperation.

'It is the only way, father. The tribes are ready for war. And if we do not lead them, they will turn to someone else who will.'

Cunobeline. though shaken by the display, remained resolute.

'An army does not make a king, Togodumnus. These men will follow you now, but when the real test comes, when ground shakes with the march of their legions and the fields run red with blood, and men scream in pain as they go to meet their gods, will they still follow?'

Togodumnus met his father's gaze, his expression unreadable.

'They will follow because they have no choice. War is coming, father. And whether you like it or not, I intend to be the one who leads us through it.'

Chapter Five

Vandal Territory

Brennus rode in silence at the rear of the column as the Vandal warriors led their remaining horses back from the lands of the Cherusci. His body ached from days on horseback, but it was the familiar weight in his heart that truly wore him down. Around him, the Vandals laughed and spoke in their guttural tongue, voices animated by the success of the horse fair. Laden with silver, weapons, and new saddles, they rode proudly, their spoils a testament to their barter skills, and, in part, to Brennus's own expertise with the animals.

The village, surrounded by rugged wooden palisades, sprawled across the plains in a loose collection of huts and animal enclosures and the returning men rode slowly through the wide entrance, where a pair of Vandal warriors stood guard, spears in hand.

The sounds of daily life surrounded them. In one corner, a group of women worked near a communal fire, their woollen shawls wrapped tightly against the breeze as they stirred large pots or mended clothing. Their dresses were simple, made of coarse fabric, dyed in muted colours of browns, greys, and the occasional faded blue. Some tended to children who played in the dirt nearby, their laughter ringing through the air.

Slaves walked between the huts, their movements brisk but methodical, carrying firewood, feeding animals, and hauling sacks of grain. Most wore rough, undyed tunics, their heads bowed as they worked, avoiding eye contact with their Vandal masters. Near the animal pens, another group of slaves tended to the livestock, sheep, goats, and a small herd of horses, while others mucked out stalls or hammered nails into newly built enclosures.

Brennus took it all in as they rode through the village. Though he had lived among the Vandals for some time, the sight of the village always struck him with a strange blend of familiarity and disquiet. For all its activity, the place was ruled by its warriors, men who lived by strength and violence, leaving the hard labour of the village to their slaves.

He shifted uncomfortably in his saddle, the familiar dread settling in his chest. Though he was not treated with the same

harshness as the other slaves, his chains were no less real. The Vandals valued his knowledge of horses and his Batavian skill with the animals granting him a certain leniency. He had his own small hut near the horse pens, and they allowed him to ride, to speak, and to work without the constant supervision many others endured. But he was still a slave.

The Vandal chieftain was waiting by the horse pens when they arrived, his broad figure wrapped in furs and his grizzled face creased with satisfaction as he surveyed the returning group. Brennus dismounted, leading his horse to the pens, when the chieftain's gruff voice halted him.

'Brennus.'

He turned, bowing his head slightly, a gesture of deference that still chafed against his pride.

Eirik eyed him, his sharp blue eyes assessing.

'Wulfstan tells me the horses sold for good silver. Tomorrow, you'll join the others on the eastern plains to round up the wild herd. We need fresh breeding stock.'

Brennus's stomach tightened. The thought of riding out again, of facing even more days and nights under the cold, watchful eyes of the Vandal overseers, sapped the little strength he had left. It seemed as though every time he neared the edge of hope, he was reminded that his captivity was endless. He had once believed he could escape, that he might find a way back to his homeland, or at least to freedom. But each passing season had eroded that dream, until all that remained was the relentless grind of survival, and the main reason he knew he could never leave. He nodded stiffly.

'I understand.'

Eirik clapped him on the shoulder, his hand heavy and patronising.

'Good. Rest well. Tomorrow will be a hard ride.'

With a final glance, the chieftain strode off, leaving Brennus to his thoughts. He turned away from the bustling camp and made his way to the small hut that he had called home for over a year. His boots crunched over the dry earth as he passed the horse pens, the familiar smell of sweat and leather mingling with the cold evening air. As he reached the door of the hut, he hesitated for a moment, his hand resting on the rough wood. Inside, the faint smell of woodsmoke and hay greeted him, and despite everything, his heart lifted. There, sitting near the low-burning fire, was the woman he had been partnered with since the Vandal patrol had fished him half dead from the river.

Her figure was slight, wrapped in a simple woollen tunic, and her dark hair was tied back loosely. She glanced up as he entered, her face softening at the sight of him.

'You're back,' she said quietly, her voice carrying a warmth that cut through the coldness of the evening.

Brennus closed the door behind him. For a moment, the weight of his captivity, the endless grind of servitude, seemed to fade, for here, in this cramped, draughty hut, surrounded by the smell of woodsmoke and hay, he had found something that made his chains bearable. The woman, his partner, though the Vandals did not recognise such bonds formally, had become his anchor. She, like him, was a captive, taken from her own people far to the east and together, they had carved out a fragile existence amidst the chaos.

Outside, the sounds of the Vandal camp faded as night fell and Brennus leaned his forehead against hers, closing his eyes as he listened to her steady breathing.

'Eirik says I'm to ride out again tomorrow,' he said quietly. 'We could be gone many days.'

The woman didn't answer, instead she handed him the bundle she was cradling in her arms, knowing it was one of the few things that could ease his burden.

A bittersweet smile crept across Brennus's face as he looked down at the reason he hadn't run with Talorcan when he'd had the chance. His newborn son gazed up at him with wide, innocent eyes, unaware of the world's harshness. Brennus's heart ached as he felt the weight of his captivity melt away, and for the fleetest of moments, he allowed himself to experience the fragile illusion of freedom.

Far to the southwest, Seneca and some of the Occultum reached the crest of a hill and reined in their horses, gazing down into the valley below. From their vantage point, they could see a Roman legion snaking its way northward, a long column of soldiers, carts, and animals stretching as far as the eye could see. The clinking of armour and the steady rhythm of marching feet drifted up on the wind, a familiar sound to the seasoned group.

'Look at them all,' said Falco quietly, 'fresh-faced and eager for glory. They'll learn soon enough.' He leaned back in his saddle, his voice laced with both amusement and a hint of bitterness.

'Most of them probably haven't seen a real fight,' said Marcus, as he watched the marching men, 'but they seem in good spirits.'

'Morale isn't going to help when we reach Britannia,' said Seneca, 'they say the tribes there are gathering, and they're not like the Gauls. They're wilder, less predictable.'

There was a long silence as the group watched the legion move steadily northward. The men below were just the first wave and in the following few months, more would follow but before then, the Occultum would make their move and become the unseen hand to guide them.

'Come on,' said Seneca finally, 'we should be getting back. Something tells me we are not long for this place. Let's move.'

A few hours later, all three men entered the camp they had used as a training base for so many months. Standing in the clearing were the men who had finally survived the long and arduous selection procedure, each exhausted and bedraggled after the final survival exercise they had endured over the past seven days. Raven stood to one side, his arms folded. He had done his best to break them, and now the training was over.

Seneca dismounted and walked over to the recruits. There were six in all, four less than there had been a few days earlier.

'Are they ready?' he asked, turning to Raven.

Raven stepped forward, his gaze sweeping over the recruits once more before answering.

'They've endured everything thrown at them,' he said.

'They'll hold.'

'Where are the others?'

'Four withdrew this morning. I told them all there were another seven days to go, and they decided it was just too much. Shame, one of them showed real promise.'

'Form a circle,' barked Falco to one side, 'face inward.'

The recruits shuffled into position, some limping heavily.

Seneca walked into the circle and walked around them, pausing to stare at each one in turn before returning to the centre.

'Well done,' he said eventually, 'you have survived. You have pushed yourselves through trials that have broken lesser men, so I will not pretend your efforts are without merit.'

Some of the recruits allowed themselves to relax, the faintest glimmer of relief crossing their faces.

'But,' Seneca continued, his tone hardening, 'survival alone is not enough.'

The brief flicker of relief vanished, and Seneca's eyes narrowed as he started walking again, his steps deliberate, his presence commanding.

'You stand on the brink of something far greater than yourselves,' he continued, 'something that is going to change the landscape of the known world. We all know it will be the legions that face the tribes of Britannia in battle but make no mistake, before they even set one single caligae on a ship, we will have paved the way for their success.' He paused, preparing the words each of them had dreamed of hearing for so many months. 'From here on in,' he continued, you are no longer legionaries, prisoners, horse traders or carpenters.

You do not belong to any unit apart from this one. We of the Occultum are not merely soldiers, nor are we simple scouts, we are the unseen hand of Rome, the hidden, the nightmare that wakes hardened warriors in the night. We operate in the shadows, in lands where the reach of the eagle has yet to stretch. You no longer exist, and you answer only to me and each other. You have proven your strength in body, but now I ask for your strength in mind, in spirit.'

He stopped in the centre of the circle, turning slowly to face them once more.

'What we do is not for glory. It is not for honour or fame, or riches, it is for the survival of Rome itself. What we do, no one will know. And if you fall, you will be forgotten by the world, but I swear to you here and now, you will not be forgotten by us, your brothers. Instead, we will grow stronger with the memory of who you were, of what you did, and we will strive to accomplish what you can no longer achieve. We are the Occultum, and that is what we do.'

The weight of his words settled heavily over the camp. No one dared to move. Raven watched, his expression unreadable, but there was a faint flicker of approval in his eyes.

'The mission we are about to embark upon,' Seneca continued, 'is more dangerous than anything you have yet faced. We will be alone, in a strange country, surrounded by enemies. There will be no reinforcements, no allies, no aid and it is highly likely that some of us, perhaps all of us, will not survive. So, if you harbour
any doubts whatsoever, this is your final chance to leave.' He paused, letting the gravity of his words sink in. The offer was clear. They could walk away, return to the legions, or to whatever lives they had lived. But the recruits remained still. Their exhaustion was etched into their very bones, yet not a single one of them moved. Seneca's eyes scanned their faces, looking for any sign of hesitation, but he found none.

'Good,' he said. 'From here on in, you will train alongside us as brothers. Get some rest.'

Without another word, he turned and walked back towards the horses. Raven lingered for a moment, his eyes meeting the recruits one last time. Then, he too turned, leaving them to their thoughts as the sun dipped lower on the horizon.

An hour or so later, Seneca stood beside his horse, brushing its coat with steady, methodical strokes. The rhythmic sound of the bristles running through the animal's dark mane was calming, a quiet reprieve after the stress of the past few months. His horse stamped the ground lightly, enjoying the attention but Seneca's mind was already focused on the mission ahead, the dangers of the north, and the men he was about to lead into the unknown. Beside him, Falco stretched, groaning as he stood up from where he had been seated, cleaning his saddle.

'Well, well, look there,' he muttered, nudging Seneca with his elbow and nodding towards the edge of the clearing.

Seneca followed his gaze. Three riders approached, their figures silhouetted against the dying light. The lead rider was unmistakably a woman, her posture straight and unyielding as she guided her horse with precision. Flanking her were two men, both clad in simple, dark tunics, their horses laden with travel bags and gear. The woman's hair, tied back in a severe knot, caught the last rays of sunlight as she rode closer, and Seneca's eyes narrowed in recognition.

'Marcia,' he murmured under his breath.

'How did she find us all the way out here?' said Falco, 'I thought this place was supposed to be a secret.'

'It is,' replied Seneca, 'but she's one of the few who knows it.' He handed the brush to Falco as the riders dismounted.

Marcia's two attendants remained close by, taking hold of the horses' reins and murmuring quietly amongst themselves. Marcia, however, strode forward with the confident ease of someone who was used to moving among men of importance.

'Marcia,' Seneca greeted, inclining his head slightly in respect. 'It is a long ride from the Hornless Bull. What brings you all this way?'

'I have news, Seneca, news that you need to know.'

He looked over at the two waiting men who had accompanied her.'

'Someone take care of those men,' he said. 'Feed them and give them a place to sleep.' He turned back to Marcia and gestured towards the large tent they used as a mess hall.

'Come. You've travelled far. You can tell me over a drink.'

Marcia followed Seneca into the tent. Several empty wooden tables lined the sides, save for one that remained laden with bread, cheese, dried meat, and jugs of ale, an ever-ready offering for the men who required constant sustenance at all hours.

Seneca gestured towards a bench at one of the far tables, and Marcia took a seat, her expression as unreadable as ever. He poured a cup of watered wine and handed it to her before sitting down opposite.

'So,' he said, 'what is so important that it brought you all the way out here, risking not just your life but the integrity of this camp?'

Marcia noted the slight air of annoyance in Seneca's voice but chose to ignore it.

'There is something you need to know,' she said

eventually, 'a few weeks ago, Talorcan arrived at the Hornless Bull. He gave me this.' She reached into the folds of her cloak and withdrew a small, folded piece of parchment, worn and creased from travel. She slid it across the table towards him.

Seneca's brow furrowed as he unfolded the parchment, scanning the rough, hastily written words. Talorcan's usual cryptic style was present, but the message was clear enough. His heart slowed as he read the final lines, the mention of Brennus cutting through him like a blade. Brennus was alive.

Seneca's hand tightened around the parchment. His old friend, thought dead for almost two years, captured by Vandals, and worse, living as a slave. The world around him seemed to dim, the camp's distant noises fading to nothing as the revelation settled in
his mind.

'Is this a joke?' he asked, his eyes locked onto Marcia's. 'A cruel jest from Talorcan?'

Marcia shook her head.

'No jest, Seneca. Talorcan saw him with his own eyes in Cherusci territory. He sent word as soon as he could.'

Seneca stood abruptly, pacing to the side of the tent. His mind raced. Brennus, one of his oldest comrades, a man he had fought with in countless battles, a man he had thought dead on the fringes of the empire, was alive, and suffering in chains. He turned back to face her.

'If Brennus is truly alive, then we cannot leave him there. We need to bring him home.'

Marcia watched, her eyes following his movements, sensing the storm brewing inside him.

'I wouldn't have brought this to you if I didn't believe it.' she said, 'I know what Brennus means to you, and to the rest of the Occultum.'

Seneca cursed under his breath, his mind torn between duty to Rome and loyalty to his brother-in-arms. One path led north, to the wilds of Britannia, where Rome's fate could be decided, the other, northeast, across the Rhine, the Weser and the Elbe rivers, into Vandal territory, somewhere where few men ever went and even fewer returned.

'We never leave any man behind,' said Seneca softly, almost as if reminding himself of their private mantra.

'No,' Marcia agreed, her voice firm. 'You don't.'

His dilemma grew heavier with each passing moment. The invasion was everything. If the Occultum failed, the conquest of Britannia could be delayed, or worse, doomed. They were to prepare the way, to sway tribes, to ensure victory before the legions even arrived. That was their duty, their purpose. Rome demanded it.

But Brennus... Brennus had fought alongside him more times than he could count and saved his life on more than one occasion. They had fought together through the worst of battles, surviving side by side when others had fallen. Could he abandon a friend, leave him to rot in chains?

'This can't be my decision alone,' said Seneca eventually. 'The men have a stake in this as much as I do. They need to know.'

Chapter Six

Gallia

Two days later, Marcia emerged from the tent she had been allocated to find the camp alive with movement. The newest recruits to the Occultum, still untried but hardened under the weight of their training, were being kitted out with their gear and Falco had provided a haphazard assortment of equipment native to the northern countries, especially Belgica and Britannia.

Each man was invited to choose whatever made them comfortable, especially the weapons that they would undoubtedly need before the invasion was over. It was important that they blended in with the locals as much as possible and that started with appearance.

'Let your hair grow,' said Raven as he walked amongst them, 'the Britons respect the strength it gives. Few cut it short and pick your boots carefully, no caligae.'

The men sifted through the pile of clothing, eventually settling on what they needed and placing it in front of them at their feet. Falco walked over and threw a pack in front of each, the sarcinae that they would carry their world in.

'Pack everything in these,' he said, 'if it doesn't fit, leave it behind. Carry only the basics and share the heavier stuff between you. One small tent between three, and one cooking pot per tent. Don't forget to allow space for extra water flasks but remember, you have to carry them wherever we go so keep the weight down.'

Marcia watched as the men prepared. Some would not return but she knew they would have been prepared well by Seneca and the Occultum. But now, her work here was done, and she knew she had to return to the Hornless Bull. She turned away and walked to the horses where her two travelling companions were already waiting.

Seneca stood a few paces away, watching her ready her horse. His face was impassive, but his eyes followed every movement she made. Behind him, Falco, Marcus and Sica stood at a respectful distance, their eyes also on Marcia. The Occultum had always regarded her with a strange mix of camaraderie and caution; she was as much a part of their world as any of them, yet always stood apart. Trusted, but distant.

Marcia mounted her horse with ease, adjusting her cloak to cover the saddle. For a moment, she simply looked at them, her eyes lingering on Seneca. There was no need for words between them now; they had said everything that mattered in the quiet, late-night conversations in the mess tent. The decision rested with him, and him alone.

'You know how to find me,' she said simply, her voice carrying through the quiet clearing. It wasn't a goodbye, not really. Marcia never said goodbye.

'Safe travels, Marcia' he replied, 'give Decimus my regards.'

She inclined her head, and with a sharp tug on the reins, she turned her horse to ride out of the camp.

'She's got more courage than half the men I've met,' muttered Falco, appearing beside Seneca. 'I've never seen her falter, no matter where we send her.'

Seneca stood silently, the weight of Marcia's message heavy on his shoulders. They had a mission, but Brennus' fate gnawed at him, unresolved. When she was finally out of sight, he exhaled and turned back to his men.

'We need to talk,' he said, 'come to the tent.'

Inside the air felt heavier. Seneca stood with his back to the others for a moment, his hands gripping the edge of the table. He stared down at the rough map of Britannia sprawled across the surface, the dark lines tracing the paths they would soon take. Finally, he turned to face them.

'It's about Brennus,' he said eventually. 'He is alive and in Vandal territory.'

At the mention of Brennus, the room seemed to tighten, the atmosphere shifting.

'That's not possible,' said Falco, 'Brennus is dead. I saw him drown.'

'Apparently not,' said Seneca, 'it seems like he survived and somehow ended up in the hands of the Vandals. He has been enslaved there and now suffers on the far side of the Elbe. Talorcan saw him himself and sent word to Marcia.'

'He must have been mistaken,' said Falco, fighting off the hope that was beginning to spark inside.

'Talorcan's information has been reliable before,' Marcus interjected. 'If he says Brennus is alive, I believe him.'

Seneca nodded.

'I believe him too. But the situation is complicated.' He gestured to the map on the table. 'The invasion of Britannia is set. If we leave to go after Brennus, we risk everything we've worked for.'

'But if we don't go,' Falco cut in, 'we're leaving him to die a slave.'

The tent fell into a heavy silence.

'If he is alive,' said Raven, eventually, 'we have to go and get him. We swore an oath to each other and if it's a choice between the invasion and Brennus, I say we find Brennus. No man gets left behind, remember?'

'What if we divide our forces?' asked Marcus. 'We have

the new recruits, and they have to be tested sometime. Some of us could go north to secure the way for the legions, while the others, those best suited, could go after Brennus.'

Seneca was quiet for a moment, letting the suggestion hang. His mind raced through the logistics of such a plan, the risks involved in splitting their already small unit in two, but a part of him knew that, had it been any of the others in his place, Brennus would already be on his way to rescue them, invasion or not.

'I've already thought long and hard about this,' said Seneca, 'and although we have a commitment to Brennus, we also have a duty to Rome. So, what I suggest is this. You four will head north and do what you have to do in Britannia. I'll take one of the new recruits and go and find Talorcan. Together, we will find Brennus and bring him home.'

'A recruit?' said Falco shaking his head. 'They're barely trained. You need someone with experience. Take me.'

'We need every experienced man heading north,' said Seneca. 'Talorcan knows the Vandal lands and with him at our side, we should be able to see it through.'

'This isn't right, Seneca,' said Falco. 'We don't split up, we go together, like we always have.'

'I know the risks, Falco. But I also know what's at stake in Britannia. If we all go for Brennus, we fail Rome and everything we've done here will be for nothing.'

Falco sighed, his frustration still visible. He crossed his arms, glancing at Seneca.

'So, who's going with you, then?'

Seneca glanced toward Raven.

'Who would you recommend, Raven, you know them better than all of us?'

'Take Canis,' replied Raven. 'He is quiet, sometimes

unapproachable but he has excelled in everything we have thrown at him. He will not let you down.'

'Canis it is,' said Seneca.

Falco muttered something under his breath but gave a begrudging nod.

'I hope you are right about this, Seneca,' said Falco. 'If you are not, we may have to rescue you next.'

The tent fell silent once more as the men absorbed what had just been laid before them. The division of their group went against everything they had trained for, everything they had sworn to uphold. But there was no escaping the reality of their situation. Seneca straightened, his hand once more resting on the map.

'I'll leave at dawn,' he said, 'you wait here until you hear from Lepidus and when the order comes, you know what to do. When I am done, I'll find you in Britannia.'

'How?' asked Falco.

'You just leave that to me,' said Seneca. 'Now go and get Canis, I have to brief him about what to expect.'

The men left the tent knowing that although the dice were loaded against him, if Brennus was to come out of this alive, he could not have wished for a better man than Seneca to try and rescue him. The plan was made. Now, all that remained was to carry it out.

Chapter Seven

Gallia

For a large part of their journey northward, the road had been relatively quiet, but as the Occultum approached Gesoriacum on the north-west coast, the air grew thick with purpose and alive with the evidence of Roman preparation. Roads were clogged with supply carts, soldiers and tents sprawled across the fields, a sea of red and brown. Legionaries drilled under the watchful eyes of their centurions and along the coast, hundreds of boats, some newly built, others hastily repurposed fishing vessels, bobbed in the estuaries, ready for the invasion. Falco's eyes swept over the coastline.

'Look at all this,' he said, shaking his head. 'I've ever seen so many boats in one place. It's like Neptune himself is gathering a fleet.'

'They're just boats,' Sica muttered, riding a few paces ahead. 'They'll burn the same as anything else.'

'It's not the ships that'll win this war,' said Marcus, 'and half these boys have never even seen battle.' His gaze shifted from the camps to the villagers pressed into service by the army. Fishermen hammered nails into hulls under the watchful eye of the Roman tradesmen, while their wives and children carried supplies.

'The legions are already taking what they need,' Raven remarked. 'They're stripping this coast bare before they even set sail.'

'It's not about need,' Marcus replied. 'It's about control. We take, they submit. Standard practice.'

Falco sighed, shaking his head.

'You sound like you're ready to deliver a speech in the

Senate, Marcus.'

'I spent over a decade in the legions,' said Marcus, 'and fought under many generals. I know how they work.'

As they rode closer to Gesoriacum, the scale of the preparations became even more clearer. The sprawling port was swarming with soldiers and craftsmen. Smoke rose from the forges, and the clang of metal against metal filled the air as blacksmiths worked day and night.

'Looks like we're late to the party,' Falco mused, eyeing the bustling scene. 'Half the empire's already here.'

'Aye,' Marcus muttered, 'and we've got the honour of going in first.' He looked at the familiar scenes around him, recognising the smells, the sounds, even the barking orders of legionary officers in the distance, and for the briefest of moments, he felt the faintest pang of nostalgia. He had been a centurion once, before the accusations, before the disgrace. And now he found himself in the company of men who operated outside the rigid structure he had known for so long. The sounds of order and military discipline floated through the air, rekindling the memories of so many years, so many battles…so many dead comrades. He fell quiet, absorbing everything around him but his thoughts were soon interrupted by Falco's booming voice.

'So, who is going to sweet-talk Lepidus when we get there?'

For a few heartbeats there was silence, and then Marcus felt the weight of their gazes slowly turn towards him.

'No,' he said, already shaking his head.

'It makes sense,' said Raven. 'You're the only one who's been through the ranks of the legions. Lepidus is a senator. He'll want to deal with someone who understands the structure, who can speak his language.'

'But you three have been part of this for far longer than me. I am still the new guy, remember? It should be one of you.'

'It has to be you, Marcus,' said Raven. 'Neither Sica or I are Roman and will draw too much attention. And it can't be Falco, this isn't about brute strength, it's politics. He'll probably insult the senator, and we'll all end up back in the Carcer Tullianum.'

'I resent that,' said Falco, without looking over. 'I'll have you know I am a highly intelligent man. A killer, yes, but I have hidden depths.'

Raven and Sica glanced at each other, controlling their urge to laugh out loud.

The group fell silent for a moment as they considered the problem. Lepidus wasn't just any senator; he was their lifeline. Without his backing, their mission would be for nothing, and Rome's plans for Britannia would hang in the balance. They all knew that Seneca was an expert when it came to navigating the delicate politics of Rome, but in his absence, someone needed to step up.

'I'm no diplomat,' said Marcus eventually, 'I was just a centurion, remember?'

'You don't need to be a diplomat,' Raven replied. 'You know how these things work better than any of us. Just listen to what he has to say and ask questions, lots of questions.'

'And if I say no?'

'Then we send Falco in and watch as he single handedly causes the collapse of the Roman Empire.'

Marcus laughed and looked over at the feigned look of hurt on Falco's face.

'So be it,' he said, finally relenting. 'I'll do it. But if this goes wrong, don't blame me.'

Decision made, they continued onward in silence,

seemingly just another four traders in the long train of supply wagons.

'We're nearly at the port,' said Raven eventually, his tone more serious. 'There'll be too many eyes on us there. We should find lodgings away from the town.'

The group veered off the main road, leaving the steady march of the supply column behind.

Up on the side of a hill, they saw a small village, its wooden houses huddled close together. On the outer edge, a bare-chested man sat on a bucket outside a taberna, plucking a chicken.

'We'll see if we can stay here for the night,' said Marcus, 'and get some rest. Tomorrow, I'll meet with Lepidus while you go and find the others.'

A few minutes later, Falco pushed the door of the tavern open, the scent of stale ale and smoke greeting them like old friends.

'This'll do nicely,' he said, and they settled into the dimly lit room as the low murmur of conversation filled the air. Tomorrow, they would receive their final orders, but tonight, to anyone looking on, they were just ordinary traders far from home. Once they were settled with drinks before them, Falco raised his cup.

'To the Occultum,' he said quietly. 'And to whatever madness comes next.'

The others exchanged glances, and despite the tension, Marcus allowed himself a small smile. He raised his own cup, tapping it against Falco's.

'To whatever comes next,' he echoed.

The following morning, Marcus stepped out of the tavern, the damp morning air still clinging to the village as the muffled

sounds of villagers waking up mixed with the distant clang of hammers from the Roman camp.

Falco was already stretching his arms, his massive frame taking up most of the doorway as Raven appeared from inside, handing him a small leather purse, the coins inside clinking as they exchanged hands.

'Don't spend it all in one place, Falco,' he said, 'spread it around a little. Too much money makes a man stand out from the crowd. And don't spend it on ale. We need dried provisions, not hangovers.'

Falco glared at Raven but without answering, he sauntered off towards the market at the far end of the village. After he had left, Raven turned to Marcus.

'While you go to meet Lepidus, me and Sica will meet the others as agreed. If they followed our instructions, they should be here by noon.'

'Tell them to lay up somewhere outside the town,' said Marcus. 'It is too risky to have us all here at the same time. And make sure they know what they are doing, I don't want any surprises before we've even begun.'

Raven smiled faintly.

'They are good men, Marcus. They just need the opportunity to prove themselves.'

Marcus turned and made his way towards the harbour, the dirt roads giving way to the cobbled streets that led to the docks. Gesoriacum was bustling even at this early hour, with the constant movement of soldiers and sailors preparing for the invasion. Supplies were being loaded off ships fresh from Rome and legionaries moved in tight formations through the streets. This wasn't just a military outpost, it was the beating heart of Rome's ambition.

As Marcus approached the harbour, he saw a small cluster of Roman officers in the distance, standing near a large galley moored to the dock. Their gleaming armour and crimson cloaks marked them as high-ranking officials, and their bodyguards stood nearby, their eyes scanning the area for any sign of threat. The scene was one of discipline and control, a stark contrast to the organised chaos of the port in general and there, at the heart of it all, stood Lepidus, the senator they had all risked their lives to save so many months before.

Tall, composed, and every bit the leader the Occultum knew him to be, Lepidus stood in conversation with two senior officers. He wore no armour, just his ornate senatorial tunic but it wasn't his attire that commanded respect, it was his presence. Even surrounded by men of high military rank, he held his ground as an equal.

For a moment, Marcus paused at the edge of the port. It was a different world from the quiet village he'd left earlier, here, every movement had purpose, every legionary was part of a greater machine, one that would soon crush Britannia beneath Roman caligae.

Marcus scratched at his beard, feeling the rough tangles against his fingers. His appearance had changed over the last few weeks, and not for the better. His hair dropped long over his shoulders, wild and unkempt and his beard thick and untrimmed. His drab tunic was worn and patched in several places, but that had been part of the plan. Better to avoid attention than draw it.

'Hold there,' barked one of the guards, stepping forward brandishing a pila. 'Where do you think you're going?'

Marcus kept his hands visible, not wanting to provoke a scene.

'I need to speak with Senator Lepidus,' he said, 'he's expecting me.'

The older guard snorted, his lips curling in amusement.

'Do you really think we're going to let some filthy beggar walk in and disturb a senator? Get back to whatever hole you crawled out of.'

Marcus forced his face to remain impassive. He had dealt with their type before, young, cocky soldiers, eager to prove themselves by belittling others. He could have knocked them both down in an instant, but that would only attract more attention, and now was not the time for that. He kept his voice calm.

'I have a message for the senator and trust me, you don't want to be the one who stops me from delivering it.'

The younger guard scoffed, taking a step closer to Marcus, his hand resting on the hilt of his gladius.

'I'll give you a message, turn around or I'll personally throw you into the sea.'

The older guard chuckled, clearly enjoying the moment.

'Go on, get out of here before we have to dirty our hands.'

Before Marcus could respond, a familiar voice cut through the noise.

'Is there a problem here?'

Lepidus strode towards them from across the dock. His eyes were sharp, scanning the scene with the calm authority of a man who was accustomed to being obeyed. He had been a legatus for many years and well used to wielding power. The guards immediately snapped to attention, though confusion flickered in their eyes.

'Apologies, Senator,' the older guard stammered. 'This man claimed he had business with you, but we didn't believe…'

Lepidus raised a hand, cutting the guard off.

'I know him,' he said, 'let him through.'

The two guards exchanged stunned glances, their previous arrogance dissolving into embarrassment. The younger one's face flushed red as he stepped aside reluctantly.

'Of course, Senator. Forgive us,' he said, bowing his head slightly.

Marcus stood still as the guards searched him for any hidden weapons, their hands brusque as they checked his tunic, his waist, and his arms. They were thorough, or at least, they thought they were and one of them even gave a smug look when he found the small dagger sheathed at Marcus's hip.

'What's this?' he sneered, pulling the knife free. 'Carrying weapons to meet a senator, eh?'

'I carry a knife everywhere,' said Marcus. 'It's for my own protection.'

'Well, you won't need it on the dock,' said the guard, tossing it into a nearby crate, 'you can pick it up on the way out.'

Marcus didn't reply. He knew better than to antagonise them further, but he couldn't help a small smile as they missed the two other knives hidden on his person. One was tucked into the shaft of his boot, the other strapped tightly to the small of his back, beneath his tunic. They waved him through, clearly rattled by Lepidus's intervention.

'You are lucky I recognised you,' said Lepidus quietly as they walked away, 'is there any need for all this?' He glanced across at Marcus's unkempt appearance.

'Apparently, it will make us fit in better when we reach

Britannia,' said Marcus, 'or so Raven tells us.'

'Where's Seneca?' asked Lepidus suddenly. 'It should have been him meeting me here.'

'He will be joining us later,' said Marcus, 'he... uh, had to be elsewhere.'

Lepidus stopped and stared at the ex-centurion.

'There is nowhere else he needs to be,' he hissed, 'his role is to be right here with me. Now, where is he?'

'I can't tell you that, Senator, it is something we need to sort out between ourselves. But believe me when I say it was unavoidable. I promise, he will join us as soon as he is able.'

'This is not good enough,' said Seneca, 'we will talk more of this later.'

They continued walking and approached the tables where the Roman officers were examining a map.

'Wait here,' said Lepidus and walked over to the table. After a brief conversation, one of the officers turned to look in his direction, and, moments later, Lepidus returned to lead Marcus over to a nearby warehouse.

'What's happening,' asked Marcus, 'who was that man?'

'That, my friend,' said Lepidus, 'is Aulus Plautius, Legatus Augusti pro Praetore, the man who will lead us into Britannia. At the moment, he is probably the most powerful man in the Empire and in a few moments, he will be joining us to give you your orders, and trust me, I hope for your sake that Seneca has trained you well.'

Chapter Eight

Germania

The journey to Oppidum Ubiorum had been smoother than expected and Seneca and Canis had made good time.

'We should reach the town by nightfall,' said Seneca, glancing over at Canis. 'Once we're there, finding Talorcan will be another matter. He comes and goes as he pleases.'

'Did I not hear Raven say that Talorcan often works for the fort as a hunter or scout?' asked Canis.

'He does. And that will be our first port of call. We will, however, have to be careful. My face is not welcome around here.'

'Why not?'

'That, my friend is a story for another day. Let's just say that I don't fancy our chances if we get caught by the local legatus. But keep in mind, Talorcan doesn't always want to be found, and we'll have to be careful not to draw too much attention while asking around. The wrong ears could get wind of our presence.'

'I understand,' replied Canis.

Seneca glanced over. The newest addition to the team had proven himself during training, fast, skilled, and a natural when it came to improvisation. But this was his first time in the field.

As they rounded a bend in the path, Seneca's senses prickled. Five men stood in the road ahead, blocking the way, the tension in their posture unmistakable. Their clothes were ragged and their hands resting on the hilts of crude swords and daggers. Bandits. The kind that preyed on travellers far from the safety of Roman patrols.

'Keep calm,' Seneca murmured to Canis, his hand subtly tightening on the reins. 'Let me do the talking.'

They slowed their horses as the men stepped forward, blocking the road. One of them, a tall man with a greasy beard, raised a hand in mock greeting. His smile was all broken teeth with no warmth.

'Hail travellers,' he called out. 'What makes you come this way away from the well-trodden routes?'

'The paths are quieter,' said Seneca, 'with fewer Roman eyes to watch us pass.'

'So, you are troublemakers then?' said the man with an amused look upon his face. 'Bandits, perhaps?'

Seneca sighed inwardly.

'We've no interest in trouble,' he said calmly. 'Let us pass, and we'll be on our way.'

The leader's grin widened.

'Oh, I'm sure you'll be on your way. But first, how about you toss down any purses you have hidden about you, eh? Lighten the load a bit. Make it easier for you to travel.'

Canis's hand drifted to his belt. Seneca shot him a warning look but kept his voice even as he addressed the bandits again.

'You don't want this. We've got nothing worth the trouble, and you've got better things to do than fight two weary travellers.'

The leader's face darkened, and he stepped closer.

'I think I'll be the judge of that.'

Seneca was about to try again when, without warning, Canis's hand flashed and a knife shot through the air, spinning in a blur before embedding itself in the throat of the bandit. The man gasped, staggering back as blood gushed from the wound, his hands clawing at his neck.

For a split second, there was silence. Then chaos erupted as the remaining four men drew their weapons and charged. Seneca cursed out loud and drew his own sword before leaping from his horse, just in time to parry a wild swing from the nearest.

'That was not the plan.' he shouted, but Canis didn't answer, he was too busy racing forward to engage the remaining three bandits.

Seneca sidestepped a thrust, spinning and slashing the man across the face with deadly precision. The bandit dropped with a howl, clutching the wound and Seneca kicked him to the ground before finishing him off with a thrust through the chest.

Canis also fought with a brutal efficiency that left no room for hesitation. He moved in quick, sharp bursts, a second knife in one hand, his sword in the other, flashing in perfect coordination as he dispatched another attacker, slicing across the man's throat before spinning to face the last two men.

One of the remaining attackers turned to run, but Canis hurled another knife after him, embedding itself deep in the back of his neck, severing his spine in two, and he dropped like a stone.

Seeing his comrades fall so quickly caused another to panic and he swung wildly at Seneca, but the veteran fighter easily
sidestepped the blow and ran him through the stomach with a clean thrust, and, just like that, the fight was over. The five bandits lay dead or dying on the road, their blood pooling in the dirt. Canis stood over the bodies, and after retrieving his knives, wiped them clean on one of their tunics.

Seneca cleaned and sheathed his sword, surveying the

scene. Despite the ease with which they had dealt with the thieves, his expression was grim. He kicked one of the corpses with the toe of his boot.

'We didn't need to kill them,' he said. 'A few words, maybe a bit of coin, and they'd have let us pass.'

'They were bandits, said Canis. 'They weren't going to let us go.'

'Maybe,' said Seneca, wiping the blood from his hands. 'But now we've got five dead men to deal with and bodies attract attention. We don't want that. Not this close to Oppidum Ubiorum.'

'Then we will hide them,' said Canis, 'and by the time they are found we will be long gone.'

Seneca nodded and stared at the young man.

'You're good with those knives,' said, grudging admiration in his voice. 'You never told us you could wield a blade like that.'

'You never asked,' said Canis simply and before Seneca could respond, he bent down to grab a body and dragged it into the undergrowth at the side of the path.

Seneca joined him and they worked quickly, dragging the bodies off the road into the undergrowth before scattered dirt over the worst of the bloodstains. There was no doubt that they would be found soon enough, but at least it gave them some time. When the last body was hidden, Seneca stepped back, surveying the now-empty road.

'You did well,' he said, mounting his horse, 'but next time, let's try talking first.'

'We'll see,' Replied Canis, mounting his own horse. 'But it depends on who's doing the talking.'

With the bodies hidden and the road clear, they set off once more towards Oppidum Ubiorum and despite the unease lingering from the skirmish, Seneca couldn't help but feel a flicker of respect for the man beside him. He was certainly an excellent fighter, but perhaps just needed to learn how to be a bit more patient, but patience, like skill, was learned in time.

As they rode into Oppidum Ubiorum, the atmosphere shifted from the quiet road they had left behind to the bustling energy of a Roman town on the frontier. The streets were crowded with merchants haggling over goods, townspeople going about their daily routines, and a mix of Roman citizens and locals who barely spared a glance at the newcomers. The town itself was a strange mix of Roman influence and native character with wooden houses standing beside more Roman-style stone buildings.

Seneca guided his horse carefully through the narrow streets, avoiding the main roads where locals and soldiers gathered in clusters. Canis followed close behind, his eyes darting around, sharp and alert, taking in the unfamiliar surroundings.

The Roman fort loomed in the distance, its walls visible just beyond the town's edge. They could have headed straight there, but Talorcan wouldn't be inside the fort, he was a man of the wild, always preferring to stay just out of reach, mingling in the shadows where eyes were less prying.

'We'll leave the horses here,' said Seneca quietly, nodding towards a small stable tucked behind a row of houses. 'We don't need attention.'

They dismounted and led their horses to the stable, and once the horses were secured, slipped back into the streets.

'If Talorcan's anywhere, he'll be in one of the taverns,' said Seneca as they moved through the winding alleys. 'It's where the serious business is done in towns like these.'

Canis kept pace beside him, his face expressionless,

though his eyes scanned every corner. They entered the first tavern, a cramped space thick with smoke and the sour smell of vomit. Mercenaries and locals filled the room, their voices a low murmur as they drank and spoke in groups. Seneca moved smoothly through the crowd, his eyes sweeping for any sign of Talorcan as Canis leaned against the wall near the entrance, watching the room with the wariness of a man who never let his guard down. Not having any luck, they left the building and headed up the narrow street, leading the way to the next tavern.

Over the next hour or so, they checked three more without any sign of Talorcan, and by the time they reached the fourth, a sense of unease had begun to settle over them.

Seneca moved to the bar, asking a few more discreet questions but the room had gone too still. He noticed it almost immediately. Conversations had dropped, and all eyes turned towards them. Canis noticed it too and his hand subtly moved to his belt, where his knife waited. Seneca held up a hand to stop him. They didn't need another fight. Not here.

A man at the corner table stood up slowly, his eyes narrowing at the two of them. He was tall, broad-shouldered, his tunic worn but his arms thick with muscle. He crossed the room, his heavy boots thudding on the floorboards, stopping just in front of Seneca.

'You don't belong here,' he said. 'And you've been asking too many questions.'

Seneca remained calm, raising his hands slightly to show he meant no harm.

'We're just looking for a friend.'

'A friend?' the man echoed with a sneer. 'You don't have friends here, Roman.' He spat the word as if it left a bad taste in his mouth.

A few others began to stand up around the room, the tension rising. Canis shifted beside Seneca, his muscles coiled, ready for a fight. But Seneca wasn't ready to let things escalate. Not yet.

'I may be Roman, but I owe no loyalty to any legion. I just need to find our comrade and we will be gone from here.'

The man shoved Seneca hard, cutting him off.

'Don't try to talk your way out of this, stranger. Why are you looking for your so-called comrade?'

A few other patrons had gathered around now, forming a loose circle. The crowd was waiting for a fight, eager to see the strangers fall. Canis's hand was already on his knife, his jaw clenched, ready for blood. But just before the first blow could be struck, a voice rang out from the far end of the room.

'That's enough.'

The crowd parted, and Talorcan stepped forward, his long black hair tied back, his pointed beard unmistakable. He moved with the grace of a hunter, his dark eyes taking in the scene with an air of casual authority. The man who had confronted them grumbled something under his breath but backed away and the rest of the crowd, sensing the situation had passed, returned to their drinks. Seneca glanced at Canis, who slowly relaxed, though his hand stayed near his knife.

'Let's go,' said Talorcan. 'You're drawing too much attention.'

Without another word, Seneca and Canis followed Talorcan back into the narrow alley. The noise from the tavern faded behind them as they moved deeper into the shadows, away from prying eyes. Once they were clear, Seneca let out a breath he hadn't realised he was holding.

'You timed that well, Talorcan. I think we might have been in some trouble there.'

'You were. That is probably the roughest tavern in the whole of the area. Lucky I found you when I did.' He looked over at Canis. 'And who are you?'

'He's one of us,' said Seneca. 'A new member of the Occultum.'

'Marcia said something about a new unit,' said Talorcan. 'Where are the others?'

'It's just us two,' said Seneca, 'the others have a different role to fulfil.'

'I assume you got my message?'

'I did, and that is why we are here. To see if we can get Brennus back. But is there somewhere else we can talk? this is just too open.'

Talorcan nodded.

'Follow me.' he said, 'I know just the place.'

As they slipped through the darkening streets, Seneca felt a sense of relief wash over him. But the tension in the air hadn't entirely lifted. Oppidum Ubiorum was full of eyes and ears, and any wrong move could bring Roman or native forces alike down on them before they even got started. But for now, they had found their man, and that was a great start.

The small, dimly lit room Talorcan led them to was tucked away at the back of a decrepit inn on the outskirts of Oppidum Ubiorum. It wasn't much, just a few wooden stools, a scarred table, and a single flickering oil lamp casting long shadows on the walls, but it was private, and that was all that mattered. Talorcan sat at the head of the table, while Canis leaned against the far wall, his eyes never leaving the door. Seneca paced slowly, his expression thoughtful, the usual calm of his features giving way to a rare tension.

'So,' he began, 'what's the situation with Brennus?

Your message said that you saw him, but he refused to acknowledge you. Is that true?'

'It is,' replied Talorcan. 'I recognised him immediately. We locked eyes and I know he recognised me too, but he shook his head and walked away, as if he wanted nothing to do with me.'

'But you say he was a slave?'

'He was not in chains if that is what you mean, he was tending to the horses. But the Vandals do not employ outsiders, they use captives, and Brennus was certainly with them.'

'Do you know how he got there?'

'No, but I assume they fished him out of the river downstream when he was washed away.'

'And you're sure of this? It couldn't have just been someone who looks like him??'

'I'm sure,' Talorcan replied. 'He is alive, Seneca, or at least he was the last time I saw him. Since I returned, I've spoken to my contacts in the villages. One of the Cherusci hunters mentioned a Vandal tribe that has a western slave, a man with exceptional skill with horses. The tribe is led by a chieftain named Wulfstan He's no ally of Rome, but he's clever. He knows that if word spreads that they're holding a Roman soldier, it could provoke a response, and they don't want that.'

'But if Brennus is part of the Occultum,' said Canis, 'there is no record of him serving with any legion.'

'We know that,' said Seneca, 'but the Vandals don't.'

'So, what's the plan? We can't just march into Vandal territory and hope they'll hand him over.'

'We're not marching anywhere,' said Seneca firmly. 'We'll have to go in quietly and see what we're dealing with first. But we need to act fast. If we wait too long, Brennus could be moved, and we'll lose track of him.'

Talorcan nodded.

'Agreed. I know where the camp is but not how long it will be there.'

Seneca stared at the wall, his mind turning over the options. They had little time to plan but the timing was crucial.

'You know these lands, Talorcan,' he said, 'what's the terrain like? Can we use it to our advantage?'

'The terrain's rough, withdense forests and deep valleys.

The Vandals know it better than we do, but we can use it to

get close without being seen. Are you alone or do you have support?'

'We don't need backup,' said Seneca, 'A small group is easier to hide.'

Canis pushed off the wall.

'I've heard enough,' he said, 'when do we leave?'

'As soon as possible,' said Seneca, standing up. 'We can't afford to waste any more time.'

'In that case, I'll gather what supplies we need,' said Talorcan, 'and meet you back here at dawn. There's a caravan leaving for the border tomorrow. We can slip in with them, posing as merchants and once we're close, we'll break off and head for the Elbe.'

And with that, the decision was made. They would venture into the heart of one of the most hostile tribes in Germania, with no back up whatsoever, just three men seeking to rescue one of their own. Somewhere out there, Brennus was waiting, and they were going to get him out…or die trying.

Chapter Nine

The Northern Sea

The fishing boat heaved and groaned beneath the weight of the storm, its battered hull cutting through the churning black waves. Marcus stood at the bow, his hands gripping the splintered rail, every muscle tensed as the boat bucked against the unrelenting sea. The salt spray stung his eyes, the cold biting deep into his bones, but his gaze remained fixed on the shadowy outline of land just visible through the driving rain. The crossing had been rough, but it was the only way they could get to the shores of Britannia unseen, and it had cost them a fortune in silver to pay a captain stupid enough to even try on such a bad night.

Falco sat against the mast. He had spent most of the last hour or so vomiting and was unusually quiet.

'How are you doing?' shouted Marcus, looking down.

'If this what they call a swift crossing,' shouted Falco, 'next time, I'll swim.'

'We're almost there,' shouted Marcus, fighting to keep his balance, 'I can see land.'

Everyone on board was desperate to reach solid ground and Marcus could sense the growing unease among the men.

Raven, crouched near the stern alongside Sica, looked up scanned the coastline, his long hair plastered to his face. 'We're nowhere near where we should be,' he called, his voice steady despite the chaos around them. 'That's not the landing site, there should be no cliffs.'

'I can see that,' Marcus shouted back, 'we'll just have to work it out when we land.'

In the centre of the ship, the newer members of the team sat in a tight huddle, bracing themselves against the relentless onslaught of wind and spray. Their cloaks clung to their soaked bodies as they crouched low, each man clutching his sarcina with both arms, knuckles white from the strain. The packs, wrapped in oiled fabric, were wedged between their knees, secured with cords tied to their wrists, a vital precaution should they be swept overboard by the savage sea. The oiled wrappings would help them stay afloat, though only for a short time, offering a fragile lifeline in the treacherous waters.

The three extra men hunkered down, each desperate for the hellish crossing to end. The heady delight and satisfaction of passing the selection process just weeks earlier had become nothing more than distant memories, and as the boat groaned under the strain of the storm, more than one of them feared they would meet their end before ever drawing a blade in anger.

'Hold fast.' Marcus shouted, as another powerful gust of wind tore at the sails.

The boat tilted dangerously as another wave crashed over the deck. Falco cursed, his usual brash humour giving way to fear and frustration.

'If we don't land soon,' he shouted, 'the sea will take us.'

As if in response, a towering wave surged toward them and in the next moment, slammed the boat into the rocky shoreline with a bone-shaking crack, throwing the men into the icy water, their cries swallowed by the roaring wind and waves.

Marcus hit the water hard, the shock of the cold nearly paralysing him. He fought to the surface, gasping for breath, desperately trying to stay afloat. Another wave hit, overwhelming him but driving him nearer to the shore. Over and over again he was driven under only to emerge once again, each time a lot weaker, but moments later, his hand hit something solid, and he clawed his way onto the jagged rocks, dragging himself out of the sea's reach. He hauled his saturated sarcina up with the tether and looked around for survivors. To one side, Raven was already pulling Sica ashore and alongside him was Falco, sputtering and cursing as he hauled Cassius up with him.

Marcus staggered to his feet, eyes scanning the shoreline. The boat was a wreck, shattered on the rocks but in the distance, he could see Atticus staggering ashore, dripping and gasping, but Drusus was nowhere to be seen. Once they had all caught their breath, they searched for hundreds of metres in each direction for any more survivors, but Drusus was gone, along with the ship's captain and his two crew.

'We can't stay here any longer,' said Raven. 'We're far from where we planned, and it's almost sunrise. We need to find somewhere to lay up until we work out where we are.'

'Up there.' Falco pointed toward a narrow ravine leading up into the cliffs. 'Looks steep, but it's better than sitting here waiting to freeze.'

With no other options, they began to climb, slipping on the wet rocks as they scrambled up the ravine, their saturated sarcinae weighing down upon them. The wind howled through the narrow gap, but they pressed on, every man focused on escaping the deadly pull of the sea below.

Sica reached the top first and turned to offer a hand to the others, helping them up one by one. When Marcus reached the top, he paused, looking out over the darkened landscape.

'We'll find shelter here,' he said, seeing a low overhang

in the cliff. 'Just for the night. At first light, we'll look for somewhere better and find out where we are.'

The men huddled beneath the rocky overhang, exhausted but alive. The storm still raged outside, the wind howling across the cliffs, but for the moment, they had found a shred of safety, and in their field of work, survival was the first victory.

By dawn, the storm had passed, leaving the landscape drenched but eerily calm. The men stirred from their makeshift shelter, the wind now a muted whisper compared to the ferocity of the night before.

'Decimus knows how to survive,' Marcus muttered, more to reassure himself than anyone else. He cast a glance at the others, faces pale, eyes hollowed by exhaustion but determined. They had made it through the night, and now they had to prepare for what came next.

The men began unwrapping their sarcinae, carefully peeling away the oiled fabric that had kept their gear dry through the storm, inspecting their weapons, and supplies with quiet efficiency. The oiled wraps, now muddy and worn, were buried in a shallow pit beneath the rocks, hidden from prying eyes.

Falco gave a sharp nod toward the rising sun.

'The gods smile on us today. We've had worse nights, eh?'

Sica, sitting cross-legged as he rechecked the edge of his blade, offered a wordless grunt. His silence said all that needed saying, they had survived by sheer chance, but they were alive, and that was always a good way to start the day.

Marcus stood, pulling his cloak tighter around him, his mind already on the next step.

'We can't stay here,' he said, 'this place is too exposed. If anyone saw the wreck or hears of it, they'll come looking.'

Raven, got to his feet.

'I'll go out and get the lay of the land. Find out where we are.'

'I'm coming with you,' Marcus replied, strapping his sword to his side. His gaze swept over the others. 'The rest of you, stay hidden. We'll be back as soon as we can.'

The two men ventured out, slipping into the dense undergrowth beyond the ravine. The land was wild and untamed, and the wind still carried the salt of the sea, but the further they moved inland, the more the landscape shifted. Raven led the way, his eyes constantly scanning for signs of life, human or otherwise. Marcus followed close behind, his senses sharpened by years of soldiering, though he knew Raven was far better at this kind of work.

The land sloped upward into a series of hills, the rocky coastline giving way to thick, marshy grasses and scattered trees. As they climbed higher, the expanse of Britannia unfurled before them, a vast and unforgiving terrain with no sign of familiar landmarks. No villages, no farms, no markers of civilisation. Just wild, empty land.

Raven paused, crouching by a cluster of low shrubs.

'I think we're further north than expected,' he murmured, running his hand over the damp earth. This is not where we were supposed to land.'

'How far off?' Marcus asked.

'Leagues.' Raven's eyes flicked toward the horizon. 'We were supposed to land in the south, but this is too far north. I think we've been blown into the lands of the Iceni.'

'Are you sure?'

'I can't be certain, but this coast seems wild and

inhabited and with those southerly winds, it makes sense. I'll know for sure when I see the cattle or hear one of the people speak. If it is Iceni land, we can breathe a little easier. Prasutagus is known to trade freely with Rome and is not as warlike as his neighbours but if it's the Trinovantes, we need to tread carefully.'

'Isn't Cunobeline the king of the Trinovantes?'

'He is. And he is also the king of the Catuvellauni. But nearer the coast, Togodumnus holds far greater sway than his father and many clans follow his lead. He is the one we need to worry about.'

'Well, let us hope that we are in the lands of the Iceni, at
least until we get our bearings.'

With the sun climbing higher, Marcus and Raven descended the hill. The wilds of Britannia stretched out before them, and for the next few hours, they saw no sign of life. By noon they were about to turn back when Raven suddenly stopped, raising a hand in warning.

'What is it?' asked Marcus.

Raven didn't answer. His eyes were fixed on the crest of the next hill. A moment later, Marcus also saw the danger, three riders appearing over the rise, their horses' hooves kicking up clods of earth as they descended toward the open valley. Celtic riders.

Marcus dropped into a crouch, motioning for Raven to follow him into the thicker grass nearby. The two men pressed themselves flat against the ground, their bodies hidden by the tall, swaying stalks. From their position, they could hear the faint clinking of bridles and the soft snorting of the horses as the riders drew nearer.

The Celts rode slowly, their sharp eyes sweeping the landscape. They were warriors, cloaked in furs, their long hair tied back with leather cords, spears held loosely in their hands. Painted designs covered their exposed skin, and they moved with the ease of men accustomed to patrolling their land.

Marcus dared not move, his breath shallow as he watched the riders come closer. If one of them looked down, even a glimpse of movement could mean discovery. His hand tightened around the hilt of his sword, though he knew full well that a confrontation would be suicide. Three mounted warriors against two on foot? They wouldn't stand a chance.

Raven lay motionless beside him, his face calm, but Marcus could see the tension in his eyes. Every second felt like an eternity as the riders approached, their horses snorting and stamping the earth just paces from where the two men lay hidden. One of the Celts tugged on his reins, his horse turning in their direction, and Marcus froze, his muscles coiled like a spring, ready to strike if they were found.

But the rider's gaze passed over them, seeing nothing but the wild grass that stretched endlessly over the hills. He spurred his horse onward and to Marcus's immense relief, the riders continued on, their pace quickening as they headed down toward the valley.

Within minutes, they were a distant blur, disappearing over the next rise, leaving nothing but the sound of the wind in their wake.

Marcus pushed himself up slightly, still half-crouched, and glanced at Raven.

'That was close.'

Raven exhaled slowly and got to his feet.

'Too close,' he said, 'but at least they were not Trinovantes.'

'You're sure?'

Raven gave a curt nod.

'Iceni. I recognised the markings.'

Marcus let out a breath, his muscles still tense from the close encounter.

'Well, at least that confirms we're not deep in enemy territory. If we're near the Iceni's lands, it means we're not as far off course as we thought.'

'Agreed,' said Raven. 'Now we know where we are, we can plan our next move. Let's get back to the others.'

The two men rose fully from the grass and began to retrace their steps. The wilds of Britannia were unforgiving, and they still had leagues to travel before they reached their comrades.

Several hours later, they arrived back at the ravine, but there was no sign of any of the others, not even a footprint.

'They've gone,' Raven muttered, his sharp eyes moving over the ground. He knelt down, brushing his hand over a patch of flattened grass. 'But not long ago.'

Marcus nodded, but there was no concern on his face. It was a common practise for the Occultum to move on when a better hiding place was available.

'Look for signs,' he said.

Raven got to his feet and both men spread out, looking for something they knew the men would have left. Raven moved to the large boulder that had sheltered them from the wind before something caught his attention, a faint series of scratches on the rock's face, barely visible to the untrained eye. He moved closer, crouching beside the stone, and ran his fingers over the markings. They were crude, hastily carved, but to Raven their meaning was clear. The symbols weren't

random. They were part of a code devised by the Occultum, a language of its own known only to those within the group. The first mark resembled an angular bird, the next
a series of jagged lines, and the final a curved line. To any other man, the scratches would have seemed like idle etchings, but to Marcus, they spoke volumes.

'They've gone west,' he said confidently, 'into the forest.

'Good, said Marcus, they must have found better cover. Let's go.'

The two men began to move, heading in the direction indicated by the markings. The terrain sloped gently upward, the tall grass giving way to patches of thick brush and stunted trees. As they neared the edge of the forest, Marcus felt the slightest release of tension. The deep woods of Britannia were untamed and filled with unseen dangers, but for now, the forest offered safety, concealment from any prying eyes that might have spotted their wrecked boat or their tracks across the open land.

Moments later, they entered the forest, the thick canopy above casting long shadows over the ground. The air was cooler here, the smell of damp earth and pine heavy around them. Marcus stayed alert, his hand never far from his sword and a hundred paces in, Raven raised his hand, signalling a stop. The tracker's eyes were sharp, his movements controlled as he listened to the faint sounds of the forest. Moments later, he cupped his hands around his mouth and mimicked the call of an owl, a soft, low hoot that echoed briefly in the stillness. For a few more heartbeats there was silence, then, from the shadows ahead, came a faint reply, another owl call, this one a little sharper, a little more deliberate. A signal. Raven's mouth twitched in a brief smile.

'They're close.'

They pushed forward again, stepping over roots and ducking beneath low branches and within minutes, Raven stopped again, staring at another unmistakeable sign, a thin branch bent at an awkward angle. It was what he had been looking for, and as he turned around, he jumped at the sight of Sica standing just a few paces away.

'Sica,' he hissed, 'you scared me to death.'

'We knew you were coming,' said Sica. 'You are out of practise, Raven, You sounded like a herd of deer racing through the forest.'

'Where are the others?' asked Marcus walking over.

'Close,' said Sica, 'follow me.'

Ten minutes later, they bent down and crawled beneath a

tangled thicket, finally emerging into a small clearing formed only a few hours earlier. All the men were sat around the perimeter, looking more relaxed than they had for many days.

'You took your time,' said Falco. 'We were thinking we might have to leave you behind and do this thing alone.'

'We had a bit of a run in,' said Marcus walking over to his sarcina. 'Nothing serious but at least we know we are in Iceni territory. He looked around approvingly. The thicket provided excellent cover and would deaden any noise they might inadvertently make. 'We will lay up here tomorrow,' he said, 'and move out at last light tomorrow.'

'Which way?' asked Sica.

'West,' said Marcus. 'Eventually we'll find a village or a farm and when we do, Raven will get directions to Venta Icenorum, the Iceni's capital.'

'The name sounds Roman,' said Cassius.

'That's because it is,' said Marcus. 'Their king,

Prasutagus, is one of the few people in these lands to be an ally of Rome. We'll head there and consolidate before we head south.'

'So be it,' said Falco and as Raven and Marcus opened their packs to get some well-earned food, Sica and Atticus left the hiding place to take first watch while the rest of the men set about settling down for the night. They had finally arrived in Britannia and after the initial few setbacks, they were now all set to carry out the mission they had trained so hard for over the last few months.

Chapter Ten

Vandal Territory

The dense forest east of the Elbe swallowed the three men in its shadow, the towering trees blocking what little morning light managed to break through the canopy. Their horses moved cautiously through the thick undergrowth, hooves muted by the damp, spongy carpet of leaves. The narrow, overgrown paths they followed were far from the well-worn roads that cut across eastern Germania, here, amidst the gnarled roots and dense undergrowth, even the smallest misstep could betray them, and that was a risk they couldn't afford to take.

Talorcan led the way, his sharp eyes sweeping the gloom between the trees, alert to any sign of movement or danger. Behind him, Seneca and Canis followed in silence, each painfully aware that death could be waiting around any corner. The Vandals were infamous for their aggression, prone to attacking strangers on sight, without warning or mercy.

Their ride through Cherusci territory had been frantic, a mad dash through lands that were semi-friendly at best. But now, as they ventured deeper into the forests near the Elbe, their pace slowed, each movement more deliberate, more calculated. They were close now, and one mistake could see them all dead.

Talorcan raised his hand, bringing them to a halt. The forest fell silent around them as he dismounted, crouching low to inspect the ground. His fingers traced a broken branch, the earth soft and freshly disturbed. His brow furrowed.

'A hunting party passed here,' he murmured, 'no more than a day ago. A small group, moving quickly.'

Seneca's gaze shifted northward, where the faint scent of smoke lingered on the breeze. His eyes narrowed.

'Fires,' he said quietly. 'We must be close.'

Talorcan nodded in agreement. Their progress since crossing the Elbe had been painfully slow, each step fraught with danger. But now, at last, they were nearing their destination, the area his contact had spoken of. It was here, somewhere in these woods, that one of the tribes kept a Roman slave, a man tasked with tending their horses.

'We need better cover,' said Seneca. 'Once we've gone firm, we'll continue on foot.'

They remounted, guiding their horses deeper into the forest. The shadows thickened, and the trees seemed to close in around them, their branches twisting together like skeletal fingers, and every rustle of leaves, every snap of a twig was magnified in the oppressive silence. The journey so far had been frantic, dangerous, and nerve-wracking, but they all knew the hardest part still lay ahead.

A few leagues away, a group of warriors made their way to the paddock at the centre of the village. Word had spread quickly that a valued brood mare had given birth, but the foal was in trouble and as they approached, they could see the Batavian horse master kneeling beside the seemingly lifeless body of the newborn. His face was slick with sweat as he worked feverishly, fighting to save its life.

Brennus' brow furrowed in deep concentration as his hands moved over the foal's legs, massaging them, coaxing blood and strength into the trembling limbs. The mother stood close by, her large eyes fixed on Brennus, but there was no fear in her gaze. She trusted him now, as did they all.

More warriors gathered, rough men clad in furs and

leather, their faces hardened by battle and weather. They watched in silence, their eyes narrowing, not in disdain, but in grudging respect. Brennus, though still a captive, had earned a measure of recognition amongst them with his skill with horses. Over a year had passed since they'd fished him from the river, and although his early days with the Vandals had been harsh, slowly but surely, things had begun to shift.

Realising he was losing the foal, Brennus moved swiftly, cupping his hands around the animal's small muzzle, sealing it completely. The warriors looked on, their brows furrowing as they watched him attempt something unexpected. Without hesitation, Brennus covered its nose with his own mouth, blowing hard into its nostrils. The onlookers shook their heads in disbelief, murmurs rippling through the crowd. When there was no response, Brennus tried again, each breath more desperate than the last.

Just as the warriors began to jeer, their voices rising in derision, a faint bleat escaped the foal's mouth. Brennus released his hold and resumed massaging its legs, pushing the blood through the small, fragile veins. Moments later, the foal cried out again, this time stronger, and kicked out with a sudden force, catching Brennus in
the side. He barely flinched, ignoring the pain, and continued until, at last, the foal began to stir.

It wobbled at first, struggling to stand, then stumbled forward. Brennus reached out, his rough hands steadying the creature, guiding it through its first attempts to balance, its tiny chest rising and falling as it drew its first proper breaths. The mare snorted softly, nudging her newborn gently with her nose and Brennus, his work done, stepped back to let mother and foal bond in peace.

A grunt of approval came from the watching warriors.

One of them, the owner of the mare, pushed his way through the group, his heavy boots crunching over the dirt. He was a large man, with a tangled beard and a perpetual scowl. He eyed Brennus for a long moment, his gaze flicking from the Batavian to the mare and her foal. Without a word, he reached into the folds of his cloak and pulled out a silver bracelet, tarnished but finely made, its surface glinting dully in the firelight.

With a grunt, he tossed it to Brennus, who caught it in one hand. The weight of the silver felt strange in his palm, and for a moment, Brennus looked at the man, surprised. It was rare for a captive to be given anything of value, and rarer still for a gesture of gratitude from one of the Vandals. The group around them remained silent, their eyes fixed on the exchange, but there was no mistaking the significance. The silver was more than payment, it was an acknowledgement.

Brennus gave a nod, his expression calm, though inside he felt the shift. He had been a prisoner for over a year, surviving by keeping his head down and his skills sharp. Now, slowly, the scales were tipping. The Vandals no longer saw him as merely a captive, but as someone of use, someone worth acknowledging.

The warrior turned and walked away, his shoulders hunched against the wind, leaving Brennus standing there, the bracelet still cool in his hand. The crowd began to disperse, their interest fading now that the spectacle was over, but Brennus felt his place among the Vandals was changing, even if they wouldn't yet admit it. He wiped the sweat from his brow, his chest still heaving from the effort of saving the foal and his eyes drifted beyond the paddock, to the far side where a familiar figure stood, watching.

There, in the shadow of a nearby hut, stood Elara, his

woman, with their child bundled in her arms. Her hair, dark and braided, caught the evening light, and even from this distance,
Brennus could see the softness in her gaze.

She had come quietly, as she often did, avoiding the gaze of the warriors who lingered nearby. She was careful, knowing his position among the tribe was still uncertain. Yet here she was, offering him the strength of her presence in this moment of quiet triumph.

Without a word, Brennus straightened and walked towards her, his body still aching from the strain of his work, but his heart lightened by the sight of her. As he drew near, Elara smiled, a small, gentle thing, but it was enough. The child in her arms stirred, a soft gurgle breaking the stillness and Brennus reached out, offering her the silver bracelet.

She stared at the gift, a flicker of surprise in her eyes. It wasn't often that anyone received such gestures from the Vandals, and she knew what it meant.

'You've earned this,' she said softly, 'it is yours to wear, not mine.'

'I want you to have it,' he said. 'Keep it in case you ever need medicine if you or the child gets ill.' The woman nodded and together, they began to walk back to the hut they shared, the bracelet tucked into Elara's hand.

As they moved away from the paddock, Brennus could feel the eyes on his back, the weight of their attention unmistakable. He glanced over his shoulder and saw Wulfstan and another warrior, Odo, a man he knew to be close to the chieftain, watching him.

The two Vandals watched him go: their gazes sharp but thoughtful. Wulfstan gave a small grunt of approval as he watched the Batavian walk away.

'He's different,' he said, scratching at his beard. 'Not like the others.'

Odo nodded slowly.

'He is. He has as a way with the horses like no one I have ever seen. There is value in such a man.'

Wulfstan looked back at the foal, now on its feet, tottering but alive.

Odo's eyes remained on Brennus, who was now disappearing into the fading light with his woman and child.

'He's been with us long enough,' he mused. 'and has earned his place, at least as far as the horses are concerned. Perhaps it is time we brought him into the fold.'

Wulfstan grunted in agreement, though there was a trace of hesitation in his voice.

'He is still a westerner and there are some who would still prefer to see his head on a spike.'

Odo shrugged, his gaze never leaving the retreating figure.

'That may be so, but you've seen how he works the horses. We'd be foolish not to think on it. To lose such a man through neglect would be an insult to the gods.'

Wulfstan slapped Odo on the back, a rare gesture of camaraderie.

'Let's give it some thought. No need to rush, but you're right. He's earned more than just a band of silver.'

As they turned back to the paddock, the foal trotted across to them, and Wulfstan watched with quiet satisfaction. They would wait and see, but one thing was clear: Brennus' place among the Vandals was changing. Slowly, but surely, the Batavian captive was becoming something more than just a slave.

Seneca and Talorcan moved through the thick forest, each footstep carefully placed, each breath measured. The undergrowth here was dense, a tangle of roots and thorns that threatened to snag and betray even the lightest tread. Canis had remained behind, tasked with minding the horses, ensuring they remained quiet and hidden deep within the woods. The Vandals would kill a man for far less than trespassing in their lands, and discovery now would mean death for them all.

As they neared the village, the sounds of the settlement drifted towards them, distant voices, the clatter of tools, and the occasional bark of a dog. Talorcan raised a hand, signalling for them to stop and Seneca froze instantly, his sharp eyes locking onto something up ahead.

Seneca motioned to a small rise in the ground, thick with brambles and ferns. It would give them the extra height they needed without exposing them to wandering eyes. Talorcan nodded, and they began to crawl, inch by inch, their bodies pressed to the earth. Every movement was deliberate, every shift in weight calculated to avoid the snapping of twigs or rustling of leaves.

They reached the rise and settled into position, burying themselves beneath the thick undergrowth. Ferns and brambles covered them completely, their bodies blending into the earth,
invisible to any who might pass by. Seneca shifted slightly, ensuring he had a clear line of sight, while Talorcan's gaze was already fixed on the village below, his sharp eyes scanning for any sign of Brennus.

They lay in silence, watching, learning the ways of the Vandal people. The village was alive with movement, a man sharpening an axe by the fire, a group of women tending to food, a few warriors returning from a hunt, carrying carcasses slung over their shoulders. Talorcan's eyes flicked from one figure to another, his mind piecing together the patterns of life in the settlement, but there was no sign of the man they sought.

'Nothing,' Talorcan whispered, his voice barely audible above the breeze.

Seneca nodded, his brow furrowed in concentration. Brennus was here, somewhere, he was sure of it. Talorcan's contact had been certain and if he wasn't visible now, they would just have to wait, watch longer, and learn more.

Hours passed as they remained hidden, the light slowly shifting from late afternoon to dusk. The shadows grew longer, the village settling into a quieter rhythm as the day's work came to an end. The central firepit was lit, and soon the smell of roasting meat filled the air, and the warriors gathered around the fire, talking in low voices, sharing jugs of ale.

'There,' Talorcan whispered suddenly.

Seneca followed his gaze and saw him. A tall man, his dark hair pulled back, stepping out from the edge of the settlement with a horse trailing behind him. Even from this distance, Seneca could see the ease with which he handled the animal, his hands moving with the confidence of someone who knew the creature well. The horse was a fine one, clearly belonging to someone of importance, and it was being led by none other than Brennus himself.

'He's alive,' Seneca murmured, his voice steady despite the rush of emotion he felt. 'But we need more time. We have to know how deep he's embedded here. See who he speaks to, what his role is.'

The two men remained in their concealed position, their eyes never leaving Brennus. They watched as he tethered the horse and spoke briefly to a passing warrior, his body language relaxed but not subservient. There was no visible sign of mistreatment, no chains, no guard trailing him, but he was still a captive, no matter how free he appeared.

Night fell, and the fire in the village burned brighter as the sky darkened and the village slowly began to settle for the night. Seneca glanced at Talorcan.

'We'll come back tomorrow. Watch again. We need to know more before we act.'

They began the slow, painful crawl back into the deeper woods before getting to their feet and heading back to where Canis and the horses awaited them. The mission was far from over, but for the first time since they had set out, Seneca felt a glimmer of hope. Brennus was alive, and soon, with the help of the gods, they would bring him home.

Chapter Eleven

The Lands of the Iceni

The journey from the coast to the Iceni capital had been long and gruelling, each step requiring patience, caution, and skill. The Occultum moved only by night, slipping through the shadows like ghosts, leaving no trace of their passage. By day, they remained hidden, using the thick woods, rocky outcrops, and abandoned ruins for cover. Every member of the team was trained in subterfuge and secrecy, and it showed in the way they navigated the hostile land, slow, methodical, and invisible.

The Britannic lands were dangerous, not just because of the tribes that roamed them, but because the terrain itself seemed to resist their forbidden presence. Raven took point, his sharp eyes able to pick out the safest routes, avoiding game trails or any sign of human passage, his senses attuned to the land, the whisper of a breeze, the snap of a twig. The moon was their only guide, its pale light filtering through the canopy as they wound their way deeper into the interior. Sometimes, they would hear distant voices, the chatter of an evening gathering in a nearby settlement or the bark of a hunting dog in the hills. At such times, they would freeze, their breaths shallow, bodies pressed against the forest floor until the danger passed. When it did, they would resume their careful pace, one foot in front of the other, always alert, always hidden.

Days passed in silence, the sun filtering weakly through the trees. The men would eat in silence, their rations sparse, their ears straining for any sound that might betray the approach of danger. They communicated with gestures, the occasional whispered word enough to keep them on task but as they drew closer to the Iceni capital, the tension grew. The forests thinned, replaced by open fields and hillforts that dotted the landscape.

Finally, on the sixth day, the walls of the Iceni capital came into view. It sat nestled on a hill, surrounded by a wooden palisade, the land around it dotted with farms and grazing fields.

Marcus signalled for the group to halt at the edge of the forest.

'Spread out,' he ordered quietly. 'Keep to the treeline but stay out of sight. Raven, Sica, you know what to do.'

An hour or so later, the two men moved through the Celtic settlement, their cloaks pulled tight against the cool and damp air. The streets were narrow, lined with earthen homes and timber-framed huts, smoke rising from the hearths within. The hum of life continued around them, the occasional murmur of voices from behind closed doors, the bleat of sheep penned in small enclosures, the clink of tools from distant workshops. Yet, they pressed forward, keeping their faces down, blending with the many people who moved about the town.

As they ventured deeper, Sica noticed something unusual amidst the rugged, native structures. Tucked between the simple dwellings were small but unmistakably Roman style buildings. They were sparse, scattered as if foreign growths in the Celtic soil, but their influence was clear. Simple brickwork, tiled roofs, and arches, small, functional structures reminiscent of the designs back in Gaul, though far less grand. It was a subtle yet undeniable testament to the Roman trade that Prasutagus, the Iceni king, had fostered for years.

Marcus exchanged a glance with Sica, the hint of

surprise mirrored in his comrade's eyes. The influence of Rome was here, even in this remote corner of Britannia.

'They've taken to Roman ways more than I'd thought,' Sica muttered under his breath.

'Prasutagus has made sure of that,' said Raven, 'trade is a powerful tool.'

They continued through the town, careful not to draw attention. The streets grew narrower, converging towards the centre. The smell of freshly baked bread mingled with the distinct, exotic aromas of spices, unfamiliar smells in these northern lands at the edge of the empire.

The square at the centre of the town was lined with traders peddling their wares, haggling with customers. Amongst them, a man stood over a collection of clay jars and woven baskets, his stock filled with spices from the distant east. Cinnamon sticks, dried saffron, and peppercorns lay carefully arranged, their value unmistakable even in the poor light.

'There,' Raven whispered, inclining his head towards the trader. 'That must be our man.'

Sica grunted in agreement, his hand instinctively brushing the hilt of his dagger as they moved towards the stall. As they approached, Raven kept his face impassive, glancing around the
square for any signs of trouble.

The trader looked up as they neared, his dark eyes scanning them quickly. He was older than Raven had expected, his face lined with years of travel and trade, yet his gaze was sharp, aware.

'Greetings, strangers,' he said, sensing another sale.

'Greetings,' replied Raven, 'Are you open for business?'

'I am always open for business,' replied the trader,

'what can I get you?'

'We seek a very rare spice from the depths of Italy,' said Raven. 'I forget the name, but I know the natives there refer to it as Eagle's Claw. Do you have it?'

For a few moments, the trader remained silent, his eyes narrowing in confusion before understanding flickered across his face.

'It is indeed a rarity,' he replied, 'but I believe I have a little left. Come with me.'

He gestured for them to follow, leading them away from the stall and deeper into the backstreets of the town. As they walked, Raven and Sica couldn't help but notice the deference shown to the trader by those they passed. He was clearly a man of influence, which made perfect sense, he was their conduit, a direct link to Prasutagus himself.

A few minutes later, they arrived at one of the Roman-style buildings they had seen earlier and stepped inside. The interior was familiar, resembling a Roman house and while not as opulent as those in the larger cities, it was clean, comfortable, and a welcome sight for both men. The trader paused, glancing back to ensure they hadn't been followed, before closing the door behind them. He then joined them in the room that served as a modest kitchen.

'Welcome,' said the man, reaching up to a shelf to retrieve an amphora of wine. 'Please, sit – you must be exhausted.' Raven and Sica sat at the table, waiting as their host poured three cups of wine before topping them up with water. Once done, he joined them at the table. 'Well, you made it,' he said, 'so here's to the future of Britannia.'

He took a sip, his eyes studying his two guests as they drained their cups in one go. 'So,' he continued, as they placed their cups back on the table, 'as you likely know, my name is

Quintus Valerius, personal advisor to King Prasutagus on all matters Roman. Which of you is Seneca?'

'I am,' Raven lied before Sica could answer. 'But how do
we know you are who you claim to be?'

'You don't,' said Quintus, with a shrug. 'But the fact that I was expecting you, and know what you want, should offer some reassurance.'

'And what do you think we want from you?' asked Sica.

'Direct access to the king,' Quintus answered. 'I don't know all the details, but if you are who I think you are, then you've come to the right man. I can arrange it. Also, the man who set this up is an old friend of mine, an ex-legatus named Lepidus. Does that ease your mind?'

Raven glanced at Sica, who gave a slight nod. It wasn't a certainty, but the facts seemed to align, and without any clear signs of deceit, they began to relax.

'Are you hungry?' asked Quintus. 'You must have travelled far.' Without waiting for a response, he stepped to the doorway and called out a name. Moments later, a young boy hurried in, his face filled with concern.

'Forgive me, lord,' the boy said, bowing his head. 'I was preparing your meal.'

'Good,' Quintus replied. 'Make enough for two more. We have guests.'

'At once, my lord,' said the boy, the relief clear in his voice as he hurried away to the kitchen.

'We cannot stay,' said Raven once the boy had left. 'We need to see Prasutagus and be gone as soon as possible.'

'You may as well stay for food,' Quintus replied, pouring himself another drink. 'I can't get you near him until tomorrow, at the earliest. He'll return just after dawn.'

'Where is he?' Sica asked.

'Who can predict the movements of a king?' Quintus shrugged. 'But there's plenty of food, and you must be famished. I could also provide provisions for your journey back to your men. How many of you are there?'

Raven and Sica exchanged a glance, their suspicions sharpened. It was the first time Quintus had said something that made them uneasy.

'What makes you think there are more of us?' asked Raven.

'Ah,' Quintus said, raising a hand in a gesture of apology. 'I realise how that might have sounded, but I'm glad to see you're so cautious. My question was clumsy but to answer your question, I
simply assumed two men would not suffice for a mission of such importance. Your strength is none of my concern and the matter is closed. Now, will you stay or not?'

Later that night, Raven and Sica slipped away from Quintus' house under the cover of darkness. They exchanged no words, each relying on instinct as they navigated the narrow streets and headed towards the distant edge of the forest.

As they neared the treeline, the looming shadows of the forest beckoned like an old ally, familiar and comforting. Yet, just before they reached the cover of the trees, both men halted abruptly, turned and dropped to the ground, their eyes fixed on the path behind them. They remained utterly still, listening intently for any sound, scanning the road for the faintest sign they had been followed.

For what seemed like an eternity, they lay in silence, the only sound the soft rustle of leaves in the breeze. Ten minutes passed, and when they were finally satisfied that no one had tracked them, Raven tapped Sica on the shoulder. Without a word, the two men rose and as they slipped into the forest's embrace, Marcus stepped out of the shadows. He gave a low whistle and waited as the rest of the Occultum slowly began to emerge from the shadows, their movements ghostly, their cloaks blending seamlessly with the dark foliage. Without speaking, Raven and Sica joined them, and the group moved as one, deeper into the heart of the forest.

Amidst the ancient trees and thick bramble, they found the spot they had chosen for the night, well-hidden, with just enough space for them to gather and rest. Once settled, they dug a small pit in the forest floor to conceal a much-needed fire, the flames providing warmth without betraying their presence. Falco retrieved a pot from his sarcina and, after filling it half with water, everyone contributed a handful of dried rations to the communal stew. Sica added a small block of something unpronounceable to the rest of the men, its pungent smell drawing curious glances and gradually, the tension began to ease as they anticipated the first hot meal they had eaten in days.

As the stew simmered, Raven relayed the details of their meeting with Quintus, explaining how they had left after agreeing to return at sunset the following day. Marcus listened intently, his
eyes narrowing slightly when Raven mentioned Quintus' strange line of questioning.

'Do you think we can trust him?' asked Marcus.

'Do we have any other option?' Raven replied. 'I believe he's the contact, but it's possible his loyalties have shifted. We won't know for certain until we meet him again tomorrow.'

'We could be walking into a trap,' said, Sica, 'he knows exactly where we'll be and when we will arrive. It's the perfect setup for an ambush.'

Marcus nodded slowly.

'True. But it's a risk we have to take. I'll give it some thought and perhaps I can come up with something to lessen the risk. You did well today, now get some food and rest. We'll work it out.' With that, he turned and walked back to the fire, where some of the men were already lying back on the soft earth, their cloaks pulled tightly around them against the chill of the night.

After the group had shared the meal, Marcus leaned back against his sarcina, his gaze distant as his comrades settled into uneasy sleep. The fire, now little more than glowing embers, cast a faint, flickering light, offering scant warmth against the cool night air. The impending meeting with Quintus and Prasutagus weighed heavily on his mind. It was, without question, the most perilous situation they had faced thus far. One wrong step, one moment of misplaced trust, could spell disaster not just for him and his men, but for their entire mission. Quintus had revealed enough to suggest he was the contact, yet his strange questioning and easy offer of aid left Marcus wary.

The risk was great, but there was no way forward without confronting it. He turned the problem over in his mind, seeking an angle, a way to lessen the danger that awaited them, until eventually, exhausted by his own racing thoughts, he allowed himself to succumb to a fitful sleep.

Chapter Twelve

Trinovante Territory

To the south, Togodumnus rode towards Camulodunum, responding to a summons carried by a rider through the mist-laden hills to the west. Word of his father's illness was no surprise, for rumours had whispered through the land for weeks, but the urgency of the call struck him with a sense of finality.

By the time he reached the seat of their father's power, his mood was foul, tinged with a hint of sadness at the impending news of his father's demise. He looked around the capital, a place he had not seen for many months.

The Roman influence was everywhere now, creeping like a shadow over the city. Coloured fabrics and strange scents of unfamiliar spices, foreign words and the occasional sound of a Latin tongue, all brought into Camulodunum by traders who slipped through their borders like hungry rats. Togodumnus felt bitterness rising in his throat. His father had allowed this, he had allowed the Trinovantes to grow too close to Rome, too comfortable in their new ways. Even now, as his father lay dying, Togodumnus could not rid himself of the anger that festered within him.

Caratacus, his elder by just a few years, rode beside him in silence. The two had met outside the city but exchanged few words, each lost in their own thoughts. Caratacus' mind was on the future, the invasion he knew was coming, but he was torn between the path of peace his father had always favoured and his brother's fiery determination to drive the Romans back into the sea. His heart fought against his mind, but here and now, such matters had no place. Not when their father was dying.

They dismounted and entered their father's hall, the old stone walls weathered and familiar around them. At the centre, their father lay on a giant bed, surrounded by his family and favoured chieftains but the once-great king, who had ruled with such strength and authority, now lay frail and sunken upon his bed, his breath shallow, his eyes distant.

Togodumnus hesitated at the threshold. He had grown distant from his father in recent years, their differences over the Romans carving a deep divide between them. Cunobeline had always sought diplomacy, compromise, a way to coexist with the
growing Roman influence, while Togodumnus seethed with the desire for resistance, for war. Now, standing on the edge of his father's final hours, that distance felt like an uncrossable chasm.

Caratacus stepped forward first, taking Cunobeline's' hand in his own.

'Father,' he said quietly. 'We are here.'

The old king's eyes fluttered open, clouded and weak, but there was a glimmer of recognition. His lips moved, but the words barely formed, the effort of speech too great. Caratacus leaned closer, his head bowed, straining to hear.

Togodumnus stood back, arms crossed, unable to move. The anger that had simmered within him now battled with something deeper, something more painful. For years, he had fought his father, over every decision, every council meeting, every conversation about Rome. But now, in this moment, none of it seemed to matter. The man who had once commanded respect and loyalty from all who knew him was slipping away, and Togodumnus was not sure he could bring himself to say goodbye.

'Come, Togodumnus,' said Caratacus, 'he needs us both.'

The younger brother hesitated, but slowly, he approached the bed, kneeling on the opposite side and for the first time in years, Togodumnus looked into his father's eyes without the burden of resentment.

Cunobeline's' eyes shifted towards him, his lips parting as if to speak. Togodumnus leaned in, hearing the faintest whisper of a word, though its meaning was lost. But the look in his father's eyes said more than words ever could, a mixture of regret, pride, and something that tugged at Togodumnus' heart in a way he had not expected.

'Rest, Father,' Togodumnus murmured, and he placed a hand on his father's shoulder, feeling the thinness of his frame, the frailty of the man who had once been larger than life.

Cunobeline's' breathing grew slower, each breath laboured and faint, until finally, the great king of the Catuvellauni and Trinovantes breathed his last and his sons, once divided by pride and ambition, were united in grief, their heads bowed as they let go of the man who had shaped both their destinies.

Chapter Thirteen

Venta Icenorum

The sun had hardly cleared the eastern horizon when Raven and Sica once more headed towards the Iceni capital, and as they descended from the wooded heights, the road through the outlaying scattering of huts around the settlement became busier, as the people went about their morning routines. The previous day they had only seen part of the town but now, in the full glare of the morning sun, they could finally take in the full scope of the settlement the wooden stakes of the palisade speaking of decades of raids and wars.

Inside the walls, the town was a bustling hive of activity. The dirt streets were uneven, worn down by years of footsteps and the passage of carts and the houses were typical of the many similar structures the two men had seen across Gaul and Germania, round structures made of wattle and daub with conical thatched roofs. The smell of smoke from hearth fires mingled with the earthy aroma of livestock and freshly cut timber and chickens pecked at the ground while pigs rooted around the wooden pens set up on the fringes of the town. Dogs wandered freely between the huts, alert but unbothered by the presence of strangers.

The marketplace itself was a swirling blend of old and new. Stalls made from rough-hewn wood were clustered in the square, where traders sold wares that ranged from simple pottery and woven goods to finer objects that seemed to have travelled from far-off lands. Amongst the local goods, a few Roman items could be seen, bronze trinkets, glass beads, and metal tools that bore the distinct precision of Roman manufacture. It was clear that trade with the empire was already underway, even if full Roman control had not yet descended upon these lands.

'They stare at you,' said Raven quietly as he glanced at a group of women who passed by, their whispers faint but unmistakable.

Sica did not reply. His eyes swept across the square, watching for any sign of hostility, and noting potential escape routes, He was used to being an outsider, used to the stares, and besides, he wasn't here for their approval. The market was a hive of activity, and though the people here were of the Iceni tribe, the atmosphere
reminded Sica of countless other towns he had walked through in faraway lands. Raven gestured with a nod towards the centre of the market.

'There,' he said, his voice barely above a whisper.

Quintas stood at his stall, his plain tunic blending in with the local crowd. His posture was relaxed, but Sica could see the tension in his shoulders, the way his eyes flicked from face to face. Quintas was no fool, he knew the risks of being here, just as Sica and Raven did.

As they approached, he turned slightly, catching their eye. His expression remained neutral, though his hand briefly twitched as though he longed to reach for the dagger hidden beneath his cloak. He gave a short nod, acknowledging their arrival but keeping the encounter casual, mindful of any unwanted attention.

'We're being watched,' Sica murmured under his breath, his sharp eyes catching a group of young men standing by a far wall. They weren't locals. Their hair was longer, their clothes worn differently, and the way they lingered with too much interest made his instincts flare.

Raven gave no sign that he had heard, but his body tensed slightly. He stepped closer to the stall, lifting a small bowl of spices to his nose as if contemplating a purchase.

'Is it done?' he asked quietly.

'The arrangements are made,' replied Quintas. 'Beneath the Oak by the river at noon. Prasutagus will meet you there.'

Raven stepped closer.

'Why can we not meet him in his halls?' he hissed

Quintas picked up a small pouch of herbs, inspecting it with forced nonchalance before continuing.

'Prasutagus may be receptive to an alliance of sorts,' he replied, 'but these are still uncertain times and until we know what offer you bring from Rome, he would rather keep his involvement away from prying eyes. But we must be cautious. There are those who would see to it that no such meeting takes place.'

Sica's eyes darkened as he followed Quintus's gaze, landing once more on the group of men loitering by the wall. Quintas nodded, lowering his voice. 'There are many such men in the town and if they suspect you are here for more than trade, they will act.'

Raven placed the spices back on the stall and glanced at the sun rising slowly over the rooftops. Noon was approaching, and with
it, the meeting that could determine the future of Rome's alliance with the Iceni. Or perhaps the trap that would destroy it.

'Let's hope he values peace more than war,' he muttered, and they began to walk away, leaving the noise of the market behind them.

Quintas watched them go with relief. Too much attention could tip the scales, and they were far from safe, but for now he had played his part, and he could breathe again. He turned away to slip back into the crowd, but before he could move, an arm wrapped around his neck and yanked him into the shadows of a narrow alleyway. For the briefest of moments, he considered fighting back, but the choke hold tightened, and he froze, his eyes wide, his heart hammering against his ribs.

'Do not move,' hissed a voice in his ear.

Quintas struggled to keep his breathing steady. There were at least three of them, maybe more, men he had not seen or sensed in the market. How could he have been so careless?

'What do you want?' he gasped.

A second man stepped in front of him, his face shadowed beneath a hood.

'You're going to tell us who those men were and what they're planning.'

Quintas clenched his teeth, resisting the urge to cry out. His mind raced, trying to find a way out of the situation, but the grip on him was firm, and the men who held him were not Iceni. Their accents were different, their clothes more worn. They were Trinovantes men, loyal to Togodumnus. He cursed under his breath. The warlord's reach was longer than he had thought.

'I don't know what you're talking about,' he said, his voice trembling despite his effort to stay calm.

The warrior stepped closer and pressed a blade against Quintus's chest.

'Lies will only make this harder for you, Roman. We've been watching you for months and know something is going on. Tell us everything you know, and we might just let you live. Deny us what we want, and we kill you right here and leave your body to attract the dogs.'

Panic surged through Quintas. His life hung in the balance, but he knew he couldn't betray Sica and Raven. He tried to twist
out of their grip, but the knife pressed harder, and he knew it would cut through at any moment. At that moment, he realised was going to die and as the instinct for survival overwhelmed him, the words spilled out before he could stop them.

'The river.' he choked out, his voice hoarse. 'They're meeting at the river... at noon. I swear it. Please... let me go...'

'Who are they?' asked another voice.

'Men from Rome,' said Quintas. 'I do know not the detail but was asked to set up a meeting.'

The pressure on the blade eased slightly, though the man behind him still held him firm. Quintas could feel his knees shaking, his entire body trembling at the thought of his imminent death.

'Who are they meeting with?'

'Prasutagus,' Quintas rasped, 'they're trying to forge an alliance. But that's all I know, I swear it. I'm only here to set it up.'

'What else?' demanded the leader. 'Tell me or I swear you will die right here.'

'I know nothing more,' gasped Quintas, desperate to stay alive. 'I swear before all the gods, you now know everything I do.'

The men exchanged glances, their faces still hidden in

shadow before the leader turned once again to Quintas.

'In that case,' he said, 'you are of no more use to us,' and with a quick thrust of his knife, he pierced the trader's heart and watched as he fell to the floor. As the light died in Quintus' eyes, he turned to his men.

'We have little time,' he said, 'we have to go.'

Outside the settlement, Raven and Sica continued along the path towards the river, the air growing cooler as the trees thickened around them.

'So, do you trust him?' asked Raven quietly, his voice barely carrying over the sound of their footsteps.

'Trust is a luxury we cannot afford right now,' said Sica, 'the situation is not good but there is little we can do other than let it run its course.'

The river came into view, its shimmering surface reflecting the midday sun. Raven scanned the surrounding area, noting the patches of woodland that hugged the river's edge, ideal for an ambush, should anyone be waiting. His eyes finally settled on a pronounced bend where the river almost doubled back on itself

before continuing its journey. A lone oak tree stood tall at the middle of the bend, a magnificent totem that reached high into the sky, its branches spreading outward as if offering protection to all who stood under it and Raven knew immediately, this was the place. He dismounted and walked over, again checking the area for potential escape routes should something go wrong, until finally, both men sat on a nearby rock and turned to look back the way they had come. All they could do now was wait.

Chapter Fourteen

The Vandal Settlement

Seneca, Talorcan and Canis took it in turn to watch the Vandal settlement from the safety of the thick undergrowth, learning the daily routines, the comings and goings of the warriors and the moments of vulnerability that came with the dusk. It was slow, frustrating work, but essential if they were to get anywhere near Brennus.

Seneca had remained focussed throughout, his mind always working, analysing each small detail, piecing together a strategy and now, after countless hours of silent observation, a plan was beginning to take shape. It was risky, but he knew there was little other choice. The Vandals were too many, the village too well fortified, so stealth, cunning and timing would be their only advantages.

Once again, they crawled back from their vantage point and retreated into the deeper parts of the forest where no man or beast ventured. The tangled undergrowth and thickets of thorny trees were just not worth the effort to most, but it was exactly the sort of landscape where the Occultum thrived.

'The situation is becoming clearer,' said Seneca eventually, 'it is definitely Brennus in there but he's not a prisoner in chains. They trust him enough to let him work with the horses and move freely around the village, and that could work in our favour.'

'In what way,' asked Talorcan.

'If he has gained their trust,' replied Seneca, 'perhaps he will be able to leave the camp without an escort, and if that is the case, we may be able to get to him without any alarm being raised.'

'Having their trust is one thing,' said Talorcan, 'but there is no way they will ever let him leave the village alone. He is just too valuable.'

'Even if he does,' said Canis, 'and assuming we manage to get away without a dozen arrows in our backs, the Vandals have stronger, faster horses and could ride these lands blindfolded if needs be. Even with a head start, our heads would be on spikes before the sun sets.'

'I agree they have the better horses,' said Seneca, 'or at least they think they do.'

'You've seen them with your own eyes, Seneca, ours would not last half a day compared to them.'

'One of them would,' said Seneca and turned to stare at Talorcan.

Talorcan stared back, realising where the conversation was going. The horse he had bought from the horse fair months earlier was a magnificent specimen and well used to the terrain, having been raised by the Vandals in these very forests and hills. He had no doubt it would hold its own against anything the Vandals had to offer but he was confused. What good would one good horse be against a hundred or more, especially when there would be four of them trying to escape?

'You will forgive me for not following your thoughts, Seneca,' he said, 'at the moment they just don't make any sense.'

'I have a plan,' said Seneca, 'it's dangerous, and relies on Brennus getting himself out of the settlement, but if we can do that, and if the gods are with us, we have an even chance of getting away.'

'That's all well and good,' said Canis, 'but where exactly do we go once he's out? As I said, the Vandals know those lands well we'd be caught before we even reached the River Weser, let alone the Rhine.'

Seneca's eyes gleamed in the firelight as he slowly shook his head.

'They won't catch us,' he said, 'because we won't be there.'

'Where will we be?' asked Canis.

'Heading east,' said Seneca, 'as fast as our horses can carry us.'

For a moment, there was silence as the statement sunk in.

'East?' Talorcan whispered, eventually. 'To where?'

'To the River Viadrus,' said Seneca, 'it's the last place anyone would think to search for us.'

Talorcan and Canis stared at Seneca in stunned silence.

'You want to split us up,' said Talorcan, as the plan became clearer. 'You want me to lead the Vandals west, on a wild chase across the Elbe, while the rest of you head into unknown lands... eastward to the Viadrus.'

'It's the only way, said Seneca. 'Once we have Brennus, if we stay together, we're as good as dead. The Vandals have faster horses, know every trail, and they'll hunt us relentlessly if they think we're heading for the Elbe. They'll expect it because it's what
anyone fleeing would do. But you, Talorcan, can give them the chase they're looking for. And while they follow you, we'll vanish in the opposite direction.'

'This is madness, Seneca,' said Canis, 'even if Talorcan manages to draw them off, no Roman has ever gone that far east or navigated the Viadrus. For all we know the lands could be barren, or filled with hostile tribes, or haunted by evil spirits.

It's a stupid idea.'

'And for those reasons, it becomes the best hope we have,' said Seneca. 'However, your understanding of the river is incorrect. There is an ancient trade route that runs all the way from the cold lands of the north to down to the Mare Nostrum. Traders call it the amber road as it is used to transport amber down to Rome in return for jewellery, furs and weapons. The river forms part of that route and although I agree little is known about it, and I know many traders never come back, but some do return, and they say that the river is vast and easily navigable. If we can reach it, we can follow it upstream to the mountains before turning west again and skirting back into Cherusci territory. It is a risk, I admit but I believe it is the only way to get away safely.'

'And what is to stop them following us?'

'Because hopefully they will still be following Talorcan towards the Elbe. He will travel fast but leave as much of a trail as possible. With a light load, and his knowledge of the area I have no doubt he can get back to the rhine alive and by the time the Vandals realise they have been tricked, we will already be halfway to the Viadrus.'

Talorcan rubbed his temples, his mind racing with the enormity of the task. It was a plan drenched in risk, but the more he thought about it, the more it made sense. Heading east was the last thing anyone would expect, and the Vandals would be so focused on the obvious path toward the Elbe that they'd never consider the alternative.

'What about Brennus?' Canis interjected, breaking the silence. 'We still don't know if he'll even go along with this. What if he's too deep with them now? What if he's not the same man you both knew?'

'That's why I need to speak to him first,' said Seneca.

'We can't make any move until I talk to him. If he's willing, we move forward. If not...' Seneca trailed off, the unspoken words hanging
in the air. They all knew what that meant. If Brennus refused, their plan was dead before it even began.

'If Brennus agrees,' said Raven, 'I'll do it. I'll ride west and make it look like we're heading for the Elbe. But you need to get him out quickly, Seneca, we are going to have to have as much of a head start as possible.'

'One more thing,' said Canis. 'Once we get Brennus and head west, how are we going to turn around and head in the opposite direction without them seeing us?'

'I've already thought of that,' said Seneca. 'There is a strategy that we use in such situations. It is dangerous and needs perfect timing, but the beauty of it is, Brennus is fully aware of it and will know exactly what we are trying to do.'

'What is it?' asked Canis.

'It's called Latebra,' said Seneca, 'and listen carefully, Canis, for it will be down to you to ensure we carry it out perfectly. Our lives depend on it.'

The following night, Seneca left the safety of the undergrowth and began his approach down to the Vandal settlement. His tunic, smeared with dung, clung uncomfortably to his skin, but the stench would help mask his scent from the dogs and horses, preventing them from raising the alarm. He moved with deliberate slowness, each step placed with care to avoid snapping twigs or rustling the undergrowth.

The wall loomed ahead, tall and imposing, its timber posts solid and fitted closely together. Seneca's pulse quickened as he neared edge of the treeline. Torches along the palisade flickered weakly, casting meagre light over the rough-hewn wood, and he lowered himself to the floor, ready to crawl over the open ground between the trees and the settlement.

He reached out with one arm, pulling his body snakelike through the grass, his pace agonizingly slow, his profile hidden to any but the most observant of watchers. Heartbeat by heartbeat, he drew nearer, silent, invisible but as he made his final approach, a faint rustle from the wall caught his attention. Seneca froze, his heart hammering in his chest. A guard's figure appeared on the walkway above, the dull glint of a spearhead briefly catching the light, but after what felt like an eternity, the guard muttered something under his breath and turned away, his footsteps fading into the distance.

Seneca exhaled silently and continued his slow crawl until he reached the palisade. He paused again, straining his ears for any indication that he had been noticed before getting back to his feet in the shadows of the wall.

He crouched low, his hand slipping quietly into the leather pouch at his waist. From within, he retrieved a bundle of steel hooks, each carefully bound in hessian twine to prevent any betraying clinks or rattles. The hooks were sharp and deadly, but it was their shape that made them unique, flattened thinner than a knife blade at the sharp end, while the opposite end had a stirrup of leather attached, a makeshift step for climbing.

Taking a deep breath, Seneca selected one of the hooks and reached upward. He felt for the narrow gap between two of the palisade's logs, his fingers working carefully, guided by touch rather than sight. Finding the crevice, he slid the hook in as delicately as possible, and with a practiced motion, he pulled it downward until the thin blade wedged itself firmly between the logs.

The leather stirrup hung loose, and Seneca tested it, applying just enough weight to ensure it was secure. The steel held fast, and he permitted himself a brief exhale, his breath barely visible in the cool night air.

Slowly, methodically, he repeated the process, his movements deliberate and precise. Each hook was placed with the utmost care, ensuring no sound betrayed his presence, and as he worked his way up the wall, his mind remained razor-sharp, his ears alert for any signs of the guards above. His hands were steady, his muscles taut but controlled, trained for this kind of slow and arduous ascent. The flicker of torchlight passed overhead, and he froze, waiting, barely daring to breathe.

No sound came from above. No alarm, and Seneca resumed his climb, until he was just below the lip of the wall. He stopped again, pressing himself flat against the wood, listening.

The faint murmurs of the guards were audible now, but they were growing distant again, their patrol taking them away from his position. He remained motionless, his mind focused on the most dangerous aspect of the climb that he still had to overcome.

Finally, he gripped the top of the logs tightly, and, with a final, controlled breath, he pulled himself up and over the wall, swinging his legs swiftly as he landed with a soft thud on the wooden platform inside the palisade. His knees bent instinctively to absorb the impact, and he remained crouched, perfectly still. His heartbeat thundered in his ears, but the night around him remained undisturbed. He strained to hear any hint of alarm, any movement that might indicate the guards had noticed his presence.

Nothing.

He allowed himself a moment of relief. The guards, no more than a hundred paces away, were turning again, their torches casting faint light in the distance, and Seneca knew he had only seconds before they would be near enough to spot him.

With no more hesitation, he crept to the edge of the platform and glanced down at the hard-packed earth below. There was no time for second-guessing, and he lowered himself silently over the side and dropped to the ground with barely a sound, landing in a crouch, before pressing himself flat against the inside of the palisade.

He knew he had much to do, and the odds were stacked against him, but it was essential that Brennus knew the plan: but first, he had to find him.

Chapter Fifteen

Vandal Territory

Seneca stared into the village from his hiding place in the shadows. He had memorised the layout from his vantage point up on the hill, but in the close darkness, with the huts looming over him, everything felt disorienting.

He moved slowly, keeping to the edges of the buildings, slipping between the narrow gaps that lay between them.

A dog barked in the distance, followed by the low murmur of voices and Seneca froze, pressing himself into the shadow of a large clay pot resting beside one of the huts. His heart hammered in his chest as he waited until the voices faded, moving away from him, and he exhaled quietly, reassured that he hadn't been discovered.

Ahead, the paddock loomed, the horses shifting restlessly in their enclosures, their hooves scraping at the dirt. He crept along the fence, keeping low to avoid being seen. The horses snorted and shuffled, but none of them reacted to his presence. Step by agonising step, Seneca made his way along the paddock, until he finally reached the far side, and there, just beyond the wooden rails, stood a small, isolated hut. Brennus' hut.

Inside the hut, a single candle burned low on a crude wooden shelf, casting flickering light over the sparse surroundings. The walls were made of rough-hewn timber, the gaps between the logs patched with mud and straw to keep the wind at bay. In one corner, a stack of furs lay on the ground, serving as a bed for Brennus, his woman, and their infant child.

Brennus lay on his back, his limbs heavy with fatigue

from the long day's tending the Vandals' prized horses. He was drifting in and out of sleep, caught in that restless space where his body craved rest, but his mind would not let him fully surrender to it.

A shadow moved in the corner of his vision, a movement so subtle that he thought it might have been a trick of the candlelight, and his body tensed instinctively, the familiar feeling of danger coursing through him like a spark of cold fire. Standing over him was a figure, the features barely discernible in the dim light. A man, tall and lean, his face smeared with blackened charcoal, blending seamlessly with the shadows of the hut

The intruder's eyes glinted in the low candlelight, and in that moment, Brennus knew this was no Vandal warrior, no villager come to disturb the night. The man's posture, his silence, and the way he moved, deliberate, calculated, spoke of someone who did not belong in this place, and he knew immediately, that there was only one group of men skilled enough to even try. The Occultum.

Brennus lay there, his heart pounding in his chest as his eyes adjusted to the sight of Seneca standing above him, the man he had fought alongside in countless campaigns, and the one man he never expected to see here, in this Gods forsaken Vandal settlement.

For a heartbeat, he wondered if this was some fevered dream, his mind playing tricks on him in his exhaustion. But the intensity in Seneca's eyes, the quiet, controlled tension in his movements, told him otherwise. This was real.

Seneca held his gaze. Without a word, he lifted a finger to his lips, commanding silence with a look of urgency. Brennus swallowed hard and glanced to his left, where his woman lay, still soundly asleep, the baby tucked into the crook of her arm.

Slowly, he shifted, his muscles groaning in protest as he rose from the furs, careful not to make a sound.

Seneca motioned toward the far side of the room, and Brennus nodded, following him silently to the rough wall of the hut, away from the candlelight and the fragile peace of his family. The two men crouched low, their backs against the timber, the sounds of the night outside barely audible over the soft crackling of the dying fire in the hearth.

For a moment, neither spoke. Brennus stared at Seneca, his mind racing to catch up with the situation. The last time they had seen each other, they had been fleeing a Cherusci war party, with little chance of survival, but here they both were, alive and in even more danger.

'What in Hades are you doing here?' Brennus finally whispered.

'I came to get you out,' replied Seneca. 'We've been watching the settlement for days, waiting for the right moment.'

Brennus felt a surge of disbelief wash over him.

'Out? Do you know what you're risking? If the Vandals find you…'

'They won't,' said Seneca, 'we've planned everything down
to the last detail. If you do as I say, we can have you out in two days and be leagues away from here before they even notice.'

Brennus shook his head slowly, still struggling to comprehend the enormity of the situation. His life here, tenuous as it was, had become something familiar, something stable. And there was his woman and child. He glanced over at them, the sight of their sleeping forms anchoring him in place.

'I have a family,' he whispered hoarsely, 'a son... I can't just abandon them.'

Seneca's eyes darted to the sleeping woman and the baby nestled in her arms.

'It matters not,' he said, 'you have to come with me. You are our brother, and your comrades have gone against the wishes of the emperor himself to come here to get you out.'

'I'm not leaving without my family,' said Brennus.

'You know we can't take them,' hissed, Seneca. 'We'll barely make it out as it is. The plan was always just about you, Brennus.'

Brennus' gaze hardened, and he shook his head.

'If I leave them, the Vandals will kill them in retribution. I can't, I won't, abandon them to that fate.'

'If you stay,' said Seneca after a long pause, 'you're as good as dead anyway. They'll turn on you eventually, whether it's tomorrow or months from now, it'll happen. You know it as well as I do.' His voice softened, a flicker of desperation creeping into his tone. 'Brennus, we can get you out of here. But we need to move, quickly.'

Brennus leaned in closer, his eyes locking with Seneca's.

'If we can't take them, Seneca, I am staying here, and we will live whatever way the Gods intend for as much time as we have been allocated.'

Seneca's gaze drifted back to the woman and child, still peacefully asleep, unaware of the danger that loomed so close. Finally, with a slow, reluctant breath, he turned back to Brennus.

'So be it,' he said, 'but if we do this, you'll need to carry your child, and your woman will have to keep up. We can't stop, Brennus. Not for anything.'

Brennus nodded.

'She's strong,' he whispered. 'We'll manage, what do you want me to do?'

An hour later, having briefed Brennus in detail, Seneca made his way back the way he came and after dodging the sentries once again, climbed back down the outside of the palisade, removing the hooks as he went. Resisting the temptation to run, he crawled once again through the long grass until at last, he was back amongst the relative safety of the trees.

'Seneca.' Talorcan whispered, emerging from the undergrowth, 'We thought you wouldn't make it. Did you speak with him?'

Seneca nodded, his breath still slightly laboured.

'He's agreed to come,' he said quietly, glancing back toward the village, 'but he won't leave without his woman and child.'

'This wasn't part of the plan,' said Talorcan.

'The plan's changed,' said Seneca. 'Brennus has been with us from the beginning and is as much part of the Occultum as any of us . I wouldn't be standing here now if it hadn't been for him, and I know many more who now sleep soundly in their beds because of something he did. We owe him this.'

Talorcan sighed, clearly weighing the risks. Finally, he nodded, though his face was grim.

'All right,' he said. 'We do it. When do we go?'

'Two days from now at last light,' said Seneca. 'Brennus will be ready and as soon as he does his part of the plan, we move.'

They both looked over to Canis. He was the newest

member of the Occultum, but he still had a say in the matter.

'I agree,' he said, 'but we move as fast as we can. It was difficult before, but now there is absolutely no room for any error whatsoever.'

Seneca glanced back toward the village, where Brennus and his family waited for their only chance of freedom.

'In that case, let's get started,' he said, 'and may the gods be with us.'

Chapter Sixteen

Britannia

Hundreds of leagues away, Raven and Sica waited beneath the oak by the river. Sica's mind returned to Quintas and the hurried conversation in the market that morning. Prasutagus had agreed to the meeting, but the manner of it, the secrecy, the location by the river, unsettled him.

'Do you think Prasutagus will come alone?' he asked.

'Not in a thousand years,' said Raven. 'He is a king after all.'

'Then we have to keep out wits about us,' said Sica. 'This whole situation stinks of treachery.'

The sound of approaching men, barely audible over the sound of the river, caught their attention and they turned to watch a group of six riders approach, all warriors and armed to the teeth.

'He looks nothing like what I expected,' said Sica, staring at the man in front.

'That's no king,' said Raven standing up. 'Be on your guard, Sica, you may have been right. This reeks of treachery.' His eyes narrowed as the six mounted men approached along the riverbank, their weapons gleaming under the midday sun, As they neared, they spread out in a semi-circle, entrapping the two men against the bend in the river.

The leader of the group pulled his horse to a stop a few paces away, his gaze blank, revealing nothing of his thoughts.

'What do we have here?' he asked. 'It looks like we have found ourselves a couple of Roman infiltrators.'

'I am no Roman,' said Raven, 'I was born in these lands, and my comrade here is a Syrian, a trader in rare spices from the east. We seek no trouble.'

The man sighed and sat back in his saddle.

'Do you know what,' he said, 'any other time, it would amuse me to listen to whatever lies you masters have had you learn, but I have been away from my tribe for a long time and yearn for the comfort of my own hearth. I actually know who you are for your friend, Quintas, told me just before I killed him. So, we will waste no more of your time and send you on your way…to meet your gods, that is.' He gave a signal, and the rest of his men drew their swords and lifted their shields, preparing to attack.

Raven's heart sank. He had feared treachery, but this was worse. They had not just been betrayed; they had already been marked for death.

The warriors rode a little closer as Raven and Sica both drew their knives, a futile but symbolic gesture against the men who had them surrounded.

'We'll take their heads back to Togodumnus as trophies,' said the leader over his shoulder, 'and let our warriors see how easily their spies were slaughtered.'

Raven's mind raced. He could already see there would be no reasoning with these men. And there was certainly no avenue of escape. Even if they jumped into the river, the slow-moving water meant they could be cut down by arrows in minutes. He and Sica were cornered.

'Do you think we can just take the arrogant one?' he asked, glancing over to Sica.

'Him and at least two more,' said Sica defiantly. 'Anything less would be shameful.'

The Trinovantes warrior raised his hand to signal the attack but before he could bring it down, a sharp whistle cut through the air, and a volley of arrows arced down from the treeline, striking the riders with deadly precision. Two men fell from their saddles with dull thuds, arrows buried deep in their chests and the leader's eyes went wide with shock as he struggled to remain on his horse, an arrow lodged in his shoulder.

The remaining riders barely had time to react before another volley rained down upon them. The man nearest to Raven toppled from his mount, clutching at the arrow piercing his side as blood poured from the wound and within moments, the once-threatening circle of enemies had been reduced to a chaotic scattering of wounded men and empty saddles.

Sica and Raven, still braced for a fight, stood frozen in confusion, their weapons ready but unused. Sica's eyes darted to Raven, uncertainty flickering across his usually unshakable features.

'What in the name of the gods?'

Before Raven could respond, the sound of hooves thundered from the trees and a new group of riders charged towards the clearing, their cloaks billowing behind them. The lead rider, a man with a regal bearing, slowed his horse as he approached
the riverbank, his expression calm but commanding, the kind of
presence that left no doubt who he was…Prasutagus, king of the Iceni.

His archers fanned out behind him, bows still in hand, but their focus was no longer on Raven and Sica. Instead, they checked the fallen warriors, seeking anything of value amongst their clothing.

Prasutagus halted his horse a few paces away, his sharp gaze sweeping over the fallen men before settling on Raven and Sica. His lips twisted into a faint smile, though there was no humour in his eyes.

'It seems we arrived just in time,' he said glancing briefly at the wounded leader writhing in pain on the ground.

Raven lowered his blade, though he remained wary.

'You saved our lives,' he said, 'and have our gratitude.'

Prasutagus inclined his head in acknowledgement.

'It seems the fates wove your thread a little longer this day,' he said, and gestured toward the dying men with a dismissive wave. 'These men are not mine and ride with those who seek the path of war, the Trinovantes.'

'The Trinovantes are still a tribe of Britannia,' said Sica, 'yet you cut them down with no hesitation.'

Prasutagus regarded him coolly for a moment before answering.

'I am a proud Briton,' he said, 'and have no love for Rome, but I am not so blinded that I would sacrifice thousands of my own people so hot-headed young men can seek the pointless glory of dying in a war they cannot win. Yes, there are battles ahead, but ones that require more than rash decisions and the spilling of Britannic blood.' He paused, his eyes narrowing slightly. 'I know who you are and why you are here, and I am willing to honour the agreement to help broker a peace between Rome and my fellow tribes, but know this, if you are here to deceive me, I will not hesitate to finish what they started.'

Raven sheathed his dagger, meeting the warlord's gaze without flinching.

'We seek no deceit, Prasutagus,' he said, 'only your aid.'

Prasutagus studied them for a long moment, then gave a slow nod.

'Then we shall speak. Come.' He turned his horse

toward the town in the distance, his archers falling in behind him.

Raven and Sica exchanged a glance. They had come perilously close to death yet again, but at last after so many weeks, they had finally made contact with the main man they had come to see.

Later that night, Raven and Sica sat in the Iceni's king's hall. Smoke curled upward, escaping through a hole in the thatched roof, while the warm glow illuminated the faces of Raven and Sica as they sat close to the hearth.

The hall was grand, befitting a king like Prasutagus. Its walls were adorned with tapestries of swirling Celtic designs, depicting scenes of hunting and battle, their vibrant colours muted in the dim light. Shields and spears lined the walls, some worn and battle-scarred, others finely decorated, crafted for ceremonial display. A collection of animal skulls hung above the hearth, their hollow eyes catching the flickering firelight. The ancient power of Britannia was palpable here, the weight of generations pressing down upon those who entered.

Yet, as Raven's gaze drifted across the hall, he couldn't help but notice the growing influence of Rome. Near the head of the hall, where Prasutagus often sat in council, stood a large Roman-style table, its marble surface shining in stark contrast to the rough-hewn furniture scattered throughout the rest of the room. On the table rested fine Roman pottery, gleaming bronze vessels, and a polished silver plate bearing the unmistakable craftsmanship of Roman artisans. There were other signs too, a small, intricately carved statue of Mars, the Roman god of war, and delicate glassware, far removed from the practical, earthen jugs of the Iceni people.

Even the large wooden chair, draped in sheepskin, where Prasutagus sat, had hints of Roman design in the carved lions' heads on the armrests.

The hall was a fusion of two worlds, the wild, untamed spirit of Britannia and the creeping order of Rome. It was a reflection of Prasutagus himself, a man torn between his ancient heritage and the pressures of the Roman Empire pressing down on his people.

Raven leaned forward, his hands stretched toward the fire for warmth. Across from him, Sica sat quietly, his sharp eyes scanning the room. This was not the hall of a king who stood firmly against Rome; it was the hall of a man walking a fine line between alliance and rebellion.

After a few moments, Prasutagus walked in, his presence commanding as he settled into the massive wooden chair opposite Raven and Sica. He stretched out his legs, the sheepskin draped over the chair rustling as he made himself comfortable. For a moment, he said nothing, simply staring into the fire, the flames dancing in his dark eyes.

'The land speaks,' said Prasutagus finally. 'And it grows restless.' He looked up, meeting Raven's gaze. 'Many of the people want war. Some of them crave it. They believe we can resist Rome, drive them out like the old days when our enemies were other tribes.'

'Do you believe that?' asked Raven.

Prasutagus leaned back in his chair, his gaze never wavering.

'I am not so foolish as to think we can defeat Rome,' he said, 'their power is vast. But I also know that bending the knee to them means more than paying tribute. It means losing our soul. I have seen what Rome does to those who do not kneel quickly enough.'

'So, where do you stand? asked Raven, 'between Rome and your people?'

Prasutagus' lips tightened into a thin line.

'I stand on the edge of a blade,' replied the king. 'Too far to one side, and we are swallowed by Rome. Too far to the other, and we are broken by war.'

'We are here to offer a way forward,' said Raven. 'A way to protect your people without losing your soul, as you say.'

'That remains to be seen,' said Prasutagus, 'what exactly do you need of me for I will not raise a single blade against fellow Britons?'

'Yet you did that exact thing just a few hours ago,' said Sica. 'Why was that different?'

'Because they came into my territory uninvited for nothing more than bloodletting. I am king of this tribe and no man gets to choose who lives and dies on my land without my approval. So, tell me what it is you want.'

'We want nothing more than a safe haven here in your lands,' said Raven. 'Our business lies elsewhere but we will need a place to base ourselves without the fear of a blade in the night, or a thousand horsemen running us down if their king changes his mind. We will be no trouble and apart from the occasional purchase of supplies or horses, you will not know we are here.'

'I can do that,' said Prasutagus, 'but what do I get in return?'

Raven glanced over to Sica before reaching beneath his cloak and retrieving a sealed scroll.

'What is this?' said Prasutagus, reaching out to take the document.

'It's the word of the emperor himself,' said Raven,

'promising you shielded status as one of the Empire's protected kingdoms. It is no secret that our legions are gathering, and this document guarantees the safety of you, your family, your people and everything that lives across the lands of the Iceni. Not only that, if any other tribe casts a covetous eye and decides to attack your lands, they will pay the price at the end of Roman blades. This document means peace and prosperity for you and your people, Prasutagus, no matter how far and how long the invasion may take.'

For a moment, silence settled over the hall. The fire crackled, and the distant sounds of the village drifted through the open doorway. Prasutagus held the scroll in his hands, his eyes scanning the seal of the emperor, its weight heavy with unspoken promises. He turned it over slowly, his fingers tracing the wax as though searching for hidden meaning beneath its surface. Then, with a sigh, he set it down on his lap, leaning forward once more toward the fire.

'Peace and prosperity,' he repeated softly, almost to himself. 'Rome's favourite song.' He looked up, meeting Raven's gaze. 'And in return for this protection, what else will they ask of me? Tribute? Taxes? Or perhaps something more... binding?'

'No more than what you already give,' Raven replied. 'They ask for stability and for your loyalty, in exchange for theirs.'

'Loyalty?' spat Prasutagus, as though the word left a bitter taste in his mouth. 'They talk of loyalty, yet they gather their legions to invade our lands, demand our resources, and turn us against each other.' He gestured towards the Roman trinkets scattered across his hall. 'Is this what loyalty looks like? Is this the future of my people, kneeling before foreign gods, drinking from glass cups while we forget how to shape our own clay?'

'What we offer, Prasutagus,' said Raven, 'is not just protection. It is a chance for you to guide your people through what is coming. You see the storm on the horizon, as do we. The Romans are here to stay. You can fight them, and be crushed beneath their legions, or you can forge a path where your people survive, where

your name is remembered not as the king who fell, but as the king who ensured his tribe's future.'

The king fell silent for a moment before replying.

'Very well. You will have your land, a place in the marshes, near the eastern edge of my territory. It is wild, untamed, and there is little there to sustain you, no crops will grow, and no cattle will thrive on its soft soil. But there is fresh water and forests, and it lies far enough from my villages that your presence will not stir unrest.'

Raven inclined his head, grateful but reserved.

'That will suffice. We need only a place to rest and plan. We have no desire to disturb your people.'

Prasutagus nodded, though his expression remained sombre.

'Do not think that I give this lightly, Raven. Your presence here is already known, and it stirs trouble in the hearts of those who still dream of rebellion. Keep your promises and do not draw more eyes to this place. I will not hesitate to revoke my hospitality if I sense that my people are at risk.'

'Understood,' said Raven, rising to his feet as Sica followed suit. 'We will stay in the shadows, and when the time comes, we will leave as quietly as we arrived.'

Prasutagus stood as well, though he did not offer his hand. Instead, he merely nodded towards the door.

'May the gods watch over you both. And remember, this is a land where even the marshes whisper to the wind.'

With that, Raven and Sica left the warmth of the hall, stepping out into the cool night air. The sky above was a deep black, the stars shimmering like distant flames as the village settled into the quiet of sleep. They made their way silently through the narrow paths that wound between the houses, and out through the settlement gates. Once they reached the cover of the trees, Sica turned to Raven, his eyes gleaming in the darkness.

'We must tread carefully. Prasutagus is a man on the edge, and we cannot push him too far. At least, not yet. You saw how easily he killed those men earlier and if he can do that to fellow tribesmen, I don't think he would have any hesitation doing the same to us.'

They moved deeper into the forest, disappearing into the night, leaving the settlement behind. Their future lay in the marshes now, far from the eyes of Romans and Britons alike.

Chapter Seventeen

Eastern Germania

Seneca crouched low behind a thick patch of bracken, his heart pounding in his chest. Everything had led to this moment. The meticulous planning, the careful coordination with Brennus, now, it was time to set it all in motion. If anything went wrong, it wouldn't just be Brennus and his family who would suffer; the men who had come to rescue him would likely meet their end as well.

His fingers felt cold as he reached into the pouch on his belt and withdrew a highly polished piece of copper, the tool that would carry the signal to his old comrade. He scanned the settlement, trying to locate Brennus amongst the Vandals. After several tense moments, he finally spotted him near a group of men at the edge of the horse paddock, appearing relaxed as he spoke with them. But Seneca could see the tension in his stance, the way his shoulders were just a little too stiff, his gaze flickering too often toward the forest.

With a steady hand, Seneca lifted the copper mirror, angling it to catch the last rays of the setting sun. The light reflected off the surface, a brief flash that danced down the hill toward the settlement below. For a heartbeat, there was no reaction, and Seneca's pulse quickened in his throat. Had Brennus seen it? Would he be able to respond without drawing attention?

A few moments later, Brennus finally shifted. He knelt down as if to adjust his boot, his fingers lingering longer than necessary on the leather straps. It was the signal. He had understood.

Seneca let out a slow breath, relief flooding through

him. The message had been received and tonight, they would make their move. He turned away and made his way back to where Talorcan and Canis waited and crouched down beside them.

'It's done,' said Seneca. 'As soon as darkness falls, we make our move. Is everything ready'

'As ready as we'll ever be,' said Talorcan, 'the horses are in place on the far side of the camp and have enough food and water for two days. Look for the crag with the face of a man.'

'Canis?' asked Seneca, 'do you know what to do?'

'I do,' said Canis, 'and I will be waiting as agreed.'

'In that case, said Seneca, there is nothing more to say. Let's get into position.'

Canis turned away and headed down to the well-trodden path that led westward towards the river Elbe. Seneca and Talorcan headed the other direction and made their way down the hill towards the settlement. The village was alive with the sounds of evening, the laughter, the clatter of pots, the distant murmur of conversation. Most of the Vandals were gathered around their fires, their attention on their evening meals, but a few guards patrolled the outskirts of the camp. Seneca's eyes flicked to the watchtower near the main gate, where two sentries stood silhouetted against the darkening sky.

The plan relied on speed and precision. Brennus would create the distraction near the opposite side of the village, drawing as many guards as possible away, and when the moment came, Seneca, and Talorcan, would move in, and make sure the gate stayed open for Brennus and his family to make their escape.

They reached the edge of the forest and crouched low, watching the village from the cover of the trees. From their position, they could see through the open gates and deep into the heart of the Vandal camp. The tension was palpable, the air thick with anticipation, and Seneca glanced at Talorcan, his eyes hard with determination.

'Wait for the signal,' he whispered. 'Once Brennus makes his move, we go.'

Inside the camp, Brennus stood in the fading light, his hands running absentmindedly over the flank of the horse he was grooming. The creature snorted and pawed at the ground, its nervous energy matching his own. His gaze shifted and his heart twisted with worry as he watched Alana approach the well, a bucket clutched in her hands, though this time containing a pile of glowing embers instead of water. She looked calm, her face betraying none of the fear he knew must be gnawing at her. She had been insistent. if they were going to escape, they had to do this together but one wrong move, one suspicious glance, and everything would come crashing down.

Brennus watched as his wife made her move. She looked around to see she wasn't being watched and with a swift flick of her hands, threw the contents of the bucket into the heart of the haystack. For a brief moment, Brennus could hardly breathe as she turned away from the growing fire and began to walk calmly back
toward the paddock. No one seemed to notice her, and the flickering flames were still too small to draw attention but had only gone a few steps when she tripped and fell headlong to the floor. Some of the women heard her fall and she blushed heavily as she got back to her feet, but there was no harm done and she hurried back to her hut.

Behind her, the fire began to spread, creeping through

the hay. Brennus' pulse hammered in his chest as he gave one last stroke to the horse's mane, then slowly backed away from the animal. He had to stay calm, act normal, at least until the fire fully took hold.

From the corner of his eye, he saw his wife slip into their hut, a final glance exchanged between them as she disappeared inside. She had done it. The fire was set. Now all that remained was to wait for the chaos to begin.

Brennus forced himself to walk slowly around the enclosure, giving the appearance of someone going about his duties. He could see the flames growing now, licking higher into the sky, smoke beginning to curl upward. He could feel the heat building, and soon enough, the first shout rang out, one of the sentries had seen the blaze.

'Fire,' the guard bellowed. 'The haystack.'

Pandemonium erupted almost instantly. Warriors rushed toward the fire, shouting orders, grabbing buckets and water skins, while others yelled for help. The settlement was thrown into disarray as everyone scrambled to contain the growing inferno, the hungry flames now sending billows of smoke swirling through the settlement.

Brennus cast one final glance at the chaos, then, under the cover of the smoke and noise, he slipped away from the horses and ran back to his hut. Moments later he re-emerged holding Elara's hand as they ran towards the gates. The fire, now roaring with intensity, had drawn everyone's attention, the flickering orange light dancing on the faces of those desperately trying to contain the flames, but Brennus' eyes were fixed on their only escape route.

The gates were just ahead, but as they approached, he could see that two guards still remained, facing inwards towards them, watching the fire and smoke climb higher into the sky at the far end of the settlement. Brennus cursed under his breath and his pulse quickened as he pulled Elara into the shadows of a nearby hut.

For a few moments, he considered trying to kill them himself, but just as he moved to step forward, a movement in the
bushes outside the gates caught his eye.

In the confusion, with their focus elsewhere, neither sentry noticed the dark shapes approaching from behind, and before the guards could react, Talorcan struck, his blade slicing across the throat of the nearest guard.

Seneca disposed of the second guard in a similar manner and as the two men lay dying on the ground, they each grabbed a victim and hurriedly dragged them into the longer grass at the side of the road.

Brennus watched the drama unfold and, wasting no more time, grabbed Elara's arm and pulled her towards the gates. Outside, Talorcan and Seneca watched them come out, Elara clutching the wrapped child to her chest with a terrified look on her face.

'Ready?' asked Seneca.

'Let's go,' said Brennus and with no further delay, they ran from the settlement to vanish into the dense forest beyond.

Back in the village, Wulfstan stood amidst the chaos, his eyes narrowed as he watched his people battle the flames. Buckets of water were being passed from hand to hand in a desperate attempt to contain the blaze, but the work was agonisingly slow. The heat from the fire licked at his face, but Wulfstan's attention was drawn to the panic and disorder swirling around him.

As he strode forward, his eyes caught sight of a

discarded bucket. He stooped to pick it up, pausing as a strange scent hit his nose. He peered inside and, instead of water, found scorch marks lining the bottom, and the faint smell of burning wood. For a moment, he stood frozen, confusion knitting his brow. Then, the realisation struck him like a hammer blow. This fire had not started on its own.

He spun around, his eyes blazing with fury as he surveyed the scene. His mind raced, seeking answers, seeking someone to blame. Before he could bark an order to his men, a slave woman approached him, her head bowed.

'My lord,' she stammered, her voice barely above a whisper, 'I saw something.'

Wulfstan's fierce gaze locked onto her.

'Speak quickly,' he snapped.

The woman swallowed hard, her eyes darting to the ground.

'There was a woman near the fire,' she murmured, 'I didn't see her face, but she fell. And when she did, she dropped this.'

Her trembling hands reached into the folds of her ragged dress and withdrew a small object. Wulfstan snatched it from her grasp, his fingers curling around the item as he brought it closer to the light. His breath caught in his throat. It was a bracelet. Simple, yet unmistakable. His heart skipped a beat. He had seen this bracelet before. It was the one gifted to Brennus.

The truth hit him with sudden, crushing force. His knuckles whitened as he clenched the bracelet tighter, the fire in his chest now a raging inferno. This fire hadn't been some random accident, it was deliberate, and Brennus was behind it.

He turned sharply, facing the men who had gathered

near the blaze.

'Bring me the horse master.'

Two men immediately ran toward Brennus's hut, but Wulfstan's eyes never left the flames as he stood there, seething, waiting for Brennus to be dragged before him. His mind raced, trying to piece together the betrayal, the audacity of it. Brennus, whom he had trusted, whom he had given privileges more than any other slave, had turned against him.

A few minutes later, the men returned.

'He's not there, my lord,' one of them reported, 'neither is he at the paddock. The woman has also gone. The hut is empty.'

Wulfstan's stomach twisted, and he stormed toward the palisade, his soldiers trailing behind him. The truth began to crystallise, but Wulfstan still struggled to accept it. There was no way Brennus could escape, not with a woman and child. It was foolish, impossible. He forced himself to search for some other explanation, something that would absolve Brennus of this madness, but as they reached the gates, the sight that greeted them crushed whatever hope remained. The gates were open, unguarded and his heart sank, a cold dread creeping into his bones.

Suddenly, a voice cut through the darkness.

'My lord, our men are here. They've been killed.'

Wulfstan's eyes snapped to the source of the voice. He walked forward and knelt beside the bodies of the two sentries. Their throats had been slit cleanly, the blood pooling beneath them. His fingers traced the wounds, and the truth hit him once more. They had been killed from behind. Brennus hadn't acted alone.

Chapter Eighteen

Britannia

The camp of the Occultum nestled amidst the jagged boulders of a sprawling rocky outcrop, hidden away within the dense forest that surrounded the waterlogged ground and fires were kept small, their light barely visible through the thick fog that curled between the trees like ghostly tendrils.

Marcus stood near one of the fires. Around him, the men of the Occultum moved silently, some sharpening weapons, others inspecting the gear they had brought with them. Their dark cloaks blended with the shadows, their presence barely noticeable among the rocks and trees. Sica crouched nearby, his fingers idly tracing the patterns in the dirt, though his mind seemed far away.

Marcus walked over to his own Sarcina, leaning against a slab of rock that protected him from the worst of the wind. They had already been here two nights, making their plans as to how to proceed, but his Sarcina was packed and ready to go in an instant should circumstances demand. They all were, and only opened to retrieve their sleeping blankets or to get some other piece of equipment as required. Two tents stood nestled amongst the higher boulders, sheltered from the worst of the weather, hidden by foliage cut from the nearby thickets. Overall, Marcus was happy with the location. There were certainly no comforts to be had but the remote location and presence of running water had made it a good choice and it was the perfect place to launch their missions across Britannia.

'Gather round,' he said quietly and one by one, the other members of the Occultum drew near, ready to receive their final orders. These were all special men, each with hidden talents, yet a collective steeliness that made them different to other men, and whilst some were more experienced than others, all had reached the demanding standards expected. These were the men who had left everything behind to join the cause, men who understood the stakes. They did not need rousing speeches, only clear orders.

'Has everyone eaten and packed their kit?' asked Marcus quietly.

The men nodded or grunted their confirmation.

'Good,' said Marcus. 'Now we need to focus on what is before us. This camp is probably the best we can hope to find while

we are here, so although it is not perfect, from now on, this is where we will be based. Saying that, when we go, we will leave no sign of us ever being here, but just remember where it is so if things go wrong, we know where to regroup.' He glanced around, meeting the eyes of each man in turn. 'We have two missions ahead of us. The first is to disrupt and destroy the forces of the Trinovante. I am not talking about direct confrontation for that way lays disaster, we will strike at their supply lines, and sow chaos in their ranks. If you think you are at risk, withdraw, we just don't have enough men to take casualties. We need to stay hidden and leave no presence that we exist, apart from the destruction we leave in our wake. Let's keep them guessing and by the time they realise what's happening, the legions will be on their way.'

Murmurs of approval rippled through the group, their faces hardening in anticipation of the coming conflict.

'The second mission,' continued Marcus, 'is more delicate. The Cantiaci to the south are wavering in their loyalty to Rome. For years, they have traded freely and benefitted from our patronage. However, we have heard that they are under immense pressure to join with the Trinovantes. The Cantiaci control most of the eastern coastline nearest to Gaul and Belgica and is the most likely area for our ships to land. As you know, the most dangerous time for any invading army is when they disembark from their ships, so if the Cantiaci join with the Trinovantes, and they are waiting for us on the shore, then it could cost hundreds of Roman lives and could even force us to turn around. We cannot risk that happening, so the second group will head further south to try and influence them.' He looked around to see if there were any question. When nobody commented, he continued.

'Raven will lead the team against the hostile tribes along with Sica, Falco and Atticus. Cassius and I will be the ones to negotiate with the Cantiaci. Each group will leave here separately and choose your own routes. Once we go, we are on our own and our paths will probably not cross again until we are done. However, if there is something that will not wait, we can leave a concealed message there,' he nodded to a rock nestled in amongst a pile of others.

If anyone needs to come back, check for messages and act accordingly if possible. Even if there is no need to return, we will all meet back here in three months at the full moon for a debrief and

update. There are many leagues to travel for all of us so allow time to get back. Those who are not here, will be assumed captured or dead.'

He looked around again, focussing on the determined faces of each man. This was what they had trained so hard for and there was nothing more they needed to know. The moment they left the camp, their methods of operation, their tactics and plans were down to them, and each was more than capable of taking the lead.

'Any questions?' he asked.

When there was no answer. He took a deep breath and gave a curt nod.

'In that case, we leave at last light.'

As the men dispersed to make their final preparations, Raven walked over to Marcus.

'The Cantiaci will be difficult to sway,' he said. 'Their position is precarious, and they fear the wrath of the Trinovantes. Would it not be better if I came with you?'

'It would,' said Marcus, 'but I need you with the others. They need to cause as much disruption as possible and then move quickly to avoid detection. You know these lands and the ways of the people, so your skills are better used there.'

'And what about the Cantiaci?'

'I accept they fear the Trinovantes,' said Marcus, 'but they have to realise that Rome is a far greater threat to their existence. We must make them see that if they agree to stay out of the conflict that is coming, they have a chance to remain free under their own rule.'

'Is that likely?'

'Who knows?' said Marcus, 'I am no politician, but it is the promise that Seneca made to me back in Gesoriacum.'

'And if they refuse?'

Marcus's gaze hardened.

'Then we remind them what happens to those who stand in the way of Rome.'

A few hours later, as the light started to fade, the men came together one last time, now separated into the two groups they had been assigned. Marcus looked around, seeing the camp had been cleared of any sign of life, including the ashes from the fires before turning to look at his comrades. Cassius had a certain air about him. His sharp eyes missed nothing, and his fox-like cunning had served him well in his former life as a merchant. Though he was more at home in the bustling markets of the Empire than in the rough terrain of Britannia, his skills in negotiation and reading people would be crucial in the days to come and would bring the sharpness of mind needed to outwit the tribe's more cunning leaders.

He turned to the second group. Sica, Raven and Falco were all seasoned members of the Occultum, and he had no concerns about any of them. All were brutal fighters and well used to operating behind enemy lines. They were the perfect choice for the task before them, while Atticus, on the other hand, was probably the weakest of them all. His survival skills were solid enough and though young, he had the promise of being an excellent scout. But his weapon skills needed sharpening and Marcus worried that he may falter if it came to close combat.

'Full moon, three months,' he said simply.

Raven nodded and with no more conversation, the two groups turned and went their separate ways. The Occultum had split, but their shared mission remained the same, to prepare the ground for the marching legions of Rome, and everything that subsequently followed.

Chapter Nineteen

Eastern Germania

Brennus tore through the dense forest, his grip tightening around Elara's trembling hand as they darted between the trees. Each step was fraught with danger, gnarled roots and jagged stones jutting up from the uneven ground. Behind them, Seneca and Talorcan urged them forward with hoarse whispers, the sounds of their heavy breathing mingling with the ominous beat of hooves in the distance.

Elara's breath came in short, desperate gasps, her fear palpable in the way she clung to Brennus. Though tears streamed down her cheeks, she made no sound, too terrified to cry out. The thudding of Wulfstan's horsemen grew louder, the pursuit relentless. They were closing in.

'I can't,' Elara whimpered, her voice cracking under the weight of despair. 'We won't make it, Brennus... we can't...'

Brennus didn't dare slow down, even as his heart pounded in his chest. He knew their only hope lay just ahead.

'We can,' he gasped, 'just a few more paces. Hold on.'

With Elara's strength fading, Brennus practically dragged her along, his legs burning from the effort. He was about to despair himself when Seneca's voice cut through the night from behind.

'Brennus. To your right...Latebra.'

Without hesitation, Brennus veered off the narrow path, plunging into a small clearing overgrown with bracken. His eyes darted wildly, searching for the hidden escape he knew must be there. 'Latebra.' he barked, frustration mounting. Then, as if by magic, a trapdoor concealed beneath the bracken hinged upward, revealing a man standing waist-deep in the hidden refuge below.

Canis, his face grim and streaked with mud, reached up to catch Elara as Brennus all but threw her and the child into his waiting arms. Brennus followed, his body collapsing against the damp earthen wall as Canis lowered the bracken-covered lid, a perfectly camouflaged lattice of ash branches and leaves.

Canis peered through a tiny gap in the lid, scanning the forest.

'Where is Seneca?' he hissed. 'He was supposed to be with you.'

'He was right behind us,' Brennus panted. 'He should be here.'

Outside, Seneca and Talorcan sprinted toward the one horse they had kept hidden in the undergrowth. Talorcan swung himself onto the saddle in one fluid motion, his eyes meeting Seneca for what might be the last time.

'Ride like the wind,' said Seneca, clapping Talorcan's leg. 'Don't stop until you reach the Rhine.'

Talorcan's face hardened.

'And you? You're going where no man I know has ever returned from.'

'Then we'll be the first,' Seneca replied, 'and the next time we meet at the Hornless Bull, I'll buy you all the ale you can drink.'

Talorcan grinned.

'I'll hold you to that,' he said, and with a sharp kick, he spurred his horse into the night, the sound of hooves crashing through the forest, intentionally loud to attract the attention of Wulfstan's men.

Seneca watched Talorcan disappear into the night

before turning back toward the clearing. He sprinted through the undergrowth, his breaths coming fast and shallow.

'Latebra.' he hissed and as the lid lifted silently, Canis reached up to pull Seneca down into the hideaway.

Inside the cramped confines of the latebra, the air was thick with tension. Brennus' heart pounded, the rhythmic thud of his pulse loud in his ears as he held Elara close. Her breathing, shallow and strained, mirrored the terror coursing through her. The child in her arms stirred restlessly, and Brennus prayed to the gods the boy wouldn't cry.

Above them, the voices of Wulfstan's men grew louder. Hooves stomped, weapons clinked, and commands were barked in frustration.

'Spread out.' one of the men called. 'Search every inch of this forest. They couldn't have gone far.'

Canis kept his eye fixed on a tiny gap in the lid, watching the flicker of torchlight as the warriors fanned out.

The forest floor crackled under the weight of the warriors' boots as they stomped across the clearing, closer to the hidden refuge with every step. Brennus could feel the vibrations through the earth
as the search continued above their heads. He knew that the hiding place was well camouflaged, but if one of the men walked directly onto it, then it was all over.

Elara's grip on his arm tightened, her body trembling with fear. He leaned in, his lips brushing her ears.

'Shhh…'

She nodded weakly, but her eyes, wide and brimming with tears, betrayed the depth of her terror.

Seneca tightened his grip on the hilt of his dagger. His eyes flicked to Brennus, then back to the lid above, his expression calm but watchful. In the years Brennus had known Seneca, he'd seen that look before, the face of a man ready for anything, even death. But not yet. Not now. Not while they still had a chance.

Outside, one of the warriors cursed loudly.

'Nothing. They can't have just vanished.'

Another soldier responded with an irritated grunt.

'The trail leads here. Keep searching. We're not leaving until we find them.'

The sound of horses shuffling filled the air, and Brennus' breath caught as a pair of boots thudded just a few feet from their hiding place. His entire body went rigid as the man stood directly above them, muttering to himself.

'Something's off,' said the warrior. 'I can feel it.'

Brennus' stomach clenched as Canis shifted slightly, his body tense, ready to spring into action if needed. But then, another voice, a familiar one, rough and commanding, cut through the night.

'Enough,' Wulfstan's voice boomed. 'They've led us on a fool's chase.'

His shadow fell across the undergrowth, and Brennus could see the flicker of his torch through the cracks in the lid.

'Mount up,' Wulfstan ordered. 'We're wasting time here.'

'My lord, there were horses here,' came a shout, 'and it looks like they are headed east.'

'Of course they are,' snarled Wulfstan, 'well, what are you waiting for? After them.'

The warriors ran to their horses and moments later, galloped out of the clearing onto the forest path, knowing their quarry could only be moments ahead. Brennus exhaled slowly, daring to hope. Perhaps Wulfstan had finally given up. Then

Came the voice again, low and cold, hovering just above the latebra.

'I'll not be made a fool, Brennus,' Wulfstan spat into the night, his words clearly meant for the hidden man. 'If you are here, I will find you. And when I do, I'll make you watch as I burn your family alive.' He turned his horse and moments later, galloped after his men.

As the last echoes of the horsemen faded, Canis carefully lifted the lid just a fraction, peering out into the clearing. Silence greeted him, nothing but the quiet rustle of leaves and the distant call of night birds.

'They're gone,' he whispered, lowering the lid once more.

Brennus let out a long, shaky breath, his muscles finally beginning to relax. Elara, still clutching the child, leaned against him, her body weak with relief. Tears spilled down her cheeks again, but this time they were tears of release, not of fear. Seneca sheathed his dagger and leaned back against the earthen wall, closing his eyes for a moment.

'Too close,' he muttered under his breath.

Brennus sat down beside him.

'They'll be back,' he warned. 'That Wulfstan isn't one to give up easily.'

'I know,' Seneca replied. 'But we've bought ourselves time and that's all we need.'

'What's the plan now? We can't stay here forever.'

Seneca stared at the roof of the hideout for a moment, his heartbeat slowing.

'We rest here until the chase dies down,' he said finally. 'Then we head back.'

'Why are we going back?' gasped Elara in the darkness. 'It's not safe there.'

'We are not going back to the settlement,' said Seneca, 'we'll head south and skirt around it. We have two horses on the other side.'

Brennus squeezed her hand.

'It's never totally safe, Elara. But by the time Wulfstan realises he's been tricked, we will be long gone.'

The small group sat in the darkness of the latebra, their breathing gradually slowing as the sounds of the night returned. They were safe, for the moment, hidden beneath the earth. But Brennus knew all too well that their escape had only just begun.

Chapter Twenty

Britannia

Togodumnus and his closest warriors rode at a steady pace through the woodland where he and his men had camped for many months. As the towering trees thinned out ahead of him, the sprawling camp of his people came into view, huts and tents scattered across the vast forest floor, smoke curling from the many small fires that dotted the landscape.

His warriors were everywhere, some sparring with each other, others gathered in clusters, laughing and boasting of battles fought and victories still to come. The sounds of swords clashing, and loud, boastful voices echoed through the camp, creating a cacophony that spoke of confidence and camaraderie. Togodumnus felt a swell of pride as he observed them. These men were the lifeblood of Britannia proud, fierce, and eager for the war that now loomed on the horizon.

As he rode deeper into the camp, his attention was drawn to a commotion nearby. Aric, one of his warlords, was berating a warrior in front of a gathered crowd. The warrior stood with his head bowed, his face set in a mixture of frustration and shame. Togodumnus pulled on the reins, bringing his horse to a halt, and watched from a short distance, curious to hear what was unfolding.

'You've failed us again,' Shouted Aric, his face twisted with anger. 'For the third time in ten days, our supply columns have been ambushed. We cannot fight without food and weapons, and still, you return empty-handed.'

The young warrior shifted uncomfortably but remained silent, his eyes fixed on the ground.

Aric continued.

'Everything burned?' Aric continued. 'Every last cart, every last weapon? Do you not understand the gravity of this? We're being bled dry, and you bring back nothing but excuses.'

Togodumnus felt a cold knot form in his stomach. Ambushed? For the third time? His unease deepened as the implications sank in. His tribe was not just facing an open enemy, they were being methodically weakened by someone unseen who struck like lightning and disappeared just as quickly.

He dismounted swiftly, his boots sinking into the soft forest
floor, and approached the scene. Aric, noticing his approach, immediately straightened, his anger replaced with a stiff formality.

'Lord Togodumnus,' Aric said, bowing his head in respect, 'I was dealing with the matter of our supply lines.'

'So, I heard,' Togodumnus replied. He turned his gaze to the young warrior, who still hadn't met his eyes. 'Tell me what happened exactly?'

'We were ambushed, my lord,' replied the warrior. 'We followed the usual route and camped in the forest west of the river. We posted extra guards but in the middle of the night, we were woken by the sound of fire as it ripped through the wagons. Everyone jumped to face the enemy, but no matter where we turned, there were none. My men raced into the trees but found no sign whatsoever. It was if we had been attacked by ghosts.'

Togodumnus stared at the man. The description was unsettlingly familiar, hit-and-run tactics, swift, deadly, and designed to leave no trace of those responsible. This was not the work of a disorganised band of raiders. It was something more deliberate, by someone who knew the ways of the forest, almost as if their own people had turned on their own.

'Do you think it may be some of the Iceni?' asked one of the warriors. 'They are known to be in the pockets of the Romans, and it would be in their interests if our resistance failed.'

'Britons attacking their own?' Aric spat in disbelief. 'No tribe would be foolish enough to weaken us when the Romans are at our door.'

Togodumnus turned back to the young warrior.

'You said this has happened three times?'

The warrior nodded, swallowing hard.

'Yes, my lord. I wasn't there but each time was the same We thought at first, it was just a band of thieves. But it's too organised. They know where we are. They know our routes.'

Togodumnus' mind raced. If these attacks continued, his warriors would be crippled long before they could even meet the Romans on the battlefield. And worse, if Britons were behind this, it meant there were enemies in the shadows, enemies who might be aligned with Rome, or working towards their own goals.

'Aric,' Togodumnus said, 'call the other warlords. This has to be stopped now before it gets any worse.'

Aric nodded, his expression grim.

'At once, my lord.'

Togodumnus turned back to the young warrior.

'You've done well to bring me this news, but next time, I expect you to return with more than just a story. If we cannot stop these attacks, we will not have the strength to fight anyone, Roman or otherwise.'

The warrior bowed his head again, chastened but relieved.

As Aric strode away to gather the other leaders, Togodumnus stood in silence, staring out over the sprawling camp. His warriors continued to laugh and boast, ignorant of the growing danger. But Togodumnus' mind was already moving, calculating, preparing. If there were enemies within Britannia, he would find them. And when he did, they would know the full fury of the Trinovantes.

Leagues away, Raven moved through the undergrowth as the four members of the Occultum slipped deeper into the Trinovantes' lands. They were still just an hour or so away from the place they had found to lay up, and although it was nothing more than a rotting fishing hut nestled at the side of a river, it was the perfect place, hidden away and forgotten, just like them. The wild growth of the forest had all but swallowed the building; the wooden beams had long since collapsed inward, and moss and ivy crept over the scattered hearth stones. To an outsider, it was nothing more than a relic of the past, but to Raven and his companions, it was their haven.

Once they reached the hut, Raven crouched down, brushing aside a curtain of vines that concealed the entrance. One by one, they slipped inside, the dark, musty interior greeting them like an old companion. It wasn't much, little more than a space to lie down and keep out of sight, but it was enough.

As soon as they were inside, Falco sat against the remains of a small wall and let out a deep sigh.

'Well, that went better than expected,' he said, as he opened his sarcina. 'Three supply columns in ten days. The Trinovantes are going to be starving soon.'

'I doubt that,' said Raven, 'but it will hurt them. We need to keep the pressure on, but we also need to be careful. We've been successful so far but if we do too much too soon, they could realise someone is targeting them.'

The men fell silent for a moment, their minds replaying the attack they'd just carried out. It had been their most ambitious strike yet, an entire column of wagons, laden with food, weapons, and supplies, bound for the Trinovantes' war camp. They had watched the convoy for days, studying its movements, waiting for the right moment to strike. And when the time came, they had infiltrated the enemy, killing the sentries who had grown complacent before moving swiftly through the temporary camp, setting fires as they went. It had been a flawless attack, and the success of it filled them all with a sense of accomplishment, even if none of them would admit it aloud. But Raven was right. The more damage they did, the more attention they would draw.

'So, what's next?' asked Atticus.

'We lay low,' said Raven. 'Let them waste their strength searching for us. Stretch them thin, then strike again. Bleed them dry with a thousand cuts.'

The group settled into silence, the rush of the nearby river filling the space where words were unnecessary.

Sica added more wood to the fire before looking up to see Falco offering the communal pot.

'Make it a good one, Sica,' he said, 'I could eat a whole cow.'

The next morning brought a bitter chill, and with it, a

relentless downpour that soaked through every layer of clothing and skin. The fishing hut, though remote and well hidden, offered little shelter from the elements, and the heavy, grey sky seemed to press down upon them. Water dripped steadily from what remained of the ceiling beams, forming pools on the dirt floor, and the fire they had struggled to keep alive overnight was now nothing more than a pile of smouldering ash.

Falco sat with his back against the wall, staring out through the gaps in the rotting wood as the rain battered the world outside. His mood mirrored the weather, sour and cold. Sica crouched near the hearth, grumbling as he attempted to light a new fire with damp tinder, while Atticus, ever watchful, sat silently by the entrance, his face pale and gaunt, a reflection of their dwindling supplies.

Raven surveyed his men with a sense of grim determination.

Their success against the Trinovantes had come at a cost. While the tribe's warriors might be growing weaker, so too were the members of the Occultum. Their supplies were almost gone, and the forest offered little in the way of sustenance. If they didn't find food soon, hunger would weaken them before their enemies ever could, but they needed more than just food, they needed warmth, and they needed a new place to hide.

Sica cursed under his breath as the fire refused to catch, his frustration mounting.

'I'm tired of this damp,' he growled, tossing the half-burnt wood aside. 'If I never see another fishing hut again, it'll be too soon.' Falco grunted in agreement but said nothing. His stomach twisted with hunger, and the cold gnawed at his bones.

'We need to find a different refuge,' said Raven, We've been focusing on the forests and the hills, but there might be small farms or outposts nearby. A few silver coins could get us enough food to last a while.'

Falco looked up.

'You're thinking of sending someone to buy provisions?'

Raven nodded.

'I'll go and take Atticus with me. I can pass as a local and will not attract too much attention, especially in this weather. We'll head south, towards the edge of the forest. There's bound to be a village or farmstead there. You and Falco scout further west, find somewhere better, maybe an old barn or another ruin.'

'Anything's better than this,' said Falco.

With the plan set, the group began to prepare, and Raven retrieved a small pouch of coins from his sarcina.

Once ready, he motioned for Atticus to follow him and the young man, though exhausted and hungry, rose without hesitation, gathering his cloak around him. Together, they slipped out of the hut and into the storm, moving quickly through the undergrowth, their feet sinking into the mud with each step.

Sica and Falco watched them go before gathering what little they had. The cold bit at their skin, but they knew they had no choice. They needed better shelter, and perhaps something more to keep the rain from soaking through to their bones. They had all chosen this path, to be shadows in a hostile land, but the cost was

beginning to show. Hunger gnawed at their spirits and bodies, but they would need more than just food and shelter. They would need luck, and, in these times, luck was as scarce as a dry place to rest.

The rain beat down relentlessly as Sica and Falco trudged through the tangled undergrowth, their cloaks plastered to their skin, offering little protection from the cold. The world around them seemed sodden, the trees dripping, the air thick with moisture. Every step felt heavier than the last, their boots sinking into the mud with each stride. Falco's breath was a steady rhythm of irritation as he muttered curses under his breath, while Sica, ever stoic, said nothing, his focus solely on the path ahead.

'This is madness,' Falco grumbled, wiping a hand across his wet face. 'We've been walking for hours. There's nothing out here.'

The truth of it was hard to argue. Every possible place they had come across had been either too close to habitation, making it too risky, or lacked basic needs like fresh water. Their search was becoming increasingly desperate, but they couldn't afford to settle for just anything.

Sica suddenly stopped and raised a hand, and Falco froze, ears straining against the sounds of the rain. At first, all they could hear was the steady drumming of water against the trees, but then, faintly, the unmistakable sound of voices drifted towards them through the storm.

'Warriors,' hissed Sica.

They dropped silently, pressing their bodies into the thick undergrowth. Peering through the gaps in the leaves, they saw five men, heavily armed, moving in a loose formation, their cloaks pulled tightly around them as they slogged through the forest. Trinovantes.

The warriors were alert, their eyes scanning the trees.

It was clear they were on patrol, likely searching for signs of the bandits that had been plaguing their tribe.

'They're hunting us,' Falco whispered, barely audible over the rain.

Sica shot him a warning glance, but didn't speak. Hearts pounded as they remained still, knowing a single wrong move could give them away. For what felt like an eternity, the warriors moved through the trees, their voices muffled by the rain. Then, finally, they disappeared from view, swallowed by the mist.

'We need to move,' said Sica, and they sprang to their feet, running silently but swiftly in the opposite direction. They moved as fast as they dared, their feet splashing through puddles, hearts hammering in their chests. The forest blurred around them, the rain and wind howling in their ears, but they didn't stop until the sounds of the patrol were far behind, and the forest seemed still once again.

Panting, Falco doubled over, his hands on his knees. 'That was too close.'

'We're not safe yet,' said Sica. 'Keep moving.'

They pushed on, the rain showing no signs of relenting and as they crested a small rise, the land beneath them changed abruptly. The trees gave way to a scarred, rocky landscape, an old quarry, long abandoned. The ground sloped steeply down into a pit, the rock walls streaked with scars from ancient mining tools, the edges of the quarry overgrown with creeping vines and brambles.

'It looks like no one's been here in years,' said Falco.

Sica pointed to the remains of a small hut near the far side of the quarry, its roof caved in, little more than a ruin.

'That might do, if we can patch it up.'

Falco shook his head.

'Too exposed,' he said, 'if anyone comes by, it's the first thing they'll see.'

As they approached, the hut revealed its full state of decay. Wooden beams had collapsed inward, and the stones of the hearth were blackened with age and rot. It would offer little more shelter than the fishing hut they'd left behind.

But then something else caught their eyes. Just beyond the hut, tucked into the hillside, a narrow, overgrown shaft sloped downward into the rock. Vines and brambles had grown thickly over the entrance, almost completely concealing it, but there was no mistaking what it was, an old mining tunnel, forgotten and choked with growth.

'What is that?' asked Falco.

'Possibly an old tin quarry,' said Sica. 'Looks like it's been abandoned for years.'

He moved to the edge of the shaft and began pulling gently at the brambles to reveal the dark entrance. The air around it was cooler, a faint draft wafting up from the depths below.

'This could be something,' he muttered, ducking low and peering inside. 'Let's see where it leads.'

Falco produced a flint and a handful of dried sheep's wool from his cloak and after nurturing a flame, lit a small candle handed
to him by Sica. Once done, the two men headed further into the shaft. It was narrow at first, barely wide enough to squeeze through, but as they descended, the tunnel widened, the rocky walls slick with moisture. The faint sound of dripping water echoed from deep within, and the air smelled of damp earth and age.

They moved cautiously, their footsteps echoing in the

quiet and, after a short while, the tunnel opened up into a series of small chambers, rough-hewn from the rock. They ran their hands along the walls, feeling the grooves left behind by ancient tools. This was where men had once worked, digging tin from the earth.

In the largest of the chambers, they found what they had been searching for. A thin stream of water trickled down one wall, seeping from the rocks above. It wasn't much, but it was fresh and clear. Falco knelt by the stream, dipping his fingers in and bringing the water to his lips.

'It's drinkable,' he said, a note of relief in his voice. 'This could work. It's hidden, it's dry, and there's water. The only thing is, there's only one way in and out, and if we are compromised, we'll be trapped in here.'

'Possibly not,' said Sica holding up the candle and watching the flame flicker. 'That breeze is coming from further inside which means there must be some sort of air shaft. Come, let's see if we can find it.'

They moved deeper into the tunnels, following the faint but steady breeze that played with the flickering candle. The air felt cooler the further they went, a promising sign, but the walls grew narrower, and the ground became uneven, forcing them to move cautiously. On either side, smaller tunnels, hardly big enough for a man to crawl through, headed off in different directions, their surfaces worn smooth by countless generations of miners. Finally, Sica stopped, holding up a hand.

'There,' he whispered, his voice barely audible over the sound of their laboured breathing. He pointed toward a dark crack in the rock above their heads. The draft of cool air was unmistakable, coming from somewhere beyond the narrow gap.

Falco looked up, peering into the fissure.

'You've got to be joking,' he muttered. 'That's barely wide enough for a dog.'

'It'll have to do,' Sica replied. 'If we're trapped, this could be our only way out. I'll check its passable.'

Without waiting for further complaints, Sica handed the candle to Falco and reached up, carefully wedging his shoulders through the opening. He grunted as he pulled himself forward, the rough stone scraping against his back and chest, but he kept moving, the promise of open air pulling him onward.

The passage felt endless, but after what seemed like an eternity, Sica's head emerged into the open. Above him, pale light filtering down through the mist and he pulled himself free, glancing around to make sure the area was clear. Satisfied, he turned and climbed back down the fissure to join Falco below.

'Well?' asked Falco, as Sica landed beside him.

'It'll do, and we can get out if we need to.' He paused and deliberately looked Falco up and down. 'At least those who do not eat too much will.'

Before Falco could react, he turned and headed back up the tunnel, still trying not to laugh at the bemused look on Falco's face.

With their escape route secured, they took a moment to rest, feeling the tension of the tunnels finally ease.

They glanced around. The chambers were deep enough to keep them concealed, and the second entrance meant it would be easy to escape if they were ever found. It wasn't perfect, but it was as good as they were going to get.

'We'll head back to the others,' said Sica. 'Let them know what we've found.'

With renewed energy, the two men began the long journey back through the rain-soaked forest, their steps lighter now that they had found what they were looking for. The quarry behind them faded into the mist, but the knowledge of what lay beneath, the hidden chambers, the fresh water, gave them a sliver of hope in the bleak, endless storm.

Further south, Raven and Atticus moved slowly, the rain continuing its merciless assault, soaking them to the bone. The narrow deer paths they followed had turned into little more than streams, and their boots squelched with every step. The wind cut through the trees, howling as it tore at their soaked cloaks, but the two men pressed on, their faces set with grim determination.

Occasionally, Atticus glanced sideways at Raven, who moved with a surety that belied the wretched conditions. It was clear he had been raised in these lands, his instincts finely attuned to the
rhythms of the forest and its people.

They had been walking for hours when Raven abruptly raised a hand, signalling for Atticus to stop. Ahead, through the rain and the thinning trees, a small farmstead came into view. The main house was simple, a typical roundhouse with a thatched roof, and beside it stood a barn, weathered but sturdy. A low stone wall ringed the property, and in the distance, a small herd of sheep huddled under the meagre shelter of a crooked tree.

They skirted the edge of the property, careful not to draw attention, and as they neared the barn, Raven's sharp eyes picked out the details, bundles of sheepskins, stacked high, ready for market. The farmer, an older man with a weathered face, moved between the barn and house, unaware of the two figures watching him from the trees.

Atticus opened his mouth to speak, but Raven silenced him with a sharp gesture. They couldn't risk approaching the farmer directly. Too dangerous, especially with Trinovantes warriors likely nearby. Instead, he made a mental note of the sheepskins and the barn's location. It could be useful later, a potential resource if they found themselves in desperate need of warmth or materials.

After watching the farmstead for a few moments more, Raven motioned for them to continue. They moved away from the property, keeping to the cover of the trees as they walked alongside a well-worn path that cut through the forest. Though the path was tempting, offering easier passage, Raven kept them off it, slipping between the trees where the foliage grew thick. They had learned the hard way that roads, even small ones, were dangerous places for men like them.

Eventually, the land began to slope downward, and in the distance, the faint outline of a village appeared through the mist. It was small, a cluster of low, wood-built houses with thatched roofs, each sending thin curls of smoke into the rainy sky. A handful of people moved about the village, cloaked against the weather, hurrying from house to house.

Raven led Atticus to a small copse of trees just outside the village, where they could observe without being seen. From their hidden vantage point, they could see the village square and the small market that had been set up despite the rain. Farmers and villagers milled about, exchanging goods and gossip, their faces mostly hidden beneath hoods.

'This is it,' Raven muttered, crouching beside Atticus. 'We'll get what we need here.' He rose to his feet, adjusting his cloak so that the hood covered his face. He glanced once more at the village, making a quick assessment of the best route, before slipping down the slope towards the outskirts and soon he was among the houses, merging with the local people going about their business.

The villagers barely glanced at him. The hoods most wore against the rain allowed him to easily blend in and he kept his head down. His eyes, however, missed nothing.

He reached the village square without incident, where the small market bustled despite the weather. Stalls were set up beneath sagging awnings, their tables laden with vegetables, smoked fish, and small barrels of ale. A butcher hacked at a carcass, his knife glistening in the rain, while nearby, a woman sold loaves of dark bread from a large basket.

Raven moved amongst the villagers with the ease of someone who had done this many times before. His cloak, drenched as it was, helped conceal him further, the hood casting shadows across his face. He moved with purpose, never lingering too long at any one place, always watching, always listening.

As he passed by a stall selling smoked meats, he paused, his eyes flicking over the wares. The vendor barely looked up from his work as Raven casually picked up a strip of cured venison.

'How much for this?' asked Raven.

'Three coins for a good cut, two for the small ones,' he replied.

Raven nodded, producing a couple of coins from his pouch and handing them over. The vendor, uninterested in conversation, took the coins and handed over the meat, already turning to his next customer.

With the venison tucked securely inside his cloak, Raven moved on through the rest of the market. He picked up a few more supplies, two loaves of bread, flour, salt and a small sack of root vegetables, always mindful of the eyes around him. Each purchase was small, nothing that would draw suspicion, but it was enough to keep them fed for a few more days. Once done, he headed back out of the village towards the copse where Atticus was waiting.

The younger man was exactly where Raven had left him, crouched beneath the dripping branches, his eyes scanning the village below.

'I've got what we need,' said Raven as he crouched beside Atticus, 'let's get back.' They headed into the trees again, following the paths back the way they had come, but after a while, Raven's pace slowed and he glanced around with a sharp eye, scanning the narrow path ahead. Finally, he stopped and headed into the undergrowth before dropping the goods he had bought from the market. He turned to Atticus, lowering his voice.

'Stay here,' he said, 'I've got one more thing to take care of.'

Atticus furrowed his brow, his hand instinctively tightening on the sack of grain he was carrying.

'What do you mean? Where are you going?'

Raven waved a hand dismissively.

'Don't worry about it. I'll be quick. Just stay out of sight.'

Before Atticus could protest further, Raven turned on his heel and disappeared down a side path.

Atticus stood there for a moment, the air around him suddenly feeling colder. He knew better than to follow, but something gnawed at him, a sense of unease he couldn't shake. He crouched low behind a patch of tall grass near the edge of the road, doing his best to stay out of sight from any passersby, but as time dragged on, he began to worry, his mind racing with possibilities. Had Raven been caught? Was he in trouble? Eventually, Atticus resolved to go after him, but just before he moved, Raven's silhouette appeared through the trees, and he was carrying a something in his arms.

Atticus stood up, relief flooding through him.

'Right,' said, Raven, looking at Atticus, 'get the supplies, now we can go.'

Atticus blinked at the pile in Raven's arms, trying to make sense of the situation.

'Sheepskins?' he said eventually, looking up. 'You disappeared for an hour for that?'

Raven chuckled and slung the sheepskins over his shoulder.

'Trust me, Atticus,' he said, 'tonight we are going to be the most popular men this side of Rome.'

Shaking his head, Atticus picked up the supplies and followed Raven back into the depths of the forest.

Chapter Twenty-One

Britannia

Marcus and Cassius approached the Cantiaci village situated near the edge of a small lake dotted with small boats. Their journey south through the rugged territories of the Iceni and Trinovantes had been longer and harsher than anticipated, marked by muddy roads, treacherous marshes, and watchful eyes. Now, at last, they had reached their destination and Marcus stared at the village ahead, assessing the threat and their own vulnerability. The thatched roofs of the roundhouses stood huddled together against the constant wind, but the place seemed eerily quiet.

'Where are the men?' Cassius muttered, his sharp eyes scanning the scene.

'They won't be far,' said Marcus. 'These people are well known for their ferocity.'

They watched for another hour or so, but eventually, Marcus knew they could wait no longer.

'We go in,' he said, standing up. 'Openly.'

With a nod of agreement, Cassius followed Marcus as they stepped out from the cover of the trees and walked toward the village. As they neared, the usual rhythm of the settlement, children running, women weaving, men sharpening tools, halted as all eyes turned to the two strangers.

Three men, tall and broad-shouldered, emerged from one of the huts to stand before them, their hair hanging in wild braids, and tattoos covering almost every piece of visible skin. One of them stepped forward, his eyes narrowing as they swept over the dishevelled pair.

'Who are you?' he demanded. 'And what do you

want?'

'We are messengers,' said Marcus, 'and here to speak with your chieftain.'

'You look like Trinovantes to me,' said one of the men, 'and smell like them too.'

'We are not Trinovantes,' Cassius cut in sharply. 'Nor are we enemies. We are friends of the Cantiaci and here purely to negotiate.'

'You ask to see our chieftain as if he is a comrade of yours,' came the reply 'so tell us his name.'

Cassius hesitated, a bead of sweat forming on his brow. They knew that the Cantiaci essentially came under the rule of the Catuvellauni, but they were also known as a fiercely independent tribe and since Cunobeline had died, he wasn't sure where their allegiances lay. The warrior stepped closer, his eyes gleaming with malice.

'You don't know, do you? He said, 'and yet you come here, claiming to be an ally.' His hand drifted to the hilt of the dagger at his belt. 'Perhaps you are spies, come to gather information for your Trinovante masters.'

Cassius opened his mouth to speak, but Marcus cut him off, picking up on the warrior's tone of voice when he mentioned the Trinovantes.

'We are not spies,' he said firmly, 'and although I know Cunobeline has passed, I admit that I do not know the name of your master. But if it is Togodumnus who leads you, then our journey has been wasted for our words are not for his ears, and we will leave you in peace.'

At the mention of Togodumnus, the three men exchanged dark looks. The tension thickened further, though their hands now hung by their sides rather than near their weapons.

'Togodumnus does not hold sway here,' said one of the men. 'His rule has been assumed by many, but the Cantiaci are a proud people, and we will decide ourselves who it is that carries the sword of kingship over us.'

'But until then, you must have a chieftain,' said Marcus. 'If he would grant us audience, we can explain fully why we are here.'

The largest man stared for a few moments longer before nodding.

'Stay here.' He walked away, leaving Marcus and Cassius under the watchful stare of his two fellow warriors. After what seemed like an age, he returned and gestured for them to follow.

'He is eating,' he said, 'but will listen to what you have to say.'

A few minutes later, Marcus and Cassius entered the chieftain's hut, the low doorway forcing them to bow as they stepped inside. Unlike the huts of other chieftains, there was no indication of wealth here, no tapestries, no ornaments of bronze or silver,

only the scent of smoke, damp earth, and something roasting over the fire. The space was small, the walls dark and bare,

with little to suggest anyone of influence resided within.

The chieftain sat cross-legged by the central hearth. He did not rise to greet them, nor did he offer even a nod of recognition. His sightless eyes seemed to stare beyond them into the dancing flames, lost in thought or memory.

'Sit,' barked the warrior, motioning to the dirt floor near the fire.

Marcus and Cassius exchanged a glance but obeyed without question, lowering themselves onto the cold, hard ground. Despite the simplicity of the surroundings, the chieftain exuded an unspoken authority. His white hair, long and tangled, fell over his shoulders in matted ropes, and his weathered face bore the marks of countless winters. His frame, though thinned by age, suggested a man who had once commanded fear and respect in equal measure. There was still something about him, something that lingered beneath the frailty of his failing body.

Beside him, an old woman worked silently. Her back was bent with age, her hands gnarled like ancient roots. She chewed on a strip of venison, softening it before passing it to the chieftain without a word. He accepted the meat absentmindedly, gnawing on it with what remained of his teeth.

Cassius shifted uneasily, his eyes scanning the room for any sign of threat or trap. It was hard to reconcile the sight before them with the stories of fierce tribal leaders who ruled with iron will. Yet, despite the chieftain's weakened state, he could sense the man's history, the power that still clung to him like the last embers of a dying fire.

After a long silence, Marcus cleared his throat and leaned slightly forward.

'We were told the chieftain was willing to speak with us,' he said.

The old man made no sign of hearing him, continuing to take chewed meat from the woman.

'Cunda does not speak unless it is needed,' said the woman, 'but he sees more than you think.'

Marcus inclined his head in acknowledgement but remained silent. Despite his outward calm, he felt the weight of the old chieftain's gaze, as though the man's sightless eyes could still pierce into his thoughts, assessing him. This was not

a place for idle words or false pretence. It would be the chieftain, and not they who
decided when this conversation would begin.

Further north, Raven, Sica and Falco sat in one of the side caverns of the abandoned tin mine. The vast network of tunnels and chambers stretched endlessly into the earth, and though the air was stale, it carried a faint breeze, ensuring the smoke from their fire dispersed harmlessly through the many caverns and shafts.

Sica crouched over the flames, carefully turning strips of cured venison on a makeshift spit, the smell of the roasting meat filling the cavern, and mixing with the earthy scent of the mine.

'Meat's nearly done,' he muttered quietly without looking up.

Falco looked over from the pile of sheepskins Marcus had stolen from the sheep farm, his arms behind his head, as he enjoyed the luxury of warmth and comfort.

'I'll have mine over here on a golden platter,' he quipped, 'and bring wine and a naked woman while you're at it.'

Sica ignored him and fished out the root vegetables from amongst the embers.

'I could get used to this,' continued Falco lazily, his voice carrying across the cavern. 'A warm fire, meat on the spit, and a proper place to sleep. Almost feels like a reward.'

'Enjoy it while you can,' said Raven from the other side of the cavern. 'It won't be long before we're on the move again.'

Falco grunted in response, rolling onto his side to face the fire.

'You always have to ruin the moment, don't you?'

Sica handed a skewer of cooked venison to Raven, then tossed another to Falco, who caught it with a grin.

'At least we won't be starving while we wait,' he said, biting into the meat with relish.

Sica turned back to the fire, prodding the remaining pieces of meat and the cavern fell silent once more, save for the occasional crackle of the fire. Finally, he stood up with a wooden bowl of meat and roasted root vegetables before heading up the tunnel to where Atticus was on guard duty.

'Food,' he said as he approached, and Atticus crawled backwards away from the brambles covering the entrance shaft. Sica took his place, looking out over the opencast mine that had once been a hive of activity and hardship.

'What do you make of this place?' asked Atticus, gesturing around them with a piece of venison. 'This mine, it looks like nobody has been here for generations.'

'Places like this,' said Sica, 'mines, quarries… they've seen more blood and suffering than any battlefield. We have many such places in my country. Slaves sent down into these places weren't expected to come back up. Tin mines especially, cruel places, worse than you can imagine.'

Atticus paused, mid-bite, and looked at Sica more closely.

'Worse than a battlefield?' he asked, raising an eyebrow.

Sica nodded, his expression grim.

'On a battlefield, you have a chance. You fight, you bleed, maybe you die, but it's quick. Here, in these mines? The death is slow. Cruel. Tin is valuable, especially to Rome. They have probably traded with these people for generations for their tin, and I wouldn't be surprised if that is one of the reasons Claudius casts a covetous eye on this island. In similar mines across the empire, they send men down into the tunnels and work them to death. Slaves mostly, some criminals. Anyone they wanted rid of without making too much of a show about it.'

Atticus shifted his stance, looking down the dark passage behind them.

'How long would they last?'

'It depends,' said Sica, shrugging. 'Some barely made it a few months. The air down there is foul, the dust chokes you, and the work...' He gestured to the rough stone walls. 'They'd carve out the rock with nothing but hammers and chisels, day after day, hour after hour. No light, save for a few flickering candles. It's no place for a man to live, but the Romans don't care about that. They care about the tin.'

Atticus wiped his mouth with the back of his hand and leaned against the wall beside Sica.

'And what's all this tin used for? Surely, it's not worth all those lives?'

'You'd be surprised,' said Sica. Tin is mixed with copper to make bronze. Without it, no bronze swords, no armour, no tools. The Romans need it for their war machine. That's why places like this exist. Britannia is rich with tin, and Rome will strip it bare. The legions won't just conquer the people; they'll strip the land itself.'

Atticus frowned, glancing at the jagged tunnel behind them.

The thought of men, shackled and broken, working in those depths sent a shiver down his spine.

'Sentenced to death, then?'

Sica nodded slowly, his face hard.

'Exactly. If a man was sent to a tin mine, he was already

dead, even if he didn't know it yet. They'd toil in the dark until their bodies gave out. Some suffocated in the dust, others were crushed when the rock walls collapsed. Few ever saw the light of day again.'

The weight of Sica's words hung in the air between them. Atticus, usually a man quick to jest or deflect with humour, found himself staring down the mine's tunnel with a newfound respect…and unease.

'And to think,' he muttered, almost to himself, 'this was the best place we could find to hide.'

Sica gave a short, humourless chuckle.

'Aye, but that's the point. No one looks for the living in a graveyard.'

Atticus was quiet for a moment, digesting the words along with the last of his meal.

'Let's hope it stays hidden, then,' he said eventually, 'I'd rather not share the fate of the poor bastards who came before us.'

'Just don't go wandering too deep into those tunnels,' said Sica, 'there's enough dead down there already.'

Atticus gave a half-smile, though it didn't quite reach his eyes.

'Trust me, I'll stay as far from those tunnels as I can.' He straightened up, his gaze hardening. 'Still, better we're here than out there. I'd rather face ghosts than Trinovantes steel any day.'

Sica gave a small nod.

'Aye,' he murmured, almost to himself. 'So would I.'

Back in the south, in the Cantiaci hut, the crackling of the fire filled the silence as the chieftain chewed, his hollow eyes seemingly locked onto the flames. Marcus felt Cassius stir beside him, the discomfort of the moment palpable, but he remained still. This was not the time to press. The old man's authority was clear, even if he had not spoken. When the chieftain was ready, they would know.

After what felt like an eternity, the woman beside Cunda wiped her hands on a scrap of cloth and leaned in to whisper

something into his ear. He did not move immediately, but after a moment, his lips parted.

'Why have you come here, Roman?' he said suddenly. The chieftain's words were slow, but Marcus sensed that every syllable carried weight, as though each was a decision unto itself.

Marcus shifted slightly but maintained his posture of respect, meeting the chieftain's gaze as best he could, despite the man's blindness. He knew the old man was still assessing him, still weighing the truth of his intentions.

'We have come to offer you a choice,' Marcus began. 'As you know, Togodumnus is rallying the tribes to resist Rome, to stand against our legions. But you, great chieftain, have a different path before you, a path that leads not to war, but to prosperity.'

The old man's expression did not change, but his head tilted ever so slightly, a sign perhaps that he was listening more closely.

'Rome has treated the Iceni with much favour,' Marcus continued. 'Prasutagus sleeps well at night knowing he will soon enjoy wealth, stability, and the freedom to rule his people as he sees fit. They already trade with us, gaining riches far beyond what these lands of Britannia can offer. But they are about to reap so much more.'

The chieftain's lips twitched, a reaction barely visible.

Whether it was amusement or disdain, Marcus could not tell. But he pressed on.

'We know that you already trade with Rome, but it has been noted that recently, your traders and ambassadors have grown fearful of the repercussions if caught by Togodumnus. We have learned that he leans on the Cantiaci to pledge your young men to fight under his banner, promising riches if you comply and war if you do not. But we are here to tell you that should you align with Togodumnus, if you fall for his false promises or listen to his misguided war talk, you will find only blood and annihilation. The legions will come, as they have done elsewhere. The resistance will be crushed, your lands burnt, your people enslaved or worse. But if you choose another way... if you choose peace... Rome will reward the Cantiaci as she has rewarded others. You will have favourable terms in trade, stability for your tribe, and the protection of an empire that spans the world.'

Silence hung in the air, heavy and oppressive. The old woman did not look up from her work, though Marcus could feel
her ears were as keen as the chieftain's. Cassius remained tense beside him, no doubt imagining the end of a sword in his gut if this did not go well.

Finally, Cunda raised a hand, slow and deliberate, as if the action itself was a tremendous effort.

'And what do you know of the Cantiaci, Roman?' he asked. 'Do you think we are like the Iceni? That we hunger for Roman riches and Roman rule?'

Marcus swallowed but did not allow the uncertainty to show on his face.

'I know that you are proud and strong,' he said. 'And that Rome does not seek to take that from you. But we offer something better than Togodumnus. He will bring you nothing but death.'

The chieftain's lips pressed together, his brow furrowing in thought. The fire crackled, sending shadows flickering across his face. For a moment, Marcus feared he had pushed too far, that the old man's pride would not allow him to entertain such an offer.

'You speak well, Roman,' he said at last. 'But words alone will not sway us. The Cantiaci do not make their decisions lightly, and I will not be the one to promise anything without deep thought. Togodumnus is a fool, but he is our kin. And kinship runs deep in these lands, deeper than the gold the Roman's so desire.'

Marcus felt a flicker of hope despite the chieftain's words.

'However,' continued Cunda, 'I will give you an answer soon enough. Until I do, you will stay here, in our village. You will eat with us, sleep under our roofs, and we will see what kind of men you truly are. Only then will I know whether to trust your words or cast them into the fire.'

Marcus nodded, though inside, a part of him recoiled at the thought of staying in this strange village, under the watchful eyes of men who might slit their throats at any moment.

'We will stay,' said Marcus. 'We are at your mercy.'

The chieftain made no further comment, simply gesturing to the warrior who had brought them in.

Marcus and Cassius rose from the dirt floor and followed the warrior out of the hut, feeling the weight of unseen eyes on them. Stepping out into the cold evening air, Marcus glanced at Cassius.

'We need to tread carefully,' he murmured, 'the

Cantiaci are a fearsome tribe known for their prowess in battle but if we can win their trust, and keep them from joining the fight, we could be
saving many Roman lives and if nothing else, that is worth taking a risk for.'

'It's not their lives that concern me at the moment,' said, Cassius, looking around at the hostile stares, 'it's ours,' and as the Cantiaci warrior led them deeper into the village, they both knew they were walking a knife edge with life and death on either side, a familiar threat for the Occultum, but unnerving, nevertheless.

Chapter Twenty-Two

Eastern Germania

The wind whipped at Talorcan's face, stinging his eyes and tearing at his cloak as he urged the horse faster, harder. Every muscle in his body screamed with the effort, but he refused to slow.

He risked a glance over his shoulder, his heart hammering against his ribs. Dark shapes moved in the distance, the Vandals were coming, a hunting pack relentless in their chase. They knew these lands far better than he did, and even with the lead he had gained, it wouldn't be long before they closed in. But he had no choice. He had to keep them away from the others.

The cold air bit at his lungs as he forced his horse to press on. The beast beneath him was lathered in sweat, its breath coming in ragged bursts, but there was no time for mercy, not now. Talorcan could still see the fear in Elara's eyes, the desperation in Brennus's grip as he held their child. He had promised them a chance, and this was it.

He ducked low against the horse's neck, his fingers gripping the reins tightly as he swerved through the thinning trees. The forest was beginning to break open, the landscape shifting to rocky hills and scattered boulders. Behind him, the distant shouts of the Vandals carried on the wind. They were gaining and he had to think. He couldn't just outrun them forever, his horse was already showing signs of slowing.

His mind raced as fast as the hooves beneath him. He knew the Vandals' reputation: ruthless warriors, skilled in ambushes and tracking. They would expect him to ride toward a known escape route, to seek cover in the forests or make a stand near the rivers. But that wasn't his plan. His only goal was to draw them far, far away from the others, from Brennus and Canis, from Seneca and Elara. They would need time, and he would give it to them, even if it cost him everything.

The trees finally broke, and Talorcan burst from the cover of the forest, galloping out into the open expanse. The terrain here was rough, the ground uneven and littered with jagged stones, but the horse was nimble, its hooves striking the earth in rapid rhythm.

The wind howled around him, carrying with it the scent of rain. Talorcan could feel it, the storm coming. Dark clouds were
gathering on the horizon, thick and heavy. Perhaps it would work in his favour. If he could just get far enough ahead, the rain might wash away his tracks, confuse the Vandals long enough for him to disappear into the wilderness.

He angled his horse toward them, spurring it on with everything he had left. The Vandals would expect him to keep running, to ride into the west, further and further until exhaustion claimed him. But Talorcan wasn't planning on running forever. He needed to think like them.

As he reached the base of the hills, he pulled hard on the reins, slowing his horse to a stop behind a cluster of boulders. The beast was panting heavily, its sides heaving with effort, but it had carried him this far, and for that, Talorcan gave a silent thanks to the gods.

He crouched low, grabbing a handful of dirt and rubbing it over the horse's flanks to dull the sheen of sweat. His heart was racing, adrenaline surging through his veins, but he forced himself to remain calm. Every step had to be calculated now, every decision weighed.

With a final glance back toward the distant forest, he

led his horse into the shadow of the hills, weaving through the rocky terrain in a wide arc. He moved quickly but carefully, making sure the Vandals would see the faint tracks leading westward. His plan was simple: lay a false trail, lead them away, then vanish. If the gods were kind, the storm would cover his tracks completely, and by the time the Vandals realised they had been deceived, he would be long gone, disappearing into the wilderness.

The ground trembled faintly as the distant sound of hooves grew louder. The Vandals were close now, their dark forms emerging from the edge of the forest, silhouetted against the grey sky. They didn't see him. Not yet.

Talorcan's pulse quickened as the first riders thundered past, their eyes fixed on the false trail leading further westward. He watched as they followed it, unaware that he was hidden among the rocks, watching them ride past. It had worked.

A few moments later, the last of the riders disappeared over the horizon, chasing a trail that led to nowhere. Talorcan remained where he was for several minutes, barely breathing, listening to the diminishing sound of hooves. When he was sure they were gone, he rose slowly, his body trembling with exhaustion and relief. He had
done it. He had gained his comrades some valuable time.

Far to the east, the fugitives stirred within the dark confines of the latebra. The air inside had grown stale, and the tight space made it difficult to move. Canis rose, his muscles aching but his senses sharp. He pushed the lid of the hideaway up just enough to peer through the gap. Satisfied that the clearing was empty, he motioned to the others.

'All clear,' he whispered.

Brennus nodded, gently shaking Elara awake. She blinked, her face pale and drawn, but the strength in her eyes hadn't faltered. She clutched their child to her chest, the boy now sleeping soundly. Seneca was already on his feet, his hand resting on the hilt of his dagger.

The night was still pitch-black as they emerged, the stars barely visible through the thick canopy overhead. The forest was alive with nocturnal sounds, but the ominous thud of hooves had faded into memory. Canis led them wordlessly, his movements sure and deliberate as he guided them eastward, away from Wulfstan's men. The path was narrow, barely discernible even to those who knew it, but Canis had marked the way the day before, when he had hidden the two spare horses.

The group moved in near silence, Brennus stayed close to Elara, his eyes constantly scanning the darkness for signs of danger. The subterfuge of the latebra had bought them precious hours, but they were still not safe, far from it.

'How much farther?' whispered Seneca.

'Not far,' replied Canis. 'If we keep this pace, we'll reach the horses by dawn.'

Elara stumbled slightly on a root, but she recovered quickly, her grip on the child never wavering. Brennus reached out to steady her, his hand brushing her arm.

'Are you alright?' he asked softly.

She nodded, her face set in determination.

'I'm fine. Keep going.'

They pressed on, the forest gradually thinning as they moved eastward, skirting the edges of the Vandal settlement, and finally, after what felt like hours, the first faint light of dawn began to creep into the sky.

'There,' Canis muttered, pointing ahead.

In the dim light, Brennus could just make out the shapes of the waiting horses, tied to a pair of low-hanging trees.

Brennus helped Elara up onto one of the horses, carefully adjusting the child in her arms before mounting behind her. Exhaustion weighed heavily on all of them, but the sight of the animals had rekindled a spark of hope.

'We ride hard,' said Seneca swinging into the saddle. 'We can't stop until we're beyond the reach of Wulfstan's men.' With a sharp kick, he urged his horse forward, and the small group galloped into the dawn. The landscape flew past them in a blur of trees and shadow, the horses' hooves pounding the earth as they pushed eastward, deeper into lands untouched by Roman legions.

As the sun rose higher, the pale light illuminated the unfamiliar terrain. The forest thinned further, and the towering trees gave way to open ground, broken only by scattered copses of birch and oak. The fugitives rode in silence, the rhythmic pounding of hooves their only companion. Brennus could feel the tension in Elara's body as she clutched their child, but she remained composed, her gaze fixed on the path ahead. Eventually, Brennus slowed his horse and raised his hand, signalling for the group to halt.

'We must rest the horses,' he said, dismounting with a grunt. 'They won't last much longer if we push them without pause.' He helped Elara down, taking the child into his arms for a moment to allow her a brief reprieve.

'We've gained some distance,' said Seneca, crouching to check the horses' hooves, 'but if we can cross the river before nightfall, we'll stand a better chance.'

Canis glanced at the sky, gauging the time. The day was still young, but the weight of the journey was already beginning to show on all of them.

'Do you think the Vandals will follow?' he asked.

Seneca stood and wiped his hands on his cloak.

'There is no doubt,' he said. 'They know these lands far better than we do, but the horses need to rest.'

'We'll walk for a while,' said Brennus. 'Once they have caught their breath, we can ride again.'

The group continued eastward, the animals following in the crisp morning air. Canis took the lead again, his keen eyes scanning the land as they pressed forward. Hours passed, and the sun climbed higher into the sky. Sweat slicked the horses' flanks, and the distance
began to blur into a haze of fatigue. At last, the glimmer of water appeared in the distance, the broad, shimmering expanse of the river they had sought.

'The Viadrus.' said Canis, with a gasp, 'we made it.'

Elara slowly approached the bank. Her eyes narrowed as she studied the rivers course. Kneeling, she dipped her hand in and brought it to her lips, tasting the water.

'This isn't the Viadrus,' she muttered, standing slowly. 'It's too small. The big river is still a half a day away.'

'Are you sure?' asked Seneca.

'I grew up in these lands,' said Elara. 'I have drunk Viadrus water since I was a babe. The river we seek is further east.'

Seneca looked back toward the forest, the trees now distant silhouettes behind them, but still too close for comfort. The sound of hooves was absent, but the fear lingered.

The group pressed eastward again, and as the last of the daylight gave way to night, a distant rush of a river came into earshot and Canis dismounted, his eyes narrowing as he surveyed the dark expanse of water ahead.

'This must be it,' he said. 'But we can't cross it tonight.

It's too dangerous.'

Brennus glanced at the river, its swift current barely visible beneath the faint starlight.

'We'll have to make camp here,' he agreed. 'The horses need rest, and so do we.'

Elara slumped onto a patch of grass, carefully adjusting her sleeping child in her arms.

'We need a fire,' said Seneca softly. 'It'll keep the cold at bay.'

Canis gathered dry twigs and branches from the nearby trees and using some dried sheep's wool from his pack, built a small fire against the trunk of a giant tree.

'At first light, we cross,' said Seneca, staring into the fire. 'On the other side we will see what the land is like before heading south. If the gods are with us, we can be back in Roman territory within the month.'

'There is another option,' said Brennus, looking up. 'Elara tells me her people are not far from here. We could go there to rest and perhaps find some help.'

'It's an option,' said Canis, 'but if we could find a boat, perhaps we could get back a lot sooner.'

'We will see what the dawn brings,' said Seneca. 'We are not safe yet but once we are across, we can breathe a little lighter.'

As the night progressed, the quiet hum of the river brought a brief sense of calm, and relief. The flames cast some fleeting warmth into their tired bodies, and they settled into the night, the pain and exhaustion easing as they rested. It had been a hard and stressful ride, but at least now they knew they were relatively safe.

But they were wrong.

On a nearby hill, hidden by the night, Wulfstan and

twelve of his men crouched low, watching the scene unfold below. His eyes gleamed as he observed the fugitives around their fire, totally unaware of his presence. He was an experienced warrior and had suspected the original trail west was just too easy to follow, and once his scouts had picked up their real trail, he had led his men east.

Now, as the group settled into uneasy rest, Wulfstan knew it was time to strike. He had tracked them this far, and there would be no escape. Not this time.

Chapter Twenty-Three

The Cantiaci Village

The fire crackled low in the Cantiaci hut, the smoke, mingling with the faint, lingering scent of whatever meal had been cooked earlier. Marcus sat cross-legged on the cold, hard ground, his back against the wall, his eyes fixed on the dying flames. His mind churned, racing through the conversation they'd had with the chieftain earlier that evening. They had made their case as best they could, but the old man had said little in response, his hollow eyes locked on the fire, his thoughts unreadable.

Across from him, Cassius sat with his arms wrapped around his knees, his posture tense and uneasy. He hadn't spoken much since they'd been led to the hut, and Marcus could sense the frustration boiling just beneath the surface. Time was slipping away, and they both knew it. Togodumnus was rallying the tribes with every passing hour, and if the Cantiaci pledged their warriors to his cause, it would only fuel the flames of rebellion that were threatening to engulf Britannia.

Marcus shifted, trying to ease the discomfort that had settled deep in his bones. The hut was small, claustrophobic even, and he could feel the weight of unseen eyes, the silent judgment of the Cantiaci warriors who patrolled the village outside. The chieftain had promised them a decision soon, but 'soon' could mean anything.

'What's on your mind?' asked Marcus.

Cassius didn't respond at first. He leaned forward, and stared at the fire as though he could conjure an answer from its depths.

'Do you ever think about what brought us here?' he asked eventually, his voice distant, as though speaking more to himself than to Marcus. 'Not just this village, this moment, but here, to this life, to the Occultum.'

Marcus raised an eyebrow, surprised by the question.

'You mean the choices we've made? I think about it all the time. I think it's impossible not to.'

Cassius smirked and poked at the fire with a stick, sending a spray of embers into the air.

'Yeah, choices. I've made more than my share of those.' He looked up at Marcus. 'They say you was a centurion.'

'I was.'

'So, you have killed a lot of men.' It was more a statement of fact rather than a question.

'We all have,' Marcus replied carefully. He could sense that Cassius was leading the conversation somewhere, though he wasn't sure where.

For a long moment, Cassius was silent again, his sharp eyes flickering in the firelight, the usual calculating glint replaced by something darker, something heavier. When he spoke, his voice was barely a whisper, as though admitting the words might change something irrevocably.

'I've killed men,' he said suddenly, 'probably a lot more than you.'

'That, my friend, is highly unlikely,' said Marcus, 'but it is not a competition. Besides, you were a merchant with a penchant of talking your way out of trouble. I know your past.'

'I wasn't always just a merchant,' Cassius said, his gaze fixed on the flames. 'Before the Occultum. Before everything.'

Marcus frowned, leaning in.

'What do you mean?'

Cassius hesitated, as if weighing whether or not to continue. Then, with a deep breath, he began.

'I've told you about the business,' he said slowly, 'the trading, the corruption that ruined me. That much was true. But that wasn't the whole of it. After I lost everything, I did what I had to do to survive. At first, I took small jobs, extortion, smuggling, that sort of thing. But that wasn't enough. There was a different kind of market, one that didn't deal in goods or gold. It dealt in lives.'

Marcus's heart skipped a beat, and he stared at Cassius, not sure if he had heard him correctly.

'What do you mean?'

'Murder,' Cassius said flatly, cutting him off. 'For money. For senators, for merchants, for anyone who had enough coin and enough enemies. People who needed a problem to disappear. If you needed someone hurt, and had a bag of silver, I was your man. Two bags would get him maimed, and a fistful of gold coins for him to become a ghost,' He looked up to see his comrade's reaction.

Marcus felt a chill crawl up his spine, his stomach tightening.

'You killed people for money?'

'I did. But do not look so indignant, am I not the same as you? The only difference is you did it in the name of Rome and for far less money than I did.'

'It's not the same,' said Marcus, 'and you know it.'

'I did what I had to do,' said Cassius. 'After Rome took everything from me, I wasn't going to live in the gutter, and I wasn't going to crawl away like a dog and let them win. So, I took the offers that came my way. At first, it was just a few, debt collectors, thieves, men who had crossed the wrong senator. But it escalated. There were always more offers.

Always more people who wanted someone dead.'

Marcus didn't speak, struggling to process what he was hearing. He knew Cassius was capable of killing, they all were, but somehow this was different.

'Why didn't you tell me this before?' he asked quietly.

'Because it doesn't matter anymore,' he said, 'that part of my life is over. I joined the Occultum because I thought it would give me a chance to belong to something, something bigger than me. To do something that wasn't... that.'

'Yet you know what we do,' said Marcus, 'and I have no doubt that there will be a lot more spilled blood before this mission is done. So how do you intend justifying more killing if you are running from your past?'

Cassius shook his head, his lips tightening into a grim line.

'I'm not running,' said Cassius, 'and those that think you can just walk away are sadly mistaken. The things you do, blood you've spilled, it sticks with you. And the people who paid for those contracts... they don't forget either.'

Marcus felt a knot of unease in his gut.

'You think they're still looking for you?'

Cassius let out a low, bitter laugh.

'I don't know. Maybe. It's not like Rome's senators are known for their forgiveness. There's always someone in power who remembers. That's why I'm here, Marcus. Not just because the Occultum gave me a way out, but because it's the only place I'm not a target.'

They sat in silence for a long moment, the weight of Cassius's confession hanging heavily in the air. Marcus tried to reconcile the man sitting across from him with the image of the cold-blooded assassin Cassius had once been. It was difficult, almost impossible, but the honesty in Cassius's eyes was undeniable.

'I'm not your judge, Cassius,' said Marcus. 'We've all done things we regret, and yes, if you want to hide them away, the Occultum is the best place to do so, apart from the grave. So put it behind you, if not for your sake, for the sake of the Occultum. We all have our burdens and don't need more. I need you to focus on why we are here and what you are doing. We are closer than any family and each of us would die for each other. That's all we ask. Do that and you will find yourself part of a unit like no other and eventually, those ghosts will fade into the background. Besides, you have a special gift, the ability to talk yourself out of any situation.'

'A survival skill,' said Cassius, 'nothing more.'

'A skill, nevertheless,' said Marcus, 'and something tells me we may need that skill if we are to survive all this, but men like the chieftain, they don't bend easily.'

Cassius met his gaze, the faintest hint of gratitude flickering in his eyes before he looked away.

'We'll see,' he said, leaning back against the wall, his voice barely audible over the crackling fire. 'We'll see.'

Two days later, Marcus and Cassius once more stood before the chieftain in his unassuming hut. The old man sat in the same place as before, his hollow eyes fixed on the fire. His age was more evident today, the weight of years pressing down on his frail frame. Beside him, the woman who had whispered in his ear during their last meeting sat silently, her eyes never leaving the Romans.

The chieftain said nothing for a long time, his bony fingers tracing patterns in the air as if weaving the thoughts in his mind. Finally, after what felt like an eternity, he spoke.

'You Romans speak well of peace,' he said. 'but peace

does not come easily to those who have known war.'

Marcus straightened, glancing at Cassius before stepping forward slightly.

'We understand, great chieftain. But peace is still possible. Rome offers you stability, protection...'

Cunda raised a hand, silencing him.

'I know what Rome offers, and I know what Togodumnus offers. He promises war, glory, a chance for our warriors to carve their names into history.

The Cantiaci have never shied from a fight. Our warriors
are strong, proud, and we have fought many battles. We do not fear Roman steel.'

His voice grew stronger, filled with the weight of his people's legacy. Marcus could feel the tension rising in the room, the pride of the Cantiaci a palpable force.

'But,' the chieftain continued, 'I am an old man. I have seen many winters, and I have seen the cost of war. Blood runs deep in these lands, and it always stains the soil. My people...'
He paused, his gaze drifting as though seeing something far beyond the flames. 'My people long for peace. They do not say it openly, but I know. They want to plant their crops without fear of fire. They want their children to grow without knowing the sound of the battle horn.'

'You are a wise man, Cunda,' said Cassius, 'and you see clearly what many others do not. War with Rome will not bring the glory Togodumnus promises. It will bring ruin. If you hold your warriors back, you will save not only your people, but your legacy.'

The chieftain's lips twitched, a flicker of something unreadable crossing his face. He leaned forward slightly, his hollow eyes searching the fire as though the flames themselves held the answer to his dilemma. After a long pause, he spoke again.

'There is one amongst my people,' he said, 'who seeks to become chieftain after I pass. He is young, strong, and favoured by many of our warriors. His name is Cadorix. He has pledged his sword to Togodumnus, and he leads many of our finest into his service. His ambitions are clear. Once I am gone, he will unite the Cantiaci under his rule and take us to war. No matter what I desire, no matter what Rome offers.'

Marcus felt the weight of the chieftain's words settle over him like a heavy cloak. The old man's meaning was clear, and a knot of tension twisted in his stomach.

'But,' the chieftain continued, 'my son has the wisdom to lead our people and prefers peace over war. He is young, and his claim is fragile, but as long as Cadorix lives, he will never rule and the Cantiaci will follow Togodumnus into the slaughter.'

The hut was deathly silent. Marcus felt his heart beating hard in his chest, the enormity of what the chieftain was asking beginning to dawn on him. He glanced at Cassius, who had gone still, his sharp eyes fixed on the old man.

'You want us to kill him,' Cassius said flatly, his voice betraying none of the shock Marcus felt coursing through his own
veins. The chieftain nodded slowly.

'If you wish for peace, if you wish for my warriors to stay behind when Togodumnus calls, then yes. Cadorix must die. Only then will my son take his rightful place as chieftain, and only then will the Cantiaci remain at peace.'

'And where will we find this man?' asked Marcus.

'He can always be found in the same place,' said the chieftain, 'at the right hand of Togodumnus.'

'You ask for the impossible,' said Marcus, his voice tight with disbelief. 'If what you say is true, he will be at the heart of the Trinovantes camp and surrounded with his best warriors.'

'Yet it would ensure peace,' Cassius interrupted. He locked eyes with Marcus, and for a moment, the weight of his past seemed to hang between them, unspoken but undeniable. Marcus knew that look. Cassius had done this before. He had taken lives when the stakes were high.

'You came here seeking a way to stop the Cantiaci from joining Togodumnus,' said the chief. 'I will not lie to you, Roman. It is a dangerous task, but if you succeed, my son will hold the Cantiaci back and you will have your peace.'

Marcus's throat tightened. He glanced at Cassius, seeing the calculation in his friend's eyes. Cassius was already thinking several steps ahead, already considering the possibilities, the risks. Marcus could see the decision forming in his mind even before he spoke.

'We'll do it,' Cassius said quietly.

Marcus felt a jolt of shock, but he forced himself to remain composed. They were playing a dangerous game and there was no time for hesitation.

The chieftain nodded slowly, his face a mask of grim acceptance.

'Very well,' he said. 'My warriors will escort you to wherever you need to be. From there, you will find Cadorix and when the deed is done, return to me. My son will be ready to take his place.'

Chapter Twenty-Four

Eastern Germania

As the first light of dawn crept over the horizon, Canis crouched by the river's edge, cupping his hands in the cool water. The camp behind him was silent, the fire reduced to smouldering embers. His companions were still asleep, their breaths slow and steady in the quiet of the early morning.

He gazed absently at a squirrel foraging nearby, its small paws darting through the undergrowth in search of food. The simple rhythm of nature seemed far removed from the dangers they had faced, and for a brief moment, Canis allowed himself to feel at ease. The cool breeze brushed his skin, and the soft murmur of the river provided a fleeting sense of peace, but the snap of a twig behind him shattered the stillness and he watched as the squirrel darted into the undergrowth, vanishing as quickly as it had appeared.

Canis's instincts kicked in and he spun around, just in time to see the glint of a raised axe, and, with a desperate twist of his body, dodged the full force of the blow. The axe glanced off the side of his head, a brutal, numbing impact that sent him sprawling, and he staggered backward, losing his footing on the slick riverbank.

The world spun as he tumbled into the rushing water and the cold hit him like a wall, shocking his senses, and the last thing he heard before the river swept him away was the savage howl of the Vandals as they descended upon his sleeping comrades.

Seneca jolted awake. Instinct took over as his hand shot to the dagger at his side, his body snapping to its feet as Chaos engulfed the camp.

Brennus was already fighting, his sword whistling through the air as he parried a Vandal's spear thrust. With a savage cry, he brought his blade down, slicing through the man's chest and the Vandal collapsed in a heap, blood pooling around his broken form.

Seneca's eyes darted across the camp. He saw another Vandal, his axe raised high, rushing toward Brennus's unprotected back. Without hesitation, he sprang forward, his dagger slicing through the air. It found its mark, sinking deep into the man's side and the Vandal let out a sharp cry before falling to the ground, his body convulsing as the life drained from him.

'Brennus.' Seneca yelled, his voice hoarse with urgency. 'We're surrounded.'

Brennus spun to face him, panting, his chest heaving from the fight. But before either man could speak further, a sudden, chilling silence descended on the camp. The Vandals, who had been advancing, halted, stepping back in unison, their eyes fixed on a figure standing in the clearing's edge.

Seneca and Brennus turned, their blood running cold.

Wulfstan stood just beyond the campfire's smouldering remains, his face twisted into a sickening grin. In his arms, he cradled the baby, gently running his fingers through the child's soft hair.

Elara lay motionless at his feet, unconscious, her body limp against the hard ground. A dark bruise had already formed on her brow, a clear sign she had been struck down. Brennus's heart lurched at the sight, panic tightening in his throat.

Wulfstan's eyes flicked to them, and his smile grew colder.

'Drop your weapons.' he said, 'or I'll crush his skull.'

Seneca's hand tightened around his dagger, his mind racing, but his eyes never left the child. Brennus, standing just a step away, trembled with fury, his body taut with barely restrained violence. His every instinct screamed at him to strike, to rip Wulfstan apart with his bare hands, if necessary, but he knew any sudden move would cost him his child. He glanced at Seneca, helplessness and desperation etched into his face.

Slowly, Brennus lowered his sword, letting it fall from his grasp. Seneca followed suit, his dagger slipping from his fingers, eyes locked on Wulfstan's every move.

'Tie them up, said Wulfstan.'

The rope bit into Seneca's wrists as Wulfstan's men bound his hands behind his back. Beside him, Brennus was similarly restrained, his face tight with barely contained rage.

Wulfstan seemed to take his time with the baby, almost cradling him mockingly before handing the child to one of his men.

'If she comes around,' he said, nodding towards the woman, 'give it back to her.'

'And if she does not?'

Wulfstan shrugged his shoulders, signifying indifference to the baby's fate. He turned to the rest of his men.

'Spread out and gather wood,' he ordered. 'I want a pyre
built right here. Let's show these people what happens to any man who betrays me.'

Brennus strained against his bonds, his eyes burning with hatred as the men shoved him to his knees. Seneca tried to keep his breathing steady, though the weight of their situation pressed down like a vice. They were powerless.

Wulfstan's men moved with a calm efficiency that turned Seneca's stomach. There was no urgency in their actions, no rush, no frenzy, just a methodical, chilling preparation for what was to come. Some tended to the horses, brushing them down and securing their gear but most dragged branches and small trees from the surrounding forest, ready to feed the pyre. Seneca swallowed the dryness in his throat and glanced at Brennus.

'We are not lost yet, my friend,' he said, 'stay strong.'

Brennus's gaze flicked towards him, but his expression was hard, unyielding.

'I'll kill him,' he hissed. 'I'll tear him apart.'

'You'll do nothing if we're tied up like cattle,' Seneca replied, a slight edge of desperation creeping into his voice. He turned his head, calling to the nearest Vandal.

'Hey. What's your name?'

The Vandal didn't respond. He didn't even glance Seneca's way, continuing instead to sharpen his blade with calm, deliberate strokes. The rasp of metal against stone sent a shiver down Seneca's spine. He shifted his weight, trying to relieve the ache in his arms, but the ropes were tight, cutting into his skin with every movement.

'We're not your enemy.' Seneca shouted, his voice rising in frustration. 'You don't have to do this,' but the Vandals carried on with their tasks as if the two captives were already dead to them.

Brennus, however, could not hold his silence. He thrashed against the ropes, fury burning in his eyes.

'Fight me like a man, Wulfstan.' he roared. 'You don't need your fire to finish this.'

Across the clearing, the pile of firewood continued to grow, thick logs and branches, dry and splintered, ready to ignite at a moment's notice. Seneca forced himself to look away from the growing pyre, his pulse pounding in his ears. He knew what was coming, but the sight of it, the sheer size of the woodpile, made it all too real. He tried again.

'You don't have to do this,' he shouted. 'Whatever you think

we've done, there's no need for this. We're not your enemy.'

One of the men paused for a moment, turning to glance at Seneca, his expression unreadable. For a fleeting second, Seneca thought he might get a response, some flicker of humanity, but the Vandal's gaze slid past him, cold and empty, as if he hadn't spoken at all.

Seneca closed his eyes briefly, feeling the weight of despair settle over him. They weren't going to reason with these men. They were beasts, merciless and eager for blood.

'This can't be how it ends,' Brennus muttered beside him. His eyes darted toward his son, now wrapped in a cloak alongside Elara.

'We're not done yet,' said Seneca through gritted teeth, 'but if we're going to get out of this, we have to think. We'll probably get one chance, one…when they least expect it.'

He searched the camp for any sign of weakness, any opportunity. His eyes fell on the horses tied near the edge of the clearing. The Vandals had tethered them loosely, clearly not expecting any resistance from their prisoners. But the horses… they could be a chance, if they could free themselves, if they could just create enough of a distraction…

As if reading his thoughts, Wulfstan's voice broke through the murmur of the camp, cold and mocking.

'You can think all you want of revenge,' he called from his place by the boulder, 'but there's no escape for you. By the time the moon shines its light onto this forsaken land, you'll be nothing but ash. Your woman... well, she'll be a plaything for my men. And the child?' He shrugged, a smirk curling his lips. 'Perhaps we'll see if he's strong enough to survive the journey back to become a slave. If not, well... the wolves have to eat too.'

Seneca's heart pounded as rage flared hot in his chest, but he forced himself to remain calm, to keep his breathing steady. Wulfstan wanted them to break, to lose control, to lash out. He refused to give him that satisfaction, but their time was running out, and unless the gods were merciful, they would soon be nothing but smouldering corpses beneath a sky indifferent to their suffering.

Two leagues downstream, Canis struggled to stay afloat, tossed like a rag doll by the surging current. His limbs flailed, desperately trying to keep his head above water, but the force of the
river was relentless. Water rushed into his mouth, filling his lungs as he gasped for air, his strength rapidly fading, his body battered against unseen rocks, pain shooting through his limbs as he was carried further and further from the camp.

Then, through the dizzying swirl of water and pain, his hand scraped against something solid, a low hanging branch jutting out over the water. Instinct took over, and he clawed at it, fingers gripping tightly as the river fought to tear him away. His nails bit into the bark, muscles screaming in protest as he hauled himself closer to the bank.

With a final, desperate heave, Canis pulled himself free from the river's grasp, his body collapsing onto the muddy shore. He lay there for several moments, his chest heaving as he struggled to catch his breath, his soaked tunic clinging to him like a second skin. The cold air stung his lungs, but it was a welcome sensation compared to the suffocating force of the water.

Blood trickled over his brow and down his face, mixing with the river water that soaked his body. Each breath was shallow and every muscle in his body burned with exhaustion. His vision swam in and out of focus, and the pounding in his head was almost unbearable and for a brief moment, he considered staying there, letting the darkness overtake him. But he knew he couldn't rest. His comrades were still out there, and Wulfstan would show no mercy. If he didn't get back to the camp soon, it would be too late.

With a groan, Canis forced himself to move. His arms trembled as he pushed himself to his knees, the pain in his head like a hammer pounding against his skull. The world tilted dangerously as he staggered to his feet, swaying unsteadily for a moment before finding his balance. His waterlogged tunic clung to him, heavy and cold, and he peeled it off, discarding the soaked garment onto the muddy ground.

Taking a deep breath, he began to move. Each step felt like agony, his legs heavy, the pain in his head throbbing with every movement. But he forced himself forward, staggering back upstream in the direction of the camp. His feet slipped on the muddy riverbank, and more than once he had to grab at low-hanging branches to keep from collapsing again. His breath came in ragged gasps, every inch of his body screaming in protest, but he pressed on.

Images flashed through his mind, Seneca and Brennus fighting for their lives, Elara with her child in her arms. He had to get back, but time was slipping through his fingers and every moment he delayed, the more danger his comrades faced.

Chapter Twenty-Five

The Lands of the Cantiaci

Marcus and Cassius followed the silent footsteps of the Cantiaci warriors, navigating through thick woods and narrow trails with the ease of men who had known these paths all their lives. The forest eventually began to thin, the dense canopy above giving way to a wide-open space, the gentle rush of water filling the still night air and at last, they reached the river separating the lands of the Cantiaci and those of the Trinovantes.

'This is as far as we go,' said one of their guides. 'Once you cross, you're on your own. The land beyond belongs to Togodumnus and his men.'

'We understand,' Marcus replied. 'Tell your chieftain we'll return when it's done.'

The warrior gave a short, stiff nod, before disappearing back into the woods, their footsteps fading quickly into the night.

As soon as they were alone, the sounds of the forest seemed to close in on them, the rush of the river now the only constant in the silence.

Marcus remained silent for a moment, his gaze fixed on the water but his thoughts far beyond it. Ever since the chieftain had given them the task, he'd been wrestling with the brutal reality of what lay ahead. Killing Cadorix wasn't just difficult, it bordered on the impossible. If the young warrior was as important to Togodumnus as they had been led to believe, he would be well-protected. Seasoned fighters, loyal and battle-hardened, would surround him, men who wouldn't let a stranger come within a sword's reach.

'We're walking into a den of wolves,' he muttered, his brow creasing. 'Cadorix isn't just another warrior, he's part of the backbone of Togodumnus's warband.'

'We need to consult with the others,' said Cassius. 'We can't do this alone.'

'I agree, said Marcus, 'so we'd better get moving.'

Without another word, the two men set off, once again heading north and into the lands of the Iceni.

To the north-west, Falco and Sica lay still, their cloaks blending seamlessly with the rocky outcrop that had been their shelter for two days. The wind whispered over the crag, carrying the sound of a pair of hungry buzzards but otherwise, the world was silent.

'Nothing,' Falco muttered under his breath, peering over the edge at the empty track below. He rolled onto his back, chewing on a dried strip of meat, his tone laced with boredom. 'Two days, and all we've seen are deer and that drunk merchant yesterday.'

Sica didn't respond immediately. He lay beside Falco, his sharp eyes never leaving the track below. His patience, as always, seemed endless. Every shift of the wind, every rustle of leaves was met with his quiet, unyielding focus.

'We leave tonight if there's still nothing,' he said.

Falco grunted in response, sitting up slightly to stretch his legs. He was about to say something more when Sica's hand shot up, a silent signal to stop.

Falco froze, his eyes fixed on the track winding through the forest below. In the distance, the faint clop of hooves reached their ears, followed by the creak of wooden wheels. He slid on his belly next to Sica, squinting down the path.

Through the mist, dark shapes emerged, figures on

horseback, leading a column of wagons.

'Well, would you look at that,' Falco whispered with a grin, his voice barely audible. 'I was starting to think we were wasting our time.'

Sica didn't reply, his focus now entirely on the supply train making its slow way down the track. The wagons were heavily laden, covered with tarpaulins, and flanked by several armed guards on horseback. The men looked rough, Trinovantes by their appearance, and their eyes constantly swept the treeline on either side of the track.

'They're expecting trouble,' Sica muttered.

'And they're well-prepared for it,' Falco added, counting the guards. 'More than I'd like to tangle with. Let's follow them, see where they're heading.'

As the supply wagons rolled further down the track, the two men melted into the trees, moving silently through the undergrowth. They trailed at a distance, staying just out of sight but close enough to keep track of their movements. d the rugged terrain with the ease of men used to such work.

By dusk, the supply train had led them deeper into Trinovantes territory. The track wound through dense forest, the light fading as the sun dipped below the horizon. As darkness fell, the supply train began to slow, and Falco and Sica crouched low behind a line of boulders, watching as the wagons came to a halt.

Through the gaps in the trees, they spotted it, a fortified village nestled in the heart of the forest. High wooden palisades surrounded the settlement, and as the wagons approached, the village gates, opened wide, swallowing them up like a ravenous beast.

Sica and Falco exchanged a glance.

'Fortified,' Falco murmured. 'This isn't just some

backwater village.'

'No,' Sica agreed, 'this is a storage compound.'

They hunkered down for the night, keeping watch from a distance as the guards patrolled the perimeter. The village was well-organised, with a constant rotation of sentries, and the faint glow of torchlight illuminated the walls.

The next day passed slowly and Falco and Sica took turns keeping watch and resting, their eyes never leaving the compound. By noon, another supply train arrived, laden with more goods, and the truth of what they were looking at began to sink in.

'This place is more than just a village,' said Falco quietly. 'They're stockpiling weapons, supplies, everything they need for war. Togodumnus is getting ready to move.'

Sica nodded.

'It's important. Too important to ignore.'

They watched for another day, confirming what they had suspected. The fortified village was a key point in the supply chain, a place where weapons and provisions were gathered and stored, ready to be distributed to the warbands preparing for battle.

As night fell once again, Sica stirred, stretching his limbs as he glanced at Falco.

'We need to get back. Raven needs to hear about this. If we can hit this place, we could cripple their supply lines.'

They moved swiftly, retreating from their position on the crag and disappearing into the forest as the night deepened around them. The journey back to the mine was long, and they moved under the cover of darkness, careful to avoid any patrols.

Just before dawn, the familiar outline of the abandoned tin mine loomed before them and they slid silently into the entrance.

Falco dropped his pack to the ground, rolling his shoulders, exhaustion creeping into his bones. Sica, however, wasted no time.

'Raven,' he called quietly, his voice echoing slightly in the dim cavern.

Raven stirred from his place by the fire, his sharp eyes narrowing as he pushed himself upright.

'You found something?'

'A fortified village,' said Sica. 'Deep in Trinovantes territory. They're using it as a storage compound for weapons and supplies. We saw two supply trains come in over the last two days.'

Raven's eyes flickered with interest.

'How well guarded?'

'Heavily,' Sica replied. 'Too many for us to hit with just the four of us. But if we could take it out, we'd deal a serious blow to Togodumnus's forces.'

'It's a big place,' said Falco, 'and they're getting ready for something big. It is a perfect target.'

Raven sat in silence for a moment, his gaze distant as he processed the information. Finally, he stood, stretching out his stiff limbs.

'I agree,' he said, 'but if this place is as important as you say, we need to tell the others. Get some rest, tomorrow we head north.'

The following day, Raven, Sica, Falco, and Atticus prepared for the long trek back into the lands of the Iceni. The air in the mine seemed heavier, as if the weight of centuries of toil and death had finally settled upon them.

Around the fire, their preparations had begun quietly.

The remains of their meal were cleared away, the fire doused until only faint wisps of smoke curled into the damp air. Each man moved with practiced efficiency, securing their belongings and making sure no trace of their presence would be left behind.

Raven and Atticus crouched near the entrance of the cavern, watching as Sica and Falco worked to conceal the mine's entrance once more, using brambles, loose rocks, and branches to ensuring that no one could tell they had ever been there.

'That should do it,' Sica muttered, wiping dirt from his hands as he stepped back, surveying their work. The entrance to the mine was now completely concealed, a wall of brambles, rocks, and foliage, blending seamlessly into the surrounding landscape.

Falco slung his sarcina over his shoulder.

'Looks like no one's been here in years,' he said.

Atticus, tightening the straps of his own pack, glanced over at Raven.

'Tell me,' he said, 'why don't we just infiltrate that compound now and do as much damage as we can before getting out?'

'Because it's too important,' said Raven. 'Even if we caused a bit of chaos, they'd be more cautious and strengthen their defences. No, if we're going to attack, we need enough men to do real damage, to cripple them properly.'

Atticus frowned, thinking it through.

'And how would Marcus and Cassius make any difference? Six of us isn't much better than four.'

Raven stood, sheathing his dagger, his eyes narrowing slightly.

'Who said anything about just the six of us?'

Atticus's confusion deepened.

'I don't understand. Where are we going to find more men?'

Raven smiled faintly, a glint of something unreadable in his eyes.

'You've come a long way since your training, Atticus' he said, shouldering his pack. 'But there's a lot you still don't know.' He turned towards the path that led into the forest. 'Now come. We need to move.'

Without further explanation, Raven strode ahead. Falco and Sica followed silently, as if Raven's cryptic words made perfect sense to them.

Atticus hesitated for a moment, then hurried after them, his mind racing. He had thought he understood these men, their mission, their tactics and had trained hard to become one of them, but now, as they moved deeper into the wilds, he realised how little he truly knew. There was more at play here than he had imagined, and whatever Raven had in mind was far bigger than a simple raid on a supply compound.

Chapter Twenty-Six

Eastern Germania

Canis crawled slowly towards the outskirts of the camp. The pyre was unmistakable, a towering mass of timber in the centre of the clearing, and the sight of it twisted his gut.

The urge to rush in was overwhelming, but Canis knew better. He was unarmed, save for the knife he still carried at his side, and he would be hopelessly outnumbered if he made a reckless move. His sword had been lost in the river, carried away by the fierce current that had nearly claimed his life and his best chance would be in the dark. He retreated deeper into the forest, putting some distance between himself and the camp. He had to think. He couldn't take on an entire band of Vandals unarmed, but there was one thing he could do, improvise.

Once hidden from view, he searched for something, anything, that could serve as a weapon.

His eyes fell on a pair of sturdy saplings nearby, each as thick as his wrist. They were straight, solid, and long enough to give him the reach he needed. Without wasting time, he drew the knife and set to work, sawing through the saplings with swift, precise strokes. His arms burned with the effort, but he pushed through, driven by the knowledge that his comrades' lives depended on him.

Once the first branch was cut, he set to work on the second. They were rough, crude weapons, nothing like the fine Roman steel he was used to wielding, but they would have to do. He began to sharpen the ends, carving them into deadly points. The work was quick, brutal, the sharp wood flaking away as he honed the tips and by the time he finished, the branches had become two crude spears, each as long as his body.

He tested their weight in his hands, feeling the balance. They would do.

With the makeshift lances ready, Canis crouched low and returned to the undergrowth surrounding the camp. The night had fully settled in now, and the camp was lit only by the glow of the small fires. Shadows danced along the edges of the clearing, and he could see Brennus bound against the pyre.

His hands tightened around the lances as he inched forward again, moving back toward the camp's edge. He could see Seneca
tied to the tree not far from the pyre, his wrists still bound behind him. His face was twisted with frustration, and Canis could see his friend's desperate attempts to break free, the futility of the effort evident in the bloodstains where the ropes bit into his skin.

Inch by inch, Canis closed the distance to Seneca. The Vandals were laughing now, dark, cruel laughter as one of them, the man holding the burning torch, made his way slowly toward the pyre, waving the flame in front of Brennus's terrified face. The others watched, eyes gleaming with anticipation.

Canis pressed the knife to the ropes binding Seneca's wrists, sawing through the thick fibres with quick, silent strokes. The tension in the ropes snapped, and Seneca's hands dropped free.

Seneca froze for a moment, his eyes wide with surprise as he glanced behind him, only to find Canis crouched low, already handing him one of the crude spears. Canis met his gaze, his face grim and determined, and in that moment, Seneca's confusion was replaced by understanding. They had one chance. He took the spear, his hands still numb from the hours of being bound, but he gripped the weapon tightly, his knuckles white as he turned his attention to the scene unfolding before them.

The torchbearer was getting closer to the pyre, each step designed to prolong Brennus's fear. The other Vandals jeered and shouted encouragements, their attention fully absorbed by the spectacle.

Canis moved quickly to Elara, her face streaked with dirt and tears. She clutched her baby tightly to her chest, rocking him gently even as terror gripped her. Canis knelt by her side, slicing through the ropes binding her feet in a single swift motion.

'When the fighting starts,' he whispered, 'take the baby and run. Don't look back. Find your people and get as far away as you can.'

Elara stared at him, her lips trembling, but she nodded.

Canis pressed a hand briefly to her shoulder, before stepping back beside Seneca, and together, they turned their eyes toward the Vandals. The torch was now inches from the pyre, the flame casting a hellish glow on Brennus's face. Every Vandal eye was fixed on the scene, their cruel laughter ringing through the night, oblivious to the two shadows that moved silently through the dark.

Canis and Seneca, their hearts pounding in unison, exchanged one last glance, and in one swift motion, Canis pulled the
knife from its sheath and sent it spinning through the air to embed itself in the back of the nearest Vandal's neck with a sickening thud. The man's body jerked violently, his hands clawing at the knife, blood pouring down his throat as he collapsed to the ground, unable to cry out.

Before the body hit the earth, both men lunged forward, cutting through the darkness like wolves amongst sheep.

The next Vandal barely had time to turn before Seneca's spear crashed into his chest with brutal force. The makeshift weapon splintered bone, and the man fell with a choked gasp, his legs crumpling beneath him as he collapsed to the ground, paralyzed.

Canis ran forward and drove his spear into the chest of the third man. The impact sent the Vandal sprawling backward, his body twisting as he hit the ground, gasping and choking as blood filled his lungs.

The chaos was swift and savage and in the span of seconds, three men lay dead or dying, their blood soaking into the earth. The other Vandals, still focused on the pyre, hadn't yet realized what was happening. But the moment of surprise was slipping away fast.

The torchbearer, his arm poised to light the pyre, turned just in time to see his comrades fall. His eyes widened in shock, but before he could react, Canis was upon him, his body a blur as he threw himself into the Vandal and the torch flew from the man's hand, landing harmlessly in the dirt. The two men struggled, but Canis was faster, his fist crashing into the man's jaw with a sickening crunch, and the Vandal's head snapped back, dazed.

Seneca was already moving toward the next guard, aiming his spear at the man's throat. The Vandal tried to raise his sword in time, but it was too late, and the sharpened point of the spear pierced his neck, and he collapsed in a gurgling heap, blood spilling down his chest.

The remaining Vandals, finally realizing what was happening, scrambled to draw their weapons. Shouts of alarm rang out across the camp, but the damage was already done. The once-confident guards now stood in shock, faced with two men who had moved like ghosts through their ranks.

Canis pulled himself up from the ground, his eyes wild, his breath coming in ragged bursts and withdrew his knife from the throat of the first guard. He spun around and swiftly cut through Brennus's binds and the Batavian stumbled towards one of the downed

warriors, his shaking hands closing around the hilt of a fallen sword. Seneca joined him and picked up an axe before they turned to face the remaining warriors side by side.

In the distance, Elara had already risen, and fled into the night, disappearing into the forest with the child, just as she had been told.

The remaining Vandals, their shock giving way to fury, began to close in, their swords gleaming in the firelight. Canis moved first, parrying the wild swing of an enemy blade, then twisting his own sword into the man's gut with a fierce grunt. The Vandal crumpled, and Canis whirled to face the next, his sword singing through the air as he deflected a heavy blow aimed at Seneca's back.

Seneca swung his axe in a vicious arc, the sharp edge biting into the neck of a second foe, blood spraying across the dirt as the man fell, clutching at the wound. Beside him, Brennus struggled to keep up, his movements slower, each step marked by the pain of his imprisonment. His limbs were heavy, his vision blurred, but he forced himself to fight, and he drove his blade into the chest of an oncoming Vandal, staggering as the man's weight fell against him.

The skirmish was swift and brutal, the clash of steel filling the air. Canis and Seneca fought like cornered wolves, their blows precise and deadly, cutting through the chaos with practised efficiency. For a moment, it seemed as if they could hold their ground, even with Brennus flagging at their side, but as the rest of the Vandals made a circle around them, Wulfstan charged forward out of the treeline, his face creased with rage and brutality and Brennus raised his sword in desperation, barely blocking Wulfstan's crushing blow. The force of it sent him reeling, his legs buckling beneath him as he crashed to the ground, his sword slipping from his grasp. His breath came in ragged gasps as he stared up at the Vandal leader looming over him, the end surely near.

Wulfstan raised his blade again, but behind him, Elara burst from the trees, her face twisted in desperation. Without thinking, she threw herself at Wulfstan, her arms wrapping around his broad throat and the Vandal staggered, caught off guard by the sudden attack.

It was only a heartbeat's distraction, but it was enough and Brennus, still on the ground, scrabbled in the dirt, finding the hilt of his sword and with a surge of raw, primal strength, drove the blade upward, tearing through flesh and muscle, up into the Vandal's guts.

Wulfstan's eyes went wide with shock and pain. His mouth opened, but no sound came out as his body jerked violently. He staggered back, dropping his sword as his hands went instinctively to the wound. Blood poured down his legs in thick rivulets, and he crumpled to the ground with a gurgling gasp, the life fading from his eyes.

Brennus rolled away, gasping for breath, his muscles trembling with exhaustion as Elara collapsed beside him, her chest heaving.

Wulfstan lay dead, his blood seeping into the earth, and the remaining Vandals, seeing their commander slain, faltered, their confidence shattered. They glanced at each other, fear creeping into their eyes before turning and fleeing into the darkness.

As the last of the Vandals disappeared, a thick, uneasy silence settled over the clearing. The only sounds were the crackling of the dying fires and the ragged breathing of the survivors. For a moment, none of them moved, as though their minds hadn't quite caught up to the brutal reality of what had just unfolded.

Elara was the first to stir, her eyes wide and unblinking. Her gaze darted to the trees where she had hidden the child, and with a strangled gasp, she took off at a run, vanishing into the darkness as quickly as she had appeared.

Seneca stood frozen, still gripping the axe, his chest heaving. His eyes swept over the battlefield, taking in the bodies scattered across the ground, the blood-soaked earth at his feet. Brennus, pale and trembling, clutched his side where bruises still ached from his imprisonment and both men exchanged a disbelieving glance.

'We're alive,' Brennus rasped, his voice hoarse with shock.

Seneca nodded, but the weight of the fight still hung over them like a storm. They were alive, yes, but barely.

A few paces away, Canis let out a low guttural moan and as his sword slipped from his fingers, he crumpled to the earth with a sickening thud.

'Canis.' Brennus shouted, rushing forward. Seneca was at his side in an instant, both men kneeling beside their fallen comrade. Their hands grabbed at his shoulders, lifting him gently, but as they turned him over, they saw something that turned their blood cold, a deep sword wound gaping in Canis's stomach, blood pooling around the jagged edges of the tear. How he had kept fighting, how he had stayed on his feet for so

long, was beyond either of them. But now,
the strength that had carried him had left his body, leaving
only the cold finality of the wound.

'It's fatal,' said Seneca as Canis's breath came in
shallow, laboured gasps. His skin was already growing pale, a
thin sheen of sweat covering his brow, but his eyes were still
open, still conscious. He knew.

They moved quickly, lifting him as gently as they could
and propping him against a nearby rock, trying to make him
as comfortable as possible. Canis grimaced, but his lips parted
in a faint, weary smile.

'Not yet,' he rasped. 'I'm…not gone yet.'

'Hold on,' said Seneca, 'just hold on.'

Seneca hurried to their discarded packs, fumbling
through the worn leather until he found the small flask of
poppy milk. His fingers trembled as he uncorked it, kneeling
beside Canis once more. Brennus placed a hand on Canis's
shoulder, steadying him as Seneca carefully brought the flask
to his lips.

'Drink this,' said Seneca softly. 'It'll help with the pain.'

Canis gave a weak nod and drank, the bitter liquid
sliding down his throat. His breathing steadied slightly, but his
eyes were dull with the knowledge of what was coming. The
poppy milk wouldn't save him, but it would ease his passing.

Seneca set the flask aside and sat beside him. Brennus
stood a few steps away, staring at his friend's face, grief etched
into his features. He had only known him a few days but
already thought of him as a brother.

Canis leaned his head back against the rock, his breath
laboured, each exhale a struggle. His eyes fluttered weakly, but
with great effort, he lifted a trembling hand toward Seneca.

'Seneca,' he rasped, his voice barely audible. 'I need to

tell you something. Something important.'

Seneca leaned in, his brow furrowed.

'Go ahead,' he said.

'Alone,' Canis gasped.

Seneca hesitated, glancing over at Brennus. With a silent nod of understanding, Brennus stepped away, disappearing into the trees to check on Elara. Seneca turned back to Canis, the man who, despite the short time they had served together, had earned his place in the brotherhood of the Occultum.

'We're alone,' said Seneca quietly, 'what do you want to say?'

Canis's breathing grew more ragged, his voice weaker with every word.

'Listen carefully,' he whispered. 'I am not... what I seem. I was sent to join your unit by men of power... to infiltrate the ranks and sabotage the campaign in Britannia.'

Seneca's heart lurched.

'What?' he gasped. 'Why? Who would do such a thing?'

'I don't know all the politics,' replied Canis, 'but the orders came from someone high in the Senate. There are those who want the campaign to fail... for their own ends. I was paid... a fortune... more than I could ever dream of. My mission was to join the Occultum... to get close.'

Seneca could barely grasp the enormity of what he was hearing.

'What was your goal? What were you meant to do?'

'I never... got my final orders,' Canis wheezed. 'That was... to come when we reached Britannia.'

'Did they threaten you?' Seneca demanded, disbelief

flooding his voice. 'Your family?'

Canis shook his head weakly.

'No. It was... my choice. For gold, for power. But...' He hesitated, his voice faltering. 'I didn't expect to bond with you... with the men. There's something... about your brotherhood. I became proud to fight alongside you.'

Seneca stared at him, torn between anger and pity.

'Why are you telling me this now?' he asked. 'I would have buried you as a true brother.'

'Because...' Canis's voice was barely a whisper now, his strength fading fast. 'There's something else. I'm not... alone.'

Seneca froze.

'What do you mean?'

'There's... another amongst you,' Canis rasped, his eyes wide with urgency. 'Another traitor...'

Seneca's blood ran cold.

'Who?' he demanded, 'tell me his name.'

But Canis's body convulsed violently, a gush of blood spilling from his mouth. His eyes widened in fear, his body shuddering as he tried to speak. His lips moved, but no sound came, and his body slumped sideways, his life slipping away before he

could say more.

'Canis.' Seneca roared, shaking him in desperation. 'Tell me. Who is it? What is his name?'

But it was too late. Canis's body went limp, his secret lost forever.

Chapter Twenty-Seven

Britannia

Marcus and Cassius approached the rendezvous in the lands of the Iceni. They had been pushing hard since leaving Cantiaci territory, avoiding the well-trodden paths and travelling only by night to remain unseen. Most of the journey had been navigated by stars and crude, worn maps etched on soft leather, maps left behind by men whose names they would never know. But now, the landscape had become familiar. They recognised the villages they passed, and it was memory and instinct that guided them towards the looming rocks ahead, barely visible in the mist.

As they reached the base of the rocky outcrop, Marcus felt a subtle shift in the air, a tension that made him pause. His hand hovered near the hilt of his sword for a moment before he relaxed, lifting his hands to his mouth and blowing softly, imitating the call of an owl.

Silence. He was about to repeat the signal when a familiar voice cut through the mist, its tone playful and low.

'Toowit–towoo,' the voice mocked, and moments later, Falco emerged from the rocks with a look of simulated disgust upon his face. 'Well look at you two,' he said, 'you look and smell like a pair of corpses that have been dug up and ravaged by wolves. You could have made an effort.'

'Falco,' said Marcus, shaking his head. 'You're going to have to learn how to sound those calls properly.'

'A bit silly if you ask me,' Falco replied, his eyes glinting in the mist. He glanced between Marcus and Cassius with mock surprise. 'I'll admit, I'm shocked you're both still alive. Especially without me there to look after you.'

'We managed well enough,' said Marcus with a sigh. 'What about you? Did you all make it back?'

'Alive and kicking,' Falco replied. He turned and gestured toward a large, strangely shaped boulder looming in the mist. 'Go left past Diana and keep going. You'll find the others at the end of the path.'

'Diana?' Cassius asked, raising an eyebrow.

'Named after one of the many women who loved me,' said Falco. 'To be fair, she was probably a bit bigger but not as good
looking.'

Cassius shook his head, bewildered, before either man could respond, Falco spoke again.

'Now go,' he said, 'your smell offends me,' and without waiting for a reply, he slipped back into the mist, vanishing as quickly as he had appeared.

'That man never fails to confuse me,' Cassius muttered, watching the fog where Falco had disappeared.

Marcus sighed, a hint of a smile still lingering on his face.

'He's a strange one, that's certain. But wait until you see him fight. Now come on, we're almost there.'

With renewed purpose, the two men continued past the towering boulder Falco had so fondly named Diana, the path ahead veiled in the shifting mist. Before long, another figure materialised from the fog, this time bearing a short sword. The figure's eyes flickered between the two bedraggled men, tense for a moment, until recognition softened his features.

'Marcus,' said Sica, lowering his sword. 'Cassius. I almost didn't recognise you.'

'Falco has already informed us that our appearance

falls short of what's expected,' Marcus replied with a faint smile.

Sica smirked.

'I'm sure he did. Come, the others are waiting.'

They followed Sica deeper into the rocky outcrop. The camp was small but well-organised, tucked into the natural crevices of the terrain. The shelter at the far end was an impressive display of their resourcefulness. Saplings and bracken formed a sturdy structure between the rocks, its roof thickly layered with undergrowth, and they had repurposed parts of one of the tents they'd brought from Gallia, using it to make the roof more resistant to the elements.

The ground had been softened with bracken, and a small fire crackled gently against the earthen wall at the far end of the shelter, its warmth radiating throughout the space. It wasn't much, but it was safe.

The smell of the food filled the air, and Marcus's stomach growled in response. Gratefully, he and Cassius removed their packs and settled onto the furs that Raven had stolen weeks earlier from the farm. Each man retrieved a wooden bowl from his sarcina and scooped out generous portions of the rich stew, the aches of many days of rough travelling melting away with each mouthful.

A few moments later, Sica joined them, helping himself to his own bowl of stew before sitting on another of the furs.

The warmth from the flames seemed to soothe their bodies, easing the tension of the long journey and for a while, they allowed the peace of the camp to wash over them, their minds free of the dangers that still lingered beyond.

At last, Marcus broke the silence.

'So,' he began, glancing over at Raven, 'we all made it back. Tell me, how went it for you?'

'We've been here for a few days now,' said Raven. 'But while we were down south, it became clear that Togodumnus is preparing for something significant. We've seen supply wagons, heavily guarded, moving weapons and provisions to at least one fortified village deep in Trinovantes territory.'

Sica nodded in agreement.

'We've confirmed it's a key storage compound. Falco and I tracked two supply wagons there ourselves. If we strike before they're fully ready, we could disrupt whatever they're planning.'

'Why would they be stockpiling so many weapons?' asked Cassius, frowning. 'There are only so many a man can wield.'

'There could be many reasons,' Marcus mused. 'They could be preparing for defensive positions, in case they need to fall back, or they might be supplying others who aren't yet ready for battle. Whatever the purpose, one thing is certain, those weapons are a potential problem for our brothers across the sea.'

'I agree,' said Raven. 'And this may not be the only cache. But they're too well-defended for the six of us to take out on our own. We'll need reinforcements.'

'We will,' said Marcus thoughtfully. 'But first, there's something else we need to address. Cunda, the chieftain of the Cantiaci, has agreed to keep his tribe out of the conflict. However, there's a condition. We must kill one of his warriors, a man named Cadorix. He's a close ally of Togodumnus and has ambitions to take control of the Cantiaci once Cunda dies. If we remove him, Cunda's son will take his place, and he's far more likely to work with Rome rather than against us.'

'That sounds simple enough,' Raven replied. 'Why didn't you do it while you were there?'

‘Because Cadorix rides with Togodumnus,’ said Marcus
grimly, ‘so if we want to get anywhere near him, we’ll have to enter the very heart of the serpent’s nest.’

Chapter Twenty-Eight

Eastern Germania

Seneca stood in the cold, grey light of early dawn, staring at the blood-soaked ground where the bodies of Vandals lay scattered. His eyes, though fixed on the carnage, were unfocused, lost in a deep well of thought. The words of Canis still echoed in his mind, a traitor in the Occultum. One of their own. But he couldn't share this with Brennus. Not yet. Not when everything was so uncertain.

Brennus stood nearby, quiet, his face still pale and bruised from the fight. Elara sat atop one of the horses, clutching her baby to her chest, eyes red from the tears she had shed in the night, but there was a strength to her gaze, a determination to survive and protect her child at all costs. After a long moment, Seneca took a deep breath and turned to Brennus.

'Help me with the bodies,' he said, already moving toward the nearest fallen Vandal.

Brennus blinked, his eyes widening slightly in surprise.

'The bodies? What do you mean?'

'We'll burn them,' Seneca replied, 'on the pyre intended for us.'

Brennus frowned, glancing at the towering stack of timber the Vandals had constructed.

'Burn them? They're our enemies, Seneca, let them rot.'

'They were warriors,' said Seneca, crouching down to lift one of the dead men. 'They died with weapons in their hands. In death, that makes them the same as us.'

Brennus hesitated but then stepped forward. Together,

they dragged the slain Vandals toward the pyre, their tunics soaked with blood and the cold morning dew.

It wasn't until Seneca reached Canis's body that Brennus stopped in his tracks. His eyes widened in shock as he watched Seneca lift the body of their fallen comrade, struggling under its weight.

'Seneca,' Brennus began, 'what are you doing?'

Seneca hefted Canis's body onto the pyre, laying him across the top of the pile. His face was hard, set in stone, his emotions buried beneath a mask of cold determination.

'Seneca.' Said Brennus, 'he was one of us. You're going to

burn him with the Vandals?'

'He was a warrior like the others,' said Seneca. 'It doesn't matter who he fought for, in death, there's no difference. His body deserves the same fate as theirs.'

Brennus stared at him, stunned.

'But he was our brother.'

'Brother or not,' Seneca cut in., 'he wasn't what we thought he was.'

Brennus swallowed, his brow furrowing in confusion. He wanted to ask more, to understand what Seneca wasn't saying, but there was something in his friend's face, something dark and unreadable, that stopped him. After a long pause, he nodded, his expression conflicted, but he said nothing more.

Seneca stood alone before the pyre, his eyes scanning the bodies. Canis lay at the top, his face pale and peaceful in death, but Seneca's heart twisted with anger and betrayal. Canis had fought alongside them, shared their victories and their struggles, but in the end, he had been something else entirely, a traitor. A pawn in some larger, unseen game.

With a deep breath, Seneca bent down and retrieved a

torch from the smaller fire, the weight of the last few hours pressing down on him.

Behind him, Brennus, Elara, and the baby were already mounted, ready to leave. The horses snorted softly in the cold air, their breath rising like mist, all watching silently as Seneca approached the pyre, the torch held in his hand.

He paused, his jaw clenched. His eyes fixed on Canis's body.

For a moment, the silence was absolute, the weight of his grief and anger pressing in on him from all sides. The betrayal was too raw, too fresh. He stared at the body of the man who had fought beside him, who had earned his trust, only to shatter it in the end. In a low voice, barely more than a whisper, Seneca cursed, his words sharp and venomous.

'May you rot in the underworld, Canis,' he muttered 'You were a traitor to Rome and those you called brother.'

And with that, he thrust the torch into the base of the pyre.

The flames took quickly, licking up the dry wood and consuming the bodies with a ferocious crackle. The fire blazed brighter, sending thick plumes of smoke into the morning sky, a final
act of cleansing for the blood that had been spilled. The faces of the
dead disappeared behind the rising flames, their forms reduced to shadow and ash.

Seneca stood there for a moment longer, his fists clenched, watching the fire rise higher and higher. Then, without another word, he turned and walked back to his horse.

Two days later the river widened and became shallower, its wide expanse cutting through the landscape like a dark, glistening ribbon. Seneca led the group to the edge of the riverbank, his eyes scanning the dark water. The ford appeared shallow enough, but the current was strong. Crossing would have to wait until morning, and the weight of exhaustion tugged at his limbs. Brennus rode up beside him, his body stiff from the long ride.

'We'll camp here for the night,' said Seneca, dismounting and moving toward a small patch of flat ground just above the waterline. 'It's too dark to cross safely.'

Brennus nodded, dismounting as well.

'I'll gather wood for the fire.'

As they set about preparing camp, Elara stood at the edge of the river, her eyes distant, as if searching for something. After a moment, she spoke, her voice soft but filled with recognition.

'This place… I know it,' she said, turning to face the others. 'I came here as a child, it is used by my people. They live ten days walk eastward on the other side of the river.'

Seneca stopped what he was doing, looking up in surprise.

'Your people? You're sure?'

Elara nodded, her expression softening for the first time since the night they had escaped.

'Yes, my people. We have many villages there and they'll welcome us. We will all be safe there.'

Brennus looked towards Seneca.

'It would be safer than continuing south without a clear destination. And they might be able to help with provisions, or at least give us a place to rest.'

Seneca stood still for a moment, staring across the river into the darkness beyond. The idea of finding refuge was tempting, at least until they got their strength back. He glanced at Elara, seeing the hope in her eyes, and he knew that her presence would ease their arrival. They had helped her, saved her and her child from the Vandals, and now she was offering them a chance to rest and regroup.

'It's a good offer,' said Seneca finally. 'But we'll need to see what the morning brings. For now, we rest. Crossing the ford in the dark is too risky.'

With that, the group settled into their evening routines. Brennus returned with wood, and soon a small fire crackled on the riverbank, casting long shadows over the water. The horses grazed nearby, tired but calm, while Elara quietly rocked her baby to sleep under the furs.

Seneca sat by the fire, staring into the flames, his thoughts far away. The idea of another traitor, someone already embedded deep within their ranks in Britannia, gnawed at him like a festering wound. He had kept this knowledge to himself, knowing that Brennus had enough to bear without the weight of this new betrayal, but the truth loomed over him like a dark cloud, impossible to ignore.

Tomorrow, they would cross the river and seek refuge with Elara's people, but tonight, the fire was warm, and for the first time in days, there was a glimmer of hope.

Seneca cast a glance toward Elara, her face now calm as she rested near her child. Her people might offer safety for a time, but he knew that the traitor, whoever he was, would have to be dealt with and by the time Seneca fell asleep, his mind was already made up and he knew exactly what was to be done.

The morning sun rose slowly as Brennus, Elara, and her child stirred from their sleep. The air was crisp, with the faint scent of damp earth and morning dew clinging to the grass around them and as they packed up their meagre belongings, a strange quiet hung over the camp, as if the land itself was holding its breath. Elara wrapped her baby tightly in a fur and mounted her horse, her eyes lingering on the river beyond. Brennus was strapping the last of the gear onto his mount when he noticed Seneca standing a little distance away, staring at the ford, his face set in a way that immediately drew concern.

'Seneca,' Brennus called, walking over. 'Everything ready?'

Seneca didn't answer at first. His eyes were fixed on the
river. Something had shifted in him during the night, though Brennus couldn't place it. Finally, he turned, his expression unreadable.

'I'm not going with you.'

Brennus blinked, his brow furrowing in confusion.

'What are you talking about? We're ready to cross. Elara's people are just a few leagues beyond the ford. We can rest there, regroup, and plan our next move.'

But Seneca shook his head, his eyes distant.

'You're crossing. You'll take Elara and her child to safety. But I'm not going with you.'

Brennus stared at him, struggling to understand.

'Why? What are you talking about? We've come this far together…'

'I need to get to Britannia,' Seneca interrupted. 'I can't afford to waste any more time. There's still a job to do.'

'Seneca, this isn't right,' said Brennus. 'We're brothers. You saved my life, I can't let you ride off alone.'

Seneca's eyes softened for a brief moment, the weight

of their shared history clear in his gaze.

'I saved your life, yes. And now I'm asking you to save her.' He nodded toward Elara. 'She needs to reach her people, and the child needs safety, a place where he can grow up without the shadow of war hanging over him. You can give them that, Brennus.'

Brennus struggled with the words, his heart warring with the decision. He glanced at Elara, at the baby nestled in her arms, and back at Seneca.

'But you... you're heading into danger alone. What's waiting for you in Britannia that's so urgent? The others are there, and you know as well as I do that they are more than capable of operating without any of us. That's how you trained us remember? A team that works well together but more than capable of continuing if his brother falls.'

Seneca could feel the weight of Canis's final confession pressing down on him, the secret he hadn't shared.

'There are things you don't know, he said, 'things I can't explain right now. But trust me, this is something I have to do.'

Brennus clenched his fists, fighting the rising frustration.

'Then let me ride with you.'

'No,' said Seneca firmly. 'This is something I have to do alone. Protect her, Brennus. Protect your son and perhaps one day,' his voice softened slightly, 'one day, we'll meet again.'

Brennus's face hardened, his eyes searching Seneca's, as if trying to find some way to change his mind. But he knew Seneca too well, there would be no changing this decision. With a heavy sigh, he stepped back, his shoulders sagging under the weight of the moment.

'I swear to you,' Brennus said, his voice hoarse with emotion, 'I'll take them to safety Seneca and one day, I'll find you again. I'll repay the debt.'

'There is no debt, Brennus. ' said Seneca. 'Just take care of them.'

With a final look, Brennus turned and mounted his horse, riding over to where Elara waited. She watched Seneca, her lips pressed into a thin line, as if she, too, understood that something had shifted. Brennus helped her steady her horse, then turned back to Seneca one last time.

'Good luck, brother,' he said quietly.

'To you as well,' Seneca replied.

Brennus turned his horse, and with Elara and her child beside him, rode toward the ford. Seneca stood where he was, watching them as they crossed the shallow waters and disappeared beyond the rise of the riverbank.

When they were gone, he turned away, his heart heavy but resolute. He walked to his horse, mounted, and gave one last look at the ford. Then, without hesitation, he dug his heels into the sides of the horse and urged it forward, heading westward, away from the river.

At first, he rode slowly, the weight of the past few days still pulling at him. But as the landscape opened up before him, the urgency returned. The distant hills stretched out like an open road, and the call of his mission, the need to uncover the traitor amongst them, pulled him forward like a relentless force. He dug his heels in deeper, and the horses broke into a gallop, the pounding of hooves echoing across the empty plains.

The road to Britannia was long, and he had no more time to waste.

Chapter Twenty-Nine

Britannia

The six men sat in the dim light of the early morning, their faces drawn with concern as they considered the weight of their situation. The campfire had long since died down to glowing embers, but no one had the mind to rekindle it. Marcus sat at the head, his sharp eyes moving between the others, Raven, Atticus, Cassius, Falco, and Sica.

'We cannot strike the cache,' Marcus began. 'We don't have the numbers to do it right, and if we fail, it will alert Togodumnus to our presence here. We need more men.'

Falco nodded, his arms crossed as he leaned back against the rock.

'Two of us tracking those wagons was one thing but hitting a fortified village… it's suicide with only the six of us.'

Cassius sat forward.

'But we've already confirmed it's a key stockpile. If we destroy it, we could significantly affect Togodumnus's ability to fight. Isn't that why we are here?'

'There is something we can do,' said Raven. 'It's a risk, but Seneca foresaw a situation just like this and put a plan in place. I don't know if it's ready yet, but Lepidus might know.'

'What plan?' Falco asked.

Raven leaned forward, resting his arms on his knees.

'Back in Gallia, those recruits who were already part of the exploratores but didn't pass the selection process for the Occultum were given another option. They could join a support unit, one that would receive additional training to back us up if we ever needed help to extract us from dangerous situations. This might be exactly the kind of situation

Seneca had in mind for them.'

Marcus nodded thoughtfully.

'It could work. But how do we know they're ready, or even suitable?'

'I selected them myself,' said Raven. 'They're men who've seen battle, but they didn't quite make it through our final tests. They're skilled, capable, just not quite enough for the Occultum. By the time we left Gallia, they were showing real promise. The only thing I don't know is if Lepidus brought them up with the invasion force. If he did, they'd be ideal to support us in the attack, well-trained and committed.'

Falco frowned.

'We have a support troop and all this time you kept it from us?'

Raven gave a small nod.

'At Seneca's instruction. He wasn't sure it was the right move, but he wanted them prepared anyway. I didn't mention it because we weren't sure they'd be ready, but now...' he paused, glancing at Marcus, 'we might need them.'

Marcus looked around the group.

'There's only one way to find out if they're available, someone has to go back and ask Lepidus.'

'Back across the sea?' said Falco incredulously. 'You can count me out.'

Sica also shook his head.

'I need to stay here. If we're scouting Togodumnus's camp, we'll need every advantage.'

'I'll go,' said Atticus, cutting into the conversation.

The group turned to look at him, surprised by the offer. Atticus had proven himself a valuable member of the Occultum, but this was no small task. The journey back to

Gesoriacum was long and fraught with danger, and the weight of such responsibility wasn't to be taken lightly.

Marcus looked at Atticus for a moment, then turned to Cassius.

'This needs to be done, but Atticus shouldn't go alone. I need Raven and Sica with me to track down Togodumnus's camp, and we can't afford to lose Falco's skill with a blade. That leaves you, Cassius. Will you go with him and see if these men Raven speaks of are ready?'

Cassius nodded without hesitation.

'If that's what you need, I'll do it. We're all in this together, right?'

'Right,' said Marcus firmly. 'That settles it.'

Falco leaned back, eyeing Marcus.

.Getting word back across the sea and back here with a force of men undetected is quite an undertaking.'

'It is,' said Marcus, 'but I'm sure that Atticus and Cassius are more than up to the task.'

'We'll leave as soon as we can,' said Cassius.

'In the meantime,' Raven continued, 'the rest of us will stay here for a few days, rest up, and then make our way to the Trinovantes' lands. We need to find Togodumnus's camp and gather as much information as we can. Once we have the men, we'll strike both targets, the weapons cache and the assassination.'

A heavy silence settled over the group. The risks were high, but this was what they had trained for, high-stakes missions in dangerous territory and every man knew what was at stake.

Raven rose slowly to his feet.

'Atticus, Cassius, we'll get you horses from the Iceni for your journey to the coast. Once you're there, find a ship to

Gesoriacum and find Lepidus. Tell him what we need and when you return, meet us in the south.'

'How will we find you?' asked Cassius.

'There's a river that borders the lands of the Trinovantes and the Iceni. South of Venta Icenorum, there's an old stone bridge connecting the two territories. Every full moon, one of us will wait there for word of your return but if we are not there within a day, head for the mine. Atticus knows thew way. Travel only by night and stay off the main roads and paths. It's crucial you remain unseen, even with reinforcements.'

'Understood,' said Cassius.

Marcus gave a nod of approval.

'Then rest up. You'll need your strength in the coming days.'

A few days later they began dismantling the camp. Every scrap of evidence that they had been there was removed, shelters disassembled, furs packed away, and the fire pit buried under a layer of earth. They worked in silence, their movements practised and efficient. Every man knew what had to be done. Sica and Falco packed the remaining supplies, while Raven ensured the last traces of their presence were erased.

Atticus and Cassius loaded their newly purchased horses, preparing for the long journey east to the coast. The urgency was clear, Lepidus had to be informed, and reinforcements were needed if they were to succeed.

As the last pieces of the camp were dismantled, Marcus approached the two men.

'Stay sharp on the road,' he said quietly. 'Keep your heads down and stay out of sight until you're on that ship.'

Cassius gripped Marcus's arm in a firm handshake. 'We'll get this done.'

'I'm sure you will,' replied Marcus. 'You've both earned your place among us, and I trust you completely.'

With that, Atticus and Cassius mounted their horses, exchanging one last glance with their comrades before turning southeast and disappearing into the mist.

As the sun dipped below the horizon, Raven, Falco, Sica, and Marcus set out southward. They had considered buying horses but decided against it, knowing they would cause too much of a trail and would be too difficult to hide.

Each of them walked in silence, their minds heavy with the knowledge of what lay ahead. This was no ordinary mission. The stakes were higher than ever before, and all of them knew there was a very real chance they would not return.

Marcus looked up at the men walking before him. Sica was as still and focused as ever, his sharp eyes scanning the path ahead, always on guard. Falco walked with a grim determination, his hand never far from the hilt of his blade, ready for whatever might come. Raven remained quiet, his thoughts no doubt running through every possible scenario they might face when they reached the enemy's camp.

'We're not fools,' said Marcus suddenly, 'none of us are. We were trained for this. And if we fall, we fall in the service of Rome.'

'I refuse to die for Rome,' said Falco, 'so if I fall, know that it will be in the service of all the women who'll miss me.'

In the distance, the faint cry of wolves echoed through the hills, a haunting sound that seemed to mirror the uncertainty of the road ahead. But despite the danger, despite the overwhelming odds, the men felt the fire of purpose burning inside them. Tomorrow, they would head into the lands of the Trinovantes, toward Togodumnus, and whether it was a one-way mission or not, they would face whatever lay ahead with the resolve of men who had been forged in the crucible of war. After all, they were the Occultum, and there was no-one better.

Chapter Thirty

Gesoriacum

Several weeks had passed since Seneca had made his decision to break away from the others, and the long trek west had worn him down. He had pressed on relentlessly, riding through hostile lands, avoiding roads and villages, and crossing forests and rivers that seemed to stretch endlessly before him. Now, as he entered the bustling port of Gesoriacum, the weariness of the journey weighed heavily on his shoulders.

The port was alive with movement, filled with the noise of final preparations for the impending invasion. Men from all corners of the Roman Empire rushed through the streets, Legionaries in Lorica Segmentata, auxiliary units, slaves carrying supplies, and artisans putting the last touches on the weapons and siege equipment. The air was thick with the scent of the sea, mingling with the acrid smell of burning wood and the metallic tang of sharpened steel. Offshore, dozens of biremes and troopships floated on the waves, awaiting their lethal cargo, thousands of soldiers, ready to sail for Britannia.

Seneca guided his tired horse through the chaotic streets, his eyes scanning the crowds. The weight of Canis's betrayal still gnawed at him, and the knowledge that a traitor remained among the ranks was like a blade hanging over his head. He had to reach Senator Lepidus, to warn him, to set things in motion.

He approached a group of soldiers loitering near a makeshift blacksmith's stall and dismounted, rubbing the tension from his aching legs. The men eyed him curiously, noting his travel-worn appearance.

'Where can I find Senator Lepidus?' asked Seneca, his

voice hoarse from days of little sleep.

One of the legionaries pointed toward a large hill overlooking the sea. At its peak stood a stone building, its white painted walls gleaming in the sun.

'You could try up there,' he said, 'it seems all the rich and powerful head that way. Wine, women, food, you name it, I have seen it all go up by the cartful. But be warned, the security is tight. You'll need more than your name to get past the gates.'

Seneca nodded his thanks, then mounted his horse once more. The villa loomed ahead, a stark contrast to the chaos of the port below. Its walls, washed in white plaster, stood out against the green of the hills, and the columns that lined the entrance gave it an air of imperious grandeur, an obvious influence of the Roman traders that had used the port for years. He urged his horse forward, his eyes narrowing as he spotted legionaries patrolling the perimeter.

'State your name and business,' one demanded, his hand resting on the pommel of his gladius.

'Gaius Octavius Seneca,' he replied. 'I've come to speak with Senator Lepidus on urgent business concerning the invasion.'

The guards exchanged a glance. The mention of the senator clearly carried weight, but that did not mean Seneca would be allowed through without scrutiny.

'Wait here,' the guard said before turning and motioning to a subordinate. The younger guard hurried off up the path to carry word to the villa. Seneca dismounted, patting his horse's neck as he waited. He could feel the eyes of the guards on him, watching him carefully.

Minutes passed before the younger guard returned,

followed by an officer dressed in the formal attire of the Roman military elite. The officer eyed Seneca appraisingly.

'You may enter,' he said curtly. 'But you will be escorted.'

Seneca nodded in agreement. He had expected no less.

The officer signalled to a pair of guards, who flanked Seneca as they made their way up the winding path toward the villa. The grandeur of the building grew more imposing with each step, the gardens meticulously maintained, the scent of flowers mingling with the sea breeze. Statues of Roman gods and heroes lined the path, imposters recently delivered from Rome, their stone faces staring down as Seneca passed.

Upon reaching the building, the guards led him through a modest entrance and into a hall. The room had been recently decorated, with frescoes depicting scenes of Roman victory and conquest, and a large mosaic of Mars, god of war, dominated the centre of the floor. Servants moved quietly through the corridors, their heads bowed, while guards stood at various points, ever watchful.

'Wait here,' said one, 'the senator will see you shortly.'

Seneca sat in a chair, leaning forward, his elbows on his knees, as the exhaustion of the journey threatened to pull him into
sleep. But his mind was racing. The invasion was clearly on the cusp of beginning, and the sight of the ships offshore had made that undeniable. Soon, Rome would move in full force against Britannia, and the outcome of that invasion could hinge on whether they were able to root out the traitor within their ranks before it was too late.

The minutes stretched on, each one feeling like an eternity. He had no idea what reception he would receive from Lepidus, but he couldn't afford to waste time with formalities.

The senator had to know what was at stake.

Finally, the door opened, and Senator Lepidus entered, his richly embroidered toga, sweeping across the floor as he approached, and the guards who had been stationed outside the door snapped to attention.

'Seneca,' gasped Lepidus, 'what are you doing here?'

The two old friends grasped wrists in recognition, but Lepidus could see the strain and exhaustion in the younger man's eyes.

'What's the matter,' he added, 'what's happened?'

'I bring news that can't wait,' said Seneca, 'we have a problem, a serious one.'

'Go on.'

'There is a traitor,' said Seneca, 'within the ranks of the Occultum itself. One who has already crossed into Britannia, working against us from the inside.'

For the first time, a flicker of concern passed over Lepidus's face. He looked around before taking Seneca by the arm and leading him through to another room and closing the door behind them.

'Sit,' he said, pointing at a table, 'explain everything. Leave nothing out.'

'I found out weeks ago in Germania,' said Seneca, taking a seat, 'one of the newer members of the group was mortally wounded and gave a dying confession.'

'Why were you in Germania in the first place?' interrupted Lepidus. 'I ordered you and your men into Britannia.'

'I know,' said Seneca, 'but there was something I had to do. I will explain everything later but for now, just be aware that one of the men who recently joined us turned out to be a traitor, planted by someone in the senate. He admitted it with his dying breath.'

'Who sent him?'

Seneca sighed, shaking his head.

'He didn't say. All I know is that his orders came from high up, from someone with influence, someone with the power to manipulate us from within.'

Lepidus's face darkened, and his fist came down hard on the table.

'This is exactly why I opposed the quick formation of these new Occultum groups, there is far too much opportunity for spies to infiltrate our ranks.'

'I understand your frustration, Senator,' said Seneca, 'but this infiltration goes far deeper than just who passed or failed the selection process. It goes deep into the heart of the senate, the people you deal with on a daily basis.'

Lepidus turned, pacing across the room, his toga sweeping behind him, his fists clenched at his sides.

'I knew this would happen,' he muttered, almost to himself. 'Too many divisions, too many moving pieces. We should never have allowed these extra units to form so quickly.'

Seneca watched him carefully, reading the senator's frustration, but he knew he had to press on.

'This isn't the time to debate the merits of the Occultum's structure, Senator. Right now, we have a much bigger problem. The second traitor is already in Britannia, and we need to find him before it's too late.'

Lepidus stopped pacing and nodded towards the closed door.

'Some of the men who will lead those legions are just through those doors,' he said, 'finalising their strategies. Plautius himself is there and he is fully aware that we have men in Britannia paving the way. How am I supposed to tell him that anything we learn could be completely compromised? We are likely to have a pugio across our throats before the sun rises.'

'Then don't tell him.'

'How can I not?' asked Lepidus. 'He is relying on my report before committing his legions.'

'Just give me some time to fix it,' said Seneca. 'Send me to Britannia to rejoin the others and I'll make this right.'

Lepidus's nostrils flared as he measured Seneca's words.

'We don't have the luxury of time, Seneca. The invasion is
just days away.'

'I'm not asking you to hold back the invasion,' Seneca interrupted. 'I know my men, and I know how they operate. A few days is all I need. Try to get me that and I'll personally deliver the traitor's head to you.'

'I don't know if I can do that,' said Lepidus. 'They are almost ready to go.'

'You have to find a way,' said Seneca, 'for all we know, the traitor can be briefing Togodumnus as we speak, telling him our tactics, the strength of our legions, the favoured landing sites, everything. If you can just give me some time, I know I can find him and when I do, I'll make him tell me exactly what he knows and what he has told them.'

Lepidus weighed the options before him. For a long moment, the room was filled only with the faint crackle of the oil lamp and the distant sounds of legionaries outside the villa, making their final preparations for the invasion.

'Very well,' he said eventually, 'Go and find your traitor but make no mistake, Seneca, the success of this invasion depends on it. Fail, and it won't just be your life on the line.'

Seneca nodded grimly. He had expected nothing less.

'You leave at dawn,' he continued, 'I'll arrange for a ship to take you across.'

'I'll need a fresh horse,' said Seneca. Marcus will have left a message with Prasutagus as to their whereabouts.'

'There's no need to speak to Prasutagus,' said Lepidus, 'just head as fast as you can to the bridge to the south of Venta Icenorum.'

'What do you mean?' asked Seneca.

'Two of your men returned from Britannia just a few days ago and requested a troop of the support exploratores we formed back in Gallia. Apparently, there's a huge arms cache they intend to destroy, and they needed more men to do it.'

Seneca's blood ran cold.

'Did you send them?'

'I had no reason not to,' said Lepidus. 'Until a few minutes ago, I thought everything was going fine.'

'How many?'

'Twenty,' said Lepidus. 'A full unit.'

'When did they sail?' Seneca's heart was pounding now, his
mind racing through the implications.

'Yesterday,' Lepidus replied. 'But if we can get you across, you should be able to get to the bridge before them. They have arranged to meet Marcus there or if not, in a disused tin mine further south.'

'Do you know where that is?'

'I don't, so make sure you get to that bridge in time. One man can travel much quicker than twenty. Sort it out, Seneca, if you hadn't been off in Germania, none of this would have happened.'

Seneca opened his mouth to protest, but the words caught in his throat. There was no use arguing. Lepidus had already turned and swept out of the room, leaving him standing alone in the dim light.

Chapter Thirty-One

Britannia

Raven moved silently, leading the group through the tangled undergrowth that bordered the forest. His eyes flicked upward briefly, checking the stars. Marcus followed just behind, his steps as quiet and measured as ever, while Falco and Sica brought up the rear, each man carrying the heavy weight of his sarcina with grim determination.

The nights had grown colder, the dampness seeping into their bones as they pushed forward, always under the cover of darkness. Each step was a calculated risk. To stay hidden, they had to avoid the main roads and tracks, which forced them through rougher terrain, thorny undergrowth, steep hills, and narrow gorges where an ambush could come at any moment.

During the day, they sheltered in dense thickets or behind natural rock formations, waiting out the sunlight. When faced with open ground, they had no choice but to wait until nightfall, lying flat and still for hours, their breaths shallow, eyes constantly scanning for any sign of movement. Food was scarce, and their rations dwindled quicker than expected. They ate only when absolutely necessary, chewing on the dried meat they had prepared back in the lands of the Iceni. When the hunger gnawed too fiercely, Raven took the risk of slipping into a nearby village, blending in with the locals to purchase food. He alone could pass unnoticed, his darker features and fluency in the local dialect making him less conspicuous.

But it wasn't always enough. On the harsher nights, they stole from the farms, small amounts of grain or vegetables, careful to leave little trace of their theft.

On the tenth night, the forest began to thin, and the terrain shifted. The familiar cover of trees and brush gave way to more open land, rolling hills dotted with occasional clusters of trees but nothing substantial to hide their presence. The distant glow of fires from villages speckled the horizon, and Raven knew they were deep into Trinovantes territory now.

They had just crested a hill when they spotted movement on a track below and Raven crouched low, signalling the others to follow. All four men dropped to the ground, their eyes fixed on the narrow path that wound through the valley. A group of riders
approached, their horses moving at a steady pace, the faint clink weapons catching the moonlight.

Raven's pulse quickened. He counted six men, all mounted, and clearly well-equipped. The sight of them confirmed what they had suspected for days, they were now deep in the heart of enemy territory. These were not simple villagers or farmers; they were Togodumnus's men, scouting the land and watching for threats.

Marcus edged closer to Raven, his voice barely a whisper.

'We're close.'

Raven nodded, his eyes tracking the riders as they disappeared into the distance.

'If those men had looked up, they'd have seen us. We need to be more careful.'

They continued, sticking to the shadows, always mindful of the tracks and signs of recent passage. The going was tough, sparser forests meant less cover, and the ground was uneven. At times, they could hear distant voices or the faint sound of barking dogs from nearby settlements, and each time, they paused, nerves on edge, waiting until the sounds faded.

As the hours dragged on, fatigue began to take its toll. Their shoulders ached from the weight of their packs, and the chill in the air seemed to seep into their very bones. But none of them complained. They were trained for this, and they had all faced worse.

When dawn broke the next morning, they found shelter in a ravine. Exhausted and cold, they ate sparingly, bits of stolen bread and a few strips of dried meat, taking turns keeping watch as the others grabbed what sleep they could.

The ravine was a place of solitude, hidden from prying eyes by the roar of the waterfall that crashed down before them. Thick vegetation grew around the edges of the cleft, and the steady mist rising from the cascade kept the rocks slick and cold. It was the perfect place to disappear, at least for a time.

Raven returned from a nearby village just after dusk, slipping quietly into the camp where Marcus, Falco, and Sica waited. He set down a rough sack of supplies, bread, dried meats, and a skin of sour wine, before pulling off his hood.

'They talk,' he said, But only in pieces. No one wants to admit where Togodumnus's men are, but I've heard enough to

know we're close.'

'What have you learned?' asked Marcus.

'A few villagers mentioned increased patrols in the area, mostly around the old trade roads. They're sending supplies to a village south of here. From the way they talk, it could be the main camp.'

'Did they mention how many men Togodumnus has with him?' asked Falco.

Raven shook his head.

'They're careful with their words, but from what I've pieced together, he has hundreds of warriors, if not more.'

Marcus slid the whetstone across his blade one last time, the scrape of steel against stone filling the narrow space.

'We need to confirm this is his main camp before we make a move,' he said. 'We'll wait a few more days. Watch the patrols and once we're sure, we make our move.'

The days that followed were filled with meticulous preparation. Raven ventured into villages under the guise of a wandering trader, speaking little but listening to everything. Meanwhile, Falco and Sica took turns monitoring the roads, counting the warriors, merchants, and occasional travellers who passed beneath their watchful eyes. At night, the group shared what they had learned, drawing ever closer to their goal and slowly, the picture became clear. Togodumnus was gathering his strength in a vast camp nestled in the heart of the valley, far from the prying eyes of Roman spies.

Finally, after more than a week of careful scouting and rest, they were ready. Their strength had returned, their supplies replenished, and the details of their plan etched in their minds. With renewed purpose, they set out for the final leg of their journey, travelling under the cover of night as they had done so many times before.

By the time they reached the ridge overlooking the valley, dawn was not far off. The stars still flickered faintly overhead, but the horizon had begun to lighten, casting a dim glow over the landscape. They crouched low as they crested the hill, taking in the sight that stretched out below them.

In the valley, the sprawling camp of Togodumnus came into view. Hundreds of campfires dotted the landscape, their orange glow flickering against the silhouettes of tents, wagons, and shelters.

Smoke curled into the sky in lazy spirals, and even from this distance, they could hear the faint murmur of voices and the clink of armour.

The camp was vast, larger than any of them had anticipated. It spread across the entire valley floor, hemmed in by dense forests on one side and jagged hills on the other. Warriors moved between the fires, their numbers almost too great to count while sentries patrolled the perimeter, their eyes scanning the surrounding landscape.

'That's it,' said Marcus quietly. 'We've found it.'

Falco crouched beside him.

'There must be thousands of them.'

'At least,' Raven replied. 'And that's only what we can see. There could be more warriors hidden in the forests or in other valleys nearby.'

'It won't be easy to get close,' said Falco. 'They have sentries posted all along the ridges. If we try to sneak in, we'll be caught before we even reach the outskirts.'

'There is a way,' said Raven, 'but we have a different problem. It looks like they are preparing to move camp and if they do, we will never get this close again. We need to decide what is more important, get to Cadorix and kill him now while we can or wait until the others come and attack the supply camp. We can't do both, Marcus, we need to make a decision.'

The four men sat in silence, the weight of their mission pressing down on them. Below them, the camp of Togodumnus sprawled out, a sea of warriors preparing for war. They had come to a fork in the road and whatever way they chose, there would be no turning back.

Chapter Thirty-Two

Britannia

Two days later, Seneca disembarked from the creaking trading ship that had carried him across the channel. The small Iceni fishing village was bustling with morning activity, fishermen hauling in their catch, women bartering over fresh goods, and the occasional trader peddling their wares. Seneca moved amongst them, his movements calm, unhurried. His horse carried a loaded pack of various metallic objects, cups, plates and bowls, all ornately decorated, typical trading goods for anyone looking to do business with one of the many tribes of Britannia. If someone stopped him to check, the contents would reinforce the illusion that he was just one more trader under the protection of Prasutagus.

He led his horse towards the edge of the village, unthreatening and inconspicuous. It was what the Occultum was good at, invisibility.

Eventually he mounted his horse, riding it slowly southward, painfully aware that he was still in sight of many people. A wooded hill loomed before him and the moment he reached the trees, he threw the bag of trading goods into the bushes before urging the horse onward with every ounce of strength he dared. There was no time for subterfuge now, no time for cautious roads or secretive detours, and the landscape flew past in a blur, windswept fields, dense patches of forest, and the occasional solitary farmstead.

The rain began to fall in earnest as he rode southward, light at first, then heavier, drumming against his hood and the horse's mane. It turned the paths slick and treacherous, but Seneca paid no mind to the discomfort. His mind was fixed on one thing alone, reaching the bridge near Venta Icenorum, before it was too late.

To the south, the four men of the Occultum crouched low on the ridge, the camp of Togodumnus sprawling below them. They had been watching for hours, eyes tracking the movement of patrols and the comings and goings of warriors, but something had changed. They had seen it in the increased patrols, the hastily assembled supply wagons, and the sense of urgency rippling through the camp like a storm about to break.

Marcus signalled to the others, and they began their silent
retreat, melting back into the shadows of the hills as the last light of day faded.

Eventually they found cover, far enough from any roads or tracks so they could speak freely without fear of being overheard.

'The situation's worse than we thought,' said Marcus. 'Those warriors aren't just preparing for some skirmish, they're readying for a full march. If we wait any longer, Togodumnus be on the road with half of the Trinovantes behind him and Cadorix will be lost to us. I think we have to leave the cache alone and go for Cadorix instead.'

'We were supposed to do both,' said Falco. 'Cripple their supplies and take out the Cantiaci leadership. That was the plan.'

'We no longer have a choice, Falco,' said Marcus. 'If the Cantiaci and Trinovantes join forces, it won't matter if we destroy every weapon in that cache, our countrymen will face an army twice the size. Killing Cadorix is the only way to stop that from happening.'

'In that case,' said Falco, 'we need a new plan. With

Togodumnus readying to march, the entire camp will be crawling with warriors. We need a way in.'

Before anyone could speak further, Raven cut through the conversation.

'I already have a plan.'

Marcus exchanged a glance with Falco.

'What do you mean, you have a plan?'

Raven pushed himself up from the rock and turned to his comrades.

'I've been thinking about it since we arrived,' he said. While you were watching the camp, I wasn't just counting men, I was studying their routines, their habits. I know how we're going to do it.'

'How?' asked Falco.

'By just walking straight through the main gates into the heart of the camp.'

The words hung in the air, met with stunned silence.

'What are you talking about?' asked Marcus. 'We can't just stroll into the middle of Togodumnus's camp.'

'That's exactly what we're going to do,' said Raven. 'Or rather, what I'm going to do. They won't expect it because no one's foolish enough to try. But I grew up here, remember? I know their
customs well enough to blend in, and no guard can recognise every face in the camp. I'll also have a perfect reason to get past them.'

'And what reason is that?'

'I'll go in as what I am... a hunter.'

'So, you plan to just walk up to the gate and tell them you're a hunter?'

Raven gave a small nod.

'Exactly. I've done it before. The trick is to walk in as

if you belong. No sneaking, no hesitation. I'll need a carcass of something to take in, preferably a deer, and tell the sentries I'm here to sell. Large camps like that always need fresh meat, and they'll be too busy to question every trader or hunter who passes through. If I look like just another man trying to trade, they'll let me in.'

Sica raised an eyebrow, shifting on his haunches.

'And you think they'll fall for it?'

Raven shrugged.

'Hunters wander. It's not unusual. The Trinovantes may be preparing for war, but they're still men. They'll want food, they'll want supplies. They won't expect anyone to walk into their camp with ill intent, especially not with their focus on the larger battle ahead.'

Falco leaned in slightly, scepticism still written across his face.

'Let's say they let you in. How do you find Cadorix? It's a big camp, and you'll have to act fast. You can't just ask around.'

'Someone like Cadorix won't be staying in a common tent,' he said. 'He'll be near the centre, likely with Togodumnus's closest men. The chieftains will have their own guards, their own fires. All I need to do is get close enough to learn their movements. I'll find him, and when night falls, I'll make my move.'

'And then what?' asked Sica. 'Once Cadorix is dead, they'll hunt you down. How do you escape?'

Raven's face hardened.

'I'll kill him quickly and leave before anyone realises. By the time they find him, I'll already be gone.'

Falco rubbed the back of his neck, still unconvinced.

'That's assuming everything goes perfectly,' he said.

'What if something goes wrong?'

'If something goes wrong, I'll adapt,' replied Raven. 'I've done it before, but we don't have time to sit here and argue about
it. Togodumnus's forces are about to move. If we delay much longer, Cadorix will march with him, and once the Cantiaci join this war, Rome's foothold in Britannia could collapse.'

A heavy silence followed, the reality of the situation sinking in. They knew Raven's plan was dangerous, almost suicidal, but it was also their only real option. They couldn't afford to waste time on the arms cache or try something more elaborate, the threat of the Cantiaci uniting with the Trinovantes overshadowed everything else. Finally, knowing they were running out of time, Marcus made a decision.

'Raven,' he began, 'I have no doubt you are more than capable of doing this, but you're not going in alone. Sica's going with you.'

Raven's face immediately darkened.

'No,' he said flatly, shaking his head. 'The fewer of us inside that camp, the smaller the risk. Two of us will draw more attention, not less.'

'Think about it, Raven,' replied Marcus, 'that camp is massive surrounded by a palisade. Hundreds of warriors, and guards everywhere. You won't have the luxury of being invisible in a place like that, so you'll need someone watching your back, someone who knows when to move, when to kill, and when to disappear.'

Raven's frustration flared, his voice rising slightly.

'I can handle it, Marcus. Getting through the gates as a hunter is simple enough. One man, no fuss. If I take Sica, it doubles the chance of something going wrong.'

'Two hunters are less suspicious than one,' Falco

interrupted.

'Perhaps so,' said Raven, 'but he's Syrian. Do you think they won't notice?'

Marcus nodded, his tone unyielding.

'They'll probably notice he looks different, but he is not going to stand out as Roman the way Falco or I would. And if something goes wrong, you'll need him to fight your way out. I can't let you do this alone, Raven. Either he goes with you, or nobody goes.'

Raven cast a glance toward Sica. The Syrian was a cold, calm killer, his skills honed to perfection in the brutal alleys of the East and the silent, bloody work of the Occultum. Assassination wasn't just something he was good at; it was what he lived for, and
if there was anyone who could handle the risks of this mission, it was him.

'So be it,' he said. 'But we do this my way. No mistakes, no unnecessary risks. We get in, find Cadorix, kill him, and get out. That's it.'

Sica nodded once, a glint of deadly resolve in his eyes.

'No mistakes,' he said, when do we go?'

'As soon as we can,' said Raven, 'but first, I have to kill a deer.'

Chapter Thirty-Three

Britannia

The camp bustled with energy, thick with the tension of warriors preparing for battle. Celtic men, their bodies painted in swirls of blue and green, moved with the confidence of those born for war. Everywhere, the clatter of weapons filled the air, spears being sharpened, swords tested with practiced swings, and the heavy thud of axes striking wood. The rhythmic pounding of hammers against anvils rang out as blacksmiths worked relentlessly, shaping iron into deadly weapons and the scent of sweat, leather, and horses mingled with the metallic tang of the forge.

Horses stamped their hooves in agitation, sensing the charged atmosphere. Some warriors took to training in small groups, clashing their wooden shields together in mock combat. Others sat by the fires, murmuring prayers to the old gods, calling for strength and victory in the days to come. Despite the tension, there was an air of savage pride, an eagerness among the men. They were ready. Togodumnus's army had gathered here for a single purpose, war, and every man in the camp knew that soon, the blood of their enemies would stain their swords.

At the heart of this deadly symphony walked Togodumnus, tall and broad-shouldered, his eyes gleaming with the fierce arrogance of a leader who knew his power. His presence commanded attention. Warriors straightened as he passed, their eyes following him with a mixture of reverence and pride. Togodumnus had united them, and his strength had forged this army into a weapon poised to defend their homeland against the unrelenting advance of Rome's legions.

Beside him walked one of his clan chieftains, an older man, his long hair tied back in a warrior's braid. The two moved purposefully through the camp, exchanging few words, their destination, the great roundhouse that he used as his command centre.

Cadorix was already there, standing near the entrance, his face drawn with a mix of anticipation and grim determination. Next to him stood another warrior from the Cantiaci, broader, rougher, and both men looked up as Togodumnus and the chieftain approached.

Without breaking stride, Togodumnus lifted a hand, beckoning them to follow as he stepped into the roundhouse. There would be no formal greetings, no hesitation. They had come to talk of war, and Togodumnus had little patience for anything else.

Inside, the flickering fire cast long shadows across the wooden walls, and the air was thick with the smell of burning oak and peat.

Togodumnus lowered himself onto a thick fur beside the fire, his eyes sharp, ever watchful. Cadorix and his companion sat across from him, their expressions guarded, revealing nothing.

A slave moved quietly around the room, carrying a wooden platter piled high with roasted meat. The wine, thick and sour, was passed from hand to hand in a plain flask, shared amongst them without ceremony. There was no need for formalities here, this was a gathering of men bound by the prospect of war.

The meat, still hot from the fire, was torn apart by rough hands, grease dripping down their fingers as they ate in silence. Each man chewed slowly, his gaze flicking now and then toward the others, weighing, measuring, gauging the strength and resolve of the man sitting opposite. The silence between them spoke more than words. It was the quiet of warriors assessing one another, each testing the limits of their trust.

Eventually, Togodumnus gave a sharp wave, dismissing the slaves. The wooden platters were whisked away, and the bones of the roasted meat tossed into the fire, sending a brief burst of embers into the air.

Cadorix shifted slightly and pulled out an ornate dagger, its hilt decorated with intricate carvings and bronze inlays. The blade caught the firelight as he offered it to Togodumnus, a gesture of allegiance and respect.

Togodumnus took the dagger with a grunt, turning it briefly in his hands. His eyes flicked over the weapon, but his interest was minimal. With a cursory glance, he set it aside, placing it on the ground beside him, the gift acknowledged but not dwelled upon. His focus was on the matter at hand.

'So, Cadorix,' he said eventually. 'Are you with us, or against us?'

In the stillness of the night, deep within an ancient stone circle a league or so away from Trinovantes camp, burning torches
flickered, casting long shadows over the towering stones that loomed around the clearing, each rock carved with the symbols of the old gods. At the centre of the circle, a group of druids moved with deliberate precision. Their chants rose and fell in rhythmic cadence, invoking the Celtic gods of war, Camulos, Taranis, and Morrigan. They beseeched the deities to favour Togodumnus's warriors in the coming conflict, to rain terror upon their enemies and bless them with unyielding strength.

The druids poured offerings of blood and wine upon the sacred stones, their ritual knives gleaming in the firelight. Animal carcasses lay on altars around them, the sacrifices made to curry favour with the gods, their lifeless forms casting grotesque shapes in the torchlight. The air itself seemed to hum with an otherworldly energy, the barrier between the mortal world and the realm of the gods thinner here, in this ancient place of power.

The druids conducting the ceremony were not ordinary men, they had come from the hallowed isle of Mona, the seat of the druidic order. Their presence signified more than mere spiritual support; it was a declaration of war against the Roman invaders, a signal that the old gods had not abandoned their people. Yet, despite the weight of their power and their influence over the tribes, there was another presence in the stone circle that overshadowed them all.

Mordred stood at the edge of the gathering, shrouded in the darkness beyond the torches, his cold eyes watching the ceremony unfold. Unlike the druids who chanted and swayed in their fervour, Mordred took no part in the rites. He needed no invocation, no pleas to the gods. Power radiated from him in a different way, a cold, calculating force that came not from faith, but from knowledge and intelligence. His gaze swept over the circle, impassive, unblinking, as though he already knew the outcome of what was to come.

He was a man who commanded fear and respect in equal measure. His influence stretched far beyond the stone circle, beyond the camp of Togodumnus, and even beyond the tribes that had gathered under the banner of war. It was whispered among the people of Britannia that Mordred held the true power, not the kings or the chieftains, not even the druids who performed their sacred rituals. It was Mordred who decided the course of events, and it was his hand that shaped the future of their world.

His warriors, chosen from the fiercest of the tribes, stood at a distance, watching the ceremony with an aloof detachment. They, like their leader, took no part in the rites. Clad in dark furs and bronze, their faces painted with the marks of death and battle, these men were not just warriors, they were something more, something other. Mystics and killers, steeped in the old ways, they moved with an eerie grace and stillness, their eyes betraying the deep connection they held with the forces that governed both life and death. They were untouchable, feared even by their own people, and they answered only to Mordred.

The ceremony ended, the chants fading into the night, but the tension remained. The druids slowly withdrew, their faces shadowed with the weight of their invocation, but even they did not dare approach Mordred.

As Mordred turned and walked away from the stone circle, his mind already working through the strategies of the coming war, it was clear that while the gods had been invoked, it was he who would wield their power. The druids had called for victory, but it would be Mordred who would decide when, and how, it was achieved.

Back in the camp, the fire crackled softly in the centre of the roundhouse as Cadorix leaned forward, his face illuminated by the flickering flames.

'You know I've pledged the Cantiaci to this fight,' Cadorix said, his eyes locking onto Togodumnus across the fire. 'The Romans have taken enough from us, and the time for waiting is over. We will crush them beneath our feet, as the old gods will it. The Cantiaci are ready, and I am ready to lead them.'

Togodumnus watched him carefully, saying nothing. His dark eyes bore into Cadorix, weighing him as a chieftain, as a warrior, and as an ally.

'But are you?' he finally replied. 'You say the Cantiaci are ready, but I see a problem, a problem that has a name…Cunda.'

Cadorix tensed at the mention of the old king's name, but he remained silent, waiting for Togodumnus to continue.

'As long as Cunda still breathes,' Togodumnus continued, 'the Cantiaci will not follow you to war. You may have ambition, Cadorix, but Cunda is their king and while he clings to life, they will not turn their backs on him to follow you.'

'Cunda is old,' replied Cadorix. 'His time is nearly over, and the gods will claim him soon enough. When he passes, the Cantiaci
will have no choice but to follow me. Then we will join forces with you and bring Rome to its knees.'

Togodumnus's lip curled in a sneer.

'And how long are we supposed to wait for that to happen, Cadorix? The Romans assemble their fleet as we speak. . We cannot wait for the gods to take their time and if you are not leading your warriors into battle when we march, then the Cantiaci will be of no use to me.'

Cadorix shifted uncomfortably, his eyes flicking to the ornate dagger he had gifted Togodumnus earlier, now lying forgotten on the floor.

'I have sworn loyalty to you, Togodumnus. The Cantiaci will fight…'

'They will fight when you are in command,' Togodumnus interrupted, his voice cutting through Cadorix's words like a blade. 'But until Cunda is dead, they are nothing. You are nothing. The Romans won't wait for your old king to die peacefully in his sleep. We can't either.'

A tense silence filled the roundhouse, broken only by the crackling fire. Cadorix clenched his fists, his mind racing. He knew where this was leading, and he didn't like it.

Togodumnus leaned forward, his voice lowering into a menacing growl.

'You know what must be done.'

Cadorix's face paled slightly. He had prepared for this moment, knowing that the time would come when Cunda's death would need to be hastened. But to murder the old king, to take his life by force, would risk everything. If the Cantiaci discovered the truth, they would never follow him.

'Cunda is a relic of a past age,' Togodumnus continued, his eyes boring into Cadorix. 'A king with no place in the war that's coming. You must kill him, Cadorix. Only then will the Cantiaci be yours to command, and only then will they be of use to me. Otherwise, they are my enemies. And if they are my enemies, you will be too.'

Cadorix's eyes widened in alarm.

'If I kill him and the tribes find out, they will turn against me. They still hold him in high regard. If they learn he's been murdered...'

'Then make sure they don't find out,' said Togodumnus,
cutting him off again. 'If you want to lead, then lead. Or I will consider you no different from him, a barrier in my way.'

Cadorix's mouth opened, but no words came out. His mind reeled with the weight of the ultimatum. It wasn't just Cunda's life at stake; it was his own survival. If he didn't lead the Cantiaci into battle, Togodumnus would see him as expendable.

Togodumnus rose from his seat abruptly, dismissing the matter with a wave of his hand.

'You have your orders, Cadorix. Either Cunda dies, or you both die. Choose wisely.'

Chapter Thirty-Four

Britannia

Seneca stood at the edge of the forest looking down at the bridge near Venta Icenorum with a growing sense of frustration. He had arrived hours earlier but there was still no sign of the Occultum or any of the newly arrived exploratores.

Knowing time was of the essence, he decided to take a risk and rode down to the edge of the river, dismounting with a sense of unease. He crouched low, brushing his hand over a patch of soft earth. Fresh hoofprints, many of them, not too deep, still sharp around the edges. They hadn't been here long, and judging by their direction, they were southward, heading back into the forest. The exploratores had passed this way, likely moving quickly towards the mine. He had missed them.

Mounting his horse again, he urged it forward, his eyes scanning the ground, now fully focused on the tracks. The signs were subtle, branches broken at an odd angle, disturbed patches of grass, and the occasional hoofprint in the mud. A slight rise in the ground revealed another clue: a few scattered branches, trampled underfoot and he felt a surge of energy, a renewed sense of purpose.

Hours passed, and the signs of passage became clearer: more broken branches, deeper hoofprints, even the occasional scrap of cloth snagged on a thorny bush. Seneca was certain he was close, and as his eyes scanned the distance ahead, looking for any sign of movement, he spotted the faint flicker of a campfire visible in the growing dusk. His breath caught, and he slowed his horse as he neared. He knew this had to be them.

As he approached the clearing, Atticus and Cassius

stepped into the open, their faces a picture of shock as they recognized their leader.

'Seneca.' Atticus called, a look of disbelief crossing his features. 'How are you here? How did you find us?'

Seneca dismounted quickly, his boots hitting the ground with a dull thud as he moved towards them. His eyes scanned the camp, and the twenty or so men gathered around their fires, all watching closely at the unexpected new arrival.

'What's the situation?' he asked, his voice taut with urgency. 'I was told you were waiting at the bridge.'

'The bridge was becoming too dangerous,' said Atticus. 'Even though we hid in the forest, there are just too many of us, especially with the horses, so we decided to move to the second rendezvous, an old tin mine in the south.'

'How far is the mine?'

'Half a day's ride, no more than that.'

'Good,' replied Seneca, in that case, he nodded to the watching exploratores, 'get them mounted. We have no time to waste.'

A few days later, the group were many leagues southward and Atticus led Seneca from the trees out into the open at the edge of the abandoned quarry. Behind them, Cassius, and the rest of the exploratores dismounted, spreading out in perfect formation, their eyes sweeping the ground ahead, ready for any threat.

Atticus moved toward the mine entrance, inspecting the ground for any recent disturbances, but the result was clear.

'It's just as we left it,' he said. 'No one's been here since we last used this place.'

Seneca looked around in frustration, feeling the eyes of

the exploratores on him, waiting for his command. They were trained for these moments where a single decision could mean the difference between life and death. They were deep in enemy territory, every moment increasing the risk of discovery.

'They could be at the arms cache,' said Atticus.

'It's possible,' said Seneca. 'Can you take us there?'

'Yes,' said Atticus. 'It's not far from here.'

Minutes later, the men rode out again, moving quickly through the forest, each man knowing that every moment spent here was another risk. Discovery meant almost certain death, But they were the exploratores, trained for operations exactly like this, where speed, stealth, and the ability to adapt at a moment's notice determined survival.

Several leagues away, Raven and Sica approached the edge of the camp, their footsteps blending with the distant murmur of the warriors gathered inside. Sica adjusted the weight of the sack slung over his shoulder. It dripped faintly, a dark stain spreading slowly along the leather strap. It was supposed to be venison, but with no time to track and hunt properly, they had killed and skinned a sheep they had stolen from a nearby farm.

They moved calmly, blending into the flow of traders and visitors coming and going. The key was to act like they belonged, like this was just another errand, another task among many before the battle. But as they passed a line of wagons, a sharp voice cut through the air.

'Wait there, strangers.'

Raven's heart skipped a beat though his expression remained calm. He turned slowly, seeing a group of warriors standing near a makeshift forge.

A guard strode forward, his eyes lingering on the bloodstained sack over Sica's shoulder before flicking back to Raven. His hand rested on the hilt of his sword, the unspoken threat hanging in the air.

'What's in the sack?' he demanded.

Raven gave a calm smile, forcing himself to remain relaxed.

'We're hunters with meat to sell to the camp cooks.'

The guard reached for the sack, ripping it open with rough hands. His nose wrinkled, and he pulled out a bloody leg of meat, inspecting it closely before looking back at Raven with a scowl.

'This isn't venison. It's mutton and Togodumnus has laid claim to every sheep farm in these lands. That means this must've been stolen.'

For a moment, Raven hesitated, feeling Sica's tension beside him. The situation was precarious, but there was still a way out. The camp was in the midst of preparing for war, supplies were stretched thin, and no one would turn away meat, no matter where it came from.

'You may be right,' he said, 'we found it wandering in the forest.' He gestured to the leg of mutton in the guard's hands. 'Tell you what, why don't you take that for yourselves? The camp cooks won't care where the rest came from and with the way things are now, everyone will be grateful for whatever we bring.'

The guard's expression softened, his scowl easing into something more calculating. He glanced at his comrades, then at the meat again, weighing the offer. Finally, he grunted, handing the sack back to Sica, but keeping the leg for himself.

'Aye, you're right,' he said, tossing the leg of mutton to one of the other warriors nearby. 'Meat's meat, and no one's gonna care where it came from.' His tone had shifted, the immediate threat fading, though his eyes still lingered on Sica.

'And him?' he asked, jerking his chin toward Sica. 'What's his story? He looks like half a savage.'

Raven gave a nonchalant shrug, his mind working quickly.

'I bought him from a slaver. Best hunter I've ever seen. Quiet, though, doesn't speak much. I've never heard him say a word.'

The guard grunted, his suspicion shifting into mild curiosity.

'Where's he from?'

Another shrug from Raven.

'Never asked. He's useful enough.'

The guard eyed Sica for another moment, as if debating whether to push the issue, but ultimately seemed to lose interest. He spat on the ground, directly at Sica's feet, the glob landing close enough to send a clear message.

'Keep him in line, then.'

Sica flinched, the movement subtle but enough to make it look as though the spit had unnerved him. He kept his gaze downcast, his shoulders slightly hunched, as if in submission, playing the part Raven had set up for him. But there was a flicker in his eyes, a restrained fury, a tightly coiled violence that only Raven would recognize.

The guard, satisfied with his intimidation, smirked.

'Go on, then. Get moving before I change my mind.' He turned away, waving them off with a dismissive gesture.

Raven nodded and began walking again, motioning for Sica to follow. As they passed, the warriors paid them little mind, more focused on the task of preparing for the coming battle than two hunters with a sack of mutton.

Sica walked beside Raven, his body still tense, but he kept his silence. Raven knew he had to be seething beneath that calm exterior, but there was no time for retaliation. There was killing to be done.

The camp grew louder as the day wore on and Raven and Sica had spent hours moving quietly among the traders, slaves, and cooks, their eyes and ears open as they gathered information. Every step they took was a calculated risk. Every question they asked had to seem casual, unnoticed by the guards constantly patrolling the camp.

The tension between them was palpable but finally, as dusk began to fall, they found their answer. A slave, weary and dull eyed from long hours of service, had spoken quietly to them, explaining how he had been tasked several times with bringing wine to Cadorix's hut.

Raven and Sica melted into the darkness as night fell. Hours passed and as midnight came and went, the camp became a quieter, more solitary place. It was the moment they had been waiting for.

Slowly, they slipped between the tents and huts, their steps silent, their breathing controlled. Raven led the way, his instincts guiding him through the darkened camp. Sica followed close behind, his body tense, every muscle primed for violence. They approached Cadorix's hut carefully, observing two guards standing outside the entrance.

After a few moments, Sica crept past Raven keeping tight to the shadows, and before the guard even knew he was there, cut his throat from behind, lowering him gently to the floor with his hand clamped firmly over his mouth. Raven followed suit with the guard standing a few paces further away, moving like a ghost to end an unsuspecting victim's life. Within seconds, both men lay dead on the floor. Neither had seen it coming and not a sound had been made. It had been a perfect kill.

Quickly, the two men dragged the bodies into the darker shadows before gently trying the door of the hut.

The door creaked softly as Raven pushed it open, the smell of stale wine and sweat hitting them as they entered. Inside, the room was dimly lit by the dying embers of a small fire, casting faint shadows over the sleeping figure of Cadorix, his chest rising and falling steadily. He was alone, unaware of the two assassins who had crept into his quarters.

Sica glided silently across the floor, seeking his second victim of the night, his hand already reaching for the man's mouth. Some primeval instinct dragged Cadorix from the depths of sleep and his eyes widened in shock, but before he could make a sound, Sica clamped his hand over the chieftain's mouth, pinning him down with surprising force and he drew the knife across Cadorix's throat
with surgical precision. For a few moments, he clung on to life, using the last of his strength to struggle, but it was too late. The deed was done, and his body soon slumped lifelessly on the bed as Sica wiped
his blade on the blanket.

Peeking through a small gap in the wooden slats of the door, Raven's stomach tightened. Not far away, another man emerged from the larger hut, tall strong imposing. The other guards immediately straightened up, reacting to his presence and judging by his appearance and garb, Raven realised it could be no other than Togodumnus himself… just standing there…within striking distance.

Sica's eyes followed Raven's, and his hand tightened

around his dagger. His body tensed, and Raven could see the hunger in his eyes, the desire to strike a crippling blow to the Celts before the Roman army had even set a single foot on Britania's soil.

'We can end it all now,' he whispered. 'All we have to do is wait until he goes back inside and do what we did here. Kill him, and the Trinovantes fall apart.'

Raven's heart raced, but he shook his head, pulling Sica back slightly.

'No,' he whispered. 'We're not here to kill Togodumnus, the plan was to take out Cadorix, divide the Cantiaci, and weaken them. If we kill him now, all the tribes of Britannia will unite, and the task will be far harder for our legions.'

Sica stared for a moment and as much as it went against his instincts, he put his blade away, ready to make their next move.

The moment passed, and outside, Togodumnus moved on, unaware of the deadly decision that had just been made. Raven and Sica watched him go but within moments, another danger appeared, another warrior walking straight towards them.

With little time to react, both men took up position against the wall and as he ducked inside, Raven lunged forward, driving his dagger into the man's throat, but it was badly timed, and the guard managed a strangled cry as he fell. It wasn't much, but it was enough and at the next hut, another warrior turned his ahead, aware that something was wrong.

'Move.' Raven hissed, and without another word, they slipped out and melted into the shadows. The camp was quiet, but within moments, the silence shattered as the guard's voice roared into the night, calling out the alarm.

Raven and Sica moved swiftly through the camp, but as they rounded a corner, two warriors stepped into their path, weapons drawn. There was no time to think, no time for subtlety.

Sica moved first, his blade flashing in the dark, silencing one of the men with a swift swipe of his blade across the man's throat and Raven followed suit, taking down the second guard with a thrust of his own blade directly through his opponent's heart. It had been sudden, efficient and lethal. More warriors passed close by, and Raven realised it would be difficult to continue with so many men running through the camp.

'We need a diversion,' he said.

Sica's looked around and eyes locked on a paddock. Walking over he quietly opened the gate, then, snatching a burning torch from a post, hurled it up onto one of the thatched rooves. Moments later, the breeze caught the flames and both men watched as the fire spread quickly with sparks igniting the rooves on nearby huts.

'Go.' Raven whispered, and they ducked back into the darkness, using the spreading confusion as cover. The fire spread behind them, lighting the sky with a fierce orange glow, and they knew it wouldn't be long before someone realized the blaze wasn't an accident. But by then, they would be long gone.

They reached the edge of the camp, the perimeter guards distracted by the spreading inferno and with the camp's attention focused on containing the fire, Raven and Sica found their way out much easier than they had anticipated. In moments, they disappeared into the forest, the sounds of chaos fading behind them as they fled into the night.

They ran as fast as they could through the darkness, knowing they had narrowly escaped death, and the camp, now a burning, screaming mess, was left far behind. Once they were clear, they paused to catch their breath, each turning and watching in awe as the fires raged higher into the night, impressed by their own work. Not only had they dispatched Cadorix but in the process had caused mayhem and confusion in the Trinovantes camp. It had been a good night's work, but they still had to get back to Marcus and Falco so quickly turned away to head back down the track to the rendezvous point.

A few leagues away, Seneca stood atop the hill, surveying the valley below. The arms cache sprawled out in the distance, a cluster of tents, wagons, and makeshift storage, surrounded by a
palisade. Men walked back and forth, horses were tied near the edge,
and several fires burned steadily within the camp. It looked peaceful, too peaceful with no signs of distress, no alarms raised, no hint of danger.

His frustration grew with every passing minute. They had hoped to find the Occultum here, or at least some indication that they had made their presence felt but there was nothing and the apparent lax attitude of the guards below suggested that they had no reason to suspect they were in any danger. Seneca inhaled deeply, eyes narrowing on the distant camp. With no sign of the Occultum, he had little choice but to wait.

'We'll set up camp in the forest,' he said, 'and take turns watching the cache. If our comrades are planning something, we'll be ready.'

The group of exploratores moved back into the cover of the forest, their horses tied carefully under the canopy of trees. They were experts at disappearing into the landscape, knowing how to remain unseen, even in close proximity to the enemy.

As the night dragged on, Seneca tried to rest, but his mind raced, his thoughts constantly returning to the fact that someone out there, amongst the men he trusted with his life, the traitor was also making deadly plans, plan that would no doubt result in many Romans dying at the hands of the celts. He had to find him, and he had to find him soon, before it was too late. Exhausted from the long day of waiting, he finally fell into a fitful sleep but after what seemed like only a few heartbeats, one of his men shook him awake.

'Seneca. Wake up.'

Seneca's eyes snapped open, his body already tensing for action.

'What is it?' he asked, pushing himself up quickly.

'There's something happening,' the man replied. 'You need to see this.'

Seneca scrambled to his feet, grabbing his sword instinctively, and followed the man to the edge of the wood. As they reached the treeline, Cassius and Atticus were already there, crouched low, their eyes fixed on the horizon.

Seneca's breath caught in his throat as he saw it, flames, high and bright, licking up into the night sky in the distance. Smoke billowed up in thick clouds, black against the star-streaked sky.

For a moment, there was only stunned silence. Then Seneca's gut twisted with a realization. It could only mean one thing.

'That's it,' he muttered, his eyes locked on the distant inferno. 'It has to be them. Get to the horses, we're moving out.'

The exploratores moved swiftly, their training kicking

in as they grabbed their weapons and mounted their horses without hesitation. Seneca led the way. his mind racing as they headed through the forest.

As they broke free from the trees and onto the open road, the smell of smoke filled the air, thick and acrid. Seneca's heart pounded in his chest. There was no doubt in his mind that his own men were responsible for whatever was happening, but whether they were still alive by the time they got there, that was another matter.

Nearer the Trinovantes camp, Falco and Marcus crouched low in the thick undergrowth alongside the agreed escape route, eyes constantly scanning the path. Raven and Sica were supposed to have met them by now, but the minutes dragged on into an anxious silence.

'Where are they?' muttered Falco under his breath. He gripped the hilt of his sword tightly, his eyes darting to Marcus.

Marcus didn't answer. He was watching the treeline. Something didn't feel right. They should have heard something by now, some signal, some movement. But the forest was unnervingly still. Moments later, the faint sound of hooves reached them, the steady rhythm growing louder as it approached. Through the thick shadows, they spotted a group of riders moving slowly through the trees. Hooded figures, cloaked in darkness, their horses barely making a sound as they moved in eerie silence.

Falco's pulse quickened. These weren't ordinary scouts or guards and there was something unsettling about their presence, the deliberate pace, the way they seemed to glide through the forest without a word. The riders were heading in the direction of the camp, straight toward the route that Falco and Marcus expected their comrades to come from.

Marcus turned to Falco, his voice barely a whisper. 'We follow.'

Without waiting for a response, Marcus slipped out of the undergrowth, his movements soundless. Falco was right behind him, both of them keeping their distance from the hooded riders as they moved deeper into the forest.

The riders slowed to a stop and dismounted with fluid movements, spreading out silently into the trees. For a moment, Marcus and Falco exchanged a confused glance. The riders were waiting for something, watching.

A few agonizing moments passed, the forest filled with the quiet rustling of the hooded figures positioning themselves in the trees. Then, in the distance, they heard the faint sound of running footsteps and Falco's eyes widened as he saw Raven and Sica, slipping through the dark woods, unaware of the danger waiting for them but before either of them could react, the trap was sprung.

The hooded figures moved swiftly, emerging from the shadows. Raven and Sica barely had time to register the ambush before they were surrounded. Spears pressed against their backs, the cold steel glinting in the faint moonlight. It was over in seconds and the two men disarmed, bound, and gagged without a single word spoken by their captors.

Falco's knuckles whitened around his sword hilt, his body tense with the urge to act. He turned to Marcus, his face hard with frustration, ready to charge in and fight, but Marcus held up a hand, his expression grim.

'There're too many,' whispered Marcus.

Falco was frustrated but he knew Marcus was right. The hooded figures outnumbered them easily, and they moved with the silent precision of trained killers. Any attempt to save Raven and Sica now would be a death sentence, for all of them.

'We follow them,' Marcus whispered, 'and wait for an opportunity.'

With a silent nod, Falco fell in line behind Marcus, watching helplessly as Raven and Sica were led deeper into the dark heart of the forest.

The forest was a blur of passing shadows as Seneca and his men rode hard, the distant glow of the burning camp growing brighter with every moment. The air was thick with the acrid scent of smoke, and even at this distance, they could hear the faint shouts of many men desperately fighting the flames consuming the camp.

As they neared a narrow stretch of the path, Seneca raised his hand, signalling for his men to slow. The horses' hooves thudded softly against the dirt as they eased into a cautious trot. Ahead, the road twisted into darkness, but something caught his attention, a faint sound. Hoofbeats, growing louder, coming from up ahead.

'Off the path,' Seneca ordered, and his men responded immediately, pulling their horses into the thick cover of the trees.

Seneca crouched low in the undergrowth, watching the path as the hoofbeats drew nearer. His breath stilled, and his grip tightened on the hilt of his sword. Moments later, a group of riders emerged from the dark, moving at a steady pace down the path away from the burning camp.

Seneca's eyes followed them as they disappeared into the night, and for a moment, the forest was silent again, the only sound the distant roar of the flames. And the shouts of panicking men. He was just about to signal his own men to mount up when another noise reached his ears, this time, the unmistakable sound of footsteps. Two men, running fast, chasing after the riders. One of the men stumbled, cursing loudly under his breath and Seneca gasped in recognition, the voice was familiar.

'Falco?'

Without thinking, he broke cover, rushing out from the trees just as the two figures reached his position. Marcus and Falco were panting heavily, their faces tense with urgency. They froze at the sight of Seneca, eyes widening with equal shock.

'Seneca.' Marcus gasped, doubling over to catch his breath. 'By the gods, what are you doing here?'

'What happened?' Seneca asked, as his men emerged cautiously from the trees behind him, equally stunned by the sudden reunion.

Marcus straightened, wiping the sweat from his brow.

'Raven and Sica...' he said, 'they've been captured. A group of hooded men dragged them off. We were tracking them, trying to figure out where they were being taken.'

'That must have been the group we just saw,' said Seneca. He turned to his men, his decision already made. 'Mount up. We're going after them.'

In moments, they were back in the saddle, and Marcus and Falco climbed up behind two of the riders. Without another word, Seneca spurred his horse forward, the shadows of his men following closely behind.

Up ahead, the journey through the forest was relentless as Raven and Sica were dragged along the narrow, winding paths, their wrists bound, their mouths gagged. The men escorting them
moved without a word, their faces shadowed beneath the

hoods of their cloaks. The only sound was the faint rustling of the leaves underfoot and the distant cries of the night creatures.

After what felt like hours, the trees parted, revealing the ancient stone circle. Torches flickered along its perimeter, casting a surreal, golden light over the clearing. A group of men clad in white robes stepped forward and Raven recognised them immediately. They were druids, the holy men who controlled the spiritual power over every tribe in Britannia. One of the druids spoke briefly with the hooded figure who had led them here.

The rest of the druids moved toward the center of the circle and began to prepare the area, lighting more torches until the entire clearing was bathed in a strange, otherworldly glow. Shadows danced across the ancient stones, and the air seemed to hum with anticipation.

Raven and Sica were tied to two trees at the edge of the circle, their bodies tight against the rough bark. They could do nothing but watch as the druids worked, their morbid fascination growing with each moment. One of the druids carried a wooden bucket filled with spring water, and as he approached the flat stone at the center of the circle, began to mutter incantations in a low, rhythmic voice. He carefully poured the water over the stone, washing it clean, his hands moving reverently over its surface.

The water dripped from the edges of the stone, pooling in the dirt below, but the druid continued his quiet chanting, as if invoking the gods to witness what was about to unfold.

At the edge of the circle, the druid warriors stood like silent sentinels, their faces obscured by the hoods of their dark cloaks. They watched with unblinking eyes, their weapons at the ready, but not a word was spoken. The atmosphere was thick with an oppressive stillness, broken only by the crackling of the torches and the steady, rhythmic chanting of the druids.

One of the druids raised his hand, signalling to the warriors and two of them approached Sica, cutting him free from the tree.

The Syrian struggled, but his hands and feet were still bound and the warriors dragged him toward the flat stone in the center of the circle, tying him down with thick ropes. His body was laid flat, his head pulled back until his throat was fully exposed, the muscles in his neck strained.

Raven's heart pounded in his chest, helpless as he watched
Sica bound to the stone, his defiance giving way to grim realization. The torches cast long, flickering shadows across his face, highlighting the sharp angle of his jaw, the clenched teeth as he bit down against the fear rising within him.

The druids worked silently, tightening the ropes until Sica's body was immobile, his chest heaving with laboured breaths. His hands twitched, fingers curling into fists, but there was nothing he could do. One of the druids leaned in, forcing Sica's head further back, exposing his neck completely. The intention was unmistakable.

Chapter Thirty-Five

Britannia

Raven's heart pounded in his chest. Across the stone circle, Sica lay helpless, bound to the sacrificial stone, his chest heaving as he glared up at his would-be executioner. The ritual blade gleamed in the flickering torchlight, raised high above the druid's head, ready to plunge downward.

The druid began to mutter under his breath, invoking the gods. Raven's breath caught, his pulse hammering in his ears. This was it. He knew there were only seconds before the blade would find Sica's throat but as he prayed to his own gods to give Sica's spirit guidance, a sharp whistle cut through the air, followed by the unmistakable thud of an arrow finding its mark. The druid's body jerked, his eyes widening in shock as the ritual blade fell from his hands, clattering to the stone as he crumpled to the ground.

For a heartbeat, the entire clearing was frozen in stunned silence before a dozen exploratores burst from the trees to fall upon the men in the stone circle, their swords gleaming in the torchlight.

The druids, caught completely off guard, scattered in panic, their chanting replaced by shouts of fear. They turned and fled, their white robes flowing behind them as they disappeared into the trees, abandoning the ceremony in a frenzied retreat.

Raven's heart raced as he watched the men charging into the clearing, knowing it could only be the support unit of exploratores they had sent for weeks earlier.

Across the stone circle, in the shadows of the trees, the leader of the druid warriors watched the scene unfold with cold calculation. His face was hidden beneath his hood, but his eyes gleamed with a dangerous light. He gave a sharp signal with his hand, and immediately, his mounted warriors urged their horses forward into the fray, their weapons drawn, ready for battle.

A clash of steel rang out through the night as the exploratores met the druid warriors head-on, and the air became thick with the sound of battle. Shadows twisted and danced across the ancient stones, as if it were some otherworldly battleground where gods and mortals clashed. The fog dulled the senses, and the sharp ring of steel seemed to echo from nowhere and everywhere at once.

Seneca stood amidst the chaos, sword in hand, his breath ragged as he scanned the swirling mist for his men. The druid warriors had appeared as if out of the fog itself, cloaked figures moving with silent precision, their blades flashing in the torchlight. It was impossible to tell how many there were, or where the next attack would come from. They melted in and out of the fog, their movements swift and deliberate, each strike meant to kill.

It was frantic, Chaos but amongst it all, one sound cut through the confusion, Falco's roar.

Falco moved like a beast unleashed, charging through the fog with a wild, raw fury that sent druid warriors staggering back. His blood-soaked face twisted into a snarl as he swung his blade with brutal force, the mist swirling around him as if alive, as if it feared him. The fog, the flickering torchlight, the death, it was his element, and he thrived in it.

A druid warrior lunged from the shadows, a wicked curved blade slicing through the mist, aiming for Falco's side. But the ex-gladiator was too quick, and he parried with a brutal upward stroke, knocking the druid off balance, before slashing downward, severing the man's arm in a spray of blood. The warrior collapsed with a scream, clutching his stump, and Falco drove his blade deep into the man's chest, silencing him forever.

Falco turned, blood dripping from his sword, eyes wild, seeking his next opponent. His breath came in hard bursts, his muscles tense and ready. The fog shifted, and another figure appeared wielding a long spear. Falco sidestepped the thrust with an almost graceful movement and in a flash, he closed the distance, his sword slashing through the air. The druid barely had time to react before Falco's blade cut through his throat, and the man crumpled to the ground in a lifeless heap.

Around him, the battle raged in a surreal blur. The fog made everything disorienting, figures emerged from the mist only to disappear again, and the flickering torches cast long, confusing shadows that played tricks on the eyes. The remaining exploratores fought with desperate efficiency, but they were hard-pressed and outnumbered.

Seneca swung his sword at a druid who darted toward him, their short blades flashing in the dim light. He parried a blow, the force of the impact vibrating through his arm, then kicked the
warrior back before driving his sword into his gut. The man groaned
and collapsed, but another emerged from the mist almost immediately, thrusting a spear toward Seneca's side. Seneca barely managed to twist out of the way, slashing at the druid's exposed arm but the man fell back to be lost again in the thickening mist.

Everywhere he turned, the battle was chaos, blades flashing, horses screaming and men grunting in pain or rage. The fog made it impossible to know how many druids there were, how many still stood. The torchlight flickered weakly, casting the entire scene in a nightmarish glow, making it feel like the land itself was turning against them.

In the middle of it all, Falco continued his rampage, cutting down druid after druid. Blood streaked his arms and face, and his eyes were wild, gleaming with the thrill of the fight. He lived for this, for the blood, the chaos, the raw, primal battle where life and death hung by a thread. He turned, seeking his next victim. He was in his element, a predator among prey, and the druids who faced him stood little chance. The mist only seemed to fuel his fury, the uncertainty of the battle sharpening his instincts, his need to kill.

But even Falco couldn't fight forever. The fog continued to thicken, and the druids fought with a terrifying calm, slipping in and out of the mist like ghosts. The exploratores were holding their ground, but the battle was slowly turning against them. Bodies littered the ground, both Roman and druid, their blood soaking into the earth beneath the ancient stones.

And then, cutting through the chaos, a sound pierced the night, a long, mournful horn echoing through the mist, and sending a shiver down Seneca's spine.

The remaining druid warriors froze for a moment, their eyes turning toward the trees, where the sound had come from, and without warning, they began to pull back, retreating into the mist as silently as they had arrived. One by one, they disappeared, leaving the bloodied, battered exploratores standing amidst the ruins of the battle.

Seneca stood panting, his sword still raised, his heart still racing. He looked around, blinking through the fog, trying to make sense of what had just happened.

'Why are they retreating?' shouted Falco, his chest

heaving, his eyes still wild with bloodlust. 'I wasn't finished.'

But the druids were gone, vanishing into the mist as quickly as they had appeared, leaving behind only the dead and the dying
in the flickering torchlight.

Seneca lowered his sword, trying to catch his breath. His mind raced with the same question Falco had asked.

Why had they stopped? What had that horn signalled?

As the tension eased, the men started to come down from the mental heights that battle often brought and made their way over to the centre of the circle to regroup. Seneca cut Sica free before striding over to release Raven, but as he arrived, he saw Marcus staring at the empty ropes that had once bound their comrade to the tree. Raven was gone.

His mind churned with conflicting emotions, rage, frustration, and a deep sense of failure. The urge to chase after the druids was overpowering. Every instinct told him to pursue them, to tear through the forest and drag Raven back from wherever they had taken him, but as much as he wanted to act, reality tempered his resolve. If they charged blindly into the night, they could easily stumble into an ambush or run into superior forces. Worse still, his men were exhausted, bloodied from the fight, and eight of his exploratores lay dead in the clearing.

Seneca exhaled sharply, pushing down his frustration.

'Gather the wounded,' he ordered, 'and take the bodies of our brothers. We can't stay here.'

His men moved quickly, and within minutes, they were again ready to ride, though this time the horses also carried the dead and the wounded.

Seneca scanned the treeline one last time, as if expecting to see some trace of Raven, some sign that they could still find him. But the forest remained dark, silent except for the soft murmurs of his own men. He turned to Marcus, who had come to stand beside him.

'We head north,' he said. We need to put as much distance as we can between us and this place before dawn. They'll be hunting us by morning.'

Marcus nodded.

'And Raven?'

'We get the men out, regroup, then we figure out what to do.'

Marcus hesitated for a moment, then clapped Seneca on the shoulder, understanding the weight of the decision. With the bodies of the fallen wrapped in their cloaks and the wounded secured into the saddles, they set off into the night. The forest closed in around them, the trees thick and foreboding as they moved swiftly away from the stone circle.

They pushed hard, riding and walking through the night, their minds focused on getting as far from the stone circle as possible. The sky above them began to lighten with the pale hues of dawn just as they came to a stop in a small clearing. The horses were exhausted, their flanks heaving, and the men were no better.

'We rest here,' said Seneca, 'just long enough to bury the dead.'

The men dug shallow graves beneath the trees, and their fallen comrades were buried side by side. There were no words spoken, only brief moments of silence as the dirt was cast over the bodies, marking their final resting place.

Once the graves were filled, Seneca gave the order to move again. The men were tired, but they didn't complain, they knew they couldn't afford to stay in one place for too long.

They pushed on until the sun was high, the forest thinning as they moved further north. Finally, after what felt like an eternity, they reached a secluded range of hills, jagged and remote, far from prying eyes. Seneca led them into a hidden cleft in the hills, a narrow valley sheltered by rocky outcrops. His men were exhausted, worn from the battle and the long ride, but they were alive. That had to count for something, even though the sting of losing Raven weighed heavily on all of them.

Marcus walked over.

'The men need rest, Seneca' he said quietly, 'they are spent.'

'I know,' Seneca replied, 'we'll stay here for a short time. Let them recover.'

'I'll sort out the watch,' said Marcus and walked away to organise the men.

A few hours later, Seneca sat at the edge of the small clearing when one of the sentries called out.

'Seneca, you need to see this.'

Seneca strode quickly to the vantage point and peered out over the open ground beyond the hills.

At first, all he saw was the vast, rolling landscape. Then, in the distance, he could see over a hundred mounted warriors, spread out in a loose formation and he knew instinctively, it wasn't a casual patrol, these men were searching for something. For them.

'They've found us,' he muttered. 'Muster the men.'

The guard raced away but Seneca stayed a moment longer, focussing on the small group leading the mounted force. A few hooded figures stood out at the head of the column, distinctly different from the other riders. The same type who had fought them in the darkness barely a few hours ago.

Without wasting another moment, he descended the rocks and strode back into the center of the small camp. The men were already packing the small number of things they had but paused to gather around him in a tight circle.

'We're being hunted,' said Seneca bluntly. 'A force of mounted men, led by druids, is closing in on us as we speak. They know where we are, and they're coming fast. We don't have the numbers to stand and fight them so, we do what we've been trained to do. We disappear.'

The men listened intently, knowing this moment had been coming since they'd left the stone circle, since Raven had been taken.

'We've been compromised,' Seneca went on. 'But as you all know we have a plan for this sort of situation, we split up, into twos and threes. Each group heads for one of the ports on the coast. Once you get a boat, you know where to head, Portus Dubris, Rutupiae or Gesoriacum.'

A heavy silence settled over the group. They had trained for this, prepared for the worst-case scenarios, but now that it was upon them, the finality of it was sobering.

'For those of you who can't make it to the coast,' Seneca continued, 'you hide. Find refuge where you can, lay low, and wait. The invasion is coming. When the legions land, make yourselves known and regroup at the landing site. Ask for Lepidus and he will guide you from there.'

Seneca's eyes scanned the faces of his men, hardened warriors, exploratores who had survived countless dangers and impossible odds. They were ready for this. It was what they did, adapt, survive, regroup.

'Stick to the plan,' said Seneca firmly. 'Use the land,

keep off the main roads, and avoid any unnecessary risks. The moment we're spotted, we're done.'

There was no time to waste. They had precious little daylight left, and they knew they had to be gone before the enemy
closed in.

'Move out,' he ordered, 'and we meet again in six months.'

With that, the group dispersed, moving with the practiced efficiency of men who had been drilled for this moment. He turned to his remaining men, the original members of the Occultum, the men he trusted more than anything else in his world. For a few moments there was an uneasy silence, and his comrades stared back, realising something was wrong.

Seneca looked each man up and down, his gaze piercing. Ever since Canis had informed him there was a traitor within the Occultum, he had hoped that it had been a mistake, or a last play on words of a man knowing he was about to die, but now, with Raven gone, that seed of doubt had only grown stronger. The druids had seemed to know their every move, from capturing Sica and Raven to knowing what direction they would be heading in. It could all be coincidence, but it was hardly likely and at last, Seneca was sure. Someone within their ranks had been feeding information to the enemy.

'Get ready to move,' he said, 'us six will stay together.'

Marcus raised an eyebrow, clearly surprised by the sudden shift in plan.

'Together? Wouldn't we have a better chance if we split into two groups like we did in Germania?'

'Ordinarily, yes,' said Seneca, 'but there are things to sort out before we can even think of heading back. We need to stay as one unit. The six of us.'

'Things?' asked Falco. 'What things?'

'It will become clearer soon enough,' said Seneca, 'but for now, let's just concentrate on staying alive. Mount up.'

As they rode out into the hills, Seneca's mind churned. Raven was gone, the druids were on their trail, and somewhere in his unit, a traitor was hiding and if he didn't find him soon, it wouldn't just be Raven they lost, it could be hundreds if not thousands of legionaries waiting to board their ships on the other side of the sea.

Chapter Thirty-Six

Britannia

Seneca and his men kept to the shadows, moving swiftly, always aware of the distant signs of pursuit. They hadn't seen a village in days, avoiding all signs of civilization, knowing that any slip could lead their pursuers directly to them. The horses were equally exhausted, their heads low, steps slow and laboured as they pressed on. They needed to break from their pursuers and as they neared the coast, the Britannic fog, heavy and cloying, rolled in yet again, but this time, almost as an unexpected ally, blanketing the forest in a veil of ghostly white. Visibility dropped to mere paces in front of them, but the fog was a welcome cover. At last, they had something working in their favour.

They rode as hard as they dared through the mist, the trees passing in ghostly shapes around them. Every branch and leaf was damp, and the sound of their hooves was muffled by the sodden earth beneath. It was gruelling, but the sense of relief among the group was palpable. For the first time in days, it felt like they had a real chance of evading their pursuers.

Seneca led them into a narrow ravine, hidden between steep rock faces and dense undergrowth. The fog still clung to the landscape, curling around the boulders and trees like tendrils of smoke.

'This will do,' he said quietly, dismounting from his horse. 'We'll stay here until it's safe to move again.'

They led the horses to a sheltered corner against the rocks, where the wind couldn't reach. The men moved slowly, their bodies weak from hunger and exhaustion, but the tension in the air began to ease. For the first time in days, they felt relatively safe.

Falco and Sica set about gathering kindling and small pieces of wood, and soon they had a modest fire going. The flames flickered low, barely visible through the fog, but it provided enough warmth to take the edge off the chill that had seeped into their bones.

'We need food,' Falco muttered, rummaging through the packs for anything edible. What they had left was meagre, some dried meat, a few roots, and some stale bread. Hardly enough to fill their stomachs, but it would have to do.

Sica took charge of the cooking, using his knife to slice the last of the food into a rough mixture. He threw it all into a pot with some water, creating a basic stew. The smell, though faint, was enough to stir their empty bellies into anticipation and they sat around the fire in silence, the firelight casting soft, dancing shadows on the rock face behind them.

Seneca stared into the flames, his mind still racing despite the momentary reprieve. The fog had given them a chance, but he knew it wouldn't last.

Sica passed the bowl of thin stew around the group, each man taking one spoonful before passing it on to the next man. It didn't last long and eventually, after a few circuits, they all watched in silence as Falco licked the sides for every last drop he could find. The heat from the food gave them a fleeting sense of comfort but they all knew this was temporary. The fog would lift, and the hunt would resume, but for now, they had warmth, food, and the safety of the ravine.

Seneca lifted his empty water flask, giving it a shake.

'There's a stream just down the slope,' said Marcus, 'I used it earlier to fill mine.'

Seneca stood up to walk down to the water's edge, the

cold water flowing softly over smooth stones as he filled his pouch. The fog was still thick around the ravine, muffling the sounds of the forest, making everything feel distant, almost dreamlike. Despite the relative safety of their temporary camp, his mind was troubled.

As he tied the neck of his flask, Marcus appeared behind him. He knelt beside Seneca without a word, scooping water into his hands and splashing it over his own head, the weariness of their journey clear in the lines etched on his face. For a few moments, neither man spoke, letting the sound of the stream fill the silence between them.

'Well,' said Marcus eventually, 'are you going to tell me what's eating at you or not?'

Seneca looked over and pondered whether he should risk telling the ex-centurion. Of all the men, his recruitment could not have been staged by anyone, but it didn't preclude him from having been bribed since. Despite the doubt, he knew he had to trust someone and after checking no one else was within earshot, proceeded to tell Marcus everything he knew.

Marcus listened in silence, his face not betraying the shock
at the accusation. When Seneca had finished, another silence fell as he absorbed the information. Finally, he spoke, his voice quiet but probing.

'And you truly believe that one of us, one of the original group, could be bought? After everything we've done together, everything we've been through?'

'We're all just mortal men, Marcus,' replied Seneca, 'and can be bought if the price is high enough. I've seen men who would kill their own brothers for enough gold, for enough power. Just because we've shared battles doesn't make us immune to that.'

Marcus's shoulders slumped slightly, the weight of Seneca's words sinking in. He looked out over the stream as the realization sunk in.

'Even me?'

'Even you,' said Seneca.

Marcus exhaled slowly, shaking his head.

'Gods, Seneca. You really think that low of us?'

'It's not about thinking low of anyone,' said Seneca, 'it's about facing the reality we're in. Someone has been feeding information to the enemy, and until we figure out who, no one is beyond suspicion.'

'You think it's Cassius or Atticus, don't you?' said Marcus. 'They're the only new ones within this inner circle.'

Seneca stood, wiping his hands on his cloak.

'They're the most obvious suspects, yes. But I'm not ruling anyone out. We've been outmanoeuvred at every turn. Maybe it is one of them, but if it's someone else, hiding in plain sight, we're all in danger. I think I need to keep my eyes open, and I think you do, too.'

'What about Raven?'

Seneca turned to look at Marcus, his brow furrowing in confusion.

'What about him?'

Marcus shifted uncomfortably, glancing back toward the camp before speaking again.

'Think about it. His disappearance... it was very convenient, don't you think?'

Seneca stared at him, the words chilling him like a cold gust of wind. He opened his mouth to object, but the longer he thought about it, the more Marcus's words gnawed at him. Convenient? Yes, it had been. In the chaos of the fight at the stone circle, Raven had vanished, his binds mysteriously cut, while the druid warriors retreated into the woods without explanation.

'What are you suggesting?' he asked, though his heart already began to sink with the implication.

'Think about it, Seneca. Raven often went out hunting alone, sometimes for hours. Who's to say he wasn't meeting someone out there, making contact with the druids? He had more than enough opportunity.'

Seneca glared in silence as Marcus's words sank in. It was true, Raven had frequently left the group to hunt. He had a knack for disappearing, for blending into the wild. At the time, it had seemed like a natural extension of his skills as a scout and hunter. But now, viewed through the lens of suspicion, it took on a more sinister edge.

'And I don't know if you have been told yet,' Marcus pressed, 'Raven stopped Sica from killing Togodumnus when they were in the camp. They had the chance to kill the most feared leader in Britannia, but Raven held him back.'

'Why would he do that?' asked Seneca.

'He claimed that killing Togodumnus would only unite all the tribes, creating an entire nation mobilising against Rome. It sounded like a reasonable reason to Sica at the time, but perhaps Raven hadn't wanted Togodumnus dead for entirely different reasons. Raven's also a Briton, remember? He knows these lands better than any of us. He knows the people, the customs, he could've been working with them this whole time.'

Seneca felt his stomach churn. He had trusted Raven, they all had. The man had been a brother to him in the field, one of his most reliable men. And yet... there were too many signs, too many pieces that, when placed together, began to form a troubling picture. Nobody had seen Raven freed from his binds, but the druid warriors had suddenly withdrawn from the fight without reason and not one of them had stayed to finish the job. That retreat had never sat right with Seneca, but he had been too focused on survival to dwell on it. Now, with Marcus's words echoing in his mind, it seemed all too clear. He nodded slowly, the pieces falling into place.

'It makes sense,' he muttered, his voice thick with disbelief. 'Too much sense.'

It was a gut-wrenching realisation. Raven's disappearance
during the battle, his ability to vanish into the wild, his connections to Britannia, the timing of the druid withdrawal, it all seemed to point at only one possibility, Raven was the traitor.

'I don't want to believe it either. ' said Marcus, 'but everything points to him. And once he was released, the warriors withdrew. Almost like they knew he wasn't really one of us anymore.'

Seneca looked toward the camp where the others sat, oblivious to the grim conversation happening by the water's edge. If Raven was the traitor, then everything had changed. Their mission, their trust, everything was tainted by that one betrayal.

'We need to tell the others,' said Marcus.

Seneca shook his head, still wrestling with the truth.

'Not yet. We need proof. Until then, we keep this between us.'

'And if we're wrong?'

'Then we'll deal with it at the time. But somehow, I don't think we are.'

The following morning, Seneca was once more at the edge of the stream, watering his horse before they continued their flight towards the coast. The fog still clung thickly to the ravine, giving it an ethereal, almost otherworldly feeling, and Seneca couldn't shake the discomfort that had settled in his chest. The shock of Raven's betrayal still gnawed at him, his thoughts churning with disappointment and anger.

The horse lifted its head, staring across the stream as it snorted, water dripping from its mouth. Seneca picked up on the horse's reaction and followed its stare, just as a voice cut through the fog just a stone's throw away.

'Seneca.'

The sound of his name echoing through the ravine cut in to him like a blade and his hand immediately flew to the hilt of his sword, his eyes scanning the swirling mist for the stranger who knew his name. Something moved and his heart missed a beat as he watched a cloaked figure slowly emerging from the fog to stand alone on the opposite bank.

Seneca's blood turned to ice. He knew at once who it was, the leader of the men who had been pursuing them.

The druid leader stood tall and motionless, his hooded face
shadowed, but there was no mistaking the quiet, terrifying authority that clung to him. The fog seemed to thicken around him, drawn to him like it was alive, swirling at his feet, as if the very elements bowed to his will.

Seneca's hand instinctively drew his sword its scabbard with a sharp hiss and again scanned the area for any sign of an ambush.

'You are alone, Roman,' said Mordred calmly, 'as am I. I have no need for warriors today.'

Seneca turned back to face him, sword at the ready, his

mind spinning. The fog drifted between them like a curtain, but Mordred's figure remained, solid and unyielding. Seneca could barely breathe, fear and disbelief battling in his chest.

'Who are you?' snapped Seneca.

'I go by many names,' said the druid, 'but most call me Mordred.'

'How did you find us?'

Mordred's lips curled into a small, knowing smile.

'You Romans may think yourselves powerful, but you are nothing in these lands. My gods... they see everything.'

Seneca's pulse quickened, his grip tightening on his sword. He had faced countless enemies before, but this was different. This felt... beyond human. He prayed silently to the gods of Rome, desperate for some kind of protection.

'You'll never take us, alive' said Seneca, his voice hardening as he forced down his fear. 'We'll never surrender.'

Mordred chuckled softly, the sound unsettling in the stillness of the ravine.

'Surrender? Oh, no, Roman. I have no interest in your surrender. You and your men are free to go.'

Seneca blinked in confusion. The cold mist swirled thickly around him, every breath he took feeling heavy, as though the fog itself pressed against his chest.

'What games are you playing, druid?' he asked warily.

Mordred raised his hand, a small, almost dismissive gesture.

'There is no game, Roman. I have already called off the hunt. Your pursuers... they are gone.'

Seneca's heart skipped a beat. None of this made sense. The druids had them cornered, why would Mordred let them slip away?

'Why?' Seneca demanded, the tip of his sword

lowering slightly. 'Why let us go?'

Mordred's eyes glinting with something dark, something ancient.

'Because I want your leaders to know of me, Roman. I want the emperor himself to speak my name. I want them to understand that it is I that rules Britannia, not them. And if they seek to take this land from me... they will have to answer to my gods.'

Seneca's breath caught in his throat. Mordred's arrogance was chilling, but there was no denying the power in his words. The druid wasn't just defying Rome, he was declaring war on it, not with an army, but with something far more terrifying.

'You expect the emperor to kneel to you?' he scoffed, trying to keep his voice steady. 'Rome will crush you and everything you believe in.'

'Crush me?' laughed the druid, 'no, Roman. Your legions may march, but they will find only death and despair in these lands. I will meet your emperor's legions, and when they see what I have to offer, they will tremble before me. Claudius will one day kneel, before me and beg forgiveness as his empire crumbles around him.'

The fog seemed to pulse around Mordred, the swirling mist growing thicker, almost suffocating and Seneca's heart pounded in his chest, fear clawing at him. His grip tightened on his sword again, and his mind raced, trying to grasp the enormity of what Mordred was saying. The emperor, Claudius himself, would have to contend with this... thing, this druid who seemed to command the very forces of nature. But there was one more question gnawing at his mind, one final thread he had to pull.

'Where is Raven?' he asked, his voice cutting through

the silence.

For a long moment, there was nothing but the soft whisper of the fog moving through the trees. Then, from the other side of the river, Mordred's voice returned, as calm and mocking as before.

'Ah, yes… your Raven.'

The fog seemed to part, revealing Mordred once more, standing at the edge of the water. Seneca's pulse quickened, dread clawing at his stomach, the strange encounter almost overwhelming.

'He will be returned to you,' said Mordred, 'and as I said, you are free to go. But freedom comes with a price.'

Seneca's heart sank at the words, his blood running cold.

'What do you mean?' he demanded, stepping closer to the riverbank. 'Return him to us, Mordred. He's still one of ours.'

A flicker of amusement danced in Mordred's eyes, barely visible through the fog.

'Of course.'

The druid raised a hand and gave a small signal. Almost immediately, one of his warriors emerged from the mist onto the riverbank, dragging something behind him. No, someone. Seneca's heart stopped as he saw the figure more clearly. It was Raven.

Stripped to the waist, his body bruised and battered, Raven stumbled forward, his hands bound tightly behind his back. The druid warrior pulled him roughly, forcing him to his knees just a few feet from the river's edge. Raven's face was gaunt, his eyes hollow, but they locked onto Seneca with a strange mixture of defiance and resignation. Blood trickled from a cut on his lip, and his dark hair clung to his sweat-streaked skin.

Seneca took an involuntary step forward, his eyes wide with shock. He had suspected Raven of betrayal, had even begun to believe it, but seeing him like this, broken and beaten, sent a wave of conflicting emotions surging through him. Traitor or not, he had known Raven for years. Fought beside him. Trusted him.

Mordred watched the scene unfold, his cold eyes glinting in the fog.

'He is yours, Seneca,' he said, almost mockingly. 'But as I told you, there is always a price.'

Before Seneca could react, the druid standing behind Raven reached down, grabbed a fistful of his hair, and yanked his head back, exposing his neck. The movement was so sudden, so brutal, that it took Seneca a heartbeat to understand what was about to happen.

'Wait.' Seneca shouted, his voice raw with horror. 'No. Stop.'

But Mordred's cruel smile only widened, and he shook his head, almost pitying.

'There must always be a price.'

The druid warrior pulled a long, curved blade from his belt, its edge gleaming in the weak light filtering through the mist, and with one swift, brutal stroke, cut deep into Raven's throat, sending spurts of blood soaring over the water. Within a few heartbeats, Raven's body crumpled to the ground, his severed head still held in the druid's grip.

For a moment, time seemed to stand still. The fog swirled
lazily around the scene, and the world became eerily quiet.

Seneca stood paralyzed, his sword dangling limply at

his side, his mind unable to process the horror of what he had just witnessed. Raven, traitor or not, was dead, executed before his very eyes. The man he had known for so long, the comrade he had fought alongside, reduced to nothing in an instant of cold, calculated violence.

Mordred, still standing across the river, met Seneca's gaze with a dark, satisfied look.

'Tell your leaders, Seneca,' he said softly, his voice carrying over the water. 'Tell them that this is what awaits them if they seek to claim Britannia. I answer to no emperor. And neither do my gods.'

Before Seneca could fully comprehend what was happening, the druid warrior pulled back his arm and hurled the severed head through the air. Time seemed to slow as it soared across the river, tumbling in the air before landing with a grotesque, wet thud at Seneca's feet.

Seneca recoiled instinctively, his stomach churning as he stared down in horror. Raven's lifeless eyes stared up at him from his bloody, bruised face, wide and accusing, the expression frozen in a macabre mixture of pain and resignation. The once-familiar face of a comrade now a grotesque reminder of betrayal and death. Blood still oozed from the neck, staining the grass red where it landed.

But before Seneca could even process the full weight of what had happened, the head rolled back down the slight incline of the bank and into the water. The current caught it immediately, pulling it downstream, the dark hair trailing in the water like a ghostly shadow.

Seneca watched, numb with shock, as it disappeared beneath the surface, the rushing water swallowing it whole. His heart pounded, the image of Raven's eyes burned into his mind.

Across the river, Mordred's voice floated back to him, barely more than a whisper in the mist.

'Remember, Roman. There is no place you can hide from me.'

And then, just like that, Mordred was gone. Swallowed by the fog, his presence vanishing as though he had never been there at all.

Seneca remained frozen by the water's edge, the world around him distant and unreal. The only thing that seemed real, the only thing that he could still feel, was the haunting image of Raven's severed head, rolling into the river, carried away by the current.

The weight of Mordred's message hung heavily in the air, suffocating. Britannia was not just land to be conquered, it was a battlefield of spirits and gods, a place where power beyond Rome's understanding waited in the mist.

Seneca stood there, rooted to the spot, his heart racing, the horror of the moment seared into his soul. He knew now that Mordred was no ordinary man. He was a force, a living symbol of the resistance that awaited them, and Rome, for all its might, would have to reckon with him.

Chapter Thirty-Seven

Britannia

Togodumnus stood in the center of his camp, the thick stench of smoke still lingering in the air from the fire that had raged for days, but despite the destruction, he stood tall, his presence commanding, his face a mask of defiance.

Around him, his chieftains gathered, murmuring their doubts. The rumours had already spread, Cadorix was dead which meant the Cantiaci would no longer be joining them. It was a bitter blow, but Togodumnus refused to let it break him. He turned to his men, his voice cutting through the low conversations.

'The Romans may think this weakens us,' he shouted, 'they may believe that without the Cantiaci, we're doomed to fail. But they are wrong.'

The chieftains fell silent, all eyes on Togodumnus.

'We are warriors.' Togodumnus bellowed, his voice swelling with fire and conviction. 'The Romans think they can bend us to their will, force us to submit. But this land, our land, belongs to us. With or without the Cantiaci, we will fight, and we will drive them back into the sea.'

A murmur of agreement rippled through the gathered leaders. Though the loss of the Cantiaci stung, Togodumnus's fire was infectious. His belief in victory, his refusal to yield, reignited their spirits. Before Togodumnus could continue, one of his scouts came running through the camp, his face pale, his breath ragged.

'Lord Togodumnus,' the man gasped, bowing quickly, 'you must come to the palisade. Quickly.'

Togodumnus frowned, his sharp eyes narrowing as he

searched the scout's face for answers.

'What is it?'

The scout swallowed hard, clearly unnerved.

'An army approaches.'

At those words, the camp fell still. Togodumnus's chieftains exchanged uneasy glances, but Togodumnus's face remained unreadable. He motioned for his leaders to follow and set off toward the palisade, his stride confident, even as a strange sense of foreboding crept into his chest.

They reached the walls quickly, and as Togodumnus climbed up to the wooden platform overlooking the surrounding land, his eyes immediately found the approaching force. A sea of warriors marched steadily toward them, their weapons glinting in the afternoon light, their numbers vast. The sight made even his most seasoned warriors murmur in unease.

At first, Togodumnus felt a cold thread of fear snake through him. But as his sharp eyes scanned the front ranks, his anxiety began to ease. He recognized the banners, the distinctive shapes of their shields. He narrowed his eyes, focusing on the figure at the head of the army, a tall man with a familiar presence, his chainmail and helm gleaming in the sunlight.

Togodumnus exhaled sharply.

'It's him,' he muttered under his breath.

'Who, my lord?' asked one of the chieftains.

'My brother,' Togodumnus growled. 'Caratacus.' He climbed down the ladder and strode through the gates, pushing them open with a forceful shove. His chieftains followed behind him, their expressions wary but determined. Outside the walls, Togodumnus marched toward the approaching army, his heart pounding, not with fear, but with frustration.

His followers halted as Togodumnus walked alone towards the oncoming army. Caratacus dismounted from his horse and strode forward to meet him, the tension between them palpable. When they were only a few paces apart, Togodumnus stopped, his eyes narrowing as he spoke.

'What are you doing here, brother? Have you come to try and stop me? To convince me to turn back, for you should know this. I will not let anyone stand in my way, and if you interfere, you will find yourself across the field from me when the battle comes.'

Caratacus didn't flinch, his gaze unwavering. For a moment, the two brothers stood in silence, the air between them thick with years of unresolved tension.

'I haven't come to fight you, Togodumnus,' he said. 'I've come to join you.'

Togodumnus blinked, his hardened expression faltering for the first time.

'What?'

Caratacus stepped closer, his eyes locking with his brother's.

'We both know what's coming,' he said, 'and although I supported our father in his approach while he was alive, I have now
had time to reconsider. If we stand divided, we will fall. But if we unite, if we fight together, we can drive them back.'

Togodumnus took a deep breath, his anger subsiding, replaced by a slow, reluctant acceptance.

'Then let us fight,' he said, 'together.'

The two brothers turned, walking side by side back towards the camp, the warriors behind them watching with a mixture of relief and anticipation. For the first time in years, the Catuvellauni and the Trinovantes were united and now that barrier had been cleared, they knew more would follow.

The die was finally cast. Rome may have their legions assembling on the far side of the northern sea, but they would not just walk into their homeland without resistance. Britannia would fight... and Rome would bleed.

Epilogue

Britannia

Many leagues away, the six men of the Occultum staggered up the final incline, their legs leaden, their faces hollow and gaunt. Weeks of fleeing the druids, hiding in forests, and sleeping under starlit skies had whittled them down to shadows of their former selves. Their horses, hardly able to move a step further, had been released days ago and food was nothing more than a memory, replaced by hunger that gnawed with each step. The salt taste of the sea lingered in the air, tantalisingly close.

At last, Seneca paused at the crest of the hill. Beside him, Atticus, Sica, Falco, Marcus, and Cassius lifted their heads, straining to catch a glimpse of whatever lay beyond. Below them, nestled in the embrace of the coast, lay a fishing village. Wisps of smoke rose lazily from small fires, and the bobbing silhouettes of boats in the harbour danced upon the waters, promising rest, sustenance, and perhaps, escape.

A murmur of relief passed through the men. Falco shut his eyes, whispering thanks to the gods, while Seneca simply closed his fist around the last dregs of his strength, staring down with grim satisfaction.

'A boat,' whispered Atticus, his voice trembling. 'We can cross to Gesoriacum, warn Plautius of the druids. We can...'

But as he spoke, Seneca looked up at Sica, who had stood silent at the edge of the group. He was pointing, his face drained of colour, and, as his finger traced a line over the horizon, dread seeped into them all.

Out at sea, hundreds of sails filled the waters as far as

the eye could reach, a white wall gliding silently towards the shore as the enormous Roman fleet rode the waves, its banners flapping in the wind.

Seneca's voice was barely a whisper, yet it carried the weight of their shared despair.

'We are too late.'

The men remained rooted atop the windswept hill, their relief dashed, their mission now a mere echo against the unyielding tide of Rome. They had been desperate to report the strength of Togodumnus to Plautius, to give him the time to plan properly,
learn about the lay of the land, to delay the invasion, but they had failed, and as the fleet crept ever closer, bringing with it the certainty of war, they knew that life would never be the same. Rome was casting a shadow that would soon drench the shores of Britannia in blood…the Roman invasion of Britannia had begun.

The End

Follow the next instalment with Seneca and the rest of the Occultum

Dark Eagle III

Rome is teetering on the edge of rebellion, the invasion of Britannia has begun and all the members of the Occultum are at risk.

The traitor's identity remains hidden, and with all his trusted agents already deployed deep behind enemy lines, Lepidus faces a crisis that threatens not only the success of the invasion but the very safety of the emperor himself.

With no one left to trust, he turns to the one man he never thought he'd need, Veteranus, an ex-legionary shrouded in infamy.

Brutal, ruthless, and once condemned to death for his savage methods, Veteranus is a wild card who bows to no authority. Now, in a desperate gamble, Lepidus must decide if this unpredictable lone wolf is the empire's last hope, or its greatest threat.

Packed with action, intrigue, and the harsh realities of war, Veteranus delves deeper into the shadowy world of Rome's covert operatives.

Author's Notes

The Invasion of Britannia

The Roman invasion of Britannia in 43 AD was a major military campaign launched by the Roman Empire under Emperor Claudius. The invasion marked the beginning of Roman rule in Britain, which lasted for nearly four centuries. The operation was both a strategic military venture and a political move designed to strengthen Claudius's position as emperor.

Before the invasion, Britannia was known to the Romans, having been explored by Julius Caesar during his expeditions in 55 and 54 BC. However, Rome had not established a lasting presence on the island. By the 1st century AD, Britannia was seen as a land of valuable resources, such as tin, lead, and agricultural products, and its tribes were known for their fierce independence. Claudius, seeking to solidify his rule and gain military prestige, decided to launch a full-scale invasion.

Emperor Claudius

Claudius came to power in 41 AD after the assassination of Caligula. Seen initially as a weak and unlikely ruler, Claudius sought to legitimize his rule through military conquest. He personally visited Britannia after the initial success of the invasion, staying for only 16 days to receive the submission of several tribes. His visit was used to solidify his political power in Rome.

Aulus Plautius

Aulus Plautius was an experienced Roman senator and general. He had previously served in various capacities throughout the empire, gaining a reputation for his administrative and military skills. Plautius led an estimated force of 40,000 men, comprising four legions and auxiliary troops, across the English Channel to begin the conquest. He successfully defeated several tribes in southeastern Britannia and established a strong foothold for Roman forces. He was later appointed the first governor of the new province of Britannia.

Caratacus

Caratacus was a leader of the Catuvellauni tribe, one of the most powerful in southeastern Britannia. He was a skilled and determined warrior who became a symbol of resistance against the Romans. Caratacus led a prolonged guerrilla campaign against the Romans, rallying various tribes to resist the invasion. Despite initial successes, he was eventually defeated and captured in 51 AD. Claudius later pardoned him, and he lived out his days in Rome.

Togodumnus

Togodumnus, like his brother Caratacus, was a key figure in the resistance against Roman forces. Togodumnus fought alongside Caratacus during the early battles of the invasion. He was killed in battle, which significantly weakened the Catuvellauni's resistance.

Cunobeline

Cunobeline, often called 'Britannorum Rex' (King of the Britons), was a dominant figure in southeastern Britannia. His capital was at Camulodunum (modern Colchester). Although Cunobeline died shortly before the invasion, his sons Caratacus and Togodumnus continued his legacy of resistance against Rome.

The Iceni

The Iceni were a Celtic tribe located in what is now Norfolk and parts of Suffolk and Cambridgeshire, England, during the Iron Age and early Roman period. The tribe initially maintained a semi-independent status under the Roman Empire after the Roman invasion of Britain in AD 43, and their king, Prasutagus, was a client ruler, who ruled as a Roman ally. Upon his death, however, the Romans annexed Iceni territory, disregarding Prasutagus' will, which had left half of his kingdom to the Romans and the other half to his daughters. This act, along with the mistreatment of his family, sparked Boudica's rebellion.

The Catuvellauni

The Catuvellauni were a powerful Celtic tribe in southeastern Britain during the late Iron Age, with their territory covering what is now Hertfordshire, Buckinghamshire, Bedfordshire, and parts of surrounding counties. Their tribal capital was initially at Verlamion (modern St Albans), later known as Verulamium under Roman rule.

The Catuvellauni became one of the most dominant tribes in southern Britain, particularly under the leadership of king Cunobeline who expanded the tribe's power significantly, conquering neighbouring tribes like the Trinovantes and establishing the Catuvellauni as a major force. He ruled from Camulodunum (modern Colchester), which became a major centre of power.

The Catuvellauni initially resisted Roman expansion during the Roman invasion of AD 43, led by Cunobeline's' sons, Caratacus and Togodumnus. They were key opponents of the Romans during the early stages of the conquest.

The Trinovantes

The Trinovantes occupied much of what is now Essex and parts of Suffolk and were one of the first tribes to come into contact with Roman forces during Julius Caesar's expeditions to Britain in 55 and 54 BC. At that time, the Trinovantes were rivals of the neighbouring Catuvellauni and during Caesar's invasions, they sided with the Romans, seeking protection from the expansionist Catuvellauni. This alliance briefly gave them a favoured position, but over time, their power declined as the Catuvellauni eventually conquered their territory.

By the time of the Roman invasion of AD 43, the Trinovantes had fallen under the control of the Catuvellauni, led by Cunobeline. After the Romans successfully defeated the native resistance, the Trinovantes became one of the first tribes to submit to Roman rule.

Also by K. M. Ashman

The Exploratores
Dark Eagle
The Hidden
Veteranus
Scarab
The Wraith
Silures
Panthera

Seeds of Empire
Seeds of Empire
Rise of the Eagle
Fields of glory

The Brotherhood
Templar Steel
Templar Stone
Templar Blood
Templar Fury
Templar Glory
Templar Legacy
Templar Loyalty

The India Summers Mysteries
The Vestal Conspiracies
The Treasures of Suleiman
The Mummies of the Reich
The Tomb Builders

The Roman Chronicles
The Fall of Britannia
The Rise of Caratacus
The Wrath of Boudicca

The Medieval Sagas
Blood of the Cross
In Shadows of Kings
Sword of Liberty
Ring of Steel

The Blood of Kings
A Land Divided
A Wounded Realm
Rebellion's Forge
The Warrior Princess
The Blade Bearer

The Road to Hastings
The Challenges of a King
The Promises of a King
The Fate of a King

The Otherworld Series
The Legacy Protocol
The Seventh God
The Last Citadel
Savage Eden
Vampire

Printed in Great Britain
by Amazon

62734624R00191